Adventures in the Ancient World: 2

Adventures in the Ancient World: 2

Morning Star

★

Cleopatra

H. Rider Haggard

Adventures in the Ancient World: 2
Morning Star & Cleopatra
by H. Rider Haggard

Leonaur is an imprint of Oakpast Ltd

ISBN: 978-1-84677-988-6 (hardcover)
ISBN: 978-1-84677-987-9 (softcover)

http://www.leonaur.com

Publisher's Notes

The views expressed in this book are not necessarily those of the publisher.

Contents

Morning Star

Dedication

My dear Budge—

Only a friendship extending over many years emboldened me, an amateur, to propose to dedicate a Romance of Old Egypt to you, one of the world's masters of the language and lore of the great people who in these latter days arise from their holy tombs to instruct us in the secrets of history and faith.

With doubt I submitted to you this story, asking whether you wished to accept pages that could not, I feared, be free from error, and with surprise in due course I read, among other kind things, your advice to me to "leave it exactly as it is." So I take you at your word, although I can scarcely think that in paths so remote and difficult I have not sometimes gone astray.

Whatever may be the shortcomings, therefore, that your kindness has concealed from me, since this tale was so fortunate as to please and interest you, its first critic, I offer it to you as an earnest of my respect for your learning and your labours.

Very sincerely yours,

H. Rider Haggard

Ditchingham.

To Doctor Wallis Budge

Keeper of Egyptian and Assyrian Antiquities

British Museum

Author's Note

It may be thought that even in a story of Old Egypt to represent a *Ka* or "Double" as remaining in active occupation of a throne, while the owner of the said "Double" goes upon a long journey and achieves sundry adventures, is, in fact, to take a liberty with Doubles. Yet I believe that this is scarcely the case. The *Ka* or Double which Wiedermann aptly calls the "Personality within the Person" appears, according to Egyptian theory, to have had an existence of its own. It did not die when the body died, for it was immortal and awaited the resurrection of that body, with which, henceforth, it would be reunited and dwell eternally. To quote Wiedermann again, "The *Ka* could live without the body, but the body could not live without the *Ka*. . . . . it was material in just the same was as the body itself." Also, it would seem that in certain ways it was superior to and more powerful than the body, since the Egyptian monarchs are often represented as making offerings to their own *Kas* as though these were gods. Again, in the story of "Setna and the Magic Book," translated by Maspero and by Mr. Flinders Petrie in his *Egyptian Tales*, the *Ka* plays a very distinct part of its own. Thus the husband is buried at Memphis and the wife in Koptos, yet the *Ka* of the wife goes to live in her husband's tomb hundreds of miles away, and converses with the prince who comes to steal the magic book.

Although I know no actual precedent for it, in the case of a particularly powerful Double, such as was given in this romance to Queen Neter-Tua by her spiritual father, Amen, the greatest of the Egyptian gods, it seems, therefore, legitimate to suppose that, in order to save her from the abomination of a forced marriage with her uncle and her father's murderer, the *Ka* would be allowed to anticipate matters a little, and to play the part recorded in these pages.

It must not be understood, however, that the fact of marriage with an uncle would have shocked the Egyptian mind, since these people, and especially their Royal Houses, made a habit of wedding their own brothers and sisters, as in this tale Mermes wed his half sister Asti.

I may add that there is authority for the magic waxen image which the sorcerer Kaku and his accomplice used to bewitch Pharaoh. In the days of Rameses III., over three thousand years ago, a plot was made to murder the king in pursuance of which such images were used. "Gods of wax. . . . for enfeebling the limbs of people," which were "great crimes of death, the great abomination of the land." Also a certain "magic roll" was brought into play which enabled its user to "employ the magic powers of the gods."

Still, the end of these wizards was not encouraging to others, for they were found guilty and obliged to take their own lives.

But even if I am held to have stretched the prerogative of the *Ka*, or of the waxen image which, by the way, has survived almost to our own time, and in West Africa, as a fetish, is still pierced with pins or nails, I can urge in excuse that I have tried, so far as a modern may, to reproduce something of the atmosphere and colour of Old Egypt, as it has appeared to a traveller in that country and a student of its records. If Neter-Tua never sat upon its throne, at least another daughter of Amen, a mighty Queen, Hatshepu, wore the crown of the Upper and the Lower Lands, and sent her embassies to search out the mysteries of Punt. Of romance also, in high places, there must have been abundance, though the short-cut records of the religious texts of the priests do not trouble themselves with such matters.

At any rate, so believing, in the hope that it may interest readers of to-day, I have ventured to discover and present one such romance, whereof the motive, we may be sure, is more ancient, by far, than the old Egyptians, namely, the triumph of true love over great difficulties and dangers. It is pleasant to dream that the gods are on the side of such lovers, and deign for their sakes to work the miracles in which for thousands of years mankind has believed, although the scientist tells us that they do not happen.

How large a part marvel and magic of the most terrible and exalted kind played in the life of Old Egypt and of the nations with which she fought and traded, we need go no further than the Book of Exodus to learn. Also all her history is full of it, since among the Egyptians it was an article of faith that the Divinity, which they worshipped under so many names and symbols, made use of such mysterious means to influence or direct the affairs of men and bring about the accomplishment of Its decrees.

H. R. H.

Chapter 1

The Plot of Abi

It was evening in Egypt, thousands of years ago, when the Prince Abi, governor of Memphis and of great territories in the Delta, made fast his ship of state to a quay beneath the outermost walls of the mighty city of Uast or Thebes, which we moderns know as Luxor and Karnac on the Nile. Abi, a large man, very dark of skin, for his mother was one of the hated Hyksos barbarians who once had usurped the throne of Egypt, sat upon the deck of his ship and stared at the setting sun which for a few moments seemed to rest, a round ball of fire, upon the bare and rugged mountains, that ring round the Tombs of the Kings.

He was angry, as the slave-women, who stood on either side fanning him, could see well enough by the scowl on his coarse face and the fire in his large black eyes. Presently they felt it also, for one of them, staring at the temples and palaces of the wonderful city made glorious by the light of the setting sun, that city of which she had heard so often, touched his head with the feathers of her fan. Thereon, as though glad of an excuse to express his ill-humour, Abi sprang up and boxed her ears so heavily that the poor girl fell to the deck.

"Awkward cat," he cried, "do that again and you shall be flogged until your robe sticks to your back!"

"Pardon, mighty Lord," she said, beginning to weep, "it was an accident; the wind caught my fan."

"So the rod shall catch your skin, if you are not more careful, Merytra. Stop that snivelling and go send Kaku the Astrologer here. Go, both, I weary of the sight of your ugly faces."

The girl rose, and with her fellow slave ran swiftly to the ladder that led to the waist of the ship.

"He called me a cat," Merytra hissed through her white teeth to her companion. "Well, if so, Sekhet the cat-headed is my godmother, and she is the Lady of Vengeance."

"Yes," answered the other, "and he said that we were both ugly—we, whom every lord who comes near the Court admires so much! Oh! I wish a holy crocodile would eat him, black pig!"

"Then why don't they buy us? Abi would sell his daughters, much more his fan-bearers—at a price."

"Because they hope to get us for nothing, my dear, and what is more, if I can manage it one of them shall, for I am tired of this life. Have your fling while you can, I say. Who knows at which corner Osiris, Lord of Death, is waiting."

"Hush!" whispered Merytra, "there is that knave of an astrologer, and he looks cross, too."

Then, hand in hand, they went to this lean and learned man and humbly bowed themselves before him.

"Master of the Stars," said Merytra, "we have a message for you. No, do not look at my cheek, please, the marks are not magical, only those of the divine fingers of the glorious hand of the most exalted Prince Abi, son of the Pharaoh happily ruling in Osiris, etc., etc., etc., of the right, royal blood of Egypt—that is on one side, and on the other of a divine lady whom Khem the Spirit, or Ptah the Creator, thought fit to dip in a vat of black dye."

"Hem!" said Kaku glancing nervously over his shoulder. Then, seeing that there was no one near, he added, "you had better be careful what you say, my dear. The royal Abi does not like to hear the colour of his late mother defined so closely. But why did he slap your face?"

She told him.

"Well," he answered, "if I had been in his place I would rather have kissed it, for it is pretty, decidedly pretty," and this learned man forgot himself so far as to wink at Merytra.

"There, Sister," said the girl, "I always told you that rough shells have sweet nuts inside of them. Thank you for your compliment, Master of learning. Will you tell us our fortune for nothing?"

"Yes, yes," he answered; "at least the fee I want will cost you nothing. Now stop this nonsense," he added, anxiously, "I gather that *he* is cross."

"I never saw him crosser, Kaku. I am glad it is you who reads the stars, not I. Listen!"

As he spoke an angry roar reached them from the high deck above.

"Where is that accursed astrologer?" said the roar.

"There, what did I tell you? Oh! never mind the rest of the papers, go at once. Your robe is full of rolls as it is."

"Yes," answered Kaku as he ran to the ladder, "but the question is, how will he like what is in the rolls?"

"The gods be with you!" cried one of the girls after him, "you will need them all."

"And if you get back alive, don't forget your promise about the fortunes," said the other.

A minute later this searcher of the heavens, a tall, hook-nosed man, was prostrating himself before Abi in his pavilion on the upper deck, so low that his Syrian-shaped cap fell from his bald head.

"Why were you so long in coming?" asked Abi.

"Because your slaves could not find me, royal Son of the Sun. I was at work in my cabin."

"Indeed, I thought I heard them giggling with you down there. What did you call me? Royal Son of the Sun? That is Pharaoh's name! Have the stars shown you——?" and he looked at him eagerly.

"No, Prince, not exactly that. I did not think it needful to search them on a matter which seems established, more or less."

"More or less," answered Abi gloomily. "What do you mean by your 'more or less'? Here am I at the turning-point of my fortunes, not knowing whether I am to be Pharaoh of the Upper and Lower Lands, or only the petty lord of a city and a few provinces in the Delta, and you satisfy my hunger for the truth with an empty dish of 'more or less.' Man, what do you mean?"

"If your Majesty will be pleased to tell his servant exactly what you desire to know, perhaps I may be able to answer the question," replied Kaku humbly.

"Majesty! Well, I desire to know by what warrant you call me 'Majesty,' who am only Prince of Memphis. Did the stars give it to you? Have you obeyed me and asked them of the future?"

"Certainly, certainly. How could I disobey? I observed them all last night, and have been working out the results till this moment; indeed, they are not yet finished. Question and I will answer."

"You will answer, yes, but what will you answer? Not the truth, I fancy, because you are a coward, though if anyone can read the truth, it is you. Man," he added fiercely, "if you dare to lie to me I will cut your head off and take it to Pharaoh as a traitor's; and your body shall lie, not in that fine tomb which you have made, but in the belly of a crocodile whence there is no resurrection. Do you understand? Then let us come to the point. Look, the sun sets there behind the Tombs of Kings, where the departed Pharaohs of Egypt take their rest till the Day of Awakening. It is a bad omen for me, I know, who wished to reach this city in the morning when Ra was in the House of Life, the East, and not in the House of Death, the West; but that accursed wind sent by Typhon, held me back and I could not. Well, let us begin at the end which must come after all. Tell me, you reader of the heavens, shall I sleep at last in that valley?"

"I think so, Prince; at least, so says your planet. Look, yonder, it springs to life above you," and he pointed to an orb that appeared at the topmost edge of the red glow of the sunset.

"You are keeping something back from me," said Abi, searching Kaku's face with his fierce eyes. "Shall I sleep in the tomb of Pharaoh, in my own everlasting house that I shall have made ready to receive me?"

"Son of Ra, I cannot say," answered the astrologer. "Divine One, I will be frank with you. Though you be wrath, yet will I tell you the truth as you command me. An evil influence is at work in your House of Life. Another star crosses and re-crosses your path, and though for a long time you seem to swallow it up, yet at the last it eclipses you—it and one that goes with it."

"What star?" asked Abi hoarsely, "Pharaoh's?"

"Nay, Prince, the star of Amen."

"Amen! What Amen?"

"Amen the god, Prince, the mighty father of the gods."

"Amen the god," repeated Abi in an awed voice. "How can a man fight against a god?"

"Say rather against two gods, for with the star of Amen goes the star of Hathor, Queen of Love. Not for many periods of thousands of years have they been together, but now they draw near to each other, and so will remain for all your life. Look," and Kaku pointed to the Eastern horizon where a faint rosy glow still lingered reflected from the western sky.

As they watched this glow melted, and there in the pure heavens, lying just where it met the distant land, seeming to rest upon the land, indeed, appeared a bright and beautiful star, and so close to it that, to the eye, they almost touched, a twin star. For a few minutes only were they seen; then they vanished beneath the line of the horizon.

"The morning star of Amen, and with it the star of Hathor," said the astrologer.

"Well, Fool, what of it?" exclaimed Abi. "They are far enough from my star; moreover, it is they that sink, not I, who ride higher every moment."

"Aye, Prince, but in a year to come they will certainly eclipse that star of yours. Prince, Amen and Hathor are against you. Look, I will show you their journeyings on this scroll and you shall see where they eat you up yonder, yes, yonder over the Valley of dead Kings, though twenty years and more must go by ere then, and take this for your comfort, during those years you shine alone," and he began to unfold a papyrus roll.

Abi snatched it from him, crumpled it up and threw it in his face.

"You cheat!" he said. "Do you think to frighten me with this nonsense about stars? Here is my star," and he drew the short sword at his side and shook it over the head of the trembling Kaku. "This sharp bronze is the star I follow, and be careful lest it should eclipse *you*, you father of lies."

"I have told the truth as I see it," answered the poor astrologer with some dignity, "but if you wish, O Prince, that in the future I should indeed prophesy pleasant things to you, why, it can be done easily enough. Moreover, it seems to me that this horoscope of yours is not so evil, seeing that it gives to you over twenty years of life and power, more by far than most men can expect—at your age. If after that come troubles and the end, what of it?"

"That is so," replied Abi mollified. "It was my ill-temper, everything has gone cross to-day. Well, a gold cup, my own, shall pay the price of it. Bear me no ill-will, I pray you, learned scribe, and above all tell me no falsehood as the message of the stars you serve. It is the truth I seek, the truth. If only she may be seen, and clasped, I care not how ill-favoured is her face."

Rejoicing at the turn which things had taken, and especially at the promise of the priceless cup which he had long coveted, Kaku bowed obsequiously. He picked up his crumpled roll and was about to retire when through the gloom of the falling night, some men mounted upon asses were seen riding over the mud flats that border the Nile at this spot, towards that bank where the ship was moored.

"The captain of my guard," said Abi, who saw the starlight gleam upon a bronze helmet, "who brings me Pharaoh's answer. Nay, go not, bide and hear it, Kaku, and give us your counsel on it, your true counsel."

So the astrologer stood aside and waited, till presently the captain appeared saluting.

"What says Pharaoh, my brother?" asked the Prince.

"Lord, he says that he will receive you, though as he did not send for you, he thinks that you can scarcely come upon any necessary errand, as he has heard long ago of your victory over the desert-dwelling barbarians, and does not want the offering of the salted heads of their officers which you bring to him."

"Good," said Abi contemptuously. "The divine Pharaoh was ever a woman in such matters, as in others. Let him be thankful that he has generals who know how to make war and to cut off the heads of his enemies in defence of the kingdom. We will wait upon him to-morrow."

"Lord," added the captain, "that is not all Pharaoh's message. He says that it has been reported to him that you are accompanied by a guard of three hundred soldiers. These soldiers he refuses to allow within the gates. He directs that you shall appear before his Majesty attended by five persons only."

"Indeed," answered Abi with a scornful laugh. "Does Pharaoh fear, then, lest I should capture him and his armies and the great city with three hundred soldiers?"

"No, Prince," answered the captain bluntly; "but I think he fears lest you should kill him and declare yourself Pharaoh as next in blood."

"Ah!" said Abi, "as next of blood. Then I suppose that there are still no children at the Court?"

"None, O Prince. I saw Ahura, the royal wife, the Lady of the Two Lands, that fairest of women, and other lesser wives and beautiful slave girls without number, but never a one of them had an infant on her breast or at her knee. Pharaoh remains childless."

"Ah!" said Abi again. Then he walked forward out of the pavilion whereof the curtains were drawn back, and stood a while upon the prow of the vessel.

By now night had fallen, and the great moon, rising from the earth as it were, poured her flood of silver light over the desert, the mountains, the limitless city of Thebes, and the wide rippling bosom of the Nile. The pylons and obelisks, glittering with copper and with gold, towered to the tender sky. In the window places of palaces and of ten thousand homes lamps shone like stars. From gardens, streets and the courts of temples floated the faint sound of singing and of music, while on the great embattled walls the watchmen called the hour from post to post.

It was a wondrous scene, and the heart of Abi swelled as he gazed upon it. What wealth lay yonder, and what power. There was the glorious house of his brother, Pharaoh, the god in human form who for all his godship had never a child to follow after him when he ascended to Osiris, as he who was sickly probably must do before so very long.

Yes, but before then a miracle might happen; in this way or in that a successor to the throne might be found and acknowledged, for were not Pharaoh and his House beloved by all the priests of Amen, and by the people, and was not he, Abi, feared and disliked because he was fierce, and the hated savage blood flowed in his veins? Oh! what evil god had put it in his father's heart to give him a princess of the Hyksos for a mother, the Hyksos, whom the Egyptians loathed, when he had the fairest women of the world from whom to choose? Well, it was done and could not be undone, though because of it he might lose his heritage of the greatest throne in all the earth. Also was it not to this fierce Hyksos blood that he owed his strength and vigour?

Why should he wait? Why should he not set his fortune on a cast? He had three hundred soldiers with him, picked men and brave, children of the sea and the desert, sworn to his House and interests. It was a time of festival, those gates were ill-guarded. Why should he not force them at the dead of night, make his way to the palace, cause Pharaoh to be gathered to his fathers, and at the dawn discover himself seated upon Pharaoh's throne? At the thought of it Abi's heart leapt in his breast, his wide nostrils spread themselves, and he erected his strong head as though already he felt upon it the weight of the double crown. Then he turned and walked back to the pavilion.

"I am minded to strike a blow," he said. "Say now, my officer, would you and the soldiers follow me into the heart of yonder city to-night to win a throne—or a grave? If it were the first, you should be the general of all my army, and you, astrologer, should become vizier, yes, after Pharaoh you two should be the greatest men in all the land."

They looked at him and gasped.

"A venturesome deed, Prince," said the captain at length; "yet with such a prize to win I think that I would dare it, though for the soldiers I cannot speak. First they must be told what is on foot, and out of so many, how know we that the heart of one or more would not fail? A word from a traitor and before this time to-morrow the embalmers, or the jackals, would be busy."

Abi heard and looked from him to his companion.

"Prince," said Kaku, "put such thoughts from you. Bury them deep. Let them rise no more. In the heavens I read something of this business, but then I did not understand, but now I see the black depths of hell opening beneath our feet. Yes, hell would be our home if we dared to lift hand against the divine person of the Pharaoh. I say that the gods themselves would fight against us. Let it be, Prince, let it be, and you shall have many years of rule, who, if you strike now, will win nothing but a crown of shame, a nameless grave, and the everlasting torment of the damned."

As he spoke Abi considered the man's face and saw that all craft had left it. This was no charlatan that spoke to him, but one in earnest who believed what he said.

"So be it," he answered. "I accept your judgment, and will wait upon my fortune. Moreover, you are both right, the thing is too dangerous, and evil often falls on the heads of those who shoot arrows at a god, especially if they have not enough arrows. Let Pharaoh live on while I make ready. Perhaps to-morrow I may work upon him to name me his heir."

The astrologer sighed in relief, nor did the captain seem disappointed.

"My head feels firmer on my shoulders than it did just now," he said: "and doubtless there are times when wisdom is better than valour. Sleep well, Prince; Pharaoh will receive you to-morrow two hours after sunrise. Have we your leave to retire?"

"If I were wise," said Abi, fingering the hilt of his sword as he spoke, "you would both of you retire for ever who know all the secret of my heart, and with a whisper could bring doom upon me."

Now the pair looked at each other with frightened eyes, and, like his master, the captain began to play with his sword.

"Life is sweet to all men, Prince," he said significantly, "and we have never given you cause to doubt us."

"No," answered Abi, "had it been otherwise I should have struck first and spoken afterwards. Only you must swear by the oath which may not be broken that in life or death no word of this shall pass your lips."

So they swore, both of them, by the holy name of Osiris, the judge and the redeemer.

"Captain," said Abi, "you have served me well. Your pay is doubled, and I confirm the promise that I made to you—should I ever rule yonder you shall be my general."

While the soldier bowed his thanks, the prince said to Kaku,

"Master of the stars, my gold cup is yours. Is there aught else of mine that you desire?"

"That slave," answered the learned man, "Merytra, whose ears you boxed just now——"

"How do you know that I boxed her ears?" asked Abi quickly. "Did the stars tell you that also? Well, I am tired of the sly hussy—take her. Soon I think she will box yours."

But when Kaku sought Merytra to tell her the glad tidings that she was his, he could not find her.

Merytra had disappeared.

Chapter 2

The Promise of the God

It was morning at Thebes, and the great city glowed in the rays of the new-risen sun. In a royal barge sat Abi the prince, splendidly apparelled, and with him Kaku, his astrologer, his captain of the guard and three other of his officers, while in a second barge followed slaves who escorted two chiefs and some fair women captured in war, also the chests of salted heads and hands, offerings to Pharaoh.

The white-robed rowers bent to their oars, and the swift boat shot forward up the Nile through a double line of ships of war, all of them crowded with soldiers. Abi looked at these ships which Pharaoh had gathered there to meet him, and thought to himself that Kaku had given wise counsel when he prayed him to attempt no rash deed, for against such surprises clearly Pharaoh was well prepared. He thought it again when on reaching the quay of cut stones he saw foot and horse-men marshalled there in companies and squadrons, and on the walls above hundreds of other men, all armed, for now he saw what would have happened to him, if with his little desperate band he had tried to pierce that iron ring of watching soldiers.

At the steps generals met him in their mail and priests in their full robes, bowing and doing him honour. Thus royally escorted, Abi passed through the open gates and the pylons of the splendid temple dedicated to the Trinity of Thebes, "the House of Amen in the Southern Apt," where gay banners fluttered from the pointed masts, up the long street bordered with tall houses set in their gardens, till he came to the palace wall. Here more guards rolled back the brazen gates which in his folly of a few hours gone he had thought that he could force, and through the avenues of blooming trees he was led to the great pillared hall of audience.

After the brightness without, that hall seemed almost dark, only a ray of sunshine flowing from an unshuttered space in the clerestory above, fell full on the end of it, and revealed the crowned Pharaoh and his queen seated in state upon their thrones of ivory and gold. Gathered round and about him also were scribes and councillors and captains, and beyond these other queens in their carved chairs and attended, each of them, by beautiful women of the household in their gala dress. Moreover, behind the thrones, and at intervals between the columns, stood the famous Nubian guard of two hundred men, the servants of the body of Pharaoh as they were called, each of them chosen for faithfulness and courage.

The centre of all this magnificence was Pharaoh, on him the sunlight beat, to him every eye was turned, and where his glance fell there heads bowed and knees were bent. A small thin man of about forty years of age with a puckered, kindly and anxious face, and a brow that seemed to sink beneath the weight of the double crown that, save for its royal snake-crest of hollow gold, was after all but of linen, a man with thin, nervous hands which played amongst the embroideries of his golden robe—such was Pharaoh, the mightiest monarch in the world, the ruler whom millions that had never seen him worshipped as a god.

Abi, the burly framed, thick-lipped, dark-skinned, round-eyed Abi, born of the same father, stared at him with wonderment, for years had passed since last they met, and in the palace when they were children a gulf had been set between the offspring of a royal mother and the child of a Hyksos concubine taken into the Household for reasons of state. In his vigour, and the might of his manhood, he stared at this weakling, the son of a brother and a sister, and the grandson of a brother and a sister. Yet there was something in that gentle eye, an essence of inherited royalty, before which his rude nature bowed. The body might be contemptible, but within it dwelt the proud spirit of the descendant of a hundred kings.

Abi advanced to the steps of the throne and knelt there, till after a little pause Pharaoh stretched out the sceptre in his hand for him to kiss. Then he spoke in his light, quick voice.

"Welcome, Prince and my brother," he said. "We quarrelled long ago, did we not, and many years have passed since we met, but Time heals all wounds and—welcome, son of my father. I need not ask if you are well," and he glanced enviously at the great-framed man who knelt before him.

"Hail to your divine Majesty!" answered Abi in his deep voice. "Health and strength be with you, Holder of the Scourge of Osiris, Wearer of the Feathers of Amen, Mortal crowned with the glory of Ra."

"I thank you, Prince," answered Pharaoh gently, "and that health and strength I need, who fear that I shall only find them when I have yielded up the Scourge of Osiris whereof you speak to him who lent it me. But enough of myself. Let us to business, afterwards we will talk of such matters together. Why have you left your government at Memphis without leave asked, to visit me here in my City of the Gates?"

"Be not wrath with me," answered Abi humbly. "A while ago, in obedience to your divine command, I attacked the barbarians who threatened your dominions in the desert. Like Menthu, god of war, I fell upon them. I took them by surprise, I smote them, thousands of them bit the dust before me. Two of their kings I captured with their women—they wait without, to be slain by your Majesty. I bring with me the heads of a hundred of their captains and the hands of five hundred of their soldiers, in earnest of the truth of my word. Let them be spread out before you. I report to your divine Majesty that those barbarians are no more, that for a generation, at least, I have made the land safe to your uttermost dominions in the north. Suffer that the heads and the hands be brought in and counted out before your Majesty, that the smell of them may rise like incense to your divine nostrils."

"No, no," said Pharaoh, "my officers shall count them without, for I love not such sights of death, and I take your word for the number. What payment do you ask for this service, my brother, for with great gifts would I reward you, who have done so well for me and Egypt?"

Before he answered Abi looked at the beautiful queen, Ahura, who sat at Pharaoh's side, and at the other royal consorts and women.

"Your Majesty," he said, "I see here many wives and ladies, but royal children I do not see. Grant—for doubtless they are in their own chambers—grant, O Pharaoh, that they may be led hither that my eyes may feed upon their loveliness, and that I may tell of them, each of them, to their cousins who await me at Memphis."

At these words a flush as of shame spread itself over the lovely face of Ahura, the royal wife, the Lady of the Two Lands; while the women turned their heads away whispering to each other bitterly, for the insult hurt them. Only Pharaoh set his pale face and answered with dignity.

"Prince Abi, to affront those whom the gods have smitten, be they kings or peasants, is an unworthy deed which the gods will not forget. You know well that I have no children. Why then do you ask me to show you their loveliness?"

"I had heard rumours, O Pharaoh," answered the Prince, "no more. Indeed, I did not believe them, for where there are so many wives I was certain that there would be some mothers. Therefore I asked to be sure before I proffered a petition which now I will make to you not for my own sake but for Egypt's and yours, O Pharaoh. Have I your leave to speak here in public?"

"Speak on," said Pharaoh sternly. "Let aught that is for the welfare of Egypt be heard by Egypt."

"Your Majesty has told me," replied Abi bowing, "that the gods, being wrath, have denied you children. Not so much as one girl of your blood have they given to you to fill your throne after you when in due season it pleases you to depart to Osiris. Were it otherwise, were there even but a single woman-child of your divine race, I would say nothing, I would be silent as the grave. But so it is, and though your queens be fair and many, so it would seem that it must remain, since the ears of the gods having been deaf to your pleadings for so long, although you have built them glorious temples and made them offerings without count, will scarcely now be opened. Even Amen your father, Amen, whose name you bear, will perform no miracle for you, O Pharaoh, who are so great that he has decreed that you shall shine alone like the full moon at night, not sharing your glory with a single star."

Now Ahura the Queen, who all this while had been listening intently, spoke for the first time in a quick angry voice, saying,

"How know you that, Prince of Memphis? Sometimes the gods relent and that which they have withheld for a space, they give. My lord lives, and I live, and a child of his may yet fill the throne of Egypt."

"It may be so, O Queen," said Abi bowing, "and for my part I pray that it will be so, for who am I that I should know the purpose of the kings of heaven? If but one girl be born of you and Pharaoh, then I take back my words and give to you that title which for many years has been written falsely upon your thrones and monuments, the title of Royal Mother."

Now Ahura would have answered again, for this sneering taunt stung her to the quick. But Pharaoh laid his hand upon her knee and said, "Continue, Prince and brother. We have heard from you that which we already know too well—that I am childless. Tell us what we do not know, the desire of your heart which lies hid beneath all these words."

"Pharaoh, it is this—I am of your holy blood, sprung of the same divine father——"

"But of a mother who was not divine," broke in Ahura; "of a mother taken from a race that has brought many a curse upon Khem, as any mirror will show you, Prince of Memphis."

"Pharaoh," went on Abi without heeding her, "you grow weak;

heaven desires you, the earth melts beneath you. In the north and in the south many dangers threaten Egypt. Should you die suddenly without an heir, barbarians will flow in from the north and from the south, and the great ones of the land will struggle for your place. Pharaoh, I am a warrior; I am built strong; my children are many; my house is built upon a rock; the army trusts me; the millions of the people love me. Take me then to rule with you and in the hearing of all the earth name me and my sons as your successors, so that our royal race may continue for generation after generation. So shall you end your days in peace and hope. I have spoken."

Now, as the meaning of this bold request sank into their hearts, all the court there gathered gasped and whispered, while the Queen Ahura in her anger crushed the lotus flower which she held in her hand and cast it to the floor. Only Pharaoh sat still and silent, his head bent and his eyes shut as though in prayer. For a minute or more he sat thus, and when he lifted his pale, pure face, there was a smile upon it.

"Abi, my brother," he said in his gentle voice, "listen to me. There are those who filled this throne before me, who on hearing such words would have pointed to you with their sceptres, whereon, Abi, those lips of yours would have grown still for ever, and you and your name and the names of all your House would have been blotted out by death. But, Abi, you were ever bold, and I forgive you for laying open the thoughts of your heart to me. Still, Abi, you have not told us all of them. You have not told us, for instance," he went on slowly, and in the midst of an intense silence, "that but last night you debated whether it would not be possible with that guard of yours to break into my palace and put me to the sword and name yourself Pharaoh—by right of blood, Abi; yes, by right of blood—my blood shed by you, my brother."

As these words left the royal lips a tumult arose in the hall, the women and the great officers sprang up, the captains stepped forward drawing their swords to avenge so horrible a sacrilege. But Pharaoh waved his sceptre, and they were still, only Abi cried in a great voice.

"Who has dared to whisper a lie so monstrous?" And he glared first at Kaku and then at the captain of his guard who stood behind him, and choked in wrath, or fear, or both.

"Suspect not your officers, Prince," went on the Pharaoh, still smiling, "for on my royal word they are innocent. Yet, Abi, a pavilion set upon the deck of a ship is no good place to plot the death of kings. Pharaoh has many spies, also, at times, the gods, to whom as you say he is so near, whisper tidings to him in his sleep. Suspect not your officers, Abi, although I think that to yonder Master of the Stars who stands behind you, I should be grateful, since, had you attempted to execute this madness, but for him I might have been forced to kill you, Abi, as one kills a snake that creeps beneath his mat. Astrologer, you shall have a gift from me, for you are a wise man. It may take the place, perhaps, of one that you have lost; was it not a certain woman slave whom your master gave to you last night—after he had punished her for no fault?"

Kaku prostrated himself before the glory of Pharaoh, understanding at last that it was the lost girl Merytra who had overheard and betrayed them. But heeding him no more, his Majesty went on.

"Abi, Prince and brother, I forgive you a deed that you purposed but did not attempt. May the gods and the spirits of our fathers forgive you also, if they will. Now as to your demand. You are my only living brother, and therefore I will weigh it. Perchance, if I should die without issue, although you are not all royal, although there flows in your veins a blood that Egypt hates; although you could plot the murder of your lord and king, it may be well that when I am gone you should fill my place, for you are brave and of the ancient race on one side, if base-born on the other. But I am not yet dead, and children may still come to me. Abi, will you be a prisoner until Osiris calls me, or will you swear an oath?"

"I will swear an oath," answered the Prince hoarsely, for he knew his shame and danger.

"Then kneel here, and by the dreadful Name swear that you will lift no hand and plot no plot against me. Swear that if a child, male or female, should be given to me, you will serve such a child truly as your lord and lawful Pharaoh. In the presence of all this company, swear, knowing that if you break the oath in letter or in spirit, then all the gods of Egypt shall pour their curse upon your head in life, and in death shall give you over to the everlasting torments of the damned."

So, having little choice, Abi swore by the Name and kissed the sceptre in token of his oath.

****

It was night. Dark and solemn was the innermost shrine of the vast temple, the "House of Amen in the Northern Apt," which we call Karnak, the very holy of holies where, fashioned of stone, and with the feathered crown upon his head, stood the statue of Amen-ra, father of the gods. Here, where none but the high-priest and the royalties of Egypt might enter, Pharaoh and his wife Ahura, wrapped in brown cloaks like common folk, knelt at the feet of the god and prayed. With tears and supplications did they pray that a child might be given to them.

There in the sacred place, lit only by a single lamp which burned from age to age, they told the story of their grief, whilst high above them the cold, calm countenance of the god seemed to stare through the gloom, as for a thousand years, in joy or sorrow, it had stared at those that went before them. They told of the mocking words of Abi who had demanded to see their children, the children that were not; they told of their terror of the people who demanded that an heir should be declared; they told of the doom that threatened their ancient house, which from Pharaoh to Pharaoh, all of one blood, for generations had worshipped in this place. They promised gifts and offerings, stately temples and wide lands, if only their desire might be fulfilled.

"Let me no more be made a mock among men," cried the beautiful queen, beating her forehead upon the stone feet of the god. "Let me bear a child to fill the seat of my lord the King, and then if thou wilt, take my life in payment."

But the god made no answer, and wearied out at length they rose and departed. At the door of the sanctuary they found the high-priest awaiting them, a wizened, aged man.

"The god gave no sign, O High-priest," said Pharaoh sadly; "no voice spoke to us."

The old priest looked at the weeping queen, and a light of pity crept into his eyes.

"To me, watching without," he said, "a voice seemed to speak, though what it said I may not reveal. Go to your palace now, O Pharaoh, and O Queen Ahura, and take your rest side by side. I think that in your sleep a sign will come to you, for Amen is pitiful, and loves his children who love him. According to that sign so speak to the Prince Abi, speak without fear or doubt, since for good or ill it shall be fulfilled."

Then like shadows, hand in hand, this royal pair glided down the vast, pillared halls till at the pylon gates, which were opened for them, they found their litters, and were borne along the great avenue of ram-headed sphinxes back to a secret door in the palace wall.

****

It was past midnight. Deep darkness and heavy silence lay upon Thebes, broken only by dogs howling at the stars and the occasional challenge of soldiers on the walls. Side by side in their golden bed the wearied Pharaoh and his queen slept heavily. Presently Ahura woke. She started up in the bed; she stared at the darkness about her with frightened eyes; she stretched out her hand and clasping Pharaoh by the arm, whispered in a thrilling voice,

"Awake, awake! I have that which I must tell you."

Pharaoh roused himself, for there was something in Ahura's voice which swept away the veils of sleep.

"What has chanced, Ahura?" he asked.

"O Pharaoh, I have dreamed a dream, if indeed it were but a dream. It seemed to me that the darkness opened, and that standing in the darkness I saw a Glory which had neither shape nor form. Yet a voice spoke from the Glory, a low, sweet voice: 'Queen Ahura, my daughter,' it said, 'I am that Spirit to whom thou and thy husband did pray this night in the sanctuary of my temple. It seemed to both of you that your prayers remained unheard, yet it was not so, as my priest knew well. Queen Ahura, thou and Pharaoh thy husband have put your trust in me these many years, and not in vain. A daughter shall be given to thee and Pharaoh, and my Spirit shall be in that child. She shall be beautiful and glorious as no woman was before her, for I clothe her with health and power and wisdom. She shall rule over the Northern and the Southern Lands; yea, for many years the double crown shall rest upon her brow, and no king that went before her, and no king that follows after her, shall be more great in Egypt. Troubles and dangers shall threaten her, but the Spirit that I give to her shall protect her in them all, and she shall tread her enemy beneath her feet. A royal lover shall come to her also, and she shall rejoice in his love and from it shall spring many kings and princes. Neter-Tua, Morning Star, shall be her name, and high-priestess of Amen—no less—shall be her office, for she is my child whom I have taken from heaven and sent down to earth; the child that I have given to Pharaoh and to thee, and I love her and appoint the good goddesses to be her companions, and command Osiris to receive her at the last.

"'Behold, in token of these things I lay my symbol on thy breast, and on her breast also shall that symbol be. When I lift it from thee and thou dost open thy eyes, then awaken Pharaoh at thy side and let these my words be written in a roll, so that none of them are forgotten.'

"Then, O Pharaoh," went on Ahura, "from the Glory there came forth a hand, and in the hand was the Symbol of Life shining as though with fire, and the hand laid it upon my breast and it burned me as though with fire, and I awoke and lo! darkness was all about me, nothing but darkness, and at my side I heard you sleeping."

Now when Pharaoh had listened to this dream, he kissed the queen and blessed her because of its good omen, and clapped his hands to summon the women of honour who slept without. They ran in bearing lights, and by the lights he saw that beneath the throat of the Queen upon her fair skin, appeared a red mark, and the shape of it was the shape of the Sign of Life; yes, there was the loop, and beneath the loop the cross.

Then Pharaoh commanded that the chief of his scribes should come to him with papyrus and writing tools, and that the high-priest of Amen should be brought swiftly from the temple. So the scribe came to the bed-chamber of the King, and in the presence of the high-priest all the words of Amen were written down, not one of them was omitted, and Pharaoh and the Queen signed the roll, and the high-priest witnessed it and, copies having been made, bore it away to hide it in the secret treasury of Amen. But the mark of the Cross of Life remained upon the breast of the Queen Ahura till the day that she died.

****

Now in the morning Pharaoh summoned his Court and commanded that the Prince Abi should be brought before him. So the Prince came and Pharaoh addressed him kindly.

"Son of my father," he said, "I have considered your request that I should take you to rule with me on the throne of Egypt, and name you and your sons to be Pharaohs after me, and it is refused. Know that it has been revealed to me and to the royal wife, Ahura, by the greatest of the gods, that a daughter shall be born to us in due season, who shall be called Morning Star of Amen, and that she and her seed shall be Pharaohs after me. Therefore rejoice with us and return to your government, Prince Abi, and be happy in our love, and in the goods and greatness that the gods have given you."

Now Abi shook with anger, for he thought that all this tale was a trick and a snare. But knowing that his peril was great there in the hand of Pharaoh, he answered only that when this Morning Star arose, his star should do it reverence, though as the words passed his lips he remembered the prophecy of his astrologer Kaku, that the Morning Star of Amen should blot out that star of his.

"You think that I speak falsely, Prince Abi, yes, that I stain my lips with lies," said Pharaoh with indignation. "Well, I forgive you this also. Go hence and await the issue and know by this sign that truth is in my heart. When the Princess Neter-Tua is born, upon her breast shall be seen the symbol of the Sign of Life. Depart now, lest I grow angry. The gifts I have promised shall follow you to Memphis."

So Abi returned to the white-walled city of Memphis and sat there sullenly, putting it about that a plot was on foot to deprive him of his heritage. But Kaku shook his head, saying in secret that the Star, Neter-Tua, would arise, for so it was decreed by Amen, father of the gods.

Chapter 3

Rames, the Princess and the Crocodile

At the appointed time to Ahura, the royal wife, was born a child, a girl with a fresh and lovely face and waving hair and eyes that from the first were blue like the summer sky at even. Also on her breast was a mole of the length of a finger nail, which mole was shaped like the holy Sign of Life.

Now Pharaoh and his house and the priests in every temple, and indeed all Egypt went mad with joy, though there were many who in secret mourned over the sex of the infant, whispering that a man and not a woman should wear the Double Crown. But in public they said nothing, since the story of this child had gone abroad and folk declared that it was sent by the gods, and divine, and that the goddesses, Isis, Nepthys, and Hathor, with Khemu, the Maker of Mankind, were seen in the birth chamber, glowing like gold. Also Pharaoh issued a decree that wherever the name of the Queen Ahura was graven in all the land, to it should be added the title "By the will of Amen, Mother of his Morning Star," and that a new hall should be built in the temple of Amen in the Northern Apt, and all about it carved the story of the coming of Prince Abi and of the vision of the Queen.

But Ahura never lived to see this glorious place, since from the hour of her daughter's birth she began to sink. On the fourteenth day, the day of purification, she bade the nurse bring the beautiful babe, and gazed at it long and blessed it, and spoke with the *Ka* or Double of the child, which she said she saw lying on her arm beside it, bidding that *Ka* protect it well through the dangers of life and death until the hour of resurrection. Then she said that she heard Amen calling to her to pay the price which she had promised for the gift of the divine child, the price of her own life, and smiled upon Pharaoh her husband, and died happily with a radiant face.

Now joy was turned to mourning, and during all the days of embalming Egypt wept for Ahura until, at length, the time came when her body was rowed across the Nile to the splendid tomb which she had made ready in the Valley of the Queens, causing masons and artists to labour at it without cease. For Ahura knew from the day of her vision that she was doomed to die, and remembered that the tombs of the dead remain as the live hands leave them, since few waste gold and toil upon the eternal house of one who is dead.

So Ahura was buried with great pomp and all her jewels, and Pharaoh, who mourned her truly, made splendid offerings in the chapel of her tomb, and having laid in the mouth of it the funeral boat in which she was borne across the Nile, he built it up for ever, and poured sand over the rock, so that none should find its place until the Day of Awakening.

Meanwhile, the infant grew and flourished, and when it was six months old, was taken to the college of the priestesses of Amen, there to be reared and taught.

****

Now on the day of the birth of the Princess Neter-Tua, there happened another birth with which our story has to do. The captain of the guard of the temple of Amen was one Mermes, who had married his own half-sister, Asti, the enchantress. As was well known, this Mermes was by right and true descent the last of that house of Pharaohs which had filled the throne of Egypt until their line was cast down generations before by the dynasty that now ruled the land, whereof the reigning Pharaoh and his daughter Neter-Tua alone remained. A long while past, in the early days of his reign, his council has whispered in Pharaoh's ear that he should kill Mermes and his sister, lest a day should come when they rebelled against him, proclaiming that they did so by right of blood. But Pharaoh, who was gentle and hated murder, instead of slaying Mermes sent for him and told him all.

Then Mermes, a noble-looking man as became the stock from which he sprang, prostrated himself and said,

"O Pharaoh, why should you kill me? It has pleased the gods to debase my House and to set up yours. Have I ever lifted up my heel against you because my forefathers were kings, or plotted with the discontent to overthrow you! See, I am satisfied with my station, which is that of a noble and a soldier in your army. Therefore let me and my half-sister, the wise lady Asti whom I purpose to marry, dwell on in peace as your true and humble servants. Dip not your hands in our innocent blood, O Pharaoh, lest the gods send a curse upon you and your House and our ghosts come back from the grave to haunt you."

When Pharaoh heard these words, his heart was moved in him, and he stretched out his sceptre for Mermes to kiss, thereby granting to him life and protection.

"Mermes," he said, "you are an honourable man, and my equal in blood if not in place. For their own purposes the gods raise up one and cast down another that at last their ends may be fulfilled. I believe that you will work no harm against me and mine, and, therefore, I will work no harm against you and your sister Asti, Mistress of Magic. Rather shall you be my friend and counsellor."

Then Pharaoh offered high rank and office to him, but Mermes would not take them, answering that if he did, envy would be stirred up against him, and in this way or that bring him to his death, since tall trees are the first to fall. So in the end Pharaoh made Mermes Captain of the Guard of Amen, and gave him land and houses enough to enable him to live as a noble of good estate, but no more. Also he became a friend of Pharaoh and one of his inner Council, to whose voice he always listened, for Mermes was a true-hearted man.

Afterwards Mermes married Asti, but like Pharaoh for a long while he remained childless, since he took no other wives. On the day of the birth of the Princess Tua, the Morning Star of Amen, however, Asti bore a son, a royal-looking child of great strength and beauty and very fair in colour, as tradition said that the kings of his race had been before him, but with black and shining eyes.

"See," said the midwife, "here is a head shaped to wear a crown."

Whereon Asti, his mother, forgetting her caution in her joy, or perhaps inspired by the gods, for from her childhood she was a prophetess, answered,

"Yes, and I think that this head and a crown will come close together," and she kissed him and named him Rames after her royal forefather, the founder of their line.

As it chanced a spy overheard this saying and reported it to the Council, and the Council urged Pharaoh to cause the boy to be put away, as they had urged in the case of his father, Mermes, because of the words of omen that Asti had spoken, and because she had given her son a royal name, naming him after the majesty of Ra, as though he were indeed the child of a king. But Pharaoh would not, asking with his soft smile whether they wished him to baptise his daughter in the blood of another infant who drew his first breath upon the same day, and adding:

"Ra sheds his glory upon all, and this high-born boy may live to be a friend in need to her whom Amen has given to Egypt. Let things befall as the gods decree. Who am I that I should make myself a god and destroy a life that they have fashioned?"

So the boy Rames lived and throve, and Mermes and Asti, when they came to hear of these things, thanked Pharaoh and blessed him.

Now the house of Mermes, as Captain of the Guard, was within the wall of the great temple of Amen, near to the palace of the priestesses of Amen where the Princess Neter-Tua was nurtured. Thus it came about that when the Queen Ahura died, the lady Asti was named as nurse to the Princess, since Pharaoh said that she should drink no milk save that of one in whose veins ran royal blood. So Asti was Tua's foster mother, and night by night she slept in her arms together with her own son, Rames. Afterwards, too, when they were weaned the babes were taught to walk and speak together, and later, as children, they became playmates.

Thus from the first these two loved each other, as brother and sister love when they are twins. But although the boy was bold and brave, this little princess always had the mastery of him, not because she was a princess and heir to the throne of Egypt—for all the high titles they gave her fell idly on her ears, nor did she think anything of the bowings of courtiers and of priests—but from some strength within herself. She it was that set the games they played, and when she talked he was obliged to listen, for although she was so sound and healthy, this Tua differed from other children.

Thus she had what she called her "silent hours" when she would suffer no one to come near her, not her ladies or her foster-mother, Asti herself, nor even Rames. Then, followed by the women at a distance, she would wander among the great columns of the temple and study the sculptures on the walls; and, since all places were open to her, Pharaoh's child, enter the sanctuaries, and stare at the gods that sat in them fashioned in granite and in alabaster. This she would do even in the solemn moonlight when mortals were afraid to approach these sacred shrines, and come thence unconcerned and smiling.

"What do you see there, O Morning Star?" asked little Rames of her once. "They are dull things, those stone gods that have never moved since the beginning of the world; also they frighten me, especially when Ra is set."

"They are not dull, and they do not frighten me," answered Tua; "they talk to me, and although I cannot understand all they say, I am happy with them."

"Talk!" he said contemptuously, "how can stones talk?"

"I do not know. I think it is their spirits that talk, telling me stories which happened before I was born and that shall happen after I am dead, yes, and after *they* seem to be dead. Now be silent—I say that they talk to me—it is enough."

"For me it would be more than enough," said the boy, "but then I am not called Child of Amen, who only worship Menthu, God of War."

****

When Rames was seven years of age, every morning he was taken to school in the temple, where the priests taught him to write with pens of reed upon tablets of wood, and told him more about the gods of Egypt than he ever wanted to hear again. During these hours, except when she was being instructed by the great ladies of the Court, or by high-priestesses, Tua was left solitary, since by the command of Pharaoh no other children were allowed to play with her, perhaps because there were none in the temple of her age whose birth was noble.

Once when he came back from his school in the evening Rames asked her if she had not been lonely without him. She answered, No, as she had another companion.

"Who is it?" he asked jealously. "Show me and I will fight him."

"No one that you can see, Rames," she replied. "Only my own *Ka*."

"Your *Ka*! I have heard of *Kas*, but I never saw one. What is it like?"

"Just like me, except that it throws no shadow, and only comes when I am quite by myself, and then, although I hear it often, I see it rarely, for it is mixed up with the light."

"I don't believe in *Kas*," exclaimed Rames scornfully, "you make them up out of your head."

A little while after this talk something happened that caused Rames to change his mind about *Kas*, or at any rate the *Ka* of Tua. In a hidden court of the temple was a deep pool of water with cemented sides, where, it was said, lived a sacred crocodile, an enormous beast that had dwelt there for hundreds of years. Rames and Tua having heard of this crocodile, often talked of it and longed to see it, but could not for there was a high wall round the tank, and in it a door of copper that was kept locked, except when once in every eight days the priests took in food to the crocodile—living goats and sheep, and sometimes a calf, none of which ever came back again.

Now one day Rames watching them return, saw the priest, who was called Guardian of the Door, put his hand behind him to thrust the key with which he had just locked the door, into his wallet, and missing the mouth of the wallet, let it fall upon the sand, then go upon his way knowing nothing of what he had done.

When he had gone in a great hurry, for he was a fat old priest and the dinner hour was at hand, Rames pounced upon the key and hid it in his robe. Then he sought out the princess and said,

"Morning Star, this evening, when I come back from school and am allowed to play with you, we can look at the wonderful beast in the tank, for look, I have the key which that fat priest will not search for till seven days are gone by, before which I can take it to him, saying that I found it in the sand, or perhaps put it back into his wallet."

When she heard this Tua's eyes shone, since above all things she desired to see this holy monster. But in the evening when the boy came running to her eagerly—for he had thought of nothing but the crocodile all day, and had bought a pigeon from a school-fellow with which to feed the brute—he found Tua in a different mood.

"I don't think that we will go to see the holy crocodile, Rames," she said, looking at him thoughtfully.

"Why not?" he asked amazed. "There is no one about, and I have put fat upon the key so that it will make no noise."

"Because my *Ka* has been with me, Rames, and told me that it is a bad act and if we do trouble will come to us."

"Oh! may the fiend Set take your *Ka*," replied the lad in a rage. "Show it to me and I will talk with it."

"I cannot, Rames, for it is *me*. Moreover, if Set took it, he would take me also, and you are wicked to wish such a thing."

Now the boy began to cry with vexation, sobbing out that she was not to be trusted, and that he had paid away his bronze knife, which Pharaoh had given him when last he visited the temple, for a pigeon to tempt the beast to the top of the water, so that they might see it, although the knife was worth many pigeons, and Pharaoh would be angry if he heard that he had parted with it.

"Why should we take the life of a poor pigeon to please ourselves?" asked Tua, softening a little at the sight of his grief.

"It's taken already," he answered. "It fluttered so that I had to sit on it to hide it from the priest, and when he had gone it was dead. Look," and he opened the linen bag he held, and showed her the dove cold and stiff.

"As you did not mean to kill it, that makes a difference," said Tua judicially. "Well, perhaps my *Ka* did not mean that we should not have one peep, and it is a pity to waste the poor pigeon, which then will have died for nothing."

Rames agreed that it would be the greatest of pities, so the two children slipped away through the trees of the garden into the shadow of the wall, along which they crept till they came to the bronze door. Then guiltily enough Rames put the great key into the lock, and with the help of a piece of wood which he had also made ready, that he set in the ring of the key to act as a lever, the two of them turning together shot back the heavy bolts.

Taking out the key lest it should betray them, they opened the door a little and squeezed themselves through into the forbidden place. No sooner had they done so than almost they wished themselves back again, for there was something about the spot that frightened them, to say nothing of the horrible smell which made Tua feel ill. It was a great tank, with a little artificial island in its centre, full of slimy water that looked almost black because of the shadow of the high walls, and round it ran a narrow stone path. At one spot in this path, however, where grew some dank-looking trees and bushes, was a slope, also of stone, and on the slope with its prow resting in the water a little boat, and in the boat, oars. But of the crocodile there was nothing to be seen.

"It is asleep somewhere," whispered Tua, "let us go away, I do not like this stench."

"Stench," answered Rames. "I smell nothing except the lilies on the water. Let us wake it up, it would be silly to go now. Surely you are not afraid, O Star."

"Oh, no! I am not afraid," answered Tua proudly. "Only wake it up quickly, please."

What Rames did not add was that it would be impossible to retreat as the door had closed behind them, and there was no keyhole on its inner side.

So they walked round the tank, but wherever it might lurk, the sleeping crocodile refused to wake.

"Let us get into the boat and look for it," suggested Rames. "Perhaps it is hiding on the island."

So he led her to the stone slope, where to her horror Tua saw the remains of the crocodile's last meal, a sight that caused her to forget her doubts and jump into the boat very quickly. Then Rames gave it a push and sprang in after her, so that they found themselves floating on the water. Now, standing in the bow, the boy took an oar and paddled round the island, but still there were no signs of the crocodile.

"I don't believe it is here at all," he said; recovering his courage.

"You might try the pigeon," suggested Tua, who, now that there was less smell, felt her curiosity returning.

This was a good thought upon which Rames acted at once. Taking the dead bird from the bag he spread out its wings to make it look as though it were alive, and threw it into the water, exclaiming, "Arise, O Holy Crocodile!"

Then with fearful suddenness, whence they knew not, that crocodile arose. An awful scaly head appeared with dull eyes and countless flashing fangs, and behind the head cubit upon cubit of monstrous form. The fangs closed upon the pigeon and everything vanished.

"That was the Holy Crocodile," said Rames abstractedly as he stared at the boiling waters, "which has lived here during the reigns of eight Pharaohs, and perhaps longer. Now we have seen it."

"Yes," answered Tua, "and I never want to see it again. Get me away quick, or I will tell your father."

Thus adjured the boy, nothing loth, seized his oar, when suddenly the ancient crocodile, having swallowed the dove, thrust up its snout immediately beneath them and began to follow the boat. Now Tua screamed aloud and said something about her *Ka*.

"Tell it to keep off the crocodile," shouted Rames as he worked the oar furiously. "Nothing can hurt a *Ka*."

But the crocodile would not be kept off. On the contrary, it thrust its grey snout and one of its claws over the stern of the boat in such a fashion that Rames could no longer work the oar, dragging it almost under water, and snapped with its horrible jaws.

"Oh! it is coming in; we are going to be eaten," cried Tua.

At that moment the boat touched the landing-place and swung round, so that its bow, where Tua was, struck the head of the crocodile, which seemed to infuriate the beast. At least, it hurled itself upon the boat, causing the fore part to heel over, fill with water, and begin to sink. Then the little lad, Rames, showed the courage that was in him. Shouting to Tua:

"Get on shore, get on shore!" he plunged past her and smote the huge reptile upon the head with the blade of his oar. It opened its hideous mouth, and he thrust the oar into it and held on.

"Leave go," cried Tua, as she scrambled to land.

But Rames would not leave go, for in his brave little heart he thought that if he did the crocodile would follow Tua and eat her. So he clung to the handle till it was wrenched from him. Indeed he did more, for seeing that the crocodile had bitten the wooden blade in two and, having dropped it, was still advancing towards the slope where it was accustomed to be fed, he leapt into the water and struck it in the eye with his little fist. Feeling the pain of the blow the monster snapped at him, and catching him by the hand began to sink back into deep water, dragging the lad after it.

Rames said nothing, but Tua, who already was at the head of the stage, looked round and saw the agony on his face.

"Help me, Amen!" she cried, and flying back, grasped Rames by his left arm just as he was falling over, then set her heels in a crack of the rock and held on. For one moment she was dragged forward till she thought that she must fall upon her face and be drowned or eaten with Rames, but the next something yielded, and she and the boy tumbled in a heap upon the stones. They rose and staggered together to the terrace. As they went Tua saw that Rames was looking at his right hand curiously; also that it was covered with blood, and that the little finger was torn off it. Then she remembered nothing further, except a sound of shouts and of heavy hammering at the copper door.

When she recovered it was to find herself in the house of Mermes with the lady Asti bending over her and weeping.

"Why do you weep, Nurse?" she asked, "seeing that I am safe?"

"I weep for my son, Princess," she answered between her sobs.

"Is he dead of his wounds, then, Asti?"

"No, O Morning Star, he lies sick in his chamber. But soon Pharaoh will kill him because he led her who will be Queen of Egypt into great danger of her life."

"Not so," said Tua, springing up, "for he saved my life."

As she spoke the door opened and in came Pharaoh himself, who had been summoned hastily from the palace. His face was white and he shook with fear, for it had been reported to him that his only child was drowned. When he saw that she lived and was not even hurt, he could not contain his joy, but casting his arms about her, sank to his knees giving thanks to the gods and the guardian spirits. She kissed him, and studying his face with her wise eyes, asked why he was so much afraid.

"Because I thought you had been killed, my daughter."

"Why did you think that, O my father, seeing that the great god, Amen, before I was born promised to protect me always, though it is true that had it not been for Rames——"

Now at the mention of this name Pharaoh was filled with rage.

"Speak not of that wicked lad," he exclaimed, "now or ever more, for he shall be scourged till he dies!"

"My father," answered Tua, springing up, "forget those words, for if Rames dies I will die also. It is I who am to blame, not he, for my *Ka* warned me not to look upon the beast, but to Rames no *Ka* spoke. Moreover, when that evil god would have eaten me it was Rames who fought with it and offered himself to its jaws in my place. Listen, my father, while I tell you all the story."

So Pharaoh listened, and when it was done he sent for Rames. Presently the boy was carried in, for he had lost so much blood that he could not walk, and was placed upon a stool before him.

"Slay me now, O Pharaoh," he said in a weak voice, "for I have sinned. Moreover, I shall die happy since my spirit gave me strength to beat off the evil beast from the Princess whom I led into trouble."

"Truly you have done wickedly," said Pharaoh, shaking his head at him, "and, therefore, perhaps, you will lose your hand and even your life. Yet, child, you have a royal heart, who first saved your playmate and then, even in my presence, take all the blame upon yourself. Therefore I forgive you, son of Mermes; moreover, I see that I was wise not to listen to those who counselled that you should be put away at birth," and bending over the boy, Pharaoh kissed him on the brow.

Also he gave orders that the greatest physicians in the land should attend upon him and purge the poison of the crocodile's teeth from his body, and when he recovered—which save for the loss of the little finger of his right hand, he did completely—he sent him a sword with a handle of gold fashioned to the shape of a crocodile, in place of the knife which he had paid away for the pigeon, bidding him use it bravely all his life in defence of her who would be his queen. Further, although he was still so young, he gave to him the high title of Count in earnest of his love and favour, and with it a name that meant Defender of the Royal Lady.

After he had gone Asti the prophetess looked at the sword which Pharaoh had given to her son.

"I see royal blood on it," she said, and handed it back to Rames.

****

But Rames and Tua were no more allowed to play together alone, for always after this the Princess was accompanied by women of honour and an armed guard. Also, within a year or two the boy was placed in charge of a general to be brought up as a soldier, a trade that he liked well enough, so that from this time forward he and Neter-Tua met but seldom. Still there was a bond between them which could not be broken by absence, for already they loved each other, and every night and morning when Tua made her petitions to Amen, after praying for Pharaoh her father, and for the spirit of her royal mother, Ahura, she prayed for Rames, and that they might meet soon. For the months when her eyes did not fall upon his face were wearisome to Tua.

Chapter 4

The Summoning of Amen

The years went by and the Princess Neter-Tua, who was called Morning Star of Amen, came at length to womanhood, and went through the ceremonies of Purification. In all Egypt there was no maiden so wise and spirited or so lovely. Tall and slender was her shape, blue as the sea were her eyes, rosy like the dawn were her cheeks, and when she did not wear it in a net of gold, her black and curling hair fell almost to her waist. Also she was very learned, for priests and priestesses taught her all things that she ought to know, together with the arts of playing on the harp and of singing and dancing, while her own excellent Spirit, that *Ka* which Amen had given her, instructed her in a deeper wisdom which she gathered unconsciously in sleep and waking dreams, as the slumbering earth gathers dew at night.

Moreover, her father, the wise old Pharaoh, opened to her the craft of statesmanship, by help of which she might govern men and overthrow her enemies. Indeed, he did more, for when her education was finished, he joined her with him in the government of Egypt, saying:

"I who always lacked bodily strength, grow aged and feeble. This mighty crown is too heavy for me to bear alone. Daughter, you must share its weight."

So the young Neter-Tua became a queen, and great was the ceremony of her coronation. The high priests and priestesses, clothed in the robes and symbols of their gods and goddesses, addressed speeches to her and blessed her in their names, giving her every good gift and promising to her eternal life. Princes and nobles made her offerings; foreign chiefs and kings bowed before her by their ambassadors. The Counts and headmen of the Two Lands swore allegiance to her, and, finally, in the presence of all the Court, Pharaoh himself set the double crown upon her brow and gave her her throne-names of "Glorious in Ra and Hathor Strong in Beauty."

So for a while Tua sat splendid on her golden seat while the people adored her, but in that triumphant hour her eyes searched for one face only, that of the tall and gallant captain, Rames, her foster-brother, and for a moment rested there content. Yes, their eyes met, those of the new-crowned Empress on her throne and of the youthful noble in the throng below. Short was the greeting, for next instant she looked away, yet more full of meaning than whole days of speech.

"The Queen does not forget what the child remembered, the goddess is still a woman," it seemed to say. And so sweet was that message that Rames staggered from the Court like one stricken by the sun.

****

Night came at last, and having dismissed her secretaries, scribes and tire-women the weary girl, now clad in simple white, sat in her chamber alone. She thought of all the splendours through which she had passed; she thought of the glories of her imperial state, of the power that she wielded, and of the proud future which stretched before her feet. But most of all she thought of the face of the young Count Rames, the playmate of her childhood, the man she loved, and wondered, ah! how she wondered, if with all her power she could ever draw him to her side. If not, of what use was this rule over millions, this dominion of her world? They called her a goddess, and in truth, at times, she believed that she was half-divine, but if so, why did her heart ache like that of any common maid?

Moreover, was she really set above the misfortunes of her race? Could a throne, however bright with gold, lift her above the sorrows of human kind? She desired to learn the truth, the very truth. Her mind was urgent, it drove her on to search out things to come, to stand face to face with them, even if they were evil. Well, she believed she had the strength, although, as yet, she had never called it to her aid.

Also this thing could not be done alone. Tua thought a while, then going to the door of her chamber she bade a woman who waited without summon to her the Lady Asti, priestess of Amen, Interpreter of Heaven. Presently Asti came, for now, as always, she was in attendance upon the new-crowned queen, a tall and noble-looking woman with fine-cut features and black hair, that although she was fifty years of age, still showed no trace of grey.

"I was in the Sanctuary when your Majesty summoned me," she said, pointing to the sacred robe she wore. "Let your Majesty pardon me, therefore, if I have been long in coming," and she bowed low before her.

But the Queen lifted her up and kissed her, saying,

"I am weary of those high titles whereof I have heard more than enough to-day. Call me Tua, O my mother, for so you have ever been to me, from whose breast I drew the milk of life."

"What ails you, my child?" asked Asti. "Was the crown too heavy for this young head of yours?" she added, stretching out her delicate hand and stroking the black and curling hair.

"Aye, Mother, the weight of it seemed to crush me with its gems and gold. I am weary and yet I cannot sleep. Tell me, why did Pharaoh summon that Council after the feast? Mermes was one of them, so you must know. And why was not I, who henceforth rule with Pharaoh, present with him?"

"Would you learn?" said Asti with a little smile. "Well, as Queen you have the right. It was because they discussed the matter of your marriage."

For a moment a light shone upon Tua's face. Then she asked anxiously:

"My marriage, and with whom?"

"Oh! many names were mentioned, Child, since she who rules Egypt does not lack for suitors."

"Tell me them quick, Asti."

So she told them, there were seven in all, the Prince of Kesh, the sons of foreign kings, great nobles, and a general of the army who claimed descent from a former Pharaoh.

As each name fell from Asti's lips Tua waved her hand, saying scornful words, such as "I know him not," "Too old," "Fat and hideous," "A foreign dog who spits upon our gods," and so forth, adding at last:

"Go on."

"That is all, Lady, no other name was mentioned, and the Council adjourned to consider these."

"No other name?"

"Do you then miss one, perchance, Tua?"

She made no answer, only her lips seemed to shape themselves to a certain sound that they did not utter. The two women looked each other in the eyes, then Asti shook her head.

"It may not be," she whispered, "for many reasons, and amongst them that by the solemn decree of long ago whereof I have told you, our blood is barred for ever from the throne. None would dare to break it, not even the Pharaoh himself. You would bring my son to his death, Tua, which such another look as you gave him in yonder hall would surely do."

"No," she answered slowly, "I would not bring him to his death, but to life and honour and—love, and one day *I* shall be Pharaoh. Only, Asti, if you betray me to him I swear that I will bring you to your death, although you are so dear."

"I shall not betray you," answered the priestess, smiling again. "In truth, most Beautiful, I do not think there is any need, even if I would. Say now, why did a certain captain turn faint and leave the hall to-day when your eyes chanced to fall on him?"

"The heat," suggested Tua, colouring.

"Yes, it was hot, but he is stronger than most men and had borne it long—like others. Still there are fires——"

"Because he was afraid of my majesty," broke in Tua hurriedly. "You know I looked very royal there, Mother."

"Yes, doubtless fear moved him—or some other passion. Yet, Beloved, put that thought from your heart as I do. When you are Pharaoh you will learn that a monarch is a slave to the people and to the law. Breathe but his name in love, and never will you see him more till you meet before Osiris."

Tua hid her eyes in her hands for a moment, then she glanced up and there was another look upon her face, a strange, new look.

"When I am Pharaoh," she answered, "there are certain matters in which I will be my own law, and if the people do not like it, they may find another Pharaoh."

Asti started at her words, and a light of joy shone in her deep eyes.

"Truly your heart is high," she said; "but, oh! if you love me—and another—bury that thought, bury it deep, or he will never live to see you placed alone upon the golden seat. Know, Lady, that already from hour to hour I fear for him—lest he should drink a poisoned cup, lest at night he should chance to stumble against a spear, lest an arrow—shot in sport—should fall against his throat and none know whence it came."

Tua clenched her hands.

"If so, there should be such vengeance as Egypt has not heard of since Mena ruled."

"Of what use is vengeance, Child, when the heart is empty and the tomb is sealed?"

Again Tua thought. Then she said:

"There are other gods besides Osiris. Now what do men call me, Mother? Nay, not my royal names."

"They call you Morning Star of Amen; they call you Daughter of Amen."

"Is that story true, Asti the Magician?"

"Aye, at least your mother dreamed the dream, for she told it to me and I have read its record, who am a priestess of Amen."

"Then this high god should love me, should he not? He should hear my prayers and give me power—he should protect those who are dear to me. Mother, they say that you, the Mistress of secret things, can open the ears of the gods and cause their mouths to speak. Mother, I command you as your Queen, call up my father Amen before me, so that I may talk with him, for I have words to which he must listen."

"Are you not afraid?" asked Asti, looking at her curiously. "He is the greatest of all the gods, and to summon him lightly is a sacrilege."

"Should a daughter fear her father?" answered Tua.

"When the divine Queen your mother and Pharaoh knelt before him in his shrine, praying that a child might be given to them, Amen did not deign to appear to them, save afterwards in a dream. Will you dare more than they? Lie down and dream, O Star of the Morning."

"Nay, I trust no dreams which change like summer clouds and pass as soon," answered the girl boldly. "If the god is my father, in the spirit or the flesh, I know not which, let him appear before me face to face. I ask his wisdom for myself and his favour for another. Call him, if you have the power, Asti. Call him even if he slay me. Better that I should die than——"

"Hush!" said Asti, laying her hand upon her lips, "speak not that name. Well, I have some skill, and for your sake—and another's—I will try, but not here. Perchance he may listen, perchance not, or, perchance, if he comes you and I must pay the price. Put on your robes, now, O Queen, and over them this veil, and follow me—if you dare."

****

Along narrow passages they crept and down many a secret-stair, till at length they came to a door at the foot of a long slope of rock. This door Asti unlocked and thrust open, then when they had entered, re-locked it behind them.

"What is this place?" whispered Tua.

"The burial crypt of the high priestesses of Amen, where it is said that the god watches. None have entered it for hard on thirty years. See here in the dust run the footsteps of those who bore the last priestess to her rest."

She held up her lamp, and by the light of it Tua saw that they were in a great cave painted with figures of the gods which had on either side of it recesses. In each of these was set a coffin with a gilded face, and behind it an alabaster statue of her who lay therein, and in front of it a table of offerings. At the head of the crypt stood a small altar of black stone, for the rest the place was empty.

Asti led Tua to a step in front of the altar and bidding her kneel, departed with the lamp which she hid away in some side chapel, so that now the darkness was intense. Presently, through the utter silence, Tua heard her creep back towards her, for although she walked so softly the dust seemed to cry beneath her feet, and her every footstep echoed round the vaulted walls. Moreover, a glow came from her, the glow of her life in that place of death. She passed Tua and knelt by the altar and the echo of her movements died away. Only it seemed to Tua that from each of the tombs to the right and to the left rose the *Ka* of her who was buried there, and drew near to watch and listen. She could not see them, she could not hear them, yet she knew that they were there and was able to count their number—thirty and two in all—while within herself rose a picture of them, each differing from the other, but all white, expectant, solemn.

Now Tua heard Asti murmuring secret invocations that she did not understand. In that place and silence they sounded weird and dreadful, and as she hearkened to them, for the first time fear crept over her. Kneeling there upon her knees she bent her head almost to the dust and put up prayers to Amen that he might be pleased to hear her and to satisfy the longings of her heart. She prayed and prayed till she grew faint and weary, while always Asti uttered her invocations. But no answer came, no deity appeared, no voice spoke. At length Asti rose, and coming to her, whispered in her ear:

"Let us depart ere the watching spirits, whose rest we have broken, grow wrath with us. The god has shut his ears."

So Tua rose, clinging to Asti, for now, she knew not why, her fear grew and deepened. For a moment she stood upon her feet, then sank to her knees again, for there at the far end of the great tomb, near to the door by which they had entered, appeared a glow upon the darkness. Slowly it took form, the form of a woman clad in the royal robes of Egypt, and bearing in its hand a sceptre. The figure of light advanced towards them, so that presently they saw its face. Tua did not know the face, though it seemed to her to be like her own, but Asti knew it, and at the sight sank to the ground.

Now the figure stood in front of them, a thing of light framed in the thick darkness, and now in a sweet, low voice it spoke.

"Hail! Queen of Egypt," it said. "Hail! Neter-Tua, Daughter of

Amen. Art thou afraid to look on the spirit of her who bore thee, thou that didst dare to summon the Father of the gods to do thy bidding?"

"I am afraid," answered Tua, shaking in all her limbs.

"And thou, Asti the Magician, art thou afraid also, who but now wast bold enough to cry to Amen-Ra—'Come from thy high heaven and make answer'?"

"It is even so, O Queen Ahura," murmured Asti.

"Woman," went on the voice, "thy sin is great, and great is the sin of this royal one at thy side. Had Amen hearkened, how would the two of you have stood before his glory, who at the sight of this shape of mine that once was mortal like yourselves, crouch choking to the earth? I tell you both that had the god arisen, as in your wickedness ye willed, there where ye knelt, there ye would have died. But he who knows all is merciful, and in his place has sent me his messenger that ye may live to look upon to-morrow's sun."

"Let Amen pardon us!" gasped Tua, "it was my sin, O Mother, for I commanded Asti and she obeyed me. On me be the blame, not on her, for I am torn with doubts and fears, for myself and for another. I would know the future."

"Why, O Queen Neter-Tua, why wouldst thou know the future? If hell yawns beneath thy feet, why wouldst thou peep through its golden doors before the time? The future is hid from mortals because, could they pierce its veil, it would crush them with its terrors. If all the woes of life and death lay open the gaze, who would dare to live and who—oh! who could dare to die?"

"Then woes await me, O thou who wast my mother?"

"How can it be otherwise? Light and darkness make the day, joy and sorrow make the life. Thou art human, be content."

"Divine also, O Ahura, if all tales be true."

"Then pay for thy divinity in tears and be satisfied. Content is the guerdon of the beast, but gods are wafted upwards on the wings of pain. How can that gold be pure which has not known the fire?"

"Thou tellest me nothing," wailed Tua, "and it is not for myself I ask. I am fair, I am Amen's daughter, and splendid is my heritage. Yet, O Dweller in Osiris, thou who once didst fill the place I hold to-day, I tell thee that I would pay away this pomp, could I but be sure that I shall not live loveless, that I shall not be given as a chattel to one whom I hate, that one—whom I do not hate—will live to call me—wife. Great dangers threaten him—and me, Amen is mighty; he is the potter that moulds the clay of men; if I be his child, if his spirit is breathed into me, oh! let him help me now."

"Let thine own faith help thee. Are not the words of Amen, which he spake concerning thee, written down? Study them and ask no more. Love is an arrow that does not miss its mark; it is the immortal fire from on high which winds and waters cannot quench. Therefore love on. Thou shalt not love in vain. Queen and Daughter, fare thee well awhile."

"Nay, nay, one word, Immortal. I thank thee, thou Messenger of the gods, but when these troubles come upon me—and another, when the sea of dangers closes o'er our heads, when shame is near and I am lonely, as well may chance, then to whom shall I turn for succour?"

"Then thou hast one within thee who is strong to aid. It was given to thee at thy birth, O Star of Amen, and Asti can call it forth. Come hither, thou Asti, and swiftly, for I must be gone, and first I would speak with thee."

Asti crept forward, and the glowing shape in the royal robe bent over her so that the light of it shone upon her face. It bent over her and seemed to whisper in her ear. Then it held out its hands towards Tua as though in blessing, and instantly was not.

****

Once more the two women stood in Tua's chamber. Pale and shaken they looked into each other's eyes.

"You have had your will, Queen," said Asti; "for if Amen did not come, he sent a messenger, and a royal one."

"Interpret me this vision," answered Tua, "for to me, at any rate, that Spirit said little."

"Nay, it said much. It said that love fails not of its reward, and what more went you out to seek?"

"Then I am glad," exclaimed Tua joyfully.

"Be not too glad, Queen, for to-night we have sinned, both of us, who dared to summon Amen from his throne, and sin also fails not of its reward. Blood is the price of that oracle."

"Whose blood, Asti? Ours?"

"Nay, worse, that of those who are dear to us. Troubles arise in Egypt, Queen."

"You will not leave me when they break, Asti?"

"I may not if I would. The Fates have bound us together till the end, and that I think is far away. I am yours as once you were mine when you lay upon my breast, but bid me no more to summon Amen from his throne."

CHAPTER 5

How Rames Fought the Prince of Kesh

Now for a whole moon there were great festivals in Thebes, and in all of these Neter-Tua, "Glorious in Ra, Hathor Strong in Beauty, Morning Star of Amen," must take her part as new-crowned Queen of Egypt. Feast followed feast, and at each of them one of the suitors of her hand was the guest of honour.

Then after it was done, Pharaoh her father and his councillors would wait upon her and ask if this man was pleasing to her. Being wise, Tua would give no direct answer, only of most of them she was rid in this way.

She demanded that the writing of the dream of her mother, Ahura, should be brought and read before her, and when it had been read she pointed out that Amen promised to her a royal lover, and that these chiefs and generals were not royal, therefore it was not of them that Amen spoke, nor did she dare to turn her eyes on one whom the god had forbidden to her.

Of others who declared that they were kings, but who, being unable to leave their countries, were represented by ambassadors, she said that not having seen them she could say nothing. When they appeared at the Court of Egypt, she would consider them.

So at length only one suitor was left, the man whom she knew well Pharaoh and his councillors desired that she should take as husband. This was Amathel, the Prince of Kesh, whose father, an aged king, ruled at Napata, a great city far to the south, situated in a land that was called an island because the river Nile embraced it in its two arms. It was said that after Egypt this country was the richest in the whole world, for there gold was so plentiful that men thought it of less value than copper and iron; also there were mines in which beautiful stones were found, and the soil grew corn in abundance.

Moreover, once in the far past, a race of Pharaohs sprung from this city of Napata, had sat on the throne of Egypt, until at length the people of Egypt, headed by the priests, had risen and overthrown them because they were foreigners and had introduced Nubian customs into the land. Therefore it was decreed by an unalterable law that none of their race should ever again wear the Double Crown. Of the descendants of these Pharaohs, Rames, Tua's playmate, was the last lawful child.

But although the Egyptians had cast them down, at heart they always grieved over the rich territory of Napata, which was lost to them, for when those Pharaohs fell Kesh declared itself independent and set up another dynasty to rule over it, of which dynasty Amathel Prince of Kesh was the heir.

Therefore they hoped that it might come back to them by marriage between Amathel and the young Queen Neter-Tua. Ever since she was born the great lords and councillors of Egypt, yes, and Pharaoh himself, seeing that he had no son to whom he might marry her after the fashion of the country, had been working to this end. It was by secret treaty that the Prince Amathel was present at the crowning of the Queen, of whose hand he had been assured on the sole condition that he came to dwell with her at Thebes. It is true that there were other suitors, but these, as all of them knew well, were but pawns in a game played to amuse the people.

The king destined to take the great queen captive was Amathel and no other. Tua knew it, for had not Asti told her, and was it not because of her fear of this man and her love for Rames that she had dared to commit the sacrilege of attempting to summon Amen from the skies? Still, as yet, the Pharaoh had not spoken to her of Amathel, nor had she met him. It was said that he had been present at her crowning in disguise, for this proud prince gave out that were she ten times Queen of Egypt, he would not pledge himself to wed as his royal wife, one who was displeasing to him, and that therefore he must see her before he pressed his suit.

Now that he had seen her in her loveliness and glory, he announced that he was well satisfied, which was but half the truth, for, in fact, she had set all his southern blood on fire, and there was nothing that he desired more than to call her wife.

On the night which had been appointed for Amathel to meet his destined bride, a feast had been prepared richer by far than any that went before. Tua, feigning ignorance, on entering the great unroofed hall lit with hundreds of torches down all its length, and seeing the multitudes at the tables, asked of the Pharaoh, her father, who was the guest that he would welcome with such magnificence which seemed worthy of a god rather than of a man.

"My daughter," answered the old monarch nervously, "it is none other than the Prince of Kesh, who in his own country they worship as divine, as we are worshipped here in Egypt, and who, in truth, is, or will be, one of the greatest of kings."

"Kesh!" she answered, "I thought that we claimed sovereignty over that land."

"Once it was ours, Daughter," said her father with a sigh, "or rather the kings of Kesh were also kings of Egypt, but their dynasty fell before my great-great-grandfather was called to the throne, and now but three of their blood are left, Mermes, Captain of the Guard of Amen; Asti, the Seer and Priestess, his wife, your foster-mother and waiting lady, and the young Count Rames, a soldier in our army, who was your playmate, and as you may remember saved you from the sacred crocodile."

"Yes, I remember," said Tua. "But then why is not Mermes King of Kesh?"

"Because the people of the city of Napata raised up another house to rule over them, of whom Amathel is the heir."

"A usurping heir, surely, my father, if there be anything in blood."

"Say not that, Tua," replied Pharaoh sharply, "for then Mermes should be Pharaoh in our place also."

Tua made no reply, only as they took their seats in the golden chairs at the head of the hall, she asked carelessly:

"Is this Prince of Kesh also a suitor for my hand, O Pharaoh?"

"What else should he be, my daughter? Did you not know it? Be gracious to him now, since it is decreed that you shall take him as a husband. Hush! answer not. He comes."

As he spoke a sound of wild music arose, and at the far end of the great hall appeared a band of players gorgeously attired, who blew horns made from small tusks of the elephant, clashed brazen cymbals and beat gilded drums. These advanced a little way up the hall and stood there playing, while after them marched a bodyguard of twenty gigantic Nubian soldiers who carried broad-bladed spears with shields of hippopotamus hide curiously worked, and were clothed in tunics and caps of leopard-skin.

Next appeared the Prince of Kesh himself, a short, stout, broad-shouldered young man, thick-featured, heavy-faced, and having large, rolling eyes. He was clad in festal garments, and hung about with heavy chains of gold fastened with clasps of glittering stones, while from his crisp, black hair rose a tall plume of nodding ostrich feathers. Fan bearers walked beside him, and the train of his long cloak was borne by two black and hideous dwarfs, full-grown men but no taller than a child of eight.

With one swift glance, while he was yet far away, Tua studied the man from head to foot, and hated him as she had never hated anyone before. Then she looked over his head, as from her raised seat upon the dais she was able to do, and saw that behind him came a second guard of picked Egyptian soldiers, and that in command of them, simply clad in his scaled armour of bronze, and wearing upon his thigh the golden-handled sword that Pharaoh had given him, was none other than the young Count Rames, her playmate and foster-brother, the man whom her heart loved. At the sight of his tall and noble form and fine-cut face rising above the coarse, squat figure of the Ethiopian prince, Tua blushed rosy red, but Pharaoh noting it, only thought, as others did, that it was because now for the first time her eyes fell upon him who would be her husband.

Why, Tua wondered, was Rames chosen to attend upon the Prince Amathel? At once the answer rose in her mind. Doubtless it had been done to gratify the pride of Amathel, not by Pharaoh, who would know nothing of such matters, but by some bribed councillor, or steward of the household. Rames was of more ancient blood than Amathel, and by right should be the King of Kesh, as he should also be Pharaoh of Egypt; therefore, to humble him he was set to wait upon Amathel.

Moreover, it was guessed that the young Queen looked kindly upon this Count Rames with whom she had been nursed, and who, like herself, was beautiful to behold. Therefore, to abase him in her eyes he had been commanded to appear walking in the train of Amathel and given charge over his sacred person at the feast.

In a moment Tua understood it all, and made a vow before her father Amen that soon or late those who had planned this outrage should pay its price, nor did she forget that promise in the after days.

Now the Prince had mounted the dais and was bowing low to Pharaoh and to her, and they must rise and bow in answer. Then Pharaoh welcomed him to Egypt in few, well-chosen words, giving him all his titles and speaking meaningly of the ancient ties which had linked their kingdoms, ties which, he prayed, might yet draw them close again.

He ceased and looked at Tua who, as Queen, had also a speech to deliver that had been given to her in writing. Although she remembered this well enough, for the roll lay beside her, never a word would she read, but turned round and bade one of her waiting-ladies bring her a fan.

So after a pause that seemed somewhat long Amathel delivered his answer that was learned by rote, for it replied to "gentle words from the lips of the divine Queen that made his heart to flower like the desert after rain," not one of which had she spoken. Thereon Tua, looking over the top of her fan, saw Rames smile grimly, while unable to restrain themselves, some of the great personages at the feast broke out laughing, and bowed down their heads to hide their merriment.

With an angry scowl the Prince turned and commanded that the gifts should be brought. Now slaves advanced bearing cups of worked gold, elephants and other beasts fashioned in gold, and golden vases full of incense, which he presented to Pharaoh on behalf of his father, the King of Kesh and himself, saying boastfully that in his country such things were common, and that he would have brought more of them had it not been for their weight.

When Pharaoh had thanked him, answering gently that Egypt too was not poor, as he hoped that he would find upon the morrow, the Prince, on his own behalf alone, offered to the Queen other presents, among them pectorals and necklaces without price fashioned of amethysts and sapphires. Also, because she was known to be the first of musicians and the sweetest-voiced lady in the land—for these were the greatest of the gifts that Tua had from Amen—he gave to her a wonderfully worked harp of ivory with golden strings, the frame of the harp being fashioned to the shape of a woman, and two black female slaves laden with ornaments, who were said to be the best singers in the Southern Land.

Now Pharaoh whispered to Tua to put on one of the necklaces, but she would not, saying that the colour of the stones did not match her white robe and the blue lotus flowers which she wore. Instead, she thanked Amathel coldly but courteously, and without looking at his gifts, told the royal Nurse, Asti, who stood behind her, to bear them away and to place them at a distance, as the perfumes that had been poured over them, oppressed her. Only, as though by an afterthought, she bade them leave the ivory harp.

Thus inauspiciously enough the feast began. At it Amathel drank much of the sweet wine of Asi or Cyprus, commanding Rames, who stood behind him, to fill his cup again and again, though whether he did this because he was nearest to him, or to lower him to the rank of a butler, Tua did not know. At least, having no choice, Rames obeyed, though cup-filling was no fitting task for a Count of Egypt and an officer of Pharaoh's guard.

When the waiting women, clad in net worked with spangles of gold, had borne away the meats, conjurers appeared who did wonderful feats, amongst other things causing a likeness of Queen Neter-Tua wearing her royal robes and having a star upon her brow, to arise out of a vase.

Then, as they had arranged, they strove to do the same for the Prince Amathel, but Asti who had more magic than all of them, watching behind Tua's chair, put out her strength and threw a spell upon them.

Behold! instead of the form of the Prince, which these conjurers summoned loudly and by name, there appeared out of the vase a monkey wearing a crown and feathers that yet resembled him somewhat, which black and hideous ape stood there for a while seeming to gibber at them, then fell down and vanished away.

Now some of the audience laughed and some were silent, but Pharaoh, not knowing whether this were a plot or an evil omen from the gods, frowned and looked anxiously at his guest. As it chanced, however, the Prince, fired with wine, was so engaged in staring at the loveliness of Tua, that he took no note of the thing, while the Queen looked upwards and seemed to see nothing. As for the conjurers, they fled from the hall, fearing for their lives, and wondering what strong spirit had entered into the vase and spoilt the trick which they had prepared.

As they went singers and dancing women hurriedly took their place, till Tua, wearying of the stare of Amathel, waved her hand and said that she wished to hear those two Nubian slaves whose voices were said to be so wonderful. So they were brought forward with their harps, and having prostrated themselves, began to play and sing very sweetly, Nubian songs melancholy and wild, whereof few could understand the meaning. So well did they sing, indeed, that when they had done, Neter-Tua said:

"You have pleased me much, and in payment I give you a royal gift. I give you your freedom, and appoint that henceforth you shall sing before the Court, if you think fit to stay here, not as slaves but for hire."

Then the two women prostrated themselves again before her Majesty and blessed her, for they knew that they could earn wealth by their gift, and the rich courtiers taking the Queen's cue, flung rings and ornaments to them, so that in a minute they got more gold than ever they had dreamed of, who were but kidnapped slaves. But Prince Amathel grew angry and said:

"Some might have been pleased to keep the priceless gift of the best singers in the world."

"Do you say that these sweet-voiced women are the best singers in the world, O Prince?" asked Tua, speaking to him for the first time. "Now if you will be pleased to listen, you provoke me to make trial of my own small skill that I may learn how far I fall short of 'the best singers in the world.'"

Then she lifted up the ivory harp with the strings of gold and swept her fingers over it, trying its notes and adjusting them with the agate screws, looking at Amathel all the while with a challenge in her lovely eyes.

"Nay, nay, my daughter," said Pharaoh, "it is scarcely fitting that a queen of Egypt should sing before all this noble company."

"Why not, my father?" she asked. "To-night we all do honour to the heir of his Majesty of Kesh. Pharaoh receives him, Pharaoh's daughter accepts his gifts, the highest in the land surround him," then she paused and added slowly, "one of blood more ancient than his own waits on him as cup-bearer, one whose race built up the throne his father fills," and she pointed to Rames, who stood near by holding the vase of wine. "Why, then, should not Egypt's queen seek to please our royal guest as best she may—since she has no other gift to give him?"

Then in the dead silence which followed this bold speech, whereof none could mistake the meaning, Neter-Tua, Morning Star of Amen, rose from her seat. Pressing the ivory harp against her young breast, she bent over it, her head crowned with the crown of Upper Egypt whereon glistened the royal *uraeus*, a snake about to strike, and swept the well-tuned strings.

Such magic was in her touch that instantly all else was forgotten, even the Pharaoh leaned back in his golden chair to listen. Softly she struck at first, then by slow degrees ever louder till the music of the harp rang through the pillared hall. Now, at length, she lifted up her heavenly voice and began to sing in a strain so wild and sweet that it seemed to pierce to the watching stars.

It was a sad and ancient love-tale that she sang, which told how a priestess of Hathor of high degree loved and was beloved by a simple scribe whom she might not wed. It told how the scribe, maddened by his passion, crept at night into the very sanctuary of the temple hoping to find her there, and for his sacrilege was slain by the angry goddess.

It told how the beautiful priestess, coming alone to make prayer in the sanctuary for strength to resist her love, stumbled over the lover's corpse and, knowing it, died of grief. It told how Hathor, goddess of love, melted by the piteous sight, breathed back life into their nostrils, and since they might not remain upon earth, wafted them to the Under-world, where they awoke and embraced and dwell on for ever and for aye, triumphant and rejoicing.

All had heard this old, old story, but none had ever heard it so divinely sung. As Tua's pure and lovely voice floated over them the listeners seemed to see that lover, daring all in his desire, creep into the solemn sanctuary of the temple. They saw Hathor appear in her wrath and smite him cold in death. They saw the beauteous priestess with her lamp, and heard her wail her life away upon her darling's corpse; saw, too, the dead borne by spirits over the borders of the world.

Then came that last burst of music thrilling and divine, and its rich, passionate notes seemed to open the heavens to their sight. There in the deep sky they perceived the awakening of the lovers and their embrace of perfect joy, and when a glory hid them, heard the victorious chant of the priestess of love sighing itself away, faint and ever fainter, till at length its last distant echoes died in the utter silence of the place of souls.

Tua ceased her music. Resting her still quivering harp upon the board, she sank back in her chair of state, outworn, trembling, while in her pale face the blue eyes shone like stars. There was stillness in the hall; the spell of that magical voice lay on the listeners; none applauded, it seemed even that none dared to move, for men remembered that this wonderful young Queen was said to be daughter of Amen, Master of the world, and thought that it had been given to them to hearken, not to a royal maiden, but to a goddess of the skies.

Quiet they sat as though sleep had smitten them, only every man of their number stared at the sweet pale face and at those radiant eyes. Drunk with passion and with wine, Amathel, Prince of Kesh, leaned his heavy head upon his hand and stared like the rest. But those eyes did not stay on him. Had he been a stone they could not have noted him less; they passed over him seeking something beyond.

Slowly he turned to see what it might be at which the Morning Star of Amen gazed, and perceived that the young captain who waited on him, he who was said to be of a race more ancient and purer than his own, he whose house had reigned in the Southern Land when his ancestors were but traffickers in gold, was also gazing at this royal singer. Yes, he bent forward to gaze as though a spell drew him, a spell, or the eyes of the Queen, and there was that upon his face which even a drunken Nubian could not fail to understand.

In the hands of Rames was the tall, golden vase of wine, and as Amathel thrust back his chair its topmost ivory bar struck the foot of the vase and tilted it, so that the red wine poured in a torrent over the Prince's head and gorgeous robes, staining him from his crest of plumes to his feet as though with blood. Up sprang the Prince of Kesh roaring with fury.

"Dog-descended slave!" he shouted. "Hog-headed brother of swine, is it thus that you wait upon my Royalty?" and with the cup in his hand he smote Rames on the face, then drew the sword at his side to kill him.

But Rames also wore a sword, that sword hafted with the golden crocodile which Pharaoh had given him long ago—that sword which Asti the foresighted had seen red with royal blood. With a wild, low cry he snatched it from its sheath, and to avoid the blow that Amathel struck at him before he could guard himself, sprang backwards from the dais to the open space in the hall that had been left clear for the dancers. After him leapt Amathel calling him "Coward," and next instant the pillars echoed, not with Tua's music but with the stern ringing of bronze upon bronze.

Now in their fear and amaze men looked up to Pharaoh, waiting his word, but Pharaoh, overcome by the horror of the scene, appeared to have swooned; at least, he lay back in his chair with his eyes shut like one asleep. Then they looked to the Queen, but Tua made no sign, only with parted lips and heaving breast watched, watched and waited for the end.

As for Rames he forgot everything save that he, a soldier and a noble of royal race, had been struck across the mouth by a black Nubian who called himself a prince. His blood boiled up in him, and through a red haze as it were, he saw Tua's glorious eyes beckoning him on to a victory. He saw and sprang as springs the lion of the desert, sprang straight at the throat of Amathel. The blow went high, an ostrich plume floated to the ground—no more, and Amathel was a sturdy fighter and had the strength of madness. Moreover, his was the longer weapon; it fell upon the scales of armour of Rames and beat him back, it fell again on his shoulder and struck him to his knee. It fell a third time, and glancing from the mail wounded him in the thigh so that the blood flowed. Now a soldier of Pharaoh's guard shouted to encourage his captain, and the Nubians shouted back, crying to their prince to slit the hog's throat.

Then Rames seemed to awake. He leapt from his knees, he smote and the blow went home, though the iron which the Nubian wore beneath his robe stayed it. He smote again more fiercely, and now it was the blood of Amathel that flowed. Then bending almost to the ground before the answering stroke, he leapt and thrust with all the strength of young limbs trained to war. He thrust and behold! between the broad shoulders of Amathel pierced from breast to back, appeared the point of the Egyptian's sword. For a moment the prince stood still, then he fell backwards heavily and lay dead.

Now, with a shout of rage the giants of the Nubian guard rushed at Rames to avenge their master's death, so that he must fly backwards before their spears, backwards into the ranks of the Pharaoh's guard. In a flash the Nubians were on them also and, how none could tell, a fearful fray began, for these soldiers hated each other, as their fathers had done before them, and there were none who could come between them, since at this feast no man bore weapons save the guards. Fierce was the battle, but the Nubians lacked a captain while Rames led veterans of Thebes picked for their valour.

The giants began to give. Here and there they fell till at length but three of them were left upon their feet, who threw down their arms and cried for mercy. Then it was for the first time that Rames understood what he had done. With bent head, his red sword in his hand, he climbed the dais and knelt before the throne of Pharaoh, saying:

"I have avenged my honour and the honour of Egypt. Slay me, O Pharaoh!"

But Pharaoh made no answer for his swoon still held him.

Then Rames turned to Tua and said:

"Pharaoh sleeps, but in your hand is the sceptre. Slay me, O Queen!"

Now Tua, who all this while had watched like one frozen into stone, seemed to thaw to life again. Her danger was past. She could never be forced to wed that coarse, black-souled Nubian, for Rames had killed him. Yonder he lay dead in all his finery with his hideous giants about him like fallen trees, and oh! in her rebellious human heart she blessed Rames for the deed.

But as she, who was trained in statecraft, knew well enough, if he had escaped the sword of Prince Amathel, it was but to fall into a peril from which there seemed to be no escape. This dead prince was the heir of a great king, of a king so great that for a century Egypt had dared to make no war upon his country, for it was far away, well-fortified and hard to come at across deserts and through savage tribes. Moreover, the man had been slain at a feast in Pharaoh's Court, and by an officer of Pharaoh's guard, which afterwards had killed his escort under the eyes of Egypt's monarchs, the hand of one of whom he sought in marriage. Such a deed must mean a bitter war for Egypt, and to those who struck the blow—death, as Rames himself knew well.

Tua looked at him kneeling before her, and her heart ached. Fiercely, despairingly she thought, throwing her soul afar to seek out wisdom and a way of escape for Rames. Presently in the blackness of her mind there arose a plan and, as ever was her fashion, she acted swiftly. Lifting her head she commanded that the doors should be locked and guarded so that none might go in or out, and that those physicians who were amongst the company should attend to the wounded, and to Pharaoh, who was ill. Then she called the High Council of the Kingdom, all of whom were gathered there about her, and spoke in a cold, calm voice, while the company flocked round to listen.

"Lords and people," she said, "the gods for their own purposes have suffered a fearful thing to come to pass. Egypt's guest and his guard have been slain before Egypt's kings, yes, at their feast and in their very presence, and it will be said far and wide that this has been done by treachery. Yet you know well, as I do, that it was no treachery, but a mischance. The divine prince who is dead, as all of you saw, grew drunken after the fashion of his people, and in his drunkenness he struck a high-born man, a Count of Egypt and an officer of Pharaoh, who to do him greater honour was set to wait upon him, calling him by vile names, and drew his sword upon him to kill him. Am I right? Did you see and hear these things?"

"Aye," answered the Council and the audience.

"Then," went on Tua, "this officer, forgetting all save his outraged honour, dared to fight for his life even against the Prince of Kesh, and being the better man, slew him. Afterwards the servants of the Prince of Kesh attacked him and Pharaoh's guard, and were conquered and the most of them killed, since none here had arms wherewith to part them. Have I spoken truth?"

"Yea, O Queen," they answered again by their spokesman. "Rames and the royal guard have little blame in the matter," and from the rest of them rose a murmur of assent.

"Now," went on Tua with gathering confidence, for she felt that all saw with her eyes, "to add to our woes Pharaoh, my father, has been smitten by the gods. He sleeps; he cannot speak; I know not whether he will live or die, and therefore it would seem that I, the duly-crowned Queen of Egypt, must act for him as was provided in such a case, since the matter is very urgent and may not be delayed. Is it your will," she added, addressing the Council, "that I should so act as the gods may show me how to do?"

"It is right and fitting," answered the Vizier, the King's companion, on behalf of all of them.

"Then, priests, lords and people," continued the Queen, "what course shall we take in this sore strait? Speaking with the voice of all of you and on your behalf, I can command that the Count Rames and all those other chosen men whom Pharaoh loves, who fought with him, shall be slain forthwith. This, indeed," she added slowly, "I should wish to do, since although Rames had suffered intolerable insult such as no high-born man can be asked to bear even from a prince, and he and all of them were but fighting to save their lives and to show the Nubians that we are not cowards here in Egypt, without doubt they have conquered and slain the heir of Kesh and his black giants who were our guests, and for this deed their lives are forfeit."

She paused watching, while although here and there a voice answered "Yes" or "They must die," from the rest arose a murmur of dissent. For in their hearts the company were on the side of Rames and Pharaoh's guards. Moreover, they were proud of the young captain's skill and courage, and glad that the Nubians, whom they hated with an ancient hate, had been defeated by the lesser men of Egypt, some of whom were their friends or relatives.

Now, while they argued among themselves Tua rose from her chair and went to look at Pharaoh, whom the physicians were attending, chafing his hands and pouring water on his brow. Presently she returned with tears standing in her beautiful eyes, for she loved her father, and said in a heavy voice:

"Alas! Pharaoh is very ill. Set the evil has smitten him, and it is hard, my people, that he perchance may be taken from us and we must bear such woe, because of the ill behaviour of a royal foreigner, for I cannot forget that it was he who caused this tumult."

The audience agreed that it was very hard, and looked angrily at the surviving Nubians, but Tua, conquering herself, continued:

"We must bear the blows that the fates rain on us, nor suffer our private grief to dull the sword of justice. Now, as I have said, even though we love them as our brothers or our husbands, yet the Count Rames and his brave comrades should perish by a death of shame, such a death as little befits the flower of Pharaoh's guard."

Again she paused, then went on in the midst of an intense silence, for even the physicians ceased from their work to hearken to her decree, as supreme judge of Egypt.

"And yet, and yet, my people, even as I was about to pass sentence upon them, uttering the doom that may not be recalled, some guardian spirit of our land sent a thought into my heart, on which I think it right to take your judgment. If we destroy these men, as I desire to destroy them, will they not say in the Southern Country and in all the nations around, that first they had been told to murder the Prince of Kesh and his escort, and then were themselves executed to cover up our crime? Will it not be believed that there is blood upon the hands of Pharaoh and of Egypt, the blood of a royal guest who, it is well known, was welcomed here with love and joy, that he might—oh! forgive me, I am but a maiden, I cannot say it. Nay, pity me not and answer not till I have set out all the case as best I may, which I fear me is but ill. It is certain that this will be said—aye, and believed, and we of Egypt all called traitors, and that these men, who after all, however evil has been their deed, are brave and upright, will be written in all the books of all the lands as common murderers, and go down to Osiris with that ill name branded on their brows. Yes, and their shame will cling to the pure hands of Pharaoh and his councillors."

Now at this picture the people murmured, and some of the noble women there began to weep outright.

"But," proceeded Tua with her pleading voice, "how if we were to take another course? How if we commanded this Count Rames and his companions to journey, with an escort such as befits the Majesty of Pharaoh, to the far city of Napata, and there to lay before the great king of that land by writings and the mouths of witnesses, all the sad story of the death of his only son? How if we sent letters to this Majesty of Kesh, saying, 'Thou hast heard our tale, thou knowest all our woe. Now judge. If thou art noble-hearted and it pleases thee to acquit these men, acquit them and we will praise thee. But if thou art wroth and stern and it pleases thee to condemn these men, condemn them, and send them back to us for punishment, that punishment which thou dost decree.' Is that plan good, my people? Can his Majesty of Kesh complain if he is made judge in his own cause? Can the kings and captains of other lands then declare that in Egypt we work murder on our guests? Tell me, who have so little wisdom, if this plan is good, as I dare to say to you, it seems to me."

Now with one voice the Council and all the guests, and especially the guards themselves who were on their trial, save Rames, who still knelt in silence before the Queen, cried out that it was very good. Yes;

they clapped their hands and shouted, vowing to each other that this young Queen of theirs was the Spirit of Wisdom come to earth, and that her excellent person was filled with the soul of a god.

But she frowned at their praises and, holding up her sceptre, sternly commanded silence.

"Such is your decree, O my Council," she cried, "and the decree of all you here present, who are the noblest of my people, and I, as I am bound by my oath of crowning, proclaim and ratify it, I, Neter-Tua, who am named Star and Daughter of Amen, who am named Glorious in Ra, who am named Hathor, Strong in Beauty, who am crowned Queen of the Upper and the Lower Land. I proclaim—write it down, O Scribes, and let it be registered this night that the decree may stand while the world endures—that two thousand of the choicest troops of Egypt shall sail up Nile, forthwith, for Kesh, and that in command of them, so that all may know his crime, shall go the young Count Rames, and with him those others who also did the deed of blood."

Now at this announcement, which sounded more like promotion than disgrace, some started and Rames looked up, quivering in all his limbs.

"I proclaim," went on Tua quickly, "that when they are come to Napata they shall kneel before its king and submit themselves to the judgment of his Majesty, and having been judged, shall return and report to us the judgment of his Majesty, that it may be carried out as his Majesty of Kesh shall appoint. Let the troops and the ships be made ready this very night, and meanwhile, save when he appears before us to take his orders as general, in token of our wrath, we banish the Count Rames from our Court and Presence, and place his companions under guard."

So spoke Tua, and the royal decree having been written down swiftly and read aloud, she sealed and signed with her sign-manual as Queen, that it might not be changed or altered, and commanded that copies of it should be sent to all the Governors of the *nomes* of Egypt, and a duplicate prepared and despatched with this royal embassy, for so she named it, to be delivered to the King of Kesh with the letters of condolence, and the presents of ceremony, and the body of Amathel, the Prince of Kesh, now divine in Osiris.

Then, at length, the doors were thrown open and the company dispersed, Rames and the guard being led away by the Council and placed in safe keeping. Also Pharaoh, still senseless but breathing quietly, was carried to his bed, and the dead were taken to the embalmers, whilst Tua, so weary that she could scarcely walk, departed to her chambers leaning on the shoulder of the royal Nurse, Asti, the mother of Rames.

Chapter 6

The Oath of Rames and of Tua

Still robed Tua lay upon a couch, for she would not seek her bed, while Asti stood near to her, a dark commanding figure.

"Your Majesty has done strange things to-night," said Asti in her quiet voice.

Tua turned her head and looked at her, then answered:

"Very strange, Nurse. You see, the gods and that troublesome son of yours and Pharaoh's sudden sickness threw the strings of Fate into my hand, and—I pulled them. I always had a fancy for the pulling of strings, but the chance never came my way before."

"It seems to me that for a beginner your Majesty pulled somewhat hard," said Asti drily.

"Yes, Nurse, so hard that I think I have pulled your son off the scaffold into a place of some honour, if he knows how to stay there, though it was the Council and the lords and the ladies, who thought that *they* pulled. You see one must commence as one means to go on."

"Your Majesty is very clever; you will make a great Queen—if you do not overpull yourself."

"Not half so clever as you were, Asti, when you made that monkey come out of the vase," answered Tua, laughing somewhat hysterically. "Oh! do not look innocent, I know it was your magic, for I could feel it passing over my head. How did you do it, Asti?"

"If your Majesty will tell me how you made the lords of Egypt consent to the sending of an armed expedition to Napata under the command of a lad, a mere captain who had just killed its heir-apparent before their eyes, which decree, if I know anything of Rames, will mean a war between Kesh and Egypt, I will tell you how I made the monkey come out of the vase."

"Then I shall never learn, Nurse, for I can't because I don't know. It came into my mind, as music comes into my throat, that is all.

Rames should have been beheaded at once, shouldn't he, for not letting that black boar tusk him? Do you think he poured the wine over Amathel's head on purpose?" and again she laughed.

"Yes, I suppose that he should have been killed, as he would have been if your Majesty had not chanced to be so fond——"

"Talking of wine," broke in Tua, "give me a cup of it. The divine Prince of Kesh who was to have been my husband—did you understand, Asti, that they really meant to make that black barbarian my husband?—I say that the divine Prince, who now sups with Osiris, drank so much that I could not touch a drop, and I am tired and thirsty, and have still some things to do to-night."

Asti went to a table where stood a flagon of wine wreathed in vine leaves, and by it cups of glass, and filling one of them brought it to Tua.

"Here's to the memory of the divine prince, and may he have left the table of Osiris before I come there. And here's to the hand that sent him thither," said Tua recklessly. Then she drained the wine, every drop of it, and threw the cup to the marble floor where it shattered into bits.

"What god has entered into your Majesty to-night?" asked Asti quietly.

"One that knows his own mind, I think," replied Tua. "There, I feel strong again, I go to visit Pharaoh. Come with me, Asti."

When Tua arrived at the bedside of Pharaoh she found that the worst of the danger was over. Fearing for his life the physicians had bled him, and now the fit had passed away and his eyes were open, although he was unable to speak and did not know her or anyone. She asked whether he would live or die, and was told that he would live, or so his doctors believed, but that for a long while he must lie quite quiet, seeing as few people as possible, and above all being troubled with no business, since, if he were wearied or excited, the fit would certainly return and kill him. So, rejoicing at this news which was better than she had expected, Tua kissed her father and left him.

"Now will your Majesty go to bed?" asked Asti when she had returned to her own apartments.

"By no means," answered Tua, "I wear Pharaoh's shoes and have much business left to do to-night. Summon Mermes, your husband."

So Mermes came and stood before her. He was still what he had been in the old days when Tua played as an infant in his house, stern, noble-looking and of few words, but now his hair had grown white and his face was drawn with grief, both for the sake of Rames, whose hot blood had brought him into so much danger, and because Pharaoh, who was his friend, lay between life and death.

Tua looked at him and loved him more than ever, for now that he was troubled some new likeness to Rames appeared upon his face which she had never seen before.

"Take heart, noble Mermes," she said gently, "they say that Pharaoh stays with us yet a while."

"I thank Amen," he answered, "for had he died, his blood would have been upon the hands of my House."

"Not so, Mermes; it would have been upon the hands of the gods. You spring from a royal line; say, what would you have thought of your son if after being struck by that fat Nubian, he had cowered at his feet and prayed for his life like any slave?"

Mermes flushed and smiled a little, then said:

"The question is rather—What would you have thought, O Queen?"

"I?" answered Tua. "Well, as a queen I should have praised him much, since then Egypt would have been spared great trouble, but as a woman and a friend I should never have spoken to him again. Honour is more than life, Mermes."

"Certainly honour is more than life," replied Mermes, staring at the ceiling, perhaps to hide the look upon his face, "and for a little while Rames seems to be in the way of it. But those who are set high have far to fall, O Queen, and—forgive me—he is my only child. Now when Pharaoh recovers——"

"Rames will be far away," broke in Tua. "Go, bring him here at once, and with him the Vizier and the chief scribe of the Council. Take this ring, it will open all doors," and she drew the signet from her finger and handed it to him.

"At this hour, your Majesty?" said Mermes in a doubtful voice.

"Have I not spoken," she answered impatiently. "When the welfare of Egypt is at stake I do not sleep."

So Mermes bowed and went, and while he was gone Tua caused Asti to smooth her hair and change her robe and ornaments for others which, although she did not say so, she thought became her better. Then she sat her down in a chair of state in her chamber of audience, and waited, while Asti stood beside her asking no questions, but wondering.

At length the doors were opened, and through them appeared Mermes and the Vizier and the chief of the scribes, both of them trying to hide their yawns, for they had been summoned from their beds who were not wont to do state business at such hours. After them limped Rames, for his wound had grown stiff, who looked bewildered, but otherwise just as he had left the feast.

Now, without waiting for the greetings of ceremony, Tua began to question the Vizier as to what steps had been taken in furtherance of her decrees, and when he assured her that the business was on foot, went into its every detail with him, as to the ships and the officers and the provisioning of the men, and so forth. Next she set herself to dictate despatches to the captains and barons who held the fortresses on the Upper Nile, communicating to them Pharaoh's orders on this matter, and the commission of Rames, whereby he, whose hands had done the ill, was put in command of the great embassy that went to make amends.

These being finished, she sent away the scribe to spend the rest of the night in writing them in duplicate, bidding him bring them to her in the early morning to be sealed. Next addressing Rames, she commanded him to start on the morrow with those troops which were ready to Takensit above the first Cataract of the Nile, which was the frontier fortress of Egypt, and there wait until the remainder of the soldiers joined them, bearing with them her presents to the King of Kesh, and the embalmed body of the Prince Amathel.

Rames bowed and said that her orders should be obeyed, and the audience being finished, still bowing and supported by Mermes, began to walk backwards towards the door, his eyes fixed upon the face of Tua, who sat with bent head, clasping the arms of her chair like one in difficulty and doubt. When he had gone a few steps she seemed to come to some determination, for with an effort she raised herself and said:

"Return, Count Rames, I have a message to give you for the King of Kesh who, unhappy man, has lost his son and heir, and it is one that no other ears must hear. Leave me a while with this captain, O Mermes and Asti, and see that none listen to our talk. Presently I will summon you to conduct him away."

They hesitated, for this thing seemed strange, then noting the look she gave them, departed through the doors behind the royal seat.

Now Rames and the Queen were left alone in that great, lighted chamber. With bent head and folded arms he stood before her while she looked at him intently, yet seemed to find no words to say. At length she spoke in a sweet, low voice.

"It is many years since we were playmates in the courts of the temple yonder, and since then we have never been alone together, have we, Rames?"

"No, Great Lady," answered Rames, "for you were born to be a queen, and I am but a humble soldier who cannot hope to consort with queens."

"Who cannot hope! Would you wish to then if you could?"

"O Queen," answered Rames, biting his lips, "why does it please you to make a mock of me?"

"It does not please me to do any such thing, for by my father Amen, Rames, I wish that we were children once more, for those were happy days before they separated us and set you to soldiering and me to statecraft."

"You have learnt your part well, Star of the Morning," said Rames, glancing at her quickly.

"Not better than you, playmate Rames, if I may judge from your sword-play this night. So it seems that we both of us are in the way of becoming masters of our trades."

"What am I to say to your Majesty? You have saved my life when it was forfeit——"

"As once you saved mine when it was forfeit, and at greater risk. Look at your hand, it will remind you. It was but tit for tat. And, friend Rames, this day I came near to being eaten by a worse crocodile than that which dwells in the pool yonder."

"I guessed as much, Queen, and the thought made me mad. Had it not been for that I should only have thrown him down. Now that crocodile will eat no more maidens."

"No," answered Tua, rubbing her chin, "he has gone to be eaten by Set, Devourer of Souls, has he not? But I think there may be trouble between Egypt and Kesh, and what Pharaoh will say when he recovers I am sure I do not know. May the gods protect me from his wrath."

"Tell me, if it pleases your Majesty, what is my fate? I have been named General of this expedition over the heads of many, I who am but a captain and a young man and an evil-doer. Am I to be killed on the journey, or am I to be executed by the King of Kesh?"

"If any kill you on the journey, Rames, they shall render me an account, be it the gods themselves, and as for the vengeance of the King of Kesh—well, you will have two thousand picked men with you and the means to gather more as you go. Listen now, for this is not in the decree or in the letters," she added, bending towards him and whispering. "Egypt has spies in Kesh, and, being industrious, I have read their reports. The people there hate the upstart race that rules them, and the king, who alone is left now that Amathel is dead, is old and half-witted, for all that family drink too much. So if the worst comes to the worst, do you think that you need be killed, you," she added meaningly, "who, if the House of Amathel were not, would by descent be King of Kesh, as, if I and my House were not, you might be Pharaoh of Egypt?"

Rames studied the floor for a little, then looked up and asked: "What shall I do?"

"It seems that is for you to find out," replied Tua, in her turn studying the ceiling. "Were I in your place, I think that, if driven to it, *I* should know what to do. One thing, however, I should *not* do. Whatever may be the judgment of the divine King of Kesh upon you, and that can easily be guessed, I should not return to Egypt with my escort, until I was quite sure of my welcome. No, I think that I should stop in Napata, which I am told is a rich and pleasant city, and try to put its affairs in order, trusting that Egypt, to which it once belonged, would in the end forgive me for so doing."

"I understand," said Rames, "that whatever happens, I alone am to blame."

"Good, and of course there are no witnesses to this talk of ours. Have you also been taking lessons in statecraft in your spare hours, Rames, much as I have tried to learn something of the art of war?"

Rames made no answer, only these two strange conspirators looked at each other and smiled.

"Your Majesty is weary. I must leave your Majesty," he said presently.

"You must be wearier than I am, Rames, with that wound, which I think has not been dressed, although it is true that we have both fought to-night. Rames, you are going on a far journey. I wonder if we shall ever meet again."

"I do not know," he answered with a groan, "but for my sake it is better that we should not. O Morning Star, why did you save me this night, who would have been glad to die? Did not that *Ka* of yours tell you that I should have been glad to die, or my mother, who is a magician?"

"I have seen nothing of my *Ka*, Rames, since we played together in the temple—ah! those were happy days, were they not? And your mother is a discreet lady who does not talk to me about you, except to warn me not to show you any favour, lest others should be jealous and murder you. Shall you then be sorry if we do not meet again? Scarcely, I suppose, since you seem so anxious to die and be rid of me and all things that we know."

Now Rames pressed his hand upon his heart as though to still its beating, and looked round him in despair. For, indeed, that heart of his felt as though it must burst.

"Tua," he gasped desperately, "can you for a minute forget that you are Queen of the Upper and the Lower Land, who perhaps will soon be Pharaoh, the mightiest monarch in the world, and remember only that you are a woman, and as a woman hear a secret and keep it close?"

"We have been talking secrets, Rames, as we used to do, you remember, long ago, and you will not tell mine which deal with the State. Why, then, should I tell yours? But be short, it grows late, or rather early, and as you know, we shall not meet again."

"Good," he answered. "Queen Neter-Tua, I, your subject, dare to love you."

"What of that, Rames? I have millions of subjects who all profess to love me."

He waved his hand angrily, and went on:

"I dare to love you as a man loves a woman, not as a subject loves a queen."

"Ah!" she answered in a new and broken voice, "that is different, is it not? Well, all women love to be loved, though some are queens and some are peasants, so why should I be angry? Rames, now, as in past days, I thank you for your love."

"It is not enough," he said. "What is the use of giving love? Love should be lent. Love is an usurer that asks high interest. Nay, not the interest only, but the capital and the interest to boot. Oh, Star! what happens to the man who is so mad as to love the Queen of Egypt?"

Tua considered this problem as though it were a riddle to which she was seeking an answer.

"Who knows?" she replied at length in a low voice. "Perhaps it costs him his life, or perhaps—perhaps he marries her and becomes Pharaoh of Egypt. Much might depend on whether the queen chanced to care about such a man."

Now Rames shook like a reed in the evening wind, and he looked at her with glowing eyes.

"Tua," he whispered, "can it be possible—do you mean that I am welcome to you, or are you but drawing me to shame and ruin?"

She made no answer to him in words, only with a certain grave deliberation, laid down the little ivory sceptre that she held, and suffering her troubled eyes to rest upon his eyes, bent forward and stretched out her arms towards him.

"Yes, Rames," she murmured into his ear a minute later, "I am drawing you to whatever may be found upon this breast of mine, love, or majesty, or shame, or ruin, or the death of one or both of us, or all of them together. Are you content to take the chances of this high game, Rames?"

"Ask it not, Tua. You know, you know!"

She kissed him on the lips, and all her heart and all her youth were in that kiss. Then, gently enough, she pushed him from her, saying:

"Stand there, I would speak with you, and as I have said, the time is short. Hearken to me, Rames, you are right; I know, as I have always known, and as you would have known also had you been less foolish than you are. You love me and I love you, for so it was decreed where souls are made, and so it has been from the beginning and so it shall be to the end. You, a gentleman of Egypt, love the Queen of Egypt, and she is yours and no other man's. Such is the decree of him who caused us to be born upon the same day, and to be nursed upon the same kind breast. Well, after all, why not? If love brings death upon us, as well may chance, at least the love will remain which is worth it all, and beyond death there is something."

"Only this, Tua, I seek the woman not a throne, and alas! through me you may be torn from your high place."

"The throne goes with the woman, Rames, they cannot be separated. But, say, something comes over me; if that happened, if I were an outcast, a wanderer, with nothing save this shape and soul of mine, and it were you that sat upon a throne, would you still love me, Rames?"

"Why ask such questions?" he replied indignantly. "Moreover, your talk is childish. What throne can I ever sit on?"

A change fell upon her at his words. She ceased to be the melting, passionate woman, and became once more the strong, far-seeing queen.

"Rames," she said, "you understand why, although it tears my heart, I am sending you so far away and into so many dangers, do you not? It is to save your life, for after what has chanced to-night in this fashion or in that here you would certainly die, as, had it not been for that plan of mine you must have died two hours ago. There are many who hate you, Rames, and Pharaoh may recover, as I pray the gods he will, and over-ride my will, for you have slain his guest who was brought here to marry me."

"I understand all of these things, Queen."

"Then awake, Rames, look to the future and understand that also, if, as I think, you have the wit. I am sending you with a strong escort, am I not? Well, that King of Kesh is old and feeble, and you have a claim upon his crown. Take it, man, and set it on your head, and as King of Kesh ask the hand of Egypt's Queen in marriage. Then who would say you nay—not Egypt's Queen, I think, or the people of Egypt who hunger for the rich Southern Land which they have lost."

So she spoke, and as these high words passed her lips she looked so splendid and so royal that, dazzled by the greatness of her majesty. Rames bowed himself before her as before the presence of a god. Then, aware that she was trying him in the balance of her judgment, he straightened himself and spoke to her as prince speaks to prince.

"Star of Amen," he said, "it is true that though here we are but your humble subjects, the blood of my father and of myself is as high as yours, and perhaps more ancient, and it is true that now yonder Amathel is dead, after my father, in virtue of those who went before us I have more right than any other to the inheritance of Kesh. Queen, I hear your words, I will take it if I can, not for its own sake, but to win you, and if I fail you will know that I died doing my best. Queen, we part and this is a far journey. Perhaps we may never meet again; at the best we must be separated for long. Queen, you have honoured me with your love, and therefore I ask a promise of you, not as a woman only, but as Queen. I ask that however strait may be the circumstances, whatever reasons of State may push you on, while I live you will take no other man to husband—no, not even if he offers you half the world in dower."

"I give it," she answered. "If you should learn that I am wed to any man upon the earth then spit upon my name as a woman, and as Queen cast me off and overthrow me if you can. Deal with me, Rames, as in such a case I will deal with you. Only be sure of your tidings ere you believe them. Now there is nothing more to say. Farewell to you, Rames, till we meet again beneath or beyond the sun. Our royal pact is made. Come, seal it and begone."

She rose and stretched out her sceptre to him, which he kissed as her faithful subject. Next, with a swift movement, she lifted the golden *uraeus* circlet from her brow and for a moment set it on his head, crowning him her king, and while it rested there she, the Queen of Egypt, bent the knee before him and did him homage. Then she cast down crown and sceptre, and as woman fell upon her lover's breast while the bright rays of morning, flowing suddenly through the eastern window-place of that splendid hall, struck upon them both, clothing them in a robe of glory and of flame.

Soon, very soon, it was done and Tua, seated there in light, watched Rames depart into the outer shadow, wondering when and how she would see him come again. For her heart was heavy within her, and even in this hour of triumphant love she greatly feared the future and its gifts.

Chapter 7

Tua Comes to Memphis

So that day Rames departed for Takensit with what ships and men could be got together in such haste. There, at the frontier post, he waited till the rest of the soldiers should join him, bringing with them the hastily embalmed body of Prince Amathel whom he had slain, and the royal gifts to the King of Kesh. Then, without a moment's delay, he sailed southwards with his little army on the long journey, fearing lest if he tarried, orders might come to him to return to Thebes. Also he desired to reach Napata before the heavy news of the death of the King's son, and without warning of the approach of Egypt's embassy.

With Tua he had no more speech, although as his galley was rowed under the walls of the palace, at a window of the royal apartments he saw a white draped figure that watched them go by. It was standing in the shadow so that he could not recognise the face, but his heart told him that this was none other than the Queen herself, who appeared there to bid him farewell.

So Rames rose from the chair in which he was seated on account of the hurt to his leg and saluted with his sword, and ordered the crew to do likewise by lifting up their oars. Then the slender figure bowed in answer, and he went on to fulfil his destiny, leaving Neter-Tua, Morning Star of Amen, to fulfil hers.

Before he sailed, however, Mermes his father and Asti his mother visited him in a place apart.

"You were born under a strange star, my son," said Mermes, "and I know not whither it will lead you, who pray that it may not be a meteor which blazes suddenly in the heavens and disappears to return no more. All the people talk of the favour the Queen has shown you who, instead of ordering you to be executed for the deed you did which robbed her of a royal husband, has set you in command of an army, you, a mere youth, and received you in secret audience, an honour granted to very few. Fate that has passed me by gives the dice to your young hand, but how the cast will fall I know not, nor shall I live to see, or so I believe."

"Speak no such evil-omened words, my father," answered Rames tenderly, for these two loved each other. "To me it seems more likely that it is I who shall not live, for this is a strange and desperate venture upon which I go, to tell to a great king the news of the death of his only son at my own hand. Mother, you are versed in the books of wisdom and can see that which is hidden to our eyes. Have you no word of comfort for us?"

"My son," answered Asti, "I have searched the future, but with all my skill it will open little of its secrets to my sight. Yet I have learned something. Great fortunes lie before you, and I believe that you and I shall meet again. But to your beloved father bid farewell."

At these words Rames turned his head aside to hide his tears, but Mermes bade him not to grieve, saying:

"Great is the mystery of our fates, my son. Some there be who tell us that we are but bubbles born of the stream to be swallowed up by the stream, clouds born of the sky to be swallowed up by the sky, the offspring of chance like the beasts and the birds, gnats that dance for an hour in the sunlight and are gone. But I believe it not, who hold that the gods clothe us with this robe of flesh for their own purpose, and that the spirit within us has been from the beginning and eternally will be. Therefore I love not life and fear not death, knowing that these are but doors leading to the immortal house that is prepared for us. The royal blood you have came to you from your mother and myself, but that our lots should have been humble, while yours, mayhap, will be splendid, does not move me to envy who perchance have been that you may be. You go forth to fulfil your fortunes which I believe are great, I bide here to fulfil mine which lead me to the tomb. I shall never see you in your power, if power comes to you, nor will your triumphant footsteps stir my sleep.

"Yet, Rames, remember that though you tread on cloth of gold and the bowed necks of your enemies, though love be your companion and diadems your crown, though flatteries float about you like incense in a shrine till, at length, you deem yourself a god, those footsteps of yours still lead to that same dark tomb and through it on to Judgment. Be great if you can, but be good as well as great. Take no man's life because you have the strength and hate him; wrong no woman because she is defenceless or can be bought. Remember that the beggar child playing in the sand may have a destiny more high than yours when all the earthly count is reckoned. Remember that you share the air you breathe with the cattle and the worm. Go your road rejoicing in your beauty and your youth and the good gifts that are given you, but know, Rames, that at the end of it I, who wait in the shadow of Osiris, I your father, shall ask an account thereof, and that beyond me stand the gods of Justice to test the web that you have woven. Now, Rames, my son, my blessing and the blessing of him who shaped us be with you, and farewell."

Then Mermes kissed him on the brow and, turning, left the room, nor did they ever meet again.

But Asti stayed awhile, and coming to him presently, looked Rames in the eyes, and said:

"Mourn not. Separations are no new thing, death is no new thing; all these sorrows have been on the earth for millions of years, and for millions of years yet shall be. Live out your life, rejoicing if the days be good, content if they be but ill, regretting nothing save your sins, fearing nothing, expecting nothing, since all things are appointed and cannot be changed."

"I hear," he answered humbly, "and I will not forget. Whether I succeed or fail you shall not be ashamed for me."

Now his mother turned to go also, but paused and said:

"I have a gift for you, Rames, from one whose name may not be spoken."

"Give it to me," he said eagerly, "I feared that it was all but a dream."

"Oh!" replied Asti scanning his face, "so there was a dream, was there? Did it fall upon you last night when the daughter of Amen, my foster-child, instructed you in secret?"

"The gift," said Rames, stretching out his hand.

Then, smiling in her quiet fashion, his mother drew from the bosom of her robe some object that was wrapped in linen and, touching her forehead with the royal seal that fastened it, gave it to Rames. With trembling fingers he broke the seal and there within the linen lay a ring which for some years, as Rames knew, Tua had worn upon the first finger of her right hand. It was massive and of plain gold, and upon the bezel of it was cut the symbol of the sun, on either side of which knelt a man and a woman crowned with the double crown of Egypt, and holding in their right hands the looped Sign of Life which they stretched up towards the glory of the sun.

"Do you know who wore that ring in long past days?" asked Asti of Rames who pressed it to his lips.

He shook his head who remembered only that Tua had worn it.

"It was your forefather and mine, Rames, the last of the royal rulers of our line, who reigned over Egypt and also over the Land of Kesh. A while ago the embalmers re-clothed his divine body in the tomb, and the Princess, who was present there with your father and myself, drew this ring off his dead hand and offered it to Mermes, who would not take it, seeing that it is a royal signet. So she wore it herself, and now for her own reasons she sends it to you, perhaps to give you authority in Kesh where that mighty seal is known."

"I thank the Queen," he murmured. "I shall wear it always."

"Then let it be on your breast till you have passed the frontier, lest some should ask questions that you find it hard to answer. My son," she went on quickly, "you dare to love this queen of ours."

"In truth I do, Mother. Did not you, who know everything, know that? Also it is your fault who brought us up together."

"Nay, my son, the fault of the gods who have so decreed. But—does she love you?"

"You are always with her, Mother, ask her yourself, if you need to ask. At least, she has sent me her own ring. Oh! Mother, Mother, guard her night and day, for if harm comes to her, then I die. Mother, queens cannot give themselves where they will as other women can; it is policy that thrusts their husbands on them. Keep her unwed, Mother. Though it should cost her her throne, still I say let her not be cast into the arms of one she hates. Protect her in her trial, if such should come; and if strength fails and the gods desert her, then hide her in the web of the magic that you have, and preserve her undefiled, for so shall I bless your name for ever."

"You fly at a rare bird, Rames, and there are many stronger hawks about besides that one you slew; yes, royal eagles who may strike down the pair of you. Yet I will do my best, who have long foreseen this hour, and who pray that before my eyes shut in death, they may yet behold you seated on the throne of your forefathers, crowned with power and with such love and beauty as have never yet been given to man. Now hide that ring upon your heart and your secret in it, as I shall, lest you should return no more to Egypt. Moreover, follow your royal Star and no other. Whatever counsel she may have given you, follow it also, stirring not to right or left, for I say that in that maiden breast of hers there dwells the wisdom of the gods."

Then holding up her hands over his head as though in blessing, Asti, too, turned and left him.

****

So Rames went and was no more seen, and by degrees the talk as to the matter of his victory over the Prince of Kesh, and as to his appointment by the whim of the maiden Queen to command the splendid embassy of atonement which she had despatched to the old King, the dead man's father, died away for lack of anything to feed on.

Tuà kept her counsel well, nor was aught known of that midnight interview with the young Count her general. Moreover, Napata was far away, so far that starting at the season when it did, the embassy could scarce return till two years had gone by, if ever it did return. Also few believed that whoever came back, Rames would be one of them, since it was said openly that so soon as he was beyond the frontiers of Egypt, the soldiers had orders to kill him and take on his body as a peace-offering.

Indeed, all praised the wit and wisdom of the Queen, who by this politic device, had rid herself of a troublesome business with as little scandal as possible, and avoided staining her own hands in the blood of a foster-brother. Had she ordered his death forthwith, they said, it would have been supposed also that she had put him away because he was of a royal race, one who, in the future, might prove a rival, or at least cause some rebellion.

Meanwhile greater questions filled the mouths of men. Would Pharaoh die and leave Neter-Tua, the young and lovely, to hold his throne, and if so, what would happen? It was a thousand years since a woman had reigned in Egypt, and none had reigned who were not wed. Therefore it seemed necessary that a husband should be found for her as soon as might be.

But Pharaoh did not die. On the contrary, though very slowly, he recovered and was stronger than he had been for years, for the fit that struck him down seemed to have cleared his blood. For some three months he lay helpless as a child, amusing himself as a child does with little things, and talking of children whom he had known in his youth, or when some of these chanced to visit him as old men, asking them to play with him with tops or balls.

Then one day came a change, and rising from his bed he commanded the presence of his Councillors, and when they came, inquired of them what had happened, and why he could remember nothing since the feast.

They put him off with soft words, and soon he grew weary and dismissed them. But after they had gone and he had eaten he sent for Mermes, the Captain of the Guard of Amen and his friend, and questioned him.

"The last thing I remember," he said, "was seeing the drunken Prince of Kesh fighting with your son, that handsome, fiery-eyed Count Rames whom some fool, or enemy, had set to wait upon him at table. It was a dog's trick, Mermes, for after all your blood is purer and more ancient than that of the present kings of Kesh. Well, the horror of the sight of my royal guest, the suitor for my daughter's hand, fighting with an officer of my own guard at my own board, struck me as a butcher strikes an ox, and after it all was blackness. What chanced, Mermes?"

"This, Pharaoh: My son killed Amathel in fair fight, then those black Nubian giants in their fury attacked your guard, but led by Rames the Egyptians, though they were the lesser men, overcame them and slew most of them. I am an old soldier, but never have I seen a finer fray——"

"A finer fray! A finer fray," gasped Pharaoh. "Why this will mean a war between Kesh and Egypt. And then? Did the Council order Rames to be executed, as you must admit he deserved, although you are his father?"

"Not so, O Pharaoh; moreover, I admit nothing, though had he played a coward's part before all the lords of Egypt, gladly would I have slain him with my own hand."

"Ah!" said Pharaoh, "there speaks the soldier and the parent. Well, I understand. He was affronted, was he not, by that bedizened black man? Were I in your place I should say as much. But—what happened?"

"Your Majesty having become unconscious," explained Mermes, "her Majesty the Queen Neter-Tua, Glorious in Ra, took command of affairs according to her Oath of Crowning. She has sent an embassy of atonement of two thousand picked soldiers to the King of Kesh, bearing with them the embalmed body of the divine Amathel and many royal gifts."

"That is good enough in its way," said Pharaoh. "But why two thousand men, whereof the cost will be very great, when a score would have sufficed? It is an army, not an embassy, and when my royal brother of Kesh sees it advancing, bearing with it the ill-omened gift of his only son's body, he may take alarm."

Mermes respectfully agreed that he might do so.

"What general is in command of this embassy, as it pleases you to call it?"

"The Count Rames, my son, is in command, your Majesty."

Now weak as he was still, Pharaoh nearly leapt from his chair:

"Rames! That young cut-throat who killed the Prince! Rames who is the last of the old rightful dynasty of Kesh! Rames, a mere captain, in command of two thousand of my veterans! Oh, I must still be mad! Who gave him the command?"

"The Queen Neter-Tua, Star of Amen, she gave him the command, O Pharaoh. Immediately after the fray in the hall she uttered her decree and caused it to be recorded in the usual fashion."

"Send for the Queen," said Pharaoh with a groan.

So Tua was summoned, and presently swept in gloriously arrayed, and on seeing her father sitting up and well, ran to him and embraced him and for a long time refused to listen to his talk of matters of State. At length, however, he made her sit by him still holding his hand, and asked her why in the name of Amen she had sent that handsome young firebrand, Rames, in command of the expedition to Kesh. Then she answered very sweetly that she would tell him. And tell him she did, at such length that before she had finished, Pharaoh, whose strength as yet was small, had fallen into a doze.

"Now, you understand," she said as he woke up with a start. "The responsibility was thrust upon me, and I had to act as I thought best. To have slain this young Rames would have been impossible, for all hearts were with him."

"But surely, Daughter, you might have got him out of the way."

"My father, that is what I have done. I have sent him to Napata, which is very much out of the way—many months' journey, I am told."

"But what will happen, Tua? Either the King of Kesh will kill him and my two thousand soldiers, or perhaps he will kill the King of Kesh as he killed his son, and seize the throne which his own forefathers held for generations. Have you thought of that?"

"Yes, my father, I thought of it, and if this last should happen through no fault of ours, would Egypt weep, think you?"

Now Pharaoh stared at Tua, and Tua looked back at Pharaoh and smiled.

"I perceive, Daughter," he said slowly, "that in you are the makings of a great queen, for within the silken scabbard of a woman's folly I see the statesman's sword of bronze. Only run not too fast lest you should fall upon that sword and it should pierce you."

Now Tua, who had heard such words before from Asti, smiled again but made no answer.

"You need a husband to hold you back," went on Pharaoh; "some great man whom you can love and respect."

"Find me such a man, my father, and I will wed him gladly," answered Tua in a sweet voice. "Only," she added, "I know not where he may be sought now that the divine Amathel is dead at the hand of the Count Rames, our general and ambassador to Kesh."

So when he grew stronger Pharaoh renewed his search for a husband meet to marry the Queen of Egypt. Now, as before, suitors were not lacking, indeed, his ambassadors and councillors sent in their names by twos and threes, but always when they were submitted to her, Tua found something against everyone of them, till at last it was said that she must be destined for a god since no mere mortal would serve her turn. But when this was reported to her, Tua only answered with a smile that she was destined to that royal lover of whom Amen had spoken to her mother in a dream; not to a god, but to the Chosen of the god, and that when she saw him, she felt sure she would know him at once and love him much.

After some months had gone by Pharaoh, quite weary of this play, asked the advice of his Council. They suggested to him that he should journey through the great cities of Egypt, both because the change might completely re-establish his divine health, and in the hope that on her travels the Queen Neter-Tua would meet someone of royal blood with whom she could fall in love. For by now it was evident to all of them that unless she did fall in love, she would not marry.

So that very night Pharaoh asked his daughter if she would undertake such a journey.

She answered that nothing would please her better, as she wearied of Thebes, and desired to see the other great cities of the land, to make herself known to those who dwell in them, and in each to be proclaimed as its future ruler. Also she wished to look upon the ocean whereof she had heard that it was so big that all the waters of the Nile flowing into it day and night made no difference to its volume.

Thus then began that pilgrimage which afterwards Tua recorded in the history of her reign on the walls of the wonderful temples that she built. Her own wish was that they should sail south to the frontiers of Egypt, since there she hoped that she might hear some tidings of Rames and his expedition, whereof latterly no certain word had come. This project, however, was over-ruled because in the south there were no great towns, also the inhabitants of the bordering desert were turbulent, and might choose that moment to attack.

So in the end they went down and not up the Nile, tarrying for a while at every great city, and especially at Atbu, the holy place where the head of Osiris is buried, and tens of thousands of the great men of Egypt have their tombs. Here Tua was crowned afresh in the very shrine of Osiris amidst the rejoicings of the people.

Then they sailed away to On, the City of the Sun, and thence to make offerings at the Great Pyramids which were built by some of the early kings who had ruled Egypt, to serve them as their tombs.

Neter-Tua entered the Pyramids to look upon the bodies of these Pharaohs who had been dead for thousands of years, and whose deeds were all forgotten, though her father would not accompany her there because the ways were so steep that he did not dare to tread them. Afterwards, with Asti and a small guard of the Arab chiefs of the desert, she mounted a dromedary and rode round them in the moonlight, hoping that she would meet the ghosts of those kings, and that they would talk with her as the ghost of her mother had done. But she saw no ghosts, nor would Asti try to summon them from their sleep, although Tua prayed her to do so.

"Leave them alone," said Asti, as they paused in the shadow of the greatest of the pyramids and stared at its shining face engraved from base to summit with many a mystic writing.

"Leave them alone lest they should be angry as Amen was, and tell your Majesty things which you do not wish to hear. Contemplate their mighty works, such as no monarch can build to-day, and suffer them to rest therein undisturbed by weaker folk."

"Do you call these mighty works?" asked Tua contemptuously, for she was angry because Asti would not try to raise the dead. "What are they after all, but so many stones put together by the labour of men to satisfy their own vanity? And of those who built them what story remains? There is none at all save some vain legends. Now if *I* live I will rear a greater monument, for history shall tell of me till time be dead."

"Perhaps, Neter-Tua, if you live and the gods will it, though for my part I think that these old stones will survive the story of most deeds."

****

On the morrow of this visit to the Pyramids Pharaoh and the Queen his daughter made their state entry into the great white-walled city of Memphis, where they were royally received by Pharaoh's brother, the Prince Abi, who was still the ruler of all this town and district. As it chanced these two had not met since Abi, many years before, came to Thebes, asking a share in the government of Egypt and to be nominated as successor to the throne.

Like every other lord and prince, he had been invited to be present at the great ceremony of the Crowning of Neter-Tua, but at the last moment sent his excuses, saying that he was ill, which seemed to be true. At any rate, the spies reported that he was confined to his bed, though whether sickness or his own will took him thither at this moment, there was nothing to show. At the time Pharaoh and his Council wondered a little that he had made no proposal for the marriage of one of his sons, of whom he had four, to their royal cousin, Neter-Tua, but decided that he had not done so because he was sure that it would not be accepted. For the rest, during all this period Abi had kept quiet in his own Government, which he ruled well and strongly, remitting his taxes to Thebes at the proper time with a ceremonial letter of homage, and even increasing the amount of them.

So it came about that Pharaoh, who by nature was kindly and unsuspicious, had long ago put away all mistrust of his brother, whose ambitions, he was sure, had come to an end with the birth of an heiress to the throne. Yet, when escorted only by five hundred of his guard, for this was a peaceful visit, Pharaoh rode into the mighty city and saw how impregnable were its walls and how strong its gates; saw also that the streets were lined with thousands of well-armed troops, doubts which he dismissed as unworthy, did creep into his heart. But if he said nothing of them, Tua, who rode in the chariot with him, was not so silent.

"My father," she said in a low voice while the crowds shouted their welcome, for they were alone in the chariot, the horses of which were led, "this uncle of mine keeps a great state in Memphis."

"Yes, Daughter, why should he not? He is its governor."

"A stranger who did not know the truth might think he was its king, my father, and to be plain, if I were Pharaoh, and had chosen to enter here, it would have been with a larger force."

"We can go away when we like, Tua," said Pharaoh uneasily.

"You mean, my father, that we can go away when it pleases the Prince your brother to open those great bronze gates that I heard clash behind us—then and not before."

At this moment their talk came to an end, for the chariot was stayed at the steps of the great hall where Abi waited to receive his royal guests. He stood at the head of the steps, a huge, coarse, vigorous man of about sixty years of age, on whose fat, swarthy face there was still, oddly enough, some resemblance to the delicate, refined-featured Pharaoh.

Tua summed him up in a single glance, and instantly hated him even more than she had hated Amathel, Prince of Kesh. Also she who had not feared the empty-headed, drunken Amathel, was penetrated with a strange terror of this man whom she felt to be strong and intelligent, and whose great, greedy eyes rested on her beauty as though they could not tear themselves away.

Now they were ascending the steps, and now Prince Abi was welcoming them to his "humble house," giving them their throne names, and saying how rejoiced he was to see them, his sovereigns, within the walls of Memphis, while all the time he stared at Tua.

Pharaoh, who was tired, made no reply, but the young Queen, staring back at him, answered:

"We thank you for your greeting, but then, my uncle Abi, why did you not meet us outside the gates of Memphis where we expected to find its governor waiting to deliver up the keys of Pharaoh's city to the officers of Pharaoh?"

Now Abi, who had thought to see some shrinking child clothed in the emblems of a queen, looked astonished at this tall and royal maiden who had so sharp a tongue, and found no words to answer her. So she swept past him and commanded to be shown where she should lodge in Memphis.

They led her to its greatest palace that had been prepared for Pharaoh and herself, a place surrounded by palm groves in the midst of the city, but having studied it with her quick eyes, she said that it did not please her. So search was made elsewhere, and in the end she chose another smaller palace that once had been a temple of Sekhet, the tiger-headed goddess of vengeance and of chastity, whereof the pylon towers fronted on the Nile which at its flood washed against them. Indeed, they were now part of the wall of Memphis, for the great unused gateway between them had been built up with huge blocks of stone.

Surrounding this palace and outside its courts, lay the old gardens of the temple where the priests of Sekhet used to wander, enclosed within a lofty limestone wall. Here, saying that the air from the river would be more healthy for him, Tua persuaded Pharaoh to establish himself and his Court, and to encamp the guards under the command of his friend Mermes, in the outer colonnades and gardens.

When it was pointed out to the Queen that, owing to the lack of dwelling-rooms, none which were fitting were left for her to occupy, she replied that this mattered nothing, since in the old pylon tower were two small chambers hollowed in the thickness of its walls, which were very pleasing to her, because of the prospect of the Nile and the wide flat lands and the distant Pyramids commanded from the lofty roof and window-places. So these chambers, in which none had dwelt for generations, were hastily cleaned out and furnished, and in them Tua and Asti her foster-mother, took up their abode.

Chapter 8

The Magic Image

That night Pharaoh and Tua rested in privacy with those members of the Court whom they had brought with them, but on the morrow began a round of festivals such as history scarcely told of in Egypt. Indeed, the feast with which it opened was more splendid than any Tua had seen at Thebes even at the time of her crowning, or on that day of blood and happiness when Amathel and his Nubian guards were slain and she and Rames declared their love. At this feast Pharaoh and the young Queen sat in chairs of gold, while the Prince Abi was placed on her right hand, and not on that of Pharaoh as he should have been as host and subject.

"I am too much honoured," said Tua, looking at him sideways. "Why do you not sit by Pharaoh, my uncle?"

"Who am I that I should take the seat of honour when my sovereigns come to visit me?" answered Abi, bowing his great head. "Let it be reserved for the high-priest of Osiris, that Holy One whom, after Ptah, we worship here above all other deities, for he is clothed with the majesty of the god of death."

"Of death," said Tua. "Is that why you put him by my father?"

"Indeed not," replied Abi, spreading out his hands, "though if a choice must be made, I would rather that he sat near one who is old and must soon be called the 'ever-living,' than at the side of the loveliest queen that Egypt has ever seen, to whom it is said that Amen himself has sworn a long life," and again he bowed.

"You mean that you think Pharaoh will soon die. Nay, deny it not, Prince Abi, I can read your thoughts, and they are ill-omened," said Tua sharply and, turning her head away, began to watch those about her.

Soon she noticed that behind Abi amongst his other officers stood a tall, grizzled man clad in the robes and cap of an astrologer, who appeared to be studying everything, and especially Pharaoh and herself, for whenever she looked round it was to find his quick, black eyes fixed upon her.

"Who is that man?" she whispered presently to Asti, who waited on her.

"The famous astrologer, Kaku, Queen. I have seen him before when he visited Thebes with the Prince before your birth. I will tell you of him afterwards. Watch him well."

So Tua watched and discovered several things, among them that Kaku observed everything that she and Pharaoh did, what they ate, to whom they spoke, and any words which fell from their lips, such as those that she had uttered about the god Osiris. All of these he noted down from time to time on his waxen tablets, doubtless that he might make use of them afterwards in his interpretation of the omens of the future.

Now, among the ladies of the Court who fanned Pharaoh and waited on him was that dancing girl of Abi's who many years before had betrayed him at Thebes, Merytra, Lady of the Footstool, now a woman of middle age, but still beautiful, of whom, although Tua disliked her, Pharaoh was fond because she was clever and witty of speech and amused him. For this reason, in spite of her history, he had advanced her to wealth and honour, and kept her about his person as a companion of his lighter hours. Something in this woman's manner attracted Tua's attention, for continually she looked at the astrologer, Kaku, who suddenly awoke to her presence and smiled as though he recognised an old friend. Then, when it was the turn of another to take her place behind Pharaoh, Merytra drew alongside of Kaku, and under shelter of her broad fan, spoke to him quickly, as though she were making some arrangement with him, and he nodded in assent, after which they separated again.

The feast wore on its weary course till, at length, the doors opened and slaves appeared bearing the mummy of a dead man, which they set upon its feet in the centre of the hall, whereon a toast-master cried:

"Drink and be merry, all ye great ones of the earth, who know not how soon ye shall come to this last lowly state."

Now this bringing in of the mummy was a very ancient rite, but one that had fallen into general disuse, so that as it chanced Tua, who had never seen it practised before, looked on it with curiosity not unmingled with disgust.

"Why is a dead king dragged from his sepulchre back into the world of life, my Uncle?" she asked, pointing to the royal emblems with which the corpse was clothed.

"It is no king, your Majesty," answered Abi, "but only the bones of some humble person, or perhaps a block of wood that wears the *uraeus* and carries the sceptre in honour of Pharaoh, our chief guest."

Now Tua frowned, and Pharaoh, who had overheard the talk, said, smiling sadly:

"A somewhat poor compliment, my brother, to one who, like myself, is old and sickly and not far from his eternal habitation. Yet why should I grumble at it who need no such reminder of that which awaits me and all of us?" and he leaned back in his chair and sighed, while Tua looked at him anxiously.

Then Abi ordered the mummy to be removed, declaring, with many apologies, that it had been brought there only because such was the ancient custom of Memphis, which, unlike Thebes, did not change its fashions. He added that this same body or figure, for he knew not which it was, having never troubled to inquire, had been looked upon by at least thirty Pharaohs, all as dead as it to-day, since it was the same that was used at the royal feasts before, long ago, the seat of government was moved to Thebes.

"If so," broke in Tua, who was angry, "it is time that it should be buried, if flesh and bone, or burned if wood. But Pharaoh is wearied. Have we your leave to depart, my Uncle?"

Without answering, Abi rose, as she thought to dismiss the company. But it was not so, for he raised a great, golden cup of wine and said:

"Before we part, my guests, let Memphis drink a welcome to the mighty Lord of the Two Lands who, for the first time in his long and glorious reign, honours it with his presence here to-day. As he said to me but now, my royal brother is weak and aged with sickness, nor can we hope that once his visit is ended, he will return again to the White-walled City. But as it chances the gods have given him a boon which they denied for long, the lovely daughter who shares his throne, and who, as we believe and pray, will reign after him when it pleases him to ascend into the kingdom of Osiris. Yet, my friends, it is evil that the safe and lawful government of Egypt should hang on one frail life. Therefore this is the toast to which I drink—that the Queen Neter-Tua, Morning Star of Amen, Hathor Strong in Beauty, who has rejected so many suitors, may before she departs from among us, find one to her liking, some husband of royal blood, skilled in the art of rule, whose strength and knowledge may serve to support her woman's weakness and inexperience in that sad hour when she finds herself alone."

Now the audience, who well understood the inner meaning and objects of this speech, rose and cheered furiously, as they had been schooled to do, emptying their cups to Pharaoh and to Tua and shouting:

"We know the man. Take him, glorious Queen, take him, Daughter of Amen, and reign for ever."

"What do they mean?" muttered Pharaoh, "I do not understand. Thank them, my daughter, my voice is weak, and let us begone."

So Tua rose when at length there was silence and, looking round her with flashing eyes, said in her clear voice that reached the furthest recesses of the hall:

"The Pharaoh, my father, and I, the Queen of the Upper and the Lower Lands, return thanks to you, our people of this city, for your loyal greetings. But as for the words that the Prince Abi has spoken, we understand them not. My prayer is that the Pharaoh may still reign in glory for many years, but if he departs and I remain, learn, O people, that you have naught to fear from the weakness and inexperience of your Queen. Learn also that she seeks no husband, nor when she seeks will she ever find one within the walls of Memphis. Rest you well, O people and you, my Uncle Abi, as now with your good leave we will do also."

Then, turning, she took her father by the hand and went without more words, leaving Abi staring at his guests while his guests stared back at him.

When Tua had reached the pylon tower, where she lodged, and her ladies had unrobed her and gone, she called Asti to her from the adjoining chamber and said:

"You are wise, my nurse, tell me, what did Abi mean?"

"If your Majesty cannot guess, then you are duller than I thought," answered Asti in her quick, dry fashion, adding; "however, I will try to translate. The Prince Abi, your noble uncle, means that he has trapped you here, and that you shall not leave these walls save as his wife."

Now fury took hold of Tua.

"How dare he speak such words?" she gasped, springing to her feet. "I, the wife of that old river-hog, my father's brother who might be my grandfather, that hideous, ancient lump of wickedness who boasts that he has a hundred sons and daughters; I, the Queen of Egypt, whose birth was decreed by Amen, I—how dare you?" and she ceased, choking in her wrath.

"The question is—how he dares, Queen. Still, that is his plot which he will carry through if he is able. I suspected it from the first, and that is why I always opposed this visit to Memphis, but you will remember that you bade me be silent, saying that you had determined to see the most ancient city in Egypt."

"You should not have been silent. You should have said what was in your mind, even if I ordered you from my presence. Neither Abi nor any of his sons proposed for my hand when the others did, therefore *I* suspected nothing——"

"After the fashion of women who have already given their hearts, Queen, and forget that they have other things to give—a kingdom, for instance. The snake does not roar like the lion, yet it is more to be feared."

"Once I am out of this place it is the snake that shall have cause to fear, Asti, for I will break its back and throw it writhing to the kites. Nurse, we must leave Memphis."

"That is not easy, Queen, since some ceremony is planned for each of the next eight days. If Pharaoh were to go away without attending them, he would anger all the people of the North which he has not visited since he was crowned."

"Then let them be angered; Pharaoh can do as he wills."

"Yes, Queen, at least, that is the saying. But do you think that Pharaoh wishes to bring about a civil war and risk his crown and yours? Listen: Abi is very strong, and under his command he has a greater army than Pharaoh can muster in these times of peace, for in addition to his trained troops, all the thousands of the Bedouin tribes of the desert look on him as lord, and at his word will fall on the wealth of Egypt like famished vultures on a fatted ox. Moreover, here you have but a guard of five hundred men, whereas Abi's regiments, summoned to do you honour, and his ships of war block the river and the southern road. How then will you leave Memphis without his good leave; how will you even send messengers to summon aid which could not reach you under fifty days?"

Now when she saw the greatness of the danger, Tua grew quite calm and answered:

"You have done wrong, Asti; if you foresaw all these things of which I never thought, you should have warned Pharaoh and his Council."

"Queen, I did warn them, and Mermes warned them also, but they would not listen, saying that they were but the idle dreams of one who strives to peep into the future and sees false pictures there. More, Pharaoh sent for me himself, and whilst thanking me and Mermes my husband, told me that he had inquired into the matter and found no cause to distrust Abi or those under his command. Moreover, he forbade me to speak to your Majesty about it, lest, being but young and a woman, you might be frightened and your pleasure spoilt."

"Who was his counsellor?" asked Tua.

"A strange one, I think, Queen. You know his waiting-woman,

Merytra, she of whom he is so fond, and who stood behind him with a fan this night."

"Aye, I know her," replied Tua, with emphasis. "She was ever whispering with that tall astrologer at the feast. But does Pharaoh take counsel with waiting-ladies of his private household?"

"With this waiting-lady, it seems, Queen. Perhaps you have not heard all her story, in the year before your birth Merytra came up the Nile with Abi. She was then quite young and very pretty; one of Abi's women. It seems that the Prince struck her for some fault, and being clever she determined to be revenged upon him. Soon she got her chance, for she heard Abi disclose to the astrologer Kaku, that same man whom you saw to-night talking with her, a plan that he had made to murder Pharaoh and declare himself king, from which Kaku dissuaded him. Having this secret and being bold, she fled at once from the ship of Abi, and that night told Pharaoh everything. But he forgave Abi, and sent him home again with honour who should have slain him for his treason. Only Merytra remained in the Court, and from that time forward Pharaoh, who trusted her and was caught by her wit and beauty, made it a habit to send for her when he wished to have news of Memphis where she was born, because she seemed always to know even the most secret things that were passing in that city. Moreover, often her information proved true."

"That is not to be wondered at, Nurse, seeing that doubtless it came from this Kaku, Abi's astrologer and magician."

"No, Queen, it is not to be wondered at, especially as she paid back secret for secret. Well, I believe that after I had warned Pharaoh of what I knew, never mind how, he sent for Merytra, who laughed the tale to scorn, and told him that Abi his brother had long ago abandoned all ambitions, being well content with his great place and power which one of his sons would inherit after him. She told him also that the troops were but assembled to do the greater honour to your Majesties who had no more loyal or loving subject than the Prince Abi, whom for her part she hated with good cause, as she loved Pharaoh and his House—with good cause. If there were any danger, she asked would she dare to put herself within the reach of Abi, the man that she had once betrayed because her heart was pure and true, and she was faithful to her king. So Pharaoh believed her, and I obeyed the orders of Pharaoh, knowing that if I did not do so he would grow angry and perhaps separate me from you, my beloved Queen and fosterling, which, now that Rames has gone, would, I think, have meant my death. Yet I fear that I have erred."

"Yes, I fear also that you have erred, Asti, but everything is forgiven to those who err through love," answered Tua kindly and kissing her. "Oh, my father, Pharaoh! What god fashioned you so weak that an evil spirit in a woman's shape can play the rudder to your policy! Leave me now, Asti, for I must sleep and call on Amen to aid his daughter. The snare is strong and cunning, but, perchance, in my dreams he will show me how it may be broke."

****

That night when the feast was ended Merytra, Pharaoh's favoured waiting-maid, did not return with the rest of the royal retinue to the temple where he lodged. As they went from the hall in state she whispered a few words into the ear of the chief Butler of the Household who, knowing that she had the royal pass to come in and out as she would, answered that the gate should be opened to her, and let her go.

So covering her head with a dark cloak Merytra slipped behind a certain statue in the ante-hall and waited till presently a tall figure, also wrapped in a dark cloak, appeared and beckoned to her. She followed it down sundry passages and up a narrow stair that seemed almost endless, until, at length, the figure unlocked a massive door, and when they had passed it, locked it again behind them.

Now Merytra found herself in a very richly furnished room lit by hanging-lamps, that evidently was the abode of one who watched the stars and practised magic, for all about were strange-looking brazen instruments and rolls of papyrus covered with mysterious signs, and suspended above the table a splendid divining ball of crystal. Merytra sank into a chair, throwing off her dark cloak.

"Of a truth, friend Kaku," she said, so soon as she had got her breath, "you dwell very near the gods."

"Yes, dear Merytra," he answered with a dry chuckle, "I keep a kind of half-way house to heaven. Perched here in my solitude I see and make note of what goes on above," and he pointed to the skies, "and retail the information, or as much of it as I think fit, to the groundlings below."

"At a price, I suppose, Kaku."

"Most certainly at a price, and I may add, a good price. No one thinks much of the physician who charges low fees. Well, you have managed to get here, and after all these years I am glad to see you again, looking almost as young and pretty as ever. Tell me your secret of eternal youth, dear Merytra."

Merytra, who was vain, smiled at this artful flattery, although, in truth, it was well deserved, for at an age when many Egyptians are old, she remained fresh and fair.

"An excellent conscience," she answered, "a good appetite and the virtuous, quiet life, which is the lot of the ladies of Pharaoh's Court—there you have the secret, Kaku. I fear that you keep too late hours, and that is why you grow white and withered like a mummy—not but that you look handsome enough in those long robes of yours," she added to gild the pill.

"It is my labours," he replied, making a wry face, for he too was vain. "My labours for the good of others, also indigestion and the draughts in this accursed tower where I sit staring at the stars, which give me rheumatism. I have got both of them now, and must take some medicine," and filling two goblets from a flask, he handed her one of them, saying, "drink it, you don't get wine like that in Thebes."

"It is very good," said Merytra when she had drunk, "but heavy. If I took much of that I think I should have 'rheumatism,' too. Now tell me, old friend, am I safe, in this place? No, not from Pharaoh, he trusts me and lets me go where I will upon his business—but from his royal brother. He used to have a long memory, and from the look of him I do not think that his temper has improved. You may remember a certain slap in the face and how I paid him back for it."

"He never knew it was you, Merytra. Being a mass of self-conceit, he thought that you ran away because he had banished you from his royal presence and presented you—to me."

"Oh, he thought that, did he! What a vain fool!"

"It was a very dirty trick you played me, Merytra," went on Kaku with indignation, for the rich wine coursing through his blood revived the sting of his loss. "You know how fond I always was of you, and indeed am still," he added, gazing at her admiringly.

"I felt that I was not worthy of so learned and distinguished a man," she replied, looking at him with her dark eyes. "I should only have hampered your life, dear Kaku, so I went into the household of that poor creature, Pharaoh, instead—Pharaoh's Nunnery we call it. But you will not explain the facts to Abi, will you?"

"No, I think not, Merytra, if we continue to get on as well as we do at present. But now you are rested, so let us come to business, for otherwise you will have to stop here all night and Pharaoh would be angry."

"Oh, to Set with Pharaoh! Though it is true that he is a good paymaster, and knows the value of a clever woman. Now, what is this business?"

The old astrologer's face grew hard and cunning. Going to the door he made sure that it was locked and drew a curtain over it. Then he took a stool and sat himself down in front of Merytra, in such a position that the light fell on her face while his own remained in shadow.

"A big business, Merytra, and by the gods I do not know that I should trust you with it. You tricked me once, you have tricked Pharaoh for years; how do I know that you will not play the same game once more and earn me an order to cut my own throat, and so lose life and soul together?"

"If you think that, Kaku, perhaps you will unlock the door and give me an escort home, for we are only wasting time."

"I don't know what to think, for you are as cunning as you are beautiful. Listen, woman," he continued in a savage whisper, and clasping her by the wrist. "If you are false, I tell you that you shall die horribly, for if the knife and poison fail, I am no charlatan, I have arts. I can make you turn loathsome to the sight and waste away, I can haunt you at nights so that you may never sleep a wink, save in full sunshine, and I will do it all and more. If I die, Merytra, we go together. Now will you swear to be true, will you swear it by the oath of oaths?"

The spy looked about her. She knew Kaku's power which was famous throughout Egypt, and that it was said to be of the most evil sort, and she feared him.

"It seems that this is a dangerous affair," she replied uneasily, "and I think that I can guess your aim. Now if I help you, Kaku, what am *I* to get?"

"Me," he answered.

"I am flattered, but what else?"

"After Pharaoh the greatest place and the most power in Egypt, as the wife of Pharaoh's Vizier."

"The wife? Doubtless from what I have heard of you, Kaku, there would be other wives to share these honours."

"No other wife—upon the oath, none, Merytra."

She thought a moment, looking at the wizened but powerful-faced old magician, then answered:

"I will take the oath and keep my share of it. See that you keep yours, Kaku, or it will be the worse for you, for women have their own evil power."

"I know it, Merytra, and from the beginning the wise have held that the spirit dwells, not in the heart or brain or liver, but in the female tongue. Now stand up."

She obeyed, and from some hidden place in the wall Kaku produced a book, or rather a roll of magical writings, that was encased in iron, the metal of the evil god, Typhon.

"There is no other such book as this," he said, "for it was written by the greatest of wizards who lived before Mena, when the god-kings ruled in Egypt, and I, myself, took it from among his bones, a terrible task for his *Ka* rose up in the grave and threatened me. He who can read in that book, as I can, has much strength, and let him beware who breaks an oath taken on that book. Now press it to your heart, Merytra, and swear after me."

Then he repeated a very terrible oath, for should it be violated it consigned the swearer to shame, sickness and misfortune in this world, and to everlasting torments in the next at the claws and fangs of beast-headed demons who dwell in the darkness beyond the sun, appointing, by name, those beings who should work the torments, and summoning them as witnesses to the bond.

Merytra listened, then said,

"You have left out your part of the oath, Friend, namely, that you promise that I shall be the only wife of Pharaoh's Vizier and hold equal power with him."

"I forgot," said Kaku, and added the words.

Then they both swore, touching their brows with the book, and as she looked up again, Merytra saw a strange, flame-like light pulse in the crystal globe that hung above her head, which became presently infiltrated with crimson flowing through it as blood might flow from a wound, till it glowed dull red, out of which redness a great eye watched her. Then the eye vanished and the blood vanished, and in place of them Queen Neter-Tua sat in glory on her throne, while the nations worshipped her, and by her side sat a man in royal robes whose face was hidden in a cloud.

"What do you see?" asked Kaku, following her gaze to the crystal.

She told him, and he pondered a while, then answered doubtfully:

"I think it is a good omen; the royal consort sits beside her. Only why was his face hidden?"

"I am sure I do not know," answered Merytra. "I think that strong, red wine of yours was doctored and has got into my head. But, come, we have sworn this oath, which I dare say will work in more ways than we guess, for such accursed swords have two edges to them. Now out with the plot, and throw a cloth over that crystal for I want to see no more pictures."

"It seems a pity since you have such a gift of vision," replied Kaku in the same dubious voice. Yet he obeyed, tying up the shining ball in a piece of mummy wrapping which he used in his spells.

"Now," he said, "I will be brief. My fat master, Abi, means to be Pharaoh of Egypt, and it seems that the best way to do so is by climbing into his niece's throne, where most men would like to sit."

"You mean by marrying her, Kaku."

"Of course. What else? He who marries the Queen, rules in right of the Queen."

"Indeed. Do you know anything of Neter-Tua?"

"As much as any other man knows; but what do you mean?"

"I mean that I shall be sorry for the husband who marries her against her will, however beautiful and high-placed she may be. I tell you that woman is a flame. She has more strength in her than all the magicians in Egypt, yourself among them. They say she is a daughter of Amen, and I believe it. I believe that the god dwells in her, and woe be to him whom she may chance to hate, if he comes to her as a husband."

"That is Abi's business, is it not? Our business, Merytra, is to get him there. Now we may take it this will not be with her consent."

"Certainly not, Kaku," she answered. "The gossip goes that she is in love with young Count Rames, who fought and killed the Prince of Kesh before her eyes, and now has gone to make amends to the king his father at the head of an army."

"That may be true, Merytra. Why not? He is her foster-brother and of royal blood, bold, too, and handsome, they say. Well, queens have no business to be in love. That is the privilege of humbler folk like you and me, Merytra. Say, is she suspicious—about Prince Abi, I mean?"

"I do not know, but Asti, her nurse and favourite lady, the wife of Mermes and mother of Rames, is suspicious enough. She is a greater magician than you are, Kaku, and if she could have had her way Pharaoh would never have set foot in Memphis. But I got your letter and over-persuaded him, the poor fool. You see he thinks me faithful to his House, and that is why I am allowed to be here to-night, to collect information."

"Ah! Well, what Asti knows the Queen will know, and she is stronger than Pharaoh, and notwithstanding all Abi's ships and soldiers, may break away from Memphis and make war upon him. So it comes to this—Pharaoh must stay here, for his daughter will not desert him."

"How will you make him stay here, Kaku? Not by——" and she glanced towards the shrouded crystal.

"Nay, no blood if it can be helped. He must not even seem to be a prisoner, it is too dangerous. But there are other ways."

"What ways? Poison?"

"Too dangerous again. Now, if he fell sick, and he has been sick before, and could not stir, it would give us time to bring about the marriage, would it not? Oh! I know that he is well at present—for him, but look here, Merytra, I have something to show you."

Then going to a chest Kaku took from it a plain box of cedar wood which was shaped like a mummy case, and, lifting off its lid, revealed within it a waxen figure of the length of a hand. This figure was beautifully fashioned to the living likeness of Pharaoh, and crowned with the double crown of Egypt.

"What is it?" asked Merytra, shrinking back. "An *ushapti* to be placed in his tomb?"

"No, woman, a magic *Ka* fashioned with many a spell out of yonder ancient roll, that can bring *him* to the tomb if it be rightly used, as you shall use it."

"I!" she exclaimed, starting. "How?"

"Thus: You, as one of Pharaoh's favourite ladies, have charge of the chamber where he sleeps. Now you must make shift to enter there alone and lay this figure in his bed, that the breath of Pharaoh may enter into it. Then take it from the bed and say these words, 'Figure, figure, I command thee by the power within thee and in the name of the Lord if Ill, that as thy limbs waste, so shall the limbs of him in whose likeness thou art fashioned waste also.' Having spoken thus, hold the legs of the image over the flame of a lamp until it be half melted, and convey the rest of it away to your own sleeping-place and hide it there. So it shall come about that during that night the nerves and muscles in the legs of Pharaoh will wither and grow useless to him, and he be paralysed and unable to stir. Afterwards, if it be needful, I will tell you more."

Now, bold though she was, Merytra grew afraid.

"I cannot do it," she said, "it is black sorcery against one who is a god, and will bring my soul to hell. Find some other instrument, or place the waxen imp in the bed of Pharaoh yourself, Kaku."

The face of the magician grew fierce and cruel.

"Come with me, Merytra," he said, and taking her by the wrist he led her to the open window-place whence he observed the stars.

So giddy was the height at the top of this lofty tower that the houses beneath looked small and far away, and the sky quite near.

"Behold Memphis and the Nile, and the wide lands of Egypt gleaming in the moonlight, and the Pyramids of the ancient kings. You wish to rule over all these, like myself—do you not, Merytra?—and if you obey me you shall do so."

"And if I do not obey?"

"Then I will throw my spell upon you, and your senses shall leave you and you shall fall headlong to that white line, which is a street, and before to-morrow morning the dogs will have picked your broken bones, so that none can know you, for you have heard too much to go hence alive unless it be to do my bidding. Oh, no! Think not to say 'I will' and afterwards deceive me, for that image which you take with you is my servant, and will keep watch on you and make report to me and to the god, its master. Now choose."

"I will obey," said Merytra faintly, and as she spoke she thought that she heard a laugh in the air outside the window.

"Good. Now hide the box beneath your cloak and drop it not, for if so that which is within will call aloud after you, and they will kill you for a sorceress. Unless my word come to you, lay the figure in Pharaoh's bed to-morrow evening, and at the hour of moonrise hold its limbs in the flame in your own chamber, and hide it away, and afterwards bring it back to me that I may enchant it afresh, if there be any need. Now come, and I will guard you to the gates of the old temple of Sekhet, where Pharaoh dwells."

Chapter 9

The Doom of Pharaoh

On the morrow when the lady Asti came to dress the Queen for that day's ceremony, she asked her if Amen had given her the wisdom that she sought.

"Not so," answered the young Queen, "all he gave me was very bad dreams, and in every one of them was mixed up that waiting woman of my father, Merytra, of whom you spoke to me. If I believed in omens I should say that she was about to bring some evil upon our House."

"It may well be so, Queen," answered Asti, "and in that case I think that she is at the work. At any rate, watching from the little window of my room, by the light of the moon I saw her return across the temple court at midnight. Moreover, it seemed to me that she was carrying something beneath her robe."

"Whence did she return?"

"From the city, I suppose. She has Pharaoh's pass, and can go in and out when she will. I have caused Mermes to question the officer of the guard, and he says that she came to the gate accompanied by a tall man wrapped in a dark cloak, who spoke with her earnestly, and left her. From this description I think it must have been the astrologer, Kaku, with whom she was talking at the feast."

"That is bad news, Nurse. What else have you to tell?"

"Only this, Queen. The gates are guarded more closely even than we thought. I tried to send out a man to Thebes this morning with a message on my own account—never mind what it was—and the sentries turned him back."

"By the gods!" exclaimed Tua, "before I have reigned a year every gate in Memphis shall be melted down for cooking vessels, and I will set their captains to work in the desert mines. Nay, such threats are foolishness, I'll not threaten, I'll strike when the time comes, but that is not yet. Can I speak with the Pharaoh?"

"No, Queen. He is up already giving audience to the nobles of Memphis, and trying cases from the Lower Land with his Counsellors; until it is time to start for this ceremony of the laying of the foundation-stone of the temple, whither you accompany him in state. Also it is as well—by to-night we may learn more. Come, let me set the crown upon your head that these dogs of Memphis may know their mistress."

****

The ceremony proved very wearisome. First there was the long chariot ride through the crowded, shouting streets, Pharaoh and Abi going in the first chariot, and Tua, attended by Abi's eldest daughter, a round-eyed lady much older than herself, in the second. Next came the office of the priests of Amen, over which Neter-Tua as daughter of Amen and high-priestess, must preside, to dedicate the temple to the glory of the god. Then the foundation deposit of little vases of offerings and models of workmen's tools, and a ring drawn from Pharaoh's hand engraved with his royal name, were blessed and set by the masons in hollows prepared for them, and the two great corner-stones let down, hiding them for ever, and declared respectively by Pharaoh and by Neter-Tua, Morning Star of Amen, Joint Sovereign of Egypt, to be well and truly laid.

Afterwards architects, those who "drew the line," exhibited plans of the temple, and received gifts from Pharaoh, and when these things were done came the mid-day feast and speeches.

At length all was over, and the great procession returned by another route to the temple of Sekhet, where Pharaoh lodged, a very tedious journey in the hot sun, since it involved a circuit of the endless walls of Memphis, with stoppages before all the temples of the gods, at each of which Pharaoh must make offerings. Nor, weary as he was, might he rest, for in the outer court of the old shrine thrones had been set up and seated on them he and Tua must hear petitions till sunset and give judgment, or postpone them for further consideration.

At last there came to an end, but, as Pharaoh, tired out, rose from his throne, Abi, his brother, who all this time had not left them, said that he also had a private petition to prefer. So they went into an inner court that had been a sanctuary, and sat down again, there being present besides the scribes only Pharaoh, the Queen, some councillors, Mermes, captain of the guard, and certain women of the royal household, among them Asti, the Queen's nurse, and Merytra, Pharaoh's favourite attendant. With Abi were his astrologer, Kaku, his two eldest sons, and a few of the great officers of his government, also the high-priests of the temples of Memphis, and three powerful chiefs of the Desert tribes.

"What is your prayer, my brother?" asked Pharaoh, as soon as the doors were closed.

"A great one, your Majesties," answered the Prince, prostrating himself, "which for the good of Egypt, and for your own good, and for my good, who reverence you as a loyal subject, I pray that you will be pleased to grant." Then he drew himself up and said slowly, "I am here to ask the hand of the glorious Queen Neter-Tua, daughter of Amen, in marriage."

Now Pharaoh stared at him, while Tua, who knew well what was coming, turned her head aside, and asked a councillor who stood near, if in the history of the land any Queen of Egypt had ever married her uncle. The councillor who was noted for his historical studies, answered that at the moment he could recall no such case.

"Then," said Tua coolly, and still addressing him, "it seems that it would be scarcely wise to create a precedent which other poor young women of the royal race might be called upon to follow."

Pharaoh caught something of the words, though Abi did not for they were spoken in a low voice, and bethought him of a way out of his difficulty.

"The Queen Neter-Tua sits at my side, and is co-regent with me of this kingdom, her mind is my mind, and what she approves it is probable I shall approve. Prefer your request to her," he said.

So Abi turned to the Queen, and laying his hands upon his heart, bowed, ogled, and began:

"A burning love of your most excellent Majesty moves me——"

"I pray you, my Uncle," interrupted Tua, "correct your words, which should begin 'A burning love of your most excellent Majesty's throne and power move me,' and so on."

Now Abi frowned while everyone else smiled, not excepting Pharaoh and the astrologer, Kaku. Again he began his speech, but so confusedly that presently Tua stopped him for the second time, saying:

"I am not deaf, most noble prince, my Uncle. I heard the words you used to Pharaoh, and even understood their import. In fact, I have already consulted our councillor here, a learned master of the law, as to the legality of such an alliance as you propose, and he gives his judgment against it."

Now Abi glared at the Councillor, a humble, dusty old man who spent all his life among rolls and chronicles.

"May it please your Majesty," this lawyer exclaimed in a thin agitated voice, "I only said there was no record of such a marriage that I can remember, though once I think a queen adopted a nephew, who afterwards became Pharaoh."

"It is the same thing, Friend," replied Tua sweetly, "for that of which there is no record in the long history of Egypt must of necessity be illegal. Still, if my uncle here wishes to adopt me, I thank him, though his lawful heirs may not, and the matter is one that can be considered."

Now, guessing that he was being played with, Abi grew angry.

"I have put a plain question to your Majesty," he said, "and perhaps I am worthy of a plain answer. As all men know, O Queen, it is time that you should be wed, and I offer myself as your husband. It is true that I am somewhat older than you are——"

"In what year was the Prince Abi born, the same as yourself, did you say?" asked Tua in an audible aside of the aged and learned Councillor, who thereon vanished behind the throne, and was seen no more.

"But," went on Abi, taking no notice of this interruption, "on the other hand I have much to offer. I rule here, your Majesties, who am also of the royal blood, and there is some disaffection in the North, especially among the great Bedouin tribes of the Desert who watch the frontier of the Kingdom. Now if this alliance comes about, and in days to be I sit upon the double throne as King-Consort of Egypt, they will be loyal, and north and south will be united more closely than they ever were before. Whereas if it does not come about——" Here Kaku, pretending to brush a fly from his face, caught his hand in Abi's robe, a signal at which his master paused.

"Go on, my Uncle, I pray you," said Tua. "If it does not come about, what then?"

"Then, Queen, there may be trouble. Nay, leave me alone, Magician, I will speak the truth, chance what may. Pharaoh, you have reigned for many years; yes, forty times has the Nile overflowed its banks since we laid our divine father in the tomb. Now, during all those years but one child has been born to you, and that after I came to Thebes to pray you to name me as your heir. Know, Pharaoh, that there are many who find this strange, and wonder whether this beautiful queen, who is called Daughter of Amen, and resembles you so little in body or in mind, sits rightfully on the throne of Egypt. If I marry her these questionings will cease. If I do not marry her the whisperings of men may grow to a wind that will blow the crown from off her head."

Now a grasp of fear and wonder rose from all who heard this bold and treasonable speech, and Tua, reddening to the eyes, bent forward as though to answer. But before ever a word had passed her lips Pharaoh sprang from his seat transformed with rage. All his patient gentleness was gone, and he looked so fierce and royal that everyone present there, even Abi himself, quailed before him.

"Is it for this that I have borne with you for so long, my brother?" he cried, rending at his robes. "Is it for this that I spared you years ago in Thebes, when your life was forfeit for your treachery? Is it for this that I have suffered you to rise to great honour, and to rule here almost as a king in my city of Memphis? Was it not enough that I should sit quiet, while you, an old man, the son of our father's barbarian slave, the loose-living despot, dare to ask for the pure hand of Egypt's Queen in marriage, you, her uncle, who might well be her grandfather also? Must I also hear your foul mouth beslime her royal birth, and the honour of her divine mother, and spit sneers at Amen, Father of the gods? Well, Amen shall deal with you when you come to the doors of his Eternal House, but here on earth I am his son and servant. Mermes, call my guards, and arrest this man and hold him safe. At Thebes, whither we depart to-morrow, he shall be judged according to our law."

Now Mermes blew a shrill call on the silver whistle that hung about his neck, and, springing forward, seized the Prince by the arm. Abi drew his sword to cut him down, and at the sight of the blade, all who were with him rushed to the door to escape, sweeping before them certain of Pharaoh's ladies, among them the waiting-woman, Merytra. But before ever they could pass it, the guards who had heard the signal of Mermes, ran in with lifted spears, driving them back again. Leaping upon Abi, they tore the sword from his hand, and threw him to the ground, huddling the rest together like frightened sheep.

"Bind this traitor and keep him safe, for to-morrow he accompanies us to Thebes," said Pharaoh.

"What of his sons, and those with him, your Majesty?" asked the officer of the guard.

"Let them go," answered Pharaoh wearily, "for they have not sinned against us. Let them go, and take warning from their master's fate."

Now, as it chanced in the confusion, Merytra had been pushed against Kaku.

"Hearken," whispered the astrologer into the woman's ear. "Do as I bid you last night, and all will yet be well. Do it or die. Do you hear me?"

"I hear, and I will obey," answered Merytra in the same low voice.

Then they were separated, for the guards took Kaku by the arm and thrust him out of the temple together with the sons of Abi.

An hour later Mermes and Asti stood before Pharaoh, and prayed him that he would depart from Memphis that very night, saying that such was the counsel also of the Queen and of his officers. But Pharaoh was tired out, and would not listen.

"To-morrow, when I have slept, will be time enough," he answered. "Moreover, shall I fly from my own city like a thief when naught is ready for our journey? Why do you press me to such a coward's act?" he added peevishly.

"For this reason, your Majesty," answered Mermes. "We are sure there is a plot to keep you here. This afternoon you could not have gone, had you tried, but to-night, Abi, being a prisoner, his people are dismayed, and having no leader will open the gates. By to-morrow one may be found, and they will be double-barred and guarded."

"What!" asked the King scornfully, "do you mean that I am a prisoner also, and here in Egypt, which I rule? Nay, good friends, at Pharaoh's word those gates will open. Or if they do not, I will pull down Memphis stone by stone, and drive out its people to share their caves with jackals. Do they think because I am kind and gentle, that I cannot lift the sword if there be need? Have they forgotten how I smote those rebels in my youth, and gave their cities to the flames, and set my yoke on Syria, that aided them. We march to-morrow, and not before. I have spoken."

Now Mermes bowed and turned to go, since when those words had passed Pharaoh's lips it was not lawful to answer them. Yet Asti dared to do so.

"O Pharaoh," she said, "be not wrath with your servant. Pharaoh, as you know, I have skill in divination, the spirits of the dead whisper at times in my ears of things that are to be. It seemed to me just now when having left the presence of the Queen, my foster-child, I stood a while alone in the darkness, that the divine Majesty of the great lady, the royal wife, Ahura, who was my friend and mistress, stood beside me and said:

"'Go, Asti, to Pharaoh, and say to Pharaoh that great danger threatens him and our royal daughter. Say to him—Fly from Memphis, lest there he should be prepared for burial, and the Star of Amen hidden by a cloud of shame. Bid him beware of one about his throne, and of that evil magician with whom she made a pact last night.'"

Now Pharaoh looked at Asti and said:

"O dreamer of dreams, interpret your own dream. Who is she about my throne of whom I should beware, and who is the magician with whom she made a pact?"

"The divine Queen did not tell me, Pharaoh," answered Asti stubbornly, "but my own skill tells me. She is Merytra, your favourite, and the magician is Kaku, whom she visited last night."

"What!" exclaimed Pharaoh, laughing. "That long-legged old astrologer with the painted cap who ran so fast when his master was taken? Why! he is nothing but a spy who has been in my pay for years; a charlatan who pretends to knowledge that he may win the secrets of his Prince. And Merytra, too, Merytra, who in bygone times warned me of this Abi's foolish plot. Asti, you are high-born and wise, one whom I love, and honour much, as does the Queen, my daughter, but you can still be jealous, as I have noted long. Asti, be not deceived, it was jealousy of Merytra that whispered in your ears, not the spirit of the divine Ahura. Now go and take your terrors with you, for this dark conspirator, Merytra, waits in my chamber to unrobe me, and talk me to sleep with her pleasant jests and gossip."

"Pharaoh has spoken, I go," said Asti in her quiet voice. "May Pharaoh's rest be sweet, and his awaking happy."

****

That night Tua could not sleep. Whenever she shut her eyes visions rose before her mind, terrifying, fantastic visions in all of which the fat and hideous Abi played a part. Thus she saw again the scene at her father's fatal feast to the Priest of Kesh, when Asti by her magic had caused the likeness of a monkey to come from the juggler's vase. Only now it was Abi who emerged from the vase, a terrible Abi, with a red sword in his hand, and Pharaoh's crown upon his head. He leapt from the mouth of the vase, he devoured her with his greedy eyes, with stealthy steps he came to seize her, and she could not stir an inch, something held her fast upon her throne.

She could bear it no more—she opened her eyes, stared at the darkness, and out of the darkness came voices, telling of death and war. She thrust her fingers into her ears, and tried to fix her thoughts on Rames, that bright-eyed, light-footed lover of hers, whom she so longed to see again, without whom she was so lonely and undefended.

"Where was Rames?" she wondered. "What fate had overtaken him? Something in her seemed to answer—Death. Oh! if Rames were dead, what should she do? Of what use was it to be Queen of Egypt, the first woman in the world, if Rames were dead?"

Loneliness, insufferable loneliness seemed to get a hold of her. She slipped from her bed, and through the doorway of her little pylon chamber. Now she was upon the narrow stair, and in face of her was that other chamber where Asti slept. Someone was talking with her! Perhaps Mermes was with his wife, and if so she could not enter. No, it was Asti's voice, and, listening, she could hear her murmuring prayers or invocations in solemn tones. She pushed open the door and entered. A little lamp burned in the room, and by its feeble light she saw the white-robed Asti, whose long hair fell about her, standing with upturned eyes and arms outstretched to Heaven. Suddenly Asti saw her also, though but dimly for she stood in the dense shadow, and knew her not.

"Advance, O thou Ghost, and declare thyself, for never was thy help more needed," she said.

"It is no ghost, but I," said Tua. "What dealings are these that you have with ghosts at this deadest hour of the night, Asti? Do not enough terrors encompass us that you must needs call on your familiar spirits to add to them?"

"I call on the spirits to save us from them, Queen, for, like you, I think that we are set in the midst of perils. This night is full of sorcery; I scent it in the air, and strive to match spell with spell. But why do you not sleep?"

"I cannot, Asti, I cannot. Fear has got hold of me. Oh! I would that we had never come to this hateful Memphis, or set eyes upon its ill-omened lord, that foul brute who seeks to make a wife of me."

"Be not afraid, Lady," said Asti, throwing her arms about Tua's slight and quivering form. "To-morrow morning we march; I have it from Pharaoh, and already the guard make preparations, while as for the accursed Abi, he is in prison."

"There is no prison that will hold him, Asti, save the grave. Oh! why did not my Father command him to be slain, as I would have done? Then, at least, we should be free of him, and he could never marry me."

"Because it was otherwise decreed, O Neter-Tua, and Pharaoh must fulfil his fate and ours, for though he is so gentle, none can turn him."

As she spoke the words, somewhere, far beneath them, arose a cry, a voice of one in dread or woe, and with it the sound of feet upon the stairs.

"What passes?" said Asti, leaping to the door.

"Pharaoh is dead or dying," answered the terrified voice without. "Let her Majesty come to Pharaoh."

They threw on their garments, they ran down the narrow stair and across the halls till they came to the chamber of Pharaoh. There upon his bed he lay and about him were the physicians of his Court. He was speechless, but his eyes were open, and he knew his daughter, for, raising his hand feebly, he beckoned to her, and pointed at his feet.

"What is it, man?" she asked of the head physician, who, by way of answer, lifted the linen on the bed, and showed her Pharaoh's legs and feet, white and withered as though with fire.

"What sickness is this?" asked Tua again.

"We know not, O Queen," answered the physician, "for in all our lives we have never seen its like. The flesh is suddenly wasted, and the limbs are paralysed."

"But I know," broke in Asti. "This is not sickness, it is sorcery. Pharaoh has been smitten by some foul spell of the Prince Abi, or of his wizards. Say, who was with him last?"

"It seems that the Lady of the Footstool, Merytra, sang him to sleep, as was her custom," answered the physician, "and left him about two hours ago, so say the guard. When I came in to see how his Majesty rested but now, I found him thus."

Now Tua lifted up her head and spoke, saying:

"My divine Father is helpless, and therefore again I rule alone in Egypt. Hear me and obey. Let the Prince Abi be brought from his prison to the inner hall, for I would question him at once. Let the waiting-woman, Merytra, be brought also under guard with drawn swords."

The officer of the watch bowed and departed to do the bidding of her Majesty, while others went to light the hall.

Soon he returned to an outer chamber whither Tua had withdrawn herself while the physicians examined Pharaoh.

"O Queen," he said, with a frightened face, "be not wrath, but the Prince Abi has gone. He has escaped out of his prison, and the waiting-woman, Merytra, is gone also."

"How came this about?" asked Tua in a cold voice.

"O Queen, the small gate was open, for people passed in and out of it continually, making preparation for to-morrow's march, it seems that about an hour ago the lady Merytra came to the gate and showed Pharaoh's signet to the officer, saying that she was on Pharaoh's business. With her went a fat man dressed in the robe of a master of camels that in the darkness the officer thought was a certain Arab of the Desert who has been to and fro about the camels. It is believed that this man was none other than the Prince Abi, dressed in the Arab's robe, and that he escaped from his cell by some secret passage which was known to him, a passage of the old priests. The Arab, whose robes he wore, cannot be found, but perhaps he is asleep in some corner."

"Bar the gates," said Tua, "and let none pass in or out. Asti, take men with you, and go search the room where Merytra slept. Perchance she has returned again."

So Asti went, and a while after re-appeared carrying something enveloped in a cloth.

"Merytra has gone, O Queen," she said in an ominous voice, "leaving this behind hidden beneath her bed," and she placed the object on a table.

"What is it? The mummy of a child?" asked Tua, shrinking back.

"Nay, Queen, the image of a man."

Then throwing aside the cloth Asti revealed the waxen figure shaped to the exact likeness of Pharaoh, or rather what remained of it, for the legs were molten and twisted, and in them could be seen the bones of ivory and the sinews of thin wire, about which they had been moulded. Also beneath the chin where the tongue would be, sharp thorns had been thrust up to the root of the mouth. The thing was life-like and horrible, and as it was, so was the dumb and stricken Pharaoh on his bed.

Neter-Tua hid her eyes for a while, and leaned against the wall, then she drew herself up and said:

"Call the physicians and the members of the Council, and those who can be spared of the officers of the guard, that everyone of them may see and bear witness to the hideous crime which has been worked against Pharaoh by his brother, the Prince Abi, and the wizard Kaku, and their accomplice, the woman Merytra."

So they were called, and came, and when they saw the dreadful thing lying in its waxen whiteness before them, they wailed and cursed those who had wrought this abominable sorcery.

"Curse them not," said Neter-Tua, "who are already accursed, and given over to the Devourer of Souls when their time shall come. Make a record of this deed, O Scribes, and do it swiftly."

So the scribes wrote the matter down, and the Queen and others who were present signed the writings as witnesses. Then Neter-Tua commanded that they should take the image and destroy it before it worked more evil, and a priest of Osiris who was present seized it and departed.

But Neter-Tua went to Pharaoh's room and knelt by his bed, watching him, for he seemed to be asleep. Presently he awoke, and looked round him wildly, moving his lips. For a while he could not speak, then of a sudden his voice burst from him in a hoarse, unnatural cry.

"They have bewitched me! I burn, I burn!" he screamed, rolling himself to and fro upon the bed. "Avenge me, my daughter, and fear nothing, for the gods are about you. I see their awful eyes. Oh! I burn, I burn!"

Then his head fell back, and the peace of death descended on his tortured brow.

Tua kissed his dead brow, and knelt at his side in prayer. After a little while she rose and said:

"It has pleased Pharaoh, the just and perfect, to depart to his everlasting habitation in Osiris. Make it known that this god is dead, and that I rule alone in Egypt. Send hither the priest of Osiris, that he may repeat the Ritual of Departing, and you, physicians, do your office."

So the priest came, but at the door Asti caught him by the hand and asked:

"How did you destroy the image of wax?"

"I burned it upon the altar in the old sanctuary of this temple," he answered.

"O, Fool!" said Asti, "you should have buried it. Know that with the enchanted thing you have burned away the life of Pharaoh also."

Then that priest fell swooning to the ground, and another had to be summoned to utter the Ritual of Departing.

Chapter 10

The Coming of the Ka

Now it was morning, and while the physicians embalmed the body of Pharaoh as best they could, Tua consulted with her officers. Long and earnest was that council, for all of them felt that their danger was very great. Abi had escaped, and if he were re-taken, none knew better than he that his death and that of all his House would be the reward of his crimes and sorceries which could only be covered up in one way—by marriage with the Queen of Egypt. Moreover, he had thousands of soldiers in the city and around it, all of them sworn to his service, whereas the royal guard was but five companies, each of a hundred men, trapped in a snare of streets and stone.

One of them suggested that they should break a way through the wall of the temple, and escape to the royal barges that lay moored on the Nile beneath them, and this plan was approved. But when they went to set about the work it was seen that these barges had been seized and were already sailing away up the river. So but two alternatives remained—to bide within the fortifications of the old temple, and send out messengers for help, or to march through the city boldly, break down the gates if these were shut against them, seize boats, and sail up the Nile for some loyal town, or if that could not be done, to take their chance in the open lands.

Now some favoured one scheme, and some the other, so that at last the decision was left with her Majesty. She thought awhile, then said:

"Here I will not stay, to be starved out as we must ere ever an army could be gathered to rescue us, and be given into the power of that vile and wicked man, the murderer of the good god, my father. Better that I should die fighting in the streets, for then at least I shall pass undefiled to join him in his eternal habitation beyond the sun. We march at midnight."

So they bowed beneath her word, and made ready while the

women of his household raised a death-wail for Pharaoh, and criers standing on the high towers proclaimed the accession of Neter-Tua, Morning-Star of Amen, Glorious in Ra, Hathor, Strong in Beauty, as sole Lord and Sovereign of the North and South, and of Egypt's subject lands. Again and again they proclaimed it, and of the multitudes who listened some cheered, but the most remained silent, fearing the vengeance of their Prince, whom the heralds summoned to do homage, but who made no sign.

Night came at last. At a signal the gates were opened, and through them, borne upon the shoulders of his Councillors, preceded by a small body of guards, and followed by his women and household, went the remains of Pharaoh, in a coffin roughly fashioned from the sycamore timbers of the temple. With solemn step and slow, they went as though they feared no harm, the priests and singers chanting some ancient, funeral hymn. Next followed the baggage bearers, and after these the royal bodyguard in the midst of whom the Queen, clad in mail, as a man, rode in a chariot, and with her the waiting-lady, Asti, wife of Mermes.

At first all went well, for the great square in front of the temple was empty. The procession of the body of Pharaoh passed it, and vanished down the street that led to the main gate, a mile away. Now the guard formed into line to enter this street also, when suddenly, barring the mouth of it, appeared great companies of men who had been hidden in other streets.

A voice cried "Halt!" and while the guards re-shaped themselves into a square about the person of the Queen, an embassy of officers, among whom were recognised the four lawful sons of Abi, advanced and demanded in the Prince's name that her Majesty should be given over to them, saying that she would be treated with all honour, and that those who accompanied her might go free.

"Answer that the Queen of Egypt does not yield herself into the hands of rebels, and of murderers; then fall on them, and slay them all," cried Neter-Tua when Mermes, her captain, had given her this message.

So he went forward and returned the answer, and next moment a flight of arrows from the Queen's guard laid low the four sons of Abi, and most of those who were with them.

Then the fight began, one of the fiercest that had been known in Egypt for many a generation. The royal regiment, it is true, was but small, but they were picked men, and mad with despair and rage. Moreover, Tua the Queen played no woman's part that night, for when these charged, striving to cut a path through the opposing hosts, she charged with them, and by the moonlight was seen standing like an angry goddess in her chariot, and loosing arrows from her bow. Also no hurt came to her or those with her, or even to the horses that drew her. It was as though she were protected by some unseen strength, that caught the sword cuts and turned aside the points of spears.

Yet it availed not, for the men of Abi were a multitude, and the royal guard but very few. Slowly, an ever-lessening band, they were pressed back, first to the walls of the old temple of Sekhet, and then within its outer court. Now all who were left of them, not fifty men under the command of Mermes, strove to hold the gate. Desperately they fought, and one by one went down to death beneath the rain of spears.

Tua had dismounted from her chariot, and leaning on her bow, for all her arrows were spent, watched the fray with Asti at her side. With a yell the troops of Abi rushed through the gate, killing as they came. Now, surrounded by all who remained to her, not a dozen men, they were driven back through the inner courts, through the halls, to the pylon stairs.

Here the last stand was made. Step by step they held the stairs, till at length there were left upon their feet only Tua, Asti and Mermes, her husband, who was sorely wounded in many places. At the little landing between the rooms of the Queen and Asti while the assailants paused a moment, the Captain Mermes, mad with grief and pain, turned and kissed his wife. Next he bowed before the Queen, saying:

"What a man may do, I have done to save your Majesty. Now I go to make report to Pharaoh, leaving you in charge of Amen, who shall protect you, and to Rames, my son, the heritage of vengeance. Farewell, O Daughter of Amen, till I see your star rise in the darkness of the Under-World, and to you, beloved wife, farewell."

Then, uttering the war-cry of his fathers, those Pharaohs who once had ruled in Egypt, the tall and noble Mermes grasped his sword in both his hands, and rushed upon the advancing foe, slaying and slaying until he himself was slain.

"Come with me, O Wife of a royal hero," said Tua to Asti, who had covered her eyes with her hand, and was leaning against the wall.

"Widow, not wife, Queen. Did you not see his spirit pass?"

Then Tua led her up more steps to the top of the pylon tower, where Asti sank down moaning in her misery. Tua walked to the outermost edge of the tower and stood there waiting the end. It was the moment of dawn. On the eastern horizon the red rim of the sun arose out of the desert in a clear sky. There upon that lofty pinnacle, clad in shining mail, and wearing a helm shaped like the crown of Lower Egypt, Tua stood in its glorious rays that turned her to a figure of fire set above a world of shadow. The thousands of the people watching from the streets below, and from boats upon the Nile, saw her, and raised a shout of wonder and of adoration.

"The Daughter of Amen-Ra!" they cried. "Behold her clad in the glory of the god!"

Soldiers crept up the stairs to the pylon roof and saw her also, while, now that the fray was ended, with them came the Prince Abi.

"Seize her," he panted, for the stairs were steep and robbed him of his breath.

But the soldiers looked and shrank back before the Majesty of Egypt, wrapped in her robe of light.

"We fear," they answered, "the ghost of Pharaoh stands before her."

Then Neter-Tua spoke, saying:

"Abi, once a Prince of Egypt and Hereditary Lord of Memphis, but now an outcast murderer, black with the blood of your King, and of many a loyal man, hear me, the anointed Queen of Egypt, hear me, O man upon whom I decree the judgment of the first and second death. Come but one step near to my Majesty, and before your eyes, and the eyes of all the multitude who watch, I hurl myself from this hideous place into the waters of the Nile. Yet ere I go to join dead Pharaoh, and side by side with him to lay our plaint against you before the eternal gods, listen to our curse upon you. From this day forward a snake shall prey upon your vitals, gnawing upwards to your heart. The spirits of Pharaoh and of all his servants whom you have slain shall haunt your sleep; never shall you know one more hour of happy rest. Through life henceforth you shall fly from a shadow, and if you climb a throne, it shall be such a one as that on which I stand encircled with the perilous depths of darkness. Thence you shall fall at last, dying by a death of shame, and the evil gods shall seize upon you, O Traitor, and drag you to the maw of the Eater-up of Souls, and therein you shall vanish for ever for aye, you and all your House, and all those who cling to you. Thus saith Neter-Tua, speaking with the voice of Amen who created her, her father and the god of gods."

Now when the soldiers heard these dreadful words, one by one they turned and crept down the stairs, till at last there were left upon the pylon roof only the Queen, Asti crouching at her feet, and the monstrous Abi, her uncle.

He looked at her, and thrice he tried to speak but failed, for the words choked in his throat. A fourth time he tried, and they came hoarsely:

"Take off your curse, O mighty Queen," he said, "and I will let you go. I am old, to-night all my lawful sons are dead; take off your curse, leave me in my Government, and though I desire you more than the throne of Egypt, O Beautiful, still I will let you go."

"Nay," answered the Queen, "I cannot if I would. It is not I who spoke, but a Spirit in my mouth. Do your worst, O son of Set. The curse remains upon you."

Now Abi shook in the fury of his fear, and answered:

"So be it, Star of Amen, having nothing more to dread I will do my worst. Pharaoh my enemy is dead, and you, his daughter, shall be my wife of your own free will, or since no man will lay a finger upon you, here in this tower you shall starve. Death is not yet; I shall have my day, it is sworn to me. Reign with me if you will, or starve without me if you will—I tell you, Daughter of Amen, that I shall have my day."

"And I tell you, Son of Set, that after the day comes the long terror of that night which knows no morrow."

Then finding no answer, he too turned and went.

When he was gone Neter-Tua stood a while looking down upon the thousands of people gathered in the great square where the battle had been fought, who stared up at her in a deadly silence. Then she descended from the coping-stone, and, taking Asti by the arm, led her from the roof to the little chamber where she had slept.

****

Six days had gone by, and Queen Neter-Tua starved in the pylon tower. Till now the water had held out for there was a good supply of it in jars, but at last it was done, while, as for food, they had eaten nothing except a store of honey which Asti took at night from the bees that hived among the topmost pylon stones. That day the honey was done also, and if had not been, without water to wash it down they could have swallowed no more of the sickly stuff. Indeed, although in after years in memory of its help, Neter-Tua chose the bee as her royal symbol, never again could she bring herself to eat of the fruit of its labours.

"Come, Nurse," said Tua, "let us go to the roof, and watch the setting of Ra, perhaps for the last time, since I think that we follow him through the Western Gates."

So they went, supporting each other up the steps, for they grew weak. From this lofty place they saw that save on the Nile side of it which was patrolled by the warships of Abi, all the temple was surrounded by a double ring of soldiers, while beyond the soldiers, on the square where the great fight had been, were gathered thousands of the people who knew that the starving Queen was wont to appear thus upon the pylon at sunset.

At the sight of her, clad in the mail which she still wore, a murmur rose from them like the murmur of the sea, followed by a deep silence since they dared not declare the pity which moved them all. In the midst of this silence, whilst the sun sank behind the Pyramids of the ancient kings, Neter-Tua lifted up her glorious voice and sang the evening hymn to Amen-Ra. As the last notes died away in the still air, again the murmur rose while the darkness gathered about the pylon, hiding her from the gaze of men.

Hand in hand as they had come, the two deserted women descended the stair to their sleeping-place.

"They dare not help us, Asti," said Tua, "let us lie down and die."

"Nay, Queen," answered Asti, "let us turn to one that giveth help to the helpless. Do you remember the words spoken by the shining spirit of Ahura the Divine?"

"I remember them, Asti."

"Queen, I have waited long, since the spell she whispered to me may be used once only, but now I am sure that the moment is at hand when that which dwells within you must be called forth to save you."

"Then call it forth, Asti," answered Tua wearily, "if you have the power. If not, oh! let us die. But say, whom would you summon? The glory of Amen or the ghost of Pharaoh, or Ahura, my mother, or one of the guardian gods?"

"None of these," answered Asti, "for I have been bidden otherwise. Lie you down and sleep, my fosterling, for I have much to do in the hours of darkness. When you awake you shall learn all."

"Aye," said Tua, "when I awake, if ever I do awake. Is it in your mind to kill me in my sleep, Asti? Is that your command? Well, if so, I shall not blame you, for then I will break this long fast of mine with Pharaoh and the divine mother, Ahura, who bore me, and together in the pleasant Fields of Peace we will wait for Rames, my lover and your son. Being a queen, they will give my burial in my father's tomb, and that is all I crave of them, and of this weary world. Sing me to rest, Nurse, as you were wont to do when I was little, and, if it be your will, tarry not long behind me."

So she laid herself down upon the bed, and, taking her hand that had grown so thin, the tall and noble Asti bent over her in the darkness, and began to sing a gentle chant or lullaby.

Tua's eyes closed, her breath came slow and deep. Then Asti the magician ceased her song and, gathering up her secret strength, put out her prayers, prayer after prayer, till at length all her soul was pure, and she dared to utter the awful spell that Ahura had whispered in her ear. At the muttered, holy words wild voices cried through the night, the solid pylon rocked, and in the city the crystal globe into which Kaku and Merytra gazed was suddenly shattered between them, and, white with terror at he knew not what, Abi sprang from his couch.

Then Asti also sank into sleep or swoon, and all was silent in that chamber, silent as the grave.

****

Neter-Tua awoke. Through the pylon window-place crept the first grey light of dawn. Her eyes searching the gloom fell first upon the dark-robed figure of Asti sleeping in a chair, her head resting upon her hand. Then a brightness drew them to the foot of her bed, and there, clothed in a faint, white light, that seemed as though it were drawn from the stars and the moon, wearing the Double Crown, and arrayed in all the royal robes of Egypt, she saw—*herself.*

Now Tua knew that she dreamed, and for a long while lay still, for it pleased her, starved and wretched as she was, a prisoner in the hands of her foes, a netted bird, to let her fancy dwell upon this splendid image of what she had been before an evil fate, speaking with the voice of Merytra, Lady of the Footstool, had beguiled dead Pharaoh to Memphis. If things had gone well with her, she should be as that image was to-day, that image which wore her crown and robes of state, yes, and her very jewels. Such were the changes of fortune even in the lives of princes whose throne seemed to be set upon a rock, princes whom the god of gods had fathered. Never before in her young life had the thing come so home to her, for until now, even through the hunger and the fear, her pride had borne her up. But in this chilly hour that precedes the dawn, the hour when, as they say, men are wont to die, it was otherwise with her. Her end was near—she knew it and understood that between the mightiest monarch in the world and the humblest peasant maid at the last there is no difference, save perchance a difference of the soul within.

Here she lay, a shadow, who must choose between a miserable end by thirst and hunger, or a loathsome marriage. And what availed it that she was called Morning-Star of Amen, she the only child of Pharaoh and of his royal wife, and that when she was dead they would grant her a state funeral, and inscribe her name among the lists of kings, while Abi, the foul usurper, sat upon her throne. Here on the bed lay what she was, there at the foot of it stood what she should be if the gods had not deserted her.

Her poor heart was filled with bitterness like a cup with vinegar, bitterness flowed through her in the place of blood. It seemed hard to die so young, she whom men named a god; to die robbed of her crown, robbed of her vengeance, and taking with her her deep, unfruitful love. Would she and Rames meet beyond the grave, she wondered? Would they wed and bear children there, who should rule as Pharaohs in the Under-world? Would Osiris redeem her mortal flesh, and Amen the Father, receive her; or would she rush down into everlasting blackness where sleep is all in all?

Oh! for one hour of strength and freedom, one short hour while at the head of her armies she rolled down upon rebellious Memphis in her might, and trod its high walls flat, and gave its palaces to the flames, and cast its accursed prince to the jaws of crocodiles. Her sunk eyes flashed at the thought of it, and her wasted bosom heaved, and lo! the eyes of that royal queen of her dreams flashed also as though in answer, and on its breast the jewels rose as though pride or anger lifted them.

Then this marvel came to pass, for the beautiful face—could her own ever have been so beautiful?—the imperial face, bent forward a little, and from the red lips came a soft voice, her own rich voice, that said:

"Speak your will, Queen, and it shall be done. I, who stand here, am your servant to command, O Morning-Star, O Amen's royal child."

Tua sat up in her bed and laughed at the vision.

"My will!" she said. "O Dream, why do you mock me? Let me think. What is my will? Well, Dream, it is that of the beggar at the gate—I desire a drink of water, and a crust of bread."

"They are there," answered the figure, pointing with the crystal sceptre in her hand to the table beside the couch.

Idly enough Tua looked, and so it was! On the table stood pure water in a silver cup, and by it cakes of bread upon a golden platter. She stretched out her hand, for surely this fantasy was pleasant, and took that ghost of a silver cup, her own cup that Pharaoh had given her as a child, and brought it to her lips and drank, and lo! water pure and cold flowed down her throat, until at length even her raging thirst was satisfied. Then she stretched out her hand again, and took the loaves of bread, and ate them hungrily till all were gone, and as she swallowed the last of them, exclaimed in bitter shame:

"Oh! what a selfish wretch am I who have drunk and eaten all, leaving nothing for my foster-mother, Asti, who lies asleep, and dies of want as I did."

"Fear not," answered the Dream. "Look, there are more for Asti." And it was true, for the silver cup brimmed once more with cold water, and on the golden platter were other cakes.

Now the Dream spoke again:

"Surely," it said, "there were other wishes in your heart, O Morning-Star, than that for human sustenance?"

"Aye, O Dream, I wished for vengeance upon Abi, the traitor, Abi the murderer of my father, who would bring me to the last shame of womanhood. I wished for vengeance upon Abi, and all who cling to him."

The bright figure bowed, stretching out its jewelled hands, and answered:

"I am your servant to obey. It shall be worked, O Queen, such vengeance as you cannot dream of, vengeance poured drop by drop like poison in his veins, the torment of disappointed love, the torment of horrible fear, the torment of power given and snatched away, the torment of a death of shame, and the everlasting torment of the Eater-up of Souls—this vengeance shall be worked upon Abi and all who cling to him. Was there not another wish in your heart, O Morning-Star, O Queen divine?"

"Aye," answered Tua, "but I may not speak it all even to myself in sleep."

"It shall be given to you, O Morning-Star. You shall find your love though far away beyond the horizon, and he shall return with you, and you twain shall rule in the Upper and the Lower Land, and in all the lands beyond with glory such as has not been known in Egypt."

Now, at length, Tua seemed to awake. She rubbed her eyes and looked. There was the sleeping Asti; there on the table beside her were the water and the bread; there at the foot of the couch, glimmering in the low lights of dawn, was the glorious figure of herself draped in the splendid robes.

"Who, and what are you?" she cried. "Are you a god or a spirit, or are you but a mocking vision caught in the web of my madness?"

"I am none of these things, O Morning-Star, I am yourself. I am that *Ka* whom our father Amen gave to you at birth to dwell with you and protect you. Do you not remember me when as a child we played together?"

"I remember," answered Tua. "You warned me of the danger of the sacred crocodile in the Temple tank, but since then I have never seen you. What gives you the strength to appear in the flesh before me, O Double?"

"The magic of Asti with which she has been endowed from on high to save you, Neter-Tua, that gives me strength. Know that although you cannot always see me, I am your eternal companion. Through life I go with you, and when you die I watch in your tomb, perfect, incorruptible, preserving your wisdom, your loveliness, and all that is yours, until the day of resurrection. I have power, I have the secret knowledge which dwells in you, although you cannot grasp it; I remember the Past, the infinite, infinite Past that you forget, I foresee the Future, the endless, endless Future that is hidden from you, to which the life you know is but as a single leaf upon the tree, but as one grain of sand in the billions of the Desert. I look upon the faces of the gods, and hear their whisperings; Fate gives me his book to read; I sleep secure in the presence of the Eternal who sent me forth, and to whom at last I return again, my journey ended, my work fulfilled, bearing you in my holy arms. O Morning-Star, the spells of Asti have clothed me in this magic flesh, the might of Amen has set me on my feet. I am here, your servant, to obey."

Now, amazed, bewildered, Tua called out:

"Awake, Nurse, awake, for I am mad. It seems to me that a messenger from on high, robed in my own flesh, stands before me and speaks with me."

Asti opened her eyes, and, perceiving the beautiful figure, rose and did obeisance to it, but said no word.

"Be seated," said the *Ka*, "and hear me, time is short. I awoke at the summons, I came forth, I am present, I endure until the spell is taken off me, and I return whence I came. O Interpreter, speak the will of her of whom I am, that I may do it in my own fashion. There is food—eat and drink, then speak."

So Asti ate and drank as Tua had done, and when she had finished and was satisfied, behold! the cup and the platter vanished away. Next in a slow, quiet voice she spoke, saying:

"O Shadow of this royal Star, by my spells incorporate, this is our case: Here we starve in misery, and without the gate Abi waits the end. If the Queen lives, he will take her who hates him to be his wife; if she dies he will seize her throne. Our wisdom is finished. What must we do to save this Star that it may shine serene until its appointed hour of setting?"

"Is that all you seek?" asked the Double, when she had finished.

"Nay," broke in Tua hurriedly, "I would not shine alone, I seek another Star to share my sky with me."

"Have you faith and will you obey?" asked the Double again. "For without faith I can do nothing."

Now Asti looked at Tua who bowed her head in assent to an unspoken question, then she answered:

"We have faith, we will obey."

"So be it," said the Shadow. "Presently Abi will come to ask whether the Queen consents to be his wife, or whether she will bide here until she dies. I who wear the fashion of the Queen will go forth and be his wife, oh! such a wife as man never had before," and as she spoke the words an awful look swept across her face, and her deep eyes flamed. "Ill goes it with the mortal man who weds a wraith that hates him and is commanded to work his woe," she added.

Now Asti and Tua understood and smiled, then the Queen said:

"So you will sit in my seat, O Shadow, and as your lord, Abi will sit on Pharaoh's throne and find it hard. But what of Egypt and my people?"

"Fear not for Egypt and your people, O Morning Star. With these it shall go well enough until you come back to claim them."

"And what of my companion and myself?" asked Tua.

The Double raised her sceptre, and pointed to the open window-space between them, beneath which, hundreds of feet beneath, ran the milky waters of the river.

"You shall trust yourselves to the bosom of Father Nile," she answered solemnly.

Now the Queen and Asti stared at each other.

"That means," said Tua, "that we must trust ourselves to Osiris, for none can fall so far and live."

"Think you so, O Star? Where, then, is that faith you promised, without which I can do nothing? Nay, I tell no more. Do my bidding, or let me go, and deal with Abi as it pleases you. Choose now, he draws near," and as she spoke the words they heard the bronze gates of the temple clash upon their hinges.

Tua shivered at the sound, then sprang from the couch, and drew herself to her full height, exclaiming:

"For my part I have chosen. Never shall it be said that Pharaoh's daughter was a coward. Better the breast of Osiris than the arms of Abi, or slow death in a dungeon. In Amen and in thee, O Double, I put my trust."

The Shadow looked from her to Asti, who answered briefly:

"Where my Lady goes there I follow, knowing that Mermes always waits. What shall we do?"

The *Ka* motioned to them to stand together in the narrow winding-place, and this they did, their arms about each other. Next she lifted her sceptre and spoke some word.

Then fire flashed before their eyes, a rush of wind beat upon their brows, and they knew no more.

Chapter 11

The Dream of Abi

On the night of the drawing-forth of the *Ka* of Neter-Tua, Kaku the wizard, and Merytra the spy, she who had been Lady of the Footstool to Pharaoh, sat together in that high chamber where Merytra had vowed her vow, and received the magic image.

"Why do you look so disturbed?" asked the astrologer of his accomplice who glanced continually over her shoulder, and seemed very ill at ease. "All has gone well. If Set himself had fashioned that image, it could not have done its work more thoroughly."

"Thoroughly, indeed," broke in Merytra in an angry voice. "You have tricked me, Wizard, I promised to help you to lame Pharaoh, not to murder him!"

"Hush! Beloved," said Kaku nervously, "murder is an ugly word, and murderers come to ugly ends—sometimes. Is it your fault if an accursed fool of a priest chose to burn the mannikin upon an altar, and thus bring this god to his lamented end?"

"No," answered Merytra, "not mine, or the priest's, but yours, and that hog, Abi's; and Set's the master of both of you. But I shall get the blame of it, for the Queen and Asti know the truth, and soon or late it will come out, and they will burn me as a sorceress, sending me to the Underworld with the blood of Pharaoh upon my hands. Pharaoh who never did me aught but good. And then, what will happen to me?"

Evidently Kaku did not know, for he rose and stood opposite to her, scratching his lean chin and smiling in a sickly, indeterminate fashion that enraged Merytra.

"Cease grinning at me like an ape of the rocks," she said, "and tell me, what is to be the end of this evil business?"

"Why trouble about ends, Fair One?" he asked. "They are always a long way off; indeed, the best philosophers hold that there is no such thing as an end. You know the sacred symbol of a snake with its tail in its mouth that surrounds the whole world, but begins where it ends, and ends where it begins. It may be seen in any tomb——"

"Cease your talk of snakes and tombs," burst in Merytra. "The thought of them makes me shudder."

"By all means, Beloved. I have always held that we Egyptians dwell too much on tombs, and—whatever it may be that lies beyond them, which after all remains a matter of doubt—fortunately. So let us turn from tombs and corpses to palaces and life. As I said just now, although we grieve over the accident of Pharaoh's death, and that of all his guard—and I may add, of Abi's four legitimate sons, things have gone well for us. To-day I have received from the Prince, in writing, my appointment as Vizier, and first King's companion, to come into force when he mounts the throne as he must do, and to-day you have received from me, with all the usual public rites and ceremonies, the name of wife, as I promised that you should. Merytra, you are the wife of the great Vizier, the pre-eminent lord, the sole Companion of the King of Egypt, a high position for one who after all during the late reign was but Pharaoh's favourite, and Lady of the Footstool."

"A footstool of silk is more comfortable to sit on than a state chair fashioned of blood-stained swords. Hearken you, Kaku! I am afraid. You say that you are the greatest of seers, and can read the future. Well, I desire to know the future, so if you are not a charlatan, show it to me."

"A charlatan! How can you suggest it, Merytra, remembering the adventure of the image?"

"That may have been an accident. Pharaoh was sickly for years, and had a stroke before. If you are not a cheat show me the future in that magic crystal. I would learn the worst, so that I may know how to meet it when it comes."

"Well, Wife, we will try, though to see such high visions the spirit should be calm, which I fear yours is not—nay, be not angry. We will try, we will try. Sit here now, and gaze, and above all be silent while I say the appropriate spells."

So the ball of crystal having been set upon the table, the pair stared into it as Kaku muttered his charms and invocations. For a long while Merytra saw nothing, till suddenly a shadow gathered in the ball, which slowly cleared away, revealing the image of dead Pharaoh clothed in his mummy wrappings. As she started back to scream the image seemed to loose its hands from the cloths that bound them, and strike outwards, whereon the crystal suddenly shattered, so that the pieces of it flew about the room, one of which struck her on the mouth, knocking out two of her front teeth, and gashing her lips.

Merytra uttered a cry, and fell backwards to the floor, while Kaku sprang from his chair as though to run away, then thought better of it, and stood still, shivering with fear.

"What was that?" said Merytra, rising from the ground, and wiping the blood from her cut mouth.

"I do not know," answered Kaku, in a quavering voice. "It would seem that the gods deny to us that knowledge of the future which you sought. Be content with the present, Merytra."

"Content with the present," she screamed, infuriated. "Look at what the present has given me—a mouthful of blood and teeth. I, who was beautiful, am spoiled for ever; I am become an old hag. Pharaoh burst the ball with his hand, and threw the pieces at me. I saw him do it, and you set him there. Wretch, I will pay you back for this evil trick," and springing at Kaku, she tore of his astrologer's cap, and the wig beneath it, and beat his bald head with them till he cried for mercy.

It was at this moment that the door opened, and through it, breathless, white with terror, half-clothed, appeared none other than the Prince Abi.

"What passes here?" he gasped, sinking into a chair. "Is this the way you conduct your midnight studies, Kaku?"

"Certainly not, most high Lord," replied the astrologer, trying to bow with his eye fixed on Merytra, who stood by him, the torn wig in her hand, in the act of striking. "Certainly not, exalted Prince. A domestic difference, that is all. This wild cat of a woman whom I have married having met with an accident, gave way to her devilish temper."

"Repeat that," exclaimed Merytra, "and I will throw you from the window-place to find out whether your sorceries can make paving-stones as soft as air. See, Lord, what he has done to me by his accursed wizardry," and she exhibited her two front teeth in her shaking hand. "I say that he set the spirit of Pharaoh whom he beguiled me to do to death, in the crystal, for I saw him there wrapped in his mummy clothes, and caused dead Pharaoh to burst the crystal and stone me with its fragments."

"Be silent, Woman," shouted Abi, "or I will have you beaten with rods, till your feet hurt more than your mouth. What is this about the spirit of Pharaoh, Kaku? Is he everywhere, for know, it is of Pharaoh, the dweller in Osiris, that I came to speak to you."

"Most exalted Ruler of the North, Son of Royal Blood, Hereditary Count who shall be King——"

"Cease your titles, Knave," exclaimed Abi, "and listen, for I need counsel, and if you cannot give it I will find one who can. Just now I lay on my bed asleep, and a dreadful vision came to me. I dreamed that I woke up, and feeling a weight on the bed beside me turned to learn what it was, and saw there the body of my brother, Pharaoh, in his death-wrappings——"

"As I saw him in the ball," broke in Merytra. "Did he pelt you also, O Abi?"

"Nay, Woman, he did worse, he spoke to me. He said—'You, my brother, to whom I forgave all your sins, you and the woman-snake that I cherished in my bosom, and your servant, the black-souled magician, her accomplice, have done me miserably to death, and set the Queen of both the Lands, Amen's royal child, to starve in yonder tower with the noble lady Asti, until she dies or takes you to be her husband—you, her uncle, who seek her beauty and my throne. Now I have a message for you from the gods, who write down these things in their eternal books against the day of judgment, when we all shall meet and plead our cause before them, Osiris the Redeemer standing on the right hand, and the Eater-up of Souls standing on the left.

"'This is the message, O Abi—Go to the Temple of Sekhet at the dawn. There you shall find that Royal Loveliness which you desire. Take it to be your wife as you desire, for it shall not say you nay. Be wedded to that Loveliness with pomp before all the eyes of Egypt, and reign by right of that Royalty, until you meet one Rames, son of Mermes, whom you also murdered, and with him a certain Beggarman who is charged with another message for you, O Abi. Ascend the Nile to Thebes, and lay this body of mine in the splendid tomb which I have made ready and sit in my seat, and do those things which that Royal Loveliness you have wed, commands to you, for It you shall obey. But hasten, hasten, Abi, to hollow for yourself a grave, and let it be near to mine, for when you are dead this my *Ka* would come to visit you, as it does to-night.'

"Then the *Ka* or the body of Pharaoh—I know not which it was—ceased from speaking, and lay there a while staring at me with its cold eyes, till at length the spirits of my four sons who are dead entered the chamber and, lifting up the shape, carried it away. I awoke, shaking like a reed in the wind, and ran hither up a thousand steps to find you brawling with this low-born slut, dead Pharaoh's worn-out shoe that in bygone years I kicked from off my foot."

Now Merytra would have answered, for she loved not such names, but the two men looked at her so fiercely that her rage died, and she was silent.

"Read me this vision, Man, and be swift, for the torment of it haunts me," went on Abi. "If you cannot I strip you of your offices, and give your carcase to the rods until you find wisdom. It was you who set me on this path, and by the gods you shall keep me safe in it or die by inches."

Now, seeing his great danger, Kaku grew cold and cunning.

"It is true, O Prince," he said, "that I set you on this path, this high and splendid path, and it is true also that from the beginning I have kept you safe in it. Had it not been for me and my counsel, long ago you would have become but a forgotten traitor. Remember that night at Thebes, when in your pride you desired to smite at the heart of Pharaoh, and how I held your hand, and remember how, many a time, my wisdom has been your guide, when left to your own rash folly you must have failed or perished. It is true also, Prince, that in the future as in the past, with me and by me you stand or fall. Yet if you think otherwise, find some wiser man to lead you, and wait the end. All the rods in Egypt cannot be broken on my back, O Abi. Now shall I speak who alone have knowledge, or will you seek another counsellor?"

"Speak on," answered Abi sullenly, "we are fish in the same net, and share each other's fortune to the end, whether it be Set's gridiron or fat Egypt's pleasure pond. Fear not, what I have promised you shall have while it is mine to give."

"Just now you promised rods," remarked Kaku, making a wry face and replacing the remains of his wig upon his bald head, "but let that pass. Now as to this dream of yours, I find its meaning good. How did Pharaoh come to you? Not as a living spirit, but in the fashion of a dead man, and who cares for dead men?"

"I do, for one, when they cut my mouth with broken crystals," interrupted Merytra, who was bathing her wounds in a basin of water.

"Would that they had cut your tongue instead of your lips, Woman," snarled Abi. "Continue, Kaku, and heed her not."

"And what was his message?" went on the magician. "Why, that you shall marry the Majesty of Egypt, and rule in her right and sit in the seat of kings. Are not these the very things that you desire, and have worked for years to win?"

"Yes, Kaku, but you forget all that about one Rames, and the tomb that I must hollow, and the rest."

"Rames? Merytra here can tell you of him, Prince. He is the madcap young Count who killed the Prince of Kesh, and was sent by Neter-Tua far to the South-lands, that the barbarians there might make an end of him without scandal. If ever he should come back with the Beggar-man and his message, which is not likely, you can answer him with the halter he deserves."

"Aye, Kaku, but how will the Queen answer him? There are stories afloat——"

"Lies, every one of them, Prince. She would have executed him at once had it not been for the influence of Mermes, and her foster-mother, Asti. This Rames has in him the royal blood of the last dynasty, and the Star of Amen is not one who will share her sky with a rival star, unless he be her lawful Lord, which is your part. If Rames or the foul Beggar brings you any message it will be that you are King of Kesh as well as of Egypt, and then you can kill him and take the heritage. A fig for Rames and its stalk for the Beggar!"

"Perhaps," replied Abi more cheerfully, "at any rate I do not fear that risk; but how about all Pharaoh's talk of tombs?"

"Being dead, Prince, it is natural that the mind of his *Ka* should run on tombs, and his own royal burial, which as a matter of policy we must give to him. Besides there the prophesy was safe, since to these same tombs all must come, especially those of us who have seen the Nile rise over sixty times—as I have," he added hastily. "When we reach the tomb it will be time to deal with its affairs; till then let us be content with life, and the good things it offers, such as thrones, and find the love of the most beautiful woman in the world, and the rest. Harvest your corn when it is ripe, Prince, and do not trouble about next year's crop or whether in his grave Pharaoh's Double eats white bread or brown. Pharaoh's daughter—or Amen's—is your business, not his ghost."

"Yes, good soothsayer," said Abi, "she is my business. But one more question. Why did that accursed mummy speak of her as 'It'—in my dream I mean—as though she were no woman, but something beyond woman?"

For a moment Kaku hesitated, for the point was hard to answer, then he replied boldly:

"Because as I believe, Prince, this Queen with whom the gods are rewarding your deserts is in truth more than woman, being Amen's very daughter, and therefore in those realms whence the dream came, she is known not as woman, but by her title of Royal Loveliness. Oh!" went on Kaku, simulating an enthusiasm that in truth did not glow within his breast, "great and glorious is your lot, King of the world, and splendid the path which I have opened to your triumphant feet. It was I who showed you how Pharaoh might be trapped in Memphis, being but a poor fool easy to deceive, and it was I—or rather Merytra yonder—who rid you of him. And now it is I, the Master whom you threatened with rods, that alone can interpret to you the happy omen of a dream which you thought fearsome. Think of the end of it, Prince, and banish every doubt. Who bore away the shape of Pharaoh? Why the spirits of your sons, thus symbolising the triumph of your House."

"At least they will have no share in it, Kaku, for they are dead," said Abi with a groan, for he had loved his sons.

"What of that, Prince? They died bravely, and we mourn them, but here again Fortune is with you, for had they lived trouble might have arisen between them and those other sons which the Queen of Egypt shall bear to you."

"Mayhap, mayhap," replied Abi, waving his hand, for the subject was painful to him, "but this Queen is not yet my wife. She is starving in yonder tower, and what am I to do? If I try to force my presence upon her, she will destroy herself as she swore, and if I leave her there any longer, being mortal, she must die. Moreover, I dare not, for even these folk of Memphis, who love me, begin to murmur. Egypt's Queen is Egypt's Queen, and they will not suffer that she should perish miserably, being beautiful and young, and one who takes all hearts. This night at sunset they gathered in tens of thousands round the tower to hear her sing that evening hymn to Ra, and afterwards marched past my palace, shouting in the darkness, 'Give food to Her Majesty, and free her, or we will.' Moreover, by now the news must have come to Thebes, and there a great army will gather to liberate or avenge her. What am I to do, Prophet?"

"Do what dead Pharaoh bade you in your dream, Prince. At the hour of dawn go to the Temple of Sekhet, where you will find the Queen become obedient to your wishes, for did not the dream declare that she will not say you nay? Then lead her to your palace, and marry her in the face of all men, and rule by right of her Majesty and of your own conquering arm."

"It can be tried," said Abi, "for then, at least, we shall learn what truth there is in dreams. But what of this Asti her companion?"

"Asti has been an ill guide to her Majesty, Prince," replied Kaku, rubbing his chin as he always did when there was mischief in his mind. "Moreover, she is advanced in years, and must be weak with grief and hunger. If she still lives Merytra here will take her in charge and care for her. You are old friends, are you not, Merytra?"

"Very," answered that lady with emphasis, "like the cat and the bird which were pets of the same master. Well, we shall have much to say to each other. Only, beware, Husband, Asti is no weakling. Your magic may be strong, but hers is stronger, for she is a great priestess and draws it from gods—not devils."

****

So it came about that at dawn Prince Abi, clad in magnificent robes, and accompanied by Councillors, among them Kaku, and by a small guard, was carried in a litter to the gates of the old temple of Sekhet, being too heavy to walk so far, and there descended. As there were none to defend them these gates were opened easily enough, and they passed through, leaving the guard without. When they came to the inner court, Abi stopped and asked where they should search.

"In one place only, your Highness," answered Kaku, "that pylon tower which overlooks the Nile, for there her Majesty starves with Asti."

"Pylon tower," grumbled Abi. "Have I not climbed enough steps this night? Still, lead on."

So they went to the narrow stair, up which the thin Kaku ran like a cat, while the officers pushed and led the huge Abi behind him. On the third landing they all halted at Abi's command.

"Hurry not," he said in a thick whisper. "Her Majesty dwells on the next floor of this hateful tower, and since Asti is with her she cannot be surprised. Beware, then, of frightening her by your sudden appearance, lest she should run to the top of the pylon, and hurl herself into the Nile, as she has sworn that she will do. Halt now, and I will call to her when I have got my breath."

So after a while he called, saying:

"O Queen, cease to starve yourself in this miserable abode, and come down to dwell in plenty with your faithful subject."

He called it once, and twice, and thrice, but there was no answer. Now Abi grew afraid.

"She must have perished," he said, "and Egypt will demand her blood at my hands. Kaku, go up and see what has happened. You are a magician, and have nothing to fear."

But the astrologer thought otherwise, and hesitated, till Abi in a rage lifted his cedar wand to strike him on the back. Then he went, step by step, slowly, pausing at each step to address prayers and praises to her Majesty of Egypt. At length he came to the door of the Queen's chamber, and kneeling down, peeped into it, to see that it was quite empty. Next he crawled across the landing to the chamber opposite, that which had been Asti's, and found it empty also. Then, made bold by fear, he ascended to the pylon roof. But here, too, there was no one to be seen. So he returned, and told Abi, who shouted:

"By Ptah, great Lord of Memphis! either she has escaped to raise Egypt on me, or she has sought death in the Nile to raise the gods upon me, which is worse. So much for your interpretation of dreams, O Cheat."

"Wait till you are sure before you call me such names, Prince," replied Kaku indignantly. "Let us search the temple, she may be elsewhere."

So they searched it court by court, and chamber by chamber, till they came to that inner hall in front of the Sanctuary where Pharaoh had set up his throne while he sojourned at Memphis. This hall was a dark place, into which light flowed only through the gratings in the clerestory, being roofed in with blocks of granite laid upon its lotus-shaped columns. Now, at the hour of sunrise, the gloom in it was still deep, so deep that the searchers felt their way from pillar to pillar, seeing nothing. Presently, however, a ray of light from the rising sun sped through the opening shaped like the eye of Osiris in the eastern wall, and as it had done for thousands of years, struck upon the shrine of the goddess, and the throne that was set in front of it, revealing the throne, and seated thereon Neter-Tua, her Majesty of Egypt.

Glorious she looked indeed, a figure of flame set in the midst of darkness. The royal robe she wore glittered in the sunlight, glittered her sceptre, her jewels, and the *uraei* on her Double Crown, but more than all of them glittered her fierce and splendid eyes. Indeed, there was something so terrible in those eyes that the beholders who discovered them thus suddenly, shrank back, whispering to each other that here sat a goddess, not a woman. For in her calmness, her proud beauty and her silence, she seemed like an immortal, one victorious who had triumphed over death, not a woman who for seven days had starved within a tower.

They shrank back, they huddled themselves together in the doorway, and there remained whispering till the growing light fell on them also. But the figure on the throne took no heed, only stared over their heads as though it were lost in mystery and thought.

At length Kaku, gathering courage, said to Abi:

"O Prince, there is your bride, such a bride as never man had before. Go now and take her," and all the others echoed:

"Go now, O Prince, and take her."

Thus adjured for very shame's sake Abi advanced, looking often behind him, till he came to the foot of the throne, and stood there bowing.

For a long while he stood bowing thus, till he grew weary indeed, for he knew not what to say. Then suddenly a clear and silvery voice spoke above him, asking:

"What do you here, Lord of Memphis? Why are you not in the cell where Pharaoh bound you? Oh! I remember—the footstool-bearer, Merytra, your paid spy, let you out, did she not? Why is she not here with Kaku the Sorcerer, who fashioned the enchanted image that did Pharaoh to death? Is it because she stays to doctor those false lips of hers that were cut last night before you went to ask yonder Kaku to interpret a certain dream which came to you?"

"How did you learn these things? Have you spies in my palace, O Queen?"

"Yes, my uncle, I have spies in your palace and everywhere. What Amen sees his daughter knows. Now you have come to lead me away to be your wife, have you not? Well, I await you, I am ready. Do it if you dare!"

"If I dare? Why should I not dare, O Queen?" asked Abi in a doubtful voice.

"Surely that question is one for you to answer, Count of Memphis and its subject *nomes*. Yet tell me this—why did the magic crystal burst asunder without cause in the chamber of Kaku last night, and why do you suppose that Kaku interpreted to you all the meaning of your dream—he who will never tell the truth unless it be beneath the rods?"

"I do not know, Queen," answered Abi, "but with Kaku I can speak later, if need be after the fashion you suggest," and he glanced at the magician wrathfully.

"No, Prince Abi, you know nothing, and Kaku knows nothing, save that rods break the backs of snakes, unless they can find a wall to hide in," and she pointed to the astrologer slinking back into the shadow. "No one knows anything save me, to whom Amen gives wisdom with sight of the future, and what I know I keep. Were it otherwise, O Abi, I could tell you things that would turn your grey hair white, and to Kaku and Merytra the spy, promise rewards that would make the torture-chamber seem a bed of down. But it is not lawful, nor would they sound pleasant in this bridal hour."

Now while Kaku between his chattering teeth muttered the words of Protection in the shadow, Abi and his courtiers stared at this terrible queen as boys seeking wild fowls' eggs in the reeds, and stumbling on a lion, stare ere they fly. Twice, indeed, the Prince turned looking towards the door and the pleasant light without, for it seemed to him that he was entering on a dark and doubtful road. Then he said:

"Your words, O Queen, cut like a two-edged sword, and methinks they leave a poison in the wound. Say now, if you are human, how it comes about that after seven days of want your flesh is not minished nor has your beauty waned. Say also who brought to you those glorious robes you wear here in this empty temple, and where is your foster-mother, Asti?"

"The gods fed me," answered the Queen gently, "and brought me these robes that I might seem the more worthy of you, O Prince. And as for Asti, I sent her to Cyprus to fetch a scent they make there and nowhere else. No, I forgot, it was yesterday she went to bring the scent from Cyprus that now is on my hair; to-day she is in Thebes, seeing to a business of mine. That is no secret, I will tell it you—it is as to the carving of all the history of his murder and betrayal in the first chamber of the Pharaoh's tomb."

Now at these magical and ill-omened words the courage of the company left them, so that they began to walk backwards towards the door, Abi going with them.

"What!" cried the Queen in a voice of sorrow that yet seemed laden with mockery. "Would you leave me here alone? Do my power and my wisdom frighten you? Alas! I cannot help them, for when the full vase is tilted the wine will run out, and when light is set behind alabaster, then the white stone must shine. Yet am I one meet to adorn the palace of the King, even such a king as you shall be, O Abi, whom Osiris loves. See, now, I will dance and sing to you as once I sang to the Prince of Kesh before the sword of Rames took away his life, so that you may judge of me, Abi, you, who have looked upon so many lovely women."

As she spoke, very slowly, so slowly that they could scarcely see her move, she glided from the throne, and standing before them, began to move her feet and body, and to chant a song.

What were the words of that song none could ever remember, but to every man there present it opened a door in his heart, and brought back the knowledge of youth. She whom he had loved best danced before him, her tender hands caressed him; the words she sang were sighs which the dead had whispered in his ears. Even to Abi, old, unwieldy and steeped in cunning, these soft visions came, although it is true that it seemed to him that this lovely singer led him to a precipice, and that when she ceased her song and appeared to vanish, to seek her he leapt into the clouds that rushed beneath.

Now the dance was done, and the last echoes of the music died away against the ancient walls whence the images of Sekhet the cat-headed watched them with her cruel smile of vengeance. The dance was done, and the beautiful dancer stood before them unflushed, unheated, but laughing gently.

"Now go, divine Prince," she said, "and you his followers, go, all of you, and leave me to my lonely house, until Pharaoh sends for me to share that new realm which he inherits beyond the West."

But they would not go and could not if they would, for some power bound them to her, while, as for Abi he scarce could take his eyes from her, but heedless of who heard them, babbled out his passion at her feet, while the rest glowered on him jealously. She listened always smiling that same smile that was so sweet, yet so inhuman. Then when he stopped exhausted, at last she spoke, saying:

"What! do you love now more greatly than you fear, as the divine Prince of Kesh loved after Amen's Star had sung to him. May your fate be happier, O noble Abi, but that, since it is not lawful that I should tell it to you, you shall discover. Abi, there shall be a royal marriage in Memphis of such joy and feasting as has not been known in the history of the Northern or the Southern Land, and for your allotted span you shall sit by the side of Egypt's Queen and shine in her light. Have you not earned the place by right of blood, O conqueror of Pharaoh, and did not Pharaoh promise it to you in your sleep? Come, the sun of this new day shines, let us walk in it, and bid farewell to shadows."

Chapter 12
The Royal Marriage

A strange rumour ran through Memphis. It was said that the Queen had yielded; it was said that she would marry the Prince Abi, that she was already at the great White House waiting to be made a bride. Men wrangled about in the streets. They swore that it could not be true, for would this high lady, the anointed Pharaoh of Egypt, take her father's murderer, and her own uncle to husband? Would she not rather die in her prison tower on which night by night they had seen her stand and sing? In their hearts they thought that she should die, for thus they had summed her up, this pure, high-hearted daughter of Amen, whom Fate had caught in an evil net. Yes, being men they held that she ought to die, and leave a story in the world, whereof Egypt could be proud for ever.

But their wives and daughters mocked at them. After all she was but a woman, they argued, and was it likely that she would throw aside the pomp of rule and the prospect of long years in order to steal away into the shadows of a forgotten tomb? Henceforth, it was true, she must take second place, for Abi would be a stern master to her. Still, any place was better than a funeral barge. She had felt the pinch of hunger yonder in that old temple; her fierce spirit had been tamed; she had kissed the rod, and after long years of waiting, Abi would be Pharaoh in Egypt.

The dispute grew hot, for even those men who rebelled against her, in their hearts had set her high, and grieved to think of her, the divine Lady, bowing her neck to the common yoke of circumstance, and selling herself for safety, and a seat on the steps of her own throne. But the women mocked on, and showed them that as they had always said, she was no better than others of her sex.

Presently the matter was settled, for heralds appeared crying throughout the city that the marriage would take place in the great hall of the White House one hour before sundown. Then the women laughed in triumph, and the men were silent.

It was the appointed hour, and that hall was filled to overflowing by all who could gain entrance there. Between the towering obelisks that stood on either side the open cedar doors, folk hung upon its steps like hiving bees; the vast square without and all the streets that led to it were black with them. Here, it is true, they could see nothing, still they fought for the merest foothold, and some of those who fell never rose again. At the head of the hall were set two thrones, the greater and the richer throne for Abi the Prince, the lesser throne for Neter-Tua the Queen. He had arranged it thus since Kaku the cunning pointed out to him that from the first he should show the people that it was he who ruled, and not Pharaoh's daughter.

It was the appointed hour, and at some signal from every temple top rang out the blare of trumpets. Thrice they sounded, and echoed into silence in that hot, still air, thus announcing that in the temple of Hathor, and the presence of the priests of all the gods, the hands of Abi and Neter-Tua had been joined in marriage.

Another rumour began to run among the crowd; like the ring set circling by a stone in water it spread from mouth to mouth, ever widening as it went.

Marvels had happened in the temple of Hathor, that was the rumour. Moreover it gave details: that the High-Priest had handed to the bride the accustomed lotus-bud, the flower of the goddess, and lo! it opened in her hand. Also, it was said, that presently the stem of it turned to a sceptre of gold, and the cup of the bloom to sapphire stones more perfect far than any from the desert mines.

Nor was this all, so went the tale, for when, as he must, the bridegroom Abi offered the white dove to Hathor in her shrine, a hawk swept through the doorway and smote it in his very hand. Yes, there in the gloom of the shrine smote it and left it dead, blood running from its beak and breast, dead upon the knees of the goddess; left it and was gone again!

Now what hawk, asked the people of each other, dare such a deed as this, unless in truth it was sent by the hawk-headed Horus, the son of Amen-Ra.

Soon these matters were forgotten for the moment, since now it was known that the royal pair were entering the great White Hall, there to show themselves to the people, and receive the homage of the nobles, chiefs, and captains. First, advancing by the covered way which led from the temple of Hathor, appeared the priests in their robes, chanting as they walked, followed by the masters of ceremonies, butlers, and heralds. Next, surrounded by his officers and guard, came the Prince Abi himself, accompanied by his vizier, Kaku, he whose magic was said to have brought Pharaoh to his end.

Not all his pomp nor the splendour of his apparel, whereof the whiteness, as many noted, was spotted with ill-omened blood, nor even the royal crown which now, for the first time, was set upon his huge, round head, could hide from those who watched that this bridegroom was ill at ease. Even as he stood there, bowing in answer to the obsequious shouts of the multitude, the sceptre in his fat hand shook, and his red lips blanched and trembled. Still he smiled and bowed on, till at length the shouting died away, and quiet fell upon the place.

Abi was forgotten, they waited the coming of the Queen, and though no herald called her advent, yet every heart of all those thousands felt that she drew near to them. Look! Yonder she stood. They had watched closely enough, yet none saw her come, doubtless because the shadows were thick. But there she stood, quite alone upon the edge of the dais in front of the two thrones, and, oh! she was different from what they had expected. Thus now she wore no gorgeous robes, but only a simple garment of purest white, cut low upon her bosom, where the red rays of the sinking sun, striking up the hall, revealed to every eye that dark mole shaped like the Cross of Life, which was her wondrous birthmark. But two ornaments adorned her, the double snakes of royalty, golden with red eyes, set in front of her tall white head-dress, which none but she might wear, the crowns of Upper and of Lower Egypt, and of all the subject lands, and in her hand a sceptre fashioned of gold, and surmounted by a lotus-bloom of sapphire, that sceptre of which rumour had told the magic tale.

Yes, she was different. They had thought to see a woman weak and pale, her eyes still red with grief, her face still stained with tears, one who had been tamed by misfortune, hunger, and the fear of death, whence she had bought herself by marriage with her conqueror. But it was not so, for never had the Star of Amen shone half so beautiful, never had they seen such majesty in those deep blue eyes that looked them through and through as though they read the secret heart of every one of them. Her tall and lovely form had not wasted, her cheeks were red with the glow of health; power and dignity flowed from her presence, fear seemed beneath her feet.

Now no voice was lifted up; they stared at her, and, smiling a little, she answered them with her calm eyes till their heads sank beneath her gaze. Then at length in the midst of that dead, oppressive silence which none dared to break, she turned, and they heard the sweep of her silken robe upon the alabaster floor.

With an effort two chamberlains stepped forward, their wands of office in their hands, to lead her to her seat, but she waved them back, and said in her clear voice:

"Nay, here I am alone; of all the millions who serve her, not one is left to lead Amen's daughter and Egypt's Queen to her rightful place. Therefore she takes it of her own strength, now and for evermore."

Then very slowly, still in the midst of silence, she mounted the greater throne that had been prepared for Abi, and there seated herself and waited.

Now murmuring rose among the courtiers and Kaku whispered into Abi's ear, while the multitude held its breath. Abi stamped his foot and issued orders which all seemed to fear to execute. At length he stepped forward, addressing the Queen in a hoarse voice.

"Lady," he said, "doubtless you know it not, but that place is mine; your seat is on my left. Be pleased to take it."

"Why so, Prince Abi?" she asked quietly.

"Lady," he answered, "because the husband takes precedence of the wife, and," he added with savage meaning, "the conqueror of the conquered."

"The conqueror of the conquered?" she repeated after him in a musing voice. "Should you not have said—the murderer of the murdered and his seed? Nay, Prince Abi, you are wrong. The sovereign of Egypt by right divine, takes precedence of her vassal, even though it has pleased the gods, whose will she has come to execute, to command her to give to him the name of husband until that will is more fully known. Come now and do homage to your Queen, and after you those slaves of yours who dared to lift the sword against her."

Then a great tumult arose, a tumult of rage and of dismay, for well nigh all in that vast place were partners in this crime, and knew that if Neter-Tua prevailed death yawned wide for them.

They shouted to Abi to take no heed of her. They shouted to him to tear her from the throne, to kill her, and seize the crown. They drew their swords and raged like an angry sea. Those who were loyal among them to Pharaoh's House, and those who feared turmoil, began to work their way backwards, and slipped by twos and threes out of the great open doors, till Tua had no friend left in all that hall. But ever as they went, others of the turbulent and the rebellious who had been concerned in the slaughter of Pharaoh's guard, took their place, pouring in from the mob without.

Wild desert-dwellers of the Bedouin tribes, who for thousands of years had been the bitter enemies of Egypt; descendants of the Hyksos, whose forefathers had ruled the land for a dozen generations, and at last been driven out; those Hyksos whose blood ran in Abi's veins, and who looked to him to lift them up again; evil-doers who had sought shelter in his regiments; hook-nosed Semites from the Lebanon; black, barbarian savages from the shores of Punt—with such as these was that hall filled.

Abi was the hope of every one of them; to him they looked for the spoils of Egypt, and before them on Abi's throne they saw a woman who stood between them and their ends, who in her ancient pride dared to demand that he, her husband, should do homage to her, and who to-morrow, if she conquered, would give them to the sword.

"Tear her to pieces!" they screamed, "the bastard whom childless Pharaoh palmed off upon the land! She is a sorceress who keeps fat on air—an evil spirit. Away with her! Or if you fear, then let us come!"

At length they had roared themselves hoarse; at length they grew still. Then Abi, who all this while had stood there hesitating, and now and again turning to hearken to Kaku who whispered in his ear, looked up at Tua and spoke.

"You see and you hear, Queen," he said. "My people mistrust you, and they are a rough people, I cannot hold them back for long. If once they get at you, very soon that sweet body of yours will be in more fragments than was Osiris after Set had handled him."

Now Tua, who hitherto had sat still and indifferent, like one who takes no heed, seemed to awake, and answered:

"A bad example, Prince, for Osiris rose again, did he not?" Then she leaned back and once more was silent.

"Do you still desire that I should do homage to you, Queen, I, your husband?" he asked presently.

"Why not?" she replied. "I have spoken. A decree of Pharaoh may not be changed, and though a woman, I am—Pharaoh."

Now Abi went white with rage, and turned to his guard to bid them drag her from the throne. But she who was watching him, suddenly lifted her sceptre and spoke in a new voice, a clear, strong voice that rang through the hall, and even reached those who were gathered on the steps without.

"There is a question between you and me, O People," she said, "and it is this—Shall I, your Queen, rule in Egypt, as my fathers ruled, or shall yonder man rule whom by the decree of Amen I have taken for husband? Now you who for the most part have the Hyksos blood running in your veins, as he has, desire that he should rule, and you have slain the good god, my father, and would make Abi king over you, and see me his handmaid, one to give him children of my royal race, no more. See, you are a multitude and my legions are far away, and I—I am alone, one lamb among the jackals, thousands and thousands of jackals who for a long while have been hungry. How, then, shall I match myself against you?"

"You cannot," shouted a wild-eyed spokesman. "Come down, lamb, and kneel before the lion, Abi, or we, the jackals, will rend you. We will not acknowledge you, we who are of the fierce Hyksos blood. While the obelisks stand that were set up by the great Hyksos Pharaoh whose descendant was Abi's mother, while the obelisks stand that are set there for all eternity, we will not acknowledge you. Come down and take your place in our lord's harem, O Pharaoh's bastard daughter."

"Ah!" Tua repeated after him, "while the obelisks stand that the Hyksos thief set up you will not acknowledge me, Pharaoh's bastard daughter!"

Then she paused and seemed to grow disturbed; she sighed, wrung her hands a little, and said in a choking voice:

"I am but one woman alone among you. My father, Pharaoh, is dead, and you bid me lay down my rank and henceforth rule only through him who trapped Pharaoh and brought him to his end. What, then, can I do?"

"Be a good maid and obey your husband, Bastard," mocked a voice, and during the roar of laughter that followed Tua looked at the speaker, an officer of Abi's, who had taken a great part in the slaughter of their escort.

Very strangely she looked at him, and those who stood by the man noted that his lips became white, and that he turned so faint that had it not been for the press about him he would have fallen. Presently he seemed to recover, and asked the priests who were near to let him join their circle, as among the outer throng the heat was too great for him to bear. Thereon one of them nodded and made room for him, and he passed in, which Tua noted also.

Now she was speaking again.

"Ill names to throw at Egypt's anointed queen, crowned and accepted by the god himself in the sanctuary of his most holy temple," she said, her eyes still resting on the brutal soldier. "Yet it is your hour, and she must bear them who has no friends in Memphis. Oh! what shall I do?" and again she wrung her hands. "Good People, it was sworn to me that Amen, greatest of the gods, set his spirit within me when I was born, and vowed that he would help me in the hour of my need. Of your grace, then, give me space to pray to Amen. Look," and she pointed before her, "yonder sinks the red ball of the sun; soon, soon it will be gone—give me until it enters the gateways of the West to pray to Amen, and then if no help comes I will bow me to your bidding, and do homage to this noble Prince of the Hyksos blood, who snared Pharaoh his brother, and by help of his magicians and of his spy, Merytra, brought him to his end."

"Yes, my people, give her the space she asks," called Abi, who feared nothing from Amen, a somewhat remote personage, and was afraid lest some tumult should happen in the course of which this lovely, new-made wife of his might be slain or injured.

So they gave her the space of time she asked. Standing up, Tua raised her arms and eyes towards heaven, and began to pray aloud:

"Hear me, Amen my Father, in the House of thy Rest, as thou hast sworn to do. O Amen my Father, thou seest my strait. Is it thy will that thy daughter should degrade herself and thee before this man who slew his king and brother, to whom thou hast commanded her to give the name of husband? If it be so, I will obey; but if it be not so, then show thy word by might or marvel, and cause him and his folk who mock my majesty and name me bastard, to bow down before me. O Amen, they deny thee in their hearts who worship other gods, as did the barbarians who begat them and threw down thy shrines in Egypt, but I know that thou sentest me forth, and in thee I put my trust, aye, even if thou slay me. Amen my Father, yonder sinks that glory in which thou dost hide thy spirit. Now, ere it be gone and night falls upon the world, declare thyself in such fashion that all men may know that indeed I am thy child; or if this be thy decree, desert me and Egypt, and leave me to my shame."

She ended her prayer and, sinking back upon the throne, rested her chin upon her hand, and gazed steadily upon the splendour of the sinking sun. Nor did she gaze alone, for every man in that vast hall turned himself about, and stared at its departing glory. There in the red light they stood, and stared, and since the place was open to the sky, the shadows of the two towering obelisks without fell on them like the shadows of swords whereof the points met together at the foot of Tua's throne. They did not believe that anything would happen, no, not even the priests believed it who here at Memphis, the city of Ptah, thought little of Amen, the god of Thebes. They thought that this piteous prayer was but a last cry of dying faith wrung from a proud and fallen woman in her wretchedness.

And yet, and yet they stared, for she had spoken with a strange certainty like one who knew the god, and was she not named Star of Amen, and were there not wondrous tales as to her birth, and had not a lotus-bloom seemed to turn to gold and jewels in the hand of this young, anointed Queen who bore the Cross of Life upon her breast? No, nothing would happen, but still they stared.

It was a very strange sunset. For days the heat had been great, but now it was fearful, also a marvellous stillness reigned in heaven and earth. Nothing seemed to stir in all the city, no dog barked, no child cried, no leaf quivered upon the tall palms; it might have been a city of the dead.

Dense clouds arose upon the sky, and moved, though no wind blew. Where the sun's rays touched them they were gold and red and purple, but above these of an inky blackness. They took strange shapes those clouds, and marshalled themselves like a host gathering for battle. There were the commanders moving quickly to and fro; there the chariots, and there the sullen lines of footmen with their gleaming spears. Now one cloud higher than the rest seemed to shoot itself across the arch of heaven, and its fashion was that of a woman with outspread hair of gold. Her feet stood upon the sun, her body bent itself athwart the sky, and upon the far horizon in the east her hands held the pale globe of the rising moon.

The watchers were frightened at this cloud. "It is Isis with the moon in her arms," said one. "Nay, it is the mother goddess Nout brooding upon the world," answered another. And though they only spoke softly, in that awful silence their voices reached Tua on the throne, and for the first time her face changed, for on it came a cold, curious smile.

Kaku began to whisper into Abi's ear, and there was fear in the eyes of both of them. He pointed with his finger at two stars, which of a sudden shone out through the green haze above the sunset glow, and then turned and looked at the Queen, urging his master eagerly. At last Abi spoke.

"Ra is set," he said. "Come, let us make an end of all this folly."

"Not yet," answered Tua quietly, "not yet awhile."

As she said the words, of a sudden, as though at a given signal, all the long lines of palm trees that grew in the rich gardens upon the river banks were seen to bow themselves towards the east, as though they did obeisance to the Queen upon her throne. Thrice they bowed thus, without a wind, and then were straight and still once more. Next the clouds rushed together as though a black pall had been drawn across the heavens, only in the west the half-hidden globe of the sun shone on through an opening in them, shone like a great and furious eye. By slow degrees it sank, till nothing was left save a little rim of fire. All the hall grew dark, and through the darkness Neter-Tua could be heard calling on the name of Amen.

"Ra is dead!" shouted a voice. "Have done, Bastard, Ra is dead!"

"Aye," she answered in a cold triumphant cry, "but Amen lives. Behold his sword, ye Traitors!"

As the words left her lips the heavens were cleft in twain by a fearful flash of lightning, and in it the people saw that once again the palm-trees bowed themselves, this time almost to the ground. Then with a roar the winds were loosed, and beneath their feet the solid earth began to heave as though a giant lifted it. Thrice it heaved like a heaving wave, and the third time through the thick cover of the darkness there rose a shriek of terror and of agony followed by the awful crash of falling stones.

Now the whole sky seemed to melt in fire, and in that fierce light was seen Tua, Star of Amen, seated on her throne, holding her sceptre to the heavens, and laughing in triumphant merriment. Well might she laugh, for the two great obelisks without the gate that the old Hyksos lion had set up there to stand "to all eternity," had fallen across the low pylons and the doors and crushed them. On to the heads of those who watched beneath they had fallen, shattering in their fall and carrying death to hundreds. Beneath the electrum cap of one of them that had been hurled from it in its descent right into the circle of the priests, lay a shapeless mass. It was that man who had mocked the Queen and turned faint beneath her gaze.

Through the western ruin of the hall those who were left alive within it fled out, a maddened mob, trampling each other to death by scores, fighting furiously to escape the vengeance of Amen and his daughter. Within the enclosure the priests lay prostrate on their faces, each praying to his god for mercy. In front of the throne, upon his knees, the royal crown shaken from his head, Abi grasped the feet of Neter-Tua and screamed to her to forgive and spare him, whilst above, shining like fire, That which sat upon the throne pointed with her sceptre at the ruin and the rout, and laughed and laughed again.

Soon all were gone save the mumbling priests, the dying, the dead, and Abi with his officers.

The clouds rolled off, the moon and the stars shone out, filling the place with gentle light. Then Tua spoke, looking down at the wretched Abi who grovelled before her.

"Say, now, Husband," she asked, "who is god in Egypt?"

"Amen your father," he gasped.

"And who is Pharaoh in Egypt?"

"You, and no other, O Queen."

"Ah!" she said, "it was over that matter that we quarrelled, did we not? which forced me, whom you thought so helpless, to find helpers. Look, there are their footsteps; they walk heavily, do they not, my Uncle?" and she nodded towards the huge fragments of the broken obelisks.

He glanced behind him at his ruined hall, at the dying and the dead. "You are Pharaoh and no other," he repeated with a shudder. "Give breath to your servant, and let him live on in your shadow."

"The first is not mine to give," she answered coldly, "though perchance it may please Amen to hold you back a little while from that place where you must settle your account with him who went before me, and his companions who died in your streets. I hope so, for you have work to do. As for the second—arise, you Priests and Officers, and see this Prince of yours do homage to the Queen of Egypt."

They rose, and clung to each other trembling, for all the heart was out of them. Then she pointed to her foot with the sceptre in her hand, and in their presence Abi knelt down and kissed her sandal. After him followed the others, the priests, the captains, the head-stewards, and the butlers, till at length came Kaku, the astrologer, who prostrated himself before her, trembling in every limb. But him she would not suffer even to touch her sandals.

"Tell me," she said, drawing back her foot, "you who are a magician, and have studied the secret writings, how does it chance that you still live on, when for lesser crimes so many lie here dead, you who are stained with the blood of Pharaoh?"

Hearing these words from which he presaged the very worst, Kaku beat his head upon the ground, babbling denials of this awful crime, and at the same time began to implore pardon for what he said he had not committed.

"Cease," she exclaimed, "and learn that your life is spared for a while, yes, and even Merytra's. Also you will retain your office of Vizier—for a while."

Now he began to pour out thanks, but she stopped him, saying:

"Thank me not, seeing that you do not know the end of this matter. Perchance it is hidden from you lest you should go mad, you and your wife, Merytra, she who was the Pharaoh's Lady of the Footstool, and sang him to sleep. Look at me, Wizard, and tell me, who am I?" and she bent down over him.

He glanced up at her, and their eyes met, nor could he turn his head away again.

"Come," she said, "as you may have learned to-night, I also have some knowledge of the hidden things. For otherwise, why did the earth shake and the everlasting pillars fall at my bidding? Now, between two of a trade there should be no secrets, so I will tell you something that perhaps you have already guessed, since I am sure that you will not repeat it even to your master or to Merytra. For I will add this—that the moment you repeat it will be the moment of your death, and the beginning of that punishment which here I withhold. Now, in the Name of the Eater-up of Souls, listen to me, O fashioner of waxen images!" and, bending down, she whispered into his ear.

Another instant, and, stark horror written on his face, the tall shape of Kaku was seen reeling backward, like to a drunken man. Indeed, had not Abi caught him he would have fallen over the edge of the dais.

"What did she tell you?" he muttered, for the Queen, who seemed to have forgotten all about him, was looking the other way.

But, making no answer, Kaku wrenched himself free and fled the place.

Chapter 13
Abi Learns the Truth

A moon had gone by, and on the first day of the new month Kaku the Vizier sat in the Hall of the Great Officers at Memphis, checking the public accounts of the city. It was not easy work, for during the past ten days twice these accounts had been sent back to him by the command of the Queen, or the Pharaoh as she called herself, with requests for information as to their items, and other awkward queries. Abi had overlooked such matters, recognising that a faithful servant was worthy of his hire—provided that he paid himself. But now it seemed that things were different, and that the amount received was the exact amount that had to be handed over to the Crown, neither more nor less. Well, there was a large discrepancy which must be made up from somewhere, or, in other words, from Kaku's private store.

In a rage he caused the two head collectors of taxes to be brought before him, and as they would not pay, bade the executioners throw them down and beat them on the feet until they promised to produce the missing sums, most of which he himself had stolen.

Then, somewhat soothed, he retired from the hall into his own office, to find himself face to face with Abi, who was waiting for him. So changed was the Prince from his old, portly self, so aged and thin and miserable did he look, that in the dusk of that chamber Kaku failed to recognise him. Thinking that he was some suppliant, he began to revile him and order him to be gone. Then the fury of Abi broke out.

Rushing at him, he seized the astrologer by the beard and smote him on the ears, saying: "Dog, is it thus that you speak to your king? Well, on you at least I can revenge myself."

"Pardon, your Majesty," said Kaku, "I did not know you in these shadows. Your Majesty is changed of late."

"Changed!" said Abi, letting him go. "Who would not be changed who suffers as I do ever since I listened to your cursed counsel, and tried to climb into the seat of Pharaoh? Before that I was happy. I had my sons, I had my wives, as many as I wished. I had my revenues and armies. Now everything has gone. My sons are dead, my women are driven away, my revenues are taken from me, my armies serve another."

"At least," suggested Kaku, "you are Pharaoh, and the husband of the most beautiful and the wisest woman in the world."

"Pharaoh!" groaned Abi. "The humblest mummy in the common city vaults is a greater king than I am, and as for the rest——" and he stopped and groaned again.

"What is the matter with your Majesty?" asked Kaku.

"The matter is that I have fallen under the influence of an evil planet."

"The Star of Amen," suggested the astrologer.

"Yes, the Star of Amen, that lovely Terror whom you call my wife. Man, she is no wife to me. Listen—there in the harem I went into the chamber where she was, none forbidding me, and found her sitting before her mirror and singing, clothed only in a thin robe of white, and her dark hair—O Kaku, never did you see such hair—which fell almost to the ground. She smiled on me, she spoke me fair, she drew me with those glittering eyes of hers—yes, she even called me husband, and sighed and talked of love, till at length I drew near to her and threw my arms about her."

"And then——"

"And then, Kaku, she was gone, and where her sweet face should have been I saw the yellow, mummied head of Pharaoh, he who is with Osiris, that seemed to grin at me. I opened my arms again, and lo! there she sat, laughing and shaking perfume from her hair, asking me, too, what ailed me that I turned so white, and if such were the way of husbands?

"Well, that was nigh a month ago, and as it began, so it has gone on. I seek my wife, and I find the mummied head of Pharaoh, and all the while she mocks me. Nor may I see the others any more, for she has caused them to be hunted hence, even those who have dwelt with me for years, saying that she must rule alone."

"Is that all?" asked Kaku.

"No, indeed, for as she torments me, so she torments every other man who comes near to her. She nets them with smiles, she bewitches them with her eyes till they go mad for love of her, and then, still smiling, she sends them about their business. Already two of them who were leaders in the great plot have died by their own hands, and another is mad, while the rest have become my secret but my bitter foes, because they love my Queen and think that I stand between her and them."

"Is that all?" asked Kaku again.

"No, not all, for my power is taken from me. I who was great, after Pharaoh the greatest in all the land, now am but a slave. From morning to night I must work at tasks I hate; I must build temples to Amen, I must dig canals, I must truckle to the common herd, and redress their grievances and remit their taxes. More, I must chastise the Bedouin who have ever been my friends, and—next month undertake a war against that King of Khita, with whom I made a secret treaty, and whose daughter that I married has been sent back to him because I loved her."

"And then?" asked Kaku.

"Oh! then when the Khita have been destroyed and made subject to Egypt, then her Majesty purposes to return in state to Thebes 'to attend to the fashioning of my sepulchre' since, so she says, this is a matter that will not bear delay. Indeed, already she makes drawings for it, horrible and mystic drawings that I cannot understand, and brings them to me to see. Moreover, Friend, know this, out of it opens another smaller tomb for *you*. Indeed, but this morning she sent an expedition to the desert quarries to bring thence three blocks of stone, one for my sarcophagus, one for yours, and one for that of your wife, Merytra. For she says that after the old fashion she purposes to honour both of you with these gifts."

At these words Kaku could no longer control himself, but began to walk up and down the room, muttering and snatching at his beard.

"How can you suffer it?" he said at length, "You who were a great prince, to become a woman's slave, to be made as dirt beneath her feet, to be held up to the mockery of those you rule, to see your wives and household driven away from you, to be tormented, to be mocked, to look on other men favoured before your eyes, to be threatened with early death. Oh! how can you suffer it? Why do you not kill her, and make an end?"

"Because," answered Abi, "because I dare not, since if I dreamed of such a thing she would guess my thought and kill *me*. Fool, do you not remember the fall of the eternal obelisks upon my captains, and what befell that man who mocked her, calling her Bastard, and sought refuge among the priests? No, I dare not lift a finger against her."

"Then, Prince, you must carry your yoke until it wears through to the marrow, which will be when that sepulchre is ready."

"Not so," answered Abi, shivering, "for I have another plan; it is of it that I am come to speak with you. Friend Kaku, *you* must kill her. Listen: you are a master of spells. The magic which prevailed against the father will overcome the daughter also. You have but to make a waxen image or two and breathe strength into them, and the thing is done, and then—think of the reward."

"Indeed I am thinking, most noble Prince," replied the astrologer with sarcasm. "Shall I tell you of that reward? It would be my death by slow torture. Moreover, it is impossible, for if you would know the truth, she cannot be killed."

"What do you mean, Fool?" asked Abi angrily. "Flesh and blood must bow to death."

A sickly smile spread itself over Kaku's thin face as he answered:

"A saying worthy of your wisdom, Prince. Certainly the experience of mankind is that flesh and blood must bow to death. Yes, yes, flesh and blood!"

"Cease grinning at me, you ape of the rocks," hissed the enraged Abi, "or I will prove as much on your mocking throat," and snatching out his sword he threatened him with it, adding: "Now tell me what you mean, or——"

"Prince," ejaculated Kaku, falling to his knees, "I may not, I cannot. Spare me, it is a secret of the gods."

"Then get you gone to the gods, you lying cur, and talk it over with them," answered Abi, lifting the sword, "for at least she will not blame me if I send you there."

"Mercy, mercy!" gasped Kaku, sprawling on the ground, while his lord held the sword above his bald head, thinking that he would choose speech rather than death.

It was at this moment, while the astrologer's fate trembled in the balance, that a sound of voices reached their ears, and above them the ring of a light, clear laugh which they knew well. Forgetting his purpose, Abi stepped to the window-place, and looked through the opening of the shutters. Presently he turned, beckoning to Kaku, and whispered:

"Come and look; there is always time for you to die."

The Vizier heard, and, creeping on his hands and knees to the window-place, raised himself and peeped through the shutter. This was what he saw. In the walled garden below, the secret garden of the palace, stood the queen Neter-Tua, and the sunlight piercing through the boughs of a flowering tree, fell in bright bars upon her beauty. She was not alone, for before her knelt a man wearing the rich robes of a noble. Kaku knew him at once, for although still young, he was

Abi's favourite captain, an officer whom he loved, and had raised to high place because of his wit and valour, having given him one of his daughters in marriage. Also he had played a chief part in the great plot against Pharaoh, and it was he who had dealt the death-blow to Mermes, the husband of the lady Asti.

Now he was playing another part, namely that of lover to the Queen, for he clasped the hem of her robe in his hands, and kissed it with his lips, and pleaded with her passionately. They could catch some of his words.

He had risked his life to climb the wall. He worshipped her. He could not live without her. He was ready to do her bidding in all things—to gather a band and slay Abi; it would be easy, for every man was jealous of the Prince, and thought him quite unworthy of her. Let her give him her love, and he would make her sole Pharaoh of Egypt again, and be content to serve her as a slave. At least let her say one kind word to him.

Thus he spoke, wildly, imploringly, like a man that is drunk with passion and knows not what he says or does, while Neter-Tua listened calmly, and now and again laughed that light, low laugh of hers.

At length he rose and strove to take her hand, but, still laughing, she waved him back, then said suddenly:

"You slew Mermes when he was weak with wounds, did you not, and he was my foster-father. Well, well, it was done in war, and you must be a brave man, as brave as you are handsome, for otherwise you would scarcely have ventured here where a word of mine would give you to your death. And now get you gone, Friend, back to my Lord's daughter who is your wife, and if you dare—tell her where you have been and why, you who are so brave a man," and once more she laughed.

Again he began his passionate implorings, begging for some token, till at length she seemed to melt and take pity on him, for stretching out her hand, she chose a flower from the many that grew near, and gave it to him, then pointed to the trees that hid the wall, among which presently he vanished, reeling in the delirium of his joy.

She watched him go, smiling very strangely, then, still smiling, looked down at the bush whence she had plucked the flower, and Kaku noted that it was one used only by the embalmers to furnish *coronals* for the dead.

But Abi noted no such thing. Forgetting his quarrel with Kaku and all else, he gasped, and foamed in his jealous rage, muttering that he would kill that captain, yes, and the false Queen, too, who dared to listen to a tale of love and give the lover flowers. Yes, were she ten times Pharaoh he would kill her, as he had the right to do, and, the naked sword still in his hand, he turned to leave the place.

"If that is your will, Lord," said Kaku in a strained voice, "bide here."

"Why, man?" asked Abi.

"Because her Majesty comes," he answered, "and this chamber is quiet and fitting. None enter it save myself."

As he spoke the words the door opened, and closed again, and before them stood Neter-Tua, Star of Amen.

In the dusk of that room the first thing that seemed to catch her eye was the bared blade in Abi's hand. For a moment she looked at it and him, also at Kaku crouching in the corner, then asked in her quiet voice:

"Why is your sword drawn, O Husband?"

"To kill you, O Wife," he answered furiously, for his rage mastered him.

She continued to look at him a little while and said, smiling in her strange fashion:

"Indeed? But why more now than at any other time? Has Kaku's counsel given you courage?"

"Need you ask, shameless woman? Does not this window-place open on to yonder garden?"

"Oh! I remember, that captain of yours—he who slew Mermes, your daughter's husband who made love to me—so well that I rewarded him with a funeral flower, knowing that you watched us. Settle your account with him as you and his wife may wish; it is no matter of mine. But I warn you that if you would take men's lives for such a fault as this, soon you will have no servants left, since they all are sinners who desire to usurp your place."

Then Abi's fury broke out. He cursed and reviled her, he called her by ill names, swearing that she should die, who bewitched all men and was the love of none, and who made him a mock and a shame in the sight of Egypt. But Neter-Tua only listened until at length he raved himself to silence.

"You talk much and do little," she said at length. "The sword is in your hand, use it, I am here."

Maddened by her scorn he lifted the weapon and rushed at her, only to reel back again as though he had been smitten by some power unseen. He rested against the wall, then again rushed and again reeled back.

"You are a poor butcher," she said at length, "after so many years of practice. Let Kaku yonder try. I think he has more skill in murder."

"Oh! your Majesty," broke in the astrologer, "unsay those cruel words, you who know that rather than lift hands against you I would die a thousand times."

"Yes," she answered gravely, "the Prince Abi suggested it to you but now, did he not, after you had suggested it to him, and you refused—for your own reasons?"

Then the sword fell from Abi's hand, and there was silence in that chamber.

"What were you talking of, Abi, before you peeped through the shutters and saw that captain of yours and me together in the garden, and why did you wish to kill this dog?" she went on presently. "Must I answer for you? You were talking of how you might be rid of me, and you wished to kill him because he did not dare to tell you why he could not do the deed, knowing that if he did so he must die. Well, since you desire to know, you shall learn, and now. Look on me, wretched Man, whom men name my husband. Look on me, accursed Slave, whom Amen has given into my hand to punish here upon the earth, until you pass to his yonder in the Under-world."

He looked up, and Kaku looked also, because he could not help it, but what they saw they never told. Only they fell down upon their faces, both of them, and groaned; beating the floor with their foreheads.

At length the icy terror seemed to be lifted from their hearts, and they dared to glance up again, and saw that she was as she had been, a most royal and lovely woman, but no more.

"What are you?" gasped Abi. "The goddess Sekhet in the flesh, or Isis, Queen of Death, or but dead Tua's ghost sent here for vengeance?"

"All of them, or none of them, as you will, though, Man, it is true that I am sent here for vengeance. Ask the Wizard yonder. He knows, and I give him leave to say."

"*She is the Double of Amen's daughter*," moaned Kaku. "She is her *Ka* set free to bring doom upon those who would have wronged her. She is a ghost armed with the might of the gods, and all we who have sinned against dead Pharaoh and her and her father Amen are given into her hand to be tormented and brought to doom."

"Where, then, is Neter-Tua, who was Queen of Egypt?" gasped Abi, rolling his great eyes. "Is she with Osiris?"

"I will tell you, Man," answered the royal Shape. "She is not dead—she lives, and is gone to seek one she loves. When she returns with him and a certain Beggar, then I shall depart and you will die, both of you, for such is the punishment decreed upon you. Until then, arise and do my bidding."

CHAPTER 14
The Boat of Ra

Tua, Star of Amen, opened her eyes. For some time already she had lain as one lies between sleep and waking, and it seemed to her that she heard the sound of dipping oars, and of water that rippled gently against the sides of a ship. She thought to herself that she dreamed. Doubtless she was in her bed in the palace at Thebes, and presently, when it was light, her ladies would come to waken her.

In the palace at Thebes! Why, now she remembered that it was months since she had seen that royal city, she who had travelled far since then, and come at last to white-walled Memphis, where many terrible things had befallen her. One by one they came into her mind; the snare, Pharaoh's murder by magic, the battle, and the slaughter of her guards, the starvation in the tower, with death on one hand, and the hateful Abi on the other; the wondrous vision of that spirit who wore her face, and said she was the guardian *Ka* given to her at birth, the words it spoke, and her dread resolve; and last of all Asti and herself standing in the lofty window niche, then a flame of fire before her face, and that fearful downward rush.

Oh! without a doubt it was over; she was dead, and these dreams and memories were such as come to the dwellers in the Under-world. Only then why did she hear the sound of lapping water, and of dipping oars?

Very slowly she opened her eyes, for Tua greatly feared what she might see. Light flowed upon her, the light of the moon which hung in a clear sky like some great lamp of gold. By it she saw that, robed all in white, she lay upon a couch in a pavilion, whereof the silken curtains were drawn back in front, and tied to gilded posts. At her side, wrapped in a grey robe, lay another figure, which she knew for Asti. It was still, so still that she was sure it must be dead, yet she knew that this was Asti. Perchance Asti dreamed also, and could hear in her dreams; at least, she would speak to her.

"Asti," she whispered, "Asti, can you hear me?"

The grey figure at her side stirred, and the head turned towards her. Then the voice of Asti, none other, answered:

"Aye, Lady, I hear and see. But say, where are we now?"

"In the Under-world, I think, Asti. Oh! that fire was death, and now we journey to the Place of Souls."

"If so, Lady, it is strange that we should still have eyes and flesh and voices as mortal women have. Let us sit up and look."

So they sat up, their arms about each other, and peered through the open curtains. Behold! they were on a ship more beautiful than any they had ever seen, for it seemed to be covered with gold and silver, while sweet odours floated from its hold. Their pavilion was set in the centre of the ship and looking aft, they perceived lines of white-clad rowers seated at their oars in the shadow of the bulwarks, and on the high stern—also robed in white—a tall steersman whose face was veiled, behind whom in the dim glimpses of the moon, they caught sight of a wide and silvery river, and on its distant banks palms and temple towers.

"It is the Boat of Ra," murmured Tua, "which bears us down the River of Death to the Kingdom behind the Sun."

Then she sank back upon her cushions, and once more fell into swoon or sleep.

Tua woke again, and lo! the sun was shining brightly, and at her side sat Asti watching her. Moreover, in front of them was set a table spread with delicate food.

"Tell me what has chanced, Nurse," she said faintly, "for I am bewildered, and know not in what world we wander."

"Our own, Queen, I think," answered Asti, "but in charge of those who are not of it, for surely this is no mortal boat, nor do mortals guide her to her port. Come, we need food. Let us eat while we may."

So they ate and drank heartily enough, and when they had finished even dared to go out of the pavilion. Looking around them they saw that they stood upon a high deck in the midst of a great ship, but that this ship was enclosed with a net of silver cords in which they could find no opening. Looking through its meshes they noted that the oars were inboard, and the great purple sails set upon the mast, also that the rowers were gone, perchance to rest beneath the deck, while on the forecastle of the ship stood the captain, white-robed and masked, and aft the steersman, also still masked, so that they could see nothing of their faces. Now, too, they were no longer sailing on a river, but down a canal bordered by banks of sand on either side, beyond which stretched desert farther than the eye could reach.

Asti studied the desert, then turned and said:

"I think I know this canal, Lady, for once I sailed it as a child. I think it is that which was dug by the Pharaohs of old, and repaired after the fall of the Hyksos kings, and that it runs from Bubastis to that bay down which wanderers sail towards the rising sun."

"Mayhap," answered Tua. "At least, this is the world that bore us and no other, and by the mercy of Amen and the power of my Spirit we are still alive, and not dead, or so it seems. Call now to the captain on yonder deck; perhaps he will tell whither he bears us in his magic ship."

So Asti called, but the captain made no sign that he saw or heard her. Next she called to the steersman, but although his veiled face was towards them, he also made no sign, so that at last they believed either that these were spirits or that they were men born deaf and dumb. In the end, growing weary of staring at this beautiful ship, at the canal and the desert beyond it, and of wondering where they were, and how they came thither, they returned to the pavilion to avoid the heat of the sun. Here they found that during their absence some hand unseen had arranged the silken bed-clothing on their couches and cleared away the fragments of their meal, resetting the beautiful table with other foods.

"Truly here is wizardry at work," said Tua, as she sank into a leather-seated ivory chair that was placed ready.

"Who doubts it?" answered Asti calmly. "By wizardry were you born; by wizardry was Pharaoh slain; by wizardry we are saved to an end that we cannot guess; by wizardry, or what men so name, does the whole world move; only being so near we see it not."

Tua thought a while, then said:

"Well, this golden ship is better than the sty of Abi the hog, nor do I believe that we journey to no purpose. Still I wonder what that spirit who named herself my *Ka* does on the throne of Egypt; also how we came on board this boat, and whither we sail."

"Wonder not, for all these things we shall learn in due season, and for my part, although I hate him I am sorry for Abi," answered Asti drily.

So they sat there in the pavilion watching the desert, over the sands of which their ship seemed to move, till at length the sun grew low, and they went to walk upon the deck. Then they returned to eat of the delicious food that was always provided for them in such plenty, and at nightfall sought their couches, and slept heavily, for they needed rest.

When they awoke again, it was daylight, though no sun shone through the skies, and their vessel rolled onward across a wide and sullen sea out of sight of land. Also the silken pavilion about them was gone, and replaced by a cabin of massive cedar wood, though of this, being sated with marvels, Tua and Asti took little note. Indeed, having neither of them been on an angry ocean before, a strange dizziness overcame them, which caused them to sleep much and think little for three whole days and nights.

At length, one evening as the sun sank, they perceived that the violent motion of the vessel had ceased with the roaring of the gale above, which for all this while had driven them onward at such fearful speed. Venturing from their cedar house, they saw that they had entered the mouth of a great river upon the banks of which grew enormous trees that sent out long crooked roots into the water, and that among these roots crouched crocodiles and other noisome reptiles. Also the white-robed oarsmen had appeared again, and, as there was no wind, rowed the ship up the river, till at length they came to a spit of sand which jutted out into the stream, and here cast anchor.

Now Tua's and Asti's desire for food returned to them, and they ate. Just as they had finished their meal, and the sun was sinking suddenly, there appeared before them two masked men, each of whom bore a basket in his hand. Asti began to question them, but like the captain and the steersman, they seemed to be deaf and dumb. At least they made no answer, only prostrated themselves humbly, and pointed towards the shore where now Tua saw a fire burning on a rock, though who had lit it she did not know.

"They mean us to leave the ship," said Asti. "Come, Queen, let us follow our fortunes, for doubtless these are high."

"As you will," answered Tua, "seeing that we should scarcely have been brought here to no end."

So they accompanied the men to the side of that splendid vessel, for now the netting that confined them had been removed, to find that a gangway had been laid from its bulwark to the shore. As they stepped on to this gangway their masked companions handed to each of them one of the baskets, then again bowed humbly and were gone. Soon they gained the bank, and scarcely had their feet touched it when the gangway was withdrawn, and the great oars began to beat the muddy water.

Round swung the ship, and for a minute hung in midstream. There stood the captain on the foredeck, and there was the steersman at the helm, and the red light of the sinking sun turned them into figures of flame. Suddenly with a simultaneous motion these men tore off their masks so that for a moment Asti and Tua saw their faces—and behold!

the face of the captain was the face of Pharaoh, Tua's father, and the face of the steersman was the face of Mermes, Asti's husband.

For one moment only did they see them, then a dark cloud hid the dying sun, and when it passed that ship was gone, whither they knew not.

The two women looked at each other, and for the first time were much afraid.

"Truly," said Tua, "we are haunted if ever mortals were, for yonder ship has ghosts for mariners."

"Aye, Lady," answered Asti, "so have I thought from the first. Still, take heart, for these ghosts once were men who loved us well, and doubtless they love us still. Be sure that for no ill purpose have we been snatched out of the hand of Abi, and brought living and unharmed by the shades of Pharaoh your sire, and Mermes my husband, to this secret shore. See, yonder burns a fire, let us go to it, and await what may befall bravely, knowing that at least it can be naught but good."

So they went to the rock and, darkness being come, sat themselves down by the fire, alongside of which lay wood for its replenishment, and near the wood soft robes of camel-hair to shield them from the cold. These robes they put on with thankfulness, and, having fed the flame, bethought them of and opened the baskets which were given to them when they left the ship. The first basket, that which Asti held, they found to contain food, cakes, dried meats and dates, as much as one woman could carry. But the second, that which had been given to Tua, was otherwise provided, for in the mouth of it lay a lovely harp of ivory with golden strings, whereof the frame was fashioned to the shape of a woman. Tua drew it out and looked at it by the light of the fire.

"It is my own harp," she said in an awed voice, "the harp that the Prince of Kesh, whom Rames slew, brought as a gift to me, to the notes of which I sang the Song of the Lovers but just before the giver died. Yes, it is my own harp that I left in Thebes. Say, now, Nurse, how came it here?"

"How came *we* here?" answered Asti shortly. "Answer my question and I will answer yours."

Then, laying down the harp, Tua looked again into her basket and found that beneath a layer of dried papyrus leaves were hidden pearls, thousands of pearls of all sizes, and of such lustre and beauty as she had never seen. They were strung upon threads of silk, all those of a like size being set upon a single thread, except the very biggest, which were as great as a finger nail, or even larger, that lay wrapped up separately in cloth at the bottom of the basket.

"Surely," said Tua, amazed, "no Queen in all the earth ever had a dower of such priceless pearls. Moreover, what good they and the harp can be to us in this forest I may not guess."

"Doubtless we shall discover in due course," answered Asti; "meanwhile, let us thank the gods for their gifts and eat."

So they ate, and then, having nothing else to do, lay down by the fire and would have slept.

But scarcely had they closed their eyes when the forest seemed to awake. First from down by the river there came dreadful roarings which they knew must be the voice of lions, for there were tame beasts of this sort in the gardens at Thebes. Next they heard the whines and wimperings of wolves and jackals, and mingled with them great snortings such as are made by the rhinoceros and the river-horse.

Nearer, nearer came these awful sounds, till at length they saw yellow eyes moving like stars in the darkness at the edge of the forest, while cross the patch of sand beneath their rock galloped swift shapes which halted and sniffed towards them. Also on the river side of them appeared huge, hog-like beasts, with gleaming tusks, and red cavernous mouths, and beyond these again, crashing through the brushwood, a gigantic brute that bore a single horn upon its snout.

"Now our end is at hand," said Tua faintly, "for surely these creatures will devour us."

But Asti only threw more wood upon the fire and waited, thinking that the flame would frighten them away. Yet it did not, for so curious, or so hungry were they, that the lions crept and crept nearer, and still more near, till at length they lay lashing their tails in the distance almost within springing distance of the rock, while on the farther side of these, like a court waiting on its monarch, gathered the hyenas and other beasts.

"They will spring presently," whispered Tua.

"Did the Spirits of the divine Pharaoh your father, and of Mermes my lord, bring us here in the Boat of Ra that we should be devoured by wild animals, like lost sheep in the desert?" asked Asti. Then, as though by an inspiration, she added, "Lady, take that harp of yours, and play and sing to it."

So Tua took the harp and swept its golden chords, and, lifting up her lovely voice, she began to sing. At first it trembled a little, but by degrees, as she forgot all save the music, it grew strong, and rang out sweetly in the silence of the forest, and the great, slow-moving river. And lo! as she sang thus, the wild brutes grew still, and seemed to listen as though they were charmed. Yes, even a snake wriggled out from between the rocks and listened, waving its crested head to and fro.

At length Tua ceased, and as the echoes died away the brutes, every one of them, turned and vanished into the forest or the river, all save the snake that coiled itself up and slept where it was. So stillness came again, and Tua and Asti slept also, nor did they wake until the sun was shining in the heavens.

Then they arose wondering, and went down over the patch of sand that was marked with the footprints of all the beasts to the river's brink, and drank and washed themselves, peering the while through the mists, for they thought that perchance they would see that golden ship with the veiled crew which had carried them from Memphis, returned and awaiting them in midstream.

But no ship was there; nothing was there except the river-horses which rose and sank, and the crocodiles on the mud-banks, and the wildfowl that flighted inward from the sea to feed. So they went back to the ashes of their fire and ate of the food in Asti's basket, and, when they had eaten, looked at each other, not knowing what to do. Then Tua said:

"Come, Nurse, let us be going. Up the river and down the river we cannot walk, for there are nothing but weeds and mud, so we must strike out through the forest, whither the gods may lead us."

Asti nodded, and, clad in the light warm clothes of camel-hair, they set the baskets upon their heads after the fashion of the peasant women of Egypt and started forward, the harp of ivory and of gold hanging upon Tua's back.

For hour after hour they marched thus through the forest, threading their path between the big boles of the trees, and heading always for the south, for that way ran the woodland glades beyond which was dense bush. Great apes chattered above them in the tree tops, and now and again some beast of prey crossed their path and vanished in the underwood, but nothing else did they see. At length, towards midday, the ground began to rise, and the trees grew smaller and farther apart, till at last they reached the edge of a sandy desert, and walked out to a little oasis, where the green grass showed them they would find water. In this oasis there was a spring, and by the edge of it they sat down and drank, and ate of their store of food, and afterwards slept a while.

Suddenly Tua, in her sleep, heard a voice, and, awaking with a start, saw a man who stood near by, leaning on a thorn-wood staff and contemplating them. He was a very strange man, apparently of great age, for his long white hair fell down upon his shoulders, and his white beard reached to his middle. Once he must have been very tall, but now he was bent with age, and the bones of his gaunt frame thrust out his ragged garments. His dark eyes also were horny, indeed it seemed as though he could scarcely see with them, for he leaned forward to peer at their faces where they lay. His face was scored by a thousand wrinkles, and almost black with exposure to the sun and wind, but yet of a marvellous tenderness and beauty. Indeed, except that it was far more ancient, and the features were on a larger and a grander scale, it reminded Tua of the face of Pharaoh after he was dead.

"My Father," said Tua, sitting up, for an impulse prompted her to name this wanderer thus, "say whence do you come, and what would you with your servants?"

"My Daughter," answered the old man in a sweet, grave voice, "I come from the wilderness which is my home. Long have I outlived all those of my generation, yes, and their children also. Therefore the wilderness and the forest that do not change are now my only friends, since they alone knew me when I was young. Be pitiful now to me, for I am poor, so poor that for three whole days no food has passed my lips. It was the smell of the meat which you have with you that led me to you. Give me of that meat, Daughter, for I starve."

"It is yours, O——" and she paused.

"I am called Kepher."

"Kepher, Kepher!" repeated Tua, for she thought it strange that a beggar-man should be named after that *scarabaeus* insect which among the Egyptians was the symbol of eternity. "Well, take and eat, O Kepher," she said, and handed him the basket that contained what was left to them of their store.

The beggar took it, and having looked up to heaven as though to ask a blessing on his meal, sat down upon the sand and began to devour the food ravenously.

"Lady," said Asti, "he will eat it all, and then we shall starve in this desert. He is a locust, not a man," she added, as another cake disappeared.

"He is our guest," answered Tua gravely, "let him take what we have to give."

For a while Asti was silent, then again she broke out into remonstrance.

"Peace, Nurse," replied Tua, "I have said that he is our guest, and the law of hospitality may not be broken."

"Then the law of hospitality will bring us to our deaths," muttered Asti.

"If so, so let it be, Nurse; at least this poor man will be filled, and for the rest, as always, we must trust to Amen our father."

Yet as she spoke the words tears gathered in her eyes, for she knew that Asti was right, and now that all the food was gone, on which with care they might have lived for two days or more, soon they would faint, and perish, unless help came to them, which was not likely in that lonesome place. Once, not so long ago, they had starved for lack of sustenance, and it was the thought of that slow pain so soon to be renewed, that brought the water to her eyes.

Meanwhile Kepher, whose appetite for one so ancient was sharp indeed, finished the contents of the basket down to the last date, and handed it back to Tua with a bow, saying:

"I thank you, Daughter; the Queen of Egypt could not have entertained me more royally," and he peered at her with his horny eyes. "I who have been empty for long, am full again, and since I cannot reward you I pray to the gods that they will do so. Beautiful Daughter, may you never know what it is to lack a meal."

At this saying Tua could restrain herself no more. A large tear from her eyes fell upon Kepher's rough hand as she answered with a little sob:

"I am glad that you are comforted with meat, but do not mock us, Friend, seeing that we are but lost wanderers who very soon must starve, since now our food is done."

"What, Daughter?" asked the old man in an astonished voice, "what? Can I believe that you gave all you had to a beggar of the wilderness, and sat still while he devoured it? And is it for this reason that you weep?"

"Forgive me, Father, but it is so," answered Tua. "I am ashamed of such weakness, but recently my friend here and I have known hunger, very sore hunger, and the dread of it moves me. Come, Asti, let us be going while our strength remains in us."

Kepher looked up at the name, then turned to Tua and said:

"Daughter, your face is fair, and your heart is perfect, since otherwise you would not have dealt with me as you have done. Still, it seems that you lack one thing—undoubting faith in the goodness of the gods. Though, surely," he added in a slow voice, "those who have passed yonder lion-haunted forest without hurt should not lack faith. Say, now, how came you there?"

"We are ladies of Egypt," interrupted Asti, "or at least this maiden is, for I am but her old nurse. Man-stealing pirates of Phoenicia seized us while we wandered on the shores of the Nile, and brought us hither in their ship, by what way we do not know. At length they put into yonder river for water, and we fled at night. We are escaped slaves, no more."

"Ah!" said Kepher, "those pirates must mourn their loss. I almost wonder that they did not follow you. Indeed, I thought that you might be other folk, for, strangely enough, as I slept in the sand last night, a certain spirit from the Under-world visited me in my dreams, and told me to search for one Asti and another lady who was with her—I cannot remember the name of that lady. But I do remember the name of the spirit, for he told it to me; it was Mermes."

Now Asti gave a little cry, and, springing up, searched Kepher's face with her eyes, nor did he shrink from her gaze.

"I perceive," she said slowly, "that you who seem to be a beggar are also a seer."

"Mayhap, Asti," he answered. "In my long life I have often noted that sometimes men are more than they seem—and women also. Perhaps you have learned the same, for nurses in great houses may note many things if they choose. But let us say no more. I think it is better that we should say no more. You and your companion—how is she named?"

"Neferte," answered Asti promptly.

"Neferte, ah! Certainly that was not the name which the spirit used, though it is true that other name began with the same sound, or so I think. Well, you and your companion, Neferte, escaped from those wicked pirates, and managed to bring certain things with you, for instance, that beautiful harp, wreathed with the royal *uraei*, and—but what is in that second basket?"

"Pearls," broke in Tua quickly.

"And a large basket of pearls. Might I see them? Oh! do not be afraid, I shall not rob those whose food I have eaten, it is against the custom of the desert."

"Certainly," answered Tua. "I never thought that you would rob us, for if you were of the tribe of thieves, surely you would be richer, and less hungry than you seem. I only thought that you were almost blind, Father Kepher, and therefore could not know the difference between a pearl and a pebble."

"My feeling still remains to me, Daughter Neferte," he answered with a little smile.

Then Tua gave him the basket. He opened it and drew out the strings of pearls, feeling them, smelling and peering at them, touching them with his tongue, especially the large single ones which were wrapped up by themselves. At length, having handled them all, he restored them to the basket, saying drily:

"It is strange, indeed, Nurse Asti, that those Syrian man-stealers attempted no pursuit of you, for here, whether they were theirs or not, are enough gems to buy a kingdom."

"We cannot eat pearls," answered Asti.

"No, but pearls will buy more than you need to eat."

"Not in a desert," said Asti.

"True, but as it chances there is a city in this desert, and not so very far away."

"Is it named Napata?" asked Tua eagerly.

"Napata? No, indeed. Yet, I have heard of such a place, the City of Gold they called it. In fact, once I visited it in my youth, over a hundred years ago."

"A hundred years ago! Do you remember the way thither?"

"Yes, more or less, but on foot it is over a year's journey away, and the path thither lies across great deserts and through tribes of savage men. Few live to reach that city."

"Yet I will reach it, or die, Father."

"Perhaps you will, Daughter Neferte, perhaps you will, but I think not at present. Meanwhile, you have a harp, and therefore it is probable that you can play and sing; also you have pearls. Now the inhabitants of this town whereof I spoke to you love music. Also they love pearls, and as you cannot begin your journey to Napata for three months, when the rain on the mountains will have filled the desert wells, I suggest that you would do wisely to settle yourselves there for a while. Nurse Asti here would be a dealer in pearls, and you, her daughter, would be a musician. What say you?"

"I say that I should be glad to settle myself anywhere out of this desert," said Tua wearily. "Lead us on to the city, Father Kepher, if you know the way."

"I know the way, and will guide you thither in payment for that good meal of yours. Now come. Follow me." And taking his long staff he strode away in front of them.

"This Kepher goes at a wonderful pace for an old man," said Tua presently. "When first we saw him he could scarcely hobble."

"Man!" answered Asti. "He is not a man, but a spirit, good or bad, I don't know which, appearing as a beggar. Could a man eat as much as he did—all our basketful of food? Does a man talk of cities that he visited in his youth over a hundred years ago, or declare that my dead husband spoke to him in his dreams? No, he is a ghost like those upon the ship."

"So much the better," answered Tua cheerfully, "since ghosts have been good friends to us, for had it not been for them I should have been dead or shamed to-day."

“That we shall find out at the end of the story,” said Asti, who was cross and weary, for the heat of the sun was great. “Meanwhile, follow on. There is nothing else to do.”

For hour after hour they walked, till at length towards evening, when they were almost exhausted, they struggled up a long rise of sand and rocks, and from the crest of it perceived a large walled town set in a green and fertile valley not very far beneath them. Towards this town Kepher, who marched at a distance in front, guided them till they reached a clump of trees on the outskirts of the cultivated land. Here he halted, and when they came up to him, led them among the trees.

“Now,” he said, “drop your veils and bide here, and if any should come to you, say that you are poor wandering players who rest. Also, if it pleases you, give me a small pearl off one of those strings, that I may go into the city, which is named Tat, and sell it to buy you food and a place to dwell in.”

“Take a string,” said Tua faintly.

“Nay, nay, Daughter, one will be enough, for in this town pearls are rare, and have a great value.”

So she gave him the gem, or rather let him take it from the silk, which he re-fastened very neatly for one who seemed to be almost blind, and strode off swiftly towards the town.

“Man or spirit, I wonder if we shall see him again?” said Asti.

Tua made no answer—she was too tired, but resting herself against the bole of a tree, fell into a doze. When she awoke again it was to see that the sun had sunk, and that before her stood the beggar Kepher, and with him two black men, each of whom led a saddled mule.

“Mount, Friends,” he said, “for I have found you a lodging.”

So they mounted, and were led to the gate of the city which at the word of Kepher was opened for them, and thence down a long street to a house built in a walled garden. Into this house they entered, the black men leading off the mules, to find that it was a well-furnished place with a table ready set in the ante-room, on which was food in plenty. They ate of it, all three of them, and when they had finished Kepher bade a woman who was waiting on them, lead them to their chamber, saying that he himself would sleep in the garden.

Thither then they went without more questions, and throwing themselves down upon beds which were prepared for them, were soon fast asleep.

Chapter 15

Tua and the King of Tat

In the morning, after Tua and Asti had put on the clean robes that lay to their hands, and eaten, suddenly they looked up and perceived that Kepher, the ancient beggar of the desert, was in the room with them, though neither of them had heard or seen him enter.

"You come silently, Friend," said Asti, looking at him with a curious eye. "A Double could not move with less noise, and—where is your shadow?" she added, staring first at the sun without, and then at the floor upon which he stood.

"I forgot it," he answered in his deep voice. "One so poor as I am cannot always afford a shadow. But look, there it is now. And for the rest, what do you know of Doubles which those who are uninstructed cannot discern? Now I have heard of a Lady in Egypt who by some chance bore your name, and who has the power, not only to see the Double, but to draw it forth from the body of the living, and furnish it with every semblance of mortal life. Also I have heard that she who reigns in Egypt to-day has such a *Ka* or Double that can take her place, and none know the difference, save that this *Ka*, which Amen gave her at her birth, works the vengeance of the gods without pity or remorse. Tell me, Friend Asti, when you were a slave-woman in Egypt did you ever hear talk of such things as these?"

Now he looked at Asti, and Asti looked at him, till at length he moved his old hands in a certain fashion, whereon she bowed her head and was silent.

But Tua, who was terrified at this talk, for she knew not what would befall them if the truth were guessed, broke in, saying:

"Welcome, Father, however it may please you to come, and with or without a shadow. Surely we have much to thank you for who have found us this fine house and servants and food—by the way, will you not eat again?"

"Nay," he answered, smiling, "as you may have guessed yesterday, I touch meat seldom; as a rule, once only in three days, and then take my fill. Life is so short that I cannot waste time in eating."

"Oh!" said Tua, "if you feel thus whose youth began more than a hundred years ago, how must it seem to the rest of us? But, Father Kepher, what are we to do in this town Tat?"

"I have told you, Maiden. Asti here will deal in pearls and other goods, and you will sing, but always behind the curtain, since here in Tat you must suffer no man to see your beauty, and least of all him who rules it. Now give me two more pearls, for I go out to buy for you other things that are needful, and after that perhaps you will see me no more for a long while. Yet if trouble should fall upon you, go to the window-place wherever you may be, and strike upon that harp of yours, and call thrice upon the name of Kepher. Doubtless there will be some listening who will hear you and bring me the news in the Desert, where I dwell who do not love towns, and then I may be able to help you."

"I thank you, my Father, and I will remember. But pardon me if I ask how can one so——" and she paused.

"So old, so ragged and so miserable give help to man or woman—that is what you would say, Daughter Neferte, is it not? Well, judge not from the outward seeming; good wine is often found in jars of common clay, and the fire hid in a rough flint can destroy a city."

"And therefore a wanderer who can swallow his own shadow can aid another wanderer in distress," remarked Tua drily. "My Father, I understand, who although I am still young, have seen many things and ere now been dragged out of deep water by strange hands."

"Such as those of Phoenician pirates," suggested Kepher. "Well, good-bye. I go to purchase what you need with the price of these pearls, and then the Desert calls me for a while. Remember what I told you, and do not seek to leave this town of Tat until the rain has fallen on the mountains, and there is water in the wells. Good-bye, Friend Asti, also; when I come again we will talk more of Doubles, until which time may the great god of Egypt—he is called Amen, is he not?—have you and your Lady in his keeping."

Then he turned and went.

"What is that man?" asked Tua when they had heard the door of the house close behind him.

"Man?" answered Asti. "I have told you that he is no man. Do men unfold their shadows like a garment? He is a god or a ghost, wearing a beggar's shape."

"Man or ghost, I like him well for he has befriended us in our need, Nurse."

"That we shall know when he has done with us," answered Asti.

An hour later, whilst they were still talking of Kepher and all the marvels that had befallen them, porters began to arrive, bearing bundles which, when opened, were found to contain silks and broideries in gold and silver thread, and leather richly worked, such as the Arabs make, and alabaster pots of ointments, and brass work from Syria, and copper jars from Cyprus, with many other goods, all very costly, and in number more than enough for a wealthy trader's store.

These goods the porters set out on the mats and shelves of the large front room of the house that opened to the street, which room seemed to have been built to receive them. Then they departed, asking no fees, and there appeared a man riding a fine white horse, who dismounted, and, bowing low towards the screen of pierced woodwork behind which Tua and Asti were hidden, laid a writing upon a little table, and rode away. When he had gone Asti opened the door in the screen and took the writing which she found she could read well enough, for it was in the Egyptian character and language.

It proved to be the title-deed of the house and garden conveyed to them jointly, and also of the rich goods which the porters had brought. At the foot of this document was written—

"Received by Kepher the Wanderer in payment of the above house and land and goods, three pearls and one full meal of meat and dates."

Then followed the seal of Kepher in wax, a finely cut *scarabaeus* holding the symbol of the sun between its two front feet.

"A proud seal for a tattered wanderer, though it is but his name writ in wax," said Tua.

But Asti only answered:

"If small pearls have such value in this city, what price will the large ones bring? Well, let us to our business, for we have time upon our hands, and cannot live upon pearls and costly stuffs."

****

So it happened that Neter-Tua, Star of Amen, Queen of Egypt, and Asti her Nurse, the Mistress of Magic, became merchants in the town of Tat.

This was the manner of their trade. For one hour in the morning, and one in the afternoon, Asti, heavily veiled, and a woman of the servants whom they had found in the house, would sit on stools amidst the goods and traffic with all comers, selling to those who would buy, and taking payment in gold dust or other articles of value, or buying from those who would sell. Then when the hour drew towards its close Tua would sweep her harp behind the screen that hid her and begin to sing, whereon all would cease from their chaffering and listen, for never before had they heard so sweet a voice. Indeed, at these times the broad street in front of their house was packed with people, for the fame of this singing of hers went through the city and far into the country that lay beyond. Then the traffic came to an end, with her song, and leaving their goods in charge of the servants, Tua and Asti departed to the back rooms of the house, and ate their meals or wandered in the large, walled garden that lay behind.

Thus the weeks went on and soon, although they sold few of the pearls, and those the smallest, for of the larger gems they said little or nothing, they began to grow rich, and to hoard up such a weight of gold in dust and nuggets, and so many precious things, that they scarcely knew what they should do with them. Still Tat seemed to be a peaceful city, or at the least none tried to rob or molest them, perhaps because a rumour was abroad that these strangers who had come out of the Unknown were under the protection of some god.

There was nothing to show how or why this rumour had arisen in the city, but on account of it, if for no other reason, these pearl-merchants, as they were called, suffered no wrong, and although they were only undefended women, whatever credit they might give, the debt was always paid. Also their servants, to whom they added as they had means, were all faithful to them. So there they remained and traded, keeping their secrets and awaiting the appointed hour of escape, but never venturing to leave the shelter of their own walls.

Now, as it happened, when they came thither the King of Tat was away making war upon another king whose country lay upon the coast, but after they had dwelt for many weeks in the place, this King, who was named Janees, returned victorious from his war and prepared to celebrate a triumph.

While he was making ready for this triumph his courtiers told him of these pearl-merchants, and, desiring pearls for his adornment on that great day, he went in disguise to the house of those who sold them. As it chanced he arrived late, and requested to see the gems just as Tua, according to her custom, was playing upon her harp. Then she began to sing, and this King Janees, who was a man of under forty years of age, listened intently to her beautiful voice, forgetting all about the pearls that he had come to buy. Her song finished, the veiled Asti rose, and bowing to all the company gathered in the street, bade her servants shut up the coffers and remove the goods.

"But I would buy pearls, Merchant, if you have such to sell," said Janees.

"Then you must return this afternoon, Purchaser," replied Asti, scanning his pale and haughty face, "for even if you were the King of Tat I would not sell to you out of my hours."

"You speak high words, Woman," exclaimed Janees angrily.

"High or low, they are what I mean," answered Asti, and went away.

The end of it was that this King Janees returned at the evening hour, led thither more by a desire to hear that lovely voice again than to purchase gems. Still he asked to see pearls, and Asti showed him some which he thrust aside as too small. Then she produced those that were larger, and again he thrust them aside, and so it went on for a long while. At length from somewhere in her clothing Asti drew two of the biggest that she had, perfect pearls of the size of the middle nail of a man's finger, and at the sight of these the eyes of Janees brightened, for such gems he had never seen before. Then he asked the price. Asti answered carelessly that it was doubtless more than he would wish to pay, since there were few such pearls in the whole world, and she named a weight in gold that caused him to step back from her amazed, for it was a quarter of the tribute that he had taken from his new-conquered kingdom.

"Woman, you jest," he said, "surely there is some abatement."

"Man," she answered, "I jest not; there is no abatement," and she replaced the pearls in her garments.

Now he grew very angry, and asked:

"Did you know that I am the King of Tat, and if I will, can take your pearls without any payment at all?"

"Are you?" asked Asti, looking at him coolly. "I should never have guessed it. Well, if you steal my goods, as you say you can, you will be King of Thieves also."

Now those who heard this saying laughed, and the King thought it best to join in their merriment. Then the bargaining went on, but before it was finished, at her appointed hour Tua began to sing behind the screen.

"Have done," said the King to Asti, "to-morrow you shall be paid your price. I would listen to that music which is above price."

So Janees listened like one fascinated, for Tua was singing her best. Step by step he drew ever nearer to the screen, though this Asti did not notice, for she was engaged in locking up her goods. At length he reached it, and thrusting his fingers through the openings in the pierced woodwork, rested his weight upon it like a man who is faint, as perhaps he was with the sweetness of that music. Then of a sudden, by craft or chance, he swung himself backward, and with him came the frail screen. Down it clattered to the floor, and lo! beyond it, unveiled, but clad in rich attire, stood Tua sweeping her harp of ivory and gold. Like sunlight from a cloud the bright vision of her beauty struck the eyes of the people gathered there, and seemed to dazzle them, since for a while they were silent. Then one said:

"Surely this woman is a queen," and another answered:

"Nay, she is a goddess," but ere the words had left his lips Tua was gone.

As for Janees the King, he stared at her open-mouthed, reeling a little upon his feet, then, as she fled, turned to Asti, saying:

"Is this Lady your slave?"

"Nay, King, my daughter, whom you have done ill to spy upon."

"Then," said Janees slowly, "I who might do less, desire to make this daughter of yours my Queen—do you understand, Merchant of Pearls—my Queen, and as a gift you shall have as much gold again as I have promised for your gems."

"Other kings have desired as much and offered more, but she is not for you or any of them," answered Asti, looking him in the face.

Now Janees made a movement as though he would strike her, then seemed to change his mind, for he replied only:

"A rough answer to a fair offer, seeing that none know who you are or whence you come. But there are eyes upon us. I will talk with you again to-morrow; till then, rest in peace."

"It is useless," began Asti, but he was already gone.

Presently Asti found Tua in the garden, and told her everything.

"Now I wish that Kepher of the Desert were at hand," said Tua nervously, "for it seems that I am in a snare, who like this Janees no better than I did Abi or the Prince of Kesh, and will never be his Queen."

"Then I think we had better fly to the wilderness and seek him there this very night, for, Lady, you know what chances to men who look upon your loveliness."

"I know what chanced to the Prince of Kesh, and what will chance to Abi at the hands of one I left behind me, I can guess; perhaps this Janees will fare no better. Still, let us go."

Asti nodded, then by an afterthought went into the house and asked some questions of the servants. Presently she returned, and said:

"It is useless; soldiers are already stationed about the place, and some of our women who tried to go out have been turned back, for they say that by the King's order none may leave our door."

"Now shall I strike upon the harp and call upon the name of Kepher, as he bade me?" asked Tua.

"I think not yet awhile, Lady. This danger may pass by or the night bring counsel, and then he would be angry if you summoned him for naught. Let us go in and eat."

So they went in, and while they sat at their food suddenly they heard a noise, and looking up, perceived by the light of the lamp that women were crowding into the room led by two eunuchs.

Tua drew a dagger from her robe and sprang up, but the head eunuch, an old, white-haired man, bowed low before her, and said:

"Lady, you can kill me if you will, for I am unarmed, but there are many more of us without, and to resist is useless. Hearken; no harm shall be done to you or to your companion, but it is the King's desire that one so royal and beautiful should be better lodged than in this place of traffic. Therefore he has commanded me to take you and all your household and all your goods to no less a place than his own palace, where he would speak with you."

"Sheathe the dagger and waste no words upon these slaves, Daughter," said Asti. "Since we have no choice, let us go."

So after they had veiled and robed, they suffered themselves to be led out and placed in a double litter with their pearls and gold, while the King's women collected all the rest of their goods and took them away together with their servants, leaving the house quite empty. Then, guarded by soldiers, they were borne through the silent streets till they came to great gates which closed behind them, and having passed up many stairs, the litter was set down in a large and beautiful room lit with silver lamps of scented oil. Here, and in other rooms beyond, they found women of the royal household and their own servants already arranging their possessions.

Soon it was done, and food and wine having been set for them, they were left alone in that room, and stood looking at each other.

"Now shall I strike and call?" said Tua, lifting the harp which she had brought with her. "Look, yonder is a window-place such as that of which Kepher spoke."

"Not yet, I think, Lady. Let us learn all our case ere we call for help," and as the words left her lips the door opened, and through it, clad in his royal robes, walked Janees the King.

Now in the centre of this great room was a marble basin filled with pure water which, perhaps, had served as the bath of the queens who dwelt there in former days, or, perhaps, was so designed for the sake of coolness in times of heat. Tua and Asti stood upon one side of this basin, and to the other came the King, so that the water lay between them. Thrice he bowed to Tua, then said:

"Lady, who, as your servants tell me, are known as Neferte, a maiden of Egypt, and for lack of the true name, doubtless this will serve, Lady, I come to ask your pardon for what must seem to you to be a grievous wrong. O Lady Neferte, this must be my excuse, that I have no choice. By fortune, good or ill, I know not which, this day I beheld your face, and now but one desire is left to me, to behold it again, and for all my life. Lady, the Goddess of Love, she, whom in Egypt you name Hathor, has made me her slave, so that I no longer think of pomp or power or wealth, or of other women, but of you and you only. Lady, I would do you no harm, for I offer you half my throne. You and you alone shall be my Queen. Speak now."

"King Janees," answered Tua, "what evil spirit has entered into you that you should wish to make a Queen of a singing-girl, the daughter of a merchant who has wandered to your city? Let me go, and keep that high place for one of the great ones of the earth. Send now to Abi, who I have heard rules as Pharaoh in Egypt, and ask a daughter of his blood, for they say that he has several; or to some of the princes of Syria, or to the King of Byblos by Lebanon, or to the lords of Kesh, or across the desert to the Emperor of Punt, and let this poor singing-girl go her ways."

"This poor singing-girl," repeated Janees after her, "who, or whose mother," and he bowed to Asti with a smile, "has pearls to sell that are worth the revenue of a kingdom; this singing-girl, the ivory figure on whose harp is crowned with the royal *uraei* of Egypt; this singing-girl whose chiselled loveliness is such as might be found perhaps among the daughters of ancient kings; this singing-girl whose voice can ravish the hearts of men and beasts! Well, Lady Neferte, I thank you for your warning, still I am ready to take my chance, hoping that my children will not be made ashamed by the blood of such a singing-girl as this, who, as I saw when that screen fell, has stamped upon her throat the holy sign they worship on the Nile."

"I am honoured," answered Tua coldly, "yet it may not be. Among my own humble folk I have a lover, and him I will wed or no man."

"You have a lover! Then hide his name from me, lest presently I should play Set to his Osiris and rend him into pieces. You shake your head, knowing doubtless that the man is great, yet I tell you that

I will conquer him and rend him into pieces for the crime of being loved by you. Listen now! I would make you my Queen, but Queen or not, mine you shall be who lie in my power. I will not force you, I will give you time. But if on the morning of the third day from this night you still refuse to share my throne, why, then you shall sit upon its footstool."

Now, in her anger, Tua threw back her veil, and met him eye to eye.

"You think me great," she said, "and truly you are right, for whatever is my rank, with me go my gods, and in their strength my innocence is great. Let me be, you petty King of Tat, lest I lift up my voice to heaven, and call down upon you the anger of the gods."

"Already, Lady, you have called down upon me the anger of a goddess, that Hathor of whom I spoke, and for the rest I fear them not. Let them do their worst. On the third night from this night, as Queen or slave, I swear that you shall be mine. This woman here, whom you call your mother, shall be witness to my oath, and to its end."

"Aye, King," broke in Asti, "I will be witness, but as to the end of that oath I do not know it yet. Would you like to learn? In my own country I was held to have something of a gift, I mean in the way of magic. It came to me, I know not whence, and it is very uncertain—at times it is my servant, and at times I can do nothing. Still, for your sake, I would try. Is it your pleasure to see that end of which you spoke, the end of your attempt to force yonder maiden to be your queen or love?"

"Aye, Woman," answered Janees, "if you have a trick, show it—why not?"

"So be it, King; but, of course, I have your word that you will not blame me if by any chance the trick should not prove to your liking—your royal word. Now stand you there, and look into this water while I pray our gods, the gods of my own country, to be gracious, and to show you what shall be your state at this same hour on the third night from now, which you say and hope shall be the night of your wedding. Sing, my Daughter, sing that old and sacred song which I have taught you. It will serve to while away the tedium of our waiting until the gods declare themselves, if such be their will."

Then Asti knelt down by the pool, and bent her head, and stretched out her hands over the water, and Tua touched the strings of her harp and began to chant very solemnly in an unknown tongue. The words of that chant were low and sweet, yet it seemed to Janees that they fell like ice upon his hot blood, and froze it within his veins. At first he kept his eyes fixed upon her beauty, but by slow degrees something drew them down to the water of the pool.

Look! A mist gathered on its blackness. It broke and cleared and there, as in a mirror, he saw a picture. He saw himself lying stripped and dead, a poor, naked corpse with wide eyes that stared to heaven, and gashed throat and sides whence the blood ran upon the marble floor of his own great hall, ruined by fire, with its scorched pillars pointing like fingers to the moon. There he lay alone, and by him stood a hound, his own hound, that lifted up its head and seemed to howl.

The last words of Tua's chant died away, and with them that picture passed. Janees leapt back from the edge of the pool, glaring at Asti.

"Sorceress!" he cried, "were you not my guest who names herself the mother of her who shall be my Queen, I swear that to-night you should die by torture in payment of this foul trick of yours."

"Yet as it is," answered Asti, "I think that I shall not die, since those who call upon the gods must not quarrel with their oracle. Moreover, I know now what you saw, and it may be nothing but a fantasy of your brain or of mine. Now let us sleep, I pray you, O King, for we are weary, and leave its secrets to the future. In three days we shall know what they may be."

Then, without another word, Janees turned and left them.

"What was it that lay in the pool, Nurse?" asked Tua. "I saw nothing."

"The shadow of a dead man, I think," answered Asti grimly. "Some jealous god has looked upon this poor King whose crime is that he desires you, and therefore he must die. Of a truth it goes ill with your lovers, O Star of Amen, and sometimes I wonder if one who is dear to me will meet with better fortune at those royal eyes of yours. If ill befalls him I think that at the last I may learn to hate you, whom from the first I cherished."

Now at the thought that she might bring death to Rames also, Tua's tears began to gather, and her voice choked in her throat.

"Say not such evil-omened words," she sobbed, "since you know well that if he is taken hence for whose sake I endure all these things, then I must follow him over the edge of the world. Moreover, you are unjust. Did I slay the Prince of Kesh, or was it another?"

"Another, Queen, but for your sake."

"And would you have had me wed Abi the hog, the murderer of my father, and of your lord? Again, was it I who but now showed this barbarian chief a shadow in the water, or was it Asti the witch, Asti the prophetess of Amen? Lastly, will the man die, if die he must, because he loves me, which, being a woman I can forgive him, or because he laid the hands of violence upon me to force me to be his queen or mistress, which I forgive him not? Oh! Asti, you know well I am not as other women are. Perchance it is true that some blood that is not human runs in me; at least I fulfil a doom laid on me before my birth, and working woe or working weal, I go as my feet are led by ghosts and gods. Why, then, do you upbraid me?" and she ceased and wept outright.

"Nay, nay, be comforted, I upbraid you not," answered Asti, drawing her to her breast. "Who am I that I should cast reproaches at Amen's Star and daughter and my Queen? I know well that the house of your fate is built, that sail you up stream or sail you down stream, you must pass its gate at last. It was fear for Rames that made me speak so bitterly, Rames my only child, if, indeed, he is left to me, for I who have so much wisdom cannot learn from man or spirit whether he lives here or with Osiris, since some black veil hangs between our souls. I fear lest the gods, grown jealous of that high love of yours, should wreak their wrath upon him who has dared to win it, and bring Rames to the grave before his time, and the thought of it rends my heart."

Now it was Tua's turn to play the comforter.

"Surely," she said, "surely, my Foster-mother, you forget the promise of Amen, King of the Gods, which he made ere I was born, to Ahura who bore me, that I should find a royal lover, and that from his love and mine should spring many kings and princes, and that this being so, Rames must live."

"Why must he live, Lady, seeing that even if he can be called royal, there are others?"

"Nay, Asti," murmured Tua, laying her head upon her breast, "for me there are no others, nor shall any child of mine be born that does not name Rames father. Whatever else is doubtful, this is sure. Therefore Rames lives, and will live, or the King of the gods has lied."

"You reason well," said Asti, and kissed her. Then she thought for a moment, and added: "Now to our work, it is the hour. Take the harp, go to the window-place, and call as the beggar-man bade you do in your need."

So Tua went to the window-place and looked down on the great courtyard beneath that was lit with the light of the moon. Then she struck on the harp, and thrice she cried aloud:

"Kepher! Kepher! Kepher!"

And each time the echo of her cry came back louder and still more loud, till it seemed as though earth and heaven were filled with the sound of the name of Kepher.

CHAPTER 16

The Beggar and the King

It was the afternoon of the third day. Tua and Asti, seated in the window-place of their splendid prison, looked through the wooden screen down into the court below, where, according to his custom at this hour, Janees the King sat in the shadow to administer justice and hear the petitions of his subjects. The two women were ill at ease, for the time of respite had almost passed.

"Night draws near," said Tua, "and with it will come Janees. Look how he eyes this window, like a hungry lion waiting to be fed. Kepher has made no sign; perchance after all he is but a wandering beggar-man filled with strange fancies, or perchance he is dead, as may well happen at his age. At least, he makes no sign, nor does Amen, to whom I have prayed so hard, send any answer to my prayers. I am forsaken. Oh! Asti, you who are wise, tell me, what shall I do?"

"Trust in the gods," said Asti. "There are still three hours to sun-down, and in three hours the gods, to whom time is nothing, can destroy the world and build it up again. Remember when we starved in the pylon tower at Memphis, and what befell us there. Remember the leap to death and the Boat of Ra, and those by whom it was captained. Remember and trust in the gods."

"I trust—in truth I trust, Asti, but yet—oh! let us talk of something else. I wonder what has chanced in Memphis since we left it in so strange a fashion? Do you think that awful *Ka* of mine queens it there with Abi for a husband? If so, I almost grieve for Abi, for she had something in her eyes which chilled my mortal blood, and yet you say she is a part of me, a spirit who cannot die, cast in my mould, and given to me at birth. I would I had another *Ka*, and that you could draw it forth again, Asti, to bewitch this Janees, and hold him while we fled. See, that case draws to an end at length. Janees is giving judgment, or rather his councillor is, for he prompts him all the time. Can you not hear his whispers? As for Janees himself, his thoughts are here, I feel his eyes burn me through this wooden screen. He is about to rise. Why! Who comes? Awake, Nurse, and look."

Asti obeyed. There in the gate of the court she saw a tall man, white-bearded, yellow-faced, horny-eyed, ancient, who, clad in a tattered robe, leaned upon his staff of thorn-wood, and stared about him blindly as though the sun bewildered him. The guards came to thrust him away, but he waved his staff, and they fell back from him as though there were power in that staff. Now his slow, tortoise-like eyes seemed to catch sight of the glittering throne, and of him who sat upon it, and with long strides he walked to the throne and halted in front of it, again leaning on his staff.

"Who is this fellow," asked Janees in an angry voice, "who stands here and makes no obeisance to the King?"

"Are you a king?" asked Kepher. "I am very blind. I thought you were but a common man such as I am, only clad in bright clothes. Tell me, what is it like to be a king, and have all things beneath your feet. Do you still hope and suffer, and fear death like a common man? Is the flesh beneath your gold and purple the same as mine beneath my rags? Do old memories torment you, memories of the dead who come no more? Can you feel griefs, and the ache of disappointment?"

"Do I sit here to answer riddles, Fool?" answered Janees angrily. "Turn the fellow out. I have business."

Now guards sprang forward to do the King's bidding, but again Kepher waved his staff, and again they fell back. Certainly it seemed as though there were power in that staff.

"Business, King," he said. "Not of the State, I think, but with one who lodges yonder," and he nodded towards the shuttered room whence Tua watched him. "Well, that is three hours hence after the sun has set, so you still have time to listen to my prayer, which you will do, as it is of this same lady with whom you have business."

"What do you know of the lady, you old knave, and of my dealings with her?" asked Janees angrily.

"Much of both, O King, for I am her father, and—shall I tell the rest?"

"Her father, you hoary liar!" broke in Janees.

"Aye, her father, and I have come to tell you that as our blood is more ancient than yours, I will not have you for a son-in-law, any more than that daughter of mine will have you for a husband."

Now some of the courtiers who heard these words laughed outright, but Janees did not laugh, his dark face turned white with rage, and he gasped for breath.

"Drag this madman forth," he shouted at length, "and cut out his insolent tongue."

Again the guards sprang forward, but before ever they reached him Kepher was speaking in a new voice, a voice so terrible that at the sound of it they stopped, leaving him untouched.

"Beware how you lay a finger on me, you men of Tat," he cried, "for how know you who dwells within these rags? Janees, you who call yourself a King, listen to the commands of a greater king, whose throne is yonder above the sun. Ere night falls upon the earth, set that maiden upon whom you would force yourself and her companion and all her goods without your southern gate, and leave them there unharmed. Such is the command of the King of kings, who dwells on high."

"And what if I mock at the command of this King?" asked Janees.

"Mock not," replied Kepher. "Bethink you of a certain picture that the lady Asti showed you in the water, and mock not."

"It was but an Egyptian trick, Wizard, and one in which I see you had a hand. Begone, I defy you and your sorceries, and your King. To-night that maid shall be my wife."

"Then, Janees, Lord of Tat, listen to the doom that I am sent to decree upon you. To-night you shall have another bride, and her name is Death. Moreover, for their sins, and because their eyes are evil, and they have rejected the worship of the gods, many of your people shall accompany you to darkness, and to-morrow another King, who is not of your House, shall rule in Tat."

Kepher ceased speaking, then turned and walked slowly down the court of judgment and through its gates, nor did any so much as lift a finger to stay him, for now about this old man there seemed to be a majesty which made them strengthless.

"Bring that wizard back and kill him here," shouted Janees presently, as the spell passed off them, and like hounds from a leash they sprang forward to do the bidding of the King.

But without the walls they could not find him. A woman had seen him here, a child had seen him there, some slaves had watched him pass yonder, and ran away because they noted that he had no shadow. At length, after many a false turn, they tracked him to the southern gate, and there the guard said that just such a beggar-man had passed through as they were about to close the gate, vanishing into the sandstorm which blew without. They followed, but so thickly blew that sand that they lost each other in their search, and but just before sundown returned to the palace singly, where in his rage the king commanded them to be beaten with rods upon their feet.

Now the darkness came, and at the appointed hour Janees, hardening his heart, went up into the chamber where dwelt Tua and Asti, leaving his guard of eunuchs at the door. The lamps were lit within that chamber, and the window-places closed, but without the desert wind howled loudly, and the air was blind with sand. On the farther side of the marble basin, as once before, Tua and Asti stood awaiting him.

"Lady," he said, "it is the appointed hour, and I seek your answer."

"King," replied Tua, "hear me, and for your own sake—not for mine. I am more than I seem. I have friends in the earth and air, did not one of them visit you to-day in yonder court? Put away this madness and let me be, for I wish you good, not evil, but if you so much as lay a finger on me, then I think that evil draws near, or at the best I die by my own hand."

"Lady," replied Janees in a cold voice, "have done with threats; I await your answer."

"King," said Tua, "for the last time I plead with you. You think that I lie to save myself, but it is not so. I would save you. Look now," and she threw back her veil and opened the wrappings about her throat. "Look at that which is stamped upon my breast, and think—is it well to offer violence to a woman who bears this holy seal?"

"I have heard of such a one," said Janees hoarsely, for the sight of her beauty maddened him. "They say that she was born in Thebes, and of a strange father, though, if so, how came she here? I am told that she reigns as Pharaoh in Egypt."

"Ask that question of your oracles, O King, but remember that rumour does not always lie, and let the daughter of that strange father go."

"There is another who claims to be your father, Lady, if by now my soldiers have not scourged him to his death—a tattered beggar-man."

"Whom those soldiers could not touch or find," broke in Asti, speaking for the first time.

"Well," went on Janees, without heeding her, "whether your father be a beggar or a god, or even if you are Hathor's self come down from heaven to be the death of men, know that I take you for my own. For the third time, answer, will you be my Queen of your own choice, or must my women drown yonder witch in this water at your feet, and drag you hence?"

Now Tua made no answer. She only let fall her veil, folded her arms upon her breast, and waited. But Asti, mocking him, cried in a loud voice, that he might hear above the howling of the hurricane without:

"Call your women, King, for the air is full of sand that chokes my throat, and I long for the water which you promise me."

Then, in his fury, Janees turned, and shouted:

"Come hither, Slaves, and do what I have commanded you."

As he spoke the door burst open, and through it, no longer clad in rags, but wearing a white robe and head-dress, walked Kepher the Wanderer, while after him, their red swords in their hands, came savage-looking chiefs, bearded, blank-faced, round-eyed, with gold chains that clanked upon their mail, captains of the Desert, men who knew neither fear nor mercy.

Janees looked and understood. He snatched out his sword, and for a moment stayed irresolute, while the great men ringed him round and waited, their eyes fixed on Kepher's face.

"Spare him, Father, if it may be so," said Tua, "since love has made him mad."

"Too late!" answered Kepher solemnly. "Those who will not accept the warning of the gods must suffer the vengeance of the gods. Janees, you who would do violence to a helpless woman, your palace burns, your city is in my keeping, and the few who stood by you are slain. Janees, to-morrow another shall rule in your place. Amen the Father has decreed your doom."

"Aye," echoed Janees heavily, "too late! Mortals cannot fight against the gods that make their sport of them. Some god commanded that I should love. Some god commands that I shall die. So be it, I am glad to die; would that I had not been born to know grief and death. Tell me, O Prophet, what evil power is there which ordains that we must be born and suffer?"

Kepher beckoned to Tua and to Asti, and they followed him, leaving Janees ringed round by those stern-faced men.

"Farewell, Lady," he called to Tua as she passed. "Here and hereafter remember this of Janees, King of Tat, that he who might have saved his life chose to die for love of you."

Then they went and saw him no more.

They passed the door of the great marble chamber about which they found guards and eunuchs lying dead; they passed down the stairways, and through the tall gates where more soldiers lay dead, and looking behind them, saw that the palace was in flames. They reached the square without, and at the command of Kepher entered into a litter, and were borne by black slaves whither they knew not.

All that night they were borne, awake or sleeping, till at length the morning came, and they descended from the litter to find themselves in an oasis of the wilderness surrounded by a vast army of the desert men. Of the city of Tat they could see nothing; like a dream it had passed out of their lives, nor did they ever hear of it and its king again. Only in the pavilion that had been provided for them they found their pearls and gold, and Tua's ivory harp.

They laid themselves down and slept, for they were very weary, only to wake when once more the day had dawned. Then they rose and ate of the food that had been placed by them, and went out of the tent. In the shadow of some palm trees stood Kepher, awaiting them, and with him certain of the stern-faced, desert chiefs, who bowed as they advanced.

"Hearken, Lady Neferte, and you, O Asti her companion," said Kepher to them, "I must depart, who, this matter finished, have my bread to beg far from here. Yet, fear not, for know that these Lords of the Desert are your servants, and for this reason were they born, that they may help you on your way. Repeat your orders," he continued, addressing the chiefs.

Then the captain of them all said:

"Wanderer, known to our fathers' grandfathers, Guardian of our race by whom we live and triumph, these are your commands: That we lead this divine Lady and her companion a journey of many moons across the deserts and mountains, till at length we bring her to the gates of the City of Gold, where our task ends. While one man of us remains alive they shall be obeyed."

"You hear," said Kepher to Tua. "Put your trust in these men. Go in peace in the day time, and sleep in peace at night, for be sure that they shall not fail you. But if they, or any other should perchance bring you into trouble, then strike upon the harp and call the name you know, as you called it in the house of Janees the mad, and I think that one will come to you. Lords of the Desert, whose great grandsires were known to me, and who live by my wisdom, this divine Lady is in your keeping. See that you guard her as you should, and when the journey is done, return and make report to me. Farewell."

Then, lifting his staff, without speaking another word to Tua or to Asti, Kepher strode away from amongst them, walking through the ranks of the Desert men who forced their camels to kneel and saluted him as he passed. Presently they saw him standing alone upon a ridge, and looking towards them for a while. Then of a sudden he was gone.

"Who is that man, O Captain, at whose bidding the wilderness swarms with tribesmen and kings are brought to doom?" asked Asti when she had watched him disappear.

"Lady," he answered, "I cannot tell you, but from the beginning he has been Master of the Desert, and those who dwell therein. At his word the sand wind blows as it blew yesterday to cover our advance, at his word the fountains spring and tribes grow great or sink to nothingness. We think that he is a spirit who moves where he lists, and executes the decrees of heaven. At the least, though they but see him from time to time, all the dwellers in the wilderness obey him, as we do, and ill does it go, as you have learned, with those dwellers in cities who know not the power which breathes beneath that tattered robe."

"I thank you," answered Asti. "I think with you that this Wanderer is a spirit, and a great one, so great that I will not name his name. Captains, my Lady is ready to march towards the City of Gold, whither you will lead us."

****

For day after day, for week after week, for month after month, they marched southward and westward across the Desert, and in the centre of their host, mounted upon camels, rode Tua and Asti veiled. Once the hillsmen attacked them in a defile of some rugged mountains, but they beat them back, and once there was a great battle with other tribes of the wilderness, who, hearing that they had a goddess among them, sought to capture her for themselves. These tribes also they defeated with slaughter, for when the fight hung in the balance Tua herself headed the charge of her horsemen, and at the sight of her in her white robes the enemy fled amazed. Once also they camped for two whole months in an oasis, waiting till rain should fall, for the country beyond lacked water. At length it came, and they went on again, on and on over the endless lands, till on a certain night they pitched their tent upon a hill.

At the first brightening of the dawn Tua and Asti went out, and there, beneath them, near to the banks of a great river, which they knew for the Nile, they saw the pyramids and the temples of Napata the Golden, the southern city of Amen, and thanked the gods who had brought them here in safety.

While they still gazed upon its glories in the red light of the rising sun the captain of the desert men appeared, and bowed before them.

"Divine Lady," he said, "woman or goddess, whichever you may be, we have fulfilled the command given to us by Kepher, the ancient King of the Wilderness. Beneath you lies Napata whither we have journeyed through so many weary months, but we would draw no nearer to its walls, who from generation to generation are sworn not to enter any city save in war. Lady, our task is done, and our men murmur to be led back to their own place, where their wives and children await them, ere, thinking that we are enemies, the people of Napata sally forth to attack us."

"It is well," answered Tua. "I thank you and the gods shall give you your reward. Leave us, and go back to your homes, but before you go, take a gift from me."

Then she sent for the gold that they had gathered in their trading in the city of Tat, and gave it to be divided among them, a great and precious treasure. Only the pearls she kept, with a little of the gold. So the captains saluted her, and in the mists of the morning they and their swarthy host stole away, and soon were hidden in a cloud of dust.

From the backs of their camels Tua and Asti watched them go like a dream of the night. Then with no word spoken between them, for their lips were sealed with hope and wonder, wrapping themselves in their dark cloaks, they rode down to the highway by the banks of the Nile, which led to the walls of Napata. Mingling with other travellers, they passed through the Field of Pyramids, and coming to the beautiful northern gate that was covered over with gold, waited there, for this gate was not yet opened. A woman who led three asses laden with green barley and vegetables, which she purposed to sell in the market-place, fell into talk with them, asking them whence they came.

Asti answered, from the city of Meroe, adding that they were singers and dealers in pearls.

"Then you have come to the right place," answered the woman, "for pearls are rare at Napata, which is so far from the sea; also it is said that the young King loves singing if it be good."

"The young King?" asked Asti. "What is his name, and where is the old king?"

"You cannot have dwelt long in Meroe, Strangers," answered the woman suspiciously, "or you would know that the old King dwells with Osiris beneath yonder pyramid, where the general of the Pharaoh of Egypt, he who rules here now, buried him after the great battle. Oh! it is a strange story, and I do not know the rights of it who sell my stuff and take little heed of such things. But at the last high Nile before one this general came with three thousand soldiers of Egypt, and the body of the Prince of Kesh, whom it seems he had slain somewhere, it is said because both of them sought the favour of the Queen of Egypt. As they tell, this was the command of that Queen—that he should submit himself to the King of Napata to be judged for his crime. This he did, and the King in his fury commanded that he should be hanged from the mast of the sacred boat of Amen. The general answered that he was ready to be hanged if the King could hang him. Then there was a war between the people of Napata and the Egyptians, aided by many of the soldiers of the city who hated their master and rebelled against his rule, which was ever cruel. The end of it was that the Egyptians and the rebels won, and the King having fallen in the fight, they crowned the Egyptian general in his place.

"His name?—Oh, I forget it, he has so many, but he is a goodly man to look at, and all love him although he is mad. See, the gates are open at last. Farewell," and dragging her asses by the halter, the peasant woman mingled with the crowd and was gone.

Tua and Asti also mingled with the crowd, and rode on up a wide street till they came to a square planted round with trees, on one side of which was built a splendid palace. Here they halted their camels, not knowing whither they should go, and as they stood irresolute the gates of the palace opened and through them came a body of horsemen clad in armour.

"See the writing on their shields," whispered Asti.

Tua looked and read, and lo! there in the royal cartouche was her own name, and after it new titles—Queen of the Upper and the Lower Land, Opener of the Gates of the South, Divine Lady of Napata by grace of Amen, Father of the Gods.

"It seems that I have subjects here," she murmured, "who elsewhere have none," then ceased.

For now through the gate rode one mounted on a splendid horse, whose shape seemed familiar to her even while he was far away.

"Who is that?" faltered Tua.

"My heart tells me it is Rames my son," answered Asti, grasping at her saddle-rope.

Chapter 17

Tua Finds Her Lover

Rames it was without a doubt; Rames grown older and stern and sad of face, but still Rames, and no other man, and oh! their eyes swam and their hearts beat at the sight of him.

"Say, shall we declare ourselves?" asked Asti.

"Nay," answered Tua, "not here and now. He would not believe, and we cannot unveil before all these men. Also, first I desire to learn more. Let him pass."

Rames rode on till he came opposite to where the two women sat on their white camels beneath a tree, when something seemed to attract his gaze to them. He looked once carelessly and turned his head away. He looked a second time, and again turned his head, though more slowly. He looked a third time, and his eyes remained fixed upon those two veiled women seated on their camels beneath the trees. Then, as though acting upon some impulse, he pulled upon his horse's bit, and rode up to them.

"Who are you, Stranger Ladies," he asked, "who own such fine camels?"

Tua bowed her head that the folds of her veil might hide her shape, but Asti answered in a feigned voice:

"Sir, both of us are merchants, and one is a harper and a singer. We have travelled hither up the Nile to the Golden City because we understand that in Napata pearls are rare, and such we have to sell. Also we were told that the new King of this city loved good singing, and my companion, who sings and harps, learned her art in Egypt, even at Thebes the holy. But who are you, Sir, that question us?"

"Lady," answered Rames, "I am an Egyptian who holds this town on behalf of the Queen of Egypt whom once I knew. Or perhaps I should say that I hold it on behalf of the Pharaoh of Egypt, since my spies tell me that the Star of Amen has taken Abi, Prince of Memphis, to husband, although they add that he finds her a masterful wife," and he laughed bitterly.

"Sir," replied Asti, "it is long since we left holy Thebes, some years indeed, and we know nothing of these things, who ply our trade from place to place. But if you are the governor of this town, show us, we pray you, as countrywomen of yours, where we may lodge in safety, and at your leisure this afternoon permit that we exhibit our pearls before you, and when that is done, and you have bought or refused them, as you may wish, that my companion should sing to you some of the ancient songs of Egypt."

"Ladies," answered Rames, "I am a soldier who would rather buy swords than pearls. Also, as it chances, I am a man who dwells alone, one in whose household no women can be found. Yet because you are of my country, or by Amen I know not why! I grant you your request. I go out to exercise this company in the arts of war, but after sundown you shall come to my palace, and I will see your wares and hear your songs. Till then, farewell. Officer," he added to a captain who had followed him, "take these Egyptians and their camels and give them a lodging in the guest-house, where they will not be molested, and at sundown bring them to me."

Then, still staring at them as though they held his eyes in their hearts, Rames departed, and the captain led them to their lodging.

****

It was the hour of sundown, and Tua, adorned in beautiful white raiment, broidered with royal purple, that she carried in her baggage on the camel, with her long hair combed out and scented, a necklace of great pearls upon her bosom, a veil flung over her head, and her harp of gold and ivory in her hand, waited to be led before Rames. Asti, his mother, waited also, but she was clad in a plain black robe, and over her head was a black veil. Presently that captain who had shown them their lodging, came to them and asked if they were ready to be led before the Viceroy of Napata.

"Viceroy?" answered Asti, "I thought he was a King."

"So he is, my good Woman," replied the captain, "but it his fancy to call himself the Viceroy of Neter-Tua, Star of Amen, wife of Abi the Usurper who rules in Egypt. A mad fancy when he might be a Pharaoh on his own account, but so it is."

"Well, Sir," said Asti, "we merchants have nothing to do with these high matters; lead us to this Pharaoh, or General, or Viceroy, with whom we hope to transact business."

So the captain conducted them to a side gate of the palace, and thence through various passages and halls, in some of which Tua recognised officers of her own whom she had commanded to accompany Rames, to an apartment of no great size, where he bade them be seated. Presently a door opened, and through it came Rames, plainly dressed in the uniform of an Egyptian general, on which they saw he wore no serpent crest or other of the outward signs of royalty. Only on his right hand that lacked the little finger, gleamed a certain royal ring, which Tua knew. With him also were several captains to whom he talked of military affairs.

Seeing the two women, he bowed to them courteously, and asked them to forgive him for having kept them waiting for him. Then he said:

"What was it that you wished to show me, Ladies? Oh! I remember, precious stones. Well, I fear me that you have brought them to a bad market, seeing that although Napata is called the City of Gold, she needs all her wealth for her own purposes, and I draw from it only a general's pay, and a sum for the sustenance of my household, which is small. Still, let me look at your wares, for if I do not buy myself, perhaps I may be able to find you a customer."

Now when they saw the young man's noble face and bearing, and heard his simple words, the hearts of Asti and Tua, his mother and his love, beat so hard within their breasts that for a while they could scarcely speak. Glad were they, indeed, that the veils they wore hid their troubled faces from his eyes, which, as in the morning, lingered on them curiously.

At length, controlling herself with an effort, Asti answered:

"Perchance, Lord, the Great Lady your wife, or the ladies your companions, will buy if you do not."

"Have I not already told you, Merchant," asked Rames angrily, "that I have no wife, and no companions that are not men?"

"You said so, Sir," she replied humbly, always speaking in her feigned voice, "yet forgive us if we believed you not, since in our journeyings my daughter and I have seen many princes, and know that such a thing is contrary to their nature. Still we will show you our wares, for surely all the men in Napata are not unmarried."

Then, without more ado, she drew out a box of scented cedar and, opening it, revealed a diadem of pearls worked into the shape of the royal *uraeus*, which they had fashioned thus at Tat, and also a few of their largest single gems.

"Beautiful, indeed," said Rames, looking at them, "though there is but one who has the right to wear this crown, the divine Queen of the Upper and the Lower Land," and he sighed.

"Nay, Lord," replied Asti, "for surely her husband might wear it also."

"It would sit but ill on the fat head of Abi, from all I hear, Lady," he broke in, laughing bitterly.

"Or," went on Asti, taking no heed of his words, "a general who had conquered a great country could usurp it, and find none to reprove him, especially if he himself happened to be of the royal blood."

Now Rames looked at her sharply.

"You speak strange words," he said, "but doubtless it is by chance. Merchant, those pearls of yours are for richer men than I am, shut them in the box again, and let the lady, your daughter, sing some old song of Egypt, for such I long to hear."

"So be it, Lord," answered Asti. "Still, keep the diadem as a gift, since it was made for you alone, and may yet be useful to you—who can know? It is the price we pay for liberty to trade in your dominions. Nay, unless you keep it my daughter shall not sing."

"Let it lie there, then, most princely Merchant, and we will talk of the matter afterwards. Now for the song."

Then, her moment come at last, Tua stood up, and holding the ivory harp beneath her veil, she swept its golden chords. Disguising her voice, as Asti had done, she began to sing, somewhat low, a short and gentle love-song, which soon came to an end.

"It is pretty," said Rames, when she had finished, "and reminds me of I know not what. But have you no fuller music at your command? If so, I would listen to it before I bid you good-night."

She bent her head and answered almost in a whisper:

"Lord, if you wish it, I will sing you the story of one who dared to set his heart too high, and of what befell him at the hands of an angry goddess."

"Sing on," he answered. "Once I heard such a story—elsewhere."

Then Tua swept her harp and sang again, but this time with all her strength and soul. As the first glorious notes floated from her lips Rames rose from his seat, and stood staring at her entranced. On went the song, and on, as she had sung it in the banqueting hall of Pharaoh at Thebes, so she sang it in the chamber of Rames at Napata. The scribe dared the sanctuary, the angry goddess smote him cold in death, the high-priestess wailed and mourned, the Queen of Love relented, and gave him back his life again. Then came that last glorious burst when, lifted up to heaven, the two lovers, forgiven, purged, chanted their triumph to the stars, and, by slow degrees, the music throbbed itself to silence.

Look! white-faced, trembling, Rames clung to a pillar in his chamber, while Tua sank back upon her chair, and the harp she held slipped from her hand down upon the floor.

"Whence came that harp?" he gasped. "Surely there are not two such in the world? Woman, you have stolen it. Nay, how can you have stolen the music, and the voice as well? Lady, forgive me, I have no thought of evil, but oh! grant me a boon. Why, I will tell you afterwards. Grant me a boon—let me look upon your face."

Tua lifted her hands, and undid the fastening of her veil, which slipped from her to her feet, showing her in the rich array of a prince of Egypt. His eyes met her beautiful eyes, and for a while they gazed upon each other like folk who dream.

"What trick is this?" he said angrily at last. "Before me stands the Star of Amen, Egypt's anointed Queen. The harp she bears was the royal gift of the Prince of Kesh, he who fell that night beneath my sword. The voice is Egypt's voice, the song is Egypt's song. Nay, how can it be? I am mad, you are magicians come to mock me, for that Star, Amen's daughter, reigns a thousand miles away with the lord she chose, Abi, her own uncle, he who, they say, murdered Pharaoh. Get you gone, Sorceress, lest I cause the priests of Amen, whereof you also make a mock, to cast you to the flames for blasphemy."

Slowly, very slowly, Tua opened the wrappings about her throat, revealing the Sign of Life that from her birth was stamped above her bosom.

"When they see this holy mark, think you that the priests of Amen will cast me to the flames, O Royal Son of Mermes?" asked Tua softly.

"Why not?" he answered. "If you have power to lie in one thing, you have power to lie in all. She who can steal the loveliness of Egypt's self, can also steal the signet of the god."

"Say, did you, O Rames, also steal that other signet on your hand, a Queen's gift, I think, that once a Pharaoh wore? Say also how did you lose the little finger of that hand? Was it perchance in the maw of a certain god that dwells in the secret pool of a temple at holy Thebes?"

So Tua spake, and waited a while, but Rames said nothing. He opened his mouth to answer, indeed, but a dumbness sealed his lips.

"Nurse," she went on presently, "I cannot persuade this Lord that I am Egypt and no other. Try you."

So Asti loosed her black veil, and let it fall about her feet. He stared at her noble features and grey hair, then, uttering a great cry of "Mother, my Mother, who they swore to me was dead in Memphis," he flung himself upon her breast, and there burst into weeping.

"Aye, Rames," said Asti presently, "your Mother, she who bore you, and no other woman, and with her one who because her royal heart loves you now as from the first, from moon to moon for two whole years has braved the dangers of the desert, and of wicked men, till at last Amen her father brings her safely to your side. Now do you believe?"

"Aye," answered Rames, "I believe."

"Then, O faithful Captain," said Tua, "take this gift from Egypt's Queen, which a while ago you thrust aside, and be its Lord and mine," and lifting the diadem of pearls crested with the royal *uraei* she set it on his brow, as once before she had done in that hour of dawn when she vowed herself to him in Thebes.

****

It was night, and all their wonderful story had been told.

"Such is our tale, Rames my Son," said Asti, "and long may you search before you find another that will match it. Now tell us yours."

"It is short, Mother," he answered. "Obeying the commands of her Majesty yonder," and he bowed towards Tua, who sat at the further side of the table at which they ate, "I travelled up the Nile to this city. As the old king, the father of the Prince of Kesh, would have slain me I attacked him first by the help of my Egyptians and his own subjects, and—well, he died. Moreover, none regretted him, for he was a bad king, and I stepped into his place, and ever since have been engaged in righting matters which they needed. Long ago I would have returned to Egypt and reported myself, only my spies told me of all that had happened there. They told me, for instance, of the murder of Pharaoh, by the witchcraft of Abi and his companions; and they told me that Pharaoh's daughter, the Star of Amen, forgetting all things and the oath she swore to me, had married her old uncle Abi that she might save her life and power."

"And you believed them, Rames?" asked Tua reproachfully.

"What else could I do but believe, Lady, seeing that those same spies swore that they had seen your Majesty seated upon your throne at Memphis, and elsewhere, and causing Abi to run to and fro like a little dog, and do your bidding in all things? How could I know that it was your Double, and not yourself that married Abi?"

"I think that Abi knows to-day," answered Tua, "since it seems that a *Ka* makes but a bad wife to any man. But now what shall we do?"

"Will you not first marry me, Lady?" suggested Rames. "Afterwards, we can think."

"Aye," she answered, "I will marry you as I have promised, but in one place only, the temple of Amen in Egypt. First win me back my throne, then ask for my hand."

"It shall be done," he answered, "though how I know not, seeing that another sits upon that throne of yours, who, perhaps, will not be willing to bid it farewell."

"We will send her a message, Son," said Asti. "Now leave us,.for we must sleep."

"Where is your messenger, Mother?" asked Rames as he went.

"Have you known me all these years, my Son, and not learned that I have servants whom you cannot see?" answered Asti.

****

It was midnight, and in their chamber of the palace of Rames, Asti and Tua knelt side by side in prayer to Amen, Father of the Gods. Then, their petitions finished, Asti rose to her feet, and once again, as in the pylon tower at Memphis, uttered the awful words that in bygone days had been spoken to her by the spirit of Ahura the divine in Osiris.

There was a sound as of whispering, a sound as of beating wings. Lo! in the shadow beyond the lamplight a mist gathered that brightened by degrees and took shape, the shape of a royal woman clad in the robes and ornaments of Egypt's Queen, whose face was as the face of Neter-Tua, only prouder and more unearthly. In silence it stood before them scanning them with its glittering eyes.

"Whence come you, O Double?" asked Asti.

"From that place where your command found me, O Mistress of Secret Things, from the house of Abi at Thebes, wherein he seems to rule as Pharaoh," the Form answered in its cold voice.

"How fares it with Abi and with Egypt, O Double?"

"With Abi it fares but ill; he wastes in toil and fear and longings, and knows no happy hour. But with Egypt it fares well. Never, O Lady of Strength, was she more great than she is to-day, for in all things I have fulfilled the commandments that were laid upon me, and now I desire to rest in that bosom whence I came," and she pointed to Tua, who stood and watched.

"Not yet, O Double, for there is still work for you to do, and then you shall be at peace till the day of the last Awakening. Hearken: Return to Thebes, and tell a false tale in the ears of Abi and his councillors. Say that Rames the Egyptian, who has seized the rule of Kesh, has declared himself Pharaoh of Egypt by right of race, and your husband by the promise of him who ruled before you whom Abi did to death. Cause this Abi to gather a great army, and to march southward to make an end of Rames. But secretly whisper into the ears of the generals of this army, that it is true the divine Pharaoh who is gone promised you in marriage to Rames with your own consent, and by the command of Amen, Father of the Gods, and of your Spirit. Whisper to them that Amen is wrath with Abi because of his crime, as he will show them in due season, and that those who rebel against him shall have his love and favour. At the Gateway of the South, whence the Nile rushes northward between great walls of rock, Rames shall meet the army of Abi. With him will come her of whom you are, and I whom you must obey; also perchance another who is greater than all of us. There at the Gateway of the South your task shall be accomplished, and you shall find the rest you seek. It is said."

"I hear the command, and it shall be done," answered the *Ka* in its cold, passionless voice. "Only, Lady of the Secrets, Doer of the Will Divine, delay not, lest, outworn, I should break back like a flame to yonder breast that is my home, slaying as I come, and leaving wreck behind me."

Then as the figure had appeared, so also it disappeared, growing faint by degrees, and vanishing away into the night out of which it came.

****

It was morning at Thebes, and Abi sat in the great hall of Pharaoh transacting business of the State, while at his side stood Kaku the Vizier. Changed were both of them, indeed, since they had plotted the death of their guest and king at Memphis, for now Abi was so worn with work and fear and wretchedness, that his royal robes hung about him in loose folds, while Kaku had become an old, old man, who trembled as he walked.

"Is the business finished, Officer?" asked Abi impatiently.

"Nay, Mighty Lord," answered Kaku, "there is still enough to keep you sitting here till noon, and after that you must receive the Council and the Embassies."

"I will not receive them. Let them wait till another day. Knave, would you work me to death, who have never known an hour's rest or peace since the happy time when I ruled as Prince of Memphis?"

"Lord," answered Kaku, bowing humbly, "weary or no you must receive them, for so it has been decreed by her Majesty the Queen, whose command may not be broken."

"The Queen!" exclaimed Abi in a low voice, rolling his hollow eyes around him as though in fear. "Oh, Kaku, would that I had never beheld the Queen. I tell you that she is not a woman, as indeed you know well, but a fiend with a heart of ice, and the venomous cunning of a snake. I am called Pharaoh, yet am but her puppet to carry out her decrees. I am called her husband, yet she is still no wife to me, or to any, although all men love her, and by that love are ofttimes brought to doom. Last night again she vanished from my side as I sat listening to her orders, and after a while, lo! there she was as before, only, as it seemed to me, somewhat weary. I asked her where she had been and she answered: 'Further than I could travel in a year to visit one she loved as much as she hated me. Now who can that be, Kaku?'"

"Rames, I think, Lord, he who has made himself King of Kesh," replied Kaku in an awed whisper. "Without a doubt she loved the man when she was a woman, though whom she loves now the evil gods know alone. We are in her power, and must work her will, for, Lord, if we do not we shall die, and I think that neither of us desires to die, since beyond that gate dead Pharaoh waits for us."

At these words Abi groaned aloud, wiping the sweat from his blanched face with the corner of his robe, and saying:

"There you speak truly. Go, call the scribes, and let us get on with the Queen's business."

Kaku turned to obey, when suddenly heralds entered the empty hall, crying:

"Her Majesty the Queen waits without with a great company, and humbly craves audience of her good lord, the divine Pharaoh of the Upper and the Lower Land."

Abi and Kaku looked at each other, and despair was in their eyes.

"Let her Majesty enter," said the King in a low voice.

The heralds retired, and presently through the cedar doors appeared the Queen in state. She was splendid to behold, splendid in her proud beauty, splendid in her dress, and in her royal ornaments. On she swept up the hall, attended by Merytra, who bore her fan and cushion, for it was her pleasure that this woman should wait upon her day and night without pause or rest, although she who had once been so handsome now was worn almost to nothingness with toil and terror. Behind Merytra came guards and high-priests, and after them the great lords of the Council, who were called the King's Companions and the generals of the army.

On she swept up the hall till reaching the foot of the throne whereon Abi sat, she motioned to Merytra to place the cushion upon its step, and knelt, saying:

"I am come as a loyal wife to make a humble prayer to Pharaoh my Lord in the presence of his Court."

"Rise and speak on, Great Lady," answered Abi. "It is not fit that you should kneel to me."

"Nay, it is most fit that Pharaoh's Queen should kneel to Pharaoh when she seeks his divine favour." Yet she rose, and, seating herself in a chair that had been brought, spoke thus:

"O Pharaoh, last night I dreamed a dream. I dreamed of the Count Rames, son of Mermes, the last of that royal race which ruled before our House in Egypt. I mean that man who slew the Prince of Kesh in this very hall, and whom, my Father being sick, I sent to Napata, to be judged by the King of Kesh, but who, it seems, overthrew that king and took his kingdom in the name of Egypt.

"I dreamed that this bold and able man, not satisfied with the rich kingdom of Kesh, has made a scheme to attack Egypt; to slay you, most glorious Lord, to proclaim himself Pharaoh by right of ancient blood, and more—to take me, your faithful wife, to be his wife, and thereby secure his throne."

"Without doubt, Queen, this turbulent Rames might think of such things," said Abi, "and so far your dream may be true; yet it should be remembered that at present he is at Napata, which is a very long way off, and has probably only a small army at his command, so why should you trouble about what he thinks?"

"O Pharaoh, that was not all my dream, for in it I saw two pictures. The first was of this bold Rames attacking Thebes, and conquering it, yes, and dragging me away to be his wife over your very corpse, O Pharaoh. The second was of you and your army meeting him at the Gate of the South Land, and slaying him, and taking possession of the kingdom of Kesh, and its golden city, and ruling them for Egypt, until you die."

"Here be two dreams, O Queen," said Abi. "Tell us now, which would you follow, for both of them cannot be right?"

"How can I know, Pharaoh, and how can you know? Yet by your side stands one who will know, for he is the first of magicians, and a chosen interpreter of the heart of the gods. Grant that he may make this matter clear," and she pointed to Kaku, who stood by the throne.

"Divine Lady," stammered Kaku, "the thing is too high for me. I have no message, I cannot tell you——"

"You were ever over-modest, Kaku," said the Queen. "Command him, O Pharaoh, to shed the light of his wisdom on us, for without doubt he knows the truth."

"Yes, yes," said Abi, "he knows it, he knows everything. Kaku, delay not, interpret the dream of her Majesty."

"I cannot, I will not," spluttered the old astrologer. "Ask my wife, the Lady Merytra there, she is wiser than I am."

"My good friend Merytra has already told me her mind," said the Queen, "now we wait for yours. A prophet must speak when the gods call on him, or," she added slowly, "he must cease to be a prophet who betrays the gods by hiding their high counsel."

Now Kaku could find no way of escape, so, since he feared the very name of Rames, within himself he determined that he would interpret the dream in the sense that Pharaoh should await the attack of this Rames at Thebes, and while every ear listened to him, thus began his tale. Yet as he spoke he felt the glittering eyes of that spirit who was called the Queen, fix themselves upon him and compel his tongue, so that he said just what he did not mean to say.

"A light shines in me," he cried, "and I see that the second vision of her Majesty is the true vision. You must go up with your army to the Gate of the South, O Pharaoh, and there meet this usurper, Rames, that these matters may be brought to their appointed end."

"Their appointed end? What appointed end?" shouted Abi.

"Doubtless that which her Majesty dreamed," answered Kaku. "At least, it is laid upon me to tell you that you must go up to the Gate of the South."

"Then I wish that the Gate of the South were laid upon you also, O Evil Prophet," exclaimed Abi. "For two years only have I ruled in Egypt, and lo! three wars have been my portion, a war against the people of Syria, a war against the desert men, and a war against the Nine Bow barbarians that invaded the Low Lands. Must I now, in my age, undertake another war against the terrible sons of Kesh also? Let this dog, Rames, come, if come he will, and I will hang him here at the gates of Thebes."

"Nay, nay, O Pharaoh," replied Kaku, "it is laid upon me to tell you that you must hang him in the desert hundreds of miles away from Thebes. That is the interpretation of the vision; that is the command of the gods."

"The gods have spoken by the mouth of their prophet," cried the Queen in a thrilling, triumphant voice. "Now Pharaoh, Priests, Councillors, and Captains of Egypt, let us make ready to travel to the Gate of the South, and there hang the dog Rames in the desert land, that thus Egypt and Egypt's King and Egypt's Queen may be freed from danger, and rest in peace, and the wealth of the City of Gold be divided amongst you all."

"Aye, aye," answered the Priests, Councillors, and Captains, the shrill voice of Kaku leading the chorus, still against his will, "let us go up at once, and let her Majesty accompany us."

"Yes," said the Queen, "I will accompany you, for though I be but a woman, shall I shrink from what Pharaoh, my dear Lord, dares? We will sail at the new moon."

****

That night Abi and Kaku stood face to face.

"What is this that you have done?" asked Abi. "Do you not remember the words which dead Pharaoh spoke in the awful vision that came to me that night at Memphis, when he bade me take the Royal Loveliness which I desired to be my wife? Do you not remember that he bade me also reign in her right until I met 'one Rames, Son of Mermes' and with him a Beggar-man who is charged with another message for me?"

"I remember," answered Kaku in a hollow voice.

"What, then, is this message, Man, that will come from Rames or the Beggar? Is it not the message of my death and yours, of us whose tombs were finished but yesterday?"

"It may be so, Lord."

"Then why did you interpret the dream of the Queen in the sense that I must hurry southwards to meet this very Rames—and my doom?"

"Because I could not help it," groaned Kaku. "That spirit who is called a Queen compelled me. Abi, there is no escape for us; we are in the net of Fate—unless, unless you dare——" and he looked meaningly at the sword that hung by Pharaoh's side.

"Nay, Kaku," he answered, "I dare not. Let us live while we may, knowing what awaits us beyond the gate."

"Aye," moaned Kaku, "beyond the Gate of the South, where we shall find Rames the Avenger, and that Beggar who is charged with a message for us."

Chapter 18
The Judgment of the Gods

Three more months had gone by, and the great host of Pharaoh was encamped beyond the southern gate, and the warships of Pharaoh were anchored thick on either bank of the Nile. There they lay prepared for battle, for spies had reported to them that the general, Rames, Lord of Kesh, was advancing northward swiftly, though with so small an army that it could easily be destroyed. Therefore Abi waited there to destroy it without further toil, nor did his terrible Queen gainsay him. She also seemed content to wait. ne evening as the sun sank it was told to them that the troops of Rames had appeared, and occupied the mountains on the right bank of the Nile, being encamped around that temple of Amen which had stood there for thousands of years.

"Good," said the Queen. "To-morrow Pharaoh will go up against him and make an end of this matter. Is it not so, Pharaoh?" and she looked at him with her glittering eyes.

"Yes, yes," answered Abi, "the sooner the better, for I am worn out, and would return to Thebes. Yet," he added in a weak, uncertain voice, "I misdoubt me of this war, I know not why. What is it that you stare at in the heavens so fixedly, O Kaku?"

Now the eyes of the Council were turned on Kaku the Vizier, and they perceived that he was much disturbed.

"Look," he said, pointing with a trembling finger towards the skies.

They looked, and saw hanging just above the evening glow a very bright and wonderful star, and near to it, another, paler star which presently it seemed to cover.

"The Star of Amen," gasped Kaku in a voice that shook, "and your star, O Pharaoh. The Star of Amen eats it up, your star goes out, and will never be seen again by living man. Oh! Abi, that which I foresaw years and years ago has come to pass. Your day is done, and your night is at hand, O Abi."

"If so," shouted Abi in his rage and terror, "be sure of this, Dog—that you shall share it."

As he spoke a sound of screams drew near, and presently into the midst of them rushed Merytra, the wife of Kaku.

"The vengeance of the gods," she screamed, "the vengeance of the gods! Listen, Abi. But now this very evening as I slept in my pavilion, who can never sleep at night, there appeared to me the spirit of dead Pharaoh, of Pharaoh whom we slew by magic, and he said: 'Tell the murderer, Abi, and the wizard-rogue, Kaku, your husband, that I summon both of them to meet me ere another sun is set, and Woman, come you with them.' Death is at our door, Abi, death and the terrible vengeance of the god!" and Merytra fell down foaming in a fit.

Now Abi went mad in the extremity of his fear.

"They are sorcerers," he shouted, "who would bewitch me. Take them and keep them safe, and let Kaku be beaten with rods till he comes to his right mind again. To-morrow, when I have slain Rames, I will hang this magician at my mast-head."

But the Queen only laughed and repeated after him:

"Yes, yes, my good Lord, to-morrow, when you have killed Rames, this magician shall hang at your mast-head. Fear not, whatever chances I will see that it is done."

****

Merytra, recovered from her madness, lay upon a bed, when a woman entered and stood over her. Looking up she saw it was the Queen.

"Hearken to me," said the Queen in an icy voice, "and tell the words I speak to Abi. The time is accomplished, and I leave him. If he would look again upon Neter-Tua, Morning Star of Amen, the Great Lady of Egypt, let him seek her in the camp of Rames. There he shall find her in the temple of Amen, which is set upon the mountain in the midst of the camp."

Then she was gone.

Merytra rose from the bed, and called to the guards to lead her to Abi. So loudly did she call, saying that she had a message for him which must not be delayed, that at length one went and told him of her words, and he came to her.

"What is it now, Sorceress?" he asked. "Have you dreamed more ill-omened dreams?"

"Nay, Pharaoh," she answered, "but the Queen has fled to Rames," and word for word she repeated what had been told her.

"It is a lie," said Abi. "How can she have fled through a triple line of guards?"

"Search, then, and see, O Pharaoh."

So Abi searched, but though none had seen her pass, and none had gone with her, the Queen could not be found.

It was midnight, and while they still searched, by the light of the moon a tall figure clad in tattered robes, who bore a thorn-wood staff in his hand, and had a white beard that fell down below his middle, was perceived walking to and fro about the camp.

"Who is that fellow?" asked Abi, and as he spoke the figure cried aloud in a great voice:

"Listen, Councillors, Captains, and Soldiers of Egypt, to the command of Amen, spoken by the lips of his messenger, Kepher the Wanderer. Lift no sword against Rames, Lord of Kesh, for he is my servant, and shall be Pharaoh over you, and husband of your Queen, and father of kings to come. Seize Abi the usurper, the murderer of Pharaoh, his brother, and Kaku the sorcerer, and Merytra the traitress, and lead them at the dawn to my temple upon yonder hill, where I will declare my commands to you in the sanctuary of the temple. So shall peace be upon you and all Egypt, and the breath of life remain in your nostrils."

Now hearing these fearful words, and remembering dead Pharaoh's prophecy of a Beggar who should bring a message to him, Abi drew his sword and rushed at the man. But ere ever he came there, the Wanderer was gone, and lo! they heard him repeating his message far away. Thither they ran also, but now the words of doom were being called upon the ships, and on their prows they saw his tall shape stand—first on this and then on that.

"It is the gods who speak," cried the priests, "let us obey the gods!" and suddenly they flung themselves upon Abi and bound him, and Kaku and Merytra they bound also, waiting for the dawn. But of the tall, white-bearded man in beggar's robes they saw and heard no more.

****

At that same time Tua slept in a chamber of the temple upon the hill, while Asti watched her. Presently a wind blew in the chamber, and Asti, looking up, became aware of a Shape that she knew well, the very shape of Tua who slept upon the bed.

"What is your will, O Double?" asked Asti.

"My will is that you give me rest," answered the *Ka*. "My task is accomplished, I am weary. Speak the secret words of power that you have, and let me return to her from whom I came, and in her bosom sleep till the great Day of Awakening."

So Asti, knowing that she was commanded so to do, uttered those secret words, and as she spoke them the glorious Shape seemed to grow faint and fade away. Only Tua rose upon her bed, stretched out her arms and sighed, fell back again and slept heavily until the morning. Then she awoke, asking what had befallen her, for she was changed.

"This has befallen, Queen. That which went forth from you by the command of Amen has returned to you again, its duty done. Rise up now and adorn yourself, for this is your day of victory and marriage."

As the sun rose Tua went forth more beautiful than the morning, and at the gates of the temple found Rames awaiting her, clad in his armour, while from the mists below came a sound as of an army approaching.

"What passes?" asked Tua, looking at him, and there was more love in her blue eyes than there is water in the Nile at flood.

"I think that Abi attacks us, Lady," he said, bowing the knee to her, "and I am fearful for you, for our men are few, and his are many."

"Be not afraid of Abi, or of anything, O Rames, though it is true that this day you must lose your liberty," she answered with a sweet and gentle smile, and he wondered at her words.

Then, before he could speak again, two of the captains of his outposts ran in and reported that without were priests and heralds, who came in peace from the army of Abi.

"Summon the officers, and let them be admitted," said Rames, "but be careful, all of you, lest this embassy should hide some trick of war. Come, Queen, it is to you that they should speak, and not to me, who am but a general of your province, Kesh," and he followed her to the inner court, where, in front of the sanctuary, was a chair, on which, at his prayer, she seated herself, as a mighty Queen should do.

Now, conducted by his own officers, the embassy entered, bearing with them three closed litters, and Tua and Rames noted that among that embassy were the greatest generals, and the most holy priests of Egypt. At a given sign they prostrated themselves before the glory of the Queen, all save the soldiers who bore the litters. Next, from among their ranks out stepped the venerable High-Priest of Amen at Thebes, and stood before Tua with bowed head till, with a motion of her hand, she commanded him to speak.

"O Morning-Star of Amen," he began, "after you left our camp last night a messenger came to us from the Father of the Gods——"

"Stay, O High-Priest," broke in Tua. "I did not leave your camp who never tarried there, and who for two long years have set no foot upon the holy soil of Egypt. No, not since I fled from Memphis to save myself from death, or what is worse—the defilement of a forced marriage with Abi, my Uncle, and Pharaoh's murderer."

Now the High-Priest turned and stared at those behind him, and all who were present stared at the Queen.

"Pardon me," he said, "but how can this thing be, seeing that for those two years we have seen your Majesty day by day living among us as the wife of Abi?"

Now Tua looked at Asti, who stood at her side, and the tall and noble Asti looked at the High-Priest, saying:

"You know me, do you not?"

"Aye, Lady," he answered, "we know you. You were the wife of Mermes, the last shoot of a royal tree, and you are the mother of the Lord Rames yonder, against whom we came out to make war. We know you well, O greatest of all the seers in Egypt, Mistress of Secret Things. But we believed that you had perished in the temple of Sekhet at Memphis, that temple where Pharaoh died. Now we understand that, being a magician, you only vanished thence."

"What bear you there?" asked Asti, glancing at the litters.

"Bring forth the prisoners," said the High-Priest.

Then the curtains were drawn, and the soldiers lifted from the litters Abi, Kaku, and Merytra, who were bound with cords, and stood them on their feet before the Queen.

"These are the very murderers of Pharaoh, my Father, who would have also brought me to shame. Why are my eyes affronted with the sight of them?" asked Tua indignantly.

"Because the Messenger of the Gods, clothed as a Beggar-man, commanded it, your Majesty," answered the High-Priest. "Now we understand that they are brought hither to be judged for the murder of Pharaoh, the good god who was your father."

"Shall a wife sit in judgment on her husband?" broke in Abi.

"Man," said Tua, "I never was your wife. How can I have been your wife, who have not seen you since the death of Pharaoh? Listen, now, all of you, to the tale of that marvel which has come to pass. At my birth—you, O High-Priest, should know it well—Amen gave to me a *Ka*, a Self within myself, to protect me in all dangers. The dangers came upon me, and Asti the Magician, my foster-mother, speaking the words that had been taught to her by the spirit of the divine Ahura who bore me, called forth that *Ka* of mine, and left it where I had been, to be the wife of Abi, such a wife, I think, as never man had before. But me, Amen, my father, rescued, and with me Asti, bearing us in the Boat of the Sun to far lands, and protecting us in many perils, till at length we came to the city of Napata, where we found a certain servant of mine whom, as it chances, I—love," and she looked at Rames and smiled.

"Meanwhile, my Shadow did the work to which it was appointed, ruling for me in Egypt, and drawing on Abi to his ruin. But last night It returned to me, and will be seen no more by men, except, perchance, in my tomb after I am dead. Judge you if my tale be true, and whether I am indeed Neter-Tua, Daughter of Amen," and opening the wrappings about her throat, she showed the holy sign that was stamped above her breast, adding:

"The High-Priest yonder should know this mark, for he saw it at my birth."

Now the aged man drew near, looked, and said:

"It is the sign. Here shines the Star of Amen and no other. Still we do not understand. Tell us the tale, O Asti."

So Asti stood forward, and told that tale, omitting nothing, and then Rames told his tale, whereto Tua the Queen added a little, and, although ere they finished the sun was high, none wearied in listening save only Abi, Kaku, and Merytra, who heard death in every word.

It was done at length, and a great silence fell upon the place, for the tongues of men were tied. Presently, the High-Priest, who all this while had stood with bent head, lifted up his eyes to heaven, crying:

"O Amen, Father of the Spirit of this Queen, show now thy will, that we may learn it and obey."

For a while there was silence, till suddenly a sound was heard in the dark sanctuary where stood the statue of the god, a sound as of a stick tapping upon the granite floor. Then the curtains of that sanctuary were drawn, and standing between them there appeared the figure of an ancient, bearded man, with stony eyes, who was clad in a beggar's robe. It was he who had met Tua and Asti in the wilderness and eaten up their food. It was he who had saved them in the palace of the desert king. It was he who but last night had walked the camp of Abi.

"I am that Messenger whom men from the beginning have called Kepher," he said. "I am the Dweller in the wilderness whom your fathers knew, and your sons shall know. I am he who seeks for charity and pays it back in life and death. I am the pen of Thoth the Recorder, I am the scourge of Osiris. I am the voice of Amen, god above the gods. Hearken you people of Egypt—not for a little end have these things come to pass, but that ye may learn that there is design in heaven, and justice upon earth, and, after justice, judgment. Pharaoh, the good servant of the gods, was basely murdered by his own kin whom he trusted. Neter-Tua, his daughter, and daughter of Amen, was condemned to shame, Rames of the royal race was sent forth to danger or to death, far from her he loved, and who loved him by that divine command which rules the hearts of men. This is the command of the gods—Let these twain be wed and take Egypt as their heritage, and call down upon it peace and greatness. But as for these murderers and wizards"—and he pointed to Abi, to Kaku, and to Merytra—"let them be placed in the sanctuary of Amen, to await what he shall send them."

So spoke Kepher the Messenger, and departed whence he came, nor in that generation did any see him more.

Then they took up Abi, Kaku, and Merytra, and cut their bonds. They threw them into the dark sanctuary before the great stone image of the god. They shut the electrum doors upon them, and left them there wailing and cursing, while the High-Priest of Amen joined the hands of Rames and of Tua, and declared them to be man and wife for ever.

Now, after these things were done, the Pharaoh and his Queen drove through the hosts of Egypt in their golden chariot, and received the homage of the hosts ere they departed northwards for Thebes. At nightfall they returned again and sat side by side at the marriage feast, and once more Tua swept her harp of ivory and gold, and sang the ancient song of him who dared much for love, and won the prize.

So in the dim, forgotten years, their joy fell on Rames and on Tua, Morning-Star of Amen, which still with them remains in the new immortal kingdom that they have won long and long ago.

****

But when in the morning Asti the wise dared to open the great doors and peer into the sanctuary of Amen, she saw a dreadful sight. For there at the feet of the effigy of the god lay Abi, who slew his brother, and Kaku the sorcerer, and Merytra the traitress, dead, slain by their own or by each other's hand, and the stony eyes of the god stared down upon them.

Cleopatra

Dedication

My dear Mother,

I have for a long while hoped to be allowed to dedicate some book of mine to you, and now I bring you this work, because whatever its shortcomings, and whatever judgment may be passed upon it by yourself and others, it is yet the one I should wish you to accept.

I trust that you will receive from my romance of "Cleopatra" some such pleasure as lightened the labour of its building up; and that it may convey to your mind a picture, however imperfect, of the old and mysterious Egypt in whose lost glories you are so deeply interested.

Your affectionate and dutiful Son,

H. Rider Haggard

January 21, 1889

Author's Note

The history of the ruin of Antony and Cleopatra must have struck many students of the records of their age as one of the most inexplicable of tragic tales. What malign influence and secret hates were at work, continually sapping their prosperity and blinding their judgment? Why did Cleopatra fly at Actium, and why did Antony follow her, leaving his fleet and army to destruction? An attempt is made in this romance to suggest a possible answer to these and some other questions.

The reader is asked to bear in mind, however, that the story is told, not from the modern point of view, but as from the broken heart and with the lips of an Egyptian patriot of royal blood; no mere beast-worshipper, but a priest instructed in the inmost mysteries, who believed firmly in the personal existence of the gods of Khem, in the possibility of communion with them, and in the certainty of immortal life with its rewards and punishments; to whom also the bewildering and often gross symbolism of the Osirian Faith was nothing but a veil woven to obscure secrets of the Sanctuary. Whatever proportion of truth there may have been in their spiritual claims and imaginings, if indeed there was any, such men as the Prince Harmachis have been told of in the annals of every great religion, and, as is shown by the testimony of monumental and sacred inscriptions, they were not unknown among the worshippers of the Egyptian Gods, and more especially of Isis.

Unfortunately it is scarcely possible to write a book of this nature and period without introducing a certain amount of illustrative matter, for by no other means can the long dead past be made to live again before the reader's eyes with all its accessories of faded pomp and forgotten mystery. To such students as seek a story only, and are not interested in the faith, ceremonies, or customs of the Mother of Religion and Civilisation, ancient Egypt, it is, however, respectfully suggested that they should exercise the art of skipping, and open this tale at its Second Book.

That version of the death of Cleopatra has been preferred which attributes her end to poison. According to Plutarch its actual manner is very uncertain, though popular rumour ascribed it to the bite of an asp. She seems, however, to have carried out her design under the advice of that shadowy personage, her physician, Olympus, and it is more than doubtful if he would have resorted to such a fantastic and uncertain method of destroying life.

It may be mentioned that so late as the reign of Ptolemy Epiphanes, pretenders of native blood, one of whom was named Harmachis, are known to have advanced their claims to the throne of Egypt. Moreover, there was a book of prophecy current among the priesthood which declared that after the nations of the Greeks the God Harsefi would create the "chief who is to come." It will therefore be seen that, although it lacks historical confirmation, the story of the great plot formed to stamp out the dynasty of the Macedonian Lagidae and place Harmachis on the throne is not in itself improbable. Indeed, it is possible that many such plots were entered into by Egyptian patriots during the long ages of their country's bondage. But ancient history tells us little of the abortive struggles of a fallen race.

The Chant of Isis and the Song of Cleopatra, which appear in these pages, are done into verse from the writer's prose by Mr. Andrew Lang, and the dirge sung by Charmion is translated by the same hand from the Greek of the Syrian Meleager.

Introduction

In the recesses of the desolate Libyan mountains that lie behind the temple and city of Abydus, the supposed burying place of the holy Osiris, a tomb was recently discovered, among the contents of which were the papyrus rolls whereupon this history is written. The tomb itself is spacious, but otherwise remarkable only for the depth of the shaft which descends vertically from the rock-hewn cave, that once served as the mortuary chapel for the friends and relatives of the departed, to the coffin-chamber beneath. This shaft is no less than eighty-nine feet in depth. The chamber at its foot was found to contain three coffins only, though it is large enough for many more. Two of these, which in all probability enclosed the bodies of the High Priest, Amenemhat, and of his wife, father and mother of Harmachis, the hero of this history, the shameless Arabs who discovered them there and then broke up.

The Arabs broke the bodies up. With unhallowed hands they tore the holy Amenemhat and the frame of her who had, as it is written, been filled with the spirit of the Hathors—tore them limb from limb, searching for treasure amidst their bones—perhaps, as is their custom, selling the very bones for a few *piastres* to the last ignorant tourist who came their way, seeking what he might destroy. For in Egypt the unhappy, the living find their bread in the tombs of the great men who were before them.

But as it chanced, some little while afterwards, one who is known to this writer, and a doctor by profession, passed up the Nile to Abydus, and became acquainted with the men who had done this thing. They revealed to him the secret of the place, telling him that one coffin yet remained entombed. It seemed to be the coffin of a poor person, they said, and therefore, being pressed for time, they had left it unviolated. Moved by curiosity to explore the recesses of a tomb as yet unprofaned by tourists, my friend bribed the Arabs to show it to him. What ensued I will give in his own words, exactly as he wrote it to me:

"I slept that night near the Temple of Seti, and started before daybreak on the following morning. With me were a cross-eyed rascal named Ali—Ali Baba I named him—the man from whom I got the ring which I am sending you, and a small but choice assortment of his fellow thieves. Within an hour after sunrise we reached the valley where the tomb is. It is a desolate place, into which the sun pours his scorching heat all the long day through, till the huge brown rocks which are strewn about become so hot that one can scarcely bear to touch them, and the sand scorches the feet. It was already too hot to walk, so we rode on donkeys, some way up the valley—where a vulture floating far in the blue overhead was the only other visitor—till we came to an enormous boulder polished by centuries of action of sun and sand. Here Ali halted, saying that the tomb was under the stone. Accordingly, we dismounted, and, leaving the donkeys in charge of a fellah boy, went up to the rock. Beneath it was a small hole, barely large enough for a man to creep through. Indeed it had been dug by jackals, for the doorway and some part of the cave were entirely silted up, and it was by means of this jackal hole that the tomb had been discovered. Ali crept in on his hands and knees, and I followed, to find myself in a place cold after the hot outside air, and, in contrast with the light, filled with a dazzling darkness. We lit our candles, and, the select body of thieves having arrived, I made an examination. We were in a cave the size of a large room, and hollowed by hand, the further part of the cave being almost free from drift-dust. On the walls are religious paintings of the usual Ptolemaic character, and among them one of a majestic old man with a long white beard, who is seated in a carved chair holding a wand in his hand.[1] Before him passes a procession of priests bearing sacred images. In the right hand corner of the tomb is the shaft of the mummy-pit, a square-mouthed well cut in the black rock. We had brought a beam of thorn-wood, and this was now laid across the pit and a rope made fast to it. Then Ali—who, to do him justice, is a courageous thief—took hold of the rope, and, putting some candles into the breast of his robe, placed his bare feet against the smooth sides of the well and began to descent with great rapidity. Very soon he had vanished into blackness, and the agitation of the cord alone told us that anything was going on below. At last the rope ceased shaking and a faint shout came rumbling up the well, an-

1 This, I take it, is a portrait of Amenemhat himself.—Editor.

nouncing Ali's safe arrival. Then, far below, a tiny star of light appeared. He had lit the candle, thereby disturbing hundreds of bats that flitted up in an endless stream and as silently as spirits. The rope was hauled up again, and now it was my turn; but, as I declined to trust my neck to the hand-over-hand method of descent, the end of the cord was made fast round my middle and I was lowered bodily into those sacred depths. Nor was it a pleasant journey, for, if the masters of the situation above had made any mistake, I should have been dashed to pieces. Also, the bats continually flew into my face and clung to my hair, and I have a great dislike of bats. At last, after some minutes of jerking and dangling, I found myself standing in a narrow passage by the side of the worthy Ali, covered with bats and perspiration, and with the skin rubbed off my knees and knuckles. Then another man came down, hand over hand like a sailor, and as the rest were told to stop above we were ready to go on. Ali went first with his candle—of course we each had a candle—leading the way down a long passage about five feet high. At length the passage widened out, and we were in the tomb-chamber: I think the hottest and most silent place that I ever entered. It was simply stifling. This chamber is a square room cut in the rock and totally devoid of paintings or sculpture. I held up the candles and looked round. About the place were strewn the coffin lids and the mummied remains of the two bodies that the Arabs had previously violated. The paintings on the former were, I noticed, of great beauty, though, having no knowledge of hieroglyphics, I could not decipher them. Beads and spicy wrappings lay around the remains, which, I saw, were those of a man and a woman.[2] The head had been broken off the body of the man. I took it up and looked at it. It had been closely shaved—after death, I should say, from the general indications—and the features were disfigured with gold leaf. But notwithstanding this, and the shrinkage of the flesh, I think the face was one of the most imposing and beautiful that I ever saw. It was that of a very old man, and his dead countenance still wore so calm and solemn, indeed, so awful a look, that I grew quite superstitious (though as you know, I am pretty well accustomed to dead people), and put the head down in a hurry. There were still some wrappings left upon the face of the second body, and I did not remove them; but she must have been a fine large woman in her day.

"'There the other mummy,' said Ali, pointing to a large and solid case that seemed to have been carelessly thrown down in a corner, for it was lying on its side.

---

2 Doubtless Amenemhat and his wife.—Editor.

"I went up to it and carefully examined it. It was well made, but of perfectly plain cedar-wood—not an inscription, not a solitary God on it.

"'Never see one like him before,' said Ali. 'Bury great hurry, he no *mafish*, no fineesh. Throw him down here on side.'

"I looked at the plain case till at last my interest was thoroughly aroused. I was so shocked by the sight of the scattered dust of the departed that I had made up my mind not to touch the remaining coffin—but now my curiosity overcame me, and we set to work.

"Ali had brought a mallet and a cold chisel with him, and, having set the coffin straight, he began upon it with all the zeal of an experienced tomb-breaker. And then he pointed out another thing. Most mummy-cases are fastened by four little tongues of wood, two on either side, which are fixed in the upper half, and, passing into mortices cut to receive them in the thickness of the lower half, are there held fast by pegs of hard wood. But this mummy case had eight such tongues. Evidently it had been thought well to secure it firmly. At last, with great difficulty, we raised the massive lid, which was nearly three inches thick, and there, covered over with a deep layer of loose spices (a very unusual thing), was the body.

"Ali looked at it with open eyes—and no wonder. For this mummy was not as other mummies are. Mummies in general lie upon their backs, as stiff and calm as though they were cut from wood; but this mummy lay upon its side, and, the wrappings notwithstanding, its knees were slightly bent. More than that, indeed, the gold mask, which, after the fashion of the Ptolemaic period, had been set upon the face, had worked down, and was literally pounded up beneath the hooded head.

"It was impossible, seeing these things, to avoid the conclusion that the mummy before us had moved with violence *since it was put in the coffin.*

"'Him very funny mummy. Him not *mafish* when him go in there,' said Ali.

"'Nonsense!' I said. 'Who ever heard of a live mummy?'

"We lifted the body out of the coffin, nearly choking ourselves with mummy dust in the process, and there beneath it half hidden among the spices, we made our first find. It was a roll of papyrus, carelessly fastened and wrapped in a piece of mummy cloth, having to all appearance been thrown into the coffin at the moment of closing.[3]

"Ali eyed the papyrus greedily, but I seized it and put it in my

3 This roll contained the third unfinished book of the history. The other two rolls were neatly fastened in the usual fashion. All three are written by one hand in the Demotic character.—Editor

pocket, for it was agreed that I was to have all that might be discovered. Then we began to unwrap the body. It was covered with very broad strong bandages, thickly wound and roughly tied, sometimes by means of simple knots, the whole working the appearance of having been executed in great haste and with difficulty. Just over the head was a large lump. Presently, the bandages covering it were off, and there, on the face, lay a second roll of papyrus. I put down my hand to lift it, but it would not come away. It appeared to be fixed to the stout seamless shroud which was drawn over the whole body, and tied beneath the feet—as a farmer ties sacks. This shroud, which was also thickly waxed, was in one piece, being made to fit the form like a garment. I took a candle and examined the roll and then I saw why it was fast. The spices had congealed and glued it to the sack-like shroud. It was impossible to get it away without tearing the outer sheets of papyrus.[4]

"At last, however, I wrenched it loose and put it with the other in my pocket.

"Then we went on with our dreadful task in silence. With much care we ripped loose the sack-like garment, and at last the body of a man lay before us. Between his knees was a third roll of papyrus. I secured it, then held down the light and looked at him. One glance at his face was enough to tell a doctor how he had died.

"This body was not much dried up. Evidently it had not passed the allotted seventy days in *natron*, and therefore the expression and likeness were better preserved than is usual. Without entering into particulars, I will only say that I hope I shall never see such another look as that which was frozen on this dead man's face. Even the Arabs recoiled from it in horror and began to mutter prayers.

"For the rest, the usual opening on the left side through which the embalmers did their work was absent; the finely-cut features were those of a person of middle age, although the hair was already grey, and the frame was that of a very powerful man, the shoulders being of an extraordinary width. I had not time to examine very closely, however, for within a few seconds from its uncovering, the unembalmed body began to crumble now that it was exposed to the action of the air. In five or six minutes there was literally nothing left of it but a wisp of hair, the skull, and a few of the larger bones. I noticed that one of the tibiae—I forget if it was the right or the left—had been fractured and very badly set. It must have been quite an inch shorter than the other.

"Well, there was nothing more to find, and now that the excite-

4 This accounts for the gaps in the last sheets of the second roll.—Editor.

ment was over, what between the heat, the exertion, and the smell of mummy dust and spices, I felt more dead than alive.

"I am tired of writing, and this ship rolls. This letter, of course, goes overland, and I am coming by 'long sea,' but I hope to be in London within ten days after you get it. Then I will tell you of my pleasing experiences in the course of the ascent from the tomb-chamber, and of how that prince of rascals, Ali Baba, and his thieves tried to frighten me into handing over the papyri, and how I worsted them. Then, too, we will get the rolls deciphered. I expect that they only contain the usual thing, copies of the 'Book of the Dead,' but there *may* be something else in them. Needless to say, I did not narrate this little adventure in Egypt, or I should have had the Boulac Museum people on my track. Good-bye, '*mafish* fineesh,' as Ali Baba always said."

In due course, my friend, the writer of the letter from which I have quoted, arrived in London, and on the very next day we paid a visit to a learned acquaintance well versed in Hieroglyphics and Demotic writing. The anxiety with which we watched him skilfully damping and unfolding one of the rolls and peering through his gold-rimmed glasses at the mysterious characters may well be imagined.

"Hum," he said, "whatever it is, this is *not* a copy of the 'Book of the Dead.' By George, what's this? Cle—Cleo—Cleopatra—Why, my dear Sirs, as I am a living man, this is the history of somebody who lived in the days of Cleopatra, *the* Cleopatra, for here's Antony's name with hers! Well, there's six months' work before me here—six months, at the very least!" And in that joyful prospect he fairly lost control of himself, and skipped about the room, shaking hands with us at intervals, and saying "I'll translate—I'll translate it if it kills me, and we will publish it; and, by the living Osiris, it shall drive every Egyptologist in Europe mad with envy! Oh, what a find! what a most glorious find!"

And O you whose eyes fall upon these pages, see, they have been translated, and they have been printed, and here they lie before you—an undiscovered land wherein you are free to travel!

Harmachis speaks to you from his forgotten tomb. The walls of Time fall down, and, as at the lightning's leap, a picture from the past starts upon your view, framed in the darkness of the ages.

He shows you those two Egypts which the silent pyramids looked down upon long centuries ago—the Egypt of the Greek, the Roman, and the Ptolemy, and that other outworn Egypt of the Hierophant, hoary with years, heavy with the legends of antiquity and the memory of long-lost honours.

He tells you how the smouldering loyalty of the land of Khem blazed up before it died, and how fiercely the old Time-consecrated Faith struggled against the conquering tide of Change that rose, like Nile at flood, and drowned the ancient Gods of Egypt.

Here, in his pages, you shall learn the glory of Isis the Many-shaped, the Executrix of Decrees. Here you shall make acquaintance with the shade of Cleopatra, that "Thing of Flame," whose passion-breathing beauty shaped the destiny of Empires. Here you shall read how the soul of Charmion was slain of the sword her vengeance smithied.

Here Harmachis, the doomed Egyptian, being about to die, salutes you who follow on the path he trod. In the story of his broken years he shows to you what may in its degree be the story of your own. Crying aloud from that dim Amenti[5] where to-day he wears out his long atoning time, he tells, in the history of his fall, the fate of him who, however sorely tried, forgets his God, his Honour, and his Country.

---

5 The Egyptian Hades or Purgatory.—Editor.

Book 1

The Preparation of Harmachis

CHAPTER 1

Of the Birth of Harmachis

By Osiris who sleeps at Abouthis, I write the truth.

I, Harmachis, Hereditary Priest of the Temple, reared by the divine Sethi, aforetime a Pharaoh of Egypt, and now justified in Osiris and ruling in Amenti. I, Harmachis, by right Divine and by true descent of blood King of the Double Crown, and Pharaoh of the Upper and Lower Land. I, Harmachis, who cast aside the opening flower of our hope, who turned from the glorious path, who forgot the voice of God in hearkening to the voice of woman. I, Harmachis, the fallen, in whom are gathered up all woes as waters are gathered in a desert well, who have tasted of every shame, who through betrayal have betrayed, who in losing the glory that is here have lost the glory which is to be, who am utterly undone—I write, and, by Him who sleeps at Abouthis, I write the truth.

O Egypt!—dear land of Khem, whose black soil nourished up my mortal part—land that I have betrayed—O Osiris!—Isis!—Horus!—ye Gods of Egypt whom I have betrayed!—O ye temples whose pylons strike the sky, whose faith I have betrayed!—O Royal blood of the Pharaohs of old, that yet runs within these withered veins—whose virtue I have betrayed!—O Invisible Essence of all Good! and O Fate, whose balance rested on my hand—hear me; and, to the day of utter doom, bear me witness that I write the truth.

****

Even while I write, beyond the fertile fields, the Nile is running red, as though with blood. Before me the sunlight beats upon the far Arabian hills, and falls upon the piles of Abouthis. Still the priests make orison within the temples at Abouthis that know me no more; still the sacrifice is offered, and the stony roofs echo back the people's prayers. Still from this lone cell within my prison-tower, I, the Word of Shame, watch thy fluttering banners, Abouthis, flaunting from thy pylon walls, and hear the chants as the long procession winds from sanctuary to sanctuary.

Abouthis, lost Abouthis! my heart goes out toward thee! For the day comes when the desert sands shall fill thy secret places! Thy Gods are doomed, O Abouthis! New Faiths shall make a mock of all thy Holies, and Centurion shall call upon Centurion across thy fortress-walls. I weep—I weep tears of blood: for mine is the sin that brought about these evils and mine for ever is their shame.

Behold, it is written hereafter.

****

Here in Abouthis I was born, I, Harmachis, and my father, the justified in Osiris, was High Priest of the Temple of Sethi. And on that same day of my birth Cleopatra, the Queen of Egypt, was born also. I passed my youth in yonder fields watching the baser people at their labours and going in and out at will among the great courts of the temples. Of my mother I knew naught, for she died when I yet hung at the breast. But before she died in the reign of Ptolemy Aulêtes, who is named the Piper, so did the old wife, Atoua, told me, my mother took a golden *uraeus*, the snake symbol of our Royalty of Egypt, from a coffer of ivory and laid it on my brow. And those who saw her do this believed that she was distraught of the Divinity, and in her madness foreshadowed that the day of the Macedonian Lagidae was ended, and that Egypt's sceptre should pass again to the hand of Egypt's true and Royal race. But when my father, the old High Priest Amenemhat, whose only child I was, she who was his wife before my mother having been, for what crime I know not, cursed with barrenness by Sekhet: I say when my father came in and saw what the dying woman had done, he lifted up his hands towards the vault of heaven and adored the Invisible, because of the sign that had been sent. And as he adored, the Hathors[6] filled my dying mother with the Spirit of Prophecy, and she rose in strength from the couch and prostrated herself thrice before the cradle where I lay asleep, the Royal asp upon my brow, crying aloud:

"Hail to thee, fruit of my womb! Hail to thee, Royal child! Hail to thee, Pharaoh that shalt be! Hail to thee, God that shalt purge the land, Divine seed of Nekt-nebf, the descended from Isis. Keep thee pure, and thou shalt rule and deliver Egypt and not be broken. But if thou dost fail in thy hour of trial, then may the curse of all

---

6 The Egyptian *Parcae* or *Fates*.—Editor.

the Gods of Egypt rest upon thee, and the curse of thy Royal forefathers, the justified, who ruled the land before thee from the age of Horus. Then in life mayst thou be wretched, and after death may Osiris refuse thee, and the judges of Amenti give judgment against thee, and Set and Sekhet torment thee, till such time as thy sin is purged, and the Gods of Egypt, called by strange names, are once more worshipped in the Temples of Egypt, and the staff of the Oppressor is broken, and the footsteps of the Foreigner are swept clean, and the thing is accomplished as thou in thy weakness shalt cause it to be done."

When she had spoken thus, the Spirit of Prophecy went out of her, and she fell dead across the cradle where I slept, so that I awoke with a cry.

But my father, Amenemhat, the High Priest, trembled, and was very fearful, both because of the words which had been said by the Spirit of the Hathors through the mouth of my mother, and because what had been uttered was treason against Ptolemy. For he knew that, if the matter should come to the ears of Ptolemy, Pharaoh would send his guards to destroy the life of the child concerning whom such things were prophesied. Therefore, my father shut the doors, and caused all those who stood by to swear upon the holy symbol of his office, and by the name of the Divine Three, and by the Soul of her who lay dead upon the stones beside them, that nothing of what they had seen and heard should pass their lips.

Now among the company was the old wife, Atoua, who had been the nurse of my mother, and loved her well; and in these days, though I know not how it had been in the past, nor how it shall be in the future, there is no oath that can bind a woman's tongue. And so it came about that by-and-by, when the matter had become homely in her mind, and her fear had fallen from her, she spoke of the prophecy to her daughter, who nursed me at the breast now that my mother was dead. She did this as they walked together in the desert carrying food to the husband of the daughter, who was a sculptor, and shaped effigies of the holy Gods in the tombs that are fashioned in the rock—telling the daughter, my nurse, how great must be her care and love toward the child that should one day be Pharaoh, and drive the Ptolemies from Egypt. But the daughter, my nurse, was so filled with wonder at what she heard that she could not keep the tale locked within her breast, and in the night she awoke her husband, and, in her turn, whispered it to him, and thereby compassed her own destruction, and the destruction of her child, my foster-brother. For the man told his friend, and the friend was a spy of Ptolemy's, and thus the tale came to Pharaoh's ears.

Now, Pharaoh was much troubled thereat, for though when he was full of wine he would make a mock of the God of the Egyptians, and swear that the Roman Senate was the only God to whom he bowed the knee, yet in his heart he was terribly afraid, as I have learned from one who was his physician. For when he was alone at night he would scream and cry aloud to the great Serapis, who indeed is no true God, and to other Gods, fearing lest he should be murdered and his soul handed over to the tormentors. Also, when he felt his throne tremble under him, he would send large presents to the temples, asking a message from the oracles, and more especially from the oracle that is at Philae. Therefore, when it came to his ears that the wife of the High Priest of the great and ancient Temple of Abouthis had been filled with the Spirit of Prophecy before she died, and foretold that her son should be Pharaoh, he was much afraid, and summoning some trusty guards—who, being Greeks, did not fear to do sacrilege—he despatched them by boat up the Nile, with orders to come to Abouthis and cut off the head of the child of the High Priest and bring it to him in a basket.

But, as it chanced, the boat in which the guards came was of deep draught, and, the time of their coming being at the lowest ebb of the river, it struck and remained fast upon a bank of mud that is opposite the mouth of the road running across the plains to Abouthis, and, as the north wind was blowing very fiercely, it was like to sink. Thereon the guards of Pharaoh called out to the common people, who laboured at lifting water along the banks of the river, to come with boats and take them off; but, seeing that they were Greeks of Alexandria, the people would not, for the Egyptians do not love the Greeks. Then the guards cried that they were on Pharaoh's business, and still the people would not, asking what was their business. Whereon a eunuch among them who had made himself drunk in his fear, told them that they came to slay the child of Amenemhat, the High Priest, of whom it was prophesied that he should be Pharaoh and sweep the Greeks from Egypt. And then the people feared to stand longer in doubt, but brought boats, not knowing what might be meant by the man's words. But there was one amongst them—a farmer and an overseer of canals—who was a kinsman of my mother's and had been present when she prophesied; and he turned and ran swiftly for three parts of an hour, till he came to where I lay in the house that is without the north wall of the great Temple. Now, as it chanced, my father was away in that part of the Place of Tombs which is to the left of the large fortress, and Pharaoh's guards, mounted on asses, were hard upon us. Then the messenger cried to the old wife, Atoua, whose tongue had brought about the evil, and told how the soldiers drew near to slay me. And they looked at each other, not knowing what to do; for, had they hid me, the guards would not have stayed their search till I was found. But the man, gazing through the doorway, saw a little child at play:

"Woman," he said, "whose is that child?"

"It is my grandchild," she answered, "the foster-brother of the Prince Harmachis; the child to whose mother we owe this evil case."

"Woman," he said, "thou knowest thy duty, do it!" and he again pointed at the child. "I command thee, by the Holy Name!"

Atoua trembled exceedingly, because the child was of her own blood; but, nevertheless, she took the boy and washed him and set a robe of silk upon him, and laid him on my cradle. And me she took and smeared with mud to make my fair skin darker, and, drawing my garment from me, set me to play in the dirt of the yard, which I did right gladly.

Then the man hid himself, and presently the soldiers rode up and asked of the old wife if this were the dwelling of the High Priest Amenemhat? And she told them yea, and, bidding them enter, offered them honey and milk, for they were thirsty.

When they had drunk, the eunuch who was with them asked if that were the son of Amenemhat who lay in the cradle; and she said "Yea—yea," and began to tell the guards how he would be great, for it had been prophesied of him that he should one day rule them all.

But the Greek guards laughed, and one of them, seizing the child, smote off his head with a sword; and the eunuch drew forth the signet of Pharaoh as warrant for the deed and showed it to the old wife, Atoua, bidding her tell the High Priest that his son should be King without a head.

And as they went one of their number saw me playing in the dirt and called out that there was more breeding in yonder brat than in the Prince Harmachis; and for a moment they wavered, thinking to slay me also, but in the end they passed on, bearing the head of my foster-brother, for they loved not to murder little children.

After a while, the mother of the dead child returned from the market-place, and when she found what had been done, she and her husband would have killed Atoua the old wife, her mother, and given me up to the soldiers of Pharaoh. But my father came in also and learned the truth, and he caused the man and his wife to be seized by night and hidden away in the dark places of the temple, so that none saw them more.

But I would to-day that it had been the will of the Gods that I had been slain of the soldiers and not the innocent child.

****

Thereafter it was given out that the High Priest Amenemhat had taken me to be as a son to him in the place of that Harmachis who was slain of Pharaoh.

CHAPTER 2

Of the Disobedience of Harmachis

And after these things Ptolemy the Piper troubled us no more, nor did he again send his soldiers to seek for him of whom it was prophesied that he should be Pharaoh. For the head of the child, my foster-brother, was brought to him by the eunuch as he sat in his palace of marble at Alexandria, flushed with Cyprian wine, and played upon the flute before his women. And at his bidding the eunuch lifted up the head by the hair for him to look on. Then he laughed and smote it on the cheek with his sandal, bidding one of the girls crown Pharaoh with flowers. And he bowed the knee, and mocked the head of the innocent child. But the girl, who was sharp of tongue—for all of this I heard in after years—said to him that "he did well to bow the knee, for this child was indeed Pharaoh, the greatest of Pharaohs, and his name was the *Osiris* and his throne was *Death*."

Aulêtes was much troubled at these words, and trembled, for, being a wicked man, he greatly feared entering into Amenti. So he caused the girl to be slain because of the evil omen of her saying; crying that he would send her to worship that Pharaoh whom she had named. And the other women he sent away, and played no more upon the flute till he was once again drunk on the morrow. But the Alexandrians made a song on the matter, which is still sung about the streets. And this is the beginning of it—

Ptolemy the Piper played
Over dead and dying;
Piped and played he well.
Sure that flute of his was made
Of the dank reed sighing
O'er the streams of Hell.
There beneath the shadows grey,
With the sisters three,

Shall he pipe for many a day.
May the Frog his butler be!
And his wine the water of that countrie
—Ptolemy the Piper!

After this the years passed on, nor did I, being very little, know anything of the great things that came to pass in Egypt; nor is it my purpose to set them out here. For I, Harmachis, having little time left to me, will only speak of those things with which I have been concerned.

And as the time went on, my father and the teachers instructed me in the ancient learning of our people, and in such matters appertaining to the Gods as it is meet that children should know. So I grew strong and comely, for my hair was black as the hair of the divine Nout, and my eyes were blue as the blue lotus, and my skin was like the alabaster within the sanctuaries. For now that these glories have passed from me I may speak of them without shame. I was strong also. There was no youth of my years in Abouthis who could stand against me to wrestle with me, nor could any throw so far with the sling or spear. And I much yearned to hunt the lion; but he whom I called my father forbade me, telling me that my life was of too great worth to be so lightly hazarded. But when I bowed before him and prayed he would make his meaning clear to me, the old man frowned and answered that the Gods made all things clear in their own season. For my part, however, I went away in wroth, for there was a youth in Abouthis who with others had slain a lion which fell upon his father's herds, and, being envious of my strength and beauty, he set it about that I was cowardly at heart, in that when I went out to hunt I only slew jackals and gazelles. Now, this was when I had reached my seventeenth year and was a man grown.

It chanced, therefore, that as I went sore at heart from the presence of the High Priest, I met this youth, who called to me and mocked me, bidding me know the country people had told him that a great lion was down among the rushes by the banks of the canal which runs past the Temple, lying at a distance of thirty stadia from Abouthis. And, still mocking me, he asked me if I would come and help him slay this lion, or would I go and sit among the old women and bid them comb my side lock? This bitter word so angered me that I was near to falling on him; but in place therefore, forgetting my father's saying, I answered that if he would come alone, I would go with him and seek this lion, and he should learn if I were indeed a coward. And at first he would not, for, as men know, it is our custom to hunt the lion in companies; so it was my hour to mock. Then he went and fetched his bow and arrows and a sharp knife. And I brought forth my heavy spear, which had a shaft of thorn-wood, and at its end a pomegranate in silver, to hold the hand from slipping; and, in silence, we went, side by side, to where the lion lay. When we came to the place, it was near sundown; and there, upon the mud of the canal-bank, we found the lion's slot, which ran into a thick clump of reeds.

"Now, thou boaster," I said, "wilt thou lead the way into yonder reeds, or shall I?" And I made as though I would lead the way.

"Nay, nay," he answered, "be not so mad! The brute will spring upon thee and rend thee. See! I will shoot among the reeds. Perchance, if he sleeps, it will arouse him." And he drew his bow at a venture.

How it chanced I know not, but the arrow struck the sleeping lion, and, like a flash of light from the belly of a cloud, he bounded from the shelter of the reeds, and stood before us with bristling mane and yellow eyes, the arrow quivering in his flank. He roared aloud in fury, and the earth shook.

"Shoot with the bow," I cried, "shoot swiftly ere he spring!"

But courage had left the breast of the boaster, his jaw dropped down and his fingers unloosed their hold so that the bow fell from them; then, with a loud cry he turned and fled behind me, leaving the lion in my path. But while I stood waiting my doom, for though I was sore afraid I would not fly, the lion crouched himself, and turning not aside, with one great bound swept over me, touching me not. He lit, and again he bounded full upon the boaster's back, striking him such a blow with his great paw that his head was crushed as an egg thrown against a stone. He fell down dead, and the lion stood and roared over him. Then I was mad with horror, and, scarce knowing what I did, I grasped my spear and with a shout I charged. As I charged the lion lifted himself up above me. He smote at me with his paw; but with all my strength I drove the broad spear into his throat, and, shrinking from the agony of the steel, his blow fell short and did no more than rip my skin. Back he fell, the great spear far in his throat; then rising, he roared in pain and leapt twice the height of a man straight into the air, smiting at the spear with his forepaws. Twice he leapt thus, horrible to see, and twice he fell upon his back. Then his strength spent itself with his rushing blood, and, groaning like a bull, he died; while I, being but a lad, stood and trembled with fear now that all cause of fear had passed.

But as I stood and gazed at the body of him who had taunted me, and at the carcass of the lion, a woman came running towards me, even the same old wife, Atoua, who, though I knew it not as yet, had offered up her flesh and blood that I might be saved alive. For she had been gathering simples, in which she had great skill, by the water's edge, not knowing that there was a lion near (and, indeed, the lions, for the most part, are not found in the tilled land, but rather in the desert and the Libyan mountains), and had seen from a distance that which I have set down. Now, when she was come, she knew me for Harmachis, and, bending herself, she made obeisance to me, and saluted me, calling me Royal, and worthy of all honour, and beloved, and chosen of the Holy Three, ay, and by the name of the Pharaoh! the Deliverer!

But I, thinking that terror had made her sick of mind, asked her of what she would speak.

"Is it a great thing," I asked, "that I should slay a lion? Is it a matter worthy of such talk as thine? There live, and have lived, men who have slain many lions. Did not the Divine Amen-hetep the Osirian slay with his own hand more than a hundred lions? Is it not written on the *scarabaeus* that hangs within my father's chamber, that he slew lions aforetime? And have not others done likewise? Why then, speakest thou thus, O foolish woman?"

All of which I said, because, having now slain the lion, I was minded, after the manner of youth, to hold it as a thing of no account. But she did not cease to make obeisance, and to call me by names that are too high to be written.

"O Royal One," she cried, "wisely did thy mother prophecy. Surely the Holy Spirit, the Knepth, was in her, O thou conceived by a God! See the omen. The lion there—he growls within the Capitol at Rome—and the dead man, he is the Ptolemy—the Macedonian spawn that, like a foreign weed, hath overgrown the land of Nile; with the Macedonian Lagidae thou shalt go to smite the lion of Rome. But the Macedonian cur shall fly, and the Roman lion shall strike him down, and thou shalt strike down the lion, and the land of Khem shall once more be free! free! Keep thyself but pure, according to the commandment of the Gods, O son of the Royal House; O hope of Khemi! be but ware of Woman the Destroyer, and as I have said, so shall it be. I am poor and wretched; yea, stricken with sorrow. I have sinned in speaking of what should be hid, and for my sin I have paid in the coin of that which was born of my womb; willingly have I paid for thee. But I have still of the wisdom of our people, nor do the Gods, in whose eyes all are equal, turn their countenance from the poor; the Divine Mother Isis hath spoken to me—but last night she spake—bidding me come hither to gather herbs, and read to thee the signs that I should see. And as I have said, so it shall come to pass, if thou canst but endure the weight of the great temptation. Come hither, Royal One!" and she led me to the edge of the canal, where the water was deep, and still and blue. "Now gaze upon that face as the water throws it back. Is not that brow fitted to bear the double crown? Do not those gentle eyes mirror the majesty of kings? Hath not the Ptah, the Creator, fashioned that form to fit the Imperial garb, and awe the glance of multitudes looking through thee to God?

"Nay, nay!" she went on in another voice—a shrill old wife's voice—"I will—be not so foolish, boy—the scratch of a lion is a venomous thing, a terrible thing; yea, as bad as the bite of an asp—it must be treated, else it will fester, and all thy days thou shalt dream of lions; ay, and snakes; and, also, it will break out in sores. But I know of it—I know. I am not crazed for nothing. For mark! everything has its balance—in madness is much wisdom, and in wisdom much madness. *La! la! la!* Pharaoh himself can't say where the one begins and the other ends. Now, don't stand gazing there, looking as silly as a cat in a crocus-coloured robe, as they say in Alexandria; but just let me stick these green things on the place, and in six days you'll heal up as white as a three-year-child. Never mind the smart of it, lad. By Him who sleeps at Philae, or at Abouthis, or at Abydus—as our divine masters have it now—or wherever He does sleep, which is a thing we shall all find out before we want to—by Osiris, I say, you'll live to be as clean from scars as a sacrifice to Isis at the new moon, if you'll but let me put it on.

"Is it not so, good folk?"—and she turned to address some people who, while she prophesied, had assembled unseen by me—"I've been speaking a spell over him, just to make a way for the virtue of my medicine—*la! la!* there's nothing like a spell. If you don't believe it, just you come to me next time your wives are barren; it's better than scraping every pillar in the Temple of Osiris, I'll warrant. I'll make 'em bear like a twenty-year-old palm. But then, you see, you must know what to say—that's the point—everything comes to a point at last. *La! la!*"

Now, when I heard all this, I, Harmachis, put my hand to my head, not knowing if I dreamed. But presently looking up, I saw a grey-haired man among those who were gathered together, who watched us sharply, and afterwards I learned that this man was the spy of Ptolemy, the very man, indeed, who had well-nigh caused me to be slain of Pharaoh when I was in my cradle. Then I understood why Atoua spoke so foolishly.

"Thine are strange spells, old wife," the spy said. "Thou didst speak of Pharaoh and the double crown and of the form fashioned by Ptah to bear it; is it not so?"

"Yea, yea—part of the spell, thou fool; and what can one swear by better nowadays than by the Divine Pharaoh the Piper, whom, and whose music, may the Gods preserve to charm this happy land?—what better than by the double crown he wears—grace to great Alexander of Macedonia? By the way, you know about everything: have they got back his *chlamys* yet, which Mithridates took to Cos? Pompey wore it last, didn't he?—in his triumph, too—just fancy Pompey in the cloak of Alexander!—a puppy-dog in a lion's skin! And talking of lions—look what this lad hath done—slain a lion with his own spear; and right glad you village folks should be to see it, for it was a very fierce lion—just see his teeth and his claws—his claws!—they are enough to make a poor silly old woman like me shriek to look at them! And the body there, the dead body—the lion slew it. Alack! he's an Osiris[7] now, the body—and to think of it, but an hour ago he was an everyday mortal like you or me! Well, away with him to the embalmers. He'll soon swell in the sun and burst, and that will save them the trouble of cutting him open. Not that they will spend a talent of silver over him anyway. Seventy days in *natron*—that's all he's likely to get. *La! la!* how my tongue does run, and it's getting dark. Come, aren't you going to take away the body of that poor lad, and the lion, too? There, my boy, you keep those herbs on, and you'll never feel your scratches. I know a thing or two for all I'm crazy, and you, my own grandson! Dear, dear, I'm glad his Holiness the High Priest adopted you when Pharaoh—Osiris bless his holy name—made an end of his son; you look so bonny. I warrant the real Harmachis could not have killed a lion like that. Give me the common blood, I say—it's so lusty."

"You know too much and talk too fast," grumbled the spy, now quite deceived. "Well, he is a brave youth. Here, you men, bear this body back to Abouthis, and some of you stop and help me skin the lion. We'll send the skin to you, young man," he went on; "not that you deserve it: to attack a lion like that was the act of a fool, and a fool deserves what he gets—destruction. Never attack the strong until you are stronger."

But for my part I went home wondering.

7 The soul when it has been absorbed in the Godhead.—Editor.

Chapter 3

Of the Rebuke Of Amenemhat

For a while as I, Harmachis, went, the juice of the green herbs which the old wife, Atoua, had placed upon my wounds caused me much smart, but presently the pain ceased. And, of a truth, I believe that there was virtue in them, for within two days my flesh healed up, so that after a time no marks remained. But I bethought me that I had disobeyed the word of the old High Priest, Amenemhat, who was called my father. For till this day I knew not that he was in truth my father according to the flesh, having been taught that his own son was slain as I have written; and that he had been pleased, with the sanction of the Divine ones, to take me as an adopted son and rear me up, that I might in due season fulfil an office about the Temple. Therefore I was much troubled, for I feared the old man, who was very terrible in his anger, and ever spoke with the cold voice of Wisdom. Nevertheless, I determined to go in to him and confess my fault and bear such punishment as he should be pleased to put upon me. So with the red spear in my hand, and the red wounds on my breast, I passed through the outer court of the great temple and came to the door of the place where the High Priest dwelt. It is a great chamber, sculptured round about with the images of the solemn Gods, and the sunlight comes to it in the daytime by an opening cut through the stones of the massy roof. But at night it was lit by a swinging lamp of bronze. I passed in without noise, for the door was not altogether shut, and, pushing my way through the heavy curtains that were beyond, I stood with a beating heart within the chamber.

The lamp was lit, for the darkness had fallen, and by its light I saw the old man seated in a chair of ivory and ebony at a table of stone on which were spread mystic writings of the words of Life and Death. But he read no more, for he slept, and his long white beard rested upon the table like the beard of a dead man. The soft light from the lamp fell on him, on the papyri and the gold ring upon his hand, where were graven the symbols of the Invisible One, but all around was shadow. It fell on the shaven head, on the white robe, on the cedar staff of priesthood at his side, and on the ivory of the lion-footed chair; it showed the mighty brow of power, the features cut in kingly mould, the white eyebrows, and the dark hollows of the deep-set eyes. I looked and trembled, for there was about him that which was more than the dignity of man. He had lived so long with the Gods, and so long kept company with them and with thoughts divine, he was so deeply versed in all those mysteries which we do but faintly discern, here in this upper air, that even now, before his time, he partook of the nature of the Osiris, and was a thing to shake humanity with fear.

I stood and gazed, and as I stood he opened his dark eyes, but looked not on me, nor turned his head; and yet he saw me and spoke.

"Why hast thou been disobedient to me, my son?" he said. "How came it that thou wentest forth against the lion when I bade thee not?"

"How knowest thou, my father, that I went forth?" I asked in fear.

"How know I? Are there, then, no other ways of knowledge than by the senses? Ah, ignorant child! was not my Spirit with thee when the lion sprang upon thy companion? Did I not pray Those set about thee to protect thee, to make sure thy thrust when thou didst drive the spear into the lion's throat! How came it that thou wentest forth, my son?"

"The boaster taunted me," I answered, "and I went."

"Yes, I know it; and, because of the hot blood of youth, I forgive thee, Harmachis. But now listen to me, and let my words sink into thy heart like the waters of Sihor into the thirsty sand at the rising of Sirius.[8] Listen to me. The boaster was sent to thee as a temptation, he was sent as a trial of thy strength, and see! it has not been equal to the burden. Therefore thy hour is put back. Hadst thou been strong in this matter, the path had been made plain to thee even now. But thou hast failed, and therefore thy hour is put back."

"I understand thee not, my father," I answered.

"What was it, then, my son, that the old wife, Atoua, said to thee down by the bank of the canal?"

Then I told him all that the old wife had said.

"And thou believest, Harmachis, my son?"

"Nay," I answered; "how should I believe such tales? Surely she is mad. All the people know her for mad."

---

8 The dog-star, whose appearance marked the commencement of the overflow of the Nile.—Editor.

Now for the first time he looked towards me, who was standing in the shadow.

"My son! my son!" he cried; "thou art wrong. She is not mad. The woman spoke the truth; she spoke not of herself, but of the voice within her that cannot lie. For this Atoua is a prophetess and holy. Now learn thou the destiny that the Gods of Egypt have given to thee to fulfil, and woe be unto thee if by any weakness thou dost fail therein! Listen: thou art no stranger adopted into my house and the worship of the Temple; thou art my very son, saved to me by this same woman. But, Harmachis, thou art more than this, for in thee and me alone yet flows the Imperial blood of Egypt. Thou and I alone of men alive are descended, without break or flaw, from that Pharaoh Nekt-nebf whom Ochus the Persian drove from Egypt. The Persian came and the Persian went, and after the Persian came the Macedonian, and now for nigh upon three hundred years the Lagidae have usurped the double crown, defiling the land of Khem and corrupting the worship of its Gods. And mark thou this: but now, two weeks since, Ptolemy Neus Dionysus, Ptolemy Aulêtes the Piper, who would have slain thee, is dead; and but now hath the Eunuch Pothinus, that very eunuch who came hither, years ago, to cut thee off, set at naught the will of his master, the dead Aulêtes, and placed the boy Ptolemy upon the throne. And therefore his sister Cleopatra, that fierce and beautiful girl, has fled into Syria; and there, if I err not, she will gather her armies and make war upon her brother Ptolemy: for by her father's will she was left joint-sovereign with him. And, meanwhile, mark thou this, my son: the Roman eagle hangs on high, waiting with ready talons till such time as he may fall upon the fat wether Egypt and rend him. And mark again: the people of Egypt are weary of the foreign yoke, they hate the memory of the Persians, and they are sick at heart of being named 'Men of Macedonia' in the markets of Alexandria. The whole land mutters and murmurs beneath the yoke of the Greek and the shadow of the Roman.

"Have we not been oppressed? Have not our children been butchered and our gains wrung from us to fill the bottomless greed and lust of the Lagidae? Have not the temples been forsaken?—ay, have not the majesties of the Eternal Gods been set at naught by these Grecian babblers, who have dared to meddle with the immortal truths, and name the Most High by another name—by the name of Serapis—confounding the substance of the Invisible? Does not Egypt cry aloud for freedom?—and shall she cry in vain? Nay, nay, for thou, my son, art the appointed way of deliverance. To thee, being sunk in eld, I have decreed my rights. Already thy name is whispered in many a sanctuary, from Abu to Athu; already priests and people swear allegiance, even by the sacred symbols, unto him who shall be declared to them. Still, the time is not yet; thou art too green a sapling to bear the weight of such a storm. But to-day thou wast tried and found wanting.

"He who would serve the Gods, Harmachis, must put aside the failings of the flesh. Taunts must not move him, nor any lusts of man. Thine is a high mission, but this thou must learn. If thou learn it not, thou shalt fail therein; and then, my curse be on thee! and the curse of Egypt, and the curse of Egypt's broken Gods! For know thou this, that even the Gods, who are immortal, may, in the interwoven scheme of things, lean upon the man who is their instrument, as a warrior on his sword. And woe be to the sword that snaps in the hour of battle, for it shall be thrown aside to rust or perchance be melted with fire! Therefore, make thy heart pure and high and strong; for thine is no common lot, and thine no mortal meed. Triumph, Harmachis, and in glory thou shalt go—in glory here and hereafter! Fail, and woe—woe be on thee!"

He paused and bowed his head, and then went on:

"Of these matters thou shalt hear more hereafter. Meanwhile, thou hast much to learn. To-morrow I will give thee letters, and thou shalt journey down the Nile, past white-walled Memphis to Annu. There thou shalt sojourn certain years, and learn more of our ancient wisdom beneath the shadow of those secret pyramids of which thou, too, art the Hereditary High Priest that is to be. And meanwhile, I will sit here and watch, for my hour is not yet, and, by the help of the Gods, spin the web of Death wherein thou shalt catch and hold the wasp of Macedonia.

"Come hither, my son; come hither and kiss me on the brow, for thou art my hope, and all the hope of Egypt. Be but true, soar to the eagle crest of destiny, and thou shalt be glorious here and hereafter. Be false, fail, and I will spit upon thee, and thou shalt be accursed, and thy soul shall remain in bondage till that hour when, in the slow flight of time, the evil shall once more grow to good and Egypt shall again be free."

I drew near, trembling, and kissed him on the brow. "May all these things come upon me, and more," I said, "if I fail thee, my father!"

"Nay!" he cried, "not me, not me; but rather those whose will I do. And now go, my son, and ponder in thy heart, and in thy secret heart digest my words; mark what thou shalt see, and gather up the dew of wisdom, making thee ready for the battle. Fear not for thyself, thou art protected from all ill. No harm may touch thee from without; thyself alone can be thine own enemy. I have said."

Then I went forth with a full heart. The night was very still, and none were stirring in the temple courts. I hurried through them, and reached the entrance to the pylon that is at the outer gate. Then, seeking solitude, and, as it were, to draw near to heaven, I climbed the pylon's two hundred steps, until at length I reached the massive roof. Here I leaned my breast against the parapet, and looked forth. As I looked, the red edge of the full moon floated up over the Arabian hills, and her rays fell upon the pylon where I stood and the temple walls beyond, lighting the visages of the carven Gods. Then the cold light struck the stretch of well-tilled lands, now whitening to the harvest, and as the heavenly lamp of Isis passed up to the sky, her rays crept slowly down to the valley, where Sihor, father of the land of Khem, rolls on toward the sea.

Now the bright beams kissed the water that smiled an answer back, and now mountain and valley, river, temple, town, and plain were flooded with white light, for Mother Isis was arisen, and threw her gleaming robe across the bosom of the earth. It was beautiful, with the beauty of a dream, and solemn as the hour after death. Mightily, indeed, the temples towered up against the face of night. Never had they seemed so grand to me as in that hour—those eternal shrines, before whose walls Time himself shall wither. And it was to be mine to rule this moonlit land; mine to preserve those sacred shrines, and cherish the honour of their Gods; mine to cast out the Ptolemy and free Egypt from the foreign yoke! In my veins ran the blood of those great Kings who await the day of Resurrection, sleeping in the tombs of the valley of Thebes. My spirit swelled within me as I dreamed upon this glorious destiny, I closed my hands, and there, upon the pylon, I prayed as I had never prayed before to the Godhead, who is called by many names, and in many forms made manifest.

"O Amen," I prayed, "God of Gods, who hast been from the beginning; Lord of Truth, who art, and of whom all are, who givest out thy Godhead and gatherest it up again; in the circle of whom the Divine ones move and are, who wast from all time the Self-begot, and who shalt be till time—hearken unto me.[9]

"O Amen—Osiris, the sacrifice by whom we are justified, Lord of the Region of the Winds, Ruler of the Ages, Dweller in the West, the Supreme in Amenti, hearken unto me.

---

9 For a somewhat similar definition of the Godhead see the funeral papyrus of Nesikhonsu, a Princess of the Twenty-first Dynasty.—Editor.

"O Isis, great Mother Goddess, mother of the Horus—mysterious Mother, Sister, Spouse, hearken unto me. If, indeed, I am the chosen of the Gods to carry out the purpose of the Gods, let a sign be given me, even now, to seal my life to the life above. Stretch out your arms towards me, O ye Gods, and uncover the glory of your countenance. Hear! ah, hear me!" And I cast myself upon my knees and lifted up my eyes to heaven.

And as I knelt, a cloud grew upon the face of the moon covering it up, so that the night became dark, and the silence deepened all around—even the dogs far below in the city ceased to howl, while the silence grew and grew till it was heavy as death. I felt my spirit lifted up within me, and my hair rose upon my head. Then of a sudden the mighty pylon seemed to rock beneath my feet, a great wind beat about my brows and a voice spoke within my heart:

"Behold a sign! Possess thyself in patience, O Harmachis!"

And as the voice spoke, a cold hand touched my hand, and left somewhat within it. Then the cloud rolled from the face of the moon, the wind passed, the pylon ceased to tremble, and the night was as the night had been.

As the light came back, I gazed upon that which had been left within my hand. It was a bud of the holy lotus new breaking into bloom, and from it came a most sweet scent.

And while I gazed behold! the lotus passed from my grasp and was gone, leaving me astonished.

CHAPTER 4

Of the Departure of Harmachis

At the dawning of the next day I was awakened by a priest of the temple, who brought word to me to make ready for the journey of which my father had spoken, inasmuch as there was an occasion for me to pass down the river to Annu el Ra. Now this is the Heliopolis of the Greeks, whither I should go in the company of some priests of Ptah at Memphis who had come hither to Abouthis to lay the body of one of their great men in the tomb that had been prepared near the resting place of the blessed Osiris.

So I made ready, and the same evening, having received letters and embraced my father and those about the temple who were dear to me, I passed down the banks of Sihor, and we sailed with the south wind. As the pilot stood upon the prow and with a rod in his hand bade the sailor-men loosen the stakes by which the vessel was moored to the banks, the old wife, Atoua, hobbled up, her basket of simples in her hand, and, calling out farewell, threw a sandal after me for good chance, which sandal I kept for many years.

So we sailed, and for six days passed down the wonderful river, making fast each night at some convenient spot. But when I lost sight of the familiar things that I had seen day by day since I had eyes to see, and found myself alone among strange faces, I felt very sore at heart, and would have wept had I not been ashamed. And of all the wonderful things I saw I will not write here, for, though they were new to me, have they not been known to men since such time as the Gods ruled in Egypt? But the priests who were with me showed me no little honour and expounded to me what were the things I saw.

On the morning of the seventh day we came to Memphis, the city of the White Hall. Here, for three days I rested from my journey and was entertained of the priests of the wonderful Temple of Ptah the Creator, and shown the beauties of the great and marvellous city.

Also I was led in secret by the High Priest and two others into the holy presence of the God Apis, the Ptah who deigns to dwell among men in the form of a bull. The God was black, and on his forehead there was a white square, on his back was a white mark shaped like an eagle, beneath his tongue was the likeness of a *scarabaeus*, in his tail were double hairs, and a plate of pure gold hung between his horns. I entered the place of the God and worshipped, while the High Priest and those with him stood aside, watching earnestly. And when I had worshipped, saying the words which had been told me, the God knelt, and lay down before me. Then the High Priest and those with him, who, as I heard in after time, were great men of Upper Egypt, approached wondering, and, saying no word, made obeisance to me because of the omen. And many other things I saw in Memphis that are too long to write of here.

On the fourth day some priests of Annu came to lead me to Sepa, my uncle, the High Priest of Annu. So, having bidden farewell to those of Memphis, we crossed the river and rode on asses two parts of a day's journey through many villages, which we found in great poverty because of the oppression of the tax-gatherers. Also, as we went, I saw for the first time the great pyramids that are beyond the image of the God Horemkhu, that Sphinx whom the Greeks name Harmachis, and the Temples of the Divine Mother Isis, Queen of the Memnonia, and the God Osiris, Lord of Rosatou, of which temples, together with the Temple of the worship of the Divine Menkau-ra, I, Harmachis, am by right Divine the Hereditary High Priest. I saw them and marvelled at their greatness and the white carven limestone, and red granite of Syene, that flashed the sun's rays back to heaven. But at this time I knew nothing of the treasure that was hid in *Her*, which is the third among the pyramids—would I had never known of it!

And so at last we came within sight of Annu, which after Memphis has been seen is no large town, but stands on raised ground, before which are lakes fed by a canal. Behind the town is the enclosed field of the Temple of the God Ra.

We dismounted at the pylon, and were met beneath the portico by a man not great of stature, but of noble aspect, having his head shaven, and with dark eyes that twinkled like the further stars.

"Hold!" he cried, in a great voice which fitted his weak body but ill. "Hold! I am Sepa, who opens the mouth of the Gods!"

"And I," I said, "am Harmachis, son of Amenemhat, Hereditary High Priest and Ruler of the Holy City Abouthis; and I bear letters to thee, O Sepa!"

"Enter," he said. "Enter!" scanning me all the while with his twinkling eyes. "Enter, my son!" And he took me and led me to a chamber in the inner hall, closed to the door, and then, having glanced at the letters that I brought, of a sudden he fell upon my neck and embraced me.

"Welcome," he cried, "welcome, son of my own sister, and hope of Khem! Not in vain have I prayed the Gods that I might live to look upon thy face and impart to thee the wisdom which perchance I alone have mastered of those who are left alive in Egypt. There are few whom it is lawful that I should teach. But thine is the great destiny, and thine shall be the ears to hear the lessons of the Gods."

And he embraced me once more and bade me go bathe and eat, saying that on the morrow he would speak with me further.

This of a truth he did, and at such length that I will forbear to set down all he said both then and afterwards, for if I did so there would be no papyrus left in Egypt when the task was ended. Therefore, having much to tell and but little time to tell it, I will pass over the events of the years that followed.

For this was the manner of my life. I rose early, I attended the worship of the Temple, and I gave my days to study. I learnt of the rites of religion and their meaning, and of the beginning of the Gods and the beginning of the Upper World. I learnt of the mystery of the movements of the stars, and of how the earth rolls on among them. I was instructed in that ancient knowledge which is called magic, and in the way of interpretation of dreams, and of the drawing nigh to God. I was taught the language of symbols and their outer and inner secrets. I became acquainted with the eternal laws of Good and Evil, and with the mystery of that trust which is held of man; also I learnt the secrets of the pyramids—which I would that I had never known. Further, I read the records of the past, and of the acts and words of the ancient kings who were before me since the rule of Horus upon earth; and I was made to know all craft of state, the lore of earth, and with it the history of Greece and Rome. Also I learnt the Grecian and Roman tongues, of which indeed I already had some knowledge—and all this while, for five long years, I kept my hands clean and my heart pure, and did no evil in the sight of God or man; but laboured heavily to acquire all things, and to prepare myself for the destiny that awaited me.

Twice every year greetings and letters came from my father Amenemhat, and twice every year I sent back my answers asking if the time had come to cease from labour. And so the days of my probation sped away till I grew faint and weary at heart, for being now a man, ay and learned, I longed to make a beginning of the life of men. And often I wondered if this talk and prophecy of the things that were to be was but a dream born of the brains of men whose wish ran before their thought. I was, indeed, of the Royal blood, that I knew: for my uncle, Sepa the Priest, showed me a secret record of the descent, traced without break from father to son, and graven in mystic symbols on a tablet of the stone of Syene. But of what avail was it to be Royal by right when Egypt, my heritage, was a slave—a slave to do the pleasure and minister to the luxury of the Macedonian Lagidae—ay, and when she had been so long a serf that, perchance, she had forgotten how to put off the servile smile of Bondage and once more to look across the world with Freedom's happy eyes?

Then I bethought me of my prayer upon the pylon tower of Abouthis and of the answer given to my prayer, and wondered if that, too, were a dream.

And one night, as, weary with study, I walked within the sacred grove that is in the garden of the temple, and mused thus, I met my uncle Sepa, who also was walking and thinking.

"Hold!" he cried in his great voice; "why is thy face so sad, Harmachis? Has the last problem that we studied overwhelmed thee?"

"Nay, my uncle," I answered, "I am overwhelmed indeed, but not of the problem; it was a light one. My heart is heavy, for I am weary of life within these cloisters, and the piled-up weight of knowledge crushes me. It is of no avail to store up force which cannot be used."

"Ah, thou art impatient, Harmachis," he answered; "it is ever the way of foolish youth. Thou wouldst taste of the battle; thou dost tire of watching the breakers fall upon the beach, thou wouldst plunge into them and venture the desperate hazard of the war. And so thou wouldst be going, Harmachis? The bird would fly the nest as, when they are grown, the swallows fly from the eaves of the Temple. Well, it shall be as thou desirest; the hour is at hand. I have taught thee all that I have learned, and methinks that the pupil has outrun his master," and he paused and wiped his bright black eyes, for he was very sad at the thought of my departure.

"And whither shall I go, my uncle?" I asked rejoicing; "back to Abouthis to be initiated into the mysteries of the Gods?"

"Ay, back to Abouthis, and from Abouthis to Alexandria, and from Alexandria to the Throne of thy fathers, Harmachis! Listen, now; things are thus: Thou knowest how Cleopatra, the Queen, fled into Syria when that false eunuch Pothinus set the will of her father Aulêtes at naught and raised her brother Ptolemy to the sole lordship of Egypt. Thou knowest also how she came back, like a Queen indeed, with a great army in her train, and lay at Pelusium, and how at this juncture the mighty Caesar, that great man, that greatest of all men, sailed with a weak company hither to Alexandria from Pharsalia's bloody field in hot pursuit of Pompey. But he found Pompey already dead, having been basely murdered by Achillas, the General, and Lucius Septimius, the chief of the Roman legions in Egypt, and thou knowest how the Alexandrians were troubled at his coming and would have slain his *lictors*. Then, as thou hast heard, Caesar seized Ptolemy, the young King, and his sister Arsinoë, and bade the army of Cleopatra and the army of Ptolemy, under Achillas, which lay facing each other at Pelusium, disband and go their ways. And for answer Achillas marched on Caesar, and besieged him straitly in the Bruchium at Alexandria, and so, for a while, things were, and none knew who should reign in Egypt. But then Cleopatra took up the dice, and threw them, and this was the throw she made—in truth, it was a bold one. For, leaving the army at Pelusium, she came at dusk to the harbour of Alexandria, and alone with the Sicilian Apollodorus entered and landed. Then Apollodorus bound her in a bale of rich rugs, such as are made in Syria, and sent the rugs as a present to Caesar. And when the rugs were unbound in the palace, behold! within them was the fairest girl on all the earth—ay, and the most witty and the most learned. And she seduced the great Caesar—even his weight of years did not avail to protect him from her charms—so that, as a fruit of his folly, he well-nigh lost his life, and all the glory he had gained in a hundred wars."

"The fool!" I broke in—"the fool! Thou callest him great; but how can the man be truly great who has no strength to stand against a woman's wiles? Caesar, with the world hanging on his word! Caesar, at whose breath forty legions marched and changed the fate of peoples! Caesar the cold! the far-seeing! the hero!—Caesar to fall like a ripe fruit into a false girl's lap! Why, in the issue, of what common clay was this Roman Caesar, and how poor a thing!"

But Sepa looked at me and shook his head. "Be not so rash, Harmachis, and talk not with so proud a voice. Knowest thou not that in every suit of mail there is a joint, and woe to him who wears the harness if the sword should search it out! For Woman, in her weakness, is yet the strongest force upon the earth. She is the helm of all things human; she comes in many shapes and knocks at many doors; she is quick and patient, and her passion is not ungovernable like that of man, but as a gentle steed that she can guide e'en where she will, and as occasion offers can now bit up and now give rein. She has a captain's eye, and stout must be that fortress of the heart in which she finds no place of vantage. Does thy blood beat fast in youth? She will outrun it, nor will her kisses tire. Art thou set toward ambition? She will unlock thy inner heart, and show thee roads that lead to glory. Art thou worn and weary? She has comfort in her breast. Art thou fallen? She can lift thee up, and to the illusion of thy sense gild defeat with triumph. Ay, Harmachis, she can do these things, for Nature ever fights upon her side; and while she does them she can deceive and shape a secret end in which thou hast no part. And thus Woman rules the world. For her are wars; for her men spend their strength in gathering gains; for her they do well and ill, and seek for greatness, to find oblivion. But still she sits like yonder Sphinx, and smiles; and no man has ever read all the riddle of her smile, or known all the mystery of her heart. Mock not! mock not! Harmachis; for he must be great indeed who can defy the power of Woman, which, pressing round him like the invisible air, is often strongest when the senses least discover it."

I laughed aloud. "Thou speakest earnestly, my uncle Sepa," I said; "one might almost think that thou hadst not come unscathed through this fierce fire of temptation. Well, for myself, I fear not woman and her wiles; I know naught of them, and naught do I wish to know; and I still hold that this Caesar was a fool. Had I stood where Caesar stood, to cool its wantonness that bale of rugs should have been rolled down the palace steps, into the harbour mud."

"Nay, cease! cease!" he cried aloud. "It is evil to speak thus; may the Gods avert the omen and preserve to thee this cold strength of which thou boastest. Oh! man, thou knowest not!—thou in thy strength and beauty that is without compare, in the power of thy learning and the sweetness of thy tongue—thou knowest not! The world where thou must mix is not a sanctuary as that of the Divine Isis. But there—it may be so! Pray that thy heart's ice may never melt, so thou shalt be great and happy and Egypt shall be delivered. And now let me take up my tale—thou seest, Harmachis, even in so grave a story woman claims her place. The young Ptolemy, Cleopatra's brother, being loosed of Caesar, treacherously turned on him. Then Caesar and Mithridates stormed the camp of Ptolemy, who took to flight across the river. But his boat was sunk by the fugitives who pressed upon it, and such was the miserable end of Ptolemy.

"Thereon, the war being ended, though she had but then borne him a son, Caesarion, Caesar appointed the younger Ptolemy to rule with Cleopatra, and be her husband in name, and he himself departed for Rome, bearing with him the beautiful Princess Arsinoë to follow his triumph in her chains. But the great Caesar is no more. He died as he had lived, in blood, and right royally. And but now Cleopatra, the Queen, if my tidings may be trusted, has slain Ptolemy, her brother and husband, by poison, and taken the child Caesarion to be her fellow on the throne, which she holds by the help of the Roman legions, and, as they say, of young Sextus Pompeius, who has succeeded Caesar in her love. But, Harmachis, the whole land boils and seethes against her. In every city the children of Khem talk of the deliverer who is to come—and thou art he, Harmachis. The time is almost ripe. The hour is nigh at hand. Go thou back to Abouthis and learn the last secrets of the Gods, and meet those who shall direct the bursting of the storm. Then act, Harmachis—act, I say, and strike home for Khem, rid the land of the Roman and the Greek, and take thy place upon the throne of thy divine fathers and be a King of men. For to this end thou wast born, O Prince!"

Chapter 5
Of the Return of Harmachis to Abouthis

On the next day I embraced my uncle Sepa, and with an eager heart departed from Annu back to Abouthis. To be short, I came thither in safety, having been absent five years and a month, being now no more a boy but a man full grown and having my mind well stocked with the knowledge of men and the ancient wisdom of Egypt. So once again I saw the old lands, and the known faces, though of these some few were wanting, having been gathered to Osiris. Now, as, riding across the fields, I came nigh to the enclosure of the Temple, the priests and people issued forth to bid me welcome, and with them the old wife, Atoua, who, but for a few added wrinkles that Time had cut upon her forehead, was just as she had been when she threw the sandal after me five long years before.

"La! la! la!" she cried; "and there thou art, my bonny lad; more bonny even than thou wert! *La!* what a man! what shoulders! and what a face and form! Ah, it does an old woman credit to have dandled thee! But thou art over-pale; those priests down there at Annu have starved thee, surely? Starve not thyself: the Gods love not a skeleton. 'Empty stomach makes empty head' as they say at Alexandria. But this is a glad hour; ay, a joyous hour. Come in—come in!" and as I lighted down she embraced me.

But I thrust her aside. "My father! where is my father?" I cried; "I see him not!"

"Nay, nay, have no fear," she answered; "his Holiness is well; he waits thee in his chamber. There, pass on. O happy day! O happy Abouthis!"

So I went, or rather ran, and reached the chamber of which I have written, and there at the table sat my father, Amenemhat, the same as he had been, but very old. I came to him and, kneeling before him, kissed his hand, and he blessed me.

"Look up, my son," he said, "let my old eyes gaze upon thy face, that I may read thy heart."

So I lifted up my head, and he looked upon me long and earnestly.

"I read thee," he said at length; "thou art pure and strong in wisdom; I have not been deceived in thee. Oh, the years have been lonely; but I did well to send thee hence. Now, tell me of thy life; for thy letters have told me little, and thou canst not know, my son, how hungry is a father's heart."

And so I told him; we sat far into the night and talked together. And in the end he bade me know that I must now prepare to be initiated into those last mysteries that are learned of the chosen of the Gods.

And so it came about that for a space of three months I prepared myself according to the holy customs. I ate no meat. I was constant in the sanctuaries, in the study of the secrets of the Great Sacrifice and of the woe of the Holy Mother. I watched and prayed before the altars. I lifted up my soul to God; ay, in dreams I communed with the Invisible, till at length earth and earth's desires seemed to pass from me. I longed no more for the glory of this world, my heart hung above it as an eagle on his outstretched wings, and the voice of the world's blame could not stir it, and the vision of its beauty brought no delight. For above me was the vast vault of heaven, where in unalterable procession the stars pass on, drawing after them the destinies of men; where the Holy Ones sit upon their burning thrones, and watch the chariot-wheels of Fate as they roll from sphere to sphere. O hours of holy contemplation! who, having once tasted of your joy could wish again to grovel on the earth? O vile flesh to drag us down! I would that thou hadst then altogether fallen from me, and left my spirit free to seek Osiris!

The months of probation passed but too swiftly, and now the holy day drew near when I was in truth to be united to the universal Mother. Never hath Night so longed for the promise of the Dawn; never hath the heart of a lover so passionately desired the sweet coming of his bride, as I longed to see Thy glorious face, O Isis! Even now that I have been faithless to Thee, and Thou art far from me, O Divine! my soul goes out to Thee, and once more I know—But as it is bidden that I should draw the veil, and speak of things which have not been told since the beginning of this world, let me pass on and reverently set down the history of that holy morn.

For seven days the great festival had been celebrated, the suffering of the Lord Osiris had been commemorated, the grief of the Mother Isis had been sung and glory had been done to the memory of the coming of the Divine Child Horus, the Son, the Avenger, the God-begot. All these things had been carried out according to the ancient rites. The boats had floated on the sacred lake, the priests had scourged themselves before the sanctuaries, and the images had been borne through the streets at night.

And now, as the sun sank on the seventh day, once more the great procession gathered to chant the woes of Isis and tell how the evil was avenged. We went in silence from the temple, and passed through the city ways. First came those who clear the path, then my father Amenemhat in all his priestly robes, and the wand of cedar in his hand. Then, clad in pure linen, I, the neophyte, followed alone; and after me the white-robed priests, holding aloft banners and emblems of the Gods. Next came those who bear the sacred boat, and after them the singers and the mourners; while, stretching as far as the eye could reach, all the people marched, clad in melancholy black because Osiris was no more. We went in silence through the city streets till at length we came to the wall of the temple and passed in. And as my father, the High Priest, entered beneath the gateway of the outer pylon, a sweet-voiced woman singer began to sing the Holy Chant, and thus she sang:

"Sing we Osiris dead, Lament the fallen head:
"The light has left the world, the world is grey.
"Athwart the starry skies
"The web of Darkness flies,
"And Isis weeps Osiris passed away.
"Your tears, ye stars, ye fires, ye rivers, shed,
"Weep, children of the Nile, weep for your Lord is dead!"

She paused in her most sweet song, and the whole multitude took up the melancholy dirge:

"Softly we tread, our measured footsteps falling
"Within the Sanctuary Sevenfold;
"Soft on the Dead that liveth are we calling:
"Return, Osiris, from thy Kingdom cold!
"Return to them that worship thee of old!"

The chorus ceased, and once again she sang:

"Within the court divine
"The Sevenfold sacred shrine
"We pass, while echoes of the
"Temple walls repeat the long lament
"The sound of sorrow sent
"Far up within the imperishable halls,

"Where, each in the other's arms, the Sisters weep,
"Isis and Nephthys, o'er His unawaking sleep."

And then again rolled forth the solemn chorus of a thousand voices:

"Softly we tread, our measured footsteps falling
"Within the Sanctuary Sevenfold;
"Soft on the Dead that liveth are we calling:
"Return, Osiris, from thy Kingdom cold!
"Return to them that worship thee of old!"

It ceased, and sweetly she took up the song:

"O dweller in the West, Lover and Lordliest,
"Thy love, thy Sister Isis, calls thee home!
"Come from thy chamber dun
"Thou Master of the Sun,
"Thy shadowy chamber far below the foam!
"With weary wings and spent
"Through all the firmament,
"Through all the horror-haunted ways of Hell,
"I seek thee near and far,
"From star to wandering star,
"Free with the dead that in Amenti dwell.
"I search the height, the deep, the lands, the skies,
"Rise from the dead and live, our Lord Osiris, rise!"

"Softly we tread, our measured footsteps falling
"Within the Sanctuary Sevenfold;
"Soft on the Dead that liveth are we calling:
"Return, Osiris, from thy Kingdom cold!
"Return to them that worship thee of old!"

Now in a strain more high and glad the singer sang:

"He wakes—from forth the prison
"We sing Osiris risen,
"We sing the child that Nout conceived and bare.
"Thine own love, Isis, waits
"The Warden of the Gates,
"She breathes the breath of Life on breast and hair,
"And in her breast and breath
"Behold! he waketh,
"Behold! at length he riseth out of rest;
"Touched with her holy hands,
"The Lord of all the Lands,

"He stirs, he rises from her breath, her breast!
"But thou, fell Typhon, fly,
"The judgment day drawn nigh,
"Fleet on thy track as flame speeds
"Horus from the sky."

"Softly we tread, our measured footsteps falling
"Within the Sanctuary Sevenfold;
"Soft on the Dead that liveth are we calling:
"Return, Osiris, from thy Kingdom cold!
"Return to them that worship thee of old!"

Once more, as we bowed before the Holy, she sang, and sent the full breath of her glad music ringing up the everlasting walls till the silence quivered with her round notes of melody, and the hearts of those who hearkened stirred strangely in the breast. And thus, as we walked, she sang the song of Osiris risen, the song of Hope, the song ofVictory:

"Sing we the Trinity, Sing we the
"Holy Three, Sing we, and praise we and worship the
"Throne, Throne that our Lord hath set—
"There peace and truth are met
"There in the Halls of the Holy alone!
"There in the shadowings
"Faint of the folded wings,
"There shall we dwell and rejoice in our rest,
"We that thy servants are!
Horus drive ill afar!
"Far in the folds of the dark of the West!"

Again, as her notes died away, thundered forth the chorus of all the voices:

"Softly we tread, our measured footsteps falling
"Within the Sanctuary Sevenfold;
"Soft on the Dead that liveth are we calling:
"Return, Osiris, from thy Kingdom cold!
"Return to them that worship thee of old!"

The chanting ceased, and as the sun sank the High Priest raised the statue of the living God and held it before the multitude that was now gathered in the court of the temple. Then, with a mighty and joyful shout of:

"Osiris our hope! Osiris! Osiris!"

the people tore their black wrappings from their dress, revealing the white robes they wore beneath, and, as one man, they bowed before the God, and the feast was ended.

But for me the ceremony was only begun, for to-night was the night of my initiation. Leaving the inner court I bathed myself, and, clad in pure linen, passed, as it is ordained, into an inner, but not the inmost, sanctuary, and laid the accustomed offerings on the altar. Then, lifting my hands to heaven, I remained for many hours in contemplation, striving, by holy thoughts and prayer, to gather up my strength against the mighty moment of my trial.

The hours sped slowly in the silence of the temple, till at length the door opened and my father Amenemhat, the High Priest, came in, clad in white, and leading by the hand the Priest of Isis. For, having been married, he did not himself enter into the mysteries of the Holy Mother.

I rose to my feet and stood humbly before them.

"Art thou ready?" said the priest, lifting the lamp he held so that its light fell upon my face. "O thou chosen one, art thou ready to see the glory of the Goddess face to face?"

"I am ready," I answered.

"Behold thee," he said again, in solemn tones, "it is no small thing. If thou wilt carry out this thy last desire, understand, royal Harmachis, that now this very night thou must die for a while in the flesh, what time thy soul shall look on spiritual things. And if thou diest and any evil shall be found within thy heart, when thou comest at last into that awful presence, woe unto thee, Harmachis, for the breath of life shall no more enter in at the gateway of thy mouth, thy body shall utterly perish, and what shall befall thy other parts, if I know, I may not say.[10] Art thou prepared to be taken to the breast of Her who Was and Is and Shall Be, and in all things to do Her holy will; for Her, while she shall so command, to put away the thought of earthly woman; and to labour always for Her glory till at the end thy life is gathered to Her eternal life?"

"I am," I answered; "lead on."

"It is well," said the priest. "Noble Amenemhat, we go hence alone."

"Farewell, my son," said my father; "be firm and triumph over things spiritual as thou shalt triumph over things earthly. He who would truly rule the world must first be lifted up above the world.

10 According to the Egyptian religion the being Man is composed of four parts: the body, the double or astral shape (*ka*), the soul (*bi*), and the spark of life sprung from the Godhead (*khou*).—Editor.

He must be at one with God, for thus only shall he learn the secrets of the Divine. But beware! The Gods demand much of those who dare to enter the circle of their Divinity. If they go back therefrom, they shall be judged of a sharper law, and scourged with a heavier rod, for as their glory is, so shall their shame be. Therefore, make thy heart strong, royal Harmachis! And when thou speedest down the ways of Night and enterest the Holies, remember that from him to whom great gifts have been given shall gifts be required again. And now—if, indeed, thy mind be fixed—go whither it is not as yet given me to follow thee. Farewell!"

For a moment as my heart weighed these heavy words, I wavered, as well as I might. But I was filled with longing to be gathered to the company of the Divine ones, and I knew that I had no evil in me, and desired to do only the thing that is just. Therefore, having with so much labour drawn the bowstring to my ear, I was fain to let fly the shaft. "Lead on," I cried with a loud voice; "lead on, thou holy Priest! I follow thee!"

And we went forth.

Chapter 6

Of the Initiation of Harmachis

In silence we passed into the Shrine of Isis. It was dark and bare—only the feeble light from the lamp gleamed faintly upon the sculptured walls, where, in a hundred effigies, the Holy Mother suckled the Holy Child.

The priest closed the doors and bolted them. "Once again," he said, "art thou ready, Harmachis?"

"Once again," I answered, "I am ready."

He spoke no more; but, having lifted up his hands in prayer, led me to the centre of the Holy, and with a swift motion put out the lamp.

"Look before thee, Harmachis!" he cried; and his voice sounded hollow in the solemn place.

I gazed and saw nothing. But from the niche that is high in the wall, where is hid that sacred symbol of the Goddess on which few may look, there came a sound as of the rattling rods of the *sistrum*.[11] And as I listened, awestruck, behold! I saw the outline of the symbol drawn as with fire upon the blackness of the air. It hung above my head, and rattled while it hung. And, as it turned, I clearly saw the face of the Mother Isis that is graven on the one side, and signifies unending Birth, and the face of her holy sister, Nephthys, that is graven on the other, and signifies the ending of all birth in Death.

Slowly it turned and swung as though some mystic dancer trod the air above me, and shook it in her hand. But at length the light went out, and the rattling ceased.

Then of a sudden the end of the chamber became luminous, and in that white light I beheld picture after picture. I saw the ancient Nile rolling through deserts to the sea. There were no men upon its banks, nor any signs of man, nor any temples to the Gods. Only wild

11 A musical instrument peculiarly sacred to Isis of which the shape and rods had a mystic significance.—Editor.

birds moved on Sihor's lonely face, and monstrous brutes plunged and wallowed in his waters. The sun sank in majesty behind the Libyan Desert and stained the waters red; the mountains towered up towards the silent sky; but in mountain, desert, and river there was no sign of human life. Then I knew that I saw the world as it had been before man was, and a terror of its loneliness entered my soul.

The picture passed and another rose up in its place. Once again I saw the banks of Sihor, and on them crowded wild-faced creatures, partaking of the nature of the ape more than of the nature of mankind. They fought and slew each other. The wild birds sprang up in affright as the fire leapt from reed huts given by foemen's hands to flame and pillage. They stole and rent and murdered, dashing out the brains of children with axes of stone. And, though no voice told me, I knew that I saw man as he was tens of thousands of years ago, when first he marched across the earth.

Yet another picture. Again I beheld the banks of Sihor; but on them fair cities bloomed like flowers. In and out their gates went men and women, passing to and fro from wide, well-tilled lands. But I saw no guards or armies, and no weapons of war. All was wisdom, prosperity, and peace. And while I wondered, a glorious Figure, clad in raiment that shone as flame, came from the gates of a shrine, and the sound of music went before and followed after him. He mounted an ivory throne which was set in a market-place facing the water: and as the sun sank called in all the multitudes to prayer. With one voice they prayed, bending in adoration. And I understood that herein was shown the reign of the Gods on earth, which was long before the days of Menes.

A change came over the dream. Still the same fair city, but other men—men with greed and evil on their faces—who hated the bonds of righteous doing, and set their hearts on sin. The evening came; the glorious Figure mounted the throne and called to prayer, but none bowed themselves in adoration.

"We are aweary of thee!" they cried. "Make Evil King! Slay him! slay him! and loose the bonds of Evil! Make Evil King!"

The glorious Shape rose up, gazing with mild eyes upon those wicked men.

"Ye know not what ye ask," he cried; "but as ye will, so be it! For if I die, by me, after much travail, shall ye once again find a path to the Kingdom of Good!"

Even as he spoke, a Form, foul and hideous to behold, leapt upon him, cursing, slew him, tore him limb from limb, and amidst the clamour of the people sat himself upon the throne and ruled. But a Shape whose face was veiled passed down from heaven on shadowy wings, and with lamentations gathered up the rent fragments of the Being. A moment she bent herself upon them, then lifted up her hands and wept. And as she wept, behold! from her side there sprang a warrior armed and with a face like the face of Ra at noon. He, the Avenger, hurled himself with a shout upon the Monster who had usurped the throne, and they closed in battle, and, struggling ever in a strait embrace, passed upward to the skies.

Then came picture after picture. I saw Powers and Peoples clad in various robes and speaking many tongues. I saw them pass and pass in millions—loving, hating, struggling, dying. Some few were happy and some had woe stamped upon their faces; but most bore not the seal of happiness nor of woe, but rather that of patience. And ever as they passed from age to age, high above in the heavens the Avenger fought on with the Evil Thing, while the scale of victory swung now here now there. But neither conquered, nor was it given to me to know how the battle ended.

And I understood that what I had beheld was the holy vision of the struggle between the Good and the Evil Powers. I saw that man was created vile, but Those who are above took pity on him, and came down to him to make him good and happy, for the two things are one thing. But man returned to his wicked way, and then the bright Spirit of Good, who is of us called Osiris, but who has many names, offered himself up for the evil-doing of the race that had dethroned him. And from him and the Divine Mother, of whom all nature is, sprang another spirit who is the Protector of us on earth, as Osiris is our justifier in Amenti.

For this is the mystery of the Osiris.

Of a sudden, as I saw the visions, these things became clear to me. The mummy cloths of symbol and of ceremony that wrap Osiris round fell from him, and I understood the secret of religion, which is Sacrifice.

The pictures passed, and again the priest, my guide, spoke to me.

"Hast thou understood, Harmachis, those things which it has been granted thee to see?"

"I have," I said. "Are the rites ended?"

"Nay, they are but begun. That which follows thou must endure alone! Behold I leave thee, to return at the morning light. Once more I warn thee. That which thou shalt see, few may look upon and live. In all my days I have known but three who dared to face this dread hour, and of those three at dawn but one was found alive. Myself, I have not trod this path. It is too high for me."

"Depart," I said; "my soul is athirst for knowledge. I will dare it."

He laid his hand upon my shoulder and blessed me. He went. I heard the door shut to behind him, the echoes of his footsteps slowly died away.

Then I felt that I was alone, alone in the Holy Place with Things which are not of the earth. Silence fell—silence deep and black as the darkness which was around me. The silence fell, it gathered as the cloud gathered on the face of the moon that night when, a lad, I prayed upon the pylon towers. It gathered denser and yet more dense till it seemed to creep into my heart and call aloud therein; for utter silence has a voice that is more terrible than any cry. I spoke; the echoes of my words came back upon me from the walls and seemed to beat me down. The stillness was lighter to endure than an echo such as this. What was I about to see? Should I die, even now, in the fullness of my youth and strength? Terrible were the warnings that had been given to me. I was fear-stricken, and bethought me that I would fly. Fly!—fly whither? The temple door was barred; I could not fly. I was alone with the Godhead, alone with the Power that I had invoked. Nay, my heart was pure—my heart was pure. I would face the terror that was to come, ay, even though I died.

"Isis, Holy Mother," I prayed. "Isis, Spouse of Heaven, come unto me, be with me now; I faint! be with me now."

And then I knew that things were not as things had been. The air around me began to stir, it rustled as the wings of eagles rustle, it took life. Bright eyes gazed upon me, strange whispers shook my soul. Upon the darkness were bars of light. They changed and interchanged, they moved to and fro and wove mystic symbols which I could not read. Swifter and swifter flew that shuttle of the light: the symbols grouped, gathered, faded, gathered yet again, faster and still more fast, till my eyes could count them no more. Now I was afloat upon a sea of glory; it surged and rolled, as the ocean rolls; it tossed me high, it brought me low. Glory was piled on glory, splendour heaped on splendour's head, and I rode above it all!

Soon the lights began to pale in the rolling sea of air. Great shadows shot across it, lines of darkness pierced it and rushed together on its breast, till, at length, I was only a Shape of Flame set like a star on the bosom of immeasurable night. Bursts of awful music gathered from far away. Miles and miles away I heard them, thrilling faintly through the gloom. On they came, nearer and more near, louder and more loud, till they swept past, above, below, around me, swept on rushing pinions, terrifying and enchanting me. They floated by, ever growing fainter, till they died in space. Then others came, and no two were akin. Some rattled as ten thousand *sistra* shaken all to tune. Some rank from the brazen throats of unnumbered clarions. Some pealed with a loud, sweet chant of voices that were more than human; and some rolled along in the slow thunder of a million drums. They passed; their notes were lost in dying echoes; and the silence once more pressed in upon me and overcame me.

The strength within me began to fail. I felt my life ebbing at its springs. Death drew near to me and his shape was *Silence*. He entered at my heart, entered with a sense of numbing cold, but my brain was still alive, I could yet think. I knew that I was drawing near the confines of the Dead. Nay, I was dying fast, and oh, the horror of it! I strove to pray and could not; there was no more time for prayer. One struggle and the stillness crept into my brain. The terror passed; an unfathomable weight of sleep pressed me down. I was dying, I was dying, and then—nothingness!

I was dead!

A change—life came back to me, but between the new life and the life that had been was a gulf and difference. Once again I stood in the darkness of the shrine, but it blinded me no more. It was clear as the light of day, although it still was black. I stood; and yet it was not I who stood, but rather my spiritual part, for at my feet lay my dead Self. There it lay, rigid and still, a stamp of awful calm sealed upon its face, while I gazed on it.

And as I gazed, filled with wonder, I was caught up on the Wings of Flame and whirled away! away! faster than the lightnings flash. Down I fell, through depths of empty space set here and there with glittering crowns of stars. Down for ten million miles and ten times ten million, till at length I hovered over a place of soft, unchanging light, wherein were Temples, Palaces, and Abodes, such as no man ever saw in the visions of his sleep. They were built of Flame, and they were built of Blackness. Their spires pierced up and up; their great courts stretched around. Even as I hovered they changed continually to the eye; what was Flame became Blackness, what was Blackness became Flame. Here was the flash of crystal, and there the blaze of gems shone even through the glory that rolls around the city which is in the Place of Death. There were trees, and their voice as they rustled was the voice of music; there was air, and, as it blew, its breath was the sobbing notes of song.

Shapes, changing, mysterious, wonderful, rushed up to meet me, and bore me down till I seemed to stand upon another earth.

"Who comes?" cried a great Voice.

"Harmachis," answered the Shapes, that changed continually. "Harmachis who hath been summoned from the earth to look upon the face of Her that Was and Is and Shall Be. Harmachis, Child of Earth!"

"Throw back the Gates and open wide the Doors!" pealed the awful Voice. "Throw back the Gates and open wide the Doors; seal up his lips in silence, lest his voice jar upon the harmonies of Heaven, take away his sight lest he see that which may not be seen, and let Harmachis, who hath been summoned, pass down the path that leads to the place of the Unchanging. Pass on, Child of Earth; but before thou goest, look up that thou mayest learn how far thou art removed from Earth."

I looked up. Beyond the glory that shone about the city was black night, and high on its bosom twinkled one tiny star.

"Behold the world that thou hast left," said the Voice, "behold and tremble."

Then my lips and eyes were sealed with silence and with darkness, so that I was dumb and blind. The Gates rolled back, the Doors swung wide, and I was swept into the city that is in the Place of Death. I was swept swiftly I know not whither, till at length I stood upon my feet. Again the great Voice pealed:

"Draw the veil of blackness from his eyes, unseal the silence on his lips, that Harmachis, Child of Earth, may see, hear, and understand, and make adoration at the Shrine of Her that Was and Is and Shall Be."

And my lips and eyes were touched once more, so that my sight and speech came back.

Behold! I stood within a hall of blackest marble, so lofty that even in the rosy light scarce could my vision reach the great groins of the roof. Music wailed about its spaces, and all adown its length stood winged Spirits fashioned in living fire, and such was the brightness of their forms that I could not look on them. In its centre was an altar, small and square, and I stood before the empty altar. Then again the Voice cried:

"O Thou that hast been, art, and shalt be; Thou who, having many names, art yet without a name; Measurer of Time; Messenger of God; Guardian of the Worlds and the Races that dwell thereon; Universal Mother born of Nothingness; Creatix uncreated; Living Splendour without Form, Living Form without Substance; Servant of the Invisible; Child of Law; Holder of the Scales and Sword of Fate; Vessel of Life, through whom all Life flows, to whom it again is gathered; Recorder of Things Done; Executrix of Decrees—*Hear!*

"Harmachis the Egyptian, who by Thy will hath been summoned from the earth, waits before Thine Altar, with ears unstopped, with eyes unsealed, and with an open heart. Hear and descend! Descend, O Many-shaped! Descend in Flame! Descend in Sound! Descend in Spirit! Hear and descend!"

****

The Voice ceased and there was silence. Then through the silence came a sound like the booming of the sea. It passed and presently, moved thereto by I know not what, I raised my eyes from my hands with which I had covered them, and saw a small dark cloud hanging over the Altar in and out of which a fiery Serpent climbed.

Then all the Spirits clad in light fell upon the marble floor, and with a loud voice adored; but what they said I could not understand. Behold! the dark cloud came down and rested on the Altar, the Serpent of fire stretched itself towards me, touched me on the forehead with its forky tongue and was gone. From within the cloud a Voice sweet and low and clear spoke in heavenly accents:

"Depart, ye Ministers, leave Me with my son whom I have summoned."

Then like arrows rushing from a bow the flame-clad Spirits leapt from the ground and sped away.

"O Harmachis," said the Voice, "be not afraid, I am She whom thou dost know as Isis of the Egyptians; but what else I am strive not thou to learn, it is beyond thy strength. For I am all things, Life is my spirit, and Nature is my raiment. I am the laughter of the babe, I am the maiden's love, I am the mother's kiss. I am the Child and Servant of the Invisible that is God, that is Law, that is Fate—though myself I be not God and Fate and Law. When winds blow and oceans roar upon the face of the Earth thou hearest my voice; when thou gazest on the starry firmament thou seest my countenance; when the spring blooms out in flowers, that is my smile, Harmachis. For I am Nature's self, and all her shapes are shapes of Me. I breathe in all that breathes. I wax and wane in the changeful moon: I grow and gather in the tides: I rise with the suns: I flash with the lightning and thunder in the storms. Nothing is too great for the measure of my majesty, nothing is so small that I cannot find a home therein. I am in thee and thou art in Me, O Harmachis. That which bade thee be bade Me also be. Therefore, though I am great and thou art little, have no fear. For we are bound together by the common bond of life—that life which flows through suns and stars and spaces, through Spirits and the souls of men, welding all Nature to a whole that, changing ever, is yet eternally the same."

I bowed my head—I could not speak, for I was afraid.

"Faithfully hast thou served Me, O my son," went on the low sweet Voice; "greatly thou hast longed to be brought face to face with Me here in Amenti; and greatly hast thou dared to accomplish thy desire. For it is no small thing to cast off the tabernacle of the Flesh and before the appointed time, if only for an hour, put on the raiment of the Spirit. And greatly, O my servant and my son, have I, too, desired to look on thee there where I am. For the Gods love those who love them, but with a wider and deeper love, and under One who is as far from Me as I am from thee, mortal, I am a God of Gods. Therefore I have caused thee to be brought hither, Harmachis; and therefore I speak to thee, my son, and bid thee commune with Me now face to face, as thou didst commune that night upon the temple towers of Abouthis. For I was there with thee, Harmachis, as I was in ten thousand other worlds. It was I, O Harmachis, who laid the lotus in thy hand, giving thee the sign which thou didst seek. For thou art of the kingly blood of my children who served Me from age to age. And if thou dost not fail thou shalt sit upon that kingly throne and restore my ancient worship in its purity, and sweep my temples from their defilements. But if thou dost fail, then shall the eternal Spirit Isis become but a memory in Egypt."

The Voice paused; and, gathering up my strength, at length I spoke aloud:

"Tell me, O Holy," I said, "shall I then fail?"

"Ask Me not," answered the Voice, "that which it is not lawful that I should answer thee. Perchance I can read that which shall befall thee, perchance it doth not please Me so to read. What can it profit the Divine, that hath all time wherein to await the issues, to be eager to look upon the blossom that is not blown, but which, lying a seed in the bosom of the earth, shall blow in its season? Know, Harmachis, that I do not shape the Future; the Future is to thee and not to Me; for it is born of Law and of the rule ordained of the Invisible. Yet thou art free to act therein, and thou shalt win or thou shalt fail according to thy strength and the measure of thy heart's purity. Thine be the burden, Harmachis, as thine in the event shall be the glory or the shame. Little do I reck of the issue, I who am but the Minister of what is written. Now hear me: I will always be with thee, my son, for my love once given can never be taken away, though by sin it may seem lost to thee. Remember then this: if thou dost triumph, thy guerdon shall be great; if thou dost fail, heavy indeed shall be thy punishment both in the flesh and in the land that thou callest Amenti. Yet this for thy comfort: shame and agony shall not be eternal. For however deep the fall from righteousness, if but repentance holds the heart, there is a path—a stony and a cruel path—whereby the height may be climbed again. Let it not be thy lot to follow it, Harmachis!

"And now, because thou hast loved Me, my son, and, wandering through the maze of fable, wherein men lose themselves upon the earth, mistaking the substance for the Spirit, and the Altar for the God, hast yet grasped a clue of Truth the Many-faced; and because I love thee and look on to the day that, perchance, shall come when thou shalt dwell blessed in my light and in the doing of my tasks: because of this, I say, it shall be given to thee, O Harmachis, to hear the Word whereby I may be summoned from the Uttermost, by one who hath communed with Me, and to look upon the face of Isis—even into the eyes of the Messenger, and not die the death.

"Behold!"

The sweet Voice ceased; the dark cloud upon the altar changed and changed—it grew white, it shone, and seemed at length to take the shrouded shape of a woman. Then the golden Snake crept from its heart once more, and, like a living diadem, twined itself about the cloudy brows.

Now suddenly a Voice called aloud the awful Word, then the vapours burst and melted, and with my eyes I saw that Glory, at the very thought of which my spirit faints. But what I saw it is not lawful to utter. For, though I have been bidden to write what I have written of this matter, perchance that a record may remain, thereon I have been warned—ay, even now, after these many years. I saw, and what I saw cannot be imagined; for there are Glories and there are Shapes which are beyond the reach of man's imagination. I saw—then, with the echo of that Word, and the memory of that sight stamped for ever on my heart, my spirit failed me, and I sank down before the Glory.

And, as I fell, it seemed that the great hall burst open and crumbled into flakes of fire round me. Then a great wind blew: there was a sound as the sound of Worlds rushing down the flood of Time—and I knew no more!

CHAPTER 7

Of the Awaking of Harmachis

Once again I woke—to find myself stretched at length upon the stone flooring of the Holy Place of Isis that is at Abouthis. By me stood the old Priest of the Mysteries, and in his hand was a lamp. He bent over me, and gazed earnestly upon my face.

"It is day—the day of thy new birth, and thou hast lived to see it, Harmachis!" he said at length. "I give thanks. Arise, royal Harmachis—nay, tell me naught of that which has befallen thee. Arise, beloved of the Holy Mother. Come forth, thou who hast passed the fire and learned what lies behind the darkness—come forth, O newly-born!"

I rose and, walking faintly, went with him, and, passing out of the darkness of the Shrines filled with thought and wonder, came once more into the pure light of the morning. And then I went to my own chamber and slept; nor did any dreams come to trouble me. But no man—not even my father—asked me aught of what I saw upon that dread night, or after what fashion I had communed with the Goddess.

After these things which have been written, I applied myself for a space to the worship of the Mother Isis, and to the further study of the outward forms of those mysteries to which I now held the key. Moreover, I was instructed in matters politic, for many great men of our following came secretly to see me from all quarters of Egypt, and told me much of the hatred of the people towards Cleopatra, the Queen, and of other things. At last the hour drew nigh; it was three months and ten days from the night when, for a while, I left the flesh, and yet living with our life, was gathered to the breast of Isis, on which it was agreed that with due and customary rites, although in utter secrecy, I should be called to the throne of the Upper and the Lower Land. So it came about that, as the solemn time drew nigh, great men of the party of Egypt gathered to the number of thirty-seven from every *nome*, and each great city of their *nome*, meeting together at Abouthis. They came in every guise—some as priests, some as pilgrims to the Shrine, and some as beggars. Among them was my uncle, Sepa, who, though he clad himself as a travelling doctor, had much ado to keep his loud voice from betraying him. Indeed, I myself knew him by it, meeting him as I walked in thought upon the banks of the canal, although it was then dusk and the great cape, which, after the fashion of such doctors, he had thrown about his head, half hid his face.

"A pest on thee!" he cried, when I greeted him by his name. "Cannot a man cease to be himself for a single hour? Didst thou but know the pains that it has cost me to learn to play this part—and now thou readest who I am even in the dark!"

And then, still talking in his loud voice, he told me how he had travelled hither on foot, the better to escape the spies who ply to and fro upon the river. But he said he should return by the water, or take another guise; for since he had come as a doctor he had been forced to play a doctor's part, knowing but little of the arts of medicine; and, as he greatly feared, there were many between Annu and Abouthis who had suffered from it.[12] And he laughed loudly and embraced me, forgetting his part. For he was too whole at heart to be an actor and other than himself, and would have entered Abouthis with me holding my hand, had I not chid him for his folly.

At length all were gathered.

It was night, and the gates of the temple were shut. None were left within them, except the thirty-seven; my father, the High Priest Amenemhat; that aged priest who had led me to the Shrine of Isis; the old wife, Atoua, who, according to ancient custom, was to prepare me for the anointing; and some five other priests, sworn to secrecy by that oath which none may break. They gathered in the second hall of the great temple; but I remained alone, clad in my white robe, in the passage where are the names of six-and-seventy ancient Kings, who were before the day of the divine Sethi. There I rested in darkness, till at length my father, Amenemhat, came, bearing a lamp, and, bowing low before me, led me by the hand forth into the great hall. Here and there, between its mighty pillars, lights were burning that dimly showed the sculptured images upon the walls, and dimly fell upon the long line of the seven-and-thirty Lords, Priests, and Princes, who, seated upon carven chairs, awaited my coming in silence. Before them, facing away from the seven Sanctuaries, a throne was set, around which stood the priests holding the sacred images and banners. As I

12 In Ancient Egypt an unskilful or negligent physician was liable to very heavy penalties.—Editor.

came into the dim and holy place, the Dignitaries rose, and bowed before me, speaking no word; while my father led me to the steps of the throne, and in a low voice bade me stand before it.

Then he spoke:

"Lords, Priests, and Princes of the ancient orders of the land of Khem—Nobles from the Upper and the Lower Country, have gathered in answer to my summons, hear me: I present to you, with such scant formality as the occasion can afford, the Prince Harmachis, by right and true descent of blood the descendant and heir of the ancient Pharaohs of our most unhappy land. He is priest of the inmost circle of the Mysteries of the Divine Isis, Master of the Mysteries—Hereditary Priest of the Pyramids, which are by Memphis, Instructed in the Solemn Rites of the Holy Osiris. Is there any among you who has aught to urge against the true line of his blood?"

He paused, and my uncle Sepa, rising from his chair, spoke: "We have made examination of the records and there is none, O Amenemhat. He is of the Royal blood, his descent is true."

"Is there any among you," went on my father, "who can deny that this royal Harmachis, by sanction of the very Gods, has been gathered to Isis, been shown the way of the Osiris, been admitted to be the Hereditary High Priest of the Pyramids which are by Memphis, and of the Temples of the Pyramids?"

Then that old priest rose who had been my guide in the Sanctuary of the Mother and made answer: "There is none; O Amenemhat; I know these things of my own knowledge."

Once more my father spoke: "Is there any among you who has aught to urge against this royal Harmachis, in that by wickedness of heart or life, by uncleanliness or falsity, it is not fit or meet that we should crown him Lord of all the Lands?"

Then an aged Prince of Memphis arose and made answer:

"We have inquired of these matters: there is none, O Amenemhat."

"It is well," said my father; "then naught is wanting in the Prince Harmachis, seed of Nekt-nebf, the Osirian. Let the woman Atoua stand forth and tell this company those things that came to pass when, at the hour of her death, she who was my wife prophesied over this Prince, being filled with the Spirit of the Hathors."

Thereon old Atoua crept forward from the shadow of the columns, and earnestly told those things that have been written.

"Ye have heard," said my father: "do you believe that the woman who was my wife spake with the Divine voice?"

"We do," they answered.

Now my uncle Sepa rose and spoke:

"Royal Harmachis, thou hast heard. Know now that we are gathered here to crown thee King of the Upper and the Lower Lands—thy holy father, Amenemhat, renouncing all his right on thy behalf. We are met, not, indeed, in that pomp and ceremony which is due to the occasion—for what we do must be done in secret, lest our lives, and the cause that is more dear to us than life, should pay the forfeit—but yet with such dignity and observance of the ancient rites as our circumstance may command. Learn, now, how this matter hangs, and if, after learning, thy mind consents thereto, then mount thy throne, O Pharaoh—and swear the oath!

"Long has Khemi groaned beneath the mailed heel of the Greek, and trembled at the shadow of the Roman's spear; long has the ancient worship of its Gods been desecrated, and its people crushed with oppression. But we believe that the hour of deliverance is at hand, and with the solemn voice of Egypt and by the ancient Gods of Egypt, to whose cause thou art of all men bound, we call upon thee, Prince, to be the sword of our deliverance. Hearken! Twenty thousand good and leal men are sworn to wait upon thy word, and at thy signal to rise as one, to put the Grecian to the sword, and with their blood and substance to build thee a throne set more surely on the soil of Khem than are its ancient pyramids—such a throne as shall even roll the Roman legions back. And for the signal, it shall be the death of that bold harlot, Cleopatra. Thou must compass her death, Harmachis, in such fashion as shall be shown to thee, and with her blood anoint the Royal throne of Egypt.

"Canst thou refuse, O our Hope? Doth not the holy love of country swell within thy heart? Canst thou dash the cup of Freedom from thy lips and bear to drink the bitter draught of slaves? The emprise is great; maybe it shall fail, and thou with thy life, as we with ours, shalt pay the price of our endeavour. But what of it, Harmachis? Is life, then, so sweet? Are we so softly cushioned on the stony bed of earth? Is bitterness and sorrow in its sum so small and scant a thing? Do we here breathe so divine an air that we should fear to face the passage of our breath? What have we here but hope and memory? What see we here but shadows? Shall we then fear to pass pure-handed where Fulfilment is and memory is lost in its own source, and shadows die in the light which cast them? O Harmachis, that man alone is truly blest who crowns his life with Fame's most splendid wreath. For, since to all the Brood of Earth Death hands his poppy-flowers, he indeed is happy to whom there is occasion given to weave them in a crown of glory. And how can a man die better than in a great endeavour to strike the gyves from his Country's limbs so that she again may stand in the face of Heaven and raise the shrill shout of Freedom, and, clad once more in a panoply of strength, trample under foot the fetters of her servitude, defying the tyrant nations of the earth to set their seal upon her brow?

"Khem calls thee, Harmachis. Come then, thou Deliverer; leap like Horus from the firmament, break her chains, scatter her foes, and rule a Pharaoh on Pharaoh's Throne—"

"Enough, enough!" I cried, while the long murmur of applause swept about the columns and up the massy walls. "Enough; is there any need to adjure me thus? Had I a hundred lives, would I not most gladly lay them down for Egypt?"

"Well said, well said!" answered Sepa. "Now go forth with the woman yonder, that she may make thy hands clean before they touch the sacred emblems, and anoint thy brow before it is encircled of the diadem."

And so I went into a chamber apart with the old wife, Atoua. There, muttering prayers, she poured pure water over my hands into a ewer of gold, and having dipped a fine cloth into oil wiped my brow with it.

"O happy Egypt!" she said; "O happy Prince, that art come to rule in Egypt! O Royal youth!—too Royal to be a priest—so shall many a fair woman think; but, perchance, for thee they will relax the priestly rule, else how shall the race of Pharaoh be carried on? O happy I, who dandled thee and gave my flesh and blood to save thee! O royal and beautiful Harmachis, born for splendour, happiness, and love!"

"Cease, cease," I said, for her talk jarred upon me; "call me not happy till thou knowest my end, and speak not to me of love, for with love comes sorrow, and mine is another and a higher way."

"Ay, ay, so thou sayest—and joy, too, that comes with love! Never talk lightly of love, my King, for it brought thee here! *La! la!* but it is always the way—'The goose on the wing laughs at crocodiles,' so goes their saying down at Alexandria; 'but when the goose is asleep on the water, it is the crocodiles that laugh.' Not but what women are pretty crocodiles. Men worship the crocodiles at Anthribis—Crocodilopolis they call it now, don't they?—but they worship women all the world over! *La!* how my tongue runs on, and thou about to be crowned Pharaoh! Did I not prophesy it to thee? Well, thou art clean, Lord of the Double Crown. Go forth!"

So I went from the chamber with the old wife's foolish talk ringing in my ears, though of a truth her folly had ever a grain of wit in it.

As I came, the Dignitaries rose once more and bowed before me. Then my father, without delay, drew near me, and placed in my hands a golden image of the divine Ma, the Goddess of Truth, and golden images of the arks of the God Amen-Ra, of the divine Mout, and the divine Khons, and spoke solemnly:

"Thou swearest by the living majesty of Ma, by the majesty of Amen-Ra, of Mout, and of Khons?"

"I swear," I said.

"Thou swearest by the holy land of Khem, by Sihor's flood, by the Temples of the Gods and the eternal Pyramids?"

"I swear."

"Remembering thy hideous doom if thou shouldst fail therein, thou swearest that thou wilt in all things govern Egypt according to its ancient laws, that thou wilt preserve the worship of its Gods, that thou wilt do equal justice, that thou wilt not oppress, that thou wilt not betray, that thou wilt make no alliance with the Roman or the Greek, that thou wilt cast out the foreign Idols, that thou wilt devote thy life to the liberty of the land of Khem?"

"I swear."

"It is well. Mount, then, the throne, that in the presence of these thy subjects, I may name thee Pharaoh."

I mounted upon the throne, of which the footstool is a Sphinx, and the canopy the overshadowing wings of Ma. Then Amenemhat drew nigh once again and placed the *Pshent* upon my brow, and on my head the Double Crown, and the Royal Robe about my shoulders, and in my hands the Sceptre and the Scourge.

"Royal Harmachis," he cried, "by these outward signs and tokens, I, the High Priest of the Temple of Ra-Men-Ma at Abouthis, crown thee Pharaoh of the Upper and Lower Land. Reign and prosper, O Hope of Khemi!"

"Reign and prosper, Pharaoh!" echoed the Dignitaries, bowing down before me.

Then, one by one, they swore allegiance, till all had sworn. And, having sworn, my father took me by the hand; he led me in solemn procession into each of the seven Sanctuaries that are in this Temple of Ra-Men-Ma, and in each I made offerings, swung incense, and officiated as priest. Clad in the Royal robes I made offerings in the Shrine of Horus, in the Shrine of Isis, in the Shrine of Osiris, in the Shrine of Amen-Ra, in the Shrine of Horemku, in the Shrine of Ptah, till at length I reached the Shrine of the King's Chamber.

Here they made their offering to me, as the Divine Pharaoh, and left me very weary—but a King.

(Here the first and smallest of the papyrus rolls comes to an end.)

Book 2

The Fall of Harmachis

Chapter 1

Of the Farewell of Amenemhat to Harmachis

Now the long days of preparation had passed, and the time was at hand. I was initiated, and I was crowned; so that although the common folk knew me not, or knew me only as Priest of Isis, there were in Egypt thousands who at heart bowed down to me as Pharaoh. The hour was at hand, and my soul went forth to meet it. For I longed to overthrow the foreigner, to set Egypt free, to mount the throne that was my heritage, and cleanse the temples of my Gods. I was fain for the struggle, and I never doubted of its end. I looked into the mirror, and saw triumph written on my brows. The future stretched a path of glory from my feet—ay, glittering with glory like Sihor in the sun. I communed with my Mother Isis; I sat within my chamber and took counsel with my heart; I planned new temples; I revolved great laws that I would put forth for my people's weal; and in my ears rang the shouts of exultation which should greet victorious Pharaoh on his throne.

But still I tarried a little while at Abouthis, and, having been commanded to do so, let my hair, that had been shorn, grow again long and black as the raven's wing, instructing myself meanwhile in all manly exercises and feats of arms. Also, for a purpose which shall be seen, I perfected myself in the magic art of the Egyptians, and in the reading of the stars, in which things, indeed, I already have great skill.

Now, this was the plan that had been built up. My uncle Sepa had, for a while, left the Temple of Annu, giving out that his health had failed him. Thence he had moved down to a house in Alexandria, to gather strength, as he said, from the breath of the sea, and also to learn for himself the wonders of the great Museum and the glory of Cleopatra's Court. There it was planned that I should join him, for there, at Alexandria, the egg of the plot was hatching. Accordingly, when at last the summons came, all things being prepared, I made ready for the journey, and passed into my father's chamber to receive his blessing before I went. There sat the old man, as once before he sat when he had rebuked me because I went out to slay the lion, his long white beard resting on the table of stone and sacred writings in his hand. When I came in he rose from his seat and would have knelt before me, crying "Hail, Pharaoh!" but I caught him by the hand.

"It is not meet, my father," I said.

"It is meet," he answered, "it is meet that I should bow before my King; but be it as thou wilt. And so thou goest, Harmachis; my blessings go with thee, O my son! And may Those whom I serve grant to me that my old eyes may, indeed, behold thee on the throne! I have searched long, striving, Harmachis, to read the future that shall be; but I can learn naught by all my wisdom. It is hid from me, and at times my heart fails. But hear this, there is danger in thy path, and it comes in the form of Woman. I have known it long, and therefore thou hast been called to the worship of the heavenly Isis, who bids her votaries put away the thought of woman till such time as she shall think well to slacken the rule. Oh, my son, I would that thou wert not so strong and fair—stronger and fairer, indeed, than any man in Egypt, as a King should be—for in that strength and beauty may lie a cause of stumbling. Beware, then, of those witches of Alexandria, lest, like a worm, some one of them creep into my heart and eat its secret out."

"Have no fear, my father," I answered, frowning, "my thought is set on other things than red lips and smiling eyes."

"It is good," he answered; "so may it befall. And now farewell. When next we meet, may it be in that happy hour when, with all the priests of the Upper Land, I move down from Abouthis to do my homage to Pharaoh on his throne."

So I embraced him, and went. Alas! I little thought how we should meet again.

****

Thus it came about that once more I passed down the Nile travelling as a man of no estate. And to such as were curious about me it was given out that I was the adopted son of the High Priest of Abouthis, having been brought up to the priesthood, and that I had at the last refused the service of the Gods, and chosen to go to Alexandria, to seek my fortune. For, be it remembered, I was still held to be the grandson of the old wife, Atoua, by all those who did not know the truth.

On the tenth night, sailing with the wind, we reached the mighty city of Alexandria, the city of a thousand lights. Above them all towered the white Pharos, that wonder of the world, from the crown of which a light like the light of the sun blazed out across the waters of the harbour to guide mariners on their way across the sea. The vessel having been cautiously made fast to the quay, for it was night, I disembarked and stood wondering at the vast mass of houses, and confused by the clamour of many tongues. For here all peoples seemed to be gathered together, each speaking after the fashion of his own land. And as I stood a young man came and touched me on the shoulder, asking me if I was from Abouthis and named Harmachis. I said "Yea." Then, bending over me, he whispered the secret pass-word into my ear, and, beckoning to two slaves, bade them bring my baggage from the ship. This they did, fighting their way through the crowd of porters who were clamouring for hire. Then I followed him down the quay, which was bordered with drinking-places, where all sorts of men were gathered, tippling wine and watching the dancing of women, some of whom were but scantily arrayed, and some not arrayed at all.

And so we went through the lamp-lit houses till at last we reached the shore of the great harbour, and turned to the right along a wide way paved with granite and bordered by strong houses, having cloisters in front of them, the like of which I had never seen. Turning once more to the right we came to a quieter portion of the city, where, except for parties of strolling revellers, the streets were still. Presently my guide halted at a house built of white stone. We passed in, and, crossing a small courtyard, entered a chamber where there was a light. And here, at last, I found my uncle Sepa, most glad to see me safe.

When I had washed and eaten, he told me that all things went well, and that as yet there was no thought of evil at the Court. Further, he said, it having come to the ears of the Queen that the Priest of Annu was sojourning at Alexandria, she sent for him and closely questioned him—not as to any plot, for of that she never thought, but as to the rumour which had reached her, that there was treasure hid in the Great Pyramid which is by Annu. For, being ever wasteful, she was ever in want of money, and had bethought her of opening the Pyramid. But he laughed at her, telling her the Pyramid was the burying-place of the divine Khufu, and that he knew nothing of its secrets. Then she was angered, and swore that so surely as she ruled in Egypt she would tear it down, stone by stone, and discover the secret at its heart. Again he laughed, and, in the words of the proverb which they have at Alexandria, told her that "Mountains live longer than Kings." Thereon she smiled at his ready answer, and let him go. Also my uncle Sepa told me that on the morrow I should see this Cleopatra. For it was her birthday (as, indeed, it was also mine), and, dressed in the robes of the Holy Isis, she would pass in state from her palace on the Lochias to the Serapeum to offer a sacrifice at the Shrine of the false God who sits in the Temple. And he said that thereafter the fashion by which I should gain entrance to the household of the Queen should be contrived.

Then, being very weary, I went to rest, but could sleep little for the strangeness of the place, the noises in the streets, and the thought of the morrow. While it was yet dark, I rose, climbed the stair to the roof of the house, and waited. Presently, the sun's rays shot out like arrows, and lit upon the white wonder of the marble Pharos, whose light instantly sank and died, as though, indeed, the sun had killed it. Now the rays fell upon the palaces of the Lochias where Cleopatra lay, and lit them up till they flamed like a jewel set on the dark, cool bosom of the sea. Away the light flew, kissing the Soma's sacred dome, beneath which Alexander sleeps, touching the high tops of a thousand palaces and temples; past the porticoes of the great museum that loomed near at hand, striking the lofty Shrine, where, carved of ivory, is the image of the false God Serapis, and at last seeming to lose itself in the vast and gloomy Necropolis. Then, as the dawn gathered into day, the flood of brightness, over brimming the bowl of night, flowed into the lower lands and streets, and showed Alexandria red in the sunrise as the mantle of a king, and shaped as a mantle. The Etesian wind came up from the north, and swept away the vapour from the harbours, so that I saw their blue waters rocking a thousand ships. I saw, too, that mighty mole the Heptastadium; I saw the hundreds of streets, the countless houses, the innumerable wealth and splendour of Alexandria set like a queen between lake Mareotis and the ocean, and dominating both, and I was filled with wonder. This, then, was one city in my heritage of lands and cities! Well, it was worth the grasping. And having looked my full and fed my heart, as it were, with the sight of splendour, I communed with the Holy Isis and came down from the roof.

In the chamber beneath was my uncle Sepa. I told him that I had been watching the sun rise over the city of Alexandria.

"So!" he said, looking at me from beneath his shaggy eyebrows; "and what thinkest thou of Alexandria?"

"I think it is like some city of the Gods," I answered.

"Ay!" he replied fiercely, "a city of the infernal Gods—a sink of corruption, a bubbling well of iniquity, a home of false faith springing from false hearts. I would that not one stone of it was left upon another stone, and that its wealth lay deep beneath yonder waters! I would that the gulls were screaming across its site, and that the wind, untainted by a Grecian breath, swept through its ruins from the ocean to Mareotis! O royal Harmachis, let not the luxury and beauty of Alexandria poison thy sense; for in their deadly air, Faith perishes, and Religion cannot spread her heavenly wings. When the hour comes for thee to rule, Harmachis, cast down this accursed city and, as thy fathers did, set up thy throne in the white walls of Memphis. For I tell thee that, for Egypt, Alexandria is but a splendid gate of ruin, and, while it endures, all nations of the earth shall march through it, to the plunder of the land, and all false Faiths shall nestle in it and breed the overthrow of Egypt's Gods."

I made no answer, for there was truth in his words. And yet to me the city seemed very fair to look on. After we had eaten, my uncle told me it was now time to set out to view the march of Cleopatra, as she went in triumph to the Shrine of Serapis. For although she would not pass till within two hours of the midday, yet these people of Alexandria have so great a love of shows and idling that had we not presently set forth, by no means could we have come through the press of the multitudes who were already gathering along the highways where the Queen must ride. So we went out to take our places upon a stand, built of timber, that had been set up at the side of the great road which pierces through the city, to the Canopic Gate. For my uncle had already purchased a right to enter there, and that dearly.

We won our way with much struggle through the great crowds that were already gathered in the streets till we reached the scaffolding of timber, which was roofed in with an awning and gaily hung with scarlet cloths. Here we seated ourselves upon a bench and waited for some hours, watching the multitude press past shouting, singing, and talking loudly in many tongues. At length soldiers came to clear the road, clad, after the Roman fashion, in breast-plates of chain-armour. After them marched heralds enjoining silence (at which the population sung and shouted all the more loudly), and crying that Cleopatra, the Queen, was coming. Then followed a thousand Cilician skirmishers, a thousand Thracians, a thousand Macedonians, and a thousand Gauls, each armed after the fashion of their country. Then passed five hundred men of those who are called the Fenced Horsemen, for both men and horses were altogether covered with mail. Next came youths and maidens sumptuously draped and wearing golden crowns, and with them images symbolising Day and Night, Morning and Noon, the Heavens and the Earth. After these walked many fair women, pouring perfumes on the road, and others scattering blooming flowers. Now there rose a great shout of "Cleopatra! Cleopatra!" and I held my breath and bent forward to see her who dared to put on the robes of Isis.

But at that moment the multitude so gathered and thickened in front of where I was that I could no longer clearly see. So in my eagerness I leapt over the barrier of the scaffolding, and, being very strong, pushed my way through the crowd till I reached the foremost rank. And as I did so, Nubian slaves armed with thick staves and crowned with ivy-leaves ran up, striking the people. One man I noted more especially, for he was a giant, and, being strong, was insolent beyond measure, smiting the people without cause, as, indeed, is the wont of low persons set in authority. For a woman stood near to me, an Egyptian by her face, bearing a child in her arms, whom the man, seeing that she was weak, struck on the head with his rod so that she fell prone, and the people murmured. But at the sight my blood rushed of a sudden through my veins and drowned my reason. I held in my hand a staff of olive-wood from Cyprus, and as the black brute laughed at the sight of the stricken woman and her babe rolling on the ground, I swung the staff aloft and smote. So shrewdly did I strike, that the tough rod split upon the giant's shoulders and the blood spurted forth, staining his trailing leaves of ivy.

Then, with a shriek of pain and fury—for those who smite love not that they be smitten—he turned and sprang at me! And all the people round gave back, save only the woman who could not rise, leaving us two in a ring as it were. On he came with a rush, and, as he came, being now mad, I smote him with my clenched fist between the eyes, having nothing else with which to smite, and he staggered like an ox beneath the first blow of the priest's axe. Then the people shouted, for they love to see a fight, and the man was known to them as a gladiator victorious in the games. Gathering up his strength, the knave came on with an oath, and, whirling his heavy staff on high, struck me in such a fashion that, had I not avoided the blow by nimbleness, I had surely been slain. But, as it chanced, the staff hit upon the ground, and so heavily that it flew in fragments. Thereon the multitude shouted again, and the great man, blind with fury, rushed at me to smite me down. But with a cry I sprang straight at his throat—for he was so heavy a man that I knew I could not hope to throw him by strength—ay, and gripped it. There I clung, though his fists battered me like bludgeons, driving my thumbs into his throat. Round and round we turned, till at length he flung himself to the earth, trusting thus to shake me off.

But I held on fast as we rolled over and over on the ground, till at last he grew faint for want of breath. Then I, being uppermost, drove my knee down upon his chest, and, as I believe, should thus have slain him in my rage had not my uncle, and others there gathered, fallen upon me and dragged me from him.

And meanwhile, though I know it not, the chariot in which the Queen sat, with elephants going before and lions led after it, had reached the spot, and had been halted because of the tumult. I looked up, and thus torn, panting, my white garments stained with the blood that had rushed from the mouth and nostrils of the mighty Nubian, I for the first time saw Cleopatra face to face. Her chariot was all of gold, and drawn by milk-white steeds. She sat in it with two fair girls, clad in Greek attire, standing one on either side, fanning her with glittering fans. On her head was the covering of Isis, the golden horns between which rested the moon's round disk and the emblem of Osiris' throne, with the *uraeus* twined around. Beneath this covering was the vulture cap of gold, the blue enamelled wings and the vulture head with gemmy eyes, under which her long dark tresses flowed towards her feet. About her rounded neck was a broad collar of gold studded with emeralds and coral. Round her arms and wrists were bracelets of gold studded with emeralds and coral, and in one hand she held the holy cross of Life fashioned of crystal, and in the other the golden rod of royalty. Her breast was bare, but under it was a garment that glistened like the scaly covering of a snake, everywhere sewn with gems. Beneath this robe was a skirt of golden cloth, half hidden by a scarf of the broidered silk of Cos, falling in folds to the sandals that, fastened with great pearls, adorned her white and tiny feet.

All this I discerned at a glance, as it were. Then I looked upon the face—that face which seduced Caesar, ruined Egypt, and was doomed to give Octavian the sceptre of the world. I looked upon the flawless Grecian features, the rounded chin, the full, rich lips, the chiselled nostrils, and the ears fashioned like delicate shells. I saw the forehead, low, broad, and lovely, the crisped, dark hair falling in heavy waves that sparkled in the sun, the arched eyebrows, and the long, bent lashes. There before me was the grandeur of her Imperial shape. There burnt the wonderful eyes, hued like the Cyprian violet—eyes that seemed to sleep and brood on secret things as night broods upon the desert, and yet as the night to shift, change, and be illumined by gleams of sudden splendour born within their starry depths. All those wonders I saw, though I have small skill in telling them. But even then I knew that it was not in these charms alone that the might of Cleopatra's beauty lay. It was rather in a glory and a radiance cast through the fleshly covering from the fierce soul within. For she was a Thing of Flame like unto which no woman has ever been or ever will be. Even when she brooded, the fire of her quick heart shone through her. But when she woke, and the lightning leapt suddenly from her eyes, and the passion-laden music of her speech chimed upon her lips, ah! then, who can tell how Cleopatra seemed? For in her met all the splendours that have been given to woman for her glory, and all the genius which man has won from heaven. And with them dwelt every evil of that greater sort, which fearing nothing, and making a mock of laws, has taken empires for its place of play, and, smiling, watered the growth of its desires with the rich blood of men. In her breast they gathered, together fashioning that Cleopatra whom no man may draw, and yet whom no man, having seen, ever can forget. They fashioned her grand as the Spirit of Storm, lovely as Lightning, cruel as Pestilence, yet with a heart; and what she did is known. Woe to the world when such another comes to curse it!

For a moment I met Cleopatra's eyes as she idly bent herself to find the tumult's cause. At first they were sombre and dark, as though they saw indeed, but the brain read nothing. Then they awoke, and their very colour seemed to change as the colour of the sea changes when the water is shaken. First, there was anger written in them; next an idle noting; then, when she looked upon the huge bulk of the man whom I had overcome, and knew him for the gladiator, something, perchance, that was not far from wonder. At the least they softened, though, indeed, her face changed no whit. But he who would read Cleopatra's mind had need to watch her eyes, for her countenance varied but a little. Turning, she said some word to her guards. They came forward and led me to her, while all the multitude waited silently to see me slain.

I stood before her, my arms folded on my breast. Overcome though I was by the wonder of her loveliness I hated her in my heart, this woman who dared to clothe herself in the dress of Isis, this usurper who sat upon my throne, this wanton squandering the wealth of Egypt in chariots and perfumes. When she had looked me over from head to the feet, she spake in a low full voice and in the tongue of Khemi which she alone had learned of all the Lagidae:

"And who and what art thou, Egyptian—for Egyptian I see thou art—who darest to smite my slave when I make progress through my city?"

"I am Harmachis," I answered boldly. "Harmachis, the astrologer, adopted son of the High Priest and Governor of Abouthis, who am come hither to seek my fortune. I smote thy slave, O Queen, because for no fault he struck down the woman yonder. Ask of those who saw, royal Egypt."

"Harmachis," she said, "the name has a high sound—and thou hast a high look;" and then, speaking to a soldier who had seen all, she bade him tell her what had come to pass. This he did truthfully, being friendly disposed towards me because I had overcome the Nubian. Thereon she turned and spoke to the girl bearing the fan who stood beside her—a woman with curling hair and shy dark eyes, very beautiful to see. The girl answered somewhat. Then Cleopatra bade them bring the slave to her. So they led forward the giant, who had found his breath again, and with him the woman whom he had smitten down.

"Thou dog!" she said, in the same low voice; "thou coward! who, being strong, didst smite down this woman, and, being a coward, wast overthrown of this young man. See, thou, I will teach thee manners. Henceforth, when thou smitest women it shall be with thy left arm. Ho, guards, seize this black slave and strike off his right hand."

Her command given, she sank back in her golden chariot, and again the cloud gathered in her eyes. But the guards seized the giant, and, notwithstanding his cries and prayers for mercy, struck off his hand with a sword upon the wood of the scaffolding and he was carried away groaning. Then the procession moved on again. As it went the fair woman with the fan turned her head, caught my eye, and smiled and nodded as though she rejoiced, at which I wondered somewhat.

The people cheered also and made jests, saying that I should soon practice astrology in the palace. But, as soon as we might, I and my uncle escaped, and made our way back to the house. All the while he rated me for my rashness; but when we came to the chamber of the house he embraced me and rejoiced greatly, because I had overthrown the giant with so little hurt to myself.

CHAPTER 2

Of the Coming of Charmion

That same night, while we sat at supper in the house, there came a knock upon the door. It was opened, and a woman passed in wrapped from head to foot in a large dark *peplos* or cloak in such fashion that her face could not be clearly seen.

My uncle rose, and as he did so the woman uttered the secret word.

"I am come, my father," she said in a sweet clear voice, "though of a truth it was not easy to escape the revels at the palace yonder. But I told the Queen that the sun and the riot in the streets had made me sick, and she let me go."

"It is well," he answered. "Unveil thyself; here thou art safe."

With a little sigh of weariness she unclasped the *peplos* and let it slip from her, giving to my sight the face and form of that beauteous girl who had stood to fan Cleopatra in the chariot. For she was very fair and pleasant to look upon, and her Grecian robes clung sweetly about her supple limbs and budding form. Her wayward hair, flowing in a hundred little curls, was bound in with a golden fillet, and on her feet were sandals fastened with studs of gold. Her cheeks blushed like a flower, and her dark soft eyes were downcast, as though with modesty, but smiles and dimples trembled about her lips.

My uncle frowned when his eyes fell upon her dress.

"Why comest thou in this garb, Charmion?" he asked sternly. "Is not the dress of thy mothers good enough for thee? This is no time or place for woman's vanities. Thou art not here to conquer, but to obey."

"Nay, be not wroth, my father," she answered softly; "perchance thou knowest not that she whom I serve will have none of our Egyptian dress; it is out of fashion. To wear it would have been to court suspicion—also I came in haste." And as she spoke I saw that all the while she watched me covertly through the long lashes which fringed her modest eyes.

"Well, well," he said sharply, fixing his keen glance upon her face, "doubtless thou speakest truth, Charmion. Be ever mindful of thy oath, girl, and of the cause to which thou art sworn. Be not light-minded, and I charge thee forget the beauty with which thou hast been cursed. For mark thou this, Charmion: fail us but one jot, and vengeance shall fall on thee—the vengeance of man and the vengeance of the Gods! To this service," he continued, lashing himself to anger as he went on till his great voice rang in the narrow room, "thou hast been bred; to this end thou hast been instructed and placed where thou art to gain the ear of that wicked wanton whom thou seemest to serve. See thou forget it not; see that the luxury of yonder Court does not corrupt thy purity and divert thy aim, Charmion," and his eyes flashed and his small form seemed to grow till it attained to dignity—nay, almost to grandeur.

"Charmion," he went on, advancing towards her with outstretched finger, "I say that at times I do not trust thee. But two nights gone I dreamed I saw thee standing in the desert. I saw thee laugh and lift thy hand to heaven, and from it fell a rain of blood; then the sky sank down on the land of Khem and covered it. Whence came the dream, girl, and what is its meaning? I have naught against thee as yet; but hearken! On the moment that I have, though thou art of my kin, and I have loved thee—on that moment, I say, I will doom those delicate limbs, which thou lovest so much to show, to the kite and the jackal, and the soul within thee to all the tortures of the Gods! Unburied shalt thou lie, and bodiless and accursed shalt thou wander in Amenti!—ay, for ever and ever!"

He paused, for his sudden burst of passion had spent itself. But by it, more clearly than before, I saw how deep a heart this man had beneath the cloak of his merriness and simplicity of mien, and how fiercely the mind within him was set upon his aim. As for the girl, she shrank from him terrified, and, placing her hands before her sweet face, began to weep.

"Nay, speak not so, my father," she said, between her sobs; "for what have I done? I know nothing of the evil wandering of thy dreams. I am no soothsayer that I should read dreams. Have I not carried out all things according to thy desire? Have I not been ever mindful of that dread oath?"—and she trembled. "Have I not played the spy and told thee all? Have I not won the heart of the Queen, so that she loves me as a sister, refusing me nothing—ay, and the hearts of those about her? Why dost thou affright me thus with thy words and threats?" and she wept afresh, looking even more beautiful in her sorrow than she was before.

"Enough, enough," he answered; "what I have said, I have said. Be warned, and affront our sight no more with this wanton dress. Thinkest thou that we would feed our eyes upon those rounded arms—we whose stake is Egypt and who are dedicated to the Gods of Egypt? Girl, behold thy cousin and thy King!"

She ceased weeping, wiping her eyes with her *chiton*, and I saw that they seemed but the softer for her tears.

"Methinks, most Royal Harmachis, and beloved Cousin," she said, as she bent before me, "that we are already made acquainted."

"Yea, Cousin," I answered, not without shamefacedness, for I had never before spoken to so fair a maid; "thou wert in the chariot with Cleopatra this day when I struggled with the Nubian?"

"Assuredly," she said, with a smile and a sudden lighting of the eyes, "it was a gallant fight and gallantly didst thou overthrow that black brute. I saw the fray and, though I knew thee not, I greatly feared for one so brave. But I paid him for my fright, for it was I who put it into the mind of Cleopatra to bid the guards strike off his hand—now, knowing who thou art, I would I had said his head." And she looked up shooting a glance at me and then smiled.

"Enough," put in my uncle Sepa, "the time draws on. Tell thou thy mission, Charmion, and be gone."

Then her manner changed; she folded her hands meekly before her and spoke:

"Let Pharaoh hearken to his handmaiden. I am the daughter of Pharaoh's uncle, the brother of his father, who is now long dead, and therefore in my veins also flows the Royal blood of Egypt. Also I am of the ancient Faith, and hate these Greeks, and to see thee set upon the throne has been my dearest hope now for many years. To this end I, Charmion, have put aside my rank and become serving-woman to Cleopatra, that I might cut a notch in which thou couldst set thy foot when the hour came for thee to climb the throne. And, Pharaoh, the notch is cut.

"This then is our plot, royal Cousin. Thou must gain an entrance to the Household and learn its ways and secrets, and, so far as may be, suborn the eunuchs and captains, some of whom I have already tempted. This done, and all things being prepared without, thou must slay Cleopatra, and, aided by me with those whom I control, in the confusion that shall ensue, throw wide the gates, and, admitting those of our party who are in waiting, put such of the troops as remain faithful to the sword and seize the Bruchium. Which being finished, within two days thou shalt hold this fickle Alexandria. At the same time those who are sworn to thee in every city of Egypt shall rise in arms, and in ten days from the death of Cleopatra thou shalt indeed be Pharaoh. This is the counsel which has been taken, and thou seest, royal Cousin, that, though our uncle yonder thinks so ill of me, I have learned my part—ay, and played it."

"I hear thee, Cousin," I answered, marvelling that so young a woman—she had but twenty years—could weave so bold a plot, for in its origin the scheme was hers. But in those days I little knew Charmion. "Go on; how then shall I gain entrance to the palace of Cleopatra?"

"Nay, Cousin, as things are it is easy. Thus: Cleopatra loves to look upon a man, and—give me pardon—thy face and form are fair. To-day she noted them, and twice she said she would she had asked where that astrologer might be found, for she held that an astrologer who could well-nigh slay a Nubian gladiator with his bare hands, must indeed be a master of the fortunate stars. I answered her that I would cause inquiry to be made. So hearken, royal Harmachis. At midday Cleopatra sleeps in her inner hall which looks over the gardens to the harbour. At that hour to-morrow, then, I will meet thee at the gates of the palace, whither thou shalt come boldly asking for the Lady Charmion. I will make appointment for thee with Cleopatra, so that she shall see thee alone when she wakes, and the rest shall be for thee, Harmachis. For much she loves to play with the mysteries of magic, and I have known her stand whole nights watching the stars and making a pretence to read them. And but lately she has sent away Dioscorides the physician, because, poor fool! he ventured on a prophecy from the conjunction of the stars, that Cassius would defeat Mark Antony. Thereon Cleopatra sent orders to the General Allienus, bidding him add the legions she had sent to Syria to help Antony to the army of Cassius, whose victory, forsooth, was—according to Dioscorides—written on the stars. But, as it chanced, Antony beat Cassius first and Brutus afterwards, and so Dioscorides has departed, and now he lectures on herbs in the museum for his bread, and hates the name of stars. But his place is empty, and thou shalt fill it, and then we will work in secret and in the shadow of the sceptre. Ay, we will work like the worm at the heart of a fruit, till the time of plucking comes, and at thy dagger's touch, royal Cousin, the fabric of this Grecian throne crumbles to nothingness, and the worm that rotted it bursts his servile covering, and, in the sight of empires, spreads his royal wings o'er Egypt."

I gazed at this strange girl once more astonished, and saw that her face was lit up with such a light as I had never seen in the eyes of woman.

"Ah," broke in my uncle, who was watching her, "ah, I love to see thee so, girl; there is the Charmion that I knew and I bred up—not the Court girl whom I like not, draped in silks of Cos and fragrant with essences. Let thy heart harden in this mould—ay, stamp it with the fervid zeal of patriot faith, and thy reward shall find thee. And now cover up that shameless dress of thine and leave us, for it grows late. To-morrow Harmachis shall come, as thou hast said, and so farewell."

Charmion bowed her head, and, turning, wrapped her dark-hued *peplos* round her. Then, taking my hand, she touched it with her lips and went without any further word.

"A strange woman!" said Sepa, when she had gone; "a most strange woman, and an uncertain!"

"Methought, my uncle," I said, "that thou wast somewhat harsh with her."

"Ay," he answered, "but not without a cause. Look thou, Harmachis; beware of this Charmion. She is too wayward, and, I fear me, may be led away. In truth, she is a very woman; and, like a restive horse, will take the path that pleases her. She has brain and fire, and she loves our cause; but I pray that the cause come not face to face with her desires, for what her heart is set on that will she do, at any cost she will do it. Therefore I frightened her now while I may: for who can know but that she will pass beyond my power? I tell thee, that in this one girl's hand lie all our lives: and if she play us false, what then? Alas! and alas! that we must use such tools as these! But it was needful: there was no other way; and yet I misdoubted me. I pray that it may be well; still, at times, I fear my niece Charmion—she is too fair, and the blood of youth runs too warm in those blue veins of hers.

"Ah, woe to the cause that builds its strength upon a woman's faith; for women are faithful only where they love, and when they love their faithlessness becomes their faith. They are not fixed as men are fixed: they rise more high and sink more low—they are strong and changeful as the sea. Harmachis, beware of this Charmion: for, like the ocean, she may float thee home; or, like the ocean, she may wreck thee, and, with thee, the hope of Egypt!"

CHAPTER 3

Of the Coming of Harmachis to the Palace

Thus it came to pass that on the next day I arrayed myself in a long and flowing robe, after the fashion of a magician or astrologer. I placed a cap on my head, about which were broidered images of the stars, and in my belt a scribe's palette and a roll of papyrus written over with magic spells and signs. In my hand I held a wand of ebony, tipped with ivory, such as is used by priests and masters of magic. Among these, indeed, I took high rank, filling my knowledge of their secrets which I had learned at Annu what I lacked in that skill which comes from use. And so with no small shame, for I love not such play and hold this common magic in contempt, I set forth through the Bruchium to the palace on the Lochias, being guided on my way by my uncle Sepa. At length, passing up the avenue of sphinxes, we came to the great marble gateway and the gates of bronze, within which is the guard-house. Here my uncle left me, breathing many prayers for my safety and success. But I advanced with an easy air to the gate, where I was roughly challenged by the Gallic sentries, and asked of my name, following, and business. I gave my name, Harmachis, the astrologer, saying that my business was with the Lady Charmion, the Queen's lady. Thereon the man made as though to let me pass in, when a captain of the guard, a Roman named Paulus, came forward and forbade it. Now, this Paulus was a large limbed man, with a woman's face, and a hand that shook from wine-bibbing. Still he knew me again.

"Why," he cried, in the Latin tongue, to one who came with him, "this is the fellow who wrestled yesterday with the Nubian gladiator, that same who now howls for his lost hand underneath my window. Curses on the black brute! I had a bet upon him for the games! I have backed him against Caius, and now he'll never fight again, and I must lose my money, all through this astrologer. What is it thou sayest?—

thou hast business with the Lady Charmion? Nay, then, that settles it. I will not let thee through. Fellow, I worship the Lady Charmion—ay, we all worship her, though she gives us more slaps than sighs. And dost thou think that we will suffer an astrologer with such eyes and such a chest as thine to cut in the game?—by Bacchus, no! She must come out to keep the tryst, for in thou shalt not go."

"Sir," I said humbly and yet with dignity, "I pray that a message may be sent to the Lady Charmion, for my business will not brook delay."

"Ye Gods!" answered the fool, "whom have we here that he cannot wait? A Caesar in disguise? Nay, be off—be off! if thou wouldst not learn how a spear-prick feels behind."

"Nay," put in the other officer, "he is an astrologer; make him prophesy—make him play tricks."

"Ay," cried the others who had sauntered up, "let the fellow show his art. If he is a magician he can pass the gates, Paulus or no Paulus."

"Right willingly, good Sirs," I answered; for I saw no other means of entering. "Wilt thou, my young and noble Lord"—and I addressed him who was with Paulus—"suffer that I look thee in the eyes; perhaps I may read what is written there?"

"Right," answered the youth; "but I wish that the Lady Charmion was the sorceress. I would stare her out of countenance, I warrant."

I took him by the hand and gazed deep into his eyes. "I see," I said, "a field of battle at night, and about it bodies stretched—among them is *thy* body, and a hyena tears its throat. Most noble Sir, thou shalt die by sword-thrusts within a year."

"By Bacchus!" said the youth, turning white to the gills, "thou art an ill-omened sorcerer!" And he slunk off—shortly afterwards, as it chanced, to meet this very fate. For he was sent on service and slain in Cyprus.

"Now for thee, great Captain!" I said, speaking to Paulus. "I will show thee how I will pass those gates without thy leave—ay, and draw thee through them after me. Be pleased to fix thy princely gaze upon the point of this wand in my hand."

Being urged by his comrades he did this, unwillingly; and I let him gaze till I saw his eyes grow empty as an owl's eyes in the sun. Then I suddenly withdrew the wand, and, shifting my countenance into the place of it, I seized him with my will and stare, and, beginning to turn round and round, drew him after me, his fierce face drawn fixed, as it were, almost to my own. Then I moved slowly backwards till I had passed the gates, still drawing him after me, and suddenly jerked my head away. He fell to the ground, to rise wiping his brow and looking very foolish.

"Art thou content, most noble Captain?" I said. "Thou seest we have passed the gates. Would any other noble Sir wish that I should show more of my skill?"

"By Taranis, Lord of Thunder, and all the Gods of Olympus thrown in, no!" growled an old Centurion, a Gaul named Brennus, "I like thee not, I say. The man who could drag our Paulus through those gates by the eye, as it were, is not a man to play with. Paulus, too, who always goes the way you don't want him—backwards, like an ass—Paulus! Why, sirrah, thou needst must have a woman in one eye and a wine-cup in the other to draw our Paulus thus."

At this moment the talk was broken, for Charmion herself came down the marble path, followed by an armed slave. She walked calm and carelessly, her hands folded behind her, and her eyes gazing at nothingness, as it were. But it was when Charmion thus looked upon nothing that she saw most. And as she came the officers and men of the guard made way for her bowing, for, as I learned afterwards, this girl, next to Cleopatra's self, wielded more power than anyone about the palace.

"What is this tumult, Brennus?" she said, speaking to the Centurion, and making as if she saw me not; "knowest thou not that the Queen sleeps at this hour, and if she be awakened it is thou who must answer for it, and that dearly?"

"Nay, Lady," said the Centurion, humbly; "but it is thus. We have here"—and he jerked his thumb towards me—"a magician of the most pestilent—um, I crave his pardon—of the very best sort, for he hath but just now, only by placing his eyes close to the nose of the worthy Captain Paulus, dragged him, the said Paulus, through the gates that Paulus swore the magician should not pass. By the same token, lady, the magician says that he has business with you—which grieves me for your sake."

Charmion turned and looked at me carelessly. "Ay, I remember," she said; "and so he has—at least, the Queen would see his tricks; but if he can do none better than cause a sot"—here she cast a glance of scorn at the wondering Paulus—"to follow his nose through the gates he guards, he had better go whence he came. Follow me, Sir Magician; and for thee, Brennus, I say, keep thy riotous crew more quiet. For thee, most honourable Paulus, get thee sober, and next time I am asked for at the gates give him who asks a hearing." And, with a queenly nod of her small head, she turned and led the way, followed at a distance by myself and the armed slave.

We passed up the marble walk which runs through the garden grounds, and is set on either side with marble statues, for the most part of heathen Gods and Goddesses, with which these Lagidae were not ashamed to defile their royal dwellings. At length we came to a beautiful portico with fluted columns of the Grecian style of art, where we found more guards, who made way for the Lady Charmion. Crossing the portico we reached a marble vestibule where a fountain splashed softly, and thence by a low doorway a second chamber, known as the Alabaster Hall, most beautiful to see. Its roof was upheld by light columns of black marble, but all its walls were panelled with alabaster, on which Grecian legends were engraved. Its floor was of rich and many-hued mosaic that told the tale of the passion of Psyche for the Grecian God of Love, and about it were set chairs of ivory and gold. Charmion bade the armed slave stay at the doorway of this chamber, so that we passed in alone, for the place was empty except for two eunuchs who stood with drawn swords before the curtain at the further end.

"I am vexed, my Lord," she said, speaking very low and shyly, "that thou shouldst have met with such affronts at the gate; but the guard there served a double watch, and I had given my commands to the officer of the company that should have relieved it. Those Roman officers are ever insolent, who, though they seem to serve, know well that Egypt is their plaything. But it is not amiss, for these rough soldiers are superstitious, and will fear thee. Now bide thou here while I go into Cleopatra's chamber, where she sleeps. I have but just sung her to sleep, and if she be awake I will call thee, for she waits thy coming." And without more words she glided from my side.

In a little time she returned, and coming to me spoke:

"Wouldst see the fairest woman in all the world, asleep?" she whispered; "if so, follow me. Nay, fear not; when she awakes she will but laugh, for she bade me be sure to bring thee instantly, whether she slept or woke. See, I have her signet."

So we passed up the beautiful chamber till we came to where the eunuchs stood with drawn swords, and these would have barred my entry. But Charmion frowned, and drawing the signet from her bosom held it before their eyes. Having examined the writing that was on the ring, they bowed, dropping their sword points and we passed through the heavy curtains broidered with gold into the resting-place of Cleopatra. It was beautiful beyond imagining—beautiful with many coloured marbles, with gold and ivory, gems and flowers—all art can furnish and all luxury can dream of were here. Here were pictures so real that birds might have pecked the painted fruits; here were statues of woman's loveliness frozen into stone; here were draperies fine as softest silk, but woven of a web of gold; here were couches and carpets such as I never saw. The air, too, was sweet with perfume, while through the open window places came the far murmur of the sea. And at the further end of the chamber, on a couch of gleaming silk and sheltered by a net of finest gauze, Cleopatra lay asleep. There she lay—the fairest thing that man ever saw—fairer than a dream, and the web of her dark hair flowed all about her. One white, rounded arm made a pillow for her head, and one hung down towards the ground. Her rich lips were parted in a smile, showing the ivory lines of teeth; and her rosy limbs were draped in so thin a robe of the silk of Cos, held about her by a jewelled girdle, that the white gleam of flesh shone through it. I stood astonished, and though my thoughts had little bent that way, the sight of her beauty struck me like a blow, so that for a moment I lost myself as it were in the vision of its power, and was grieved at heart because I must slay so fair a thing.

Turning suddenly from the sight, I found Charmion watching me with her quick eyes—watching as though she would search my heart. And, indeed, something of my thought must have been written on my face in a language that she could read, for she whispered in my ear:

"Ay, it is pity, is it not? Harmachis, being but a man, methinks that thou wilt need all thy ghostly strength to nerve thee to the deed!"

I frowned, but before I could frame an answer she touched me lightly on the arm and pointed to the Queen. A change had come upon her: her hands were clenched, and about her face, all rosy with the hue of sleep, gathered a cloud of fear. Her breath came quick, she raised her arms as though to ward away a blow, then with a stifled moan sat up and opened the windows of her eyes. They were dark, dark as night; but when the light found them they grew blue as the sky grows blue before the blushing of the dawn.

"Caesarion?" she said; "where is my son Caesarion?—Was it then a dream? I dreamed that Julius—Julius who is dead—came to me, a bloody toga wrapped about his face, and having thrown his arms about his child led him away. Then I dreamed I died—died in blood and agony; and one I might not see mocked me as I died. *Ah!* who is that man?"

"Peace, Madam! peace!" said Charmion. "It is but the magician Harmachis, whom thou didst bid me bring to thee at this hour."

"Ah! the magician—that Harmachis who overthrew the giant? I remember now. He is welcome. Tell me, Sir Magician, can thy magic mirror call forth an answer to this dream? Nay, how strange a thing is Sleep, that wrapping the mind in a web of darkness, straightly compels it to its will! Whence, then, come those images of fear rising on the horizon of the soul like some untimely moon upon a midday sky? Who grants them power to stalk so lifelike from Memory's halls, and, pointing to their wounds, thus confront the Present with the Past? Are they, then, messengers? Does the half-death of sleep give them foothold in our brains, and thus upknit the cut thread of human kinship? That was Caesar's self, I tell thee, who but now stood at my side and murmured through his muffled robe warning words of which the memory is lost to me. Read me this riddle, thou Egyptian Sphinx,[13] and I'll show thee a rosier path to fortune than all thy stars can point. Thou hast brought the omen, solve thou its problem."

"I come in a good hour, most mighty Queen," I answered, "for I have some skill in the mysteries of Sleep, that is, as thou hast rightly guessed, a stair by which those who are gathered to Osiris may from time to time enter at the gateways of our living sense, and, by signs and words that can be read of instructed mortals, repeat the echoes of that Hall of Truth which is their habitation. Yes, Sleep is a stair by which the messengers of the guardian Gods may descend in many shapes upon the spirit of their choice. For, O Queen, to those who hold the key, the madness of our dreams can show a clearer purpose and speak more certainly than all the acted wisdom of our waking life, which is a dream indeed. Thou didst see great Caesar in his bloody robe, and he threw his arms about the Prince Caesarion and led him hence. Hearken now to the secret of thy vision. It was Caesar's self thou sawest coming to thy side from Amenti in such a guise as might not be mistaken. When he embraced the child Caesarion he did it for a sign that to him, and him alone, had passed his greatness and his love. When he seemed to lead him hence he led him forth from Egypt to be crowned in the Capitol, crowned the Emperor of Rome and Lord of all the Lands. For the rest, I know not. It is hid from me."

Thus, then, I read the vision, though to my sense it had a darker meaning. But it is not well to prophesy evil unto Kings.

Meanwhile Cleopatra had risen, and, having thrown back the gnat gauze, was seated upon the edge of her couch, her eyes fixed upon my face, while her fingers played with her girdle's jewelled ends.

"Of a truth," she cried, "thou art the best of all magicians, for thou readest my heart, and drawest a hidden sweet out of the rough shell of evil omen!"

---

13 Alluding to his name. Harmachis was the Grecian title of the divinity of the Sphinx, as Horemkhu was the Egyptian.—Editor.

"Ay, O Queen," said Charmion, who stood by with downcast eyes, and I thought that there was bitter meaning in her soft tones; "may no rougher words ever affront thy ears, and no evil presage tread less closely upon its happy sense."

Cleopatra placed her hands behind her head and, leaning back, looked at me with half-shut eyes.

"Come, show us of thy magic, Egyptian," she said. "It is yet hot abroad, and I am weary of those Hebrew Ambassadors and their talk of Herod and Jerusalem. I hate that Herod, as he shall find—and will have none of the Ambassadors to-day, though I yearn a little to try my Hebrew on them. What canst thou do? Hast thou no new trick? By Serapis! if thou canst conjure as well as thou canst prophesy, thou shalt have a place at Court, with pay and perquisites to boot, if thy lofty soul does not scorn perquisites."

"Nay," I answered, "all tricks are old; but there are some forms of magic to be rarely used, and with discretion, that may be new to thee, O Queen! Art thou afraid to venture on the charm?"

"I fear nothing; go on and do thy worst. Come, Charmion, and sit by me. But, stay, where are all the girls?—Iras and Merira?—they, too, love magic."

"Not so," I said; "the charms work ill before so many. Now behold!" and, gazing at the twain, I cast my wand upon the marble and murmured a spell. For a moment it was still, and then, as I muttered, the rod slowly began to writhe. It bent itself, it stood on end, and moved of its own motion. Next it put on scales, and behold it was a serpent that crawled and fiercely hissed.

"Fie on thee!" cried Cleopatra, clapping her hands; "callest thou that magic? Why, it is an old trick that any wayside conjurer can do. I have seen it a score of times."

"Wait, O Queen," I answered, "thou hast not seen all." And, as I spoke, the serpent seemed to break in fragments, and from each fragment grew a new serpent. And these, too, broke in fragments and bred others, till in a little while the place, to their glamoured sight, was a seething sea of snakes, that crawled, hissed, and knotted themselves in knots. Then I made a sign, and the serpents gathered themselves round me, and seemed slowly to twine themselves about my body and my limbs, till, save my face, I was wreathed thick with hissing snakes.

"Oh, horrible! horrible!" cried Charmion, hiding her countenance in the skirt of the Queen's garment.

"Nay, enough, Magician, enough!" said the Queen: "thy magic overwhelms us."

I waved my snake-wrapped arms, and all was gone. There at my feet lay the black wand tipped with ivory, and naught beside.

The two women looked upon each other and gasped with wonder. But I took up the wand and stood with folded arms before them.

"Is the Queen content with my poor art?" I asked most humbly.

"Ay, that I am, Egyptian; never did I see its like! Thou art Court astronomer from this day forward, with right of access to the Queen's presence. Hast thou more of such magic at thy call?"

"Yea, royal Egypt; suffer that the chamber be a little darkened, and I will show thee one more thing."

"Half am I afraid," she answered; "nevertheless do thou as this Harmachis says, Charmion."

So the curtains were drawn and the chamber made as though the twilight were at hand. I came forward, and stood beside Cleopatra. "Gaze thou there!" I said sternly, pointing with my wand to the empty space where I had been, "and thou shalt behold that which is in thy mind."

Then for a little space was silence, while the two women gazed fixedly and half fearful at the spot.

And as they gazed a cloud gathered before them. Very slowly it took shape and form, and the form it took was the form of a man, though as yet he was but vaguely mapped upon the twilight, and seemed now to grow and now to melt away.

Then I cried with a loud voice:

"Spirit, I conjure thee, *appear!*"

And as I cried the Thing, perfect in every part, leapt into form before us, suddenly as the flash of day. His shape was the shape of royal Caesar, the toga thrown about his face, and on his form a vestment bloody from a hundred wounds. An instant so he stood, then I waved my wand and he was gone.

I turned to the two women on the couch, and saw Cleopatra's lovely face all clothed in terror. Her lips were ashy white, her eyes stared wide, and all the flesh was shaking on her bones.

"Man!" she gasped; "man! who and what art thou who canst bring the dead before our eyes?"

"I am the Queen's astronomer, magician, servant—what the Queen wills," I answered, laughing. "Was this the form that was on the Queen's mind?"

She made no answer, but, rising, left the chamber by another door.

Then Charmion rose also and took her hands from her face, for she, too, had been stricken with dread.

"How dost thou these things, royal Harmachis?" she said. "Tell me; for of a truth I fear thee."

"Be not afraid," I answered. "Perchance thou didst see nothing but what was in my mind. All things are shadows. How canst thou, then, know their nature, or what is and what only seems to be? But how goes it? Remember, Charmion, this sport is played to an end."

"It goes well," she said. "By to-morrow morning's dawn these tales will have gone round, and thou wilt be more feared than any man in Alexandria. Follow me, I pray thee."

CHAPTER 4

Of the Ways of Charmion

On the following day I received the writing of my appointment as Astrologer and Magician-in-Chief to the Queen, with the pay and perquisites of that office, which were not small. Rooms were given me in the palace, also, through which I passed at night to the high watch-tower, whence I looked on the stars and drew their auguries. For at this time Cleopatra was much troubled about matters political, and not knowing how the great struggle among the Roman factions would end, but being very desirous to side with the strongest, she took constant counsel with me as to the warnings of the stars. These I read to her in such manner as best seemed to fit the high interest of my ends. For Antony, the Roman Triumvir, was now in Asia Minor, and, rumour ran, very wroth because it had been told him that Cleopatra was hostile to the Triumvirate, in that her General, Serapion, had aided Cassius. But Cleopatra protested loudly to me and others that Serapion had acted against her will. Yet Charmion told me that, as with Allienus, it was because of a prophecy of Dioscorides the unlucky that the Queen herself had secretly ordered Serapion so to do. Still, this did not save Serapion, for to prove to Antony that she was innocent she dragged the General from the sanctuary and slew him. Woe be to those who carry out the will of tyrants if the scale should rise against them! And so Serapion perished.

Meanwhile all things went well with us, for the minds of Cleopatra and those about her were so set upon affairs abroad that neither she nor they thought of revolt at home. But day by day our party gathered strength in the cities of Egypt, and even in Alexandria, which is to Egypt as another land, all things being foreign there. Day by day, those who doubted were won over and sworn to the cause by that oath which cannot be broken, and our plans of action more firmly laid. And every other day I went forth from the palace to take counsel with my uncle Sepa, and there at his house met the Nobles and the great priests who were for the party of Khem.

I saw much of Cleopatra, the Queen, and I was ever more astonished at the wealth and splendour of her mind, that for richness and variety was as a woven cloth of gold throwing back all lights from its changing face. She feared me somewhat, and therefore wished to make a friend of me, asking me of many matters that seemed to be beyond the province of my office. I saw much of the Lady Charmion also—indeed, she was ever at my side, so that I scarce knew when she came and when she went. For she would draw nigh with that soft step of hers, and I would turn to find her at hand and watching me beneath the long lashes of her downcast eyes. There was no service that was too hard for her, and no task too long; for day and night she laboured for me and for our cause.

But when I thanked her for her loyalty, and said it should be had in mind in that time which was at hand, she stamped her foot, and pouted with her lips, like an angry child, saying that, among all the things which I had learned, this had I not learned—that Love's service asked no payment, and was its own guerdon. And I, being innocent in such matters, and, foolish that I was, holding the ways of women as of small account, read her sayings in the sense that her services to the cause of Khem, which she loved, brought with them their own reward. But when I praised so fine a spirit, she burst into angry tears and left me wondering. For I knew nothing of the trouble at her heart. I knew not then that, unsought, this woman had given me her love, and that she was rent and torn by pangs of passion fixed like arrows in her breast. I did not know—how should I know it, who never looked upon her otherwise than as an instrument of our joint and holy cause? Her beauty never stirred me—no, not even when she leaned over me and breathed upon my hair, I never thought of it otherwise than as a man thinks of the beauty of a statue. What had I to do with such delights, I who was sworn to Isis and dedicate to the cause of Egypt? O ye Gods, bear me witness that I am innocent of this thing which was the source of all my woe and the woe of Khem!

How strange a thing is this love of woman, that is so small in its beginning and in its ends so great! See, at the first it is as the little spring of water welling from a mountain's heart. And at the last what is it? It is a mighty river that floats *argosies* of joy and makes wide lands to smile. Or, perchance, it is a torrent to wash in a flood of ruin across the fields of Hope, bursting in the barriers of design, and bringing to tumbled nothingness the tenement of man's purity and the temples of his faith. For when the Invisible conceived the order of the universe He set this seed of woman's love within its plan, that by its most unequal growth is doomed to bring about equality of law. For now it lifts the low to heights untold, and now it brings the noble to the level of the dust. And thus, while Woman, that great surprise of nature, is, Good and Evil can never grow apart. For still She stands, and, blind with love, shoots the shuttle of our fate, and pours sweet water into the cup of bitterness, and poisons the wholesome breath of life with the doom of her desire. Turn this way and turn that, She is at hand to meet thee. Her weakness is thy strength, her might is thy undoing. Of her thou art, to her thou goest. She is thy slave, yet holds thee captive; at her touch honour withers, locks open, and barriers fall. She is infinite as ocean, she is variable as heaven, and her name is the Unforeseen. Man, strive not to escape from Woman and the love of woman; for, fly where thou wilt, She is yet thy fate, and whate'er thou buildest thou buildest it for her!

And thus it came to pass that I, Harmachis, who had put such matters far from me, was yet doomed to fall by the thing I held of no account. For, see, this Charmion: she loved me—why, I know not. Of her own thought she learned to love me, and of her love came what shall be told. But I, knowing naught, treated her like a sister, walking as it were hand in hand with her towards our common end.

And so the time passed on, till, at length, all things were made ready.

It was the night before the night when the blow should fall, and there were revellings in the palace. That very day I had seen Sepa, and with him the captains of a band of five hundred men, who should burst into the palace at midnight on the morrow, when I had slain Cleopatra the Queen, and put the Roman and the Gallic legionaries to the sword. That very day I had suborned the Captain Paulus who, since I drew him through the gates, was my will's slave. Half by fear and half by promises of great reward I had prevailed upon him, for the watch was his, to unbar that small gate which faces to the East at the signal on the morrow night.

All was made ready—the flower of Freedom that had been five-and-twenty years in growth was on the point of bloom. Armed companies were gathering in every city from Abu to Athu, and spies looked out from their walls, awaiting the coming of the messenger who should bring tidings that Cleopatra was no more and that Harmachis, the royal Egyptian, had seized the throne.

All was prepared, triumph hung in my hand as a ripe fruit to the hand of the plucker. Yet as I sat at the royal feast my heart was heavy, and a shadow of coming woe lay cold within my mind. I sat there in a place of honour, near the majesty of Cleopatra, and looked down the lines of guests, bright with gems and garlanded with flowers, marking those whom I had doomed to die. There before me lay Cleopatra in all her beauty, which thrilled the beholder as he is thrilled by the rushing of the midnight gale, or by the sight of stormy waters. I gazed on her as she touched her lips with wine and toyed with the chaplet of roses on her brow, thinking of the dagger beneath my robe that I had sworn to bury in her breast. Again, and yet again, I gazed and strove to hate her, strove to rejoice that she must die—and could not. There, too, behind her—watching me now, as ever, with her deep-fringed eyes—was the lovely Lady Charmion. Who, to look at her innocent face, would believe that she was the setter of that snare in which the Queen who loved her should miserably perish? Who would dream that the secret of so much death was locked in her girlish breast? I gazed, and grew sick at heart because I must anoint my throne with blood, and by evil sweep away the evil of the land. At that hour I wished, indeed, that I was nothing but some humble husbandman, who in its season grows and in its season garners the golden grain! Alas! the seed that I had been doomed to sow was the seed of Death, and now I must reap the red fruit of the harvest!

"Why, Harmachis, what ails thee?" said Cleopatra, smiling her slow smile. "Has the golden skein of stars got tangled, my astronomer? or dost thou plan some new feat of magic? Say what is it that thou dost so poorly grace our feast? Nay, now, did I not know, having made inquiry, that things so low as we poor women are far beneath thy gaze, why, I should swear that Eros had found thee out, Harmachis!"

"Nay, that I am spared, O Queen," I answered. "The servant of the stars marks not the smaller light of woman's eyes, and therein is he happy!"

Cleopatra leaned herself towards me, looking on me long and steadily in such fashion that, despite my will, the blood fluttered at my heart.

"Boast not, thou proud Egyptian," she said in a low voice which none but I and Charmion could hear, "lest perchance thou dost tempt me to match my magic against thine. What woman can forgive that a man should push us by as things of no account? It is an insult to our sex which Nature's self abhors," and she leaned back again and laughed most musically. But, glancing up, I saw Charmion, her teeth on her lip and an angry frown upon her brow.

"Pardon, Royal Egypt," I answered coldly, but with such wit as I could summon, "before the Queen of Heaven even stars grow pale!" This I said of the moon, which is the sign of the Holy Mother whom Cleopatra dared to rival, naming herself Isis come to earth.

"Happily said," she answered, clapping her white hands. "Why, here's an astronomer who has wit and can shape a compliment! Nay, such a wonder must not pass unnoted, lest the Gods resent it. Charmion, take this rose-chaplet from my hair and set it upon the learned brow of our Harmachis. He shall be crowned *King of Love*, whether he will it or not."

Charmion lifted the chaplet from Cleopatra's brows and, bearing it to where I was, with a smile set it upon my head yet warm and fragrant from the Queen's hair, but so roughly that she pained me somewhat. She did this because she was wroth, although she smiled with her lips and whispered, "An omen, royal Harmachis." For though she was so very much a woman, yet, when she was angered or suffered jealousy, Charmion had a childish way.

Having thus fixed the chaplet, she curtsied low before me, and with the softest tone of mockery named me, in the Greek tongue, "Harmachis, King of Love." Then Cleopatra laughed and pledged me as "King of Love," and so did all the company, finding the jest a merry one. For in Alexandria they love not those who live straitly and turn aside from women.

But I sat there, a smile upon my lips, and black wrath in my heart. For, knowing who and what I was, it irked me to think myself a jest for the frivolous nobles and light beauties of Cleopatra's Court. But I was chiefly angered against Charmion, because she laughed the loudest, and I did not then know that laughter and bitterness are often the veils with which a sore heart wraps its weakness from the world. "An omen" she said it was—that crown of flowers—and so it proved indeed. For I was fated to barter the Double Diadem of the Upper and the Lower Land for a wreath of passion's roses that fade before they fully bloom, and Pharaoh's ivory bed of state for the pillow of a faithless woman's breast.

"King of Love!" they crowned me in their mockery; ay, and King of Shame! And I, with the perfumed roses on my brow—I, by descent and ordination the Pharaoh of Egypt—thought of the imperishable halls of Abouthis and of that other crowning which on the morrow should be consummate.

But still smiling, I pledged them back, and answered with a jest. For rising, I bowed before Cleopatra and craved leave to go. "Venus," I said, speaking of the planet that we know as Donaou in the morning and Bonou in the evening, "was in the ascendant. Therefore, as new-crowned King of Love, I must now pass to do my homage to its Queen." For these barbarians name Venus Queen of Love.

And so amidst their laughter I withdraw to my watch-tower, and, dashing that shameful chaplet down amidst the instruments of my craft, made pretence to note the rolling of the stars. There I waited, thinking on many things that were to be, until Charmion should come with the last lists of the doomed and the messages of my uncle Sepa, whom she had seen that evening.

At length the door opened softly, and she came jewelled and clad in her white robes, as she had left the feast.

CHAPTER 5

Of the Coming of Cleopatra to the Chamber of Harmachis

"At length thou art come, Charmion," I said. "It is over-late."

"Yea, my Lord; but by no means could I escape Cleopatra. Her mood is strangely crossed to-night. I know not what it may portend. Strange whims and fancies blow across it like light and contrary airs upon a summer sea, and I cannot read her purpose."

"Well, well; enough of Cleopatra. Hast thou seen our uncle?"

"Yes, Royal Harmachis."

"And hast thou the last lists?"

"Yes; here they are," and she drew them from her bosom. "Here is the list of those who, after the Queen, must certainly be put to the sword. Among them thou wilt note is the name of that old Gaul Brennus. I grieve for him, for we are friends; but it must be. It is a heavy list."

"It is so," I answered conning it; "when men write out their count they forget no item, and our count is long. What must be must be. Now for the next."

"Here is the list of those to be spared, as friendly or uncertain; and here that of the towns which will certainly rise as soon as the messenger reaches their gates with tidings of the death of Cleopatra."

"Good. And now"—and I paused—"and now as to the manner of Cleopatra's death. How hast thou settled it? Must it be by my own hand?"

"Yea, my Lord," she answered, and again I caught that note of bitterness in her voice. "Doubtless Pharaoh will rejoice that his should be the hand to rid the land of this false Queen and wanton woman, and at one blow break the chains which gall the neck of Egypt."

"Talk not thus, girl," I said; "thou knowest well that I do not rejoice, being but driven to the act by deep necessity and the pressure of my vows. Can she not, then, be poisoned? Or can no one of the eunuchs be suborned to slay her? My soul turns from this bloody work! Indeed, I marvel, however heavy be her crimes, that thou canst speak so lightly of the death by treachery of one who loves thee!"

"Surely Pharaoh is over-tender, forgetting the greatness of the moment and all that hangs upon this dagger-stroke that shall cut the thread of Cleopatra's life. Listen, Harmachis. *Thou* must do the deed, and *thou* alone! Myself I would do it, had my arm the strength; but it has not. It cannot be done by poison, for every drop she drinks and every morsel that shall touch her lips is strictly tasted by three separate tasters, who cannot be suborned. Nor may the eunuchs of the guard be trusted. Two, indeed, are sworn to us; but the third cannot be come at. He must be cut down afterwards; and, indeed, when so many men must fall, what matters a eunuch more or less? Thus it shall be, then. To-morrow night, at three hours before midnight thou dost cast the final augury of the issue of the war. And then thou wilt, as is agreed, descend alone with me, having the signet, to the outer chamber of the Queen's apartment. For the vessel bearing orders to the Legions sails from Alexandria at the following dawn; and alone with Cleopatra, since she wills that the thing be kept secret as the sea, thou wilt read the message of the stars. And as she pores over the papyrus, then must thou stab her in the back, so that she dies; and see thou that thy will and arm fail thee not! The deed being done—and indeed it will be easy—thou wilt take the signet and pass out to where the eunuch is—for the others will be wanting. If by any chance there is trouble with him—but there will be no trouble, for he dare not enter the private rooms, and the sounds of death cannot reach so far—thou must cut him down. Then I will meet thee; and, passing on, we will come to Paulus, and it shall be my care to see that he is neither drunk nor backward, for I know how to hold him to the task. And he and those with him shall throw open the side gate, when Sepa and the five hundred chosen men who are in waiting shall pour in and cast themselves upon the sleeping legionaries, putting them to the sword. Why, the thing is easy so thou rest true to thyself, and let no womanish fears creep into thy heart. What is this dagger's thrust? It is nothing, and yet upon it hang the destinies of Egypt and the world."

"Hush!" I said. "What is that?—I hear a sound."

Charmion ran to the door, and, gazing down the long, dark passage, listened. In a moment she came back, her finger on her lips. "It is the Queen," she whispered hurriedly; "the Queen who mounts the stair alone. I heard her bid Iras to leave her. I may not be found alone with thee at this hour; it has a strange look, and she may suspect. What wants she here? Where can I hide?"

I glanced round. At the further end of the chamber was a heavy curtain that hid a little place built in the thickness of the wall which I used for the storage of rolls and instruments.

"Haste thee—there!" I said, and she glided behind the curtain, which swung back and covered her. Then I thrust the fatal scroll of death into the bosom of my robe and bent over the mystic chart. Presently I heard the sweep of woman's robes and there came a low knock upon the door.

"Enter, whoever thou art," I said.

The latch lifted, and Cleopatra swept in, royally arrayed, her dark hair hanging about her and the sacred snake of royalty glistening on her brow.

"Of a truth, Harmachis," she said with a sigh, as she sank into a seat, "the path to heaven is hard to climb! Ah! I am weary, for those stairs are many. But I was minded, my astronomer, to see thee in thy haunts."

"I am honoured overmuch, O Queen!" I said bowing low before her.

"Art thou now? And yet that dark face of thine has a somewhat angry look—thou art too young and handsome for this dry trade, Harmachis. Why, I vow thou hast cast my wreath of roses down amidst thy rusty tools! Kings would have cherished that wreath along with their choicest diadems, Harmachis! and thou dost throw it away as a thing of no account! Why, what a man art thou! But stay; what is this? A lady's kerchief, by Isis! Nay, now, my Harmachis, how came *this* here? Are our poor kerchiefs also instruments of thy high art? Oh, fie, fie!—have I caught thee, then? Art thou indeed a fox?"

"Nay, most royal Cleopatra, nay!" I said, turning; for the kerchief which had fallen from Charmion's neck had an awkward look. "I know not, indeed, how the frippery came here. Perhaps, some one of the women who keeps the chamber may have let it fall."

"Ah! so—so!" she said dryly, and still laughing like a rippling brook. "Yes, surely, the slave-women who keep chambers own such toys as this, of the very finest silk, worth twice its weight in gold, and broidered, too, in many colours. Why, myself I should not shame to wear it! Of a truth it seems familiar to my sight." And she threw it round her neck and smoothed the ends with her white hand. "But there; doubtless, it is a thing unholy in thine eyes that the scarf of thy beloved should rest upon my poor breast. Take it, Harmachis; take it, and hide it in thy bosom—nigh thy heart indeed!"

I took the accursed thing, and, muttering what I may not write, stepped on to the giddy platform whence I watched the stars. Then, crushing it into a ball, I threw it to the winds of heaven.

At this the lovely Queen laughed once more.

"Nay, think now," she cried; "what would the lady say could she see her love-gauge thus cast to all the world? Mayhap, Harmachis, thou wouldst deal thus with my wreath also? See, the roses fade; cast it forth," and, stooping, she took up the wreath and gave it to me.

For a moment, so vexed was I, I had a mind to take her at her word and send the wreath to join the kerchief. But I thought better of it.

"Nay," I said more softly, "it is a Queen's gift, and I will keep it," and, as I spoke, I saw the curtain shake. Often since that night I have sorrowed over those simple words.

"Gracious thanks be to the King of Love for this small mercy," she answered, looking at me strangely. "Now, enough of wit; come forth upon this balcony—tell me of the mystery of those stars of thine. For I always loved the stars, that are so pure and bright and cold, and so far away from our fevered troubling. There I would wish to dwell, rocked on the dark bosom of the night, and losing the little sense of self as I gazed for ever on the countenance of yon sweet-eyed space. Nay—who can tell, Harmachis?—perhaps those stars partake of our very substance, and, linked to us by Nature's invisible chain, do, indeed, draw our destiny with them as they roll. What says the Greek fable of him who became a star? Perchance it has truth, for yonder tiny sparks may be the souls of men, but grown more purely bright and placed in happy rest to illume the turmoil of their mother-earth. Or are they lamps hung high in the heavenly vault that night by night some Godhead, whose wings are Darkness, touches with his immortal fire so that they leap out in answering flame? Give me of thy wisdom and open these wonders to me, my servant, for I have little knowledge. Yet my heart is large, and I would fill it, for I have the wit, could I but find the teacher."

Thereon, being glad to find footing on a safer shore, and marvelling somewhat to learn that Cleopatra had a place for lofty thoughts, I spoke and willingly told her such things as are lawful. I told her how the sky is a liquid mass pressing round the earth and resting on the elastic pillars of the air, and how above is the heavenly ocean Nout, in which the planets float like ships as they rush upon their radiant way. I told her many things, and amongst them how, through the certain never-ceasing movement of the orbs of light, the planet Venus, that was called Donaou when she showed as the Morning Star, became the planet Bonou when she came as the sweet Star of Eve. And while I stood and spoke watching the stars, she sat, her hands clasped upon her knee, and watched my face.

"Ah!" she broke in at length, "and so Venus is to be seen both in the morning and the evening sky. Well, of a truth, she is everywhere, though she best loves the night. But thou lovest not that I should use these Latin names to thee. Come, we will talk in the ancient tongue of Khem, which I know well; I am the first, mark thou, of all the Lagidae who know it. And now," she went on, speaking in my own tongue, but with a little foreign accent that did but make her talk more sweet, "enough of stars, for, when all is said, they are but fickle things, and perhaps may even now be storing up an evil hour for thee or me, or for both of us together. Not but what I love to hear thee speak of them, for then thy face loses that gloomy cloud of thought which mars it and grows quick and human. Harmachis, thou art too young for such a solemn trade; methinks that I must find thee a better. Youth comes but once; why waste it in these musings? It is time to think when we can no longer act. Tell me how old art thou, Harmachis?"

"I have six-and-twenty years, O Queen," I answered, "for I was born in the first month of Shomou, in the summer season, and on the third day of the month."

"Why, then, we are of an age even to a day," she cried, "for I too have six-and-twenty years, and I too was born on the third day of the first month of Shomou. Well, this may we say: those who begot us need have no shame. For if I be the fairest woman in Egypt, methinks, Harmachis, that there is in Egypt no man more fair and strong than thou, ay, or more learned. Born of the same day, why, 'tis manifest that we were destined to stand together, I, as the Queen, and thou, perchance, Harmachis, as one of the chief pillars of my throne, and thus to work each other's weal."

"Or maybe each other's woe," I answered, looking up; for her sweet speeches stung my ears and brought more colour to my face than I loved that she should see there.

"Nay, never talk of woe. Be seated here by me, Harmachis, and let us talk, not as Queen and subject, but as friend to friend. Thou wast angered with me at the feast to-night because I mocked thee with yonder wreath—was it not so? Nay, it was but a jest. Didst thou know how heavy is the task of monarchs and how wearisome are their hours, thou wouldst not be wroth because I lit my dullness with a jest. Oh, they weary me, those princes and those nobles, and those stiff-necked pompous Romans. To my face they vow themselves my slaves, and behind my back they mock me and proclaim me the servant of their Triumvirate, or their Empire, or their Republic, as the wheel of Fortune turns, and each rises on its round! There is never a man among them—nothing but fools, parasites, and puppets—never a man since with their coward daggers they slew that Caesar whom all the world in arms was not strong enough to tame. And I must play off one against the other, if maybe, by so doing, I can keep Egypt from their grip. And for reward, what? Why, this is my reward—that all men speak ill of me—and, I know it, my subjects hate me! Yes, I believe that, woman though I am, they would murder me could they find a means!"

She paused, covering her eyes with her hand, and it was well, for her words pierced me so that I shrank upon the seat beside her.

"They think ill of me, I know it; and call me wanton, who have never stepped aside save once, when I loved the greatest man of all the world, and at the touch of love my passion flamed indeed, but burnt a hallowed flame. These ribald Alexandrians swear that I poisoned Ptolemy, my brother—whom the Roman Senate would, most unnaturally, have forced on me, his sister, as a husband! But it is false: he sickened and died of fever. And even so they say that I would slay Arsinoë, my sister—who, indeed, would slay me!—but that, too, is false! Though she will have none of me, I love my sister. Yes, they all think ill of me without a cause; even thou dost think ill of me, Harmachis.

"O Harmachis, before thou judgest, remember what a thing is envy!—that foul sickness of the mind which makes the jaundiced eye of pettiness to see all things distraught—to read Evil written on the open face of Good, and find impurity in the whitest virgin's soul! Think what a thing it is, Harmachis, to be set on high above the gaping crowd of knaves who hate thee for thy fortune and thy wit; who gnash their teeth and shoot the arrows of their lies from the cover of their own obscureness, whence they have no wings to soar; and whose hearts' quest it is to drag down thy nobility to the level of the groundling and the fool!

"Be not, then, swift to think evil of the Great, whose every word and act is searched for error by a million angry eyes, and whose most tiny fault is trumpeted by a thousand throats, till the world shakes with echoes of their sin! Say not: 'It is thus, 'tis certainly thus'—say, rather: 'May it not be otherwise? Have we heard aright? Did she this thing of her own will?' Judge gently, Harmachis, as wert thou I thou wouldst be judged. Remember that a Queen is never free. She is, indeed, but the point and instrument of those forces politic with which the iron books of history are graved. O Harmachis! be thou my friend—my friend and counsellor!—my friend whom I can trust indeed!—for here, in this crowded Court, I am more utterly alone than any soul that breathes about its corridors. But *thee* I trust; there is faith written in those quiet eyes, and I am minded to lift thee high, Harmachis. I can no longer bear my solitude of mind—I must find one with whom I may commune and speak that which lies within my heart. I have faults, I know it; but I am not all unworthy of thy faith, for there is good grain among the evil seed. Say, Harmachis, wilt thou take pity on my loneliness and befriend me, who have lovers, courtiers, slaves, dependents, more thick than I can count, but never one single *friend*?" and she leant towards me, touching me lightly, and gazed on me with her wonderful blue eyes.

I was overcome; thinking of the morrow night, shame and sorrow smote me. *I*, her friend!—*I*, whose assassin dagger lay against my breast! I bent my head, and a sob or a groan, I know not which, burst from the agony of my heart.

But Cleopatra, thinking only that I was moved beyond myself by the surprise of her graciousness, smiled sweetly, and said:

"It grows late; to-morrow night when thou bringest the auguries we will speak again, O my friend Harmachis, and thou shalt answer me." And she gave me her hand to kiss. Scarce knowing what I did, I kissed it, and in another moment she was gone.

But I stood in the chamber, gazing after her like one asleep.

CHAPTER 6

Of the Words and Jealousy of Charmion

I stood still, plunged in thought. Then by hazard as it were I took up the wreath of roses and looked on it. How long I stood so I know not, but when next I lifted up my eyes they fell upon the form of Charmion, whom, indeed, I had altogether forgotten. And though at the moment I thought but little of it, I noted vaguely that she was flushed as though with anger, and beat her foot upon the floor.

"Oh, it is thou, Charmion!" I said. "What ails thee? Art thou cramped with standing so long in thy hiding-place? Why didst not thou slip hence when Cleopatra led me to the balcony?"

"Where is my kerchief?" she asked, shooting an angry glance at me. "I let fall my broidered kerchief."

"Thy kerchief!—why, didst thou not see? Cleopatra twitted me about it, and I flung it from the balcony."

"Yes, I saw," answered the girl, "I saw but too well. Thou didst fling away my kerchief, but the wreath of roses—that thou wouldst not fling away. It was 'a Queen's gift,' forsooth, and therefore the royal Harmachis, the Priest of Isis, the chosen of the Gods, the crowned Pharaoh wed to the weal of Khem, cherished it and saved it. But my kerchief, stung by the laughter of that light Queen, he cast away!"

"What meanest thou?" I asked, astonished at her bitter tone. "I cannot read thy riddles."

"What mean I?" she answered, tossing up her head and showing the white curves of her throat. "Nay, I mean naught, or all; take it as thou wilt. Wouldst know what I mean, Harmachis, my cousin and my Lord?" she went on in a hard, low voice. "Then I will tell thee—thou art in danger of the great offence. This Cleopatra has cast her fatal wiles about thee, and thou goest near to loving her, Harmachis—to loving her whom to-morrow thou must slay! Ay, stand and stare at that wreath in thy hand—the wreath thou couldst not send to join my kerchief—sure Cleopatra wore it but to-night! The perfume of the hair of Caesar's mistress—Caesar's and others'—yet mingles with the odour of its roses! Now, prithee, Harmachis, how far didst thou carry the matter on yonder balcony? for in that hole where I lay hid I could not hear or see. 'Tis a sweet spot for lovers, is it not?—ay, and a sweet hour, too? Venus surely rules the stars to-night?"

All of this she said so quietly and in so soft and modest a way, though her words were not modest, and yet so bitterly, that every syllable cut me to the heart, and angered me till I could find no speech.

"Of a truth thou hast a wise economy," she went on, seeing her advantage: "to-night thou dost kiss the lips that to-morrow thou shalt still for ever! It is frugal dealing with the occasion of the moment; ay, worthy and honourable dealing!"

Then at last I broke forth. "Girl," I cried, "how darest thou speak thus to me? Mindest thou who and what I am that thou loosest thy peevish gibes upon me?"

"I mind what it behoves thee to be," she answered quick. "What thou art, that I mind not now. Surely thou knowest alone—thou and Cleopatra!"

"What meanest thou?" I said. "Am I to blame if the Queen—"

"The Queen! What have we here? Pharaoh owns a Queen!"

"If Cleopatra wills to come hither of a night and talk—"

"Of stars, Harmachis—surely of stars and roses, and naught beside!"

After that I know not what I said; for, troubled as I was, the girl's bitter tongue and quiet way drove me well-nigh to madness. But this I know: I spoke so fiercely that she cowered before me as she had cowered before my uncle Sepa when he rated her because of her Grecian garb. And as she wept then, so she wept now, only more passionately and with great sobs.

At length I ceased, half-shamed but still angry and smarting sorely. For even while she wept she could find a tongue to answer with—and a woman's shafts are sharp.

"Thou shouldst not speak to me thus!" she sobbed; "it is cruel—it is unmanly! But I forget thou art but a priest, not a man—except, mayhap, for Cleopatra!"

"What right hast thou?" I said. "What canst thou mean?"

"What right have I?" she asked, looking up, her dark eyes all aflood with tears that ran down her sweet face like the dew of morning down a lily's heart. "What right have I? O Harmachis! art thou blind? Didst thou not know by what right I speak thus to thee?

Then I must tell thee. Well, it is the fashion in Alexandria! By that first and holy right of woman—by the right of the great love I bear thee, and which, it seems, thou hast no eyes to see—by the right of my glory and my shame. Oh, be not wroth with me, Harmachis, nor set me down as light, because the truth at last has burst from me; for I am not so. I am what thou wilt make me. I am the wax within the moulder's hands, and as thou dost fashion me so I shall be. There breathes within me now a breath of glory, blowing across the waters of my soul, that can waft me to ends more noble than ever I have dreamed afore, if thou wilt be my pilot and my guide. But if I lose thee, then I lose all that holds me from my worse self—and let shipwreck come! Thou knowest me not, Harmachis! thou canst not see how big a spirit struggles in this frail form of mine! To thee I am a girl, clever, wayward, shallow. But I am more! Show me thy loftiest thought and I will match it, the deepest puzzle of thy mind and I will make it clear. Of one blood we are, and love can ravel up our little difference and make us grow one indeed. One end we have, one land we love, one vow binds us both. Take me to thy heart, Harmachis, set me by thee on the Double Throne, and I swear that I will lift thee higher than ever man has climbed. Reject me, and beware lest I pull thee down! And now, putting aside the cold delicacy of custom, stung to it by what I saw of the arts of that lovely living falsehood, Cleopatra, which for pastime she practises on thy folly, I have spoken out my heart, and answer thou!" And she clasped her hands and, drawing one pace nearer, gazed, all white and trembling, on my face.

For a moment I stood struck dumb, for the magic of her voice and the power of her speech, despite myself, stirred me like the rush of music. Had I loved the woman, doubtless she might have fired me with her flame; but I loved her not, and I could not play at passion. And so thought came, and with thought that laughing mood, which is ever apt to fashion upon nerves strained to the point of breaking. In a flash, as it were, I bethought me of the way in which she had that very night forced the wreath of roses on my head, I thought of the kerchief and how I had flung it forth. I thought of Charmion in the little chamber watching what she held to be the arts of Cleopatra, and of her bitter speeches. Lastly, I thought of what my uncle Sepa would say of her could he see her now, and of the strange and tangled skein in which I was enmeshed. And I laughed aloud—the fool's laughter that was my knell of ruin!

She turned whiter yet—white as the dead—and a look grew upon her face that checked my foolish mirth. "Thou findest, then, Harmachis," she said in a low, choked voice, and dropping the level of her eyes, "thou findest cause of merriment in what I have said?"

"Nay," I answered; "nay, Charmion; forgive me if I laughed. It was rather a laugh of despair; for what am I to say to thee? Thou hast spoken high words of all thou mightest be: is it left for me to tell thee what thou art?"

She shrank, and I paused.

"Speak," she said.

"Thou knowest—none so well!—who I am and what my mission is: thou knowest—none so well!—that I am sworn to Isis, and may, by law Divine, have naught to do with thee."

"Ay," she broke in, in her low voice, and with her eyes still fixed upon the ground—"ay, and I know that thy vows are broken in spirit, if not in form—broken like wreaths of cloud; for, Harmachis—*thou lovest Cleopatra!*"

"It is a lie!" I cried. "Thou wanton girl, who wouldst seduce me from my duty and put me to an open shame!—who, led by passion or ambition, or the love of evil, hast not shamed to break the barriers of thy sex and speak as thou hast spoken—beware lest thou go too far! And if thou wilt have an answer, here it is, put straightly, as thy question. Charmion, outside the matter of my duty and my vows, thou art *naught* to me!—nor for all thy tender glances will my heart beat one pulse more fast! Hardly art thou now my friend—for, of a truth, I scarce can trust thee. But, once more: beware! To me thou mayest do thy worst; but if thou dost dare to lift a finger against our cause, that day thou diest! And now, is this play done?"

And as, wild with anger, I spoke thus, she shrank back, and yet further back, till at length she rested against the wall, her eyes covered with her hand. But when I ceased she dropped her hand, glancing up, and her face was as the face of a statue, in which the great eyes glowed like embers, and round them was a ring of purple shadow.

"Not altogether done," she answered gently; "the arena must yet be sanded!" This she said having reference to the covering up of the bloodstains at the gladiatorial shows with fine sand. "Well," she went on, "waste not thine anger on a thing so vile. I have thrown my throw and I have lost. *Vae victis!*—ah! *Vae victis!* Wilt thou not lend me the dagger in thy robe, that here and now I may end my shame? No? Then one word more, most royal Harmachis: if thou canst, forget my folly; but, at the least, have no fear from me. I am now, as ever, thy servant and the servant of our cause. Farewell!"

And she went, leaning her hand against the wall. But I, passing to my chamber, flung myself upon my couch, and groaned in bitterness of spirit. Alas! we shape our plans, and by slow degrees build up our house of Hope, never counting on the guests that time shall bring to lodge therein. For who can guard against—the Unforeseen?

At length I slept, and my dreams were evil. When I woke the light of the day which should see the red fulfilment of the plot was streaming through the casement, and the birds sang merrily among the garden palms. I woke, and as I woke the sense of trouble pressed in upon me, for I remembered that before this day was gathered to the past I must dip my hands in blood—yes, in the blood of Cleopatra, who trusted me! Why could I not hate her as I should? There had been a time when I looked on to this act of vengeance with somewhat of a righteous glow of zeal. And now—and now—why, I would frankly give my royal birthright to be free from its necessity! But, alas! I knew that there was no escape. I must drain this cup or be for ever cast away. I felt the eyes of Egypt watching me, and the eyes of Egypt's Gods. I prayed to my Mother Isis to give me strength to do this deed, and prayed as I had never prayed before; and oh, wonder! no answer came. Nay, how was this? What, then, had loosed the link between us that, for the first time, the Goddess deigned no reply to her son and chosen servant? Could it be that I had sinned in heart against her? What had Charmion said—that I loved Cleopatra? Was this sickness love? Nay! a thousand times nay!—it was but the revolt of Nature against an act of treachery and blood. The Goddess did but try my strength, or perchance she also turned her holy countenance from murder?

I rose filled with terror and despair, and went about my task like a man without a soul. I conned the fatal lists and noted all the plans—ay, in my brain I gathered up the very words of that proclamation of my Royalty which, on the morrow, I should issue to the startled world.

"Citizens of Alexandria and dwellers in the land of Egypt," it began, "Cleopatra the Macedonian hath, by the command of the Gods, suffered justice for her crimes—"

All these and other things I did, but I did them as a man without a soul—as a man moved by a force from without and not from within. And so the minutes wore away. In the third hour of the afternoon I went as by appointment fixed to the house where my uncle Sepa lodged, that same house to which I had been brought some three months gone when I entered Alexandria for the first time. And here I found the leaders of the revolt in the city assembled in secret conclave to the number of seven. When I had entered, and the doors were barred, they prostrated themselves, and cried, "Hail, Pharaoh!" but I bade them rise, saying that I was not yet Pharaoh, for the chicken was still in the egg.

"Yea, Prince," said my uncle, "but his beak shows through. Not in vain hath Egypt brooded all these years, if thou fail not with that dagger-stroke of thine to-night; and how canst thou fail? Nothing can now stop our course to victory!"

"It is on the knees of the Gods," I answered.

"Nay," he said, "the Gods have placed the issue in the hands of a mortal—in thy hands, Harmachis!—and there it is safe. See: here are the last lists. Thirty-one thousand men who bear arms are sworn to rise when the tidings come to them. Within five days every citadel in Egypt will be in our hands, and then what have we to fear? From Rome but little, for her hands are full; and, besides, we will make alliance with the Triumvirate, and, if need be, buy them off. For of money there is plenty in the land, and if more be wanted thou, Harmachis, knowest where it is stored against the need of Khem, and outside the Roman's reach of arm. Who is there to harm us? There is none. Perchance, in this turbulent city, there may be struggle, and a counter-plot to bring Arsinoë to Egypt and set her on the throne. Therefore Alexandria must be severely dealt with—ay, even to destruction, if need be. As for Arsinoë, those go forth to-morrow on the news of the Queen's death who shall slay her secretly."

"There remains the lad Caesarion," I said. "Rome might claim through Caesar's son, and the child of Cleopatra inherits Cleopatra's rights. Here is a double danger."

"Fear not," said my uncle; "to-morrow Caesarion joins those who begat him in Amenti. I have made provision. The Ptolemies must be stamped out, so that no shoot shall ever spring from that root blasted by Heaven's vengeance."

"Is there no other means?" I asked sadly. "My heart is sick at the promise of this red rain of blood. I know the child well; he has Cleopatra's fire and beauty and great Caesar's wit. It were shame to murder him."

"Nay, be not so chicken-hearted, Harmachis," said my uncle, sternly. "What ails thee, then? If the lad is thus, the more reason that he should die. Wouldst thou nurse up a young lion to tear thee from the throne?"

"Be it so," I answered, sighing. "At least he is spared much, and will go hence innocent of evil. Now for the plans."

We sat long taking counsel, till at length, in face of the great emergency and our high emprise, I felt something of the spirit of former days flow back into my heart. At the last all was ordered, and so ordered that it could scarce miscarry, for it was fixed that if by any chance I could not come to slay Cleopatra on this night, then the plot should hang in the scale till the morrow, when the deed must be done upon occasion. For the death of Cleopatra was the signal. These matters being finished, once more we stood and, our hands upon the sacred symbol, swore the oath that may not be written. And then my uncle kissed me with tears of hope and joy standing in his keen black eyes. He blessed me, saying that he would gladly give his life, ay, and a hundred lives, if they were his, if he might but live to see Egypt once more a nation, and me, Harmachis, the descendant of its royal and ancient blood, seated on the throne. For he was a patriot indeed, asking nothing for himself, and giving all things to his cause. And I kissed him in turn, and thus we parted. Nor did I ever see him more in the flesh who has earned the rest that as yet is denied to me.

So I went, and, there being yet time, walked swiftly from place to place in the great city, taking note of the positions of the gates and of the places where our forces must be gathered. At length I came to that quay where I had landed, and saw a vessel sailing for the open sea. I looked, and in my heaviness of heart longed that I were aboard of her, to be borne by her white wings to some far shore where I might live obscure and die forgotten. Also I saw another vessel that had dropped down the Nile, from whose deck the passengers were streaming. For a moment I stood watching them, idly wondering if they were from Abouthis, when suddenly I heard a familiar voice beside me.

"*La! la!*" said the voice. "Why, what a city is this for an old woman to seek her fortune in! And how shall I find those to whom I am known? As well look for the rush in the papyrus-roll.[14] Begone! thou knave! and let my basket of simples lie; or, by the Gods, I'll doctor thee with them!"

I turned, wondering, and found myself face to face with my foster-nurse, Atoua. She knew me instantly, for I saw her start, but in the presence of the people she checked her surprise.

"Good Sir," she whined, lifting her withered countenance towards me, and at the same time making the secret sign. "By thy dress thou shouldst be an astronomer, and I was specially told to avoid astronomers as a pack of lying tricksters who worship their own star only; and, therefore, I speak to thee, acting on the principle of contraries, which is law to us women. For surely in this Alexandria, where all

14 Papyrus was manufactured from the pith of rushes. Hence Atoua's saying.—Editor.

things are upside down, the astronomers may be the honest men, since the rest are clearly knaves." And then, being by now out of earshot of the press, "Royal Harmachis, I am come charged with a message to thee from thy father Amenemhat."

"Is he well?" I asked.

"Yes, he is well, though waiting for the moment tries him sorely."

"And his message?"

"It is this. He sends greeting to thee and with it warning that a great danger threatens thee, though he cannot read it. These are his words: 'Be steadfast and prosper.'"

I bowed my head and the words struck a new chill of fear into my soul.

"When is the time?" she asked.

"This very night. Where goest thou?"

"To the house of the honourable Sepa, Priest of Annu. Canst thou guide me thither?"

"Nay, I may not stay; nor is it wise that I should be seen with thee. Hold!" and I called a porter who was idling on the quay, and, giving him a piece of money, bade him guide the old wife to the house.

"Farewell," she whispered; "farewell till to-morrow. Be steadfast and prosper."

Then I turned and went my way through the crowded streets, where the people made place for me, the astronomer of Cleopatra, for my fame had spread abroad.

And even as I went my footsteps seemed to beat *Be steadfast, Be steadfast, Be steadfast,* till at last it was as though the very ground cried out its warning to me.

Chapter 7

Of the Veiled Words of Charmion

It was night, and I sat alone in my chamber, waiting the moment when, as it was agreed, Charmion should summon me to pass down to Cleopatra. I sat alone, and there before me lay the dagger that was to pierce her. It was long and keen, and the handle was formed of a sphinx of solid gold. I sat alone, questioning the future, but no answer came. At length I looked up, and Charmion stood before me—Charmion, no longer gay and bright, but pale of face and hollow-eyed.

"Royal Harmachis," she said, "Cleopatra summons thee, presently to declare to her the voices of the stars."

So the hour had fallen!

"It is well, Charmion," I answered. "Are all things in order?"

"Yea, my Lord; all things are in order: well primed with wine, Paulus guards the gates, the eunuchs are withdrawn save one, the legionaries sleep, and already Sepa and his force lie hid without. Nothing has been neglected, and no lamb skipping at the shamble doors can be more innocent of its doom than is Queen Cleopatra."

"It is well," I said again; "let us be going," and rising, I placed the dagger in the bosom of my robe. Taking a cup of wine that stood near, I drank deep of it, for I had scarce tasted food all that day.

"One word," Charmion said hurriedly, "for it is not yet time: last night—ah, last night—" and her bosom heaved, "I dreamed a dream that haunts me strangely, and perchance thou also didst dream a dream. It was all a dream and 'tis forgotten: is it not so, my Lord?"

"Yes, yes," I said; "why troublest thou me thus at such an hour?"

"Nay, I know not; but to-night, Harmachis, Fate is in labour of a great event, and in her painful throes mayhap she'll crush me in her grip—me or thee, or the twain of us, Harmachis. And if that be so—well, I would hear from thee, before it is done, that 'twas naught but a dream, and that dream forgot—"

"Yes, it is all a dream," I said idly; "thou and I, and the solid earth, and this heavy night of terror, ay, and this keen knife—what are these but dreams, and with what face shall the waking come?"

"So now, thou fallest in my humour, Royal Harmachis. As thou sayest, we dream; and while we dream yet can the vision change. For the fantasies of dreams are wonderful, seeing that they have no stability, but vary like the vaporous edge of sunset clouds, building now this thing, and now that; being now dark and heavy, and now alight with splendour. Therefore, before we wake to-morrow tell me one word. Is that vision of last night, wherein I *seemed* to be quite shamed, and thou didst *seem* to laugh upon my shame, a fixed fantasy, or can it, perchance, yet change its countenance? For remember, when that waking comes, the vagaries of our sleep will be more unalterable and more enduring than are the pyramids. Then they will be gathered into that changeless region of the past where all things, great and small—ay, even dreams, Harmachis, are, each in its own semblance, frozen to stone and built into the Tomb of Time immortal."

"Nay, Charmion," I replied, "I grieve if I did pain thee; but over that vision comes no change. I said what was in my heart and there's an end. Thou art my cousin and my friend, I can never be more to thee."

"It is well—'tis very well," she said; "let it be forgotten. And now on from dream—to dream," and she smiled with such a smile as I had never seen her wear before; it was sadder and more fateful than any stamp that grief can set upon the brow.

For, though being blinded by my own folly and the trouble at my heart I knew it not, with that smile, the happiness of youth died for Charmion the Egyptian; the hope of love fled; and the holy links of duty burst asunder. With that smile she consecrated herself to Evil, she renounced her Country and her Gods, and trampled on her oath. Ay, that smile marks the moment when the stream of history changed its course. For had I never seen it on her face Octavianus had not bestridden the world, and Egypt had once more been free and great.

And yet it was but a woman's smile!

"Why lookest thou thus strangely, girl?" I asked.

"In dreams we smile," she answered. "And now it is time; follow thou me. Be firm and prosper, Royal Harmachis!" and bending forward she took my hand and kissed it. Then, with one strange last look, she turned and led the way down the stair and through the empty halls.

In the chamber that is called the Alabaster Hall, the roof of which is upborne by columns of black marble, we stayed. For beyond was the private chamber of Cleopatra, the same in which I had seen her sleeping.

"Abide thou here," she said, "while I tell Cleopatra of thy coming," and she glided from my side.

I stood for long, mayhap in all the half of an hour, counting my own heart-beats, and, as in a dream, striving to gather up my strength to that which lay before me.

At length Charmion came back, her head held low and walking heavily.

"Cleopatra waits thee," she said: "pass on, there is no guard."

"Where do I meet thee when what must be done is done?" I asked hoarsely.

"Thou meetest me here, and then to Paulus. Be firm and prosper. Harmachis, fare thee well!"

And so I went; but at the curtain I turned suddenly, and there in the midst of that lonely lamplit hall I saw a strange sight. Far away, in such a fashion that the light struck full upon her, stood Charmion, her head thrown back, her white arms outstretched as though to clasp, and on her girlish face a stamp of anguished passion so terrible to see that, indeed, I cannot tell it! For she believed that I, whom she loved, was passing to my death, and this was her last farewell to me.

But I knew naught of this matter; so with another passing pang of wonder I drew aside the curtains, gained the doorway, and stood in Cleopatra's chamber. And there, upon a silken couch at the far end of the perfumed chamber, clad in wonderful white attire, rested Cleopatra. In her hand was a jewelled fan of ostrich plumes, with which she gently fanned herself, and by her side was her harp of ivory, and a little table whereon were figs and goblets and a flask of ruby-coloured wine. I drew near slowly through the soft dim light to where the Wonder of the World lay in all her glowing beauty. And, indeed, I have never seen her look so fair as she did upon that fatal night. Couched in her amber cushions, she seemed to shine as a star on the twilight's glow. Perfume came from her hair and robes, music fell from her lips, and in her heavenly eyes all lights changed and gathered as in the ominous opal's disc.

And this was the woman whom, presently, I must slay!

Slowly I drew near, bowing as I came; but she took no heed. She lay there, and the jewelled fan floated to and fro like the bright wing of some hovering bird.

At length I stood before her, and she glanced up, the ostrich-plumes pressed against her breast as though to hide its beauty.

"What! friend; art thou come?" she said. "It is well; for I grew lonely here. Nay; 'tis a weary world! We know so many faces, and there are so few whom we love to see again. Well, stand not there so mute, but be seated." And she pointed with her fan to a carven chair that was placed near her feet.

Once more I bowed and took the seat.

"I have obeyed the Queen's desire," I said, "and with much care and skill worked out the lessons of the stars; and here is the record of my labour. If the Queen permits, I will expound it to her." And I rose, in order that I might pass round the couch and, as she read, stab her in the back.

"Nay, Harmachis," she said quietly, and with a slow and lovely smile. "Bide thou where thou art, and give me the writing. By Serapis! thy face is too comely for me to wish to lose the sight of it!"

Checked in this design, I could do nothing but hand her the papyrus, thinking to myself that while she read I would arise suddenly and plunge the dagger to her heart. She took it, and as she did so touched my hand. Then she made pretence to read. But she read no word, for I saw that her eyes were fixed upon me over the edge of the scroll.

"Why placest thou thy hand within thy robe?" she asked presently; for, indeed, I clutched the dagger's hilt. "Is thy heart stirred?"

"Yea, O Queen," I said; "it beats high."

She gave no answer, but once more made pretence to read, and the while she watched me.

I took counsel with myself. How should I do the hateful deed? If I flung myself upon her now she would see me and scream and struggle. Nay, I must wait a chance.

"The auguries are favourable, then, Harmachis?" she said at length, though this she must have guessed.

"Yes, O Queen," I answered.

"It is well," and she cast the writing on the marble. "The ships shall sail. For, good or bad, I am weary of weighing chances."

"This is a heavy matter, O Queen," I said. "I had wished to show upon what circumstance I base my forecast."

"Nay, not so, Harmachis; I have wearied of the ways of stars. Thou hast prophesied; that is enough for me; for, doubtless, being honest, thou hast written honestly. Therefore, save thou thy reasons and we'll be merry. What shall we do? I could dance to thee—there are none who can dance so well!—but it would scarce be queenly. Nay, I have it.

I will sing." And, leaning forward, she raised herself, and, bending the harp towards her, struck some wandering chords. Then her low voice broke out in perfect and most sweet song.

And thus she sang:

Night on the sea, and night upon the sky,
And music in our hearts, we floated there,
Lulled by the low sea voices, thou and I,
And the wind's kisses in my cloudy hair:
And thou didst gaze on me and call me fair—
Enfolded by the starry robe of night—
And then thy singing thrilled upon the air,
Voice of the heart's desire and Love's delight.

Adrift, with starlit skies above,
With starlit seas below,
We move with all the suns that move,
With all the seas that flow;
For bond or free, Earth, Sky, and Sea,
Wheel with one circling will,
And thy heart drifteth on to me,
And only time stands still.

Between two shores of Death we drift,
Behind are things forgot:
Before the tide is driving swift
To lands beholden not.
Above, the sky is far and cold;
Below, the moaning sea
Sweeps o'er the loves that were of old,
But, oh, Love! kiss thou me.

Ah, lonely are the ocean ways,
And dangerous the deep,
And frail the fairy barque that strays
Above the seas asleep!
Ah, toil no more at sail nor oar,
We drift, or bond or free;
On yon far shore the breakers roar,
But, oh, Love! kiss thou me.

And ever as thou sangest I drew near,
Then sudden silence heard our hearts that beat,
For now there was an end of doubt and fear,
Now passion filled my soul and led my feet;

Then silent didst thou rise thy love to meet,
Who, sinking on thy breast, knew naught but thee,
And in the happy night I kissed thee,
Sweet; Ah, Sweet! between the starlight and the sea.

The last echoes of her rich notes floated down the chamber, and slowly died away; but in my heart they rolled on and on. I have heard among the women-singers at Abouthis voices more perfect than the voice of Cleopatra, but never have I heard one so thrilling or so sweet with passion's honey-notes. And indeed it was not the voice alone, it was the perfumed chamber in which was set all that could move the sense; it was the passion of the thought and words, and the surpassing grace and loveliness of that most royal woman who sang them. For, as she sang, I seemed to think that we twain were indeed floating alone with the night, upon the starlit summer sea. And when she ceased to touch the harp, and, rising, suddenly stretched out her arms towards me, and with the last low notes of song yet quivering upon her lips, let fall the wonder of her eyes upon my eyes, she almost drew me to her. But I remembered, and would not.

"Hast thou, then, no word of thanks for my poor singing, Harmachis?" she said at length.

"Yea, O Queen," I answered, speaking very low, for my voice was choked; "but thy songs are not good for the sons of men to hear—of a truth they overwhelm me!"

"Nay, Harmachis; there is no fear for thee," she said laughing softly, "seeing that I know how far thy thoughts are set from woman's beauty and the common weakness of thy sex. With cold iron we may safely toy."

I thought within myself that coldest iron can be brought to whitest heat if the fire be fierce enough. But I said nothing, and, though my hand trembled, I once more grasped the dagger's hilt, and, wild with fear at my own weakness, set myself to find a means to slay her while yet my sense remained.

"Come hither, Harmachis," she went on, in her softest voice. "Come, sit by me, and we will talk together; for I have much to tell thee," and she made place for me at her side upon the silken seat.

And I, thinking that I might so more swiftly strike, rose and seated myself some little way from her on the couch, while, flinging back her head, she gazed on me with her slumberous eyes.

Now was my occasion, for her throat and breast were bare, and, with a mighty effort, once again I lifted my hand to clutch the dagger-hilt. But, more quick than thought, she caught my fingers with her own and gently held them.

"Why lookest thou so wildly, Harmachis?" she said. "Art sick?"

"Ay, sick indeed!" I gasped.

"Then lean thou on the cushions and rest thee," she answered, still holding my hand, from which the strength had fled. "The fit will surely pass. Too long hast thou laboured with thy stars. How soft is the night air that flows from yonder casement heavy with the breath of lilies! Hark to the whisper of the sea lapping against the rocks, that, though it is faint, yet, being so strong, doth almost drown the quick cool fall of yonder fountain. List to Philomel; how sweet from a full heart of love she sings her message to her dear! Indeed it is a lovely night, and most beautiful is Nature's music, sung with a hundred voices from wind and trees and birds and ocean's wrinkled lips, and yet sung all to tune. Listen, Harmachis: I have guessed something concerning thee. Thou, too, art of a royal race; no humble blood pours in those veins of thine. Surely such a shoot could spring but from the stock of Princes? What! gazest thou at the leaf-mark on my breast? It was pricked there in honour of great Osiris, whom with thee I worship. See!"

"Let me hence," I groaned, striving to rise; but my strength had gone.

"Nay, not yet awhile. Thou wouldst not leave me yet? thou *canst* not leave me yet. Harmachis, hast thou never loved?"

"Nay, nay, O Queen! What have I to do with love? Let me hence!—I am faint—I am fordone!"

"Never to have loved—'tis strange! Never to have known some woman-heart beat all in tune to thine—never to have seen the eyes of thy adored aswim with passion's tears, as she sighed her vows upon thy breast!—Never to have loved!—never to have lost thyself in the mystery of another's soul; nor to have learned how Nature can overcome our naked loneliness, and with the golden web of love of twain weave one identity! Why, it is never to have lived, Harmachis!"

And ever as she murmured she drew nearer to me, till at last, with a long, sweet sigh, she flung one arm about my neck, and gazed upon me with blue, unfathomable eyes, and smiled her dark, slow smile, that, like an opening flower, revealed beauty within beauty hidden. Nearer she bent her queenly form, and still more near—now her perfumed breath played upon my hair, and now her lips met mine.

And woe is me! In that kiss, more deadly and more strong than the embrace of Death, were forgotten Isis, my heavenly Hope, Oaths, Honour, Country, Friends, all things—all things save that Cleopatra clasped me in her arms, and called me Love and Lord.

"Now pledge me," she sighed; "pledge me one cup of wine in token of thy love."

I took the draught, and I drank deep; then too late I knew that it was drugged.

I fell upon the couch, and, though my senses still were with me, I could neither speak nor rise.

But Cleopatra, bending over me, drew the dagger from my robe.

"*I've won!*" she cried, shaking back her long hair. "I've won, and for the stake of Egypt, why, 'twas a game worth playing! With this dagger, then, thou wouldst have slain me, O my Royal Rival, whose myrmidons even now are gathered at my palace gate? Art still awake? Now what hinders me that I should not plunge it to *thy* heart?"

I heard and feebly pointed to my breast, for I was fain to die. She drew herself to the full of her imperial height, and the great knife glittered in her hand. Down it came till its edge pricked my flesh.

"Nay," she cried again, and cast it from her, "too well I like thee. It were pity to slay such a man! I give thee thy life. Live on, lost Pharaoh! Live on, poor fallen Prince, blasted by a woman's wit! Live on, Harmachis—to adorn my triumph!"

****

Then sight left me; and in my ears I only heard the song of the nightingale, the murmur of the sea, and the music of Cleopatra's laugh of victory. And as I sank away, the sound of that low laugh still followed me into the land of sleep, and still it follows me through life to death.

CHAPTER 8

Of the Awaking of Harmachis

Once more I woke; it was to find myself in my own chamber. I started up. Surely, I, too, had dreamed a dream? It could be nothing but a dream? It could not be that I woke to know myself a *traitor!* That the opportunity had gone for ever! That I had betrayed the cause, and that last night those brave men, headed by my uncle, had waited in vain at the outer gate! That Egypt from Abu to Athu was even now waiting—waiting in vain! Nay, whatever else might be, this could not be! Oh, it was an awful dream which I had dreamed! a second such would slay a man. It were better to die than face such another vision sent from hell. But, though the thing was naught but a hateful fantasy of a mind o'er-strained, where was I now? Where was I now? I should be in the Alabaster Hall, waiting till Charmion came forth.

Where was I? and O ye Gods! what was that dreadful thing, whose shape was the shape of a man?—that thing draped in bloodstained white and huddled in a hideous heap at the foot of the couch on which I seemed to lie?

I sprang at it with a shriek, as a lion springs, and struck with all my strength. The blow fell heavily, and beneath its weight the thing rolled over upon its side. Half mad with terror, I rent away the white covering; and there, his knees bound beneath his hanging jaw, was the naked body of a man—and that man the Roman Captain Paulus! There he lay, through his heart a dagger—my dagger, handled with the sphinx of gold!—and pinned by its blade to his broad breast a scroll, and on the scroll, writing in the Roman character. I drew near and read, and this was the writing:

Harmachidi salvere ego sum quem subdere noras
paulus romanus disce hinc quid prodere prosit.

"Greeting, Harmachis! I was that Roman Paulus whom thou didst suborn. Learn now how blessed are traitors!"

Sick and faint I staggered back from the sight of that white corpse stained with its own blood. Sick and faint I staggered back, till the wall stayed me, while without the birds sang a merry greeting to the day. So it was no dream, and I was lost! lost!

I thought of my aged father, Amenemhat. Yes, the vision of him flashed into my mind, as he would be, when they came to tell him his son's shame and the ruin of all his hopes. I thought of that patriot priest, my uncle Sepa, waiting the long night through for the signal which never came. Ah, and another thought followed swift! How would it go with them? I was not the only traitor. I, too, had been betrayed. By whom? By yonder Paulus, perchance. If it were Paulus, he knew but little of those who conspired with me. But the secret lists had been in my robe. O Osiris! they were gone! and the fate of Paulus would be the fate of all the patriots in Egypt. And at this thought my mind gave way. I sank and swooned even where I stood.

My sense came back to me, and the lengthening shadows told me that it was afternoon. I staggered to my feet; the corpse of Paulus was still there, keeping its awful watch above me. I ran desperately to the door. It was barred, and without I heard the tramp of sentinels. As I stood they challenged and grounded their spears. Then the bolts were shot back, the door opened, and radiant, clad in royal attire, came the conquering Cleopatra. She came alone, and the door was shut behind her. I stood like one distraught; but she swept on till she was face to face with me.

"Greeting, Harmachis," she said, smiling sweetly. "So, my messenger has found thee!" and she pointed to the corpse of Paulus. "*Pah!* he has an ugly look. *Ho!* guards!"

The door was opened, and two armed Gauls stepped across the threshold.

"Take away this carrion," said Cleopatra, "and fling it to the kites. Stay, draw that dagger from his traitor breast." The men bowed low, and the knife, rusted red with blood, was dragged from the heart of Paulus and laid upon the table. Then they seized him by the head and body and staggered thence, and I heard their heavy footfalls as they bore him down the stairs.

"Methinks, Harmachis, thou art in an evil case," she said, when the sound of the footfalls had died away. "How strangely the wheel of Fortune turns! But for that traitor," and she nodded towards the door through which the corpse of Paulus had been carried, "I should now be as ill a thing to look on as he is, and the red rust on yonder knife would have been gathered from *my* heart."

So it was Paulus who had betrayed me.

"Ay," she went on, "and when thou camest to me last night, I *knew* that thou camest to slay. When, time upon time, thou didst place thy hand within thy robe, I knew that it grasped a dagger hilt, and that thou wast gathering thy courage to the deed which thou didst little love to do. Oh! it was a strange wild hour, well worth the living, and I wondered greatly, from moment to moment, which of us twain would conquer, as we matched guile with guile and force to force!

"Yea, Harmachis, the guards tramp before thy door, but be not deceived. Did I not know that I hold thee to me by bonds more strong than prison chains—did I not know that I am hedged from ill at thy hands by a fence of honour harder for thee to pass than all the spears of all my legions, thou hadst been dead ere now, Harmachis. See, here is thy knife," and she handed me the dagger; "now slay me if thou canst," and she drew near, tore open the bosom of her robe, and stood waiting with calm eyes.

"Thou canst not slay me," she went on; "for there are things, as I know well, that no man—no man such as thou art—may do and live: and this is the chief of them—to slay the woman who is all his own. Nay, stay thy hand! Turn not that dagger against thy breast, for if thou mayst not slay me, by how much more mayst thou not slay thyself, O thou forsworn Priest of Isis! Art thou, then, so eager to face that outraged Majesty in Amenti? With what eyes, thinkest thou, will the Heavenly Mother look upon Her son, who, shamed in all things and false to his most sacred vow, comes to greet Her, his life-blood on his hands? Where, then, will be the space for thy atonement?—if, indeed, thou mayest atone!"

Then I could bear no more, for my heart was broken. Alas! it was too true—I dared not die! I was come to such a pass that I did not even dare to die! I flung myself upon the couch and wept—wept tears of blood and anguish.

But Cleopatra came to me, and, seating herself beside me, she strove to comfort me, throwing her arms about my neck.

"Nay, love, look up," she said; "all is not lost for thee, nor am I angered against thee. We did play a mighty game; but, as I warned thee, I matched my woman's magic against thine, and I have conquered. But I will be open with thee. Both as Queen and woman thou hast my pity—ay, and more; nor do I love to see thee plunged in sorrow. It was well and right that thou shouldst strive to win back that throne my fathers seized, and the ancient liberty of Egypt. Myself as lawful Queen had done the same, nor shrunk from the deed of darkness to which I was sworn. Therein, then, thou hast my sympathy, that ever goes out to what is great and bold. It is well also that thou shouldst grieve over the greatness of thy fall. Therein, then, as woman—as loving woman—thou hast my sympathy. Nor is all lost. Thy plan was foolish—for, as I hold, Egypt could never have stood alone—for though thou hadst won the crown and country—as without a doubt thou must have done—yet there was the Roman to be reckoned with. And for thy hope learn this: I am little known. There is no heart in this wide land that beats with a truer love for ancient Khem than does this heart of mine—nay, not thine own, Harmachis. Yet I have been heavily shackled heretofore—for wars, rebellions, envies, plots, have hemmed me in on every side, so that I might not serve my people as I would. But thou, Harmachis, shalt show me how. Thou shalt be my counsellor and my love. Is it a little thing, Harmachis, to have won the heart of Cleopatra; that heart—fie on thee!—that thou wouldst have stilled? Yes, *thou* shalt unite me to my people and we will reign together, thus linking in one the new kingdom and the old and the new thought and the old. So do all things work for good—ay, for the very best: and thus, by another and a gentler road, thou shalt climb to Pharaoh's throne.

"See thou this, Harmachis: thy treachery shall be cloaked about as much as may be. Was it, then, thy fault that a Roman knave betrayed thy plans? that, thereon, thou wast drugged, thy secret papers stolen and their key guessed? Will it, then, be a blame to thee, the great plot being broken and those who built it scattered, that thou, still faithful to thy trust, didst serve thee of such means as Nature gave thee, and win the heart of Egypt's Queen, that, through her gentle love, thou mightest yet attain thy ends and spread thy wings of power across the land of Nile? Am I an ill-counsellor, thinkest thou, Harmachis?"

I lifted my head, and a ray of hope crept into the darkness of my heart; for when men fall they grasp at feathers. Then, I spoke for the first time:

"And those with me—those who trusted me—what of them?"

"Ay," she answered, "Amenemhat, thy father, the aged Priest of Abouthis; and Sepa, thy uncle, that fiery patriot, whose great heart is hid beneath so common a shell of form; and—"

I thought she would have said Charmion, but she named her not.

"And many others—oh, I know them all!"

"Ay!" I said, "what of them?"

"Hear now, Harmachis," she answered, rising and placing her hand upon my arm, "for thy sake I will show mercy to them. I will do no more than must be done. I swear by my throne and by all the Gods of Egypt that not one hair of thy aged father's head shall be harmed by me; and, if it be not too late, I will also spare thy uncle Sepa, ay, and the others. I will not do as did my forefather, Epiphanes, who, when the Egyptians rose against him, dragged Athinis, Pausiras, Chesuphus, and Irobasthus, bound to his chariot—not as Achilles dragged Hector, but yet living—round the city walls. I will spare them all, save the Hebrews, if there be any Hebrews; for the Jews I hate."

"There are no Hebrews," I said.

"It is well," she said, "for no Hebrew will I ever spare. Am I then, indeed, so cruel a woman as they say? In thy list, Harmachis, were many doomed to die; and I have but taken the life of one Roman knave, a double traitor, for he betrayed both me and thee. Art thou not overwhelmed, Harmachis, with the weight of mercy which I give thee, because—such are a woman's reasons—thou pleasest me, Harmachis? Nay, by Serapis!" she added with a little laugh, "I'll change my mind; I will not give thee so much for nothing. Thou shalt buy it from me, and the price shall be a heavy one—it shall be a kiss, Harmachis."

"Nay," I said, turning from that fair temptress, "the price is too heavy; I kiss no more."

"Bethink thee," she answered, with a heavy frown. "Bethink thee and choose. I am but a woman, Harmachis, and one who is not wont to sue to men. Do as thou wilt; but this I say to thee—if thou dost put me away, I will gather up the mercy I have meted out. Therefore, most virtuous priest, choose thou between the heavy burden of my love and the swift death of thy aged father and of all those who plotted with him."

I glanced at her and saw that she was angered, for her eyes shone and her bosom heaved. So, I sighed and kissed her, thereby setting the seal upon my shame and bondage. Then, smiling like the triumphant Aphrodite of the Greeks, she went thence, bearing the dagger with her.

I knew not yet how deeply I was betrayed; or why I was still left to draw the breath of life; or why Cleopatra, the tiger-hearted, had grown merciful. I did not know that she feared to slay me, lest, so strong was the plot and so feeble her hold upon the Double Crown, the tumult that might tread hard upon the tidings of my murder should shake her from the throne—even when I was no more. I did not know that because of fear and the weight of policy only she showed scant mercy to those whom I had betrayed, or that because of cunning and not for the holy sake of woman's love—though, in truth, she liked me well enough—she chose rather to bind me to her by the fibres of my heart. And yet I will say this in her behalf: even when the danger-cloud had melted from her sky she kept faith, nor, save Paulus and one other, did any suffer the utmost penalty of death for their part in the great plot against Cleopatra's crown and dynasty. But they suffered many other things.

And so she went, leaving the vision of her glory to strive with the shame and sorrow in my heart. Oh, bitter were the hours that could not now be made light with prayer. For the link between me and the Divine was snapped, and Isis communed with Her Priest no more. Bitter were the hours and dark, but ever through their darkness shone the starry eyes of Cleopatra, and came the echo of her whispered love. For not yet was the cup of sorrow full. Hope still lingered in my heart, and I could almost think that I had failed to some higher end, and that in the depths of ruin I should find another and more flowery path to triumph.

For thus those who sin deceive themselves, striving to lay the burden of their evil deeds upon the back of Fate, striving to believe their wickedness may compass good, and to murder Conscience with the sharp plea of Necessity. But it can avail nothing, for hand in hand down the path of sin rush Remorse and Ruin, and woe to him they follow! Ay, and woe to me who of all sinners am the chief!

Chapter 9

Of the Imprisonment of Harmachis

For a space of eleven days I was thus kept prisoned in my chamber; nor did I see anyone except the sentries at my doors, the slaves who in silence brought me food and drink, and Cleopatra's self, who came continually. But, though her words of love were many, she would tell me nothing of how things went without. She came in many moods—now gay and laughing, now full of wise thoughts and speech, and now passionate only, and to every mood she gave some new-found charm. She was full of talk as to how I should help her make Egypt great, and lessen the burdens on the people, and fright the Roman eagles back. And, though at first I listened heavily when she spoke thus, by slow advance as she wrapped me closer and yet more close in her magic web, from which there was no escape, my mind fell in time with hers. Then I, too, opened something of my heart, and somewhat also of the plans that I had formed for Egypt. She seemed to listen gladly, weighing them all, and spoke of means and methods, telling me how she would purify the Faith and repair the ancient temples—ay, and build new ones to the Gods. And ever she crept deeper into my heart, till at length, now that every other thing had gone from me, I learned to love her with all the unspent passion of my aching soul. I had naught left to me but Cleopatra's love, and I twined my life about it, and brooded on it as a widow over her only babe. And thus the very author of my shame became my all, my dearest dear, and I loved her with a strong love that grew and grew, till it seemed to swallow up the past and make the present a dream. For she had conquered me, she had robbed me of my honour, and steeped me to the lips in shame, and I, poor fallen, blinded wretch, I kissed the rod that smote me, and was her very slave.

Ay, even now, in those dreams which still come when Sleep unlocks the secret heart, and sets its terrors free to roam through the opened halls of Thought, I seem to see her royal form, as erst I saw it, come with arms outstretched and Love's own light shining in her eyes, with lips apart and flowing locks, and stamped upon her face the look of utter tenderness that she alone could wear. Ay, still, after all the years, I seem to see her come as erst she came, and still I wake to know her an unutterable lie!

And thus one day she came. She had fled in haste, she said, from some great council summoned concerning the wars of Antony in Syria, and she came, as she had left the council, in all her robes of state, the sceptre in her hand, and on her brow the *uraeus* diadem of gold. There she sat before me, laughing; for, wearying of them, she had told the envoys to whom she gave audience in the council that she was called from their presence by a sudden message come from Rome; and the jest seemed merry to her. Suddenly she rose, took the diadem from her brow, and set it on my hair, and on my shoulders her royal mantle, and in my hand the sceptre, and bowed the knee before me. Then, laughing again, she kissed me on the lips, and said I was indeed her King. But, remembering how I had been crowned in the halls of Abouthis, and remembering also that wreath of roses of which the odour haunts me yet, I rose, pale with wrath, and cast the trinkets from me, asking how she dared to mock me—her caged bird. And I think there was that about me which startled her, for she fell back.

"Nay, Harmachis," she said, "be not wroth! How knowest thou that I mock thee? How knowest thou that thou shalt not be Pharaoh in fact and deed?"

"What meanest thou?" I said. "Wilt thou, then, wed me before Egypt? How else can I be Pharaoh now?"

She cast down her eyes. "Perchance, love, it is in my mind to wed thee," she said gently. "Listen," she went on: "Thou growest pale, here, in this prison, and thou dost eat little. Gainsay me not! I know it from the slaves. I have kept thee here, Harmachis, for thy own sake, that is so dear to me; and for thy own sake, and thy honour's sake, thou must still seem to be my prisoner. Else wouldst thou be shamed and slain—ay, murdered secretly. But I can meet thee here no more! therefore to-morrow I shall free thee in all, save in the name, and thou shalt once more be seen at Court as my astronomer. And I will give this reason—that thou hast cleared thyself; and, moreover, that thy auguries as regards the war have been auguries of truth—as, indeed, they have, though for this I have no cause to thank thee, seeing that thou didst suit thy prophecies to fit thy cause. Now, farewell; for

I must return to those heavy-browed ambassadors; and grow not so sudden wroth, Harmachis, for who knows what may come to pass betwixt thee and me?"

And, with a little nod, she went, leaving it on my mind that she had it in her heart to wed me openly. And of a truth, I believe that, at this hour, such was her thought. For, if she loved me not, still she held me dear, and as yet she had not wearied of me.

On the morrow Cleopatra came not, but Charmion came—Charmion, whom I had not seen since that fatal night of ruin. She entered and stood before me, with pale face and downcast eyes, and her first words were words of bitterness.

"Pardon me," she said, in her gentle voice, "in that I dare to come to thee in Cleopatra's place. Thy joy is not delayed for long, for thou shalt see her presently."

I shrank at her words, as well I might, and, seeing her vantage, she seized it.

"I come, Harmachis—Royal no more!—I come to say that thou art free! Thou art free to face thine own infamy, and see it thrown back from every eye which trusted thee, as shadows are from water. I come to tell thee that the great plot—the plot of twenty years and more—is at its utter end. None have been slain, indeed, unless it is Sepa, who has vanished. But all the leaders have been seized and put in chains, or driven from the land, and their party is broken and scattered. The storm has melted before it burst. Egypt is lost, and lost for ever, for her last hope is gone! No longer may she struggle—now for all time she must bow her neck to the yoke, and bare her back to the rod of the oppressor!"

I groaned aloud. "Alas, I was betrayed!" I said. "Paulus betrayed us."

"Thou wast betrayed? Nay, thou thyself wast the betrayer! How came it that thou didst not slay Cleopatra when thou wast alone with her? Speak, thou forsworn!"

"She drugged me," I said again.

"O Harmachis!" answered the pitiless girl, "how low art thou fallen from that Prince whom once I knew!—thou who dost not scorn to be a liar! Yea, thou wast drugged—drugged with a love-philtre! Yea, thou didst sell Egypt and thy cause for the price of a wanton's kiss! Thou Sorrow and thou Shame!" she went on, pointing her finger at me and lifting her eyes to my face, "thou Scorn!—thou Outcast!—and thou Contempt! Deny if it thou canst. Ay, shrink from me—knowing what thou art, well mayst thou shrink! Crawl to Cleopatra's feet, and kiss her sandals till such time as it pleases her to trample thee in thy kindred dirt; but from all honest folk *shrink!—shrink!*"

My soul quivered beneath the lash of her bitter scorn and hate, but I had no words to answer.

"How comes it," I said at last in a heavy voice, "that thou, too, art not betrayed, but art still here to taunt me, thou who once didst swear that thou didst love me? Being a woman, hast thou no pity for the frailty of man?"

"My name was not on the lists," she said, dropping her dark eyes. "Here is an opportunity: betray me also, Harmachis! Ay, it is because I once loved thee—dost thou, indeed, remember it?—that I feel thy fall the more. The shame of one whom we have loved must in some sort become our shame, and must ever cling to us, because we blindly held a thing so base close to our inmost heart. Art thou also, then, a fool? Wouldst thou, fresh from thy royal wanton's arms, come to me for comfort—to *me* of all the world?"

"How know I," I said, "that it was not thou who, in thy jealous anger, didst betray our plans? Charmion, long ago Sepa warned me against thee, and of a truth now that I recall—"

"It is like a traitor," she broke in, reddening to her brow, "to think that all are of his family, and hold a common mind! Nay, I betrayed thee not; it was that poor knave, Paulus, whose heart failed him at the last, and who is rightly served. Nor will I stay to hear thoughts so base. Harmachis—royal no more!—Cleopatra, Queen of Egypt, bids me say that thou art free, and that she waits thee in the Alabaster Hall."

And shooting one swift glance through her long lashes she curtsied and was gone.

****

So once more I came and went about the Court, though but sparingly, for my heart was full of shame and terror, and on every face I feared to see the scorn of those who knew me for what I was. But I saw nothing, for all those who had knowledge of the plot had fled, and Charmion had spoken no word, for her own sake. Also, Cleopatra had put it about that I was innocent. But my guilt lay heavy on me, and made me thin and wore away the beauty of my countenance. And though I was free in name, yet I was ever watched; nor might I stir beyond the palace grounds.

And at length came the day which brought with it Quintus Dellius, that false Roman knight who ever served the rising star. He bore letters to Cleopatra from Marcus Antonius, the Triumvir, who, fresh from the victory of Philippi, was now in Asia wringing gold from the subject kings with which to satisfy the greed of his legionaries.

Well I mind me of the day. Cleopatra, clad in her robes of state, attended by the officers of her Court, among whom I stood, sat in the great hall on her throne of gold, and bade the heralds admit the Ambassador of Antony, the Triumvir. The great doors were thrown wide, and amidst the blare of trumpets and salutes of the Gallic guards the Roman came in, clad in glittering golden armour and a scarlet cloak of silk, and followed by his suite of officers. He was smooth-faced and fair to look upon, and with a supple form; but his mouth was cold, and false were his shifting eyes. And while the heralds called out his name, titles, and offices, he fixed his gaze on Cleopatra—who sat idly on her throne all radiant with beauty—as a man who is amazed. Then when the heralds had made an end, and he still stood thus, not stirring, Cleopatra spoke in the Latin tongue:

"Greeting to thee, noble Dellius, envoy of the most mighty Antony, whose shadow lies across the world as though Mars himself now towered up above us petty Princes—greeting and welcome to our poor city of Alexandria. Unfold, we pray thee, the purpose of thy coming."

Still the crafty Dellius made no answer, but stood as a man amazed.

"What ails thee, noble Dellius, that thou dost not speak?" asked Cleopatra. "Hast thou, then, wandered so long in Asia that the doors of Roman speech are shut to thee? What tongue hast thou? Name it, and We will speak in it—for all tongues are known to Us."

Then at last he spoke in a soft full voice: "Oh, pardon me, most lovely Egypt, if I have thus been stricken dumb before thee: but too great beauty, like Death himself, doth paralyse the tongue and steal our sense away. The eyes of him who looks upon the fires of the midday sun are blind to all beside, and thus this sudden vision of thy glory, royal Egypt, overwhelmed my mind, and left me helpless and unwitting of all things else."

"Of a truth, noble Dellius," answered Cleopatra, "they teach a pretty school of flattery yonder in Cilicia."

"How goes the saying here in Alexandria?" replied the courtly Roman: "'The breath of flattery cannot waft a cloud,'[15] does it not? But to my task. Here, royal Egypt, are letters under the hand and seal of the noble Antony treating of certain matters of the State. Is it thy pleasure that I should read them openly?"

"Break the seals and read," she answered.

Then bowing, he broke the seals and read:

"The *Triumviri Reipublicae Constituendae*, by the mouth of Marcus Antonius, the Triumvir, to Cleopatra, by grace of the Roman Peo-

15 In other words, what is Divine is beyond the reach of human praise.—Editor.

ple Queen of Upper and Lower Egypt, send greeting. Whereas it has come to our knowledge that thou, Cleopatra, hast, contrary to thy promise and thy duty, both by thy servant Allienus and by thy servant Serapion, the Governor of Cyprus, aided the rebel murderer Cassius against the arms of the most noble Triumvirate. And, whereas it has come to our knowledge that thou thyself wast but lately making ready a great fleet to this end. We summon thee that thou dost without delay journey to Cilicia, there to meet the noble Antony, and in person make answer concerning these charges which are laid against thee. And we warn thee that if thou dost disobey this our summons it is at thy peril. Farewell."

The eyes of Cleopatra flashed as she hearkened to these high words, and I saw her hands tighten on the golden lions' heads whereon they rested.

"We have had the flattery," she said; "and now, lest we be cloyed with sweets, we have its antidote! Listen thou, Dellius: the charges in that letter, or, rather, in that writ of summons, are false, as all folk can bear us witness. But it is not now, and it is not to thee, that We will make defence of our acts of war and policy. Nor will We leave our kingdom to journey into far Cilicia, and there, like some poor suppliant at law, plead our cause before the Court of the Noble Antony. If Antony would have speech with us, and inquire concerning these high matters, the sea is open, and his welcome shall be royal. Let him come thither! That is our answer to thee and to the Triumvirate, O Dellius!"

But Dellius smiled as one who would put away the weight of wrath, and once more spoke:

"Royal Egypt, thou knowest not the noble Antony. He is stern on paper, and ever he sets down his thoughts as though his stylus were a spear dipped in the blood of men. But face to face with him, thou, of all the world, shalt find him the gentlest warrior that ever won a battle. Be advised, O Egypt! and come. Send me not hence with such angry words, for if thou dost draw Antony to Alexandria, then woe to Alexandria, to the people of the Nile, and to thee, great Egypt! For then he will come armed and breathing war, and it shall go hard with thee, who dost defy the gathered might of Rome. I pray thee, then, obey this summons. Come to Cilicia; come with peaceful gifts and not in arms. Come in thy beauty, and tricked in thy best attire, and thou hast naught to fear from the noble Antony." He paused and looked at her meaningly; while I, taking his drift, felt the angry blood surge into my face.

Cleopatra, too, understood, for I saw her rest her chin upon her hand and the cloud of thought gathered in her eyes. For a time she sat thus, while the crafty Dellius watched her curiously. And Charmion, standing with the other ladies by the throne, she also read his meaning, for her face lit up, as a summer cloud lights in the evening when the broad lightning flares behind it. Then once more it grew pale and quiet.

At length Cleopatra spoke. "This is a heavy matter," she said, "and therefore, noble Dellius, we must have time to let our judgment ripen. Rest thou here, and make thee as merry as our poor circumstances allow. Thou shalt have thy answer within ten days."

The envoy thought awhile, then replied smiling: "It is well, O Egypt; on the tenth day from now I will attend for my answer, and on the eleventh I sail hence to join Antony my Lord."

Once more, at a sign from Cleopatra, the trumpets blared, and he withdrew bowing.

CHAPTER 10

Of the Trouble of Cleopatra

That same night Cleopatra summoned me to her private chamber. I went, and found her much troubled in mind; never before had I seen her so deeply moved. She was alone, and, like some trapped lioness, walked to and fro across the marble floor, while thought chased thought across her mind, each, as clouds scudding over the sea, for a moment casting its shadow in her deep eyes.

"So thou art come, Harmachis," she said, resting for a while, as she took my hand. "Counsel me, for never did I need counsel more. Oh, what days have the Gods measured out to me—days restless as the ocean! I have known no peace from childhood up, and it seems none shall I know. Scarce by a very little have I escaped thy dagger's point, Harmachis, when this new trouble, that, like a storm, has gathered beneath the horizon's rim, suddenly bursts over me. Didst mark that tigerish fop? Well should I love to trap him! How soft he spoke! Ay, he purred like a cat, and all the time he stretched his claws. Didst hear the letter, too? it has an ugly sound. I know this Antony. When I was but a child, budding into womanhood, I saw him; but my eyes were ever quick, and I took his measure. Half Hercules and half a fool, with a dash of genius veining his folly through. Easily led by those who enter at the gates of his voluptuous sense; but if crossed, an iron foe. True to his friends, if, indeed, he loves them; and ofttimes false to his own interest. Generous, hardy, and in adversity a man of virtue; in prosperity a sot and a slave to woman. That is Antony. How deal with such a man, whom fate and opportunity, despite himself, have set on the crest of fortune's wave? One day it will overwhelm him; but till that day he sweeps across the world and laughs at those who drown."

"Antony is but a man," I answered, "and a man with many foes; and, being but a man, he can be overthrown."

"Ay, he can be overthrown; but he is one of three, Harmachis. Now that Cassius hath gone where all fools go, Rome has thrown out a hydra head. Crush one, and another hisses in thy face. There's Lepidus, and with him, that young Octavianus, whose cold eyes may yet with a smile of triumph look on the murdered forms of empty, worthless Lepidus, of Antony, and of Cleopatra. If I go not to Cilicia, mark thou! Antony will knit up a peace with these Parthians, and, taking the tales they tell of me for truth—and, indeed, there is truth in them—will fall with all his force on Egypt. And how then?"

"How then? Why, then we'll drum him back to Rome."

"Ah, thou sayest so, and, perchance, Harmachis, had I not won that game we played together some twelve days gone, thou, being Pharaoh, mightest well have done this thing, for round thy throne old Egypt would have gathered. But Egypt loves not me nor my Greek blood; and I have but now scattered that great plot of thine, in which half the land was meshed. Will these men, then, arise to succour me? Were Egypt true to me, I could, indeed, hold my own against all the force that Rome may bring; but Egypt hates me, and had as lief be ruled by the Roman as the Greek. Still I might make defence had I the gold, for with money soldiers can be bought to feed the maw of mercenary battle. But I have none; my treasuries are dry, and though there is wealth in the land, yet debts perplex me. These wars have brought me ruin, and I know not how to find a talent. Perchance, Harmachis, thou who art, by hereditary right, Priest of the Pyramids," and she drew near and looked me in the eyes, "perchance, if long descended rumour does not lie, thou canst tell me where I can touch the gold to save thy land from ruin, and thy Love from the grasp of Antony? Say, is it so?"

I thought a while, and then I answered:

"And if such a tale were true, and if I could show thee treasure stored by the mighty Pharaohs of the most far-off age against the needs of Khem, how can I know that thou wouldst indeed make use of that wealth to those good ends?"

"Is there, then, a treasure?" she asked curiously. "Nay, fret me not, Harmachis; for of a truth the very name of gold at this time of want is like the sight of water in the desert."

"I believe," I said, "that there is such a treasure, though I myself have never seen it. But I know this, that if it still lie in the place where it was set, it is because so heavy a curse will rest upon him who shall lay hands on it wickedly and for selfish ends, that none of those Pharaohs to whom it has been shown have dared to touch it, however sore their need."

"So," she said, "they were cowardly aforetime, or else their need was not great. Wilt thou show me this treasure, then, Harmachis?"

"Perhaps," I answered, "I will show it to thee if it still be there, when thou hast sworn that thou wilt use it to defend Egypt from this Roman Antony and for the welfare of her people."

"I swear it!" she said earnestly. "Oh, I swear by every God in Khem that if thou showest me this great treasure, I will defy Antony and send Dellius back to Cilicia with sharper words than those he brought. Yes, I'll do more, Harmachis: so soon as may be, I will take thee to husband before all the world, and thou thyself shalt carry out thy plans and beat off the Roman eagles."

Thus she spoke, gazing at me with truthful, earnest eyes. I believed her, and for the first time since my fall was for a moment happy, thinking that all was not lost to me, and that with Cleopatra, whom I loved thus madly, I might yet win my place and power back.

"Swear it, Cleopatra!" I said.

"I swear, beloved! and thus I seal my oath!" and she kissed me on the forehead. And I, too, kissed her; and we talked of what we would do when we were wed, and how we should overcome the Roman.

And thus I was again beguiled; though I believe that, had it not been for the jealous anger of Charmion—which, as shall be seen, was ever urging her forward to fresh deeds of shame—Cleopatra would have wedded me and broken with the Roman. And, indeed, in the issue, it had been better for her and Egypt.

We sat far into the night, and I revealed to her somewhat of that ancient secret of the mighty treasure hid beneath the mass of *Her.* Thither, it was agreed, we should go on the morrow, and the second night from now attempt its search. So, early on the next day, a boat was secretly made ready, and Cleopatra entered it, veiled as an Egyptian lady about to make a pilgrimage to the Temple of Horemkhu. And I also entered, cloaked as a pilgrim, and with us ten of her most trusted servants disguised as sailors. But Charmion went not with us. We sailed with a fair wind from the Canopic mouth of the Nile; and that night, pushing on with the moon, we reached Sais at midnight, and here rested for a while. At dawn we once more loosed our craft, and all that day sailed swiftly, till, at last, at the third hour from the sunset, we came in sight of the lights of that fortress which is called Babylon. Here, on the opposite bank of the river, we moored our ship safely in a bed of reeds.

Then, on foot and secretly, we set out for the pyramids, which were at a distance of two leagues, Cleopatra, I and one trusted eunuch, for we left the other servants with the boat. Only I caught an ass for Cleopatra to ride that was wandering in a tilled field, and threw a cloak upon it. She sat on it and I led the ass by paths I knew, the eunuch following us on foot. And, within little more than an hour, having gained the great causeway, we saw the mighty pyramids towering up through the moonlit air and aweing us to silence. We passed on in utter silence, through the haunted city of the dead, for all around us stood the solemn tombs, till at length we climbed the rocky hill, and stood in the deep shadow of Khufu Khut, the splendid Throne of Khufu.

"Of a truth," whispered Cleopatra, as she gazed up the dazzling marble slope above her, everywhere blazoned over with a million mystic characters—"of a truth, there were Gods ruling in Khem in those days, and not men. This place is sad as Death—ay, and as mighty and far from man. Is it here that we must enter?"

"Nay," I answered, "it is not here. Pass on."

I led the way through a thousand ancient tombs, till we stood in the shadow of Ur the Great, and gazed at his red heaven-piercing mass.

"Is it here that we must enter?" she whispered once again.

"Nay," I answered, "it is not here. Pass on."

We passed on through many more tombs, till we stood in the shadow of *Her*,[16] and Cleopatra gazed astonished at its polished beauty, which for thousands of years, night by night, had mirrored back the moon, and at the black girdle of Ethiopian stone that circled its base about. For this is the most beautiful of all pyramids.

"Is it that we must enter?" she said.

I answered, "It is here."

We passed round between the Temple of the Worship of his Divine Majesty, Menkau-ra, the Osirian, and in the base of the pyramid till we came to the north side. Here in the centre is graved the name of Pharaoh Menkau-ra, who built the pyramid to be his tomb, and stored his treasure in it against the need of Khem.

"If the treasure still remains," I said to Cleopatra, "as it remained in the days of my great-great-grandfather, who was Priest of this Pyramid before me, it is hid deep in the womb of the mass before thee, Cleopatra; nor can it be come by without toil, danger, and terror of mind. Art thou prepared to enter—for thou thyself must enter and must judge?"

"Canst thou not go in with the eunuch, Harmachis, and bring the treasure forth?" she said, for a little her courage began to fail her.

"Nay, Cleopatra," I answered, "not even for thee and for the weal of Egypt can I do this thing, for of all sins it would be the greatest sin.

16 The "Upper," now known as the Third Pyramid.—Editor.

But it is lawful for me to do this. I, as hereditary holder of the secret, may, upon demand, show to the ruling monarch of Khem the place where the treasure lies, and show also the warning that is written. And if on seeing and reading, the Pharaoh deems that the need of Khem is so sore and strait that it is lawful for him to brave the curse of the Dead and draw forth the treasure, it is well, for on his head must rest the weight of this dread deed. Three monarchs—so say the records that I have read—have thus dared to enter in the time of need. They were the Divine Queen Hatshepsu, that wonder known to the Gods alone; her Divine brother Tahutimes Men-Kheper-ra; and the Divine Rameses Mi-amen. But of these three Majesties, not one when they saw dared to touch; for, though sharp their need, it was not great enough to consecrate the act. So, fearing lest the curse should fall upon them, they went hence sorrowing."

She thought a little, till at last her spirit overcame her fear.

"At the least I will see with mine own eyes," she said.

"It is well," I answered. Then, stones having been piled up by me and the eunuch who was with us on a certain spot at the base of the pyramid, to somewhat more than the height of a man, I climbed on them and searched for the secret mark, no larger than a leaf. I found it with some trouble, for the weather and the rubbing of the wind-stirred sand had worn even the Ethiopian stone. Having found it, I pressed on it with all my strength in a certain fashion. Even after the lapse of many years the stone swung round, showing a little opening, through which a man might scarcely creep. As it swung, a mighty bat, white in colour as though with unreckoned age, and such as I had never seen before for bigness, for his measure was the measure of a hawk, flew forth and for a moment hovered over Cleopatra, then sailed slowly up and up in circles, till at last he was lost in the bright light of the moon.

But Cleopatra uttered a cry of terror, and the eunuch, who was watching, fell down in fear, believing it to be the guardian Spirit of the pyramid. And I, too, feared, though I said nothing. For even now I believe that it was the Spirit of Menkau-ra, the Osirian, who, taking the form of a bat, flew forth from his holy House in warning.

I waited a while, till the foul air should clear from the passage. Then I drew out the lamps, kindled them, and passed them, to the number of three, into the entrance of the passage. This done, I went to the eunuch, and, taking him aside, I swore him by the living spirit of Him who sleeps at Abouthis that he should not reveal those things which he was about to see.

This he swore, trembling sorely, for he was very much afraid. Nor, indeed, did he reveal them.

This done, I clambered through the opening, taking with me a coil of rope, which I wound around my middle, and beckoned to Cleopatra to come. Making fast the skirt of her robe, she came, and I drew her through the opening, so that at length she stood behind me in the passage which is lined with slabs of granite. After her came the eunuch, and he also stood in the passage. Then, having taken counsel of the plan of the passage that I had brought with me, and which, in signs that none but the initiated can read, was copied from those ancient writings that had come down to me through one-and-forty generations of my predecessors, the Priests of this Pyramid of *Her*, and of the worship of the Temple of the Divine Menkau-ra, the Osirian, I led the way through that darksome place towards the utter silence of the tomb. Guided by the feeble light of our lamps, we passed down the steep incline, gasping in the heat and the thick, stagnated air. Presently we had left the region of the masonry and were slipping down a gallery hewn in the living rock. For twenty paces or more it ran steeply. Then its slope lessened and shortly we found ourselves in a chamber painted white, so low that I, being tall, had scarcely room to stand; but in length four paces, and in breadth three, and cased throughout with sculptured panels. Here Cleopatra sank upon the floor and rested awhile, overcome by the heat and the utter darkness.

"Rise!" I said. "We must not linger here, or we faint."

So she rose, and passing hand in hand through that chamber, we found ourselves face to face with a mighty door of granite, let down from the roof in grooves. Once more I took counsel of the plan, pressed with my foot upon a certain stone, and waited. Then, suddenly and softly, I know not by what means, the mass heaved itself from its bed of living rock. We passed beneath, and found ourselves face to face with a second door of granite. Again I pressed on a certain spot, and this door swung wide of itself, and we went through, to find ourselves face to face with a third door, yet more mighty than the two through which we had won our way. Following the secret plan, I struck this door with my foot upon a certain spot, and it sank slowly as though at a word of magic till its head was level with the floor of rock. We crossed and gained another passage which, descending gently for a length of fourteen paces, led us into a great chamber, paved with black marble, more than nine cubits high, by nine cubits broad, and thirty cubits long. In this marble floor was sunk a great sarcophagus of granite, and on its lid were graved the name and titles of the Queen of Menkau-ra. In this chamber, too, the air was purer, though I know not by what means it came thither.

"Is the treasure here?" gasped Cleopatra.

"Nay," I answered; "follow me," and I led the way to a gallery, which we entered through an opening in the floor of the great chamber. It had been closed by a trap-door of stone, but the door was open. Creeping along this shaft, or passage, for some ten paces, we came at length to a well, seven cubits in depth. Making fast one end of the rope that I had brought about my body and the other to a ring in the rock, I was lowered, holding the lamp in my hand, till I stood in the last resting-place of the Divine Menkau-ra. Then the rope was drawn up, and Cleopatra, being made fast to it, was let down by the eunuch, and I received her in my arms. But I bade the eunuch, sorely against his will, since he feared to be left alone, await our return at the mouth of the shaft. For it was not lawful that he should enter whither we went.

Chapter 11

Of the Tomb of the Divine Menkau-Ra

We stood within a small arched chamber, paved and lined with great blocks of the granite stone of Syene. There before us—hewn from a single mass of basalt shaped like a wooden house and resting on a sphinx with a face of gold—was the sarcophagus of the Divine Menkau-ra.

We stood and gazed in awe, for the weight of the silence and the solemnity of that holy place seemed to crush us. Above us, cubit over cubit in its mighty measure, the pyramid towered up to heaven and was kissed of the night air. But we were deep in the bowels of the rock beneath its base. We were alone with the dead, whose rest we were about to break; and no sound of the murmuring air, and no sight of life came to dull the awful edge of solitude. I gazed on the sarcophagus; its heavy lid had been lifted and rested at its side, and around it the dust of ages had gathered thick.

"See," I whispered, pointing to a writing, daubed with pigment upon the wall in the sacred symbols of ancient times.

"Read it, Harmachis," answered Cleopatra, in the same low voice; "for I cannot."

Then I read: "I, Rameses Mi-amen, in my day and in my hour of need, visited this sepulchre. But, though great my need and bold my heart, I dared not face the curse of Menkau-ra. Judge, O thou who shalt come after me, and, if thy soul is pure and Khem be utterly distressed, take thou that which I have left."

"Where, then, is the treasure?" she whispered. "Is that Sphinx-face of gold?"

"Even there," I answered, pointing to the sarcophagus. "Draw near and see."

And she took my hand and drew near.

The cover was off, but the painted coffin of the Pharaoh lay in the depths of the sarcophagus. We climbed the Sphinx, then I blew the dust from the coffin with my breath and read that which was written on its lid. And this was written:

"Pharaoh Menkau-ra, the Child of Heaven.

"Pharaoh Menkau-ra, Royal Son of the Sun.

"Pharaoh Menkau-ra, who didst lie beneath the heart of Nout.

"Nout, thy Mother, wraps thee in the spell of Her holy name.

"The name of thy Mother, Nout, is the mystery of Heaven.

"Nout, thy Mother, gathers thee to the number of the Gods.

"Nout, thy Mother, breathes on thy foes and utterly destroys them.

"O Pharaoh Menkau-ra, who livest for ever!"

"Where, then, is the treasure?" she asked again. "Here, indeed, is the body of the Divine Menkau-ra; but the flesh even of Pharaohs is not gold, and if the face of this Sphinx be gold how may we move it?"

For answer I bade her stand upon the Sphinx and grasp the upper part of the coffin while I grasped its foot. Then, at my word, we lifted, and the lid of the case, which was not fixed, came away, and we set it upon the floor. And there in the case was the mummy of Pharaoh, as it had been laid three thousand years before. It was a large mummy, and somewhat ungainly. Nor was it adorned with a gilded mask, as is the fashion of our day, for the head was wrapped in clothes yellow with age, which were made fast with pink flaxen bandages, under which were pushed the stems of lotus-blooms. And on the breast, wreathed round with lotus-flowers, lay a large plate of gold closely written over with sacred writing. I lifted up the plate, and, holding it to the light, I read:

"I, Menkau-ra, the Osirian, aforetime Pharaoh of the Land of Khem, who in my day did live justly and ever walked in the path marked for my feet by the decree of the Invisible, who was the beginning and is the end, speak from my tomb to those who after me shall for an hour sit upon my Throne. Behold, I, Menkau-ra, the Osirian, having in the days of my life been warned of a dream that a time will come when Khem shall fear to fall into the hands of strangers, and her monarch shall have great need of treasure wherewith to furnish armies to drive the barbarian back, have out of my wisdom done this thing. For it having pleased the protecting Gods to give me wealth beyond any Pharaoh who has been since the days of Horus—thousands of cattle and geese, thousands of calves and asses, thousands of measures of corn, and hundreds of measures of gold and gems; this wealth I have used sparingly, and that which remains I have bartered for precious stones—even for emeralds, the most beautiful and largest that are in the world. These stones, then, I have stored up against that day of the need of Khem. But because as there have been, so there shall be, those who do wickedly on the earth, and who, in the lust of gain, might seize this wealth that I have stored, and put it to their uses; behold, thou Unborn One, who in the fullness of time shalt stand above me and read this that I have caused to be written, I have stored the treasure thus—even among my bones. Therefore, O thou Unborn One, sleeping in the womb of Nout, I say this to thee! If thou indeed hast need of riches to save Khem from the foes of Khem, fear not and delay not, but tear me, the Osirian, from my tomb, loose my wrappings and rip the treasure from my breast, and all shall be well with thee; for this only I do command, that thou dost replace my bones within my hollow coffin. But if the need be passing and not great, or if there be guile in thy heart, then the curse of Menkau-ra be on thee! On thee be the curse that shall smite him who breaks in upon the dead! On thee be the curse that follows the traitor! On thee be the curse that smites him who outrages the Majesty of the Gods! Unhappy shalt thou live, in blood and misery shalt thou die, and in misery shalt thou be tormented for ever and for ever! For, Wicked One, there in Amenti we shall come face to face!

"And to the end of the keeping of this secret, I, Menkau-ra, have set up a Temple of my Worship, which I have built upon the eastern side of this my House of Death. It shall be made known from time to time to the Hereditary High Priest of this my Temple. And if any High Priest that shall be do reveal this secret to another than the Pharaoh, or Her who wears the Pharaoh's crown and is seated upon the throne of Khem, accursed be he also. Thus have I, Menkau-ra, the Osirian, written. Now to thee, who, sleeping in the womb of Nout, yet shall upon a time stand over me and read, I say, judge thou! and if thou judgest evilly, on thee shall fall this the curse of Menkau-ra from which there is no escape. Greeting and farewell."

"Thou hast heard, O Cleopatra," I said solemnly; "now search thy heart; judge thou, and for thine own sake judge justly."

She bent her head in thought.

"I fear to do this thing," she said presently. "Let us hence."

"It is well," I said, with a lightening of the heart, and bent down to lift the wooden lid. For I, too, feared.

"And yet, what said the writing of the Divine Menkau-ra?—it was emeralds, was it not? And emeralds are now so rare and hard to come by. Ever did I love emeralds, and I can never find them without a flaw."

"It is not a matter of what thou dost love, Cleopatra," I said; "it is a matter of the need of Khem and of the secret meaning of thy heart, which thou alone canst know."

"Ay, surely, Harmachis; surely! And is not the need of Egypt great? There is no gold in the treasury, and how can I defy the Roman if I have no gold? And have I not sworn to thee that I will wed thee and defy the Roman; and do I not swear it again—yes, even in this solemn hour, with my hand upon dead Pharaoh's heart? Why, here is that occasion of which the Divine Menkau-ra dreamed. Thou seest it is so, for else Hatshepsu or Rameses or some other Pharaoh had drawn forth the gems. But no; they left them to come to this hour because the time was not yet come. Now it must be come, for if I take not the gems the Roman will surely seize on Egypt, and then there will be no Pharaoh to whom the secret may be told. Nay, let us away with fears and to the work. Why dost look so frightened? Having pure hearts, there is naught to fear, Harmachis."

"Even as thou wilt," I said again; "it is for thee to judge, since if thou judgest falsely on thee will surely fall the curse from which there is no escape."

"So, Harmachis, take Pharaoh's head and I will take his—Oh, what an awful place is this!" and suddenly she clung to me. "Methought I saw a shadow yonder in the darkness! Methought that it moved toward us and then straightway vanished! Let us be going! Didst thou see naught?"

"I saw nothing, Cleopatra; but mayhap it was the Spirit of the Divine Menkau-ra, for the spirit ever hovers round its mortal tenement. Let us, then, be going; I shall be right glad to go."

She made as though to start, then turned back again and spoke once more.

"It was naught—naught but the mind that, in such a house of Horror, bodies forth those shadowy forms of fear it dreads to see. Nay, I must look upon these emeralds; indeed, if I die, I must look! Come—to the work!" and stooping, she with her own hands lifted from the tomb one of the four alabaster jars, each sealed with the graven likeness of the heads of the protecting Gods, that held the holy heart and entrails of the Divine Menkau-ra. But nothing was found in these jars, save only what should be there.

Then together we mounted on the Sphinx, and with toil drew forth the body of the Divine Pharaoh, laying it on the ground. Now Cleopatra took my dagger, and with it cut loose the bandages which held the wrappings in their place, and the lotus-flowers that had been set in them by loving hands, three thousand years before, fell down upon the pavement. Then we searched and found the end of the outer bandage, which was fixed in at the hinder part of the neck. This we cut loose, for it was glued fast. This done, we began to unroll the wrappings of the holy corpse. Setting my shoulders against the sarcophagus, I sat upon the rocky floor, the body resting on my knees, and, as I turned it, Cleopatra unwound the cloths; and awesome was the task. Presently something fell out; it was the sceptre of the Pharaoh, fashioned of gold, and at its end was a pomegranate cut from a single emerald.

Cleopatra seized the sceptre and gazed on it in silence. Then once more we went on with our dread business. And ever as we unwound, other ornaments of gold, such as are buried with Pharaohs, fell from the wrappings—collars and bracelets, models of *sistra*, an inlaid axe, and an image of the holy Osiris and of the holy Khem. At length all the bandages were unwound, and beneath we found a covering of coarsest linen; for in those very ancient days the craftsmen were not so skilled in matters pertaining to the embalming of the body as they are now. And on the linen was written in an oval, "Menkau-ra, Royal Son of the Sun." We could in no wise loosen this linen, it held so firm on to the body. Therefore, faint with the great heat, choked with mummy dust and the odour of spices, and trembling with fear of our unholy task, wrought in that most lonesome and holy place, we laid the body down, and ripped away the last covering with the knife. First we cleared Pharaoh's head, and now the face that no man had gazed on for three thousand years was open to our view. It was a great face, with a bold brow, yet crowned with the royal *uraeus*, beneath which the white locks, stained yellow by the spices, fell in long, straight wisps. Not the cold stamp of death, and not the slow flight of three thousand years, had found power to mar the dignity of those shrunken features. We gazed on them, and then, made bold with fear, stripped the covering from the body. There at last it lay before us, stiff, yellow, and dread to see; and on the left side, above the thigh, was the cut through which the embalmers had done their work, but it was sewn up so deftly that we could scarcely find the mark.

"The gems are within," I whispered, for I felt that the body was very heavy. "Now, if thy heart fail thee not, thou must make an entry to this poor house of clay that once was Pharaoh," and I gave her the dagger—the same dagger which had drunk the life of Paulus.

"It is too late to doubt," she answered, lifting her white beauteous face and fixing her blue eyes all big with terror upon my own. She took the dagger, and with set teeth the Queen of this day plunged it into the dead breast of the Pharaoh of three thousand years ago. And even as she did so there came a groaning sound from the opening to the shaft where we had left the eunuch! We leapt to our feet, but heard no more, and the lamp-light still streamed down through the opening.

"It is nothing," I said. "Let us make an end."

Then with much toil we hacked and rent the hard flesh open, and as we did so I heard the knife point grate upon the gems within.

Cleopatra plunged her hand into the dead breast and drew forth somewhat. She held it to the light, and gave a little cry, for from the darkness of Pharaoh's heart there flashed into light and life the most beauteous emerald that ever man beheld. It was perfect in colour, very large, without a flaw, and fashioned to a *scarabaeus* form, and on the under side was an oval, inscribed with the divine name of Menkau-ra, Son of the Sun.

Again, again, and yet again, she plunged in her hand and drew emeralds from Pharaoh's breast bedded there in spices. Some were fashioned and some were not; but all were perfect in colour without a flaw, and in value priceless. Again and again she plunged her white hand into that dread breast, till at length all were found, and there were one hundred and forty and eight of such gems as are not known in the world. The last time that she searched she brought forth not emeralds, indeed, but two great pearls, wrapped in linen, such as never have been seen. And of these pearls more hereafter.

So it was done, and all the mighty treasure lay glittering in a heap before us. There it lay, and there, too, lay the regalia of gold, the spiced and sickly-scented wrappings, and the torn body of white-haired Pharaoh Menkau-ra, the Osirian, the ever living in Amenti.

We rose, and a great awe fell upon us, now that the deed was done and our hearts were no more upborne by the rage of search—so great an awe, indeed, that we could not speak. I made a sign to Cleopatra. She grasped the head of Pharaoh and I grasped his feet, and together we lifted him, climbed the Sphinx, and placed him once more within his coffin. I piled the torn mummy cloths over him and on them laid the lid of the coffin.

And now we gathered up the great gems, and such of the ornaments as might be carried with ease, and I hid them as many as I could, in the folds of my robe. Those that were left Cleopatra hid upon her breast. Heavily laden with the priceless treasure, we gave one last look at the solemn place, at the sarcophagus and the Sphinx on which it rested, whose gleaming face of calm seemed to mock us with its everlasting smile of wisdom. Then we turned and went from the tomb.

At the shaft we halted. I called to the eunuch, who stayed above, and methought a faint mocking laugh answered me. Too smitten with terror to call again, and fearing that, should we delay, Cleopatra would certainly swoon, I seized the rope, and being strong and quick mounted by it and gained the passage. There burnt the lamp: but the eunuch I saw not. Thinking, surely, that he was a little way down the passage, and slept—as, in truth, he did—I bade Cleopatra make the rope fast about her middle, and with much labour, drew her up. Then, having rested awhile, we moved with the lamps to seek for the eunuch.

"He was stricken with terror and has fled, leaving the lamp," said Cleopatra. "O ye Gods! who is *that* seated there?"

I peered into the darkness, thrusting out the lamps, and this was what their light fell on—this at the very dream of which my soul sickens! There, facing us, his back resting against the rock, and his hands splayed on either side upon the floor, sat the eunuch—*dead!* His eyes and mouth were open, his fat cheeks dropped down, his thin hair yet seemed to bristle, and on his countenance was frozen such a stamp of hideous terror as well might turn the beholder's brain. And lo! fixed to his chin, by its hinder claws, hung that grey and mighty bat, which, flying forth when we entered the pyramid, vanished in the sky, but, returning, had followed us to its depths. There it hung upon the dead man's chin slowly rocking itself to and fro, and we could see the fiery eyes shining in its head.

Aghast, utterly aghast, we stood and stared at the hateful sight; till presently the bat spread his huge wings and, losing his hold, sailed to us. Now he hovered before Cleopatra's face, fanning her with his white wings. Then with a scream, like a woman's shriek of fury, the accursed Thing flittered on, seeking his violated tomb, and vanished down the well into the sepulchre. I fell against the wall. But Cleopatra sank in a heap upon the floor, and, covering her head with her arms, she shrieked till the hollow passages rang with the echoes of her cries, that seemed to grow and double and rush along the depths in volumes of shrill sound.

"Rise!" I cried, "rise and let us hence before the Spirit shall return to haunt us! If thou dost suffer thyself to be overwhelmed in this place thou art lost for ever."

She staggered to her feet, and never may I forget the look upon her ashy face or in her glowing eyes. Seizing lamps with a rush, we passed the dead eunuch's horrid form, I holding her by the hand. We gained the great chamber, where was the sarcophagus of the Queen of Menkau-ra, and traversed its length. We fled along the passage. What if the Thing had closed the three mighty doors? No; they were open, and we sped through them; the last only did I stay to close. I touched the stone, as I knew how, and the great door crashed down, shutting us off from the presence of the dead eunuch and the Horror that had hung upon the eunuch's chin. Now we were in the white chamber with the sculptured panels, and now we faced the last steep ascent. Oh that last ascent! Twice Cleopatra slipped and fell upon the polished floor. The second time—it was when half the distance had been done—she let fall her lamp, and would, indeed, have rolled down the slide had I not saved her. But in doing thus I, too, let fall my lamp that bounded away into shadow beneath us, and we were in utter darkness. And perchance about us, in the darkness, hovered that awful Thing!

"Be brave!" I cried; "O love, be brave, and struggle on, or both are lost! The way, though steep, is not far; and, though it be dark, we can scarce come to harm in this straight shaft. If the gems weight thee, cast them away!"

"Nay," she gasped, "that I will not; this shall not be endured to no end. I die with them!"

Then it was that I saw the greatness of this woman's heart; for in the dark, and notwithstanding the terrors we had passed and the awfulness of our state, she clung to me and clambered on up that dread passage. On we clambered, hand in hand, with bursting hearts, till there, by the mercy or the anger of the Gods, at length we saw the faint light of the moon, creeping through the little opening in the pyramid. One struggle more, now the hole was gained, and like a breath from heaven, the sweet night air played upon our brows. I climbed through, and, standing on a pile of stones, lifted and dragged Cleopatra after me. She fell to the ground and then sank down upon it motionless.

I pressed upon the turning stone with trembling hands. It swung to and caught, leaving no mark of the secret place of entry. Then I leapt down and, having pushed away the pile of stones, looked on Cleopatra. She had swooned, and notwithstanding the dust and grime upon her face, it was so pale that at first I believed she must be dead. But placing my hand upon her heart I felt it stir beneath; and, being spent, I flung myself down beside her upon the sand, to gather up my strength again.

CHAPTER 12

Of the Coming Back of Harmachis

Presently I lifted myself, and, laying the head of Egypt's Queen upon my knee, strove to call her back to life. How fair she seemed, even in her disarray, her long hair streaming down her breast! how deadly fair she seemed in the faint light—this woman the story of whose beauty and whose sin shall outlive the solid mass of the mighty pyramid that towered over us! The heaviness of her swoon had smoothed away the falseness of her face, and nothing was left but the divine stamp of Woman's richest loveliness, softened by shadows of the night and dignified by the cast of deathlike sleep. I gazed upon her and all my heart went out to her; it seemed that I did but love her more because of the depth of the treasons to which I had sunk to reach her, and because of the terrors we had outfaced together. Weary and spent with fears and the pangs of guilt, my heart sought hers for rest, for now she alone was left to me. She had sworn to wed me also, and with the treasure we had won we would make Egypt strong and free her from her foes, and all should yet be well. Ah! could I have seen the picture that was to come, how, and in what place and circumstance, once again this very woman's head should be laid upon my knee, pale with that cast of death! Ah! could I have seen!

I chafed her hand between my hands. I bent down and kissed her on the lips, and at my kiss she woke. She woke with a little sob of fear—a shiver ran along her delicate limbs, and she stared upon my face with wide eyes.

"Ah! it is thou!" she said. "I mind me—thou hast saved me from that horror-haunted place!" And she threw her arms about my neck, drew me to her and kissed me. "Come, love," she said, "let us be going! I am sore athirst, and—ah! so very weary! The gems, too, chafe my breast! Never was wealth so hardly won! Come, let us be going from the shadow of this ghostly spot! See the faint lights glancing from the wings of Dawn. How beautiful they are, and how sweet to behold! Never, in those Halls of Eternal Night, did I think to look upon the blush of dawn again! Ah! I can still see the face of that dead slave, with the Horror hanging to his beardless chin! Bethink thee!—there he'll sit for ever—there—with the Horror! Come; where may we find water? I would give an emerald for a cup of water!"

"At the canal on the borders of the tilled land below the Temple of Horemkhu—it is close by," I answered. "If any see us, we will say that we are pilgrims who have lost our way at night among the tombs. Veil thyself closely, therefore, Cleopatra; and beware lest thou dost show aught of those gems about thee."

So she veiled herself, and I lifted her on to the ass which was tethered near at hand. We walked slowly through the plain till we came to the place where the symbol of the God Horemkhu,[17] fashioned as a mighty Sphinx (whom the Greeks call Harmachis), and crowned with the royal crown of Egypt, looks out in majesty across the land, his eyes ever fixed upon the East. As we walked the first arrow of the rising sun quivered through the grey air, striking upon Horemkhu's lips of holy calm, and the Dawn kissed her greeting to the God of Dawn. Then the light gathered and grew upon the gleaming sides of twenty pyramids, and, like a promise from Life to Death, rested on the portals of ten thousand tombs. It poured in a flood of gold across the desert sand—it pierced the heavy sky of night, and fell in bright beams upon the green of fields and the tufted crest of palms. Then from his horizon bed royal Ra rose up in pomp and it was day.

Passing the temple of granite and of alabaster that was built before the days of Khufu, to the glory of the Majesty of Horemkhu, we descended the slope, and came to the banks of the canal. There we drank; and that draught of muddy water was sweeter than all the choicest wine of Alexandria. Also we washed the mummy dust and grime from our hands and brows and made us clean. As she bathed her neck, stooping over the water, one of the great emeralds slipped from Cleopatra's breast and fell into the canal, and it was but by chance that at length I found it in the mire. Then, once more, I lifted Cleopatra onto the beast, and slowly, for I was very weary, we marched back to the banks of Sihor, where our craft was. And having at length come thither, seeing no one save some few peasants going out to labour on the lands, I turned the ass loose in that same field where we had found him, and we boarded the craft while the crew were yet sleeping. Then,

17 That is, "Horus on the horizon"; and signifies the power of Light and Good overcoming the power of Darkness and Evil incarnate in his enemy, Typhon.—Editor.

waking them, we bade them make all sail, saying that we had left the eunuch to sojourn a while behind us, as in truth we had. So we sailed, having first hidden away the gems and such of the ornaments of gold as we could bring to the boat.

We spent four days and more in coming to Alexandria, for the wind was for the most part against us; and they were happy days! At first, indeed, Cleopatra was somewhat silent and heavy at heart, for what she had seen and felt in the womb of the pyramid weighed her down. But soon her Imperial spirit awoke and shook the burden from her breast, and she became herself again—now gay, now learned; now loving, and now cold; now queenly, and now altogether simple—ever changing as the winds of heaven, and as the heaven, deep, beauteous, and unsearchable!

Night after night for those four perfect nights, the last happy hours I ever was to know, we sat hand in hand upon the deck and heard the waters lap the vessel's side, and watched the soft footfall of the moon as she trod the depths of Nile. There we sat and talked of love, talked of our marriage and all that we would do. Also I drew up plans of war and of defence against the Roman, which now we had the means to carry out; and she approved them, sweetly saying that what seemed good to me was good to her. And so the time passed all too swiftly.

Oh those nights upon the Nile! their memory haunts me yet! Yet in my dreams I see the moonbeams break and quiver, and hear Cleopatra's murmured words of love mingle with the sound of murmuring waters. Dead are those dear nights, dead is the moon that lit them; the waters which rocked us on their breast are lost in the wide salt sea, and where we kissed and clung there lips unborn shall kiss and cling! How beautiful was their promise, doomed, like an unfruitful blossom, to wither, fall, and rot! and their fulfilment, ah, how drear! For all things end in darkness and in ashes, and those who sow in folly shall reap in sorrow. Ah! those nights upon the Nile!

And so at length once more we stood within the hateful walls of that fair palace on the Lochias, and the dream was done.

****

"Whither hast thou wandered with Cleopatra, Harmachis?" Charmion asked of me when I met her by chance on that day of return. "On some new mission of betrayal? Or was it but a love-journey?"

"I went with Cleopatra upon secret business of the State," I answered sternly.

"So! Those who go secretly, go evilly; and foul birds love to fly at night. Not but what thou art wise, for it would scarce beseem thee, Harmachis, to show thy face openly in Egypt."

I heard, and felt my passion rise within me, for I could ill bear this fair girl's scorn.

"Hast thou never a word without a sting?" I asked. "Know, then, that I went whither thou hadst not dared to go, to gather means to hold Egypt from the grasp of Antony."

"So," she answered, looking up swiftly. "Thou foolish man! Thou hadst done better to save thy labour, for Antony will grasp Egypt in thy despite. What power hast thou to-day in Egypt?"

"That he may do in my despite; but in despite of Cleopatra that he cannot do," I said.

"Nay, but with the *aid* of Cleopatra he can and will do it," she answered with a bitter smile. "When the Queen sails in state up Cydnus stream she will surely draw this coarse Antony thence to Alexandria, conquering, and yet, like thee, a slave!"

"It is false! I say that it is false! Cleopatra goes not to Tarsus, and Antony comes not to Alexandria; or, if he come, it will be to take the chance of war."

"Now, thinkest thou thus?" she answered with a little laugh. "Well, if it please thee, think as thou wilt. Within three days thou shalt know. It is pretty to see how easily thou art fooled. Farewell! Go, dream on Love, for surely Love is sweet."

And she went, leaving me angered and troubled at heart.

****

I saw Cleopatra no more that day, but on the day which followed I saw her. She was in a heavy mood, and had no gentle word for me. I spake to her of the defence of Egypt, but she put the matter away.

"Why dost thou weary me?" she said with anger; "canst thou not see that I am lost in troubles? When Dellius has had his answer tomorrow then we will speak of these matters."

"Ay," I said, "when Dellius has had his answer; and knowest thou that but yesterday, Charmion—whom about the palace they name the 'Keeper of the Queen's secrets'—Charmion swore that the answer would be 'Go in peace, I come to Antony!'"

"Charmion knows nothing of my heart," said Cleopatra, stamping her foot in anger, "and if she talk so freely the girl shall be scourged out of my Court, as is her desert. Though, in truth," she added, "she has more wisdom in that small head of hers than all my privy councillors—ay, and more wit to use it. Knowest thou that I have sold a portion of those gems to the rich Jews of Alexandria, and at a great price, ay, at five thousand *sestertia* for each one?[18] But a few, in truth, for they could not buy more as yet. It was rare to see their eyes when they fell upon them: they grew large as apples with avarice and wonder. And now leave me, Harmachis, for I am weary. The memory of that dreadful night is with me yet."

I bowed and rose to go, and yet stood wavering.

"Pardon me, Cleopatra; it is of our marriage."

"Our marriage! Why, are we not indeed already wed?" she answered.

"Yes; but not before the world. Thou didst promise."

"Ay, Harmachis, I promised; and to-morrow, when I have rid me of this Dellius, I will keep my promise, and name thee Cleopatra's Lord before the Court. See that thou art in thy place. Art content?"

And she stretched out her hand for me to kiss, looking on me with strange eyes, as though she struggled with herself. Then I went; but that night I strove once more to see Cleopatra, and could not. "The Lady Charmion was with the Queen," so said the eunuchs, and none might enter.

****

On the morrow the Court met in the great hall one hour before mid-day, and I went thither with a trembling heart to hear Cleopatra's answer to Dellius, and to hear myself also named King-consort to the Queen of Egypt. It was a full and splendid Court; there were councillors, lords, captains, eunuchs, and waiting-women, all save Charmion. The house passed, but Cleopatra and Charmion came not. At length Charmion entered gently by a side entrance, and took her place among the waiting-ladies about the throne. Even as she did so she cast a glance at me, and there was triumph in her eyes, though I knew not over what she triumphed. I little guessed that she had but now brought about my ruin and sealed the fate of Egypt.

Then presently the trumpets blared, and, clad in her robes of state, the *uraeus* crown upon her head, and on her breast, flashing like a star, that great emerald *scarabaeus* which she had dragged from dead Pharaoh's heart, Cleopatra swept in splendour to her throne, followed by a glittering guard of Northmen. Her lovely face was dark, dark were her slumberous eyes, and none might read their message, though all that Court searched them for a sign of what should come. She seated herself slowly as one who may not be moved, and spoke to the chief of the heralds in the Greek tongue:

18 About forty thousand pounds of our money.—Editor.

"Does the Ambassador of the noble Antony wait?"

The herald bowed low and made assent.

"Let him come in and hear our answer."

The doors were flung wide, and, followed by his train of knights, Dellius, clad in his golden armour and his purple mantle, walked with cat-like step up the great hall, and made obeisance before the throne.

"Most Royal and Beauteous Egypt," he said, in his soft voice, "as thou hast graciously been pleased to bid me, thy servant, I am here to take thy answer to the letter of the noble Antony the Triumvir, whom to-morrow I sail to meet at Tarsus, in Cilicia. And I will say this, Royal Egypt, craving pardon the while for the boldness of my speech—bethink thee well before words that cannot be unspoken fall from those sweet lips. Defy Antony, and Antony will wreck thee. But, like thy mother Aphrodite, rise glorious on his sight from the bosom of the Cyprian wave, and for wreck he will give thee all that can be dear to woman's royalty—Empire, and pomp of place, cities and the sway of men, fame and wealth, and the Diadem of rule made sure. For mark: Antony holds this Eastern World in the hollow of his warlike hand; at his will kings are, and at his frown they cease to be."

And he bowed his head and, folding his hands meekly on his breast, awaited answer.

For a while Cleopatra answered not, but sat like the Sphinx Horemkhu, dumb and inscrutable, gazing with lost eyes down the length of that great hall.

Then, like soft music, her answer came; and trembling I listened for Egypt's challenge to the Roman:

"Noble Dellius,—We have bethought us much of the matter of thy message from great Antony to our poor Royalty of Egypt. We have bethought us much, and we have taken counsel from the oracles of the Gods, from the wisest among our friends, and from the teachings of our heart, that ever, like a nesting bird, broods over our people's weal. Sharp are the words that thou has brought across the sea; methinks they had been better fitted to the ears of some petty half-tamed prince than to those of Egypt's Queen. Therefore we have numbered the legions that we can gather, and the triremes and the galleys wherewith we may breast the sea, and the moneys which shall buy us all things wanting to our war. And we find this, that, though Antony be strong, yet has Egypt naught to fear from the strength of Antony."

She paused, and a murmur of applause of her high words ran down the hall. Only Dellius stretched out his hand as though to push them back. Then came the end!

"Noble Dellius,—Half are we minded there to bid our tongue stop, and, strong in our fortresses of stone, and our other fortresses built of the hearts of men, abide the issue. And yet thou shalt not go thus. We are guiltless of those charges against us that have come to the ears of noble Antony, and which now he rudely shouts in ours; nor will we journey into Cilicia to answer them."

Here the murmur arose anew, while my heart beat high in triumph; and in the pause that followed, Dellius spoke once more.

"Then, Royal Egypt, my word to Antony is word of War?"

"Nay," she answered; "it shall be one of Peace. Listen; we said that we would not come to make answer to these charges, nor will we. But"—and she smiled for the first time—"we will gladly come, and that swiftly, in royal friendship to make known our fellowship of peace upon the banks of Cydnus."

I heard, and was bewildered. Could I hear aright? Was it thus that Cleopatra kept her oaths? Moved beyond the hold of reason, I lifted up my voice and cried:

"O Queen, *remember!*"

She turned upon me like a lioness, with a flashing of the eyes and a swift shake of her lovely head.

"Peace, Slave!" she said; "who bade thee break in upon our counsels? Mind thou thy stars, and leave matters of the world to the rulers of the world!"

I sank back shamed, and, as I did so, once more I saw the smile of triumph on the face of Charmion, followed by what was, perhaps, the shadow of pity for my fall.

"Now that yon brawling charlatan," said Dellius, pointing at me with his jewelled finger, "has been rebuked, grant me leave, O Egypt, to thank thee from my heart for these gentle words—"

"We ask no thanks from thee, noble Dellius; nor lies it in thy mouth to chide our servant," broke in Cleopatra, frowning heavily; "we will take thanks from the lips of Antony alone. Get thee to thy master, and say to him that before he can make ready a fitting welcome our keels shall follow in the track of thine. And now, farewell! Thou shalt find some small token of our bounty upon thy vessel."

Dellius bowed thrice and withdrew, while the Court stood waiting the Queen's word. And I, too, waited, wondering if she would yet make good her promise, and name me Royal Spouse there in the face of Egypt. But she said nothing. Only, still frowning heavily, she rose, and, followed by her guards, left the throne, and passed into the Alabaster Hall. Then the Court broke up, and as the lords and councillors went by they looked on me with mockery. For though none knew all my secret, nor how it stood between me and Cleopatra, yet they were jealous of the favour shown me by the Queen, and rejoiced greatly at my fall. But I took no heed of their mocking as I stood dazed with misery and felt the world of Hope slip from beneath my feet.

Chapter 13

Of the Reproach of Harmachis

And at length, all being gone, I, too, turned to go, when a eunuch struck me on the shoulder and roughly bade me wait on the presence of the Queen. An hour past this fellow would have crawled to me on his knees; but he had heard, and now he treated me—so brutish is the nature of such slaves—as the world treats the fallen, with scorn. For to come low after being great is to learn all shame. Unhappy, therefore, are the Great, for they may fall!

I turned upon the slave with so fierce a word that, cur-like, he sprang behind me; then I passed on to the Alabaster Hall, and was admitted by the guards. In the centre of the hall, near the fountain, sat Cleopatra, and with her were Charmion and the Greek girl Iras, and Merira and other of her waiting-ladies. "Go," she said to these, "I would speak with my astrologer." So they went, and left us face to face.

"Stand thou there," she said, lifting her eyes for the first time. "Come not nigh me, Harmachis: I trust thee not. Perchance thou hast found another dagger. Now, what hast thou to say? By what right didst thou dare to break in upon my talk with the Roman?"

I felt the blood rush through me like a storm; bitterness and burning anger took hold of my heart. "What hast *thou* to say, Cleopatra?" I answered boldly. "Where is thy vow, sworn on the dead heart of Menkau-ra, the ever-living? Where now thy challenge to this Roman Antony? Where thy oath that thou wouldest call me 'husband' in the face of Egypt?" and I choked and ceased.

"Well doth it become Harmachis, who never was forsworn, to speak to me of oaths!" she said in bitter mockery. "And yet, O thou most pure Priest of Isis; and yet, O thou most faithful friend, who never didst betray thy friends; and yet, O thou most steadfast, honourable, and upright man, who never bartered thy birthright, thy country, and thy cause for the price of a woman's passing love—by what token knowest thou that my word is void?"

"I will not answer thy taunts, Cleopatra," I said, holding back my heart as best I might, "for I have earned them all, though not from thee. By this token, then, I know it. Thou goest to visit Antony; thou goest, as said that Roman knave, 'tricked in thy best attire,' to feast with him whom thou shouldst give to vultures for their feast. Perhaps, for aught I know, thou art about to squander those treasures that thou hast filched from the body of Menkau-ra, those treasures stored against the need of Egypt, upon wanton revels which shall complete the shame of Egypt. By these things, then, I know that thou art forsworn, and I, who, loving thee, believed thee, tricked; and by this, also, that thou who didst but yesternight swear to wed me, dost to-day cover me with taunts, and even before that Roman put me to an open shame!"

"To wed thee? and I did swear to wed thee? Well, and what is marriage? Is it the union of the heart, that bond beautiful as gossamer and than gossamer more light, which binds soul to soul, as they float through the dreamy night of passion, a bond to be, perchance, melted in the dews of dawn? Or is it the iron link of enforced, unchanging union whereby if sinks the one the other must be dragged beneath the sea of circumstance, there, like a punished slave, to perish of unavoidable corruption?[19] Marriage! *I* to marry! *I* to forget freedom and court the worst slavery of our sex, which, by the selfish will of man, the stronger, still binds us to a bed grown hateful, and enforces a service that love mayhap no longer hallows! Of what use, then, to be a Queen, if thereby I may not escape the evil of the meanly born? Mark thou, Harmachis: Woman being grown hath two ills to fear—Death and Marriage; and of these twain is Marriage the more vile; for in Death we may find rest, but in Marriage, should it fail us, we must find hell. Nay, being above the breath of common slander that enviously would blast those who of true virtue will not consent to stretch affection's links, I *love*, Harmachis; but I *marry* not!"

"And yesternight, Cleopatra, thou didst swear that thou wouldst wed me, and call me to thy side before the face of Egypt!"

"And yesternight, Harmachis, the red ring round the moon marked the coming of the storm, and yet the day is fair! But who knows that the tempest may not break to-morrow? Who knows that I have not chosen the easier path to save Egypt from the Roman? Who knows, Harmachis, that thou shalt not still call me wife?"

---

19 Referring to the Roman custom of chaining a living felon to the body of one already dead.—Editor.

Then I no longer could bear her falsehood, for I saw that she but played with me. And so I spoke that which was in my heart:

"Cleopatra!" I cried, "thou didst swear to protect Egypt, and thou art about to betray Egypt to the Roman! Thou didst swear to use the treasures that I revealed to thee for the service of Egypt, and thou art about to use them to be her means of shame—to fashion them as fetters for her wrists! Thou didst swear to wed me, who loved thee, and for thee gave all, and thou dost mock me and reject me! Therefore I say—with the voice of the dread Gods I say it!—that on *thee* shall fall the curse of Menkau-ra, whom thou hast robbed indeed! Let me go hence and work out my fate! Let me go, O thou fair Shame! thou living Lie! whom I have loved to my doom, and who hast brought upon me the last curse of doom! Let me hide myself and see thy face no more!"

She rose in her wrath, and she was terrible to see.

"Let thee go to stir up evil against me! Nay, Harmachis, thou shalt not go to build new plots against my throne! I say to thee that thou, too, shalt come to visit Antony in Cilicia, and there, perchance, I will let thee go!" And ere I could answer, she had struck upon the silver gong that hung near her.

Before its rich echo had died away, Charmion and the waiting-women entered from one door, and from the other, a file of soldiers—four of them of the Queen's bodyguard, mighty men, with winged helmets and long fair hair.

"Seize that traitor!" cried Cleopatra, pointing to me. The captain of the guard—it was Brennus—saluted and came towards me with drawn sword.

But I, being mad and desperate, and caring little if they slew me, flew straight at his throat, and dealt him such a heavy blow that the great man fell headlong, and his armour clashed upon the marble floor. As he fell I seized his sword and *targe*, and, meeting the next, who rushed on me with a shout, caught his blow upon the shield, and in answer smote with all my strength. The sword fell where the neck is set into the shoulder, and, shearing through the joints of his harness, slew him, so that his knees were loosened and he sank down dead. And the third, as he came, I caught upon the point of my sword before he could strike, and it pierced him and he died. Then the last rushed on me with a cry of "Taranis!" and I, too, rushed on him, for my blood was aflame. Now the women shrieked—only Cleopatra said nothing, but stood and watched the unequal fray. We met, and I struck with all my strength, and it was a mighty blow, for the sword shore through the iron shell and shattered there, leaving me weaponless. With a shout of triumph the guard swung up his sword and smote down upon my head, but I caught the blow with my shield. Again he smote, and again I parried; but when he raised his sword a third time I saw this might not endure, so with a cry I hurled my buckler at his face. Glancing from his shield it struck him on the breast and staggered him. Then, before he could gain his balance, I rushed in beneath his guard and gripped him round the middle.

For a full minute the tall man and I struggled furiously, and then, so great was my strength in those days, I lifted him like a toy and dashed him down upon the marble floor in such fashion that his bones were shattered so that he spoke no more. But I could not save myself and fell upon him, and as I fell the Captain Brennus, whom I had smitten to earth with my fist, having once more found his sense, came up behind me and smote me upon the head and shoulders with the sword of one of those whom I had slain. But I being on the ground, the blow did not fall with all its weight, also my thick hair and broidered cap broke its force; and thus it came to pass that, though sorely wounded, the life was yet whole in me. But I could struggle no more.

Then the cowardly eunuchs, who had gathered at the sound of blows and stood huddled together like a herd of cattle, seeing that I was spent, threw themselves upon me, and would have butchered me with their knives. But Brennus, now that I was down, would strike no more, but stood waiting. And the eunuchs had surely slain me, for Cleopatra watched like one who watches in a dream and made no sign. Already my head was dragged back, and their knife-points were at my throat, when Charmion, rushing forward, threw herself upon me and, calling them "Dogs!" desperately thrust her body before them in such fashion that they could not smite. Now Brennus with an oath seized first one and then another and cast them from me.

"Spare his life, Queen!" he cried in his barbarous Latin. "By Jupiter, he is a brave man! Myself felled like an ox in the shambles, and three of my boys finished by a man without armour and taken unawares! I grudge them not to such a man! A boon, Queen! spare his life, and give him to me!"

"Ay, spare him! spare him!" cried Charmion, white and trembling.

Cleopatra drew near and looked upon the dead and him who lay dying as I had dashed him to the ground, and on me, her lover of two days gone, whose wounded head rested now on Charmion's white robes.

I met the Queen's glance. "Spare not!" I gasped; "*vae victis!*" Then a flush gathered on her brow—methinks it was a flush of shame!

"Dost after all love this man at heart, Charmion," she said with a little laugh, "that thou didst thrust thy tender body between him and the knives of these sexless hounds?" and she cast a look of scorn upon the eunuchs.

"Nay!" the girl answered fiercely; "but I cannot stand by to see a brave man murdered by such as these."

"Ay!" said Cleopatra, "he is a brave man, and he fought gallantly; I have never seen so fierce a fight even in the games at Rome! Well, I spare his life, though he is weak of me—womanish weak. Take him to his own chamber and guard him there till he is healed or—dead."

Then my brain reeled, a great sickness seized upon me, and I sank into the nothingness of a swoon.

****

Dreams, dreams, dreams! without end and ever-changing, as for years and years I seemed to toss upon a sea of agony. And through them a vision of a dark-eyed woman's tender face and the touch of a white hand soothing me to rest. Visions, too, of a royal countenance bending at times over my rocking bed—a countenance that I could not grasp, but whose beauty flowed through my fevered veins and was a part of me—visions of childhood and of the Temple towers of Abouthis, and of the white-haired Amenemhat, my father—ay, and an ever-present vision of that dread hall in Amenti, and of the small altar and the Spirits clad in flame! There I seemed to wander everlastingly, calling on the Holy Mother, whose memory I could not grasp; calling ever and in vain! For no cloud descended upon the altar, only from time to time the great Voice pealed aloud: "Strike out the name of Harmachis, child of Earth, from the living Book of Her who Was and Is and Shall Be! *Lost! lost! lost!*"

And then another voice would answer:

"Not yet! not yet! Repentance is at hand; strike not out the name of Harmachis, child of Earth, from the living Book of Her who Was and Is and Shall Be! By suffering may sin be wiped away!"

I woke to find myself in my own chamber in the tower of the palace. I was so weak that I scarce could lift my hand, and life seemed but to flutter in my breast as flutters a dying dove. I could not turn my head; I could not stir; yet in my heart there was a sense of rest and of dark trouble done. The light from the lamp hurt my eyes: I shut them, and, as I shut them, heard the sweep of a woman's robes upon the stair, and a swift, light step that I knew well. It was that of Cleopatra!

She entered and drew near. I felt her come! Every pulse of my poor frame beat an answer to her footfall, and all my mighty love and hate rose from the darkness of my death-like sleep, and rent me in their struggle! She leaned over me; her ambrosial breath played upon my face: I could hear the beating of her heart! Lower she leaned, till at last her lips touched me softly on the brow.

"Poor man!" I heard her murmur. "Poor, weak, dying Man! Fate hath been hard to thee! Thou wert too good to be the sport of such a one as I—the pawn that I must move in my play of policy! Ah, Harmachis! thou shouldst have ruled the game! Those plotting priests could give thee learning; but they could not give thee knowledge of mankind, nor fence thee against the march of Nature's law. And thou didst love me with all thy heart—ah! well I know it! Manlike, thou didst love the eyes that, as a pirate's lights, beckoned thee to shipwrecked ruin, and didst hang doting on the lips which lied thy heart away and called thee 'slave'! Well; the game was fair, for thou wouldst have slain me; and yet I grieve. So thou dost die? and this is my farewell to thee! Never may we meet again on earth; and, perchance, it is well, for who knows, when my hour of tenderness is past, how I might deal with thee, didst thou live? Thou dost die, they say—those learned long-faced fools, who, if they let thee die, shall pay the price. And where, then, shall we meet again when my last throw is thrown? We shall be equal there, in the kingdom that Osiris rules. A little time, a few years—perhaps to-morrow—and we shall meet; then, knowing all I am, how wilt thou greet me? Nay, here, as there, still must thou worship me! for injuries cannot touch the immortality of such a love as thine. Contempt alone, like acid, can eat away the love of noble hearts, and reveal the truth in its pitiful nakedness. Thou must still cling to thee, Harmachis; for, whatever my sins, yet I am great and set above thy scorn. Would that I could have loved thee as thou lovest me! Almost I did so when thou slewest those guards; and yet—not quite.

"What a fenced city is my heart, that none can take it, and, even when I throw the gates wide, no man may win its citadel! Oh, to put away this loneliness and lose me in another's soul! Oh, for a year, a month, an hour to quite forget policy, peoples, and my pomp of place, and be but a loving woman! Harmachis, fare thee well! Go join great Julius whom thy art called up from death before me, and take Egypt's greetings to him. Ah well! I fooled thee, and I fooled Caesar—perchance before all is done Fate will find me, and myself I shall be fooled. Harmachis, fare thee well!"

She turned to go, and as she turned I heard the sweep of another dress and the light fall of another woman's foot.

"Ah! it is thou, Charmion. Well, for all thy watching the man dies."

"Ay," she answered, in a voice thick with grief. "Ay, O Queen, so the physicians say. Forty hours has he lain in stupor so deep that at times his breath could barely lift this tiny feather's weight, and hardly could my ear, placed against his breast, take notice of the rising of his heart. I have watched him now for ten long days, watched him day and night, till my eyes stare wide with want of sleep, and for faintness I can scarce keep myself from falling. And this is the end of all my labour! The coward blow of that accursed Brennus has done its work, and Harmachis dies!"

"Love counts not its labour, Charmion, nor can it weight its tenderness on the scale of purchase. That which it has it gives, and craves for more to give and give, till the soul's infinity be drained. Dear to thy heart are these heavy nights of watching; sweet to thy weary eyes is that sad sight of strength brought so low that it hangs upon thy weakness like a babe to its mother's breast! For, Charmion, thou dost love this man who loves thee not, and now that he is helpless thou canst pour thy passion forth over the unanswering darkness of his soul, and cheat thyself with dreams of what yet might be."

"I love him not, as thou hast proof, O Queen! How can I love one who would have slain thee, who art as my heart's sister? It is for pity that I nurse him."

She laughed a little as she answered, "Pity is love's own twin, Charmion. Wondrous wayward are the paths of woman's love, and thou hast shown thine strangely, that I know. But the more high the love, the deeper the gulf whereinto it can fall—ay, and thence soar again to heaven, once more to fall! Poor woman! thou art thy passion's plaything: now tender as the morning sky, and now, when jealousy grips thy heart, more cruel than the sea. Well, thus are we made. Soon, after all this troubling, nothing will be left thee but tears, remorse, and—memory."

And she went forth.

Chapter 14

Of the Tender Care of Charmion

Cleopatra went, and for a while I lay silent, gathering up my strength to speak. But Charmion came and stood over me, and I felt a great tear fall from her dark eyes upon my face, as the first heavy drop of rain falls from a thunder cloud.

"Thou goest," she whispered; "thou goest fast whither I may not follow! O Harmachis, how gladly would I give my life for thine!"

Then at length I opened my eyes, and spoke as best I could:

"Restrain thy grief, dear friend," I said, "I live yet; and, in truth, I feel as though new life gathered in my breast!"

She gave a little cry of joy, and I never saw aught more beautiful than the change that came upon her weeping face! It was as when the first lights of the day run up the pallor of that sad sky which veils the night from dawn. All rosy grew her lovely countenance; her dim eyes shone out like stars; and a smile of wonderment, more sweet than the sudden smile of the sea as its ripples wake to brightness beneath the kiss of the risen moon, broke through her rain of tears.

"Thou livest!" she cried, throwing herself on her knees beside my couch. "Thou livest—and I thought thee gone! Thou art come back to me! Oh! what say I? How foolish is a woman's heart! 'Tis this long watching! Nay; sleep and rest thee, Harmachis!—why dost thou talk? Not one more word, I command thee straitly! Where is the draught left by that long-bearded fool? Nay thou shalt have no draught! There, sleep, Harmachis; sleep!" and she crouched down at my side and laid her cool hand upon my brow, murmuring, "*Sleep! sleep!*"

And when I woke there she was still, but the lights of dawn were peeping through the casement. There she knelt, one hand upon my forehead, and her head, in all its disarray of curls, resting upon her outstretched arm.

"Charmion," I whispered, "have I slept?"

Instantly she was wide awake, and, gazing on me with tender eyes, "Yea, thou hast slept, Harmachis."

"How long, then, have I slept?"

"Nine hours."

"And thou hast held thy place there, at my side, for nine long hours?"

"Yes, it is nothing; I also have slept—I feared to waken thee if I stirred."

"Go, rest," I said; "it shames me to think of this thing. Go rest thee, Charmion!"

"Vex not thyself," she answered; "see, I will bid a slave watch thee, and to wake me if thou needest aught; I sleep there, in the outer chamber. Peace—I go!" and she strove to rise, but, so cramped was she, fell straightway on the floor.

I can scarcely tell the sense of shame that filled me when I saw her fall. Alas! I could not stir to help her.

"It is naught," she said; "move not, I did but catch my foot. There!" and she rose, again to fall—"a pest upon my awkwardness! Why—I must be sleeping. 'Tis well now. I'll send the slave;" and she staggered thence like one overcome with wine.

And after that, I slept once more, for I was very weak. When I woke it was afternoon, and I craved for food, which Charmion brought me.

I ate. "Then I die not," I said.

"Nay," she answered, with a toss of her head, "thou wilt live. In truth, I did waste my pity on thee."

"And thy pity saved my life," I said wearily, for now I remembered.

"It is nothing," she answered carelessly. "After all, thou art my cousin; also, I love nursing—it is a woman's trade. Like enough I had done as much for any slave. Now, too, that the danger is past, I leave thee."

"Thou hadst done better to let me die, Charmion," I said after a while, "for life to me can now be only one long shame. Tell me, then, when sails Cleopatra for Cilicia?"

"She sails in twenty days, and with such pomp and glory as Egypt has never seen. Of a truth, I cannot guess where she has found the means to gather in this store of splendour, as a husbandman gathers his golden harvest."

But I, knowing whence the wealth came, groaned in bitterness of spirit, and made no answer.

"Goest thou also, Charmion?" I asked presently.

"Ay, I and all the Court. Thou, too—thou goest."

"I go? Nay, why is this?"

"Because thou art Cleopatra's slave, and must march in gilded chains behind her chariot; because she fears to leave thee here in Khem; because it is her will, and there is an end."

"Charmion, can I not escape?"

"Escape, thou poor sick man? Nay, how canst thou escape? Even now thou art most strictly guarded. And if thou didst escape, whither wouldst thou fly? There's not an honest man in Egypt but would spit on thee in scorn!"

Once more I groaned in spirit, and, being so very weak, I felt the tears roll adown my cheek.

"Weep not!" she said hastily, and turning her face aside. "Be a man, and brave these troubles out. Thou hast sown, now must thou reap; but after harvest the waters rise and wash away the rotting roots, and then seed-time comes again. Perchance, yonder in Cilicia, a way may be found, when once more thou art strong, by which thou mayst fly—if in truth thou canst bear thy life apart from Cleopatra's smile; then in some far land must thou dwell till these things are forgotten. And now my task is done, so fare thee well! At times I will come to visit thee and see that thou needest nothing."

So she went, and I was nursed thenceforward, and that skilfully, by the physician and two women-slaves; and as my wound healed so my strength came back to me, slowly at first, then most swiftly. In four days from that time I left my couch, and in three more I could walk an hour in the palace gardens; another week and I could read and think, though I went no more to Court. And at length one afternoon Charmion came and bade me make ready, for the fleet would sail in two days, first for the coast of Syria, and thence to the gulf of Issus and Cilicia.

Thereon, with all formality, and in writing, I craved leave of Cleopatra that I might be left, urging that my health was so feeble that I could not travel. But a message was sent to me in answer that I must come.

And so, on the appointed day, I was carried in a litter down to the boat, and together with that very soldier who had cut me down, the Captain Brennus, and others of his troop (who, indeed, were sent to guard me), we rowed aboard a vessel where she lay at anchor with the rest of the great fleet. For Cleopatra was voyaging as though to war in much pomp, and escorted by a fleet of ships, among which her galley, built like a house and lined throughout with cedar and silken hangings, was the most beautiful and costly that the world has ever seen. But I went not on this vessel, and therefore it chanced that I did not see Cleopatra or Charmion till we landed at the mouth of the river Cydnus.

The signal being made, the fleet set sail; and, the wind being fair, we came to Joppa on the evening of the second day. Thence we sailed slowly with contrary winds up the coast of Syria, making Caesarea, and Ptolemais, and Tyrus, and Berytus, and past Lebanon's white brow crowned with his crest of cedars, on to Heraclea and across the gulf of Issus to the mouth of Cydnus. And ever as we journeyed, the strong breath of the sea brought back my health, till at length, save for a line of white upon my head where the sword had fallen, I was almost as I had been. And one night, as we drew near Cydnus, while Brennus and I sat alone together on the deck, his eye fell upon the white mark his sword had made, and he swore a great oath by his heathen Gods. "An thou hadst died, lad," he said, "methinks I could never again have held up my head! Ah! that was a coward stroke, and I am shamed to think that it was I who struck it, and thou on the ground with thy back to me! Knowest thou that when thou didst lie between life and death, I came every day to ask tidings of thee? and I swore by Taranis that if thou didst die I'd turn my back upon that soft palace life and then away for the bonny North."

"Nay, trouble not, Brennus," I answered; "it was thy duty."

"Mayhap! but there are duties that a brave man should not do—nay, not at the bidding of any Queen who ever ruled in Egypt! Thy blow had dazed me or I had not struck. What is it, lad?—art in trouble with this Queen of ours? Why art thou dragged a prisoner upon this pleasure party? Knowest thou that we are strictly charged that if thou dost escape our lives shall pay the price?"

"Ay, in sore trouble, friend," I answered; "ask me no more."

"Then, being of the age thou art, there's a woman in it—that I swear—and, perchance, though I am rough and foolish, I might make a guess. Look thou, lad, what sayest thou? I am weary of this service of Cleopatra and this hot land of deserts and of luxury, that sap a man's strength and drain his pocket; and so are others whom I know of. What sayest thou: let's take one of these unwieldy vessels and away to the North? I'll lead thee to a better land than Egypt—a land of lake and mountain, and great forests of sweet-scented pine; ay, and find thee a girl fit to mate with—my own niece—a girl strong and tall, with wide blue eyes and long fair hair, and arms that could crack thy ribs were she of a mind to hug thee! Come, what sayest thou? Put away the past, and away for the bonny North, and be a son to me."

For a moment I thought, and then sadly shook my head; for though I was sorely tempted to be gone, I knew that my fate lay in Egypt, and I might not fly my fate.

"It may not be, Brennus," I answered. "Fain would I that it might be, but I am bound by a chain of destiny which I cannot break, and in the land of Egypt I must live and die."

"As thou wilt, lad," said the old warrior. "I should have dearly loved to marry thee among my people, and make a son of thee. At the least, remember that while I am here thou hast Brennus for a friend. And one thing more; beware of that beauteous Queen of thine, for, by Taranis, perhaps an hour may come when she will hold that thou knowest too much, and then—" and he drew his hand across his throat. "And now good night; a cup of wine, then to sleep, for to-morrow the foolery—"

****

(Here several lengths of the second roll of papyrus are so broken as to be undecipherable. They seem to have been descriptive of Cleopatra's voyage up the Cydnus to the city of Tarsus.)

****

"And—(the writing continues)—to those who could take joy in such things, the sight must, indeed, have been a gallant one. For the stern of our galley was covered with sheets of beaten gold, the sails were of the scarlet of Tyre, and the oars of silver touched the water to a measure of music. And there, in the centre of the vessel, beneath an awning ablaze with gold embroidery, lay Cleopatra, attired as the Roman Venus (and surely Venus was not more fair!), in thin robes of whitest silk, bound in beneath her breast with a golden girdle delicately graven over with scenes of love. All about her were little rosy boys, chosen for their beauty, and clad in naught save downy wings strapped upon their shoulders, and on their backs Cupid's bow and quiver, who fanned her with fans of plumes. Upon the vessel's decks, handling the cordage, that was of silken web, and softly singing to the sound of harps and the beat of oars, were no rough sailors, but women lovely to behold, some robed as Graces and some as Nereids—that is, scarce robed at all, except in their scented hair. And behind the couch, with drawn sword, stood Brennus, in splendid armour and winged helm of gold; and by him others—I among them—in garments richly worked, and knew that I was indeed a slave! On the high poop also burned censers filled with costliest incense, of which the fragrant steam hung in little clouds about our wake."

Thus, as in a dream of luxury, followed by many ships, we glided on towards the wooded slopes of Taurus, at whose foot lay that ancient city Tarshish. And ever as we came the people gathered on the banks and ran before us, shouting: "Venus is risen from the sea! Venus hath come to visit Bacchus!" We drew near to the city, and all its people—everyone who could walk or be carried—crowded down in thousands to the docks, and with them came the whole army of Antony, so that at length the Triumvir was left alone upon the judgment seat.

Dellius, the false-tongued, came also, fawning and bowing, and in the name of Antony gave the "Queen of Beauty" greeting, bidding her to a feast that Antony had made ready. But she made high answer, and said, "Forsooth, it is Antony who should wait on us; not we on Antony. Bid the noble Antony to our poor table this night—else we dine alone."

Dellius went, bowing to the ground; the feast was made ready; and then at last I set eyes on Antony. He came clad in purple robes, a great man and beautiful to see, set in the stout prime of life, with bright eyes of blue, and curling hair, and features cut sharply as a Grecian gem. For he was great of form and royal of mien, and with an open countenance on which his thoughts were so clearly written that all might read them; only the weakness of the mouth belied the power of the brow. He came attended by his generals, and when he reached the couch where Cleopatra lay he stood astonished, gazing on her with wide-opened eyes. She, too, gazed on him earnestly; I saw the red blood run up beneath her skin, and a great pang of jealousy seized upon my heart. And Charmion, who saw all beneath her downcast eyes, saw this also and smiled. But Cleopatra spoke no word, only she stretched out her white hand for him to kiss; and he, saying no word, took her hand and kissed it.

"Behold, noble Antony!" she said at last in her voice of music, "thou hast called me, and I am come."

"Venus has come," he answered in his deep notes, and still holding his eyes fixed upon her face. "I called a woman—a Goddess hath risen from the deep!"

"To find a God to greet her on the land," she laughed with ready wit. "Well, a truce to compliments, for being on the earth even Venus is ahungered. Noble Antony, thy hand."

The trumpets blared, and through the bowing crowd Cleopatra, followed by her train, passed hand in hand with Antony to the feast.

(Here there is another break in the papyrus.)

CHAPTER 15

Of the Feast of Cleopatra

On the third night the feast was once more prepared in the hall of the great house that had been set aside to the use of Cleopatra, and on this night its splendour was greater even than on the nights before. For the twelve couches that were set about the table were embossed with gold, and those of Cleopatra and Antony were of gold set with jewels. The dishes also were all of gold set with jewels, the walls were hung with purple cloths sewn with gold, and on the floor, covered with a net of gold, fresh roses were strewn ankle-deep, that as the slaves trod them sent up their perfume. Once again I was bidden to stand, with Charmion and Iras and Merira, behind the couch of Cleopatra, and, like a slave, from time to time call out the hours as they flew. And there being no help, I went wild at heart; but this I swore—it should be for the last time, since I could not bear that shame. For though I would not yet believe what Charmion told me—that Cleopatra was about to become the Love of Antony—yet I could no more endure this ignominy and torture. For from Cleopatra now I had no words save such as a Queen speaks to her slave, and methinks it gave her dark heart pleasure to torment me.

Thus it came to pass that I, the Pharaoh, crowned of Khem, stood among eunuchs and waiting-women behind the couch of Egypt's Queen while the feast went merrily and the wine-cup passed. And ever Antony sat, his eyes fixed upon the face of Cleopatra, who from time to time let her deep glance lose itself in his, and then for a little while their talk died away. For he told her tales of war and of deeds that he had done—ay, and love-jests such as are not meet for the ears of women. But she took offence at nothing; rather, falling into his humour, she would cap his stories with others of a finer wit, but not less shameless.

At length, the rich meal being finished, Antony gazed at the splendour around him.

"Tell me, then, most lovely Egypt," he said; "are the sands of Nile compact of gold, that thou canst, night by night, thus squander the ransom of a King upon a single feast? Whence comes this untold wealth?"

I bethought me of the tomb of the Divine Menkau-ra, whose holy treasure was thus wickedly wasted, and looked up so that Cleopatra's eye caught mine; but, reading my thoughts, she frowned heavily.

"Why, noble Antony," she said, "surely it is nothing! In Egypt we have our secrets, and know whence to conjure riches at our need. Say, what is the value of this golden service, and of the meats and drinks that have been set before us?"

He cast his eyes about, and hazarded a guess.

"Maybe a thousand *sestertia*."[20]

"Thou hast understated it by half, noble Antony! But such as it is I will give it thee and those with thee as a free token of my friendship. And more will I show thee now: I myself will eat and drink ten thousand *sestertia* at a draught."

"That cannot be, fair Egypt!"

She laughed, and bade a slave bring her white vinegar in a glass. When it was brought she set it before her and laughed again, while Antony, rising from his couch, drew near and set himself at her side, and all the company leant forward to see what she would do. And this she did. She took from her ear one of those great pearls which last of all had been drawn from the body of the Divine Pharaoh; and before any could guess her purpose she let it fall into the vinegar. Then came silence, the silence of wonder, and slowly the priceless pearl melted in the strong acid. When it was melted she lifted the glass and shook it, then drank the vinegar, to the last drop.

"More vinegar, slave!" she cried; "my meal is but half finished!" and she drew forth the second pearl.

"By Bacchus, no! that shalt thou not!" cried Antony, snatching at her hands; "I have seen enough;" and at that moment, moved to it by I know not what, I called aloud:

"The hour falls, O Queen!—*the hour of the coming of the curse of Menkau-ra!*"

An ashy whiteness grew upon Cleopatra's face, and she turned upon me furiously, while all the company gazed wondering, not knowing what the words might mean.

"Thou ill-omened slave!" she cried. "Speak thus once more and thou shalt be scourged with rods!—ay, scourged like an evildoer—that I promise thee, Harmachis!"

20 About eight thousand pounds of English money.—Editor.

"What means the knave of an astrologer?" asked Antony. "Speak, sirrah! and make clear thy meaning, for those who deal in curses must warrant their wares."

"I am a servant of the Gods, noble Antony. That which the Gods put in my mind that must I say; nor can I read their meaning," I answered humbly.

"Oh, oh! thou servest the Gods, dost thou, thou many-coloured mystery?" This he said having reference to my splendid robes. "Well, I serve the Goddesses, which is a softer cult. And there's this between us: that though what they put in my mind I say, neither can I read their meaning," and he glanced at Cleopatra as one who questions.

"Let the knave be," she said impatiently; "to-morrow we'll be rid of him. Sirrah, begone!"

I bowed and went; and, as I went, I heard Antony say: "Well, he may be a knave—for that all men are—but this for thy astrologer: he hath a royal air and the eye of a King—ay, and wit in it."

Without the door I paused, not knowing what to do, for I was bewildered with misery. And, as I stood, someone touched me on the hand. I glanced up—it was Charmion, who in the confusion of the rising of the guests, had slipped away and followed me.

For in trouble Charmion was ever at my side.

"Follow me," she whispered; "thou art in danger."

I turned and followed her. Why should I not?

"Whither go we?" I asked at length.

"To my chamber," she said. "Fear not; we ladies of Cleopatra's Court have small good fame to lose; if anyone by chance should see us, they'll think that it is a love-tryst, and such are all the fashion."

I followed, and, presently, skirting the crowd, we came unseen to a little side entrance that led to a stair, up which we passed. The stair ended in a passage; we turned down it till we found a door on the left hand. Charmion entered silently, and I followed her into a dark chamber. Being in, she barred the door and, kindling tinder to a flame, lit a hanging lamp. As the light grew strong I gazed around. The chamber was not large, and had but one casement, closely shuttered. For the rest, it was simply furnished, having white walls, some chests for garments, an ancient chair, what I took to be a tiring table, on which were combs, perfumes, and all the frippery that pertains to woman, and a white bed with a broidered coverlid, over which was hung a gnat-gauze.

"Be seated, Harmachis," she said, pointing to the chair. I took the chair, and Charmion, throwing back the gnat-gauze, sat herself upon the bed before me.

"Knowest thou what I heard Cleopatra say as thou didst leave the banqueting-hall?" she asked presently.

"Nay, I know not."

"She gazed after thee, and, as I went over to her to do some service, she murmured to herself: 'By Serapis, I will make an end! I will wait no longer: to-morrow he shall be strangled!'"

"So!" I said, "it may be; though, after all that has been, I can scarce believe that she will murder me."

"Why canst thou not believe it, thou most foolish of men? Dost forget how nigh thou wast to death there in the Alabaster Hall? Who saved thee then from the knives of the eunuchs? Was it Cleopatra? Or was it I and Brennus? Stay, I will tell thee. Thou canst not yet believe it, because, in thy folly, thou dost not think it possible that the woman who has but lately been as a wife to thee can now, in so short a time, doom thee to be basely done to death. Nay, answer not—I know all; and I tell thee this: thou hast not measured the depth of Cleopatra's perfidy, nor canst thou dream the blackness of her wicked heart. She had surely slain thee in Alexandria had she not feared that thy slaughter being noised abroad might bring trouble on her. Therefore has she brought thee here to kill thee secretly. For what more canst thou give her? She has thy heart's love, and is wearied of thy strength and beauty. She has robbed thee of thy royal birthright and brought thee, a King, to stand amidst the waiting-women behind her at her feasts; she has won from thee the great secret of the holy treasure!"

"Ah, thou knowest that?"

"Yes, I know all; and to-night thou seest how the wealth stored against the need of Khem is being squandered to fill up the wanton luxury of Khem's Macedonian Queen! Thou seest how she has kept her oath to wed thee honourably. Harmachis—at length thine eyes are open to the truth!"

"Ay, I see too well; and yet she swore she loved me, and I, poor fool, I believed her!"

"She swore she loved thee!" answered Charmion, lifting her dark eyes: "now I will show thee how she loves thee. Knowest thou what was this house? It was a priest's college; and, as thou wottest, Harmachis, priests have their ways. This little room aforetime was the room of the Head Priest, and the chamber that is beyond and below was the gathering-place of the other priests. The old slave who keeps the house told me all this, and also she revealed what I shall show thee. Now, Harmachis, be silent as the dead, and follow me!"

She blew out the lamp, and by the little light that crept through the shuttered casement led me by the hand to the far corner of the room. Here she pressed upon the wall, and a door opened in its thickness. We entered, and she closed the spring. Now we were in a little chamber, some five cubits in length by four in breadth; for a faint light struggled into the closet, and also the sound of voices, I knew not whence. Loosing my hand, she crept to the end of the place, and looked steadfastly at the wall; then crept back and, whispering "Silence!" led me forward with her. Then I saw that there were eyeholes in the wall, which pierced it, and were hidden on the farther side by carved work in stone. I looked through the hole that was in front of me, and I saw this: six cubits below was the level of the floor of another chamber, lit with fragrant lamps, and most richly furnished. It was the sleeping-place of Cleopatra, and there, within ten cubits of where we stood, sat Cleopatra on a gilded couch, and by her side sat Antony.

"Tell me," Cleopatra murmured—for this place was so built that every word spoken in the room below came to the ears of the listener above—"tell me, noble Antony, wast pleased with my poor festival?"

"Ay," he answered in his deep soldier's voice, "ay, Egypt, I have made feasts, and been bidden to feasts, but never saw I aught like thine; and I tell thee this, though I am rough of tongue and unskilled in pretty sayings such as women love, thou wast the richest sight of all that splendid board. The red wine was not so red as thy beauteous cheek, the roses smelt not so sweet as the odour of thy hair, and no sapphire there with its changing light was so lovely as thy eyes of ocean blue."

"What! Praise from Antony! Sweet words from the lips of him whose writings are so harsh! Why, it is praise indeed!"

"Ay," he went on, "it was a royal feast, though I grieve that thou didst waste that great pearl; and what meant that hour-calling astrologer of thine, with his ill-omened talk of the curse of Menkau-ra?"

A shadow fled across her glowing face. "I know not; he was lately wounded in a brawl, and methinks the blow has crazed him."

"He seemed not crazed, and there was that about his voice which rings in my ears like some oracle of fate. So wildly, too, he looked upon thee, Egypt, with those piercing eyes of his, like one who loved and yet hated through the love."

"He is a strange man, I tell thee, noble Antony, and a learned. Myself, at times, I almost fear him, for he is deeply versed in the ancient arts of Egypt. Knowest thou that the man is of royal blood, and once he plotted to slay me? But I won him over, and slew him not, for he had the key to secrets that I fain would learn; and, indeed, I loved his wisdom, and to listen to his deep talk of all hidden things."

"By Bacchus, I grow jealous of the knave! And now, Egypt?"

"And now I have sucked his knowledge dry, and have no more cause to fear him. Didst thou not see that I have made him stand these three nights a slave amid my slaves, and call aloud the hours as they fled in festival. No captive King marching in thy Roman triumphs can have suffered pangs so keen as that proud Egyptian Prince when he stood shamed behind my couch."

Here Charmion laid her hand on mine and pressed it, as though in tenderness.

"Well, he shall trouble us no more with his words of evil omen," Cleopatra went on slowly; "to-morrow morn he dies—dies swiftly and in secret, leaving no trace of what his fate has been. On this is my mind fixed; of a truth, noble Antony, it is fixed. Even as I speak the fear of this man grows and gathers in my breast. Half am I minded to give the word even now, for I breathe not freely till he be dead," and she made as though to rise.

"Let it be till morning," he said, catching her by the hand; "the soldiers drink, and the deed will be ill done. 'Tis pity too. I love not to think of men slaughtered in their sleep."

"In the morning, perchance, the hawk may have flown," she answered, pondering. "He hath keen ears, this Harmachis, and can summon things to aid him that are not of the earth. Perchance, even now he hears me in the spirit; for, of a truth, I seem to feel his presence breathing round me. I could tell thee—but no, let him be! Noble Antony, be my tiring-woman and loose me this crown of gold, it chafes my brow. Be gentle, hurt me not—so."

He lifted the *uraeus* crown from her brows, and she shook loose her heavy weight of hair that fell about her like a garment.

"Take back thy crown, royal Egypt," he said, speaking low, "take it from my hand; I will not rob thee of it, but rather set it more firmly on that beauteous brow."

"What means my Lord?" she asked, smiling and looking into his eyes.

"What mean I? Why then, this: thou camest hither at my bidding to make answer of the charges laid against thee as to matters politic. And knowest thou, Egypt, that hadst thou been other than thou art thou hadst not gone back to queen it on the Nile; for of this I am sure, the charges against thee are true in fact. But, being what thou art—and look thou! never did Nature serve a woman better!—I forgive thee all. For the sake of thy grace and beauty I forgive thee that which had not been forgiven to virtue, or to patriotism, or to the dignity of age! See now how good a thing is woman's wit and loveliness, that can make kings forget their duty and cozen even blindfolded Justice to peep ere she lifts her sword! Take back thy crown, O Egypt! It is now my care that, though it be heavy, it shall not chafe thee."

"These are royal words, most notable Antony," she made answer; "gracious and generous words, such as befit the Conqueror of the world! And touching my misdeeds in the past—if misdeeds there have been—I say this, and this alone—then I knew not Antony. For, knowing Antony, who could sin against him? What woman could lift a sword against one who must be to all women as a God—one who, seen and known, draws after him the whole allegiance of the heart, as the sun draws flowers? And what more can I say and not cross the bounds of woman's modesty? Why, only this—set that crown upon my brow, great Antony, and I will take it as a gift from thee, by the giving made doubly dear, and to thy uses I will guard it.

"There, now I am thy vassal Queen, and through me all old Egypt that I rule does homage to Antony the Triumvir, who shall be Antony the Emperor of Rome and Khem's Imperial Lord!"

And, having set the crown upon her locks, he stood gazing on her, grown passionate in the warm breath of her living beauty, till at length he caught her by both hands and drawing her to him kissed her thrice, saying:

"Cleopatra, I love thee, Sweet—I love thee as I never loved before." She drew back from his embrace, smiling softly; and as she did so the golden circlet of the sacred snakes fell, being but loosely set upon her brow, and rolled away into the darkness beyond the ring of light.

I saw the omen, and even in the bitter anguish of my heart knew its evil import. But these twain took no note.

"Thou lovest me?" she said, most sweetly; "how know I that thou lovest me? Perchance it is Fulvia whom thou lovest—Fulvia, thy wedded wife?"

"Nay, it is not Fulvia, 'tis thou, Cleopatra, and thou alone. Many women have looked favourably upon me from my boyhood up, but to never a one have I known such desire as to thee, O thou Wonder of the World, like unto whom no woman ever was! Canst thou love me, Cleopatra, and to me be true, not for my place or power, not for that which I can give or can withhold, not for the stern music of my legion's tramp, or for the light that flows from my bright Star of Fortune; but for myself, for the sake of Antony, the rough captain, grown old in camps? Ay, for the sake of Antony the reveller, the frail, the unfixed of purpose, but who yet never did desert a friend, or rob a poor man, or take an enemy unawares? Say, canst thou love me, Egypt? Oh! if thou wilt, why, I am more happy than though I sat to-night in the Capitol at Rome crowned absolute Monarch of the World!"

And, ever as he spoke, she gazed on him with wonderful eyes, and in them shone a light of truth and honesty such as was strange to me.

"Thou speakest plainly," she said, "and thy words are sweet to mine ears—they would be sweet, even were things otherwise than they are, for what woman would not love to see the world's master at her feet? But things being as they are, why, Antony, what can be so sweet as thy sweet words? The harbour of his rest to the storm-tossed mariner—surely that is sweet! The dream of Heaven's bliss which cheers the poor ascetic priest on his path of sacrifice—surely that is sweet! The sight of Dawn, the rosy-fingered, coming in his promise to glad the watching Earth—surely that is sweet! But, ah! not one of these, nor all dear delightful things that are, can match the honey-sweetness of thy words to me, O Antony! For thou knowest not—never canst thou know—how drear my life hath been, and empty, since thus it is ordained that in love only can woman lose her solitude! And I have *never* loved—never might I love—till this happy night! Ay, take me in thy arms, and let us swear a great vow of love—an oath that may not be broken while life is in us! Behold! Antony! now and for ever I do vow most strict fidelity unto thee! Now and for ever I am thine, and thine alone!"

****

Then Charmion took me by the hand and drew me thence.

"Hast seen enough?" she asked, when we were once more within the chamber and the lamp was lit.

"Yea," I answered; "my eyes are opened."

Chapter 16

Of the Plan of Charmion

For some while I sat with bowed head, and the last bitterness of shame sank into my soul. This, then, was the end. For this I had betrayed my oaths; for this I had told the secret of the pyramid; for this I had lost my Crown, my Honour, and, perchance, my hope of Heaven! Could there be another man in the wide world so steeped in sorrow as I was that night? Surely not one! Where should I turn? What could I do? And even through the tempest of my torn heart the bitter voice of jealousy called aloud. For I loved this woman, to whom I had given all; and she at this moment—she was—Ah! I could not bear to think of it; and in my utter agony, my heart burst in a river of tears such as are terrible to weep!

Then Charmion drew near me, and I saw that she, too, was weeping.

"Weep not, Harmachis!" she sobbed, kneeling at my side. "I cannot endure to see thee weep. Oh! why wouldst thou not be warned? Then hadst thou been great and happy, and not as now. Listen, Harmachis! Thou didst hear what that false and tigerish woman said—to-morrow she hands thee over to the murderers!"

"It is well," I gasped.

"Nay: it is not well. Harmachis, give her not this last triumph over thee. Thou hast lost all save life: but while life remains, hope remains also, and with hope the chance of vengeance."

"Ah!" I said, starting from my seat. "I had not thought of that. Ay—the chance of vengeance! It would be sweet to be avenged!"

"It would be sweet, Harmachis, and yet this—Vengeance is an arrow that in falling oft pierces him who shot it. Myself—I know it," and she sighed. "But a truce to talk and grief. There will be time for us twain to grieve, if not to talk, in all the heavy coming years. Thou must fly—before the coming of the light must thou fly. Here is a plan. To-morrow, ere the dawn, a galley that but yesterday came from Alexandria, bearing fruit and stores, sails thither again, and its captain is known to me, but to thee he is not known. Now, I will find thee the garb of a Syrian merchant, and cloak thee, as I know how, and furnish thee with a letter to the captain of the galley. He shall give thee passage to Alexandria; for to him thou wilt seem but as a merchant going on the business of thy trade. Brennus is officer of the guard to-night, and Brennus is a friend to me and thee. Perhaps he will guess somewhat; or, perhaps, he will not guess; at the least, the Syrian merchant shall safely pass the lines. What sayest thou?"

"It is well," I answered wearily; "little do I reck the issue."

"Rest thou, then, here, Harmachis, while I make these matters ready; and, Harmachis, grieve not overmuch; there are others who should grieve more heavily than thou." And she went, leaving me alone with my agony which rent me like a torture-bed. Had it not been for that fierce desire of vengeance which from time to time flashed across my tormented mind as the lightning over a midnight sea, methinks my reason had left me in that dark hour. At length I heard her footstep at the door, and she entered, breathing heavily, for she bore a sack of clothing in her arms.

"It is well," she said: "here is the garb with spare linen, and writing-tablets, and all things needful. I have seen Brennus also, and told him that a Syrian merchant would pass the guard an hour before the dawn. And though he made pretence of sleep, I think he understood, for he answered, yawning, that if they but had the pass-word, 'Antony,' fifty Syrian merchants might go through about their lawful business. And here is the letter to the captain—thou canst not mistake the galley, for she is moored along to the right—a small galley, painted black, as thou dost enter on the great quay, and, moreover, the sailors make ready for sailing. Now I will wait here without, while thou dost put off the livery of thy service and array thyself."

When she was gone I tore off my gorgeous garments and spat upon them and trod them on the ground. Then I put on the modest robe of a merchant, and bound the tablets round me, on my feet the sandals of untanned hide, and at my waist the knife. When it was done Charmion entered once again and looked on me.

"Too much art thou still the royal Harmachis," she said; "see, it must be changed."

Then she took scissors from her tiring-table, and, bidding me be seated, she cut off my locks, clipping the hair close to the head. Next she found stains of such sort as women use to make dark the eyes, and mixed them cunningly, rubbing the stuff on my face and hands and on the white mark in my hair where the sword of Brennus had bitten to the bone.

"Now thou art changed—somewhat for the worse, Harmachis," she said, with a dreary laugh, "scarce myself should I know thee. Stay, there is one more thing," and, going to a chest of garments, she drew thence a heavy bag of gold.

"Take thou this," she said; "thou wilt have need of money."

"I cannot take thy gold, Charmion."

"Yes, take it. It was Sepa who gave it to me for the furtherance of our cause, and therefore it is fitting that thou shouldst spend it. Moreover, if I want money, doubtless Antony, who is henceforth my master, will give me more; he is much beholden to me, and this he knows well. There, waste not the precious time in haggling o'er the pelf—not yet art thou all a merchant, Harmachis;" and, without more words, she thrust the pieces into the leather bag that hung across my shoulders. Then she made fast the sack containing the spare garments, and, so womanly thoughtful was she, placed in it an alabaster jar of pigment, with which I might stain my countenance afresh, and, taking the broidered robes of my office that I had cast off, hid them in the secret passage. And so at last all was made ready.

"Is it time that I should go," I asked.

"Not yet a while. Be patient, Harmachis, for but one little hour more must thou endure my presence, and then, perchance, farewell for ever."

I made a gesture signifying that this was no time for sharp words.

"Forgive me my quick tongue," she said; "but from a salt spring bitter waters well. Be seated, Harmachis; I have heavier words to speak to thee before thou goest."

"Say on," I answered; "words, however heavy, can move me no more."

She stood before me with folded hands, and the lamp-light shone upon her beauteous face. I noticed idly how great was its pallor and how wide and dark were the rings about the deep black eyes. Twice she lifted her white face and strove to speak, twice her voice failed her; and when at last it came it was in a hoarse whisper.

"I cannot let thee go," she said—"I cannot let thee go unwitting of the truth.

"*Harmachis, 'twas I who did betray thee!*"

I sprang to my feet, an oath upon my lips; but she caught me by the hand.

"Oh, be seated," she said—"be seated and hear me; then, when thou hast heart, do to me as thou wilt. Listen. From that evil moment when, in the presence of thy uncle Sepa, for the second time I set eyes upon thy face, I loved thee—how much, thou canst little guess. Think upon thine own love for Cleopatra, and double it, and double it again, and perchance thou mayst come near to my love's mighty sum. I loved thee, day by day I loved thee more, till in thee and for thee alone I seemed to live. But thou wast cold—thou wast worse than cold! thou didst deal with me not as a breathing woman, but rather as the instrument to an end—as a tool with which to grave thy fortunes. And then I saw—yes, long before thou knewest it thyself—thy heart's tide was setting strong towards that ruinous shore whereon to-day thy life is broken. And at last that night came, that dreadful night when, hid within the chamber, I saw thee cast my kerchief to the winds, and with sweet words cherish my Royal Rival's gift. Then—oh, thou knowest—in my pain I betrayed the secret that thou wouldst not see, and thou didst make a mock of me, Harmachis! Oh! the shame of it—thou in thy foolishness didst make a mock of me! I went thence, and within me were rising all the torments which can tear a woman's heart, for now I was sure that thou didst love Cleopatra! Ay, and so mad was I, even that night I was minded to betray thee: but I thought—not yet, not yet; to-morrow he may soften. Then came the morrow, and all was ready for the bursting of the great plot that should make thee Pharaoh. And I too came—thou dost remember—and again thou didst put me away when I spake to thee in parables, as something of little worth—as a thing too small to claim a moment's weighty thought. And, knowing that this was because—though thou knewest it not—thou didst love Cleopatra, whom now thou must straightway slay, I grew mad, and a wicked Spirit entered into me, possessing me utterly, so that I was myself no longer, nor could control myself. And because thou hadst scorned me, I did this, to my everlasting shame and sorrow!—I passed into Cleopatra's presence and betrayed thee and those with thee, and our holy cause, saying that I had found a writing which thou hadst let fall and read all this therein."

I gasped and sat silent; and gazing sadly at me she went on:

"When she understood how great was the plot, and how deep its roots, Cleopatra was much troubled; and, at first, she would have fled to Sais or taken ship and run for Cyprus, but I showed her that the ways were barred. Then she said she would cause thee to be slain, there, in the chamber, and I left her so believing; for, at that hour, I was glad that thou shouldst be slain—ay, even if I wept out my heart upon thy grave, Harmachis. But what said I just now?—Vengeance is an arrow that oft falls on him who looses it. So it was with me; for between my going and thy coming Cleopatra hatched a deeper plan. She feared that to slay thee would only be to light a fiercer fire of revolt; but she saw that to bind thee to her, and, having left men awhile in doubt, to show thee faithless, would strike the imminent danger at its roots and wither it. This plot once formed, being great, she dared its doubtful issue, and—need I go on? Thou knowest, Harmachis, how she won; and thus the shaft of vengeance that I loosed fell upon my own head. For on the morrow I knew that I had sinned for naught, that the burden of my betrayal had been laid on the wretched Paulus, and that I had but ruined the cause to which I was sworn and given the man I loved to the arms of wanton Egypt."

She bowed her head awhile, and then, as I spoke not, once more went on:

"Let all my sin be told, Harmachis, and then let justice come. See now, this thing happened. Half did Cleopatra learn to love thee, and deep in her heart she bethought her of taking thee to wedded husband. For the sake of this half love of hers she spared the lives of those in the plot whom she had meshed, bethinking her that if she wedded thee she might use them and thee to draw the heart of Egypt, which loves not her nor any Ptolemy. And then, once again she entrapped thee, and in thy folly thou didst betray to her the secret of the hidden wealth of Egypt, which to-day she squanders to delight the luxurious Antony; and, of a truth, at that time she purposed to make good her oath and marry thee. But on the very morn when Dellius came for answer she sent for me, and telling me all—for my wit, above any, she holds at price—demanded of me my judgment whether she should defy Antony and wed thee, or whether she should put the thought away and come to Antony. And I—now mark thou all my sin—I, in my bitter jealousy, rather than I would see her thy wedded wife and thou her loving lord, counselled her most strictly that she should come to Antony, well knowing—for I had had speech with Dellius—that if she came, this weak Antony would fall like a ripe fruit at her feet, as, indeed, he has fallen. And but now I have shown thee the issue of the scheme. Antony loves Cleopatra and Cleopatra loves Antony, and thou art robbed, and matters have gone well for me, who of all women on the earth to-night am the wretchedest by far. For when I saw how thy heart broke but now, my heart seemed to break with thine, and I could no longer bear the burden of my evil deeds, but knew that I must tell them and take my punishment.

"And now, Harmachis, I have no more to say; save that I thank thee for thy courtesy in hearkening, and this one thing I add. Driven by my great love I have sinned against thee unto death! I have ruined thee,

I have ruined Khem, and myself also I have ruined! Let death reward me! Slay thou me, Harmachis—I will gladly die upon thy sword; ay, and kiss its blade! Slay thou me and go; for if thou slayest me not, myself I will surely slay!" And she threw herself upon her knees, lifting her fair breast toward me, that I might smite her with my dagger. And, in my bitter fury, I was minded to strike; for, above all, I thought how, when I was fallen, this woman, who herself was my cause of shame, had scourged me with her whip of scorn. But it is hard to slay a fair woman; and, even as I lifted my hand to strike, I remembered that she had now twice saved my life.

"Woman! thou shameless woman!" I said, "arise! I slay thee not! Who am I, that I should judge thy crime, that, with mine own, doth overtop all earthly judgment?"

"Slay me, Harmachis!" she moaned; "slay me, or I slay myself! My burden is too great for me to bear! Be not so deadly calm! Curse me, and slay!"

"What was it that thou didst say to me just now, Charmion—that as I had sown so I must reap? It is not lawful that thou shouldst slay thyself; it is not lawful that I, thine equal in sin, should slay thee because through thee I sinned. As *thou* hast sown, Charmion, so must *thou* also reap. Base woman! whose cruel jealousy has brought all these woes on me and Egypt, live—live on, and from year to year pluck the bitter fruit of crime! Haunted be thy sleep by visions of thy outraged Gods, whose vengeance awaits thee and me in their dim Amenti! Haunted be thy days by memories of that man whom thy fierce love brought to shame and ruin, and by the sight of Khem a prey to the insatiate Cleopatra and a slave to Roman Antony."

"Oh, speak not thus, Harmachis! Thy words are sharper than any sword; and more surely, if more slowly, shall they slay! Listen, Harmachis," and she grasped my robe: "when thou wast great, and all power lay within thy grasp, thou didst reject me. Wilt reject me now that Cleopatra hast cast thee from her—now that thou art poor and shamed and with no pillow to thy head? Still am I fair, and still I worship thee. Let me fly with thee, and make atonement for my lifelong love. Or, if this be too great a thing to ask, let me be but as thy sister and thy servant—thy very slave, so that I may still look upon thy face, and share thy trouble and minister to thee. O Harmachis, let me but come and I will brave all things and endure all things, and nothing but Death himself shall stay me from thy side. For I do believe that the love that sank me to so low a depth, dragging thee with me, can yet lift me to an equal height, and thee with me!"

"Wouldst tempt me to fresh sin, woman? And dost thou think, Charmion, that in some hovel where I must hide, I could bear, day by day, to look upon thy fair face, and seeing, remember that those lips betrayed me? Not thus easily shalt thou atone! This I know even now: many and heavy shall be thy lonely days of penance! Perchance that hour of vengeance yet may come, and perchance thou shalt live to play thy part in it. Thou must still abide in the Court of Cleopatra; and, while thou art there, if I yet live, I will from time to time find means to give thee tidings. Perhaps a day may dawn when once more I shall need thy service. Now, swear that, in this event, thou wilt not fail me a second time."

"I swear, Harmachis!—I swear! May everlasting torments, too hideous to be dreamed—more hideous, even, by far, than those that wring me now—be my portion if I fail thee in one jot or tittle—ay, though I wait a lifetime for thy word!"

"It is well; see that thou keep the oath—not twice may we betray. I go to work out my fate; abide thou to work out thine. Perchance our divers threads will once more mingle ere the web be spun. Charmion, who unasked didst love me—and who, prompted by that gentle love of thine, didst betray and ruin me—fare thee well!"

She gazed wildly upon my face—she stretched out her arms as though to clasp me; then, in the agony of her despair, she cast herself at length and grovelled upon the ground.

I took up the sack of clothing and the staff and gained the door, and, as I passed it, I threw one last glance upon her. There she lay, with arms outstretched—more white than her white robes—her dark hair streaming about her, and her fair brows hidden in the dust.

And thus I left her, nor did I again set my eyes upon her till nine long years had come and gone.

(Here ends the second and largest roll of papyrus.)

Book 3

The Vengeance of Harmachis

CHAPTER 1

Of the Escape of Harmachis from Tarsus

I made my way down the stair in safety, and presently stood in the courtyard of that great house. It was but an hour from dawn, and none were stirring. The last reveller had drunk his fill, the dancing-girls had ceased their dancing, and silence lay upon the city. I drew near the gate, and was challenged by an officer who stood on guard, wrapped in a heavy cloak.

"Who passes," said the voice of Brennus.

"A merchant, may it please you, Sir, who, having brought gifts from Alexandria to a lady of the Queen's household, and, having been entertained of the lady, now departs to his galley," I answered in a feigned voice.

"Umph!" he growled. "The ladies of the Queen's household keep their guests late. Well; it is a time of festival. The pass-word, Sir Shopkeeper? Without the pass-word you must needs return and crave the lady's further hospitality."

"'*Antony*,' Sir; and a right good word, too. Ah! I've wandered far, and never saw I so goodly a man or so great a general. And, mark you, Sir! I've travelled far, and seen many generals."

"Ay; *Antony* is the word! And Antony is a good general in his way—when it is a sober way, and when he cannot find a skirt to follow. I've served with Antony—and against him, too; and know his points. Well, well; he's got an armful now!"

And all this while that he was holding me in talk, the sentry had been pacing to and fro before the gate. But now he moved a little way to the right, leaving the entrance clear.

"Fare thee well, Harmachis, and begone!" whispered Brennus, leaning forward and speaking quickly. "Linger not. But at times bethink thee of Brennus who risked his neck to save thine. Farewell, lad, I would that we were sailing North together," and he turned his back upon me and began to hum a tune.

"Farewell, Brennus, thou honest man," I answered, and was gone. And, as I heard long afterwards, when on the morrow the hue and cry was raised because the murderers could not find me, though they sought me everywhere to slay me, Brennus did me a service. For he swore that as he kept his watch alone an hour after midnight he saw me come and stand upon the parapet of the roof, that then I stretched out my robes and they became wings on which I floated up to Heaven, leaving him astonished. And all those about the Court lent ear to this history, believing in it, because of the great fame of my magic; and they wondered much what the marvel might portend. The tale also travelled into Egypt, and did much to save my good name among those whom I had betrayed; for the more ignorant among them believed that I acted not of my will, but of the will of the dread Gods, who of their own purpose wafted me into Heaven. And thus to this day the saying runs that "*When Harmachis comes again Egypt shall be free.*" But alas, Harmachis comes no more! Only Cleopatra, though she was much afraid, doubted her of the tale, and sent an armed vessel to search for the Syrian merchant, but not to find him, as shall be told.

****

When I reached the galley of which Charmion had spoken, I found her about to sail, and gave the writing to the captain, who conned it, looking on me curiously, but said nothing.

So I went aboard, and immediately we dropped swiftly down the river with the current. And having come to the mouth of the river unchallenged, though we passed many vessels, we put out to sea with a strong favouring wind that before night freshened to a great gale. Then the sailor men, being much afraid, would have put about and run for the mouth of Cydnus again, but could not because of the wildness of the sea. All that night it blew furiously, and by dawn our mast was carried away, and we rolled helplessly in the trough of the great waves. But I sat wrapped in a cloak, little heeding; and because I showed no fear the sailors cried out that I was a wizard, and sought to cast me into the sea, but the captain would not. At dawn the wind slackened, but ere noon it once more blew in terrible fury, and at the fourth hour from noon we came in sight of the rocky coast of that cape in the island of Cyprus which is called Dinaretum, where is a mountain named Olympus, and thither-wards we drifted swiftly.

Then, when the sailors saw the terrible rocks, and how the great waves that smote on them spouted up in foam, once more they grew much afraid, and cried out in their fear. For, seeing that I still sat unmoved, they swore that I certainly was a wizard, and came to cast me forth as a sacrifice to the Gods of the sea. And this time the captain was overruled, and said nothing. Therefore, when they came to me I rose and defied them, saying, "Cast me forth, if ye will; but if ye cast me forth ye shall perish."

For in my heart I cared little, having no more any love of life, but rather a desire to die, though I greatly feared to pass into the presence of my Holy Mother Isis. But my weariness and sorrow at the bitterness of my lot overcame even this heavy fear; so that when, being mad as brute beasts, they seized me and, lifting me, hurled me into the raging waters, I did but utter one prayer to Isis and made ready for death. But it was fated that I should not die; for, when I rose to the surface of the water, I saw a spar of wood floating near me, to which I swam and clung. And a great wave came and swept me, riding, as it were, upon the spar, as when a boy I had learned to do in the waters of the Nile, past the bulwarks of the galley where the fierce-faced sailors clustered to see me drown. And when they saw me come mounted on the wave, cursing them as I came, and saw, too, that the colour of my face had changed—for the salt water had washed way the pigment, they shrieked with fear and threw themselves down upon the deck. And within a very little while, as I rode toward the rocky coast, a great wave poured into the vessel, that rolled broadside on, and pressed her down into the deep, whence she rose no more.

So she sank with all her crew. And in that same storm also sank the galley which Cleopatra had sent to search for the Syrian merchant. Thus all traces of me were lost, and of a surety she believed that I was dead.

But I rode on toward the shore. The wind shrieked and the salt waves lashed my face as, alone with the tempest, I rushed upon my way, while the sea-birds screamed about my head. I felt no fear, but rather a wild uplifting of the heart; and in the stress of my imminent peril the love of life seemed to waken again. And so I plunged and drifted, now tossed high toward the lowering clouds, now cast into the deep valleys of the sea, till at length the rocky headland loomed before me, and I saw the breakers smite upon the stubborn rocks, and through the screaming of the wind heard the sullen thunder of their fall and the groan of stones sucked seaward from the beach. On! high-throned upon the mane of a mighty billow—fifty cubits beneath me the level of the hissing waters; above me the inky sky!

It was done! The spar was torn from me, and, dragged downwards by the weight of the bag of gold and the clinging of my garments, I sank struggling furiously.

Now I was under—the green light for a moment streamed through the waters, and then came darkness, and on the darkness pictures of the past. Picture after picture—all the long scene of life was written here. Then in my ears I only heard the song of the nightingale, the murmur of the summer sea, and the music of Cleopatra's laugh of victory, following me softly and yet more soft as I sank away to sleep.

****

Once more my life came back, and with it a sense of deadly sickness and of aching pain. I opened my eyes and saw a kind face bending over me, and knew that I was in the room of a builded house.

"How came I hither?" I asked faintly.

"Of a truth, Poseidon brought thee, Stranger," answered a rough voice in barbarous Greek; "we found thee cast high upon the beach like a dead dolphin and brought thee to our house, for we are fisher-folk. And here, methinks, thou must lie a while, for thy left leg is broken by the force of the waves."

I strove to move my foot and could not. It was true, the bone was broken above the knee.

"Who art thou, and how art thou named?" asked the rough-bearded sailor.

"I am an Egyptian traveller whose ship has sunk in the fury of the gale, and I am named Olympus," I answered, for these people called a mountain that we had sighted Olympus, and therefore I took the name at hazard. And as Olympus I was henceforth known.

Here with these rough fisher-folk I abode for the half of a year, paying them a little out of the sum of gold that had come safely ashore upon me. For it was long before my bones grew together again, and then I was left somewhat of a cripple; for I, who had been so tall and straight and strong, now limped—one limb being shorter than the other. And after I recovered from my hurt, I still lived there, and toiled with them at the trade of fishing; for I knew not whither I should go or what I should do, and, for a while, I was fain to become a peasant fisherman, and so wear my weary life away. And these people entreated me kindly, though, as others, they feared me much, holding me to be a wizard brought hither by the sea. For my sorrows had stamped so strange an aspect on my face that men gazing at me grew fearful of what lay beneath its calm.

There, then, I abode, till at length, one night as I lay and strove to sleep, great restlessness came upon me, and a mighty desire once more to see the face of Sihor. But whether this desire was of the Gods or born of my own heart, not knowing, I cannot tell. So strong was it, at the least, that before it was dawn I rose from my bed of straw and clothed myself in my fisher garb, and, because I had no wish to answer questions, thus I took farewell of my humble hosts. First I placed some pieces of gold on the well-cleaned table of wood, and then taking a pot of flour I strewed it in the form of letters, writing:

"This gift from Olympus, the Egyptian, who returns into the sea."

Then I went, and on the third day I came to the great city of Salamis, that is also on the sea. Here I abode in the fishermen's quarters till a vessel was about to sail for Alexandria, and to the captain of this vessel, a man of Paphos, I hired myself as a sailor. We sailed with a favouring wind, and on the fifth day I came to Alexandria, that hateful city, and saw the light dancing on its golden domes.

Here I might not abide. So again I hired myself out as a sailor, giving my labour in return for passage, and we passed up the Nile. And I learned from the talk of men that Cleopatra had come back to Alexandria, drawing Antony with her and that they lived together with royal state in the palace on the Lochias. Indeed, the boatmen already had a song thereon, which they sang as they laboured at the oar. Also I heard how the galley that was sent to search for the vessel which carried the Syrian merchant had foundered with all her crew, and the tale that the Queen's astronomer, Harmachis, had flown to Heaven from the roof of the house at Tarsus. And the sailors wondered because I sat and laboured and would not sing their ribald song of the loves of Cleopatra. For they, too, began to fear me, and mutter concerning me among themselves. Then I knew that I was a man accursed and set apart—a man whom none might love.

On the sixth day we drew nigh to Abouthis, where I left the craft, and the sailors were right glad to see me go. And, with a breaking heart, I walked through the fertile fields, seeing faces that I knew well. But in my rough disguise and limping gait none knew me. At length, as the sun sank, I came near to the great outer pylon of the temple; and here I crouched down in the ruins of a house, not knowing why I had come or what I was about to do. Like a lost ox I had strayed from far, back to the fields of my birth, and for what? If my father, Amenemhat, still lived, surely he would turn his face from me. I dared not go into the presence of my father. I sat hidden there among the broken rafters, and idly watched the pylon gates, to see if, perchance, a face I knew should issue from them. But none came forth or entered in, though the great gates stood wide; and then I saw that herbs were growing between the stones, where no herbs had grown for ages. What could this be? Was the temple deserted? Nay; how could the worship of the eternal Gods have ceased, that for thousands of years had, day by day, been offered in the holy place? Was, then, my father dead? It well might be. And yet, why this silence? Where were the priests: where the worshippers?

I could bear the doubt no more, but as the sun sank red I crept like a hunted jackal through the open gates, and on till I reached the first great Hall of Pillars. Here I paused and gazed around me—not a sight, not a sound, in the dim and holy place! I went on with a beating heart to the second great hall, the hall of six-and-thirty pillars where I had been crowned Lord of all the Lands: still not a sight or a sound! Thence, half fearful of my own footfall, so terribly did it echo in the silence of the deserted Holies, I passed down the passage of the names of the Pharaohs towards my father's chamber. The curtain still swung over the doorway; but what would there be within?—also emptiness? I lifted it, and noiselessly passed in, and there in his carven chair at the table on which his long white beard flowed, sat my father, Amenemhat, clad in his priestly robes. At first I thought that he was dead, he sat so still; but at length he turned his head, and I saw that his eyes were white and sightless. He was blind, and his face was thin as the face of a dead man, and woeful with age and grief.

I stood still and felt the blind eyes wandering over me. I could not speak to him—I dared not speak to him; I would go and hide myself afresh.

I had already turned and grasped the curtain, when my father spoke in a deep, slow voice:

"Come hither, thou who wast my son and art a traitor. Come hither, thou Harmachis, on whom Khem builded up her hope. Not in vain, then, have I drawn thee from far away! Not in vain have I held my life in me till I heard thy footfall creeping down these empty Holies, like the footfall of a thief!"

"Oh! my father," I gasped, astonished. "Thou art blind: how knowest thou me?"

"How do I know thee?—and askest thou that who hast learned of our lore? Enough, I know thee and I brought thee hither. Would, Harmachis, that I knew thee not! Would that I had been blasted of the Invisible ere I drew thee down from the womb of Nout, to be my curse and shame, and the last woe of Khem!"

"Oh, speak not thus!" I moaned; "is not my burden already more than I can bear? Am I not myself betrayed and utterly outcast? Be pitiful, my father!"

"Be pitiful!—be pitiful to thee who hast shown so great pity? It was thy pity which gave up noble Sepa to die beneath the hands of the tormentors!"

"Oh, not that—not that!" I cried.

"Ay, traitor, that!—to die in agony, with his last poor breath proclaiming thee, his murderer, honest and innocent! Be pitiful to thee, who gavest all the flower of Khem as the price of a wanton's arms!—thinkest thou that, labouring in the darksome desert mines, those noble ones in thought are pitiful to thee, Harmachis? Be pitiful to thee, by whom this Holy Temple of Abouthis hath been ravaged, its lands seized, its priests scattered, and I alone, old and withered, left to count out its ruin—to thee, who hast poured the treasures of *Her* into thy leman's lap, who hast forsworn Thyself, thy Country, thy Birthright, and thy Gods! Yea, thus am I pitiful: Accursed be thou, fruit of my loins!—Shame be thy portion, Agony thy end, and Hell receive thee at the last! Where art thou? Yea, I grew blind with weeping when I heard the truth—sure, they strove to hide it from me. Let me find thee that I may spit upon thee, thou Renegade! thou Apostate! thou Outcast!"—and he rose from his seat and staggered like a living Wrath toward me, smiting the air with his wand. And as he came with outstretched arms, awful to see, suddenly his end found him, and with a cry he sank down upon the ground, the red blood streaming from his lips. I ran to him and lifted him; and as he died, he babbled:

"He was my son, a bright-eyed lovely boy, and full of promise as the Spring; and now—and now—oh, would that he were dead!"

Then came a pause and the breath rattled in his throat.

"Harmachis," he gasped, "art there?"

"Yea, father."

"Harmachis, atone!—atone! Vengeance can still be wreaked—forgiveness may still be won. There's gold; I've hidden it—Atoua—she can tell thee—ah, this pain! Farewell!"

And he struggled faintly in my arms and was dead.

****

Thus, then, did I and my holy father, the Prince Amenemhat, meet together for the last time in the flesh, and for the last time part.

Chapter 2

Of the Last Misery of Harmachis

I crouched upon the floor gazing at the dead body of my father, who had lived to curse me, the utterly accursed, while the darkness crept and gathered round us, till at length the dead and I were alone in the black silence. Oh, how tell the misery of that hour! Imagination cannot dream it, nor words paint it forth. Once more in my wretchedness I bethought me of death. A knife was at my girdle, with which I might cut the thread of sorrow and set my spirit free. Free? ay, free to fly and face the last vengeance of the Holy Gods! Alas! and alas! I did not dare to die. Better the earth with all its woes than the quick approach of those unimagined terrors that, hovering in dim Amenti, wait the advent of the fallen.

I grovelled on the ground and wept tears of agony for the lost unchanging past—wept till I could weep no more; but no answer came from the silence—no answer but the echoes of my grief. Not a ray of hope! My soul wandered in a darkness more utter than that which was about me—I was forsaken of the Gods and cast out of men. Terror took hold upon me crouching in that lonely place hard by the majesty of the awful Dead. I rose to fly. How could I fly in this gloom?—And where should I fly who had no place of refuge? Once more I crouched down, and the great fear grew on me till the cold sweat ran from my brow and my soul was faint within me. Then, in my last despair, I prayed aloud to Isis, to whom I had not dared to pray for many days.

"O Isis! Holy Mother!" I cried; "put away Thy wrath, and of Thine infinite pity, O Thou all-pitiful, hearken to the voice of the anguish of him who was Thy son and servant, but who by sin hath fallen from the vision of Thy love. O throned Glory, who, being in all things, hast of all things understanding and of all griefs knowledge, cast the weight of Thy mercy against the scale of my evil-doing, and make the balance equal. Look down upon my woe, and measure it; count up the sum of my repentance and take Thou note of the flood of sorrow that sweeps my soul away. O Thou Holy, whom it was given to me to look upon face to face, by that dread hour of commune I summon Thee; I summon Thee by the mystic word. Come, then, in mercy, to save me; or, in anger, to make an end of that which can no more be borne."

And, rising from my knees, I stretched out my arms and dared to cry aloud the Word of Fear, to use which unworthily is death.

Swiftly the answer came. For in the silence I heard the sound of the shaken *sistra* heralding the coming of the Glory. Then, at the far end of the chamber, grew the semblance of the horned moon, gleaming faintly in the darkness, and betwixt the golden horns rested a small dark cloud, in and out of which the fiery serpent climbed.

My knees waxed loose in the presence of the Glory, and I sank down before it.

Then spake the small, sweet Voice within the cloud:

"Harmachis, who wast my servant and my son, I have heard thy prayer, and the summons that thou hast dared to utter, which on the lips of one with whom I have communed, hath power to draw Me from the Uttermost. No more, Harmachis, may we be one in the bond of Love Divine, for thou hast put Me away of thine own act. Therefore, after this long silence I come, Harmachis, clothed in terrors, and, perchance, ready for vengeance, for not lightly can Isis be drawn from the halls of Her Divinity."

"Smite, Goddess!" I answered. "Smite, and give me over to those who wreak Thy vengeance; for I can no longer bear the burden of my woe!"

"And if thou canst not bear thy burden here, upon this upper earth," came the soft reply, "how then shalt thou bear the greater burden that shall be laid upon thee there, coming defiled and yet unpurified into my dim realm of Death, that is Life and Change unending? Nay, Harmachis, I smite thee not, for not all am I wroth that thou hast dared to utter the awful Word which calls Me down to thee. Hearken, Harmachis; I praise not, and I reproach not, for I am the Minister of Reward and Punishment and the Executrix of Decrees; and if I give, I give in silence; and if I smite, in silence do I smite. Therefore, I will add naught to thy burden by the weight of heavy words, though through thee it has come to pass that soon shall Isis, the Mother-Mystery, be but a memory in Egypt. Thou hast sinned, and heavy shall be thy punishment, as I did warn thee, both in the flesh and in my kingdom of Amenti. But I told thee that there is a road of repentance, and surely thy feet are set thereon, and therein must thou walk with a humble heart, eating of the bread of bitterness, till such time as thy doom be measured."

"Have I, then, no hope, O holy?"

"That which is done, Harmachis, is done, nor can its issues be altered. Khem shall no more be free till all its temples are as the desert dust; strange Peoples shall, from age to age, hold her hostage and in bonds; new Religions shall arise and wither within the shadow of her pyramids, for to every World, Race, and Age the countenances of the Gods are changed. This is the tree that shall spring from thy seed of sin, Harmachis, and from the sin of those who tempted thee!"

"Alas! I am undone!" I cried.

"Yea, thou art undone; and yet shall this be given to thee: thy Destroyer thou shalt destroy—for so, in the purpose of my justice, it is ordained. When the sign comes to thee, arise, go to Cleopatra, and in such manner as I shall put into thy heart do Heaven's vengeance upon her! And now for thyself one word, for thou hast put Me from thee, Harmachis, and no more shall I come face to face with thee till, cycles hence, the last fruit of thy sin hath ceased to be upon this earth! Yet, through the vastness of the unnumbered years, remember thou this: the Love Divine is Love Eternal, which cannot be extinguished, though it be everlastingly estranged. Repent, my son; repent and do well while there is yet time, that at the dim end of ages thou mayest once more be gathered unto Me. Still, Harmachis, though thou seest Me not; still, when the very name by which thou knowest Me has become a meaningless mystery to those who shall be after thee; still I, whose hours are eternal—I, who have watched Universes wither, wane, and, beneath the breath of Time, melt into nothingness; again to gather, and, re-born, thread the maze of space—still, I say, I shall companion thee. Wherever thou goest, in whatever form of life thou livest, there I shall be! Art thou wafted to the farthest star, art thou buried in Amenti's lowest deep—in lives, in deaths, in sleeps, in wakings, in remembrances, in oblivions, in all the fevers of the outer Life, in all the changes of the Spirit—still, if thou wilt but atone and forget Me no more, I shall be with thee, waiting thine hour of redemption. For this is the nature of Love Divine, wherewith it loves that which partakes of its divinity and by the holy tie hath once been bound to it. Judge then, Harmachis: was it well to put this from thee to win the dust of earthly woman? And, now, dare not again to utter the Word of Power till these things are done! Harmachis, for this season, fare thee well!"

****

As the last note of the sweet Voice died away, the fiery snake climbed into the heart of the cloud. Now the cloud rolled from the horns of light, and was gathered into the blackness. The vision of the crescent moon grew dim and vanished. Then, as the Goddess passed, once more came the faint and dreadful music of the shaken *sistra*, and all was still.

I hid my face in my robe, and even then, though my outstretched hand could touch the chill corpse of that father who had died cursing me, I felt hope come back into my heart, knowing that I was not altogether lost nor utterly rejected of Her whom I had forsaken, but whom I yet loved. And then weariness overpowered me, and I slept.

****

I woke, the faint lights of dawn were creeping from the opening in the roof. Ghastly they lay upon the shadowy sculptured walls and ghastly upon the dead face and white beard of my father, the gathered to Osiris. I started up, remembering all things, and wondering in my heart what I should do, and as I rose I heard a faint footfall creeping down the passage of the names of the Pharaohs.

"*La! La! La!*" mumbled a voice that I knew for the voice of the old wife, Atoua. "Why, 'tis dark as the House of the Dead! The Holy Ones who built this Temple loved not the blessed sun, however much they worshipped him. Now, where's the curtain?"

Presently it was drawn, and Atoua entered, a stick in one hand and a basket in the other. Her face was somewhat more wrinkled, and her scanty locks were somewhat whiter than aforetime, but for the rest she was as she had ever been. She stood and peered around with her sharp black eyes, for as yet she could see nothing because of the shadows.

"Now where is he?" she muttered. "Osiris—glory to His name—send that he has not wandered in the night, and he blind! Alack! that I could not return before the dark. Alack! and alack! what times have we fallen on, when the Holy High Priest and the Governor, by descent, of Abouthis, is left with one aged crone to minister to his infirmity! O Harmachis, my poor boy, thou hast laid trouble at our doors! Why, what's this? Surely he sleeps not, there upon the ground?—'twill be his death! Prince! Holy Father! Amenemhat! awake, arise!" and she hobbled towards the corpse. "Why, how is it! By Him who sleeps, he's dead! untended and alone—*dead! dead!*" and she sent her long wail of grief ringing up the sculptured walls.

"Hush! woman, be still!" I said, gliding from the shadows.

"Oh, what art thou?" she cried, casting down her basket. "Wicked man, hast thou murdered this Holy One, the only Holy One in Egypt? Surely the curse will fall on thee, for though the Gods do seem to have forsaken us now in our hour of trial, yet is their arm long, and certainly they will be avenged on him who hath slain their anointed!"

"Look on me, Atoua," I cried.

"Look! ay, I look—thou wicked wanderer who hast dared this cruel deed! Harmachis is a traitor and lost far away, and Amenemhat his holy father is murdered, and now I'm all alone without kith or kin. I gave them for him. I gave them for Harmachis, the traitor! Come, slay me also, thou wicked one!"

I took a step toward her, and she, thinking that I was about to smite her, cried out in fear:

"Nay, good Sir, spare me! Eighty and six, by the Holy Ones, eighty and six, come next flood of Nile, and yet I would not die, though Osiris is merciful to the old who served him! Come no nearer—help! help!"

"Thou fool, be silent," I said; "knowest thou me not?"

"Know thee? Can I know every wandering boatman to whom Sebek grants to earn a livelihood till Typhon claims his own? And yet—why, 'tis strange—that changed countenance!—that scar!—that stumbling gait! It is thou, Harmachis!—'tis thou, O my boy! Art come back to glad mine old eyes? I hoped thee dead! Let me kiss thee?—nay, I forget. Harmachis is a traitor, ay, and a murderer! Here lies the holy Amenemhat, murdered by the traitor, Harmachis! Get thee gone! I'll have none of traitors and of parricides! Get thee to thy wanton!—it is not thou whom I did nurse."

"Peace! woman; peace! I slew not my father—he died, alas!—he died even in my arms."

"Ay, surely, and cursing thee, Harmachis! Thou hast given death to him who gave thee life! *La! la!* I am old, and I've seen many a trouble; but this is the heaviest of them all! I never liked the looks of mummies; but I would I were one this hour! Get thee gone, I pray thee!"

"Old nurse, reproach me not! Have I not enough to bear?"

"Ah! yes, yes!—I did forget! Well; and what is thy sin? A woman was thy bane, as women have been to those before thee, and shall be to those after thee. And what a woman! *La! la!* I saw her, a beauty such as never was—an arrow pointed by the evil Gods for destruction! And thou, a young man bred as a priest—an ill training—a very ill training! 'Twas no fair match. Who can wonder that she mastered thee? Come, Harmachis; let me kiss thee! It is not for a woman to be hard on a man because he loved our sex too much. Why, that is but nature; and Nature knows her business, else she had made us otherwise. But here is an evil case. Knowest thou that this Macedonian Queen of thine hath seized the temple lands and revenues, and driven away the priests—all, save the holy Amenemhat, who lies here, and whom she left, I know not why; ay, and caused the worship of the Gods to cease within these walls. Well, he's gone!—he's gone! and indeed he is better with Osiris, for his life was a sore burden to him. And hark thou, Harmachis: he hath not left thee empty-handed; for, so soon as the plot failed, he gathered all his wealth, and it is large, and hid it—where, I can show thee—and it is thine by right of descent."

"Talk not to me of wealth, Atoua. Where shall I go and how shall I hide my shame?"

"Ah! true, true; here mayst thou not abide, for if they found thee, surely they would put thee to the dreadful death—ay, to the death by the waxen cloth. Nay, I will hide thee, and, when the funeral rites of the holy Amenemhat have been performed, we will fly hence, and cover us from the eyes of men till these sorrows are forgotten. *La! la!* it is a sad world, and full of trouble as the Nile mud is full of beetles. Come, Harmachis, come."

Chapter 3
Of the Message of Charmion

These things then came to pass. For eighty days I was hidden of the old wife, Atoua, while the body of the Prince, my father, was made ready for burial by those skilled in the arts of embalming. And when at last all things were done in order, I crept from my hiding-place and made offerings to the spirit of my father, and placing lotus-flowers on his breast went thence sorrowing. And on the following day, from where I lay hid, I saw the Priests of the Temple of Osiris and of the holy shrine of Isis come forth, and in slow procession bear his painted coffin to the sacred lake and lay it beneath the funeral tent in the consecrated boat. I saw them celebrate the symbol of the trial of the dead, and name him above all men just, and then bear him thence to lay him by his wife, my mother, in the deep tomb that he had hewn in the rock near to the resting-place of the Holy Osiris, where, notwithstanding my sins, I, too, hope to sleep ere long. And when all these things were done and the deep tomb sealed, the wealth of my father having been removed from the hidden treasury and placed in safety, I fled, disguised, with the old wife, Atoua, up the Nile till we came to Tápé,[1] and here in this great city I lay a while, till a place could be found where I should hide myself.

And such a place I found. For to the north of the great city are brown and rugged hills, and desert valley blasted of the sun, and in this place of desolation the Divine Pharaohs, my forefathers, hollowed out their tombs in the solid rock, the most part of which are lost to this day, so cunningly have they been hidden. But some are open, for the accursed Persians and other thieves broke into them in search of treasure. And one night—for by night only did I leave my hiding-place—just as the dawn was breaking on the mountain tops, I wandered alone in this sad valley of death, like to which there is no other, and presently

1 Thebes.—Editor.

came to the mouth of a tomb hidden amid great rocks, which afterwards I knew for the place of the burying of the Divine Rameses, the third of that name, now long gathered to Osiris. And by the faint light of the dawn creeping through the entrance I saw that it was spacious and that within were chambers.

On the following night, therefore, I returned, bearing lights, with Atoua, my nurse, who ever ministered faithfully to me as when I was little and without discretion. And we searched the mighty tomb and came to the great Hall of the Sarcophagus of granite, in which the Divine Rameses sleeps, and saw the mystic paintings on the walls: the symbol of the Snake unending, the symbol of Ra resting upon the *Scarabaeus*, the symbol of Ra resting upon Nout, the symbol of the Headless men, and many others, whereof, being initiated, well I read the mysteries. And opening from the long descending passage I found chambers in which were paintings beautiful to behold, and of all manner of things. For beneath each chamber is entombed the master of the craft of which the paintings tell, he who was the chief of the servants of that craft in the house of this Divine Rameses. And on the walls of the last chamber—on the left-hand side, looking toward the Hall of the Sarcophagus—are paintings exceedingly beautiful, and two blind harpers playing upon their bent harps before the God Mou; and beneath the flooring these harpers, who harp no more, are soft at sleep. Here, then, in this gloomy place, even in the tomb of the Harpers and the company of the dead, I took up my abode; and here for eight long years I worked out my penance and made atonement for my sin. But Atoua, because she loved to be near the light, abode in the chamber of the Boats—that is, the first chamber on the right-hand side of the gallery looking toward the Hall of the Sarcophagus.

And this was the manner of my life. On every second day the old wife, Atoua, went forth and brought water from the city and such food as is necessary to keep the life from failing, and also tapers made from fat. And one hour at the time of sunrise and one hour at the time of sunset I did go forth also to wander in the valley for my health's sake and to save my sight from failing in the great darkness of the tomb. But the other hours of the day and night, except when I climbed the mountain to watch the course of the stars, I spent in prayer and meditation and sleep, till the cloud of sin lifted from my heart and once more I drew near to the Gods, though with Isis, my heavenly Mother, I might speak no more. And I grew exceedingly wise also, pondering on all those mysteries to which I held the key. For abstinence and prayer and sorrowful solitude wore away the grossness of my flesh, and with the eyes of the Spirit I learned to look deep into the heart of things till the joy of Wisdom fell like dew upon my soul.

Soon the rumour was wafted about the city that a certain holy man named Olympus abode in solitude in the tombs of the awful Valley of the Dead; and hither came people bearing sick that I might cure them. And I gave my mind to the study of simples, in which Atoua instructed me; and by lore and the weight of my thought I gained great skill in medicine, and healed many sick. And thus ever, as time went on, my fame was noised abroad; for it was said that I was also a magician and that in the tombs I had commune with the Spirits of the Dead. And this, indeed, I did—though it is not lawful for me to speak of these matters. Thus, then, it came to pass that no more need Atoua go forth to seek food and water, for the people brought it—more than was needful, for I would receive no fee. Now at first, fearing lest some in the hermit Olympus might know the lost Harmachis, I would only meet those who came in the darkness of the tomb. But afterwards, when I learned how it was held through all the land that Harmachis was certainly no more, I came forth and sat in the mouth of the tomb, and ministered to the sick, and at times calculated nativities for the great. And thus my fame grew continually, till at length folk journeyed even from Memphis and Alexandria to visit me; and from them I learned how Antony had left Cleopatra for a while, and, Fulvia being dead, had married Octavia, the sister of Caesar. Many other things I learned also.

And in the second year I did this: I despatched the old wife, Atoua, disguised as a seller of simples, to Alexandria, bidding her seek out Charmion, and, if yet she found her faithful, reveal to her the secret of my way of life. So she went, and in the fifth month from her sailing returned, bearing Charmion's greetings and a token. And she told me that she had found means to see Charmion, and, in talk, had let fall the name of Harmachis, speaking of me as one dead; at which Charmion, unable to control her grief, wept aloud. Then, reading her heart—for the old wife was very clever, and held the key of knowledge—she told her that Harmachis yet lived, and sent her greetings. Thereon Charmion wept yet more with joy, and kissed the old wife, and made her gifts, bidding her tell me that she had kept her vow, and waited for my coming and the hour of vengeance. So, having learned many secrets, Atoua returned again to Tápé.

And in the following year messengers came to me from Cleopatra, bearing a sealed roll and great gifts. I opened the roll, and read this in it:

"Cleopatra to Olympus, the learned Egyptian who dwells in the Valley of Death by Tápé—

"The fame of thy renown, O learned Olympus, hath reached our ears. Tell thou, then, this to us, and if thou tellest aright greater honour and wealth shalt thou have than any in Egypt: How shall we win back the love of noble Antony, who is bewitched of cunning Octavia, and tarries long from us?"

Now, in this I saw the hand of Charmion, who had made my renown known to Cleopatra.

All that night I took counsel with my wisdom, and on the morrow wrote my answer as it was put into my heart to the destruction of Cleopatra and Antony. And thus I wrote:

"Olympus the Egyptian to Cleopatra the Queen—

"Go forth into Syria with one who shall be sent to lead thee; thus shalt thou win Antony to thy arms again, and with him gifts more great than thou canst dream."

And with this letter I dismissed the messengers, bidding them share the presents sent by Cleopatra among their company.

So they went wondering.

But Cleopatra, seizing on the advice to which her passion prompted her, departed straightway with Fonteius Capito into Syria, and there the thing came about as I had foretold, for Antony was subdued of her and gave her the greater part of Cilicia, the ocean shore of Arabia Nabathaea, the balm-bearing provinces of Judaea, the province of Phoenicia, the province of Coele-Syria, the rich isle of Cyprus, and all the library of Pergamus. And to the twin children that, with the son Ptolemy, Cleopatra had borne to Antony, he impiously gave the names of "Kings, the Children of Kings"—of Alexander Helios, as the Greeks name the sun, and of Cleopatra Selene, the moon, the long-winged.

These things then came to pass.

Now on her return to Alexandria Cleopatra sent me great gifts, of which I would have none, and prayed me, the learned Olympus, to come to her at Alexandria; but it was not yet time, and I would not. But thereafter she and Antony sent many times to me for counsel, and I ever counselled them to their ruin, nor did my prophecies fail.

****

Thus the long years rolled away, and I, the hermit Olympus, the dweller in a tomb, the eater of bread and the drinker of water, by strength of the wisdom that was given me of the avenging Power, became once more great in Khem. For I grew ever wiser as I trampled the desires of the flesh beneath my feet and turned my eyes to heaven.

At length eight full years were accomplished. The war with the Parthians had come and gone, and Artavasdes, King of Armenia, had been led in triumph through the streets of Alexandria. Cleopatra had visited Samos and Athens; and, by her counselling, the noble Octavia had been driven, like some discarded concubine, from the house of Antony at Rome. And now, at the last, the measure of the folly of Antony was full even to the brim. For this Master of the World had no longer the good gift of reason; he was lost in Cleopatra as I had been lost. Therefore, in the event, Octavianus declared war against him.

And as I slept upon a certain day in the chamber of the Harpers, in the tomb of Pharaoh that is by Tápé, there came to me a vision of my father, the aged Amenemhat, and he stood over me, leaning on his staff, and spoke, saying:

"Look forth, my son."

Then I looked forth, and with the eyes of my spirit saw the sea, and two great fleets grappling in war hard by a rocky coast. And the emblems were those of Octavian, and of the other those of Cleopatra and Antony. The ships of Antony and Cleopatra bore down upon the ships of Caesar, and drove them on, for victory inclined to Antony.

I looked again. There sat Cleopatra in a gold-decked galley watching the fight with eager eyes. Then I cast my Spirit on her so that she seemed to hear the voice of dead Harmachis crying in her ear.

"*Fly, Cleopatra,*" it seemed to say, "*fly or perish!*"

She looked up wildly, and again she heard my Spirit's cry. Now a mighty fear took hold of her. She called aloud to the sailors to hoist the sails and make signal to her fleet to put about. This they did wondering but little loath, and fled in haste from the battle.

Then a great roar went up from friend and foe.

"Cleopatra is fled! Cleopatra is fled!" And I saw wreck and red ruin fall upon the fleet of Antony and awoke from my trance.

The days passed, and again a vision of my father came to me and spoke, saying:

"Arise, my son!—the hour of vengeance is at hand! Thy plots have not failed; thy prayers have been heard. By the bidding of the Gods, as she sat in her galley at the fight of Actium, the heart of Cleopatra was filled with fears, so that, deeming she heard thy voice bidding her fly or perish, she fled with all her fleet. Now the strength of Actium is broken on the sea. Go forth, and as it shall be put into thy mind, so do thou."

In the morning I awoke, wondering, and went to the mouth of the tomb, and there, coming up the valley, I saw the messengers of Cleopatra, and with them a Roman guard.

"What will ye with me now?" I asked, sternly.

"This is the message of the Queen and of great Antony," answered the Captain, bowing low before me, for I was much feared by all men. "The Queen commands thy presence at Alexandria. Many times has she sent, and thou wouldst not come; now she bids thee to come, and that swiftly, for she has need of thy counsel."

"And if I say Nay, soldier, what then?"

"These are my orders, most holy Olympus; that I bring thee by force."

I laughed aloud. "By force, thou fool! Use not such talk to me, lest I smite thee where thou art. Know, then, that I can kill as well as cure!"

"Pardon, I beseech thee!" he answered, shrinking. "I say but those things that I am bid."

"Well, I know it, Captain. Fear not; I come."

So on that very day I departed, together with the aged Atoua. Ay, I went as secretly as I had come; and the tomb of the Divine Rameses knew me no more. And with me I took all the treasures of my father, Amenemhat, for I was not minded to go to Alexandria empty-handed and as a suppliant, but rather as a man of much wealth and condition. Now, as I went, I learned that Antony, following Cleopatra, had, indeed, fled from Actium, and knew that the end drew nigh. For this and many other things had I foreseen in the darkness of the tomb of Tápé, and planned to bring about.

****

Thus, then, I came to Alexandria, and entered into a house which had been made ready for me at the palace gates.

And that very night Charmion came to me—Charmion whom I had not seen for nine long years.

CHAPTER 4

Of the Commands of Cleopatra

Clad in my plain black robe, I sat in the guest-chamber of the house that had been made ready for me. I sat in a carven lion-footed chair, and looked upon the swinging lamps of scented oil, the pictured tapestries, the rich Syrian rugs—and, amidst all this luxury, bethought me of that tomb of the Harpers which is at Tápé, and of the nine long years of dark loneliness and preparation. I sat; and crouched upon a rug near to the door, lay the aged Atoua. Her hair was white as snow, and shrivelled with age was the wrinkled countenance of the woman who, when all deserted me, had yet clung to me, in her great love forgetting my great sins. Nine years! nine long years! and now, once again, I set my foot in Alexandria! Once again in the appointed circle of things I came forth from the solitude of preparation to be a fate to Cleopatra; and this second time I came not forth to fail.

And yet how changed the circumstance! I was out of the story: my part now was but the part of the sword in the hands of Justice; I might no more hope to make Egypt free and great and sit upon my lawful throne. Khem was lost, and lost was I, Harmachis. In the rush and turmoil of events, the great plot of which I had been the pivot was covered up and forgotten; scarce a memory of it remained. The curtain of dark night was closing in upon the history of my ancient Race; its very Gods were tottering to their fall; I could already, in the spirit, hear the shriek of the Roman eagles as they flapped their wings above the furthest banks of Sihor.

Presently I roused myself and bade Atoua go seek a mirror and bring it to me, that I might look therein.

And I saw this: a face shrunken and pallid, on which no smile came; great eyes grown wan with gazing into darkness looking out beneath the shaven head, emptily, as the hollow eye-pits of a skull; a wizened halting form wasted by abstinence, sorrow, and prayer; a long wild beard of iron grey; thin blue-veined hands that ever trembled like a leaf; bowed shoulders and lessened limbs. Time and grief had done their work indeed; scarce could I think myself the same as when, the Royal Harmachis—in all the splendour of my strength and youthful beauty—I first had looked upon the woman's loveliness that did destroy me. And yet within me burned the same fire as of yore; yet I was not changed, for time and grief have no power to alter the immortal spirit of man. Seasons may come and go; Hope, like a bird, may fly away; Passion may break its wings against the iron bars of Fate; Illusions may crumble as the cloudy towers of sunset flame; Faith, as running water, may slip from beneath our feet; Solitude may stretch itself around us like the measureless desert sand; Old Age may creep as the gathering night over our bowed heads grown hoary in their shame—yea, bound to Fortune's wheel, we may taste of every turn of chance—now rule as Kings, now serve as Slaves; now love, now hate; now prosper, and now perish. But still, through all, we are the same; for this is the marvel of Identity.

****

And as I sat and thought these things in bitterness of heart, there came a knocking at the door.

"Open, Atoua!" I said.

She rose and did my bidding; and a woman entered, clad in Grecian robes. It was Charmion, still beautiful as of old, but sad faced now and very sweet to see, with a patient fire slumbering in her downcast eyes.

She entered unattended; and, speaking no word, the old wife pointed to where I sat, and went.

"Old man," she said, addressing me, "lead me to the learned Olympus. I come upon the Queen's business."

I rose, and, lifting my head, looked upon her.

She gazed, and gave a little cry.

"Surely," she whispered, glancing round, "surely thou art not that—" And she paused.

"That Harmachis whom once thy foolish heart did love, O Charmion? Yes, I am he and what thou seest, most fair lady. Yet is Harmachis dead whom thou didst love; but Olympus, the skilled Egyptian, waits upon thy words!"

"Cease!" she said, "and of the past but one word, and then—why, let it lie. Not well, with all thy wisdom, canst thou know a true woman's heart, if thou dost believe, Harmachis, that it can change with the changes of the outer form, for then assuredly could no love follow its beloved to that last place of change—the Grave. Know thou, learned Physician, I am of that sort who, loving once, love always, and being not beloved again, go virgin to the death."

She ceased, and having naught to say, I bowed my head in answer. Yet though I said nothing and though this woman's passionate folly had been the cause of all our ruin, to speak truth, in secret I was thankful to her who, wooed of all and living in this shameless Court, had still through the long years poured out her unreturned love upon an outcast, and who, when that poor broken slave of Fortune came back in such unlovely guise, held him yet dear at heart. For what man is there who does not prize that gift most rare and beautiful, that one perfect thing which no gold can buy—a woman's unfeigned love?

"I thank thee that thou dost not answer," she said; "for the bitter words which thou didst pour upon me in those days that long are dead, and far away in Tarsus, have not lost their poisonous sting, and in my heart is no more place for the arrows of thy scorn, new venomed through thy solitary years. So let it be. Behold! I put it from me, that wild passion of my soul," and she looked up and stretched out her hands as though to press some unseen presence back, "I put it from me—though forget it I may not! There, 'tis done, Harmachis; no more shall my love trouble thee. Enough for me that once more my eyes behold thee, before sleep seals thee from their sight. Dost remember how, when I would have died by thy dear hand, thou wouldst not slay, but didst bid me live to pluck the bitter fruit of crime, and be accursed by visions of the evil I had wrought and memories of thee whom I have ruined?"

"Ay, Charmion, I remember well."

"Surely the cup of punishment has been filled. Oh! couldst thou see into the record of my heart, and read in it the suffering that I have borne—borne with a smiling face—thy justice would be satisfied indeed!"

"And yet, if report be true, Charmion, thou art the first of all the Court, and therein the most powerful and beloved. Does not Octavianus give it out that he makes war, not on Antony, nor even on his mistress, Cleopatra, but on Charmion and Iras?"

"Yes, Harmachis, and think that it has been to me thus, because of my oath to thee, to be forced to eat the bread and do the tasks of one whom so bitterly I hate!—one who robbed me of thee, and who, through the workings of my jealousy, brought me to be that which I am, brought thee to shame, and all Egypt to its ruin! Can jewels and riches and the flattery of princes and nobles bring happiness to such a one as I, who am more wretched than the meanest scullion wench? Oh, I have often wept till I was blind; and then, when the hour came, I must arise and tire me, and, with a smile, go do the bidding of the Queen and that heavy Antony. May the Gods grant me to see them dead—ay, the twain of them!—then myself I shall be content to die! Thy lot has been hard, Harmachis; but at least thou have been free, and many is the time that I have envied thee the quiet of thy haunted cave."

"I do perceive, O Charmion, that thou art mindful of thy oaths; and it is well, for the hour of vengeance is at hand."

"I am mindful, and in all things I have worked for thee in secret—for thee, and for the utter ruin of Cleopatra and the Roman. I have fanned his passion and her jealousy, I have egged her on to wickedness and him to folly, and of all have I caused report to be brought to Caesar. Listen! thus stands the matter. Thou knowest how went the fight at Actium. Thither went Cleopatra with her fleet, sorely against the will of Antony. But, as thou sentest me word, I entreated him for the Queen, vowing to him, with tears, that, did he leave her, she would die of grief; and he, poor slave, believed me. And so she went, and in the thick of the fight, for what cause I know not, though perchance thou knowest, Harmachis, she made signal to her squadron, and, putting about fled from the battle, sailing for Peloponnesus. And now, mark the end! When Antony saw that she was gone, he, in his madness, took a galley, and deserting all, followed hard after her, leaving his fleet to be shattered and sunk, and his great army in Greece, of twenty legions and twelve thousand horse, without a leader. And all this no man would believe, that Antony, the smitten of the Gods, had fallen so deep in shame. Therefore for a while the army tarried, and but now to-night comes news brought by Canidius, the General, that, worn with doubt and being at length sure that Antony had deserted them, the whole of his great force has yielded to Caesar."

"And where, then, is Antony?"

"He has built him a habitation on a little isle in the Great Harbour and named it Timonium; because, forsooth, like Timon, he cries out at the ingratitude of mankind that has forsaken him. And there he lies smitten by a fever of the mind, and thither thou must go at dawn, so wills the Queen, to cure him of his ills and draw him to her arms; for he will not see her, nor knows he yet the full measure of his woe. But first my bidding is to lead thee instantly to Cleopatra, who would ask thy counsel."

"I come," I answered, rising. "Lead thou on."

And so we passed the palace gates and along the Alabaster Hall, and presently once again I stood before the door of Cleopatra's chamber, and once again Charmion left me to warn her of my coming.

Presently she came back and beckoned to me. "Make strong thy heart," she whispered, "and see that thou dost not betray thyself, for still are the eyes of Cleopatra keen. Enter!"

"Keen, indeed, must they be to find Harmachis in the learned Olympus! Had I not willed it, thyself thou hadst not known me, Charmion," I made answer.

Then I entered that remembered place and listened once more to the plash of the fountain, the song of the nightingale, and the murmur of the summer sea. With bowed head and halting gait I came, till at length I stood before the couch of Cleopatra—that same golden couch on which she had sat the night she overcame me. Then I gathered my strength, and looked up. There before me was Cleopatra, glorious as of old, but, oh! how changed since that night when I saw Antony clasp her in his arms at Tarsus! Her beauty still clothed her like a garment; the eyes were yet deep and unfathomable as the blue sea, the face still splendid in its great loveliness. And yet all was changed. Time, that could not touch her charms, had stamped upon her presence such a look of weary grief as may not be written. Passion, beating ever in that fierce heart of hers, had written his record on her brow, and in her eyes shone the sad lights of sorrow.

I bowed low before this most royal woman, who once had been my love and destruction, and yet knew me not.

She looked up wearily, and spoke in her slow, well remembered voice: "So thou art come at length, Physician. How callest thou thyself?—Olympus? 'Tis a name of promise, for surely now that the Gods of Egypt have deserted us, we do need aid from Olympus. Well, thou hast a learned air, for learning does not with beauty. Strange, too, there is that about thee which recalls what I know not. Say, Olympus, have we met before?"

"Never, O Queen, have my eyes fallen on thee in the body," I answered in a feigned voice. "Never till this hour, when I come forth from my solitude to do thy bidding and cure thee of thy ills!"

"Strange! and even in the voice—Pshaw! 'tis some memory that I cannot catch. In the body, thou sayest? then, perchance, I knew thee in a dream?"

"Ay, O Queen; we have met in dreams."

"Thou art a strange man, who talkest thus, but, if what I hear be true, one well learned; and, indeed, I mind me of thy counsel when thou didst bid me join my Lord Antony in Syria, and how things befell according to thy word. Skilled must thou be in the casting of nativities and in the law of auguries, of which these Alexandrian fools have little knowledge. Once I knew such another man, one Harmachis," and she sighed: "but he is long dead—as I would I were also!—and at times I sorrow for him."

She paused, while I sank my head upon my breast and stood silent.

"Interpret me this, Olympus. In the battle at that accursed Actium, just as the fight raged thickest and Victory began to smile upon us, a great terror seized my heart, and thick darkness seemed to fall before my eyes, while in my ears a voice, ay, the voice of that long dead Harmachis, cried '*Fly! fly, or perish!*' and I fled. But from my heart the terror leapt to the heart of Antony, and he followed after me, and thus was the battle lost. Say, then, what God brought this evil thing about?"

"Nay, O Queen," I answered, "it was no God—for wherein hast thou angered the Gods of Egypt? Hast thou robbed the temples of their Faith? Hast thou betrayed the trust of Egypt? Having done none of these things, how, then, can the Gods of Egypt be wroth with thee? Fear not, it was nothing but some natural vapour of the mind that overcame thy gentle soul, made sick with the sight and sound of slaughter; and as for the noble Antony, where thou didst go needs must that he should follow."

And as I spoke, Cleopatra turned white and trembled, glancing at me the while to find my meaning. But I well knew that the thing was of the avenging Gods, working through me, their instrument.

"Learned Olympus," she said, not answering my words; "my Lord Antony is sick and crazed with grief. Like some poor hunted slave he hides himself in yonder sea-girt Tower and shuns mankind—yes, he shuns even me, who, for his sake, endure so many woes. Now, this is my bidding to thee. To-morrow, at the coming of the light, do thou, led by Charmion, my waiting-lady, take boat and row thee to the Tower and there crave entry, saying that ye bring tidings from the army. Then he will cause you to be let in, and thou, Charmion, must break this heavy news that Canidius bears; for Canidius himself I dare not send. And when his grief is past, do thou, Olympus, soothe his fevered frame with thy draughts of value, and his soul with honeyed words, and draw him back to me, and all will yet be well. Do thou this, and thou shalt have gifts more than thou canst count, for I am yet a Queen and yet can pay back those who serve my will."

"Fear not, O Queen," I answered, "this thing shall be done, and I ask no reward, who have come hither to do thy bidding to the end."

So I bowed and went and, summoning Atoua, made ready a certain potion.

Chapter 5

Of the Drawing Forth of Antony

Ere it was yet dawn Charmion came again, and we walked to the private harbour of the palace. There, taking boat, we rowed to the island mount on which stands the Timonium, a vaulted tower, strong, small, and round. And, having landed, we twain came to the door and knocked, till at length a grating was thrown open in the door, and an aged eunuch, looking forth, roughly asked our business.

"Our business is with the Lord Antony," said Charmion.

"Then it is no business, for Antony, my master, sees neither man nor woman."

"Yet will he see us, for we bring tidings. Go tell him that the Lady Charmion brings tidings from the army."

The man went, and presently returned.

"The Lord Antony would know if the tidings be good or ill, for, if ill, then will he none of it, for with evil tidings he has been overfed of late."

"Why—why, it is both good and ill. Open, slave, I will make answer to thy master!" and she slipped a purse of gold through the bars.

"Well, well," he grumbled, as he took the purse, "the times are hard, and likely to be harder; for when the lion's down who will feed the jackal? Give thy news thyself, and if it do but draw the noble Antony out of this hall of Groans, I care not what it be. Now the palace door is open, and there's the road to the banqueting-chamber."

We passed on, to find ourselves in a narrow passage, and, leaving the eunuch to bar the door, advanced till we came to a curtain. Through this entrance we went, and found ourselves in a vaulted chamber, ill-lighted from the roof. On the further side of this rude chamber was a bed of rugs, and on them crouched the figure of a man, his face hidden in the folds of his toga.

"Most noble Antony," said Charmion drawing near, "unwrap thy face and hearken to me, for I bring thee tidings."

Then he lifted up his head. His face was marred by sorrow; his tangled hair, grizzled with years, hung about his hollow eyes, and white on his chin was the stubble of an unshaven beard. His robe was squalid, and his aspect more wretched than that of the poorest beggar at the temple gates. To this, then, had the love of Cleopatra brought the glorious and renowned Antony, aforetime Master of half the World!

"What will ye with me, Lady," he asked, "who would perish here alone? And who is this man who comes to gaze on fallen and forsaken Antony?"

"This is Olympus, noble Antony, that wise physician, the skilled in auguries, of whom thou hast heard much, and whom Cleopatra, ever mindful of thy welfare, though but little thou dost think of hers, has sent to minister to thee."

"And, can thy physician minister to a grief such as my grief? Can his drugs give me back my galleys, my honour, and my peace? Nay! Away with thy physician! What are thy tidings?—quick!—out with it! Hath Canidius, perchance, conquered Caesar? Tell me but that, and thou shalt have a province for thy guerdon—ay! and if Octavianus be dead, twenty thousand *sestertia* to fill its treasury. Speak—nay—speak not! I fear the opening of thy lips as never I feared an earthly thing. Surely the wheel of fortune has gone round and Canidius has conquered? Is it not so? Nay—out with it! I can no more!"

"O noble Antony," she said, "steel thy heart to hear that which I needs must tell thee! Canidius is in Alexandria. He has fled far and fast, and this is his report. For seven whole days did the legions wait the coming of Antony, to lead them to victory, as aforetime, putting aside the offers of the envoys of Caesar. But Antony came not. And then it was rumoured that Antony had fled to Taenarus, drawn thither by Cleopatra. The man who first brought that tale to the camp the legionaries cried shame on—ay, and beat him to the death! But ever it grew, until at length there was no more room to doubt; and then, O Antony, thy officers slipped one by one away to Caesar, and where the officers go there the men follow. Nor is this all the story; for thy allies—Bocchus of Africa, Tarcondimotus of Cilicia, Mithridates of Commagene, Adallas of Thrace, Philadelphus of Paphlagonia, Archelaus of Cappadocia, Herod of Judaea, Amyntas of Galatia, Polemon of Pontus, and Malchus of Arabia—all, all have fled or bid their generals fly back to whence they came; and already their ambassador's crave cold Caesar's clemency."

"Hast done thy croakings, thou raven in a peacock's dress, or is there more to come?" asked the smitten man, lifting his white and trembling face from the shelter of his hands. "Tell me more; say that Egypt's dead in all her beauty; say that Octavianus lowers at the Canopic gate; and that, headed by dead Cicero, all the ghosts of Hell do audibly shriek out the fall of Antony! Yea, gather up every woe that can o'erwhelm those who once were great, and loose them on the hoary head of him whom—in thy gentleness—thou art still pleased to name 'the noble Antony'!"

"Nay, my Lord, I have done."

"Ay, and so have I done—done, quite done! It is altogether finished, and thus I seal the end," and snatching a sword from the couch, he would, indeed, have slain himself had I not sprung forward and grasped his hand. For it was not my purpose that he should die as yet; since had he died at that hour Cleopatra had made her peace with Caesar, who rather wished the death of Antony than the ruin of Egypt.

"Art mad, Antony? Art, indeed, a coward?" cried Charmion, "that thou wouldst thus escape thy woes, and leave thy partner to face the sorrow out alone?"

"Why not, woman? Why not? She would not be long alone. There's Caesar to keep her company. Octavianus loves a fair woman in his cold way, and still is Cleopatra fair. Come now, thou Olympus! thou hast held my hand from dealing death upon myself, advise me of thy wisdom. Shall I, then, submit myself to Caesar, and I, Triumvir, twice Consul, and aforetime absolute Monarch of all the East, endure to follow in his triumph along those Roman ways where I myself have passed in triumph?"

"Nay, Sire," I answered. "If thou dost yield, then art thou doomed. All last night I questioned of the Fates concerning thee, and I saw this: when thy star draws near to Caesar's it pales and is swallowed up; but when it passes from his radiance, then bright and big it shines, equal in glory to his own. All is not lost, and while some part remains, everything may be regained. Egypt can yet be held, armies can still be raised. Caesar has withdrawn himself; he is not yet at the gates of Alexandria, and perchance may be appeased. Thy mind in its fever has fired thy body; thou art sick and canst not judge aright. See, here, I have a potion that shall make thee whole, for I am well skilled in the art of medicine," and I held out the phial.

"A potion, thou sayest man!" he cried. "More like it is a poison, and thou a murderer, sent by false Egypt, who would fain be rid of me now that I may no more be of service to her. The head of Antony is the peace offering she would send to Caesar—she for whom I have lost all! Give me thy draught. By Bacchus! I will drink it, though it be the very elixir of Death!"

"Nay, noble Antony; it is no poison, and I am no murderer. See, I will taste it, if thou wilt," and I held forth the subtle drink that has the power to fire the veins of men.

"Give it me, Physician. Desperate men are brave men. There!—Why, what is this? Yours is a magic draught! My sorrows seem to roll away like thunder-clouds before the southern gale, and the spring of Hope blooms fresh upon the desert of my heart. Once more I am Antony, and once again I see my legions' spears asparkle in the sun, and hear the thunderous shout of welcome as Antony—beloved Antony—rides in pomp of war along his deep-formed lines! There's hope! there's hope! I may yet see the cold brows of Caesar—that Caesar who never errs except from policy—robbed of their victor bays and crowned with shameful dust!"

"Ay," cried Charmion, "there still is hope, if thou wilt but play the man! O my Lord! come back with us; come back to the loving arms of Cleopatra! All night she lies upon her golden bed, and fills the hollow darkness with her groans for 'Antony!' who, enamoured now of Grief, forgets his duty and his love!"

"I come! I come! Shame upon me, that I dared to doubt her! Slave, bring water, and a purple robe: not thus can I be seen of Cleopatra. Even now I come."

****

In this fashion, then, did we draw Antony back to Cleopatra, that the ruin of the twain might be made sure.

****

We led him up the Alabaster Hall and into Cleopatra's chamber, where she lay, her cloudy hair about her face and breast, and tears flowing from her deep eyes.

"O Egypt!" he cried, "behold me at thy feet!"

She sprang from the couch. "And art thou here, my love?" she murmured; "then once again are all things well. Come near, and in these arms forget thy sorrows and turn my grief to joy. Oh, Antony, while love is left to us, still have we all!"

And she fell upon his breast and kissed him wildly.

****

That same day, Charmion came to me and bade me prepare a poison of the most deadly power. And this at first I would not do, fearing that Cleopatra would therewith make an end of Antony before his time. But Charmion showed me that this was not so, and told me also for what purpose was the poison. Therefore I summoned Atoua, the skilled in simples, and all that afternoon we laboured at the deadly work. And when it was done, Charmion came once more, bearing with her a chaplet of fresh roses, that she bade me steep in the poison.

This then I did.

That night at the great feast of Cleopatra, I sat near Antony, who was at her side, and wore the poisoned wreath. Now as the feast went on, the wine flowed fast, till Antony and the Queen grew merry. And she told him of her plans, and of how even now her galleys were being drawn by the canal that leads from Bubastis on the Pelusiac branch of the Nile, to Clysma at the head of the Bay of Heroopolis. For it was her design, should Caesar prove stubborn, to fly with Antony and her treasure down the Arabian Gulf, where Caesar had no fleet, and seek some new home in India, whither her foes might not follow. But, indeed, this plan came to nothing, for the Arabs of Petra burnt the galleys, incited thereto by a message sent by the Jews of Alexandria, who hated Cleopatra and were hated of her. For I caused the Jews to be warned of what was being done.

Now, when she had made an end of telling him, the Queen called on him to drink a cup with her, to the success of this new scheme, bidding him, as she did so, steep his wreath of roses in the wine, and make the draught more sweet. This, then, he did, and it being done, she pledged him. But when he was about to pledge her back, she caught his hand, crying "*Hold!*" whereat he paused, wondering. Now, among the servants of Cleopatra was one Eudosius, a steward; and this Eudosius, seeing that the fortunes of Cleopatra were at an end, had laid a plan to fly that very night to Caesar, as many of his betters had done, taking with him all the treasure in the palace that he could steal. But this design being discovered to Cleopatra, she determined to be avenged upon Eudosius.

"Eudosius," she cried, for the man stood near; "come hither, thou faithful servant! Seest thou this man, most noble Antony; through all our troubles he has clung to us and been of comfort to us. Now, therefore, he shall be rewarded according to his deserts and the measure of his faithfulness, and that from thine own hand. Give him thy golden cup of wine, and let him drink a pledge to our success; the cup shall be his guerdon."

And still wondering, Antony gave it to the man, who, stricken in his guilty mind, took it, and stood trembling. But he drank not.

"Drink! thou slave; drink!" cried Cleopatra, half rising from her seat and flashing a fierce look on his white face. "By Serapis! so surely as I yet shall sit in the Capitol at Rome, if thou dost thus flout the Lord Antony, I'll have thee scourged to the bones, and the red wine poured upon thy open wounds to heal them! *Ah!* at length thou drinkest! Why, what is it, good Eudosius? art sick? Surely, then, this wine must be as the water of jealousy of those Jews, that has power to slay the false and strengthen the honest only. Go, some of you, search this man's room; methinks he is a traitor!"

Meanwhile the man stood, his hands to his head. Presently he began to tremble, and then fell, clutching at his bosom, as though to tear out the fire in his heart. He staggered, with livid, twisted face and foaming lips, to where Cleopatra lay watching him with a slow and cruel smile.

"Ah, traitor! thou hast it now!" she said. "Prithee, is death sweet?"

"Thou wanton!" yelled the dying man, "thou hast poisoned me! Thus mayst thou also perish!" and with one shriek he flung himself upon her. She saw his purpose, and swift and supple as a tiger sprang to one side, so that he did but grasp her royal cloak, tearing it from its emerald clasp. Down he fell upon the ground, rolling over and over in the purple *chiton*, till presently he lay still and dead, his tormented face and frozen eyes peering ghastly from its folds.

"Ah!" said the Queen, with a hard laugh, "the slave died wondrous hard, and fain would have drawn me with him. See, he has borrowed my garment for a pall! Take him away and bury him in his livery."

"What means Cleopatra?" said Antony, as the guards dragged the corpse away; "the man drank of my cup. What is the purpose of this most sorry jest?"

"It serves a double end, noble Antony! This very night that man would have fled to Octavianus, bearing of our treasure with him. Well, I have lent him wings, for the dead fly fast! Also this: thou didst fear that I should poison thee, my Lord; nay, I know it. See now, Antony, how easy it were that I should slay thee if I had the will. That wreath of roses which thou didst steep within the cup is dewed with deadly bane. Had I, then, a mind to make an end of thee, I had not stayed thy hand. O Antony, henceforth trust me! Sooner would I slay myself than harm one hair of thy beloved head! See, here come my messengers! Speak, what did ye find?"

"Royal Egypt, we found this. All things in the chamber of Eudosius are made ready for flight, and in his baggage is much treasure."

"Thou hearest?" she said, smiling darkly. "Think ye, my loyal servants all, that Cleopatra is one with whom it is well to play the traitor? Be warned by this Roman's fate!"

****

Then a great silence of fear fell upon the company, and Antony sat also silent.

Chapter 6

Of the Poisonings of Cleopatra

Now I, Harmachis, must make speed with my task, setting down that which is permitted as shortly as may be, and leaving much untold. For of this I am warned, that Doom draws on and my days are well-nigh sped. After the drawing forth of Antony from the Timonium came that time of heavy quiet which heralds the rising of the desert wind. Antony and Cleopatra once again gave themselves up to luxury, and night by night feasted in splendour at the palace. They sent ambassadors to Caesar; but Caesar would have none of them; and, this hope being gone, they turned their minds to the defence of Alexandria. Men were gathered, ships were built, and a great force was made ready against the coming of Caesar.

And now, aided by Charmion, I began my last work of hate and vengeance. I wormed myself deep into the secrets of the palace, counselling all things for evil. I bade Cleopatra keep Antony gay, lest he should brood upon his sorrows: and thus she sapped his strength and energy with luxury and wine. I gave him of my draughts—draughts that sank his soul in dreams of happiness and power, leaving him to wake to a heavier misery. Soon, without my healing medicine he could not sleep, and thus, being ever at his side, I bound his weakened will to mine, till at last he would do little if I said not "It is well." Cleopatra, also grown very superstitious, leaned much upon me; for I prophesied falsely to her in secret.

Moreover, I wove other webs. My fame was great throughout Egypt, for during the long years that I had dwelt in Tápé it had spread through all the land. Therefore many men of note came to me, both for their health's sake and because it was known that I had the ear of Antony and the Queen; and, in these days of doubt and trouble, they were fain to learn the truth. All these men I worked upon with doubtful words, sapping their loyalty; and I caused many to fall away, and yet none could bear an evil report of what I had said. Also, Cleopatra sent me to Memphis, there to move the Priests and Governors that they should gather men in Upper Egypt for the defence of Alexandria. And I went and spoke to the priests with such a double meaning and with so much wisdom that they knew me to be one of the initiated in the deeper mysteries. But how I, Olympus the physician, came thus to be initiated none might say. And afterwards they sought me secretly, and I gave them the holy sign of brotherhood; and thereunder bade them not to ask who I might be, but send no aid to Cleopatra. Rather, I said, must they make peace with Caesar, for by Caesar's grace only could the worship of the Gods endure in Khem. So, having taken counsel of the Holy Apis, they promised in public to give help to Cleopatra, but in secret sent an embassy to Caesar.

Thus, then, it came to pass that Egypt gave but little aid to its hated Macedonian Queen. Thence from Memphis I came once more to Alexandria, and, having made favourable report, continued my secret work. And, indeed, the Alexandrians could not easily be stirred, for, as they say in the marketplace, "The ass looks at its burden and is blind to its master." Cleopatra had oppressed them so long that the Roman was like a welcome friend.

Thus the time passed on, and every night found Cleopatra with fewer friends than that which had gone before, for in evil days friends fly like swallows before the frost. Yet she would not give up Antony, whom she loved; though to my knowledge Caesar, by his freedman, Thyreus, made promise to her of her dominions for herself and for her children if she would but slay Antony, or even betray him bound. But to this her woman's heart—for still she had a heart—would not consent, and, moreover, we counselled her against it, for of necessity we must hold him to her, lest, Antony escaping or being slain, Cleopatra might ride out the storm and yet be Queen of Egypt. And this grieved me, because Antony, though weak, was still a brave man, and a great; and, moreover, in my own heart I read the lesson of his woes. For were we not akin in wretchedness? Had not the same woman robbed us of Empire, Friends, and Honour? But pity has no place in politics, nor could it turn my feet from the path of vengeance it was ordained that I should tread. Caesar drew nigh; Pelusium fell; the end was at hand. It was Charmion who brought the tidings to the Queen and Antony, as they slept in the heat of the day, and I came with her.

"Awake!" she cried. "Awake! This is no time for sleep! Seleucus hath surrendered Pelusium to Caesar, who marches straight on Alexandria!"

With a great oath, Antony sprang up and clutched Cleopatra by the arm.

"Thou hast betrayed me—by the Gods I swear it! Now thou shalt pay the price!" And snatching up his sword he drew it.

"Stay thy hand, Antony!" she cried. "It is false—I know naught of this!" And she sprang upon him, and clung about his neck, weeping. "I know naught, my Lord. Take thou the wife of Seleucus and his little children, whom I hold in guard, and avenge thyself. O Antony, Antony! why dost thou doubt me?"

Then Antony threw down his sword upon the marble, and, casting himself upon the couch, hid his face, and groaned in bitterness of spirit.

But Charmion smiled, for it was she who had sent secretly to Seleucus, her friend, counselling him to surrender forthwith, saying that no fight would be made at Alexandria. And that very night Cleopatra took all her great store of pearls and emeralds—those that remained of the treasure of Menkau-ra—all her wealth of gold, ebony, ivory, and cinnamon, treasure without price, and placed it in the mausoleum of granite which, after our Egyptian fashion, she had built upon the hill that is by the Temple of the Holy Isis. These riches she piled up upon a bed of flax, that, when she fired it, all might perish in the flame and escape the greed of money-loving Octavianus. And she slept henceforth in this tomb, away from Antony; but in the daytime she still saw him at the palace.

But a little while after, when Caesar with all his great force had already crossed the Caponic mouth of the Nile and was hard on Alexandria, I came to the palace, whither Cleopatra had summoned me. There I found her in the Alabaster Hall, royally clad, a wild light in her eyes, and, with her, Iras and Charmion, and before her guards; and stretched here and there upon the marble, bodies of dead men, among whom lay one yet dying.

"Greeting, thou Olympus!" she cried. "Here is a sight to glad a physician's heart—men dead and men sick unto death!"

"What doest thou, O Queen?" I said affrighted.

"What do I? I wreak justice on these criminals and traitors; and, Olympus, I learn the ways of death. I have caused six different poisons to be given to these slaves, and with an attentive eye have watched their working. That man," and she pointed to a Nubian, "he went mad, and raved of his native deserts and his mother. He thought himself a child again, poor fool! and bade her hold him close to her breast and save him from the darkness which drew near. And that Greek, he shrieked, and, shrieking, died. And this, he wept and prayed for pity, and in the end, like a coward, breathed his last. Now, note the Egyptian yonder, he who still lives and groans; first he took the draught—the deadliest draught of all, they swore—and yet the slave so dearly loves his life he will not leave it! See, he yet strives to throw the poison from him; twice have I given him the cup and yet he is athirst. What a drunkard we have here! Man, man, knowest thou not that in death only can peace be found? Struggle no more, but enter into rest." And even as she spoke, the man, with a great cry, gave up the spirit.

"There!" she cried, "at length the farce is played—away with those slaves whom I have forced through the difficult gates of Joy!" and she clapped her hands. But when they had borne the bodies thence she drew me to her, and spoke thus:

"Olympus, for all thy prophecies, the end is at hand. Caesar must conquer, and I and my Lord Antony be lost. Now, therefore, the play being well-nigh done, I must make ready to leave this stage of earth in such fashion as becomes a Queen. For this cause, then, I do make trial of these poisons, seeing that in my person I must soon endure those agonies of death that to-day I give to others. These drugs please me not; some wrench out the soul with cruel pains, and some too slowly work their end. But thou art skilled in the medicines of death. Now, do thou prepare me such a draught as shall, pangless, steal my life away."

And as I listened the sense of triumph filled my bitter heart, for I knew now that by my own hand should this ruined woman die and the justice of the Gods be done.

"Spoken like a Queen, O Cleopatra!" I said. "Death shall cure thy ills, and I will brew such a wine as shall draw him down a sudden friend and sink thee in a sea of slumber whence, upon this earth, thou shalt never wake again. Oh! fear not Death: Death is thy hope; and, surely, thou shalt pass sinless and pure of heart into the dreadful presence of the Gods!"

She trembled. "And if the heart be not altogether pure, tell me—thou dark man—what then? Nay, I fear not the Gods! for if the Gods of Hell be men, there I shall Queen it also. At the least, having once been royal, royal I shall ever be."

And, as she spoke, suddenly from the palace gates came a great clamour, and the noise of joyful shouting.

"Why, what is this?" she said, springing from her couch.

"Antony! Antony!" rose the cry; "Antony hath conquered!"

She turned swiftly and ran, her long hair streaming on the wind. I followed her, more slowly, down the great hall, across the courtyards, to the palace gates. And here she met Antony, riding through them, radiant with smiles and clad in his Roman armour. When he saw her he leapt to the ground, and, all armed as he was, clasped her to his breast.

"What is it?" she cried; "is Caesar fallen?"

"Nay, not altogether fallen, Egypt: but we have beat his horsemen back to their trenches, and, like the beginning, so shall be the end, for, as they say here, 'Where the head goes, the tail will follow.' Moreover, Caesar has my challenge, and if he will but meet me hand to hand, the world shall soon see which is the better man, Antony or Octavian." And even as he spoke and the people cheered there came the cry of "A messenger from Caesar!"

The herald entered, and, bowing low, gave a writing to Antony, bowed again, and went. Cleopatra snatched it from his hand, broke the silk and read aloud:

"Caesar to Antony, greeting.

"This answer to thy challenge: Can Antony find no better way of death than beneath the sword of Caesar? Farewell!"

And thereafter they cheered no more.

****

The darkness came, and before it was midnight, having feasted with his friends who to-night went over his woes and to-morrow should betray him, Antony went forth to the gathering of the captains of the land-forces and of the fleet, attended by many, among whom was I.

When all were come together, he spoke to them, standing bareheaded in their midst, beneath the radiance of the moon. And thus he most nobly spoke:

"Friends and companions in arms! who yet cling to me, and whom many a time I have led to victory, hearken to me now, who to-morrow may lie in the dumb dust, disempired and dishonoured. This is our design: no longer will we hang on poised wings above the flood of war, but will straightway plunge, perchance thence to snatch the victor's diadem, or, failing, there to drown. Be now but true to me, and to your honour's sake, and you may still sit, the most proud of men, at my right hand in the Capitol of Rome. Fail me now, and the cause of Antony is lost and so are ye. To-morrow's battle must be hazardous indeed, but we have stood many a time and faced a fiercer peril, and ere the sun had sunk, once more have driven armies like desert sands before our gale of valour and counted the spoil of hostile kings. What have we to fear? Though allies be fled, still is our array as strong as

Caesar's! And show we but as high a heart, why, I swear to you, upon my princely word, to-morrow night I shall deck yonder Canopic gate with the heads of Octavian and his captains!

"Ay, cheer, and cheer again! I love that martial music which swells, not as from the indifferent lips of clarions, now 'neath the breath of Antony and now of Caesar, but rather out of the single hearts of men who love me. Yet—and now I will speak low, as we do speak o'er the bier of some beloved dead—yet, if Fortune should rise against me and if, borne down by the weight of arms, Antony, the soldier, dies a soldier's death, leaving you to mourn him who ever was your friend, this is my will, that, after our rough fashion of the camp, I here declare to you. You know where all my treasure lies. Take it, most dear friends; and, in the memory of Antony, make just division. Then go to Caesar and speak thus: 'Antony, the dead, to Caesar, the living, sends greeting; and, in the name of ancient fellowship and of many a peril dared, craves this boon: the safety of those who clung to him and that which he hath given them.'

"Nay, let not my tears—for I must weep—overflow your eyes! Why, it is not manly; 'tis most womanish! All men must die, and death were welcome were it not so lone. Should I fall, I leave my children to your tender care—if, perchance, it may avail to save them from the fate of helplessness. Soldiers, enough! to-morrow at the dawn we spring on Caesar's throat, both by land and sea. Swear that ye will cling to me, even to the last issue!"

"We swear!" they cried. "Noble Antony, we swear!"

"It is well! Once more my star grows bright; to-morrow, set in the highest heaven, it yet may shine the lamp of Caesar down! Till then, farewell!"

He turned to go. As he went they caught his hand and kissed it; and so deeply were they moved that many wept like children; nor could Antony master his grief, for, in the moonlight, I saw tears roll down his furrowed cheeks and fall upon that mighty breast.

And, seeing all this, I was much troubled. For I well knew that if these men held firm to Antony all might yet go well for Cleopatra; and though I bore no ill-will against Antony, yet he must fall, and in that fall drag down the woman who, like some poisonous plant, had twined herself about his giant strength till it choked and mouldered in her embrace.

Therefore, when Antony went I went not, but stood back in the shadow watching the faces of the lords and captains as they spoke together.

"Then it is agreed!" said he who should lead the fleet. "And this we swear to, one and all, that we will cling to noble Antony to the last extremity of fortune!"

"Ay! ay!" they answered.

"Ay! ay!" I said, speaking from the shadow; "cling, and *die!*"

They turned fiercely and seized me.

"Who is he?" quoth one.

"'Tis that dark-faced dog, Olympus!" cried another. "Olympus, the magician!"

"Olympus, the traitor!" growled another; "put an end to him and his magic!" and he drew his sword.

"Ay! slay him; he would betray the Lord Antony, whom he is paid to doctor."

"Hold a while!" I said in a slow and solemn voice, "and beware how ye try to murder the servant of the Gods. I am no traitor. For myself, I abide the event here in Alexandria, but to you I say, Flee, flee to Caesar! I serve Antony and the Queen—I serve them truly; but above all I serve the Holy Gods; and what they make known to me, that, Lords, I do know. And I know this: that Antony is doomed, and Cleopatra is doomed, for Caesar conquers. Therefore, because I honour you, noble gentlemen, and think with pity on your wives, left widowed, and your little fatherless children, that shall, if ye hold to Antony, be sold as slaves—therefore, I say, cling to Antony if ye will and die; or flee to Caesar and be saved! And this I say because it is so ordained of the Gods."

"The Gods!" they growled; "what Gods? Slit the traitor's throat, and stop his ill-omened talk!"

"Let him show us a sign from his Gods or let him die: I do mistrust this man," said another.

"Stand back, ye fools!" I cried. "Stand back—free mine arms—and I will show you a sign;" and there was that in my face which frightened them, for they freed me and stood back. Then I lifted up my hands and putting out all my strength of soul searched the depths of space till my Spirit communed with the Spirit of my Mother Isis. Only the Word of Power I uttered not, as I had been bidden. And the holy mystery of the Goddess answered to my Spirit's cry, falling in awful silence upon the face of the earth. Deeper and deeper grew the terrible silence; even the dogs ceased to howl, and in the city men stood still afeared. Then, from far away, there came the ghostly music of the *sistra*. Faint it was at first, but ever as it came it grew more loud, till the air shivered with the unearthly sound of terror. I said naught, but pointed with my hand toward the sky. And behold! bosomed upon the air, floated a vast veiled Shape that, heralded by the swelling music of the *sistra*, drew slowly near, till its shadow lay upon us. It came, it passed, it went toward the camp of Caesar, till at length the music died away, and the awful Shape was swallowed in the night.

"It is Bacchus!" cried one. "Bacchus, who leaves lost Antony!" and, as he spoke, there rose a groan of terror from all the camp.

But I knew that it was not Bacchus, the false God, but the Divine Isis who deserted Khem, and, passing over the edge of the world, sought her home in space, to be no more known of men. For though her worship is still upheld, though still she is here and in all Earths, Isis manifests herself no more in Egypt. I hid my face and prayed, but when I lifted it from my robe, lo! all had fled and I was alone.

CHAPTER 7

Of the Brewing of the Draught of Death

On the morrow, at dawn, Antony came forth and gave command that his fleet should advance against the fleet of Caesar, and that his cavalry should open the land-battle with the cavalry of Caesar. Accordingly, the fleet advanced in a triple line, and the fleet of Caesar came out to meet it. But when they met, the galleys of Antony lifted their oars in greeting, and passed over to the galleys of Caesar; and they sailed away together. And the cavalry of Antony rode forth beyond the Hippodrome to charge the cavalry of Caesar; but when they met, they lowered their swords and passed over to the camp of Caesar, deserting Antony. Then Antony grew mad with rage and terrible to see. He shouted to his legions to stand firm and wait attack; and for a little while they stood. One man, however—that same officer who would have slain me on the yesternight—strove to fly; but Antony seized him with his own hand, threw him to the earth, and, springing from his horse, drew his sword to slay him. He held his sword on high, while the man, covering his face, awaited death. But Antony dropped his sword and bade him rise.

"Go!" he said. "Go to Caesar, and prosper! I did love thee once. Why, then, among so many traitors, should I single thee out for death?"

The man rose and looked upon him sorrowfully. Then, shame overwhelming him, with a great cry he tore open his shirt of mail, plunged his sword into his own heart and fell down dead. Antony stood and gazed at him, but he said never a word. Meanwhile the ranks of Caesar's legions drew near, and so soon as they crossed spears the legions of Antony turned and fled. Then the soldiers of Caesar stood still mocking them; but scarce a man was slain, for they pursued not.

"Fly, Lord Antony! fly!" cried Eros, his servant, who alone with me stayed by him. "Fly ere thou art dragged a prisoner to Caesar!"

So he turned and fled, groaning heavily. I went with him, and as we rode through the Canopic gate, where many folk stood wondering, Antony spoke to me:

"Go, thou, Olympus; go to the Queen and say: 'Antony sends greeting to Cleopatra, who hath betrayed him! To Cleopatra he sends greeting and farewell!'"

And so I went to the tomb, but Antony fled to the palace. When I came to the tomb I knocked upon the door, and Charmion looked forth from the window.

"Open," I cried, and she opened.

"What news, Harmachis?" she whispered.

"Charmion," I said, "the end is at hand. Antony is fled!"

"It is well," she answered; "I am aweary."

And there on her golden bed sat Cleopatra.

"Speak, man!" she cried.

"Antony has fled, his forces are fled, Caesar draws near. To Cleopatra the great Antony sends greeting and farewell. Greeting to Cleopatra who betrayed him, and farewell."

"It is a lie!" she screamed; "I betrayed him not! Thou, Olympus, go swiftly to Antony and answer thus: 'To Antony, Cleopatra, who hath not betrayed him, sends greeting and farewell. Cleopatra is no more.'"

And so I went, following out my purpose. In the Alabaster Hall I found Antony pacing to and fro, tossing his hands toward heaven, and with him Eros, for of all his servants Eros alone remained by this fallen man.

"Lord Antony," I said, "Egypt bids thee farewell. Egypt is dead by her own hand."

"Dead! dead!" he whispered, "and is Egypt dead? and is that form of glory now food for worms? Oh, what a woman was this! E'en now my heart goes out towards her. And shall she outdo me at the last, I who have been so great; shall I become so small that a woman can overtop my courage and pass where I fear to follow? Eros, thou hast loved me from a boy—mindest thou how I found thee starving in the desert, and made thee rich, giving thee place and wealth? Come, now pay me back. Draw that sword thou wearest and make an end of the woes of Antony."

"Oh, Sire," cried the Greek, "I cannot! How can I take away the life of godlike Antony?"

"Answer me not, Eros; but in the last extreme of fate this I charge thee. Do thou my bidding, or begone and leave me quite alone! No more will I see thy face, thou unfaithful servant!"

Then Eros drew his sword and Antony knelt before him and bared his breast, turning his eyes to heaven. But Eros, crying "I cannot! oh, I cannot!" plunged the sword to his own heart, and fell dead.

Antony rose and gazed upon him. "Why, Eros, that was nobly done," he said. "Thou art greater than I, yet I have learned thy lesson!" and he knelt down and kissed him.

Then, rising of a sudden, he drew the sword from the heart of Eros, plunged it into his bowels, and fell, groaning, on the couch.

"O thou, Olympus," he cried, "this pain is more than I can bear! Make an end of me, Olympus!"

But pity stirred me, and I could not do this thing.

Therefore I drew the sword from his vitals, staunched the flow of blood, and, calling to those who came crowding in to see Antony die, I bade them summon Atoua from my house at the palace gates. Presently she came, bringing with her simples and life-giving draughts. These I gave to Antony, and bade Atoua go with such speed as her old limbs might to Cleopatra, in the tomb, and tell her of the state of Antony.

So she went, and after a while returned, saying that the Queen yet lived and summoned Antony to die in her arms. And with her came Diomedes. When Antony heard, his ebbing strength came back, for he was fain to look upon Cleopatra's face again. So I called to the slaves—who peeped and peered through curtains and from behind pillars to see this great man die—and together, with much toil, we bore him thence till we came to the foot of the Mausoleum.

But Cleopatra, being afraid of treachery, would no more throw wide the door; so she let down a rope from the window and we made it fast beneath the arms of Antony. Then did Cleopatra, who the while wept most bitterly, together with Charmion and Iras the Greek, pull on the rope with all their strength, while we lifted from below till the dying Antony swung in the air, groaning heavily, and the blood dropped from his gaping wound. Twice he nearly fell to earth: but Cleopatra, striving with the strength of love and of despair, held him till at length she drew him through the windowplace, while all who saw the dreadful sight wept bitterly, and beat their breasts—all save myself and Charmion.

When he was in, once more the rope was let down, and, with some aid from Charmion, I climbed into the tomb, drawing up the rope after me. There I found Antony, laid upon the golden bed of Cleopatra; and she, her breast bare, her face stained with tears, and her hair streaming wildly about him, knelt at his side and kissed him, wiping the blood from his wounds with her robes and hair. And let all my shame be written: as I stood and watched her the old love awoke once more within me, and mad jealousy raged in my heart because—though I could destroy these twain—I could not destroy their love.

"O Antony! my Sweet, my Husband, and my God!" she moaned. "Cruel Antony, hast thou the heart to die and leave me to my lonely shame? I will follow thee swiftly to the grave. Antony, awake! awake!"

He lifted up his head and called for wine, which I gave him, mixing therein a draught that might allay his pain, for it was great. And when he had drunk he bade Cleopatra lie down on the bed beside him, and put her arms about him; and this she did. Then was Antony once more a man; for, forgetting his own misery and pain, he counselled her as to her own safety: but to this talk she would not listen.

"The hour is short," she said; "let us speak of this great love of ours that hath been so long and may yet endure beyond the coasts of Death. Mindest thou that night when first thou didst put thine arms about me and call me 'Love'? Oh! happy, happy night! Having known that night it is well to have lived—even to this bitter end!"

"Ay, Egypt, I mind it well and dwell upon its memory, though from that hour fortune has fled from me—lost in my depth of love for thee, thou Beautiful. I mind it!" he gasped; "then didst thou drink the pearl in wanton play, and then did that astrologer of thine call out his hour—'The hour of the coming of the curse of Menkau-ra.' Through all the after-days those words have haunted me, and now at the last they ring in my ears."

"He is long dead, my love," she whispered.

"If he be dead, then I am near him. What meant he?"

"He is dead, the accursed man!—no more of him! Oh! turn and kiss me, for thy face grows white. The end is near!"

He kissed her on the lips, and for a little while so they stayed, to the moment of death, babbling their passion in each other's ears, like lovers newly wed. Even to my jealous heart, it was a strange and awful thing to see.

****

Presently, I saw the Change of Death gather on his face. His head fell back.

"Farewell, Egypt; farewell!—I die!"

Cleopatra lifted herself upon her hands, gazed wildly on his ashen face, and then, with a great cry, she sank back swooning.

****

But Antony yet lived, though the power of speech had left him.

Then I drew near and, kneeling, made pretence to minister to him. And as I ministered I whispered in his ear:

"Antony," I whispered, "Cleopatra was my love before she passed from me to thee. I am Harmachis, that astrologer who stood behind thy couch at Tarsus; and I have been the chief minister of thy ruin.

"*Die, Antony!—the curse of Menkau-ra hath fallen!*"

He raised himself, and stared upon my face. He could not speak, but, gibbering, he pointed at me. Then with a groan his spirit fled.

Thus did I accomplish my revenge upon Roman Antony, the World-loser.

****

Thereafter, we recovered Cleopatra from her swoon, for not yet was I minded that she should die. And taking the body of Antony, Caesar permitting, I and Atoua caused it to be most skilfully embalmed after our Egyptian fashion, covering the face with a mask of gold fashioned like to the features of Antony. Also I wrote upon his breast his name and titles, and painted his name and the name of his father within his inner coffin, and drew the form of the Holy Nout folding her wings about him.

Then with great pomp Cleopatra laid him in that sepulchre which had been made ready, and in a sarcophagus of alabaster. Now, this sarcophagus was fashioned so large that place was left in it for a second coffin, for Cleopatra would lie by Antony at the last.

These things then happened. And but a little while after I learned tidings from one Cornelius Dolabella, a noble Roman who waited upon Caesar, and, moved by the beauty that swayed the souls of all who looked upon her, had pity for the woes of Cleopatra. He bade me warn her—for, as her physician, it was allowed me to pass in and out of the tomb where she dwelt—that in three days she would be sent away to Rome, together with her children, save Caesarion, whom Octavian had already slain, that she might walk in the triumph of Caesar. Accordingly I went in, and found her sitting, as now she always sat, plunged in a half stupor, and before her that blood-stained robe with which she had staunched the wounds of Antony. For on this she would continually feast her eyes.

"See how faint they grow, Olympus," she said, lifting her sad face and pointing to the rusty stains, "and he so lately dead! Why, Gratitude could not fade more fast. What is now thy news? Evil tidings is writ large in those dark eyes of thine, which ever bring back to me something that still slips my mind."

"The news is ill, O Queen," I answered. "I have this from the lips of Dolabella, who has it straight from Caesar's secretary. On the third day from now Caesar will send thee and the Princes Ptolemy and Alexander and the Princess Cleopatra to Rome, there to feast the eyes of the Roman mob, and be led in triumph to that Capitol where thou didst swear to set thy throne!"

"Never, never!" she cried, springing to her feet. "Never will I walk in chains in Caesar's triumph! What must I do? Charmion, tell me what I can do!"

And Charmion, rising, stood before her, looking at her through the long lashes of her downcast eyes.

"Lady, thou canst die," she said quietly.

"Ay, of a truth I had forgotten; I can die. Olympus, hast thou the drug?"

"Nay; but if the Queen wills it, by to-morrow morn it shall be brewed—a drug so swift and strong that not the Gods themselves can hold him who drinks it back from sleep."

"Let it be made ready, thou Master of Death!"

I bowed, and withdrew myself; and all that night I and old Atoua laboured at the distilling of the deadly draught. At length it was done, and Atoua poured it into a crystal phial, and held it to the light of the fire; for it was white as the purest water.

"*La! la!*" she sang, in her shrill voice; "a drink for a Queen! When fifty drops of that water of my brewing have passed those red lips of hers, thou wilt indeed be avenged of Cleopatra, O Harmachis! Ah, that I could be there to see thy Ruin ruined! *La! la!* it would be sweet to see!"

"Vengeance is an arrow that oft-times falls upon the archer's head," I answered, bethinking me of Charmion's saying.

Chapter 8

Of the Death of Cleopatra

On the morrow Cleopatra, having sought leave of Caesar, visited the tomb of Antony, crying that the Gods of Egypt had deserted her. And when she had kissed the coffin and covered it with lotus-flowers she came back, bathed, anointed herself, put on her most splendid robes, and, together with Iras, Charmion, and myself, she supped. Now as she supped her spirit flared up wildly, even as the sky lights up at sunset; and once more she laughed and sparkled as in bygone years, telling us tales of feasts which she and Antony had eaten of. Never, indeed, did I see her look more beauteous than on that last fatal night of vengeance. And thus her mind drew on to that supper at Tarsus when she drank the pearl.

"Strange," she said; "strange that at the last the mind of Antony should have turned back to that night among all the nights and to the saying of Harmachis. Charmion, dost thou remember Harmachis the Egyptian?"

"Surely, O Queen," she answered slowly.

"And who, then, was Harmachis?" I asked; for I would learn if she sorrowed o'er my memory.

"I will tell thee. It is a strange tale, and now that all is done it may well be told. This Harmachis was of the ancient race of the Pharaohs, and, having, indeed, been crowned in secret at Abydus, was sent hither to Alexandria to carry out a great plot that had been formed against the rule of us royal Lagidae. He came and gained entry to the palace as my astrologer, for he was very learned in all magic—much as thou art, Olympus—and a man beautiful to see. Now this was his plot—that he should slay me and be named Pharaoh. In truth it was a strong one, for he had many friends in Egypt, and I had few. And on that very night when he should carry out his purpose, yea, at the very hour, came Charmion yonder, and told the plot to me; saying that she had chanced upon its clue. But, in after days—though I have said little thereon to thee, Charmion—I misdoubted me much of that tale of thine; for, by the Gods! to this hour I believe that thou didst love Harmachis, and because he scorned thee thou didst betray him; and for that cause also hast all thy days remained a maid, which is a thing unnatural. Come, Charmion, tell us; for naught matters now at the end."

Charmion shivered and made answer: "It is true, O Queen; I also was of the plot, and because Harmachis scorned me I betrayed him; and because of my great love for him I have remained unwed." And she glanced up at me and caught my eyes, then let the modest lashes veil her own.

"So! I thought it. Strange are the ways of women! But little cause, methinks, had that Harmachis to thank thee for thy love. What sayest thou, Olympus? Ah, and so thou also wast a traitor, Charmion? How dangerous are the paths which Monarchs tread! Well, I forgive thee, for thou hast served me faithfully since that hour.

"But to my tale. Harmachis I dared not slay, lest his great party should rise in fury and cast me from the throne. And now mark the issue. Though he must murder me, in secret this Harmachis loved me, and something thereof I guessed. I had striven a little to draw him to me, for the sake of his beauty and his wit; and for the love of man Cleopatra never strove in vain. Therefore when, with the dagger in his robe, he came to slay me, I matched my charms against his will, and need I tell you, being man and woman, how I won? Oh, never can I forget the look in the eyes of that fallen prince, that forsworn priest, that discrowned Pharaoh, when, lost in the poppied draught, I saw him sink into a shameful sleep whence he might no more wake with honour! And, thereafter—till, in the end, I wearied of him, and his sad learned mind, for his guilty soul forbade him to be gay—a little I came to care for him, though not to love. But he—he who loved me—clung to me as a drunkard to the cup which ruins him. Deeming that I should wed him, he betrayed to me the secret of the hidden wealth of the pyramid of *Her*—for at the time I much needed treasure—and together we dared the terrors of the tomb and drew it forth, even from dead Pharaoh's breast. See, this emerald was a part thereof!"—and she pointed to the great *scarabaeus* that she had drawn from the holy heart of Menkau-ra.

"And because of what was written in the tomb, and of that Thing which we saw in the tomb—ah, pest upon it! why does its memory haunt me now?—and also because of policy, for I would fain have won the love of the Egyptians, I was minded to marry this Harmachis and declare his place and lineage to the world—ay, and by his aid hold Egypt from the Roman. For Dellius had then come to call me to Antony, and after much thought I determined to send him back with sharp words. But on that very morning, as I tired me for the Court, came Charmion yonder, and I told her this, for I would see how the matter fell upon her mind. Now mark, Olympus, the power of jealousy, that little wedge which yet has strength to rend the tree of Empire, that secret sword which can carve the fate of Kings! This she could in no wise bear—deny it, Charmion, if thou canst, for now it is clear to me!—that the man she loved should be given to me as husband—me, whom *he* loved! And therefore, with more skill and wit than I can tell, she reasoned with me, showing that I should by no means do this thing, but journey to Antony; and for that, Charmion, I thank thee, now that all is come and gone. And by a very little, her words weighed down my scale of judgment against Harmachis, and I went to Antony. Thus it is through the jealous spleen of yonder fair Charmion and the passion of a man on which I played as on a lyre, that all these things have come to pass. For this cause Octavian sits a King in Alexandria; for this cause Antony is discrowned and dead; and for this cause I, too, must die to-night! Ah! Charmion! Charmion! thou hast much to answer, for thou hast changed the story of the world; and yet, even now—I would not have it otherwise!"

She paused awhile, covering her eyes with her hand; and, looking, I saw great tears upon the cheek of Charmion.

"And of this Harmachis," I asked; "where is he now, O Queen?"

"Where is he? In Amenti, forsooth—making his peace with Isis, perchance. At Tarsus I saw Antony, and loved him; and from that moment I loathed the sight of the Egyptian, and swore to make an end of him; for a lover done with should be a lover dead. And, being jealous, he spoke some words of evil omen, even at that Feast of the Pearl; and on the same night I would have slain him, but before the deed was done, he was gone."

"And whither was he gone?"

"Nay; that know not I. Brennus—he who led my guard, and last year sailed North to join his own people—Brennus swore he saw him float to the skies; but in this matter I misdoubted me of Brennus, for methinks he loved the man. Nay, he sank off Cyprus, and was drowned; perchance Charmion can tell us how?"

"I can tell thee nothing, O Queen; Harmachis is lost."

"And well lost, Charmion, for he was an evil man to play with—ay, although I bettered him I say it! Well he served my purpose; but I loved him not, and even now I fear him; for it seemed to me that I heard his voice summoning me to fly, through the din of the fight at Actium. Thanks be to the Gods, as thou sayest, he is lost, and can no more be found."

****

But I, listening, put forth my strength, and, by the arts I have, cast the shadow of my Spirit upon the Spirit of Cleopatra so that she felt the presence of the lost Harmachis.

"Nay, what is it?" she said. "By Serapis! I grow afraid! It seems to me that I feel Harmachis here! His memory overwhelms me like a flood of waters, and he these ten years dead! Oh! at such a time it is unholy!"

"Nay, O Queen," I answered, "if he be dead then he is everywhere, and well at such a time—the time of thy own death—may his Spirit draw near to welcome thine at its going."

"Speak not thus, Olympus. I would see Harmachis no more; the count between us is too heavy, and in another world than this more evenly, perchance should we be matched. Ah, the terror passes! I was but unnerved. Well the fool's story hath served to wile away the heaviest of our hours, the hour which ends in death. Sing to me, Charmion, sing, for thy voice is very sweet, and I would soothe my soul to sleep. The memory of that Harmachis has wrung me strangely! Sing, then, the last song I shall hear from those tuneful lips of thine, the last of so many songs."

"It is a sad hour for song, O Queen!" said Charmion; but, nevertheless, she took her harp and sang. And thus she sang, very soft and low, the dirge of the sweet-tongued Syrian Meleager:

Tears for my lady dead, Heliodore!
Salt tears and strange to shed,
Over and o'er;
Go tears and low lament
Fare from her tomb,
Wend where my lady went,
Down through the gloom—
Sighs for my lady dead,
Tears do I send,
Long love remembered,
Mistress and friend!

Sad are the songs we sing,
Tears that we shed,
Empty the gifts we bring—
Gifts to the dead!
Ah, for my flower, my Love,
Hades hath taken,
Ah, for the dust above,
Scattered and shaken!
Mother of blade and grass,
Earth, in thy breast
Lull her that gentlest was,
Gently to rest!

The music of her voice died away, and it was so sweet and sad that Iras began to weep and the bright tears stood in Cleopatra's stormy eyes. Only I wept not; my tears were dry.

"'Tis a heavy song of thine, Charmion," said the Queen. "Well, as thou saidst, it is a sad hour for song, and thy dirge is fitted to the hour. Sing it over me once again when I lie dead, Charmion. And now farewell to music, and on to the end. Olympus, take yonder parchment and write what I shall say."

I took the parchment and the reed, and wrote thus in the Roman tongue: "Cleopatra to Octavianus, greeting.

"This is the state of life. At length there comes an hour when, rather than endure those burdens that overwhelm us, putting off the body we would take wing into forgetfulness. Caesar, thou hast conquered: take thou the spoils of victory. But in thy triumph Cleopatra cannot walk. When all is lost, then we must go to seek the lost. Thus in the desert of Despair the brave do harvest Resolution. Cleopatra hath been great as Antony was great, nor shall her fame be minished in the manner of her end. Slaves live to endure their wrong; but Princes, treading with a firmer step, pass through the gates of Wrong into the Royal Dwellings of the Dead. This only doth Egypt ask of Caesar—that he suffer her to lie in the tomb of Antony. Farewell!"

This I wrote, and having sealed the writing, Cleopatra bade me go find a messenger, despatch it to Caesar, and then return. So I went, and at the door of the tomb I called a soldier who was not on duty, and, giving him money, bade him take the letter to Caesar. Then I went back, and there in the chamber the three women stood in silence, Cleopatra clinging to the arm of Iras, and Charmion a little apart watching the twain.

"If indeed thou art minded to make an end, O Queen," I said, "the time is short, for presently Caesar will send his servants in answer to thy letter," and I drew forth the phial of white and deadly bane and set it upon the board.

She took it in her hand and gazed thereon. "How innocent it seems!" she said; "and yet therein lies my death. 'Tis strange."

"Ay, Queen, and the death of ten other folk. No need to take so long a draught."

"I fear," she gasped—"how know I that it will slay outright? I have seen so many die by poison and scarce one has died outright. And some—ah, I cannot think on them!"

"Fear not," I said, "I am a master of my craft. Or, if thou dost fear, cast this poison forth and live. In Rome thou mayst still find happiness; ay, in Rome, where thou shalt walk in Caesar's triumph, while the laughter of the hard-eyed Latin women shall chime down the music of thy golden chains."

"Nay, I will die, Olympus. Oh, if one would but show the path."

Then Iras loosed her hand and stepped forward. "Give me the draught, Physician," she said. "I go to make ready for my Queen."

"It is well," I answered; "on thy own head be it!" and I poured from the phial into a little golden goblet.

She raised it, curtsied low to Cleopatra, then, coming forward, kissed her on the brow, and Charmion she also kissed. This done, tarrying not and making no prayer, for Iras was a Greek, she drank, and, putting her hand to her head, instantly fell down and died.

"Thou seest," I said, breaking in upon the silence, "it is swift."

"Ay, Olympus; thine is a master drug! Come now, I thirst; fill me the bowl, lest Iras weary in waiting at the gates!"

So I poured afresh into the goblet; but this time, making pretence to rinse the cup, I mixed a little water with the bane, for I was not minded that she should die before she knew me.

Then did the Royal Cleopatra, taking the goblet in her hand, turn her lovely eyes to heaven and cry aloud:

"O ye Gods of Egypt! who have deserted me, to you no longer will I pray, for your ears are shut unto my crying and your eyes blind to my griefs! Therefore, I make entreaty of that last friend whom the Gods, departing, leave to helpless man. Sweep hither, Death, whose winnowing wings enshadow all the world, and give me ear! Draw nigh, thou King of Kings! who, with an equal hand, bringest the fortunate head of one pillow with the slave, and by thy spiritual breath dost waft the bubble of our life far from this hell of earth! Hide me where winds blow not and waters cease to roll; where wars are done and Caesar's legions cannot march! Take me to a new dominion, and crown me Queen of Peace! Thou art my Lord, O Death, and in thy kiss I have conceived. I am in labour of a Soul: see—it stands new-born upon the edge of Time! Now—now—go, Life! Come, Sleep! Come, Antony!"

And, with one glance to heaven, she drank, and cast the goblet to the ground.

****

Then at last came the moment of my pent-up vengeance, and of the vengeance of Egypt's outraged Gods, and of the falling of the curse of Menkau-ra.

"What's this?" she cried; "I grow cold, but I die not! Thou dark physician, thou hast betrayed me!"

"Peace, Cleopatra! Presently shalt thou die and know the fury of the Gods! *The curse of Menkau-ra hath fallen!* It is finished! Look upon me, woman! Look upon this marred face, this twisted form, this living mass of sorrow! *Look! look!* Who am I?"

She stared upon me wildly.

"Oh! oh!" she shrieked, throwing up her arms; "at last I know thee! By the Gods, thou art Harmachis!—Harmachis risen from the dead!"

"Ay, Harmachis risen from the dead to drag thee down to death and agony eternal! See, thou Cleopatra; *I* have ruined thee as thou didst ruin me! I, working in the dark, and helped of the angry Gods, have been thy secret spring of woe! I filled thy heart with fear at Actium; I held the Egyptians from thy aid; I sapped the strength of Antony; I showed the portent of the Gods unto thy captains! By my hand at length thou diest, for I am the instrument of Vengeance! Ruin I pay thee back for ruin, Treachery for treachery, Death for death! Come hither, Charmion, partner of my plots, who betrayed me, but, repenting, art the sharer of my triumph, come watch this fallen wanton die!"

Cleopatra heard, and sank back upon the golden bed, groaning "And thou, too, Charmion!"

A moment so she sat, then her Imperial spirit burnt up glorious before she died. She staggered from the bed, and, with arms outstretched, she cursed me.

"Oh! for one hour of life!" she cried—"one short hour, that therein I might make thee die in such fashion as thou canst not dream, thou and that false paramour of thine, who betrayed both me and thee! And thou didst love me! Ah, *there* I have thee still! See, thou subtle, plotting priest"—and with both hands she rent back the royal robes from her bosom—"see, on this fair breast once night by night thy head was pillowed, and thou didst sleep wrapped in these same arms. Now, put away their memory *if thou canst!* I read it in thine eyes—that mayst thou not! No torture which I bear can, in its sum, draw nigh to the rage of that deep soul of thine, rent with longings never, never to be reached! Harmachis, thou slave of slaves, from thy triumph-depths I snatch a deeper triumph, and conquered yet I conquer! I spit upon thee—I defy thee—and, dying, doom thee to the torment of thy deathless love! O Antony! I come, my Antony!—I come to thy own dear arms! Soon I shall find thee, and, wrapped in a love undying and divine, together we will float through all the depths of space, and, lips to lips and eyes to eyes, drink of desires grown more sweet with every draught! Or if I find thee not, then I shall sink in peace down the poppied ways of Sleep: and for me the breast of Night, whereon I shall be softly cradled, will yet seem thy bosom, Antony! Oh, I die!—come, Antony—and give me peace!"

Even in my fury I had quailed beneath her scorn, for home flew the arrows of her winged words. Alas! and alas! it was *true*—the shaft of my vengeance fell upon my own head; never had I loved her as I loved her now. My soul was rent with jealous torture, and thus I swore she should not die.

"Peace!" I cried; "what peace is there for thee? Oh! ye Holy Three, hear now my prayer. Osiris, loosen Thou the bonds of Hell and send forth those whom I shall summon! Come Ptolemy, poisoned of thy sister Cleopatra; come Arsinoë, murdered in the sanctuary by thy sister Cleopatra; come Sepa, tortured to death of Cleopatra; come Divine Menkau-ra, whose body Cleopatra tore and whose curse she braved for greed; come one, come all who have died at the hands of Cleopatra! Rush from the breast of Nout and greet her who murdered you! By the link of mystic union, by the symbol of the Life, Spirits, I summon you!"

Thus I spoke the spell; while Charmion, affrighted, clung to my robe, and the dying Cleopatra, resting on her hands, swung slowly to and fro, gazing with vacant eyes.

Then the answer came. The casement burst asunder, and on flittering wings that great bat entered which last I had seen hanging to the eunuch's chin in the womb of the pyramid of *Her*. Thrice it circled round, once it hovered o'er dead Iras, then flew to where the dying woman stood. To her it flew, on her breast it settled, clinging to that emerald which was dragged from the dead heart of Menkau-ra. Thrice the grey Horror screamed aloud, thrice it beat its bony wings, and lo! it was gone.

Then suddenly within that chamber sprang up the Shapes of Death. There was Arsinoë, the beautiful, even as she had shrunk beneath the butcher's knife. There was young Ptolemy, his features twisted by the poisoned cup. There was the majesty of Menkau-ra, crowned with the *uraeus* crown; there was grave Sepa, his flesh all torn by the torturer's hooks; there were those poisoned slaves; and there were others without number, shadowy and dreadful to behold! who, thronging that narrow chamber, stood silently fixing their glassy eyes upon the face of her who slew them!

****

"Behold! Cleopatra!" I said. "*Behold thy peace, and die!*"

"Ay!" said Charmion. "Behold and die! thou who didst rob me of my honour, and Egypt of her King!"

****

She looked, she saw the awful Shapes—her Spirit, hurrying from the flesh, mayhap could hear words to which my ears were deaf. Then her face sank in with terror, her great eyes grew pale, and, shrieking, Cleopatra fell and died: passing, with that dread company, to her appointed place.

****

Thus, then, I, Harmachis, fed my soul with vengeance, fulfilling the justice of the Gods, and yet knew myself empty of all joy therein. For though that thing we worship doth bring us ruin, and Love being more pitiless than Death, we in turn do pay all our sorrow back; yet we must worship on, yet stretch out our arms towards our lost Desire, and pour our heart's blood upon the shrine of our discrowned God.

For Love is of the Spirit, and knows not Death.

Chapter 9

Of the Doom of Harmachis

Charmion unclasped my arm, to which she had clung in terror.

"Thy vengeance, thou dark Harmachis," she said, in a hoarse voice, "is a thing hideous to behold! O lost Egypt, with all thy sins thou wast indeed a Queen!

"Come, aid me, Prince; let us stretch this poor clay upon the bed and deck it royally, so that it may give its dumb audience to the messengers of Caesar as becomes the last of Egypt's Queens."

I spoke no word in answer, for my heart was very heavy, and now that all was done I was weary. Together, then, we lifted up the body and laid it on the golden bed. Charmion placed the *uraeus* crown upon the ivory brow, and combed the night-dark hair that showed never a thread of silver, and, for the last time, shut those eyes wherein had shone all the changing glories of the sea. She folded the chill hands upon the breast whence Passion's breath had fled, and straightened the bent knees beneath the broidered robe, and by the head set flowers. And there at length Cleopatra lay, more splendid now in her cold majesty of death than in her richest hour of breathing beauty!

We drew back and looked on her, and on dead Iras at her feet.

"It is done!" quoth Charmion; "we are avenged, and now, Harmachis, dost follow by this same road?" And she nodded towards the phial on the board.

"Nay, Charmion. I fly—I fly to a heavier death! Not thus easily may I end my space of earthly penance."

"So be it, Harmachis! And I, Harmachis—I fly also, but with swifter wings. My game is played. I, too, have made atonement. Oh! what a bitter fate is mine, to have brought misery on all I love, and, in the end, to die unloved! To thee I have atoned; to my angered Gods I have atoned; and now I go to find a way whereby I may atone to Cleopatra in that Hell where she is, and which I must share! For she loved me well, Harmachis; and, now that she is dead, methinks that, after thee, I loved her best of all. So of her cup and the cup of Iras I will surely drink!" And she took the phial, and with a steady hand poured what was left of the poison into the goblet.

"Bethink thee, Charmion," I said; "yet mayst thou live for many years, hiding these sorrows beneath the withered days."

"Yet I may, but I will not! To live the prey of so many memories, the fount of an undying shame that night by night, as I lie sleepless, shall well afresh from my sorrow-stricken heart!—to live torn by a love I cannot lose!—to stand alone like some storm-twisted tree, and, sighing day by day to the winds of heaven, gaze upon the desert of my life, while I wait the lingering lightning's stroke—nay, that will not I, Harmachis! I had died long since, but I lived on to serve thee; now no more thou needest me, and I go. Oh, fare thee well!—for ever fare thee well! For not again shall I look again upon thy face, and there I go thou goest not! For thou dost not love me who still dost love that queenly woman thou hast hounded to the death! Her thou shalt never win, and I thee shall never win, and this is the bitter end of Fate! See, Harmachis: I ask one boon before I go and for all time become naught to thee but a memory of shame. Tell me that thou dost forgive me so far as thine is to forgive, and in token thereof kiss me—with no lover's kiss, but kiss me on the brow, and bid me pass in peace."

And she drew near to me with arms outstretched and pitiful trembling lips and gazed upon my face.

"Charmion," I answered, "we are free to act for good or evil, and yet methinks there is a Fate above our fate, that, blowing from some strange shore, compels our little sails of purpose, set them as we will, and drives us to destruction. I forgive thee, Charmion, as I trust in turn to be forgiven, and by this kiss, the first and the last, I seal our peace." And with my lips I touched her brow.

She spoke no more; only for a little while she stood gazing on me with sad eyes. Then she lifted the goblet, and said:

"Royal Harmachis, in this deadly cup I pledge thee! Would that I had drunk of it ere ever I looked upon thy face! Pharaoh, who, thy sins outworn, yet shalt rule in perfect peace o'er worlds I may not tread, who yet shalt sway a kinglier sceptre than that I robbed thee of, for ever, fare thee well!"

She drank, cast down the cup, and for a moment stood with the wide eyes of one who looks for Death. Then He came, and Charmion the Egyptian fell prone upon the floor, dead. And for a moment more I stood alone with the dead.

I crept to the side of Cleopatra, and, now that none were left to see, I sat down on the bed and laid her head upon my knee, as once before it had been laid in that night of sacrilege beneath the shadow of the everlasting pyramid. Then I kissed her chill brow and went from the House of Death—avenged, but sorely smitten with despair!

****

"Physician," said the officer of the Guard as I went through the gates, "what passes yonder in the Monument? Methought I heard the sounds of death."

"Naught passes—all hath passed," I made reply, and went.

And as I went in the darkness I heard the sound of voices and the running of the feet of Caesar's messengers.

Flying swiftly to my house I found Atoua waiting at the gates. She drew me into a quiet chamber and closed the doors.

"Is it done?" she asked, and turned her wrinkled face to mine, while the lamplight streamed white upon her snowy hair. "Nay, why ask I—I know that it is done!"

"Ay, it is done, and well done, old wife! All are dead! Cleopatra, Iras, Charmion—all save myself!"

The aged woman drew up her bent form and cried: "Now let me go in peace, for I have seen my desire upon thy foes and the foes of Khem. *La! la!*—not in vain have I lived on beyond the years of man! I have seen my desire upon thy enemies—I have gathered the dews of Death, and thy foe hath drunk thereof! Fallen is the brow of Pride! the Shame of Khem is level with the dust! Ah, would that I might have seen that wanton die!"

"Cease, woman! cease! The Dead are gathered to the Dead! Osiris holds them fast, and everlasting silence seals their lips! Pursue not the fallen great with insults! Up!—let us fly to Abouthis, that all may be accomplished!"

"Fly thou, Harmachis!—Harmachis, fly—but I fly not! To this end only I have lingered on the earth. Now I untie the knot of life and let my spirit free! Fare thee well, Prince, the pilgrimage is done! Harmachis, from a babe have I loved thee, and love thee yet!—but no more in this world may I share thy griefs—I am spent. Osiris, take thou my Spirit!" and her trembling knees gave way and she sank to the ground.

I ran to her side and looked upon her. She was already dead, and I was alone upon the earth without a friend to comfort me!

Then I turned and went, no man hindering me, for all was confusion in the city, and departed from Alexandria in a vessel I had made ready. On the eighth day, I landed, and, in the carrying out of my purpose, travelled on foot across the fields to the Holy Shrine of Abouthis. And here, as I knew, the worship of the Gods had been lately set up again in the Temple of the Divine Sethi: for Charmion had caused Cleopatra to repent of her decree of vengeance and to restore the lands that she had seized, though the treasure she restored not. And the temple having been purified, now, at the season of the Feast of Isis, all the High Priests of the ancient Temples of Egypt were gathered together to celebrate the coming home of the Gods into their holy place.

I gained the city. It was on the seventh day of the Feast of Isis. Even as I came the long array wended through the well-remembered streets. I joined in the multitude that followed, and with my voice swelled the chorus of the solemn chant as we passed through the pylons into the imperishable halls. How well known were the holy words:

"Softly we tread, our measured footsteps falling Within the Sanctuary Sevenfold; Soft on the Dead that liveth are we calling: 'Return, Osiris, from thy Kingdom cold! Return to them that worship thee of old!'"

And then, when the sacred music ceased, as aforetime on the setting of the majesty of Ra, the High Priest raised the statue of the living God and held it on high before the multitude.

With a joyful shout of

"Osiris! our hope, Osiris! Osiris!"

the people tore the black wrappings from their dress, showing the white robes beneath, and, as one man, bowed before the God.

Then they went to feast each at his home; but I stayed in the court of the temple.

Presently a priest of the temple drew near, and asked me of my business. And I answered him that I came from Alexandria, and would be led before the council of the High Priests, for I knew that the Holy Priests were gathered together debating the tidings from Alexandria.

Thereon the man left, and the High Priests, hearing that I was from Alexandria, ordered that I should be led into their presence in the Hall of Columns—and so I was led in. It was already dark, and between the great pillars lights were set, as on that night when I was crowned Pharaoh of the Upper and the Lower Land. There, too, was the long line of Dignitaries seated in their carven chairs, and taking counsel together. All was the same; the same cold images of Kings and Gods gazed with the same empty eyes from the everlasting walls. Ay, more; among those gathered there were five of the very men who, as leaders of the great plot, had sat here to see me crowned, being the only conspirators who had escaped the vengeance of Cleopatra and the clutching hand of Time.

I took my stand on the spot where once I had been crowned and made me ready for the last act of shame with such bitterness of heart as cannot be written.

"Why, it is the physician Olympus," said one. "He who lived a hermit in the Tombs of Tápé, and who but lately was of the household of Cleopatra. Is it, then, true that the Queen is dead by her own hand, Physician?"

"Yea, holy Sirs, I am that physician; also Cleopatra is dead by *my* hand."

"By thy hand? Why, how comes this?—though well is she dead, forsooth, the wicked wanton!"

"Your pardon, Sirs, and I will tell you all, for I am come hither to that end. Perchance among you there may be some—methinks I see some—who, nigh eleven years ago, were gathered in this hall to secretly crown one Harmachis, Pharaoh of Khem?"

"It is true!" they said; "but how knowest thou these things, thou Olympus?"

"Of the rest of those seven-and-thirty nobles," I went on, making no answer, "are two-and-thirty missing. Some are dead, as Amenemhat is dead; some are slain, as Sepa is slain; and some, perchance, yet labour as slaves within the mines, or live afar, fearing vengeance."

"It is so," they said: "alas! it is so. Harmachis the accursed betrayed the plot, and sold himself to the wanton Cleopatra!"

"It is so," I went on, lifting up my head. "Harmachis betrayed the plot and sold himself to Cleopatra; and, holy Sirs—*I am that Harmachis!*"

The Priests and Dignitaries gazed astonished. Some rose and spoke; some said naught.

"I am that Harmachis! I am that traitor, trebly steeped in crime!—a traitor to my Gods, a traitor to my Country, a traitor to my Oath! I come hither to say that I have done this. I have executed the Divine vengeance on her who ruined me and gave Egypt to the Roman. And now that, after years of toil and patient waiting, this is accomplished by my wisdom and the help of the angry Gods, behold I come with all my shame upon my head to declare the thing I am, and take the traitor's guerdon!"

"Mindest thou of the doom of him who hath broke the oath that may not be broke?" asked he who first had spoken, in heavy tones.

"I know it well," I answered; "I court that awful doom."

"Tell us more of this matter, thou who wast Harmachis."

So, in cold clear words, I laid bare all my shame, keeping back nothing. And ever as I spoke I saw their faces grow more hard, and knew that for me there was no mercy; nor did I ask it, nor, had I asked, could it have been granted.

When, at last, I had done, they put me aside while they took counsel. Then they drew me forth again, and the eldest among them, a man very old and venerable, the Priest of the Temple of the Divine Hatshepu at Tápé, spoke, in icy accents:

"Thou Harmachis, we have considered this matter. Thou hast sinned the threefold deadly sin. On thy head lies the burden of the woe of Khem, this day enthralled of Rome. To Isis, the Mother Mystery, thou hast offered the deadly insult, and thou hast broken thy holy oath. For all of these sins there is, as well thou knowest, but one reward, and that reward is thine. Naught can it weigh in the balance of our justice that thou hast slain her who was thy cause of stumbling; naught that thou comest to name thyself the vilest thing who ever stood within these walls. On thee also must fall the curse of Menkau-ra, thou false priest! thou forsworn patriot! thou Pharaoh shameful and discrowned! Here, where we set the Double Crown upon thy head, we doom thee to the doom! Go to thy dungeon and await the falling of its stroke! Go, remembering what thou mightest have been and what thou art, and may those Gods who through thy evil doing shall perchance ere long cease to be worshipped within these holy temples, give to thee that mercy which we deny! Lead him forth!"

****

So they took me and led me forth. With bowed head I went, looking not up, and yet I felt their eyes burn upon my face.

Oh! surely of all my shames this is the heaviest!

Chapter 10

Of the Last Writing of Harmachis

They led me to the prison chamber that is high in the pylon tower and here I wait my doom. I know not when the sword of Fate shall fall. Week grows to week, and month to month, and still it is delayed. Still it quivers unseen above my head. I know that it will fall, but when I know not. Perchance, I shall wake in some dead hour of midnight to hear the stealthy steps of the slayers and be hurried forth. Perchance, they are now at hand. Then will come the secret cell! the horror! the nameless coffin! and at last it will be done! Oh, let it come! let it come swiftly!

All is written; I have held back nothing—my sin is sinned—my vengeance is finished. Now all things end in darkness and in ashes, and I prepare to face the terrors that are to come in other worlds than this. I go, but not without hope I go: for, though I see Her not, though no more She answers to my prayers, still I am aware of the Holy Isis, who is with me for evermore, and whom I shall yet again behold face to face. And then at last in that far day I shall find forgiveness; then the burden of my guilt will roll from me and innocency come back and wrap me round, bringing me holy Peace.

Oh! dear land of Khem, as in a dream I see thee! I see Nation after Nation set its standard on thy shores, and its yoke upon thy neck! I see new Religions without end calling out their truths upon the banks of Sihor, and summoning thy people to their worship! I see thy temples—thy holy temples—crumbling in the dust: a wonder to the sight of men unborn, who shall peer into thy tombs and desecrate the great ones of thy glory! I see thy mysteries a mockery to the unlearned, and thy wisdom wasted like waters on the desert sands! I see the Roman Eagles stoop and perish, their beaks yet red with the blood of men, and the long lights dancing down the barbarian spears that follow in their wake! And then, at last, I see Thee once more great, once more free, and having once more a knowledge of thy Gods—ay, thy Gods with a changed countenance, and called by other names, but still thy Gods!

The sun sinks over Abouthis. The red rays of Ra flame on temple roofs, upon green fields, and the wide waters of father Sihor. So as a child I watched him sink; just so his last kiss touched the further pylon's frowning brow; just that same shadow lay upon the tombs. All is unchanged! I—I only am changed—so changed, and yet the same!

Oh, Cleopatra! Cleopatra! thou Destroyer! if I might but tear thy vision from my heart! Of all my griefs, this is the heaviest grief—still must I love thee! Still must I hug this serpent to my heart! Still in my ears must ring that low laugh of triumph—the murmur of the falling fountain—the song of the nightinga—

> (Here the writing on the third roll of papyrus abruptly ends. It would almost seem that the writer was at this moment broken in upon by those who came to lead him to his doom.)

www.ingramcontent.com/pod-product-compliance
Lightning Source LLC
LaVergne TN
LVHW050914080826
845145LV00001B/84

* 9 7 8 1 8 4 6 7 7 9 8 7 9 *